FALLEN

ALSO BY LINDA CASTILLO

Sworn to Silence

Pray for Silence

Breaking Silence

Gone Missing

Her Last Breath

The Dead Will Tell

After the Storm

Among the Wicked

Down a Dark Road

A Gathering of Secrets

Shamed

Outsider

A Simple Murder (A Kate Burkholder Story Collection)

FALLEN

A KATE BURKHOLDER NOVEL

Linda Castillo

MINOTAUR
BOOKS
NEW YORK

First published in the United States by Minotaur Books, an imprint of St. Martin's Publishing Group

FALLEN. Copyright © 2021 by Linda Castillo. All rights reserved. Printed in the United States of America. For information, address St. Martin's Publishing Group, 120 Broadway, New York, NY 10271.

www.minotaurbooks.com

Designed by Omar Chapa

The Library of Congress Cataloging-in-Publication Data is available upon request.

ISBN 978-1-250-14292-4 (hardcover)
ISBN 978-1-250-82803-3 (international, sold outside the U.S., subject to rights availability)
ISBN 978-1-250-14294-8 (ebook)

Our books may be purchased in bulk for promotional, educational, or business use. Please contact your local bookseller or the Macmillan Corporate and Premium Sales Department at 1-800-221-7945, extension 5442, or by email at MacmillanSpecialMarkets@macmillan.com.

First Edition: 2021

10 9 8 7 6 5 4 3 2 1

This book is dedicated to all of my wonderful friends at the Dover Public Library in Dover, Ohio. Thank you for hosting such lovely (and fun!) events for the last eleven years. You always go above and beyond and it means a lot. Seeing you and your patrons has become a tradition I cherish more than you know. Your library is my home away from home when I'm on the road, and I very much appreciate each and every one of you.

FALLEN

CHAPTER 1

She knew coming back after so many years would be difficult, especially when she'd left so much hurt behind when she departed. She'd hurt the people she loved, never wasting a moment on the notion of regret. She'd sullied relationships that should have meant the world to her. She'd blamed others when misfortune reared its head, never admitting she might've been wrong. Mistakes had always been the one thing she was good at, and she'd made them in spades.

Once upon a time she'd called Painters Mill home. She'd belonged here, been part of the community, and she'd never looked too far beyond the cornfields, the quaint farmhouses and winding back roads. Once, this little town had been the center of her universe. It was the place where her family still lived—a family she hadn't been part of for twelve years. Like it or not, her connection to this place and its people ran deep—too deep, in her opinion—and it was a link she could no longer deny no matter how hard she tried.

This saccharine little town with its all-American main street and pastoral countryside hadn't always been kind. In the eyes of the seventeen-year-old girl she'd been, Painters Mill was a place of brutal lessons, rules she couldn't abide by, and crushing recriminations by people who, like her, possessed the power to hurt.

It took years for her to realize all the suffering and never-lived-up-to expectations were crap. Like her *mamm* always said: Time is a relevant thing and life is a cruel teacher. It was one of few things her mother had been right about.

Painters Mill hadn't changed a lick. Main Street, with its charming storefronts and Amish tourist shops, still dominated the historic downtown. The bucolic farms and back roads were still dotted with the occasional buggy or hay wagon. Coming back was like entering a time warp. It was as if she'd never been gone, and everything that had happened since was nothing more than a dream. The utter sameness of this place unsettled her in ways she hadn't expected.

The Willowdell Motel sure hadn't changed. Same trashy façade and dusty gravel parking lot. Inside, the room was still dressed in the same god-awful orange carpet. Same bad wall art. Same shoddily concealed cigarette smoke and the vague smell of moldy towels. It was a place she shouldn't have known at the age of seventeen.

If life had taught her one lesson that stood out above the rest, it was to look forward, not back. To focus on goals instead of regrets. It took a lot of years and even more sacrifice, but she'd clawed her way out of the cesspit she'd made of her life. She'd done well—better than she ever imagined possible—and she'd forged a good life for herself. Did any of that matter now? Was it enough?

Tossing her overnight bag onto the bed, Rachael Schwartz figured she'd waited long enough to make things right. The time had come for her to rectify the one wrong that still kept her up nights. The one bad decision she hadn't been able to live down. The one that, for years now, pounded at the back of her brain with increasing intensity. She didn't know how things would turn out or if she'd get what she wanted. The one thing she *did* know was that she had to try. However this turned out, good or bad or somewhere in between, she figured she would simply have to live with it.

The knock on the door came at two A.M. Even as she threw the covers aside and rolled from the bed, she knew who it was. A smile touched her mouth as she crossed to the door. Recognition kicked when she checked the peephole. The quiver of pleasure that followed didn't quite cover the ping of trepidation. She swung open the door.

"Well, it's about damn time," she said.

A faltering smile followed by a flash of remembrance. "I didn't think I'd ever see you again."

She grinned. "No such luck."

"Sorry about the time. Can I come in?"

"I think you'd better. We've a lot to discuss." Stepping back, she motioned her visitor inside. "I'll get the light."

Her heart strummed as she started for the night table next to the bed. All the words she'd practiced saying for months now tumbled in her brain like dice. Something not quite right, but then what had she expected?

"I hope you brought the wine," she said as she bent to turn on the lamp.

The blow came out of nowhere. A sunburst of white light and sound, like a stick of dynamite igniting in her head. A splintering of pain. Her knees hit the floor. Shock and confusion rattled through her.

She reached out, grabbed the night table. A sound escaped her as she struggled to her feet, teetered left. She turned, spotted the bat, saw the other things she'd missed before. Dark intent. Buried rage. Dear God, how could she have been so naive?

The bat came down again. Air whooshed. She staggered right, tried to escape it. Not fast enough. The blow landed hard on her shoulder. Her clavicle snapped. The lightning bolt of pain took her breath. Mewling, she turned, tried to run, fell to her knees.

Footsteps behind her. More to come. She swiveled, raised her hands to protect herself. The bat struck her forearm. An explosion of pain. The shock pulsing like a strobe.

"Don't!" she cried.

Her attacker drew back. Teeth clenched. The dead eyes of a taxidermist's glass. The bat struck her cheekbone, the force snapping her head back. She bit her tongue, tasted blood. Darkness crowded her vision. The sensation of falling into space. The floor rushed up, struck her shoulder. The scrape of carpet against her face. The knowledge that she was injured badly. That it wasn't going to stop. That she'd made a serious miscalculation.

The shuffle of feet on carpet. The hiss of a labored breath. Fighting dizziness, she reached for the bed, fisted the bedsheet, tried to pull herself up. The bat struck the mattress inches from her hand. Still a chance to get away. Terrible sounds tore from her throat as she threw herself onto the bed, scrabbled across. On the other side, she grabbed the lamp, yanked the cord from the wall.

The bat slammed against her back. A sickening wet-meat punch that rent the air from her lungs. An electric shock ran the length of her spine. Unconsciousness beckoned. She swiveled, tried to swing the lamp, but she was too injured and it clattered to the floor.

"Get away!" she cried.

She rolled off the bed, tried to land on her feet. Her legs buckled and she went down. She looked around. A few feet away, the door stood open. Pale light spilling in. If she could reach it . . . Freedom, she thought. Life. She crawled toward it, pain running like a freight train through her body.

A sound to her left. Shoes against carpet. Legs coming around the bed. Blocking her way. "No!" she screamed, a primal cry of outrage and terror. No time to brace.

The bat struck her ribs with such force she was thrown onto her side. An animalistic sound ripped from her throat. Pain piled atop pain. She opened her mouth, tried to suck in air, swallowed blood.

A wheeze escaped her as she rolled onto her back. The face that stared down at her was a mindless machine. Flat eyes filled with unspeakable purpose. No intellect. No emotion. And in that instant, she knew she was going to die. She knew her life was going to end here in this dirty motel and there wasn't a goddamn thing she could do to help herself.

See you in hell, she thought.

She didn't see the next blow coming.

CHAPTER 2

The winters are endless in northeastern Ohio. People are stuck indoors for the most part. The sun doesn't show itself for weeks on end. When the relentless cold and snow finally break and the first tinge of green touches the fields, spring fever hits with the force of a pandemic.

My name is Kate Burkholder and I'm the chief of police in Painters Mill, Ohio. Founded in 1815, it's a pretty little township of about 5,300 souls that sits in the heart of Amish country. I was born Plain, but unlike the majority of Amish youths, I left the fold when I was eighteen. In nearby Columbus, I earned my GED and a degree in criminal justice, and I eventually found my way into law enforcement. But after I'd been in the big city a few years, my roots began to call, and when the town council courted me for the position of chief I returned and never looked back.

This morning, I'm in the barn with my significant other, John Tomasetti, who is an agent with the Ohio Bureau of Criminal Investigation. We met in the course of a murder investigation shortly after I became chief, and after a rocky start we began the most unlikely of relationships. Much to our surprise, it grew into something genuine and lasting, and for the first time in my adult life I'm unabashedly happy.

We're replacing some of the siding on the exterior of the barn. Tomasetti made a trip to the lumberyard earlier for twenty tongue-and-groove timbers and a couple of gallons of paint. As we unload supplies from the truck, a dozen or so Buckeye hens peck and scratch at the dirt floor.

Our six-acre farm is a work in progress, mainly because we're do-it-yourselfers and as with most endeavors in this life, there's a learning curve. We're hoping to replace the siding this coming weekend. Next weekend, we prime and paint. The weekend after that, weather permitting, we might just get started on the garden.

"I hear you finally got another dispatcher hired," Tomasetti says as he slides a board from the truck bed and drops it onto the stack on the ground.

"She started last week," I tell him. "Going to be a good fit."

"Bet Mona's happy about that."

Thinking of my former dispatcher—who is now Painters Mill's first full-time female officer—I smile. "She's not the only one," I say. "The chief actually gets to take the occasional day off."

He's standing in the truck bed now, holding a gallon of paint in each hand, looking down at me. "I like her already."

I drop the final board onto the stack and look up at him. "Anyone ever tell you you look good in those leather gloves?" I ask.

"I get that a lot," he says.

He's in the process of stepping down when my cell phone vibrates against my hip. I glance at the screen to see DISPATCH pop up on the display. I answer with, "Hey, Lois."

"Chief." Lois Monroe is my first-shift dispatcher. She's a self-assured woman, a grandmother, a crossword-puzzle whiz kid, and an experienced dispatcher. Judging by her tone, something has her rattled.

"Mona took a call from the manager out at the Willowdell Motel. She just radioed in saying there's a dead body in one of the rooms."

In the back of my mind I wonder if the death is from natural causes—a heart attack or slip-fall—or, worse-case scenario, a drug overdose. A phenomenon that's happening far too often these days, even in small towns like Painters Mill.

"Any idea what happened?" I ask.

"She says it's a homicide, Chief, and she sounds shook. Says it's a bad scene."

It's not the kind of call I'm used to taking.

"I'm on my way," I say. "Tell Mona to secure the scene. Protect any possible evidence. No one goes in or out. Get an ambulance out there and call the coroner."

It takes me twenty minutes to reach the motel. I took the time to throw on my uniform and equipment belt, and made the drive from Wooster in record time.

The Willowdell Motel is a Painters Mill icon of sorts. The sign in front touts MID-CENTURY MODERN with CLEAN ROOMS and a SPARKLING POOL in an effort to lure tourists looking to spend a few days relaxing in Amish country. The locals don't see the place with such optimism, especially when the pool isn't quite so sparkling, the façade is in dire need of fresh paint, and the rooms haven't been renovated since the 1980s.

I pull into the gravel lot to find Mona's cruiser parked next to the office, the overheads flashing. She's exited the vehicle and is standing outside room 9 talking to a heavyset man wearing camo pants and a golf shirt. I've met him at some point, but I don't recall his name.

Likely, the manager. I park the Explorer next to her cruiser and pick up my radio mike. "Ten-twenty-three," I say, letting Dispatch know I've arrived on scene.

I get out and approach them. Mona glances my way, looks unduly relieved to see me. She's twenty-six years old and has been a full-time officer for a few weeks. She's as enamored with law enforcement now as she was on her first day on the job. Despite her lack of experience, she's a good cop; she's motivated, has good instincts, and she's willing to work any shift, which is a plus when you only have five officers in the department.

I take her measure as we exchange a handshake. She's pale-faced; her hand is shaking and cold in mine. Mona is no shrinking violet. Like most of my officers, she prefers action over boredom, and she's never investigated a crime that didn't intrigue her in some way. This morning, she's stone-faced and I'm pretty sure I see a fleck of vomit on her sleeve.

"What do you have?" I ask.

"Deceased female." She motions with her eyes to room 9. "She's on the floor. Chief, there's blood everywhere. I have no idea what happened." She glances over her shoulder at the man who's straining to hear our every word, and lowers her voice. "It looks like there was one hell of a struggle. I can't tell if she was stabbed or shot or . . . something else."

I turn my attention to the man. "You the manager?"

"Doug Henry." He taps the MANAGER badge clipped to his shirt. "I'm the one called 911."

"Any idea what happened?" I ask. "Did you see anything?"

"Well, checkout is at eleven. Maid isn't here today, so I gotta clean. I called the room around ten thirty. No one picked up, so I waited until eleven and knocked on the door. When she didn't answer, I used my key." He blows out a long breath. "I ain't never seen anything like that in my life and I used to work down to the slaughterhouse. There's blood everywhere. Stuff knocked over. I got the hell out of there and called you guys."

"Who is the room registered to?" I ask.

"Last name is Schwartz," he tells me.

It's a common name in this part of Ohio, both Amish and English. If memory serves me, we have at least two families here in Painters Mill with that last name. "First name?"

"I can go look it up for you," he offers.

"I'd appreciate it." I turn my attention to Mona. "You clear the room?"

Grimacing, she shakes her head. "Once I saw her, I figured this was more than I could handle and got out."

"Anyone else been in the room?"

"Just me."

"Coroner and ambulance en route?"

She nods. "Sheriff's Office, too."

I start toward room 9. "Let's clear the room," I tell her. "Make sure there's no one else inside. Quick in and out."

I go through the door first. "Stay cognizant of evidence. Don't touch anything."

"Roger that."

It takes a moment for my eyes to adjust to the dimly lit interior. I smell the blood before I see it. The dark, unpleasant smell of metal and sulfur. A few feet away, a red-black pool the size of a dinner plate is soaked into the carpet. A smear on the bedspread. Spatter on the headboard and wall. A finer spray on the ceiling. On the other side of the bed, I see the victim's hands.

"Clear the bathroom," I tell Mona. "Eyes open."

I feel the familiar quiver in my gut as I move to the bed—that primal aversion to violent death. No matter how many times I see it, I always get that shaky feeling in the pit of my stomach, that shortness of breath. I round the foot of the bed and get my first look at the body. The victim is female. Lying on her stomach. Legs splayed. One arm beneath her. The other arm is outstretched, clawlike hand clutching carpet, as if she'd been trying to drag herself to the door. She's wearing a pink T-shirt and panties. Socks.

I wish for better light as I approach. I pull my mini Maglite from my utility belt, flick it on. The beam tells a horrific tale. A lamp lies on the floor, shade crushed, the cord ripped from the wall. Whatever happened to this woman, she fought back, didn't make it easy for the son of a bitch to do this to her.

Good girl, a little voice whispers in the back of my brain.

"Bathroom is clear," comes Mona's voice.

"Blood?"

"No."

I glance over my shoulder, see her silhouetted against the light slanting in from the door. My mind has jumped ahead to the preservation of evidence; I'm keenly aware that I'm in the process of contaminating that evidence. No way around it.

"Go outside and get the scene taped off," I tell her, hearing the stress in my voice. "No one comes in. No vehicles except the coroner."

"Ten-four."

I'm no stranger to violence or the unspeakable things human beings are capable of doing to each other. Even so, for an instant I can't catch my breath.

The woman's head is turned away from me, her chin tilted at an unnatural angle. I see strawberry-blond hair matted with blood, the scalp laid open, a small red mouth at the back of her head. Green-blue fingernail

11

polish. Gold bracelet. Pretty hands. And I'm reminded that just hours ago, this woman cared about such mundane things as a manicure and jewelry.

Careful not to disturb the scene, I sidle around to the other side of the woman. I know immediately she's dead. The left side of her face has been destroyed. Cheekbone caved in. Eyeball dislodged from its socket. Nose an unrecognizable flap of skin. Tongue protruding through broken teeth. A string of blood and drool dribbling onto the carpet to form a puddle the size of a fist.

I shift the beam of my flashlight to her face. Recognition flickers uneasily in my gut, the stir of some long-forgotten memory. A punch of dread follows, because at that moment I do not want to know her. But I do and the rush of nausea that follows sends me back a step.

Bending, I put my hands on my knees, and blow out a breath. "Damn."

I choke out a sound I don't recognize, end it with a cough. Giving myself a quick mental shake, I straighten, look around the room. A high-end purse with leather fringe has been tossed haphazardly onto the chair. An overnight bag sits on the floor in front of the cubbyhole closet. I go to the chair, pluck a pen from my pocket, and use it to flip open the flap. Inside, I see a leather wallet, a cosmetic case, a comb, perfume. I pull out the wallet. I notice several twenty-dollar bills as I open it and I know that whoever did this didn't do it for money.

Her driver's license stares at me from its clear-faced pocket. The floor tilts beneath my feet when I see the name. Rachael Schwartz. The dread bubbling inside me burgeons as I stare down at the photo of the pretty young woman with strawberry-blond hair and her trademark almost-smile. It's the kind of smile that shouts *I'm going places and if you can't keep up you will be left behind!* But then that was Rachael. Hard to handle. High emotion and higher drama. Even as a kid, she was prone to making mistakes and then defending her position even when she was wrong, which was often. If you hurt her or angered her, she lashed out with inordinate ferocity. Faults aside, her love was fierce and pure. I know all of those things because I was one of the few Amish who understood her, though I never said as much aloud.

Closing my eyes, I bank the rise of emotion, shove it back into its hole. "Son of a bitch," I whisper.

I knew Rachael Schwartz since she was in diapers. She was seven years younger than me, the middle child of a Swartzentruber family here in Painters Mill. The Swartzentruber sect is an Old Order subgroup and its members adhere to the timeworn traditions in the strictest sense. They eschew much of the technology other sects allow, such as the use of gravel for long lanes, indoor plumbing, and even the use of a slow-moving-vehicle sign for their buggies. The Schwartzes had five kids and I babysat them a few times when I was a teenager. Her *mamm* and *datt* still live in the old farmhouse off of Hogpath Road.

I lost track of Rachael over the years. I heard she left Painters Mill at some point, before I returned here as chief. She was the only girl I'd ever met who was worse at being Amish than me.

Using my cell, I snap a photo of the license in case I need to reference the information later.

"Chief?"

I startle, turn to face Mona, hoping my face doesn't reflect the riot of emotions banging around inside me. "You get the crime scene tape up?" I ask.

"Yes, ma'am." Something flickers in her eyes. She cocks her head. "You know her?"

I sigh, shake my head. "Not well, but . . ." I don't know how to finish the sentence, so I let the words trail off.

Mona gives me a moment; then her gaze flicks to the purse. "Anything?"

"Driver's license. Cash." I acknowledge the thought that's been nudging at the back of my mind. "No cell phone. Have you seen one?"

"No."

I use the pen to go through the scant items inside, then drop the wallet back into the purse.

By the time I've finished, I've got my head on straight. I start toward Mona. "I'm going to call BCI," I say, referring to the Ohio Bureau of Criminal Investigation. "Get a CSU out here. In the interim, we need to canvass, starting with the motel rooms. Check with the manager to see which ones are occupied. Start with the rooms closest to this one and work your way out. Talk to everyone. See if they saw or heard anything unusual."

"You got it."

We exit the room. On the sidewalk outside the door, I stop, draw a deep breath, let it out, draw in another. "Get Glock out here, too," I say, referring to Rupert "Glock" Maddox, my most experienced officer. "We got four vehicles here in the parking lot. I'll find out which one belongs to her and we'll get it cordoned off, too."

"Got it, Chief."

Pulling out my cell, I call Dispatch. Usually, we communicate via radio. Because I don't want Rachael's name floating around on the airwaves in case someone is listening to a police scanner, I opt for my cell.

"Run Rachael Schwartz through LEADS," I tell Lois, referring to the Law Enforcement Automated Data System, which is a database administered by the Ohio State Highway Patrol and allows law enforcement to share criminal justice information. "Check for warrants. Phone number. Known associates. Whatever you can find." I glance down at the photo on my phone and recite the address off her license. "Check property records, too. Find out who owns the property where she lives."

"Roger that."

I hit END and turn to the motel manager, who's standing a few feet away, smoking a cigarette. "She dead?" he asks.

I nod. "Can you tell me which rooms are occupied?"

"Two. Four. Seven. And nine."

I nod at Mona and she starts toward the room two doors down.

"Do you know which vehicle belongs to Schwartz?" I ask the manager.

He looks down at the paper in his hand. "Let's see if she included the info on her check-in form. Here we go." He motions toward the Lexus parked a couple of spaces down from the room. "Right there."

"Was she alone?" I ask.

"I didn't see anyone else. No other name on the form. And she only requested one key."

I nod, look around, spot the security camera tucked under the eave a few yards away. "Are your security cameras working?"

"Far as I know."

"I need to take a look," I say. "Can you get the recordings for me?"

"I think so."

"What time did she check in?"

He glances down at the form in his hand. "A little after eight P.M. yesterday."

I nod. "Would you mind sticking around for a while in case I have some more questions?"

"I'll be here until five."

I thank him and hit the speed dial for Tomasetti.

CHAPTER 3

"I figured you wouldn't be able to go long without hearing the sound of my voice."

I manage a pretty decent rendition of a laugh. But Tomasetti's an astute man—or maybe I'm not as good at my seasoned-cop equanimity as I think, because he asks, "What's wrong?"

"There's been a homicide," I tell him. "At the motel."

A beat of silence and then, "What do you need?"

"A CSU, for starters."

"Shooting? Stabbing? Domestic? What do you have?"

"Not sure. Beating, I think. Hard to tell because there's a lot of trauma. Victim is female. Thirty years old."

"I'll get someone down there ASAP." He waits, reluctant to end the call, knowing there's more. "What else, Kate?"

"Tomasetti, this girl . . . she was Amish once. I mean, years ago. I heard she left." I stumble over my words, jumble them, take a moment and clear my throat. "I knew her. I mean, when she was a kid. Growing up."

"Any idea who might've done it?"

"No. I haven't seen her in years." I look around, hating it that my thoughts are in disarray, that some distant connection is getting in the way. "Whoever did this . . . it's bad. There was an incredible amount of violence."

"Killer knew her."

"Probably." I scrub a hand over my face. "I need to tell her parents."

"Hang tight. I'll be there as soon as I can."

I've just ended the call when the crunch of tires in gravel draws my gaze. I look up to see a Holmes County Sheriff's Office cruiser pull into the lot, overheads flashing, and park behind my Explorer. I've met Dane "Fletch" Fletcher a dozen times in the years I've been chief. We've worked traffic accidents together. Defused a couple of domestic disputes. A bar fight at the Brass Rail. Last summer, we participated in a fundraiser for the 4-H club and spent most of the day in a dunk tank while squealing preteens threw a softball to hit the drop button. He's a decent cop with a laid-back personality and a sense of humor I appreciate a little more than I should.

"Hey, Fletch," I say, crossing to him.

He greets me with a handshake. "Heard you've got a dead body on your hands."

I lay out what little I know. "BCI is on the way."

"Hell of a way to close out the week. County is here to help if you need us, Kate."

The Willowdell Motel is inside the township limits of Painters Mill. But I work closely with the sheriff's office. We have a good relationship, and depending on manpower and workload, our boundaries sometimes overlap.

He scratches his head, his eyes on the open door of room 9. "Victim?"

I give him the rundown on Rachael Schwartz, sticking to the facts, tucking all those other gnarly emotions back into their hole.

"Formerly Amish, huh?" He rubs his hand over his chin. "Damn. Back to visit the family?"

"Maybe." I sigh, look around. "I did a cursory search of the room. There's a purse with an ID. Money still inside, so this wasn't a robbery. I didn't find a cell. We'll get a closer look once BCI gets here." I'm relieved when my thoughts begin to settle, my cop's mind clicking back into place.

I work a pair of gloves from the pouch on my utility belt and slip them on as I approach the Lexus parked a few yards from room 9. It's a newish sedan with a gleaming red finish and sleek lines that speak of affluence and prosperity.

I'm aware of the deputy behind me, craning his neck to see inside the vehicle. "Nice wheels for an Amish lady," he comments.

"Formerly Amish."

I'm reluctant to touch anything, but in the forefront of my mind the knowledge that a killer is walking free in my town pushes me to do just that. I open the driver's-side door. The interior is warm and smells of leather and perfume, all of it laced with the vague aroma of fast food. There's a wadded-up McDonald's bag on the floor of the back seat. A pretty floral jacket draped over the passenger seatback. A pair of royal-blue high heels lie on the passenger-side floor. Leaning in, careful not to touch anything else, I open the console. Inside, I see a couple of audiobooks, a pack of Marlboros, loose change, and a travel-size bottle of ibuprofen. No cell phone. I'm about to close the console when I spot the folded piece of paper tucked into the cellophane cover of the cigarette pack. Using my cell, I take a couple of photos. Then I pluck the note from the pack and unfold it. A single address is written in blue ink and underlined twice.

FALLEN

"Hello," I say. I set the note on the seat, pull out my cell, and snap another photo.

"What's that?"

I turn to find Fletch standing behind me, craning his head. "Not sure," I tell him. "An address."

He squints at the paper. "Huh."

Fletch is a good enough cop to know that the fewer people inside the crime scene tape, the better. I nudge him to give me some space. "Do you have cones and tape?" I ask, referring to typical traffic equipment.

He catches my drift. "You want me to cordon off the parking lot?"

"That would be a big help. On the outside chance we can pick up tread marks or footwear imprints."

"Whatever you need, Chief."

Leaving the note on the seat, I circle around to the front of the vehicle and do a similar search of the passenger side, but find nothing of interest.

I've just closed the door when the coroner's Escalade pulls up and parks a few yards away.

I pull out my cell and call Dispatch.

"Hey, Chief."

"I need you to look up an address." I pull out my cell, call up the photo of the note, and recite the address. "Find out who lives there and get their information. Run them through LEADS and check for warrants."

"Give me two minutes."

"Thanks."

I end the call and look around. Mona and Glock are talking to a tattooed-up couple who'd spent the night in a room two doors down. They can't seem to stop looking at the door to room 9. Even from twenty feet away, I see shock and curiosity on their faces.

Because Painters Mill is a small town, it's not unusual for me to be acquainted with the people I deal with in the course of my job, whether they're victim or perpetrator or somewhere in between. This is different. I didn't know Rachael Schwartz well. In fact, I hadn't thought of her in years. Not since hearing about the tell-all book she wrote about the Amish two or three years ago, anyway. Even then, it was only a passing thought. A shake of the head. I didn't read the book.

But I knew her as a child—and she made an impression. She was a lively, outspoken girl, both of which set her apart from other Amish kids. She was precocious, questioning of authority, and argumentative—all of which worked to her detriment. As she entered her teens those traits burgeoned into disrespect for her elders and disdain for her brethren, which caused tremendous problems for everyone involved, but especially for Rachael.

Last I heard—likely in the course of a conversation with one of the local Amish—Rachael had left the fold and fled Painters Mill some twelve or thirteen years ago. Where did she go? Aside from authoring the book, how did she spend the last years of her life? Why was she back in town? Who hated her with such passion that they beat her to an unrecognizable heap?

The questions nag, like an irritated nerve beneath a rotting tooth. And I know in the coming days, I'm going to do everything in my power to get the answers I need, even if I don't like what comes back at me.

CHAPTER 4

Rhoda and Dan Schwartz live on a narrow dirt track a mile or so off of Hogpath Road just outside Painters Mill. The couple is a pillar of the Amish community and has been for as long as I can remember. Now that her children are grown and married, Rhoda has gone back to teaching school at the two-room schoolhouse down the road. Dan runs the dairy farm with the help of his eldest son. They're decent, hardworking people, good neighbors. All of that said, they were quick to condemn me when I got into trouble as a teenager. I wonder if their intolerance played a role in their daughter's leaving the fold.

The death of a child is the worst news a parent can receive. It's the kind of slow agony they take with them to the grave. It changes the order of their world. Steals the joy from their lives, their hope for the future. Generally speaking, the Amish are stoic when faced with grief, in part because of their faith and their belief in eternal life. Even so, when it comes to the loss of a child, there is nothing that will spare them that brutal punch of pain.

Dread lies in my gut like a stone as I make the turn and barrel up the lane. The Schwartz farmhouse is an old two-story structure that's been added onto several times over the decades. The brick façade is crumbling in places. The front porch isn't quite straight. But the white paint is fresh and the garden in the side yard with its picket fence and freshly turned earth is magazine-cover perfect.

I park in the gravel area at the back of the house next to an old manure spreader and follow the flagstone walkway to the front. I find Rhoda on the wraparound porch. She's on her knees, half a dozen clay pots scattered on sheets of *The Budget* newspaper, and a bag of potting soil leaning against the column. She's a pleasant-looking woman of about fifty, her silver-brown hair tucked into her *kapp,* and a quick smile that reveals dimples she passed on to her daughter.

"Hi, Rhoda," I say as I ascend the steps.

She looks up from her work. "Katie Burkholder! Well, I'll be." She gets to her feet, brushes her hands on her skirt. "*Wie bischt du heit?*" How are you today?

Her expression is friendly and open, but she's surprised to see me, wondering why I'm here, in uniform. I'm loath to tear her world apart and I experience a wave of hatred for the son of a bitch who took her daughter's life.

She reaches for my hand and squeezes. "How's your family, Katie?" She's got short nails, her palms callused. "Is that sister of yours *ime familye weg* again?" The Amish have an aversion to the word "pregnant," instead using their own phrase, "in the family way." "That Sarah, always holding us in suspense."

I look into her eyes and for the first time I notice she also passed their blue-green irises on to Rachael, too, and an uneasy sensation of her coming grief tightens my chest.

"I'm afraid this is an official visit, Rhoda." I squeeze her hand. "Is Dan home?"

Her smile falters. Something in my expression or tone has given her pause. She cocks her head, the initial tinge of worry entering her eyes. "Is everything all right?"

"Where's Dan?" I repeat.

"He's inside," she tells me. "I made fried bologna sandwiches for lunch. I suspect he's sneaking a second one about now. If you'd like to stay, we can get caught up on things."

She's nervous and blabbering now. She knows I've news to bear, that it's not good. A hundred scenarios are surely running through her mind, as if she'd always known her daughter's antics would catch up with her one day and lead to this moment.

"The man eats like a horse, I tell you," she says in *Deitsch*.

I want to wrap my arms around her, silence her chatter, hold her while she comes apart, absorb some of the pain I'm about to inflict. But there's no way I can do any of those things, so I brush past her and open the door. "Mr. Schwartz?" I call out. "Dan, it's Kate Burkholder."

Dan Schwartz appears in the doorway that separates the living room from the kitchen, a sandwich in hand. He's wearing a straw flat-brimmed hat. Blue work shirt. Brown trousers. Suspenders. His face splits into a grin at the sight of me. He's still missing the eyetooth I recall from my youth. He's never gotten it fixed.

"*Wie geht's alleweil?*" How goes it now? At the sight of me and his wife, his expression falls. "*Was der schinner is letz?*" What in the world is wrong?

"It's Rachael," I tell them. "She's dead. I'm sorry."

"What?" Choking out a desperate-sounding laugh, Rhoda raises her hand, takes a step back, as if she's realized I'm a carrier of some deadly contagion. "*Sell is nix as baeffzes.*" That's nothing but trifling talk.

23

Dan reaches for his wife, misses, stumbles closer and grasps her hand in his. He says nothing. But I see the slash of pain lay him open. While the Amish live by their belief in the divine order of things and life beyond death, they are human beings first and foremost, and their pain rips a hole in my heart.

"Rachael?" Rhoda brings her hand to her face, places it over her mouth as if to prevent the scream building inside her from bursting out. "No. That can't be. I would have known."

"Are you sure?" Dan asks me.

"She's gone," I tell them. "Last night. I'm sorry."

"But . . . how?" he asks. "She's young. What happened to her?"

I almost ask them to sit down, realize I'm procrastinating, a feeble attempt to spare them that second brutal punch. But I know that delaying bad news is one thing a cop can never do. When notifying next of kin, you tell them. Straightforward. No frills. No beating around the bush. You lay down the facts. You express your sympathy. You distance yourself enough to ask the questions that need to be asked.

Because I don't have the official cause or manner of death, I tell them what I can. "All I know is that her body was found around eleven o'clock this morning."

The Amish man raises his gaze to mine. Tears shimmer in his eyes, but he doesn't let them fall. "Was it an accident? A car?" His mouth tightens. "Or drugs? What?"

I'm not doing a very good job of relaying the facts. My mind is clouded by my own emotions, the things I saw, the things I know about their daughter. "She was found in a room at the Willowdell Motel," I tell him. "We don't know exactly what happened, but there was some physical trauma. The police are investigating."

Rhoda Schwartz presses both hands to her cheeks. Tears well in her eyes and spill. "*Mein Gott.*" My God.

24

Dan looks at me, blinking rapidly, trying to absorb. "What kind of trauma?"

I can tell by the way he's looking at me that he already suspects that his daughter's antics, her lifestyle, finally caught up with her.

"I believe Rachael was murdered," I tell them.

"Someone . . . took her life?" Rhoda chokes out a sound that's part sob, part whimper. "Who would do such a thing? Why would they do that?"

Dan looks away, silent. The muscles in his jaws work. His eyes glitter with tears, but still they do not fall.

After a moment, he raises his gaze to mine. "Rachael was here? In Painters Mill?"

"You didn't know she was in town?" I let my gaze slide from Dan to Rhoda, the question aimed at both of them.

Both shake their heads.

"Do you have any idea why she was here?" I ask.

Rhoda doesn't even seem to hear the question. She's turned away, wrapped her arms around herself, blind and deaf, cocooned in her own misery. From where I stand, I can see her shoulders shaking as she silently sobs.

"We didn't know," Dan tells me.

"When's the last time you saw her?" I ask.

Dan lowers his gaze to the floor, so I turn my attention to Rhoda.

The woman looks at me as if she'd forgotten I was in the room. Her face has gone pale. Her nose glows red. She blinks as if bringing me back into view. "Right before Christmas, a year ago, I think."

That Rachael hadn't seen her parents in almost a year and a half tells me a great deal about the relationship. "Last time you talked to her, did she mention any problems? Was she troubled in any way?"

The Amish woman shakes her head. "She seemed same as always. A little lost maybe. But you know how that goes. She left the fold. That's what happens."

"Do you stay in touch with her?" I ask. "Did she call or write?"

"I talked to her on her birthday," the Amish woman tells me. "I called her. From the pay phone shack down the road there. Been a year ago now."

"How did she seem last time you talked to her?" I ask. "Did she mention what was going on in her life? Was she having any problems? Anything unusual or worrisome?"

"She was fine." The Amish woman's face screws up. Leaning forward, she buries her face in her hands.

I give her a moment and press on. "How was your relationship with her overall?"

"As well as can be expected," Rhoda tells me. "Bishop Troyer put her under the *bann,* you know. I never lost hope that she'd find her way back to us, back to the Amish way."

For the first time I see guilt on their faces, mingling with the grief, as if they've just realized they should have softened their stance and stayed closer to their daughter in spite of the rules.

"Did she stay in touch with anyone else here in Painters Mill?" I ask.

"She was always close with Loretta Bontrager," Rhoda tells me.

I don't know Loretta personally, but the image of a quiet little Amish girl drifts through my memory. Back then, her last name was Weaver and she was the polar opposite of Rachael. While Rachael was loud and outspoken, Loretta was reserved and shy. No one could quite figure out how they became best friends. Loretta still lives in Painters Mill; I see her around town on occasion. She's married now with children of her own.

I pull the notebook from my pocket and write down her name.

"They've been friends since they were little things," Dan says.

26

"Don't know if they see each other much anymore," Rhoda adds. "But if Rachael kept in touch with anyone here in Painters Mill besides us, it would be Loretta."

I nod, my mind already moving in the next direction. "Was there anyone else she was close to?"

"We wouldn't know about that," Dan tells me.

"Did she have a boyfriend?" I ask.

Dan drops his gaze, deferring to his wife.

"She was private about such things," the Amish woman says quietly.

I nod, realizing she likely doesn't know, and I shift gears. "Did she ever mention any problems with anyone? Any arguments?"

The man shakes his head, his eyes on the floor, mouth working.

But it's Rhoda who answers the question. "If she did, she never spoke of it. Not to us."

"Probably didn't want to worry us, you know," Dan adds. "She was thoughtful that way."

"Thoughtful" is the one word I wouldn't use to describe Rachael Schwartz. "Do you know any of her friends in Cleveland?" I ask.

The couple exchange a look.

Dan shakes his head. "We don't know anything about her life there." Disapproval rings hard in his voice.

"Do you have any idea where she worked?" I ask. "How she was making a living?"

"Worked at some fancy restaurant," Rhoda tells me.

"Do you know the name of it?"

"No." Shaking her head, Rhoda looks down at her hands. "And she wrote that book, you know. All those lies." She clucks her mouth. "Amish men having their way with women in the back seat of their buggies. Good Lord."

"Chafed a lot of hides here in Painters Mill." Dan grimaces, shame

27

darkening his features. "We knew nothing good would come of her being in the city."

"Evil goings-on," Rhoda adds. "We tried to tell her, but she was a headstrong girl, didn't listen. You know how she was." She shakes her head. "She would have been safer here. Gotten married. Had a family. Stayed close to God."

I don't point out to them that from all indications Rachael was murdered right here in Painters Mill, likely by someone who knew her. Someone filled with rage, a complete lack of control, no conscience to speak of, and the capacity to do it again.

CHAPTER 5

The Willowdell Motel is crawling with law enforcement when I arrive. In an effort to preserve any possible tire tread evidence, all official vehicles have relocated to the road shoulder in front of the motel. I see Glock's cruiser. An SUV from the Holmes County Sheriff's Office. An Ohio State Highway Patrol Dodge Charger. The only vehicles inside the perimeter are the BCI crime scene unit truck and the Holmes County Coroner's van.

I pick up my radio and hail Dispatch. "Anything come back on Schwartz?"

"Two DUIs in the last four years," Lois tells me. "Both out of Cuyahoga County. She pled no contest both times. Hot-check charge six years ago. Paid a fine. Last summer she was arrested for domestic violence. Charge was later dropped."

A ping sounds in the back of my brain. "Does Prince Charming have a name?"

"Jared Moskowski. Thirty-two years old. No record. Never been

29

arrested." She rattles off a Cleveland address. "Get this: Moskowski was the complainant on the domestic," she says.

Most often in the course of a domestic dispute, it's the female who gets roughed up by a male partner and makes the call. Knowing what I do about Rachael Schwartz, I'm not surprised that she was at least as much an instigator as a victim. Even so, I'll make sure Tomasetti takes a hard look at Moskowski.

I'm about to thank her and end the call when she pipes back up. "Oh, and I got a line on that address you gave me."

"Shoot."

"It's not a residence, but a business. A bar called The Pub."

"You're a font of interesting information this afternoon," I tell her.

"Internet connection helps a little."

As I park behind Glock's cruiser, I wonder if Rachael is still involved with Moskowski. I wonder if their relationship is volatile. I think about the bar in Wooster and I wonder why Rachael would write down the address when she lives in Cleveland, which is about an hour's drive away. Did she have plans to meet someone? Or did she meet with them on the drive to Painters Mill from Cleveland? Was there an argument? Did that someone follow her to Painters Mill and confront her in that motel room?

I spot Tomasetti's Tahoe several yards away and start toward it. I find him leaning against the hood, talking on his cell. Upon noticing my approach, he ends the call.

"You talked to the family?" he asks.

I nod, wondering if traces of the conversation are still evident on my face. "They took it pretty hard."

He's looking at me a little too closely, his eyes seeing more than I want him to see. "Hard on you, too, evidently."

"And here I thought I was getting pretty good at my tough-guy façade." I make the statement lightly, but it doesn't ring true.

"How well did you know her?"

"I didn't, really. Not as an adult." I struggle to put my finger on the flicker of pain in my chest. "The first time I saw Rachael Schwartz, she was still in diapers."

"Long time."

"She was too damn young to die."

I'm exasperated that I can't hold his gaze. Maybe because I know he sees all the things I'd rather not deal with at the moment. That my emotions are too close to the surface. He watches me, saying nothing, and in that instant, the silence strips me bare.

"I knew her when she was a kid. That's what's so tough about this. Of all the Schwartz kids, Rachael is the one that . . . made an impression. She was vivacious. A mischief-maker. She loved to laugh. Trouble was never too far away." I don't know why I'm telling him all of that, but it feels important and the words come out in a rush.

"Connections," he says.

"Too many probably."

He sighs. "Looks like trouble found *her* this time."

"You going to assist with the case?" I ask. "I mean, officially?"

"I'm your guy."

I look toward the motel room. In my mind's eye, I see the way Rachael Schwartz looked dead on the floor. The extent of damage to her body. Her face.

"Tomasetti, the level of violence . . ."

"Yeah."

"It was . . . over-the-top. Personal, I think, and passionate."

I tell him about the domestic dispute, but he already knows. "I got an address for Moskowski," he tells me. "Detectives are on their way to pick him up."

Typically, and since this is my case, I'd be part of the interview process. But because this investigation involves multiple agencies, and Moskowski lives in Cleveland, which is light-years out of my jurisdiction, Tomasetti will be the one to conduct the initial Q and A.

I hold his gaze, wrestling with what needs to be said and what doesn't. "Rachael Schwartz . . . she wasn't exactly the poster child for an Amish girl."

He cocks his head, knowing there's more, waits.

"She got into trouble a lot. I mean, growing up. She made a lot of mistakes. Broke the rules. If her penchant for finding trouble followed her into adulthood . . ." I'm mixing potentially helpful information with extraneous crap, so I take a moment, dial it back. "I'm not saying she was a bad person. She wasn't. Just sort of . . . full-bore."

"I've been around long enough to know that most people are little bit of both," he says gently.

"I don't want her to be just another young woman who ended up dead because she made some bad decisions. She wasn't perfect, but she deserved the chance to live her life."

He watches a state trooper get into his vehicle and pull out, gives me a moment to settle. It's a small thing. But it's one of a thousand reasons why I love him. John Tomasetti knows my weaknesses. All of them. He gets it. He gets me. And he's good at letting things be.

"Are we talking about a specific bad decision?" he asks.

"Domestic violence incident aside." I tell him about the book. "It made quite a stir here in Painters Mill. Some people weren't happy with her."

"Anyone in particular?"

"The Amish. Others, I'm sure. I'll do a little digging and let you know when I get a name."

He nods. "So she's likely made a few enemies over the years."

"Probably."

He nods toward the motel. "The manager came through with the CCTV. It's not good. Too dark. Too far away. Angle is bad." He shrugs. "I put our IT guys on it, so we'll see."

Movement at the door of room 9 draws my attention. A technician with the coroner's office clad in protective gear is wheeling a gurney from the van to the walkway outside the room.

"Before I go . . ." I tell him about the piece of paper in the vehicle with the scrawled address. "It's a bar in Wooster. The Pub. I thought I'd run up that way as soon as I get some time."

His eyes narrow on mine. "Wooster is about the midway point between Cleveland and Painters Mill. You thinking she met someone on her way down?"

"Maybe."

I'm only giving him part of my attention now. Doc Coblentz is standing just inside the doorway of the motel room, typing something into his iPad. The last thing I want to do is go back in there. But my need for information—my need to hear the coroner's preliminary thoughts—overrides my misgivings.

"I've got to go."

He looks past me, watches the technician kick down the brake on the gurney. "You've got this, right?"

The smile I give him feels tight and phony on my face, so I lose it, let him see the truth—that this has me a hell of a lot more shaken than I want to be.

"I just want to get this right," I tell him.

"You will."

There are too many people around for a kiss goodbye or any such nonsense, so I brush my fingertips across his hand and start for the door.

I nod at the deputy as I duck beneath the crime scene tape. My boots crunch against gravel as I walk toward room 9. I pause at the doorway and find Doc Coblentz standing over Rachael Schwartz's body. Clad in protective gear—face mask, disposable gown, a hair cap even though he's bald, and shoe covers—he looks like a cross between the Michelin man and the Pillsbury doughboy.

His technician, also clad in protective gear, punches something into an iPad.

"Doc," I say.

Doc Coblentz turns, looks at me over the top of his eyeglasses, and I can't help but notice that even in the face of such a heinous crime, his expression is serene. Unlike me, he's not shaken or angry or outraged. Not for the first time I wonder how he does it, dealing with the dead as often as he does, and I'm reminded that he is first and foremost a man of medicine. A pediatrician—a healer of children. When it comes to his role as coroner, he is a scientist with a puzzle to solve.

"Come on in, Kate," he says. "I'm about to release the scene to all those anxious-looking BCI boys out there and all their high-tech gadgets."

I cross to him, trying not to notice the stink of blood and urine and other smells I don't want to think about. "Can you tell me what happened to her?" I ask.

"I can speculate."

"I'll take whatever you can give me."

He looks down at the victim and sighs. "Preliminarily, and simply judging by the trauma, I would say she was beaten to death."

"Fists? Weapon?"

"Blunt object more than likely."

I force myself to look at the body, grapple to put what I see into words. "What about the . . . wounds?" I ask. "Is it possible she was also stabbed or slashed?"

"Force of impact," he tells me. "Which basically means she was struck with such force that it broke the skin, laid it open. As far as I can see, there are no incised wounds. Or gunshot wounds for that matter. As I'm sure you're aware, my assessment could change once I get her on the table."

I nod, shuddering inwardly. "Any idea of the time of death?"

"Well, she's in full rigor, which sets in at about two hours after death and completes at about eight hours. Depending on several factors, in this case the ambient temp and rate of decomp, full rigor ends after eighteen to twenty hours."

I calculate the equation, recall the manager telling me she checked in at about eight P.M. last night. "So, it's safe to say this probably happened sometime during the night."

The coroner shrugs. "Or very early this morning."

I look around, take in the obvious signs of a struggle. I think about the cash, the possibility that this was drug related, and I ask, "Can you tell if she was moved? After she was killed?"

Doc Coblentz nods at the technician, who has come over to stand next to us. In tandem, both men kneel and ease their gloved hands beneath the victim's shoulder and hip and lift her several inches. Beneath her, the carpet is wet with urine. I squat for a better look. My eyes are drawn immediately to the purple-black flesh that had been pressed against the carpeted floor.

"As you can see," the doc says, "she's almost into full lividity. Once the heart stops beating, gravity sets in and the blood settles to the lowest part of the body and pools. That happens at approximately twelve hours." The men ease the body back to the floor. "I would venture to say she died shortly before or after she fell or was pushed or placed here on the floor."

"Any chance you can narrow down the time of death, Doc?"

He makes a sound that's part growl, part sigh. "Tough to do at this

35

point, Kate. Once I get her to the morgue, I'll get a core body temp. That said, and taking all of the usual caveats into consideration, judging by the extent of rigor and livor, I'm guessing she died somewhere between eleven P.M. and five A.M."

A hundred more questions fly at my brain, but I set them aside for later because I know he won't be able to give me definitive answers. I straighten, and start toward the door. For the first time I'm aware that my face is hot, the back of my neck damp with sweat. The room feels small and claustrophobic. The air is thick and stinking of bodily fluids.

Outside, I swallow the spit that's pooled at the back of my throat and take a deep breath of fresh air.

I don't speak to anyone as I make my way toward the Explorer. I can't get the picture of Rachael Schwartz's brutalized body out of my head. Her skin laid open. Her face destroyed. Eye bulging from its socket. Her body broken beyond words.

I reach the Explorer, yank open the door, and slide behind the wheel, take a moment to compose myself. With a murder investigation spooling and the clock ticking, I need to be focused on my job. On finding the person responsible and bringing him to justice. Instead, my thoughts are scattered. I'm outraged and saddened and furious at once. That a woman I knew as a child is dead. That it happened in the town whose residents I swore to serve and protect.

"Not on my watch," I whisper.

Putting the vehicle in gear, I pull out of the gravel lot and head toward town.

CHAPTER 6

I met Rachael Schwartz for the first time when she was a newborn. The birth of a baby is a momentous occasion for all families, but it's an especially big event when you're Amish. After the new mom has had a few days to rest, the Amish women in the community come calling to see the new addition. Most bring a covered dish or two, help out with any chores that need to be done, and share a cup of *siess kaffi* or sweet coffee.

At the age of seven, I wasn't particularly interested in babies, but I recall my *mamm* dragging me over to the Schwartz farm, where I spent an hour watching her coddle and coo over a crying, red-faced infant that smelled of sour milk and stomach gas. Rachael didn't make a good first impression.

In a peripheral sort of way, I watched her grow up. Because of our age difference, we didn't play together or spend time. But all Amish children attend worship and mingle afterward—and squeeze in some playtime if possible. As her personality developed, I took notice, because for once someone else was getting into trouble instead of me.

The Amish generally have no use for babysitters. Most of the time and regardless of the occasion they take the baby with them, whether it's to worship, a wedding, or a funeral. When I was thirteen, Rhoda and Dan Schwartz had to travel to Pennsylvania. My *mamm* offered up my babysitting services, perhaps in the hope of reinforcing my own understanding of responsibility and Amish gender roles. Babysitting a herd of kids was not my idea of time well spent. But I hadn't yet discovered the power of argument, and so, by well-meaning parents hoping the experience might somehow help me find my missing maternal instinct, I was thrown to the wolves. It should have been pure misery for a girl like me—a tomboy who didn't quite conform or know how to fit in. How unlikely that another girl who was every bit as fallible as me would turn an unbearably mundane babysitting assignment into something unexpected.

Generally speaking, Amish kids are pretty well behaved, with a good work ethic and an early-to-bed-early-to-rise routine that make them easy to manage. Rachael was a rule-breaker with a penchant for trouble and a talent for fun.

She was the girl whose dress was perpetually stained, her *kapp* never quite straight, her gap-toothed smile beaming mischief. She was perpetual motion meets chaos. The kid who talked too much and had a temper when she didn't get her way—and might even mete out some revenge if you crossed her. But she was also a curious child who asked too many questions, especially about topics she didn't necessarily need to know, and she was rarely satisfied with the answers she got. The one who preferred baseball to dolls, and whose favorite food was strawberry ice cream. She was a prankster. Sometimes those pranks weren't very nice. I was a victim myself a time or two, but I quickly realized: You could get mad, but you couldn't stay that way, because Rachael always found a way to make you laugh, even when you didn't want to.

Rhoda and Dan were going to be gone for three days, which meant this hell-world I'd stepped into was going to last a while. It was on that second day I learned just how alike Rachael and I really were.

I was in the kitchen, making bologna sandwiches, when eight-year-old Danny burst in, breathless and sweating, his voice infused with panic. "Rachael got her head cut off!" he cried. "I think she's drowning!"

That got my attention. I dropped the spatula, ran to him, knelt in front of him. "What happened?" I asked. "Where is she?"

"She rolled down the hill!" the boy cried. "The barrel hit a tree and it bounced over the bob-wire and went in the crick!"

My babysitting skills may have been lacking, but I was responsible enough to experience a moment of terror. I grabbed his hand. "Show me!"

We dashed out the back door, ran to the barn, through the stalls and equipment area, and exited through the rear pens. From there, we sprinted across the pasture, huffing and puffing. Danny yelped when he lost his hat, but he didn't go back for it. Another fifty yards and the land swept down at a steep angle. At the base of the hill, two Amish boys were climbing over a five-strand barbed-wire fence. A fifty-five-gallon drum was wedged between the strands. Beyond, the green-blue water of Painters Creek snaked eastward, its murky surface dappled with sunlight slanting down through the trees.

"Where is she?" I cried as I started down the hill, running too fast, especially with an eight-year-old boy in tow.

"She flew out of the barrel!" he cried.

The answer didn't make any sense, so I kept going. Having heard us, the boys, on the other side of the fence now, spun toward me. Breathless with panic. Faces sweaty and red.

"*Vo is Rachael?*" I called out to them. Where is Rachael?

"*Sie fall im vassah!*" her older brother shouted. She fell in the water.

I noticed that one end of the barrel had been cut off and removed. And a horrific picture emerged. The boys had been getting inside the barrel and rolling down the hill, which was far too steep for such a game. Somehow, six-year-old Rachael had gotten involved.

I reached the fence and vaulted it without slowing, my eyes skimming the water's surface. "I don't see her!"

"She rolled down the hill in the barrel!" The neighbor boy, Samuel Miller, stuttered every word. "It hit the fence and she fell out! Went in the water!"

I stumbled down the steep bank, tripping over the tangle of tree roots. A couple of feet from the water's edge, I slipped in mud and plunged into the water. A crush of cold. The smell of fish and mud. Deep water. Over my head. I surfaced, sputtering.

"Rachael!" Treading water, I looked around, felt around for her with my legs.

"Where is she?" Even as I shouted the words, I heard a cough. I swiveled, spotted the small form crawling onto the rocky shoal on the opposite bank. Rachael, blue dress soaked and torn. On her hands and knees. Her *kapp* tugged down over one ear. One shoe missing.

I dog-paddled toward her. My feet made contact with the rocky bottom and I rushed to her. "Rachael!"

She sat on the rocks, her legs splayed in front of her. Her face was eggshell pale. Eyes huge. Expression shaken. A scrape on her chin. A drop of watery blood dangled beneath her nose.

I thought about the barbed wire and envisioned a gaping wound in need of stitches. Every single awful scenario scrolled through my mind at a dizzying speed.

"Are you hurt?" I heaved myself from the water and started toward her, my dress dripping, shoes squeaking with every step.

The girl looked up at me and blinked. I braced, expecting a wail and tears. Instead, she wiped blood from her nose with a hand that was rock steady. A grin overtook her face. A laugh burst from her mouth.

"You're not going to tattle on me, are you, Katie?" She frowned at the smear of blood on her hand. "I want to do it again."

CHAPTER 7

Ben and Loretta Bontrager own a good-size dairy operation on a sixty-two-acre spread a few miles outside Painters Mill. I've known Loretta since she was a youngster, too shy to speak, and hiding behind the skirt of her *mamm*'s dress. She was the polar opposite of Rachael and yet somehow the two girls became best friends. While Rachael was the gregarious live wire, Loretta was the quiet and obedient follower.

Aside from the occasional wave in town, I haven't spoken to Loretta in years. I met her husband, Ben, for the first time two years ago when he ran into some problems for selling unpasteurized milk, which is illegal in the state of Ohio. He readily agreed to cease operations and there was never a need for me to come back. Until now.

I've just turned in to the lane of the Bontrager farm when I glance across the pasture to my right and spot the horse and rider. It's common to see people riding horses here in Painters Mill. We've got a few cowboys, the local 4-H club; even Amish kids partake on occasion. This particular equestrian rides like poetry and takes the horse into a circle at an easy lope. Horse and rider are one, a ballad of perfect balance and animal beauty that's so captivating, I stop the Explorer to take it in.

After a moment, the rider spots me, slows the animal, and trots toward me. I almost can't believe my eyes when I realize this rider is not only Amish, but female. She's bareback, sneaker-clad feet dangling. Her skirt is hiked up to her knees and I see a pair of trousers underneath. She clutches a tuft of mane with one hand, and with the other grips the reins, which look like old leather lines that have been cut short for riding. The horse's head is high, nostrils flared, foam at the corners of its mouth.

"Nicely done," I call out to her.

The girl runs her hand over the animal's shoulder, but not before I see the flash of pride in her eyes. "He's a good horse," she tells me.

I get out and walk over to the fence that runs alongside the lane. She's eleven or twelve years old, with big brown eyes, a sprinkling of freckles on a sunburned nose, and dark hair tucked messily into a *kapp*. A tiny bow peeks out at me from the base of the head covering, and I smile. That bow, which is not approved by the *Ordnung*, is a symbol of a girl's individuality, a sign of independence, and a small way to set herself apart from her *mamm*.

The horse is a Standardbred, the most common breed used for buggies. Most are worked so much in the course of day-to-day transportation, they're rarely used for riding. Most are never trained for anything but driving.

"You're a good rider," I tell her.

The girl lifts a shoulder, lets it drop, looks down at her dangling foot.

"Who trained him to ride under saddle like that?" I ask.

"I reckon I did."

She mumbles the response in a way that tells me it's an achievement

43

she probably shouldn't admit to, and I wonder if she's been warned to stay off the horse. It wouldn't be the first time an Amish girl was disallowed to partake in an activity a boy would have every right in which to excel.

"You should enter him in the Annie Oakley Days horse show," I tell her.

Her eyes light up. I see pride in their depths, and I hope she holds on to that as she grows into adulthood.

"What's your name?" I ask.

"Fannie Bontrager."

"Ben and Loretta are your parents?"

"*Ja.*"

"Are they home?"

Nodding, she points toward the house.

I round the front of the Explorer and open the door. Look across the hood at her. "Enjoy the rest of your ride, Fannie."

Beaming a grin, she wheels the horse around, and lopes away.

Shaking my head, I get back into the Explorer and continue on.

The Bontrager farmhouse is a two-story frame structure with fresh white paint, double redbrick chimneys, and a gleaming metal roof. I drive past a ramshackle German-style bank barn and a muddy pen where a gaggle of Holstein cows encircle a round bale of hay. I park at the rear of the house and take a narrow concrete sidewalk to the front porch. I've barely knocked when the door swings open.

Loretta Bontrager wears a gray dress with a matching *halsduch,* or "cape"; an organdy *kapp;* and a pair of nondescript oxfords. She's got a dishcloth in one hand, a soapy sponge in the other, her attention lingering on whatever she'd been cleaning.

She does a double take at the sight of me. "Katie Burkholder?" Stepping aside, she ushers me inside. "What a surprise."

I go through the door and extend my hand. "It's been a while."

"I'll say." She drops the sponge into a bucket full of suds, dries her hands with the dish towel, and grasps my hand. "Time has a way of slipping by, doesn't it? Too fast if you ask me."

"I met your daughter on my way up the lane," I tell her.

"Probably on that horse again, eh?"

"She's a good rider."

"Like her *datt,* I guess." She shakes her head. "Keeping her off that horse is like trying to keep the wool off a sheep."

She cocks her head, polite, wondering why I'm here. "*Witt du kaffi?*" Would you like coffee?

"I can't stay," I tell her.

Something in my voice must have alerted her that I'm not here for a friendly chat and she goes still.

"Loretta, I'm afraid I've got some bad news. It's Rachael Schwartz. She's dead."

The Amish woman's smile falters as if for an instant she thinks the words are some cruel joke. "What?" She sways, reaches out and sets her hand against the wall. "But . . . *Rachael*? Gone? How can that be?"

"I'm sorry. I know you were close."

She steadies herself, lets her hand slide from the wall, and faces me. "Rachael," she whispers. "She's so young and healthy. How?"

"She was murdered," I tell her. "Sometime last night."

"Oh . . . no." The words come out on a gasp. "Someone—" She cuts off the sentence as if she can't bring herself to finish. "Do her *mamm* and *datt* know?"

"I just talked to them."

She makes a sound that's part sympathy, part pain. "Poor Rhoda and Dan. My heart is broken for them." Tears shimmer in her eyes when

45

she raises her gaze to mine. "I can't understand this, Katie. Who would do such a thing? And *why*?"

"I don't know. We're looking into it." I pause, give her a moment. "I understand you kept in touch with her. I was hoping you might be able to shed some light on her life. The people she knew. Do you have a few minutes to answer some questions?"

"Of course." But she looks as if she's grappling for strength that isn't there, for the control she can't quite reach. "Whatever you need . . . however I can help, just ask."

I pull my notebook from my pocket. "When's the last time you saw her?"

She looks down at the floor, thinking, and then raises her gaze to mine. "Over a year, I think. We met a couple of times at a little diner between Painters Mill and Cleveland, just to stay in touch and get caught up on things. I missed her so much after she moved away." She shakes her head. "I must have sent her a hundred letters that first year, but you know Rachael. She wasn't much of a letter writer."

"Did you visit her in Cleveland?"

She shakes her head. "I had Fannie by then and it was tough to get away with a new baby and all. You know how it is."

"When's the last time you talked to her?" I ask.

"A few months, I think."

"Did she mention any problems? Anything unusual or troubling in her life? Arguments or disagreements with anyone? A boyfriend maybe?"

The Amish woman considers a moment, then tightens her mouth. "She didn't mention any problems. But you know how Rachael was. Such a happy-go-lucky girl." Her brows furrow. "The only thing that stands out about the last time I talked to her is that she seemed a little . . . lost. Lonely. Homesick, maybe."

"How so?"

"Reminiscing, I guess. Asking about her parents and such. Like she missed them." She emits a sound of dismay. "Like they would have anything to do with her."

My cop's antennae go up. "Bad blood?" I ask.

She waves off the notion. "Nothing like that. It's just that Dan and Rhoda were tough on her. You know how the Amish are. Hardest on the ones they love the most."

I nod, remembering my own rebellion against the rules and the hard line my parents took to rein me in. "Did she have a good relationship with her parents?"

"They never accepted her leaving. They wanted her to come back. Get married. Have lots of children." A wistful smile plays at the corners of her mouth. "Of course, Rachael didn't want any of those things." Loretta shrugs. "It makes me sad to say it, Katie, especially now. But I think they saw her as fallen. Like maybe she was so far gone there was no way to bring her back."

Neither Rhoda nor Dan had mentioned that aspect of their relationship with their daughter. Their grief had been genuine and deep. Even so, I was Amish once. I've been a cop long enough to know that sometimes it's those troubled, passionate bonds that push people to the edge of their tolerance.

"Did she stay in touch with anyone else here in Painters Mill?"

"Not that I know of."

"Did you know she was in town?"

Her eyes widen. "She was here? You mean—" She bites off the word. I see her mind work through the implications. "Katie . . . it happened *here*? In Painters Mill?"

"I believe so."

"Oh, dear Lord." Raising her hands to her face, she swipes at the

47

tears with her fingertips. "I always thought of the city as a place of sin. A place that wasn't always good or safe for her. To think it happened *here.*" She presses a hand against her chest. "Did you get them?" she asks. "The person who did it?"

"We haven't made an arrest yet."

"That's a scary thing. I mean, knowing they're still out there."

I nod. "Loretta, can you think of anyone else Rachael might've come here to see?"

"Other than her parents . . ." Her expression turns troubled. "She wasn't exactly on the best terms with the Amish community."

I know where she's going, but I say nothing, wait for her to continue.

"The book, you know. She wrote all those terrible things about the Amish. Some of them thought badly of her. A few washed their hands of her completely. The elders knew she wasn't going to come back. Katie, no one said as much, but I don't think they *wanted* her back."

Misconceptions about *meidung* or excommunication abound. Most non-Amish people believe the *bann* is a form of punishment. It's not. Shunning is intended to be redemptive and bring fallen individuals back into the fold. In most cases, it works because when you're Amish, your family is the center of your universe. Without them, you are cast adrift in a world you're not prepared to handle.

"Did anyone in particular want her permanently excommunicated?" I ask.

"It was gossip mostly. You know how the Amish are. Rachael didn't talk about it. But I know it hurt her." Loretta smiles, reflective, but fresh tears glitter in her eyes. "You remember how she was. *En frei geisht.*" A free spirit. "She loved to laugh. She loved to love. She loved people. She loved life with all of its gifts. It was hard not to love her. But when she got mad . . ." She hefts a laugh. "You knew it. She did everything with such . . . *eahnsht.*" Zeal. "One of the reasons she didn't fit in, I suppose. She just couldn't follow the rules. That was why she left, you know. That was why I worried about her."

"Because she was a *druvvel-machah*?" I ask. Troublemaker.

"Because she never held back. Rachael was full speed ahead at a hundred miles an hour, even if she didn't know exactly where she was going. She was vocal and her opinions weren't always popular, especially among the Amish. Then she wrote that book and it just made everything worse."

I recall the stir it made here in Painters Mill. It was some kind of tell-all that was touted as nonfiction. For those of us who are familiar with the Amish, it was glaringly obvious the book was little more than a sensationalized hit piece rife with fiction.

I ask for her take anyway. "How so?"

"Well, she trashed that clan down Killbuck way. The Anabaptist group. They call themselves Amish, but they're not. *Maulgrischt*," she says, using the *Deitsch* term for "pretend Christian."

I'm familiar with Amos Gingerich and his followers. I see them on occasion at the farmers' market, selling vegetables, woodworking novelties, and plants and trees from a small nursery they run on their property. They call themselves the Killbuck Amish. They don't adhere to any *Ordnung* that I know of. The Amish refuse to claim them. In fact, a good number of the group's members are those who've been excommunicated from other church districts. Gingerich takes them in and, rumor has it, indoctrinates them into a community that's more cultlike than Amish. Last I heard there were thirty or so members who live in a communelike compound, a praxis more in tune with the Hutterites than Amish. While most members get around via horse and buggy, the community shares a single vehicle and has several phones on the farm.

The citizens of Painters Mill ignore them for the most part, but rumors abound. Things like the men taking more than one wife. That the children are at risk. A few years ago, the sheriff's office and Children Services got involved because someone claimed the kids were being separated from their parents and forced to work. The investigation that followed was inconclusive, but it put them on my cop's radar.

"Katie, you asked me if anyone ever threatened Rachael." She gives a single resolute nod. "You might take a look at Amos Gingerich. I think he threatened her once."

I take out my notebook and write down the name. "What kind of threat?"

"Well, you know she stayed with them awhile. After she was put under the *bann*. She didn't leave on good terms." She lowers her voice. "Rachael told me he mentioned some of the awful stories in *Martyrs Mirror*—you know, the way they tortured and killed the Christians way back when. It gave me the shivers, but Rachael just laughed. She wasn't too worried about it. I didn't think of it again until now."

Martyrs Mirror is a fixture in most Amish homes. My parents weren't readers, but my *mamm* kept a copy on a table in the living room. Over a thousand pages in length, the ancient tome details the horrors committed against Christians, especially the Anabaptists. I read the book as a kid—stories of men and women being burned at the stake, decapitated, drowned, and buried alive. The brutality and injustice left an impression, not only about faith and martyrdom, but the kinds of cruelties human beings are capable of.

"Do you know why he threatened her?" I ask.

She grimaces. "Rachael devoted an entire chapter to Gingerich and the Killbuck clan. She trashed them. Called him a polygamist—and accused him of worse."

"Like what?"

"I don't know it to be true, but she told me some of the men were taking wives as young as fourteen and fifteen years of age. Too young, you know. I told her to let it go. Go on with her life and forget about them. But Rachael was headstrong. Said those girls deserved to be heard. She told me later that her publisher made her change the names, to keep the lawyers out of it, I guess, but everyone knew. Amos Gingerich was not happy about it."

I think about the scrap of paper in her car with the address scribbled on it. "Do you know if Rachael knew anyone in Wooster? Or from the Wooster area?"

Her brows draw together. "Not that I recall."

"What about men? Did she have a man in her life? A boyfriend that you know of?"

Up until now, Loretta has been aghast and struggling to accept the news of her friend's death. Her reactions have been genuine, her demeanor stunned. My question effectively shuts her down, and my cop's gut takes note. Something there, I think, and I wait.

"Rachael is . . . was the best friend I ever had. I loved her like a sister. I don't want to say anything unkind." For a moment, the Amish woman wrestles with some internal foe, then raises her gaze to mine. "She was a wild one, Katie. As a teenager, she liked boys. As a woman, she liked her men. Maybe a little too much."

"Anyone in particular?" I ask.

The Amish woman presses her lips together. "She knew I didn't approve, so she didn't talk too much about it. But there were men. A lot of them."

"Do you have a name?"

She shakes her head. "All I know is that there was always a man in her life and every single one of them seemed to be wrong for her."

CHAPTER 8

Summer 2008

Loretta had never disobeyed her parents. Not once in all of her sixteen years. She'd never lied to them. Never shirked her responsibilities. Never conceived the notion of misleading them in any way. Tonight, all of that was going to change.

She'd laughed the first time she heard the expression "Amish rager." A few of the older Amish boys were talking about it at a singing she'd attended last year. She'd only caught snatches of the conversation. From what she gathered, a rager was a huge outdoor party, held in a barn or field, and isolated from the prying eyes of the adults. There was music and alcohol and, sometimes, the English showed up. It was the kind of gathering that would entail a lot of rule breaking that would undoubtedly get back to parents—and maybe even the bishop. At the time, such an idea had seemed profane and forbidden—something she would never get involved in.

What a difference a year made. Loretta was sixteen now—almost grown up—and her initial disdain for the idea of attending a rager had transformed into something closer to curiosity. Leave it to her best friend to bring that far-off temptation into sharp focus and test all the sensibilities she'd lived by the entirety of her life.

Last church Sunday, when the preaching service was over and all the adults were talking, Rachael had come to her, breathless and flushed, her eyes alight.

"There's a rager this weekend," she whispered, as they'd set out knives, cups, and saucers.

Rachael was so pretty. She was long-limbed with a sun-kissed complexion, and thick lashes over eyes the color of a summer storm. She already had a womanly figure, unlike Loretta, who was built like a broomstick. Her smile was as bright as the sun—and so contagious you couldn't help but smile back, even when you knew she was going to get you into trouble. This afternoon she was vibrating with energy Loretta knew would lead to no good.

"That's just plain silly," Loretta told her as she set a paper napkin on the table. "Mamm and Datt will never allow it."

Rachael rolled her eyes. "You're such a *bottelhinkel*." It was the *Deitsch* term for a worn-out hen that was ready for the stewpot. "We're not going to tell them!"

The thought of attending a rager appealed more than Loretta wanted to admit. But she knew it was an invitation for trouble. "Are you sure it's a good idea?" she said.

Looking left and right, Rachael took her hand and pulled her to the hall, out of earshot of the older women who were bringing out pies. "Ben Bontrager is going to be there."

Loretta's heart quivered at the mention of Ben Bontrager. She'd been half in love with him since she was six years old. He didn't know it yet, but she was going to marry him. They were going to live on a big farm and have dozens of children and too many animals to count.

"I don't think I can go," Loretta said.

"You have to!" Rachael whispered. "Ben is on *rumspringa*. I heard there are going to be some loose English girls there. You can't let him . . . you know."

Loretta wasn't dense; she knew boys were different from girls. They couldn't always control their urges. The thought of Ben giving in to some floozy *Englischer* crushed her.

"What do I tell Mamm and Datt?" she asked.

"Don't tell them anything, silly girl."

"How will I get out of the house without them knowing?"

Looking past her to make sure no one was listening, Rachael lowered her voice. "Sneak out your bedroom window. It's right over the porch. I'll meet you at the end of the lane at midnight. We'll go to the rager, stay for an hour, just long enough for you to see Ben, and then we'll go home. No one will ever know."

No one will ever know.

Famous last words.

A week ago, sneaking out of the house had seemed like such an exciting idea. Now, Loretta wasn't so sure.

Lying in her bed, she checked the alarm clock on the table for the hundredth time. It was eleven forty-five. The house had been quiet for some time. Her parents had retired to their room hours ago. Loretta knew her *mamm* liked to read before she went to sleep. But the light was out now. Time to go.

Rising, Loretta reached for her pillow and arranged it beneath the covers so if someone peeked in, they'd see the silhouette of her sleeping form. Satisfied, she crossed to the window. Her hands shook as she slid it open. The warm summer night greeted her as she stepped over the sill and onto the roof over the porch.

Careful not to make a sound, she lowered herself onto her rear and crab-walked down the slick metal to the nearest branch. Rising, she used the branch for balance and worked her way to the fork in the trunk. From there, she climbed down and jumped the last four feet.

The thump of her shoes hitting the ground seemed inordinately loud in the silence of the night. Certain someone must have heard, she looked around, heart pounding. But there was no one there. No lantern light inside. No movement in the kitchen window. Nothing but the sound of the bullfrogs from the pond and crickets all around.

Loretta launched herself into a run. She cut through the yard, the dew wet on her shoes. Upon reaching the gravel lane, she cut right and sprinted toward the road. Her feet pounded the gravel, her breaths echoed off the blackberry bushes that grew alongside the lane. She was nearly to the end when the shadowy figure stepped out in front of her.

Loretta yelped.

"Shhh!"

At the sight of her friend, relief flooded her with such force that her legs went weak. "You scared the jeepers out of me!"

Giggling, Rachael grabbed her hand. "Quiet or someone will hear you."

Rachael was wearing English clothes. Jeans. Tank top. Fancy sandals that showed her toes—which were painted pink. Suddenly, Loretta felt frumpy. "I look like a *bottelhinkel*."

Stepping back, Rachael set her chin on her fingers and gave her a critical look. "At least we can fix your hair." Without waiting for her assent, Rachael untied the strings of her *kapp*, and removed it. Tucking it into the bushes so Loretta could pick it up later, she removed the bobby pins from Loretta's hair, then used her fingertips to muss it.

"There. Now you're gorgeous!"

"My hair looks like straw."

"Phooey." Rachael motioned toward the road. "Come on. We don't want to be late."

Only when they were well past the mailbox did Loretta notice the buggy. Her steps faltered as recognition kicked. "Who's that?" she asked, knowing full well who it was.

"He's just going to drive us," Rachael said.

The boy in question leaned against the wheel of his buggy, smoking a cigarette, watching them. "About damn time," he drawled.

Levi Yoder was twenty years old. A nice-looking Amish boy from a good family. But Loretta had heard the stories. He'd been caught smoking and drinking. Worst of all, he'd been caught going out with loose English girls. Just last Sunday at worship, she'd caught him looking at her. Beneath all that good-Amish-boy charm, he had a dark side.

"You didn't mention someone driving us," she whispered.

Before Rachael could respond, Levi tossed the cigarette onto the road and approached them. "Told you she'd chicken out," he said.

"No one's chickening out," Rachael snapped, a challenge in her voice. He grinned.

Loretta didn't like him, but she had to admit he looked good in English clothes. Blue jeans. T-shirt. Cowboy boots. He'd let his hair grow and if she wasn't mistaken, he was sprouting a goatee.

A shiver spread through her when his eyes landed on her. "You going to introduce me to your friend?" he asked Rachael.

"Nope." Rachael started for the buggy. "She has zero interest and you're just our ride."

He pressed his hand to his chest. "Cut a guy off at the knees why don't you?"

Feeling conspicuous, Loretta followed her friend.

Levi reached into the buggy and tore two cans of beer from a six-pack. He handed one to Rachael, who took it without thanking him as she climbed in.

Loretta reached the buggy and he held out a can of beer. "I remember you now. You're Rhoda and Dan's girl. The little skinny thing, never says a word."

Face burning, she looked down at her dress. She didn't know what to say or how to react. All she knew was that she didn't like the way he was looking at her.

"Here you go." Taking her hand, he helped her into the buggy.

Loretta slid onto the seat beside her friend.

Levi leaned in and eased the beer into her hand. "You grew up nice," he murmured.

"Cut it out, Levi," Rachael said. "We need smokes, too."

Climbing into the buggy, he pulled the pack from his shirt pocket, tapped one out, offered it to Rachael. "You're wound tight tonight, aren't you?"

She laughed. "You have no idea, Amish boy. Let's go. We don't have much time."

CHAPTER 9

There's one bookstore in Painters Mill. Beerman's Books has been a Main Street fixture for as long as I can remember. The owner, Barbara Beerman, has run the place since I was a kid. When my *mamm* came into town to pick up fabric at the store next door, I would sneak in to browse the kinds of books my parents didn't want me to read. I wasn't exactly a bookworm, but I loved being transported to exotic places. If I could break the rules in the process, all the better.

Beerman's Books is two blocks down from the police station. It's a small, narrow space that smells of patchouli and bergamot, books and dust, and coffee from the station next to the "reading nook," which is basically an antique chair, lamp, and side table where bookish types can kick back and read before buying.

The bell on the door jingles cheerfully when I enter. Barbara looks up from her place at the counter, an ancient-looking tome open in front of her. "Hi, Chief Burkholder. What can I do for you?"

I cross to the counter, aware of the resident cat skulking between the shelves. "I'm looking for the book written by Rachael Schwartz," I tell her.

"Ah. You and everyone else. I heard about the murder. Do you guys know who did it yet?"

"We're working on it."

She nods. "Well, we have her book." She pushes herself to her feet and rounds the counter. "The tourists love it so much we have a tough time keeping it in stock."

"Have you read it?" I ask.

"The day it was released. Talk about tell-all. Rachael Schwartz didn't pull any punches."

"So I've heard."

"Apparently, she wasn't fond of her brethren."

"Did she name names?" I ask.

She shakes her head. "There's an author note in the beginning of the book saying the names were changed to 'protect' the identities of people depicted. The Amish aren't the most litigious people, but the publisher was worried about potential lawsuits nonetheless, I suppose." She leads me to an aisle and starts down it. "That said, Painters Mill is a small town. A few days after the book was released an Amish guy came in and bought all six books. Said he was going to burn them." She clucks. "I told him I would order more, but he didn't seem to care."

Midway down the aisle, she bends and pulls out a good-size trade paperback. "Here we go." Straightening, she looks at the spine. "*AMISH NIGHTMARE: How I Escaped the Clutches of Righteousness.*"

"I'll take two copies," I tell her.

"Double the fun." She grins. "I'll ring you up."

The things I've learned about Rachael Schwartz in the last hours nag at me on the drive back to the Willowdell Motel. By all indications, she lived her life with a no-holds-barred abandon. She wasn't afraid to push boundaries or get too close to the edge. She wasn't afraid to step on toes. In fact, she seemed to thrive on controversy even though it caused her some degree of unhappiness. She was social, with a multitude of relationships, not all of which were auspicious. I think about the level of violence of the attack and I wonder who hated her enough to beat her with such savagery. Conventional wisdom tells me it was someone she knew. Did he follow her here from Cleveland? Or did she meet her killer here in Painters Mill?

It's late afternoon when I pull into the parking lot of the motel. As usual when I'm dealing with a serious case, I feel the ever-present tick of the clock, reminding me how crucial these first hours are in terms of solving of the crime. Five hours have passed since the discovery of Schwartz's body, and the parking lot is still abuzz with law enforcement vehicles. The BCI crime scene unit truck is parked outside room 9, the rear door standing open. A technician clad in white Tyvek carries a cardboard box from the room and loads it onto the truck. I spot Tomasetti standing next to his Tahoe talking on his cell and I head that way.

He drops the phone into his jacket pocket as I approach. "You're a sight for sore eyes," I tell him.

"That's what all the female chiefs of police tell me," he replies.

There are too many people around for a too-personal greeting, so we settle for a quick touching of hands. "Anything new?" I ask.

"CSU is about to wrap it up. They got some prints we'll expedite through AFIS. A lot of blood evidence. If we're lucky, some of it will belong to the perpetrator and we'll get some DNA."

"Weapon?"

"We searched the room. Dumpster in the back lot. Treed area in the rear. It's not here."

"Did you find a cell phone?"

"Behind the night table. Probably got knocked off during the struggle. I couriered it to the lab in London," he tells me, referring to the BCI lab near Columbus. "We'll go through it with a fine-tooth comb."

"I don't know anything about her life in Cleveland," I say. "Anything on known associates?"

"Detectives are on scene at her residence now." He glances down at his cell phone, where he's jotted notes. "She lives in a townhome in the Edgewater district. Lake view. Heated floors. Swanky."

"Finances?"

"Still looking."

We fall silent, the information churning. "She live alone?" I ask.

He hits a button on his phone, swipes the screen. "She lives with Andrea June Matson. Thirty-two years old. No record. Evidently, they're business partners and own a restaurant downtown. The Keyhole. Matson is currently unaccounted for, but we're looking."

"Any problems between them?"

"Cops have never been called to the residence or the restaurant, but detectives are canvassing now and will be talking to friends and family to see what pops."

"How did you find Matson?"

"I answered Schwartz's cell when it rang," he tells me. "It was Matson on the other end. She didn't like it when I couldn't put Schwartz on the phone and hung up on me. Evidently, she didn't believe me when I told her I was with BCI. Get this: The last call Schwartz made was to Matson. That was around midnight. We're triangulating towers now."

"I want to talk to her," I say.

"You and everyone else. I put out an APB. We'll get her." He cocks his head. "Anything on your end?"

I hit the highlights of my conversations with Rachael's parents and Loretta Bontrager and tell him about the book.

"Sounds like she lived an interesting life," he responds.

"Maybe a little too interesting," I tell him. "Anything on Moskowski?"

"They picked him up without incident." He glances at his watch. "I need to get up to Cleveland."

Part of me wants to be there for the interview, not only with Moskowski, but with Matson. While a lover is always at the top of a cop's suspect list, a business partner comes in on a fast second. Those two people aside, Rachael Schwartz left plenty of unresolved problems right here in Painters Mill.

"Chief Burkholder!"

Both of us look up to see Steve Ressler jogging toward us. He's a tall red-haired man clad in khaki slacks that are a couple of inches too short, a blue polo shirt tight enough to show ribs, and glow-in-the-dark white sneakers. Steve is the publisher of *The Advocate,* Painters Mill's weekly newspaper. The paper has a decent circulation, mainly because Ressler is good at what he does. He's old-school and covers stories with journalistic integrity and an unfailing adherence to the facts, even when they're hard to come by. He's a type A personality, a stickler for deadlines, and he rarely accepts "no comment" for an answer.

"What can you tell me about the murder, Chief? Do you have anyone in custody? Do you have a suspect?" The questions fly in a flurry, his eyes darting to the motel room door where the coroner technician rolls a gurney laden with a black body bag.

"All I can tell you is that we have a deceased female. Her name is Rachael Schwartz."

He scribbles the name furiously. "Can you confirm it was a murder?"

he asks. "Suicide? I heard it was murder. If that's the case, should the residents of Painters Mill be concerned for their safety?"

"The coroner has not ruled on manner or cause of death yet."

He gives me a spare-me-the-pat-rejoinder roll of his eyes. "Can you confirm that the victim was Amish?"

"Formerly Amish."

More scribbling. "Anything else you can tell me, Chief?"

"Just that the Ohio Bureau of Criminal Investigation will be assisting my department. I'll put out a press release shortly."

"Don't keep me waiting too long," Ressler says as he walks away.

The crush of gravel beneath tires draws my attention. I look up to see a sleek Audi sedan barrel into the lot. Going too fast. Not some lost tourist looking for a room or a local curious about all the law enforcement vehicles. Tomasetti notices, too, and without speaking we watch the vehicle skid to a stop a scant foot from the crime scene tape. The driver's-side door flies open and a stylishly dressed woman clambers out, big sunglasses, cell phone pressed to her ear, and looks around as if not quite sure where she's landed.

Mona, whom I charged with securing the scene, strides toward the woman. "Ma'am? Can I help you?"

"What's going on here?" The woman lifts the crime scene tape and ducks under it.

"Ma'am. Stop." Mona rushes to her. "You can't do that!"

In tandem, Tomasetti and I start toward them.

"Excuse me?" Spotting us, the woman calls out, "I'm looking for Rachael Schwartz."

"That's either a reporter or Matson," Tomasetti murmurs.

"My money's on Matson," I tell him. "Journalists can't afford clothes like that."

"Or the car."

Mona grasps the woman's arm, stopping her. "This is a crime scene, ma'am. You need to wait outside the caution tape."

"I'm looking for Rachael Schwartz." The woman's voice shakes. She's noticed all the law enforcement vehicles—and the coroner's van. "I need to know what's going on."

She's wearing a black skirt and jacket that contrast nicely with artfully highlighted blond hair. Silky pink blouse that's open at the throat. A body that regularly sees the inside of a gym.

"The police are investigating an incident." Gripping her arm, Mona ushers her toward the crime scene tape.

"Incident? What incident?" The woman twists away. "I think Rachael was staying at this motel." She thrusts a painted nail toward the door of room 9. "What in the hell is going on in there?"

Tomasetti and I reach them. I hold up my badge and identify myself. "Ma'am, what's your name?" I ask.

She looks at me as if I'm some insect that's landed on her arm and she's thinking about crushing me with a slap. "Are you in charge? For God's sake! Someone tell me what the hell is going on. I need to see Rachael Schwartz and I need to see her right now."

She's agitated, edging toward hysterics. She doesn't seem to notice when Tomasetti takes her arm. "Come with me," he says as he guides her toward the perimeter tape.

Mona hooks a finger around the yellow tape and holds it up as the three of us duck beneath it.

Realizing what's happening, the woman chokes out a sound of dismay and twists away. "Please tell me something didn't happen to her."

I take her other arm. I'm aware of Tomasetti standing on the other side of her, not touching her. Mona stands guard at the caution tape, watching us. Backup if we need it.

"What's your name?" I repeat.

"Andrea . . . Andy Matson." She stutters the name, her attention fastened to the doorway of room 9. "Please tell me she's not hurt."

"What's your relationship with Rachael Schwartz?" I ask.

"She's my business partner. My roommate. For God's sake, she's my best friend." She tries to wrench her arm from my grip, but I don't let her go.

"I've been trying to reach her all day. Rachael *always* answers her phone. Last time I called, some dude picked up. Said he was with BCI. I knew something was wrong . . . so I just got in my car and drove." The words tumble out in a rush.

Breathless, she thrusts her hand toward the motel, where the technician with the coroner's office is closing the double doors of the van. "I arrive to see that!"

She tears her eyes from the van, divides her attention between me and Tomasetti. "You guys are scaring the hell out of me."

"Rachael Schwartz is dead," I tell her.

"Dead?" She recoils as if I struck her. "But . . . that's crazy. She can't be . . . I just saw her yesterday. I talked to her last night. She was fine." She pauses to catch her breath. "What happened to her?"

"The coroner hasn't made an official determination yet, but we believe someone gained access to her room sometime during the night and killed her."

"Oh my God." Breaths hissing, she bends at the hip, sets her hands on her knees. "Rachael. Shit. Shit."

"Do you need to sit down?" I ask.

She spits on the ground, shakes her head.

I give her a moment, watching her for any telltale signs of deception, but she gives me nothing.

Feeling the tick of the clock, I touch her shoulder. "Ms. Matson, I know this is a bad time, but I need to ask you some questions."

Straightening, she blows out a breath, her expression dark, mascara beginning to run. "Who did it?"

"We don't know. We're looking. It would be a big help if you could help us fill in some blanks."

Her reaction seems genuine. Shock, after all, is difficult to fake. But I've been around long enough to know certain individuals are masterful at deception. It's too early in the game for me to tell, so I proceed with caution.

"When's the last time you saw her?" I ask.

"Yesterday morning. I passed her in the hall when she was on her way to get coffee. I was on my way to the shower."

"When's the last time you talked to her?" Tomasetti asks.

"Last night. On the phone. Late." She sets her thumb and forefinger to the bridge of her nose. "I gave her hell because I didn't know she was spending the night here. I'm like, oh, thanks for telling me."

As if remembering harsh words between them, she closes her eyes. "I was a shit. I didn't know that would be the last time we . . ." She doesn't finish the sentence.

"Was Rachael having any problems with anyone?" I ask. "Any arguments or disagreements? Did she have any volatile relationships?"

"Who *wasn't* she having problems with?" Choking out a sound that's part laugh, part sob, she lowers her face into her hands. "Every relationship she had was volatile. That's just the way she was."

Tomasetti makes a sound of irritation. "Straight answers would be a big help about now."

She raises her head. Misery boils in her eyes. "Look, all I'm saying is that for better or for worse, Rachael spoke her mind. Didn't hold back. That was one of the things I loved about her. I mean, the girl was on fire and burning hot, you know? She lived and breathed controversy. Anyone who disagreed with her? She ate them for lunch." She makes the statement with a fondness that tells me she's probably a bit of a rabble-rouser herself. "I told her one day it was going to catch up with her, but she just laughed."

"Who was she close to?" I pull out my notebook and pen.

"Jared Moskowski."

I feel Tomasetti's eyes on me, but I don't look at him. "Boyfriend?"

"Fuck buddy," she says. "And he's a jealous, insecure, and petty son of a bitch. Rachael was too much for him to handle and he knew it."

"Did they fight?"

"All the time."

"Did he ever hit her?" Tomasetti asks. "Or physically abuse her?"

"Not that I saw, but their relationship was . . . screwed up." She shrugs. "He wasn't man enough to handle her."

"Did they fight about anything in particular?" I ask.

"The frickin' weather, for God's sake. All I know is they didn't get along. They were always pissed at each other." She presses her lips together. "I don't know why she was so crazy about him."

She turns her eyes on me, outrage flashing, her mouth tight. "Did he do it?"

I ignore the question. "Is there anyone else Rachael didn't get along with?"

The woman's brows draw together. "I guess you know she used to be Amish. She's from Painters Mill. Her parents are religious fanatics and shunned her or whatever the hell they do." Resentment rings hard in the laugh that follows. "For God's sake, even the Amish were pissed at her."

"What about you?" Tomasetti asks.

She looks at him as if the question is a personal affront. "Are you kidding me?" Her gaze flicks to me. "She's dead and you two bozos are looking at me? That's rich."

"You can answer the question here, or we can do it at the police station," I tell her. "Your choice."

"Look, Rachael and I were friends. *Real* friends. We were roommates. Business partners. So yeah, there was some occasional conflict." Her eyes fasten onto mine, unshed tears glittering. "I'll be the first to tell you she was difficult. But I loved her anyway. She was like a sister to me, and you're a damn fool if you waste any time looking at me."

"How did you meet her?"

"I was the style editor at a boutique magazine in Cleveland and wrote a piece on how Rachael went from Amish girl to restaurateur. We met for drinks, got to talking. It didn't take long for me to realize she was one of the most ambitious and fascinating women I'd ever met." She smiles as if remembering. "I told her that her story would make a compelling book." She lifts her shoulders, lets them drop. "She had the story. I knew how to write. The rest is history."

"You cowrote the book?" I ask.

"I *wrote* the book," she corrects.

"Your name isn't on the cover," Tomasetti points out.

Her smile turns brittle. "Well, it should have been, but then that was Rachael for you. She wanted the limelight. I ended up in the acknowledgments."

"Big of her," he says. "Did you get angry about that?"

Matson rolls her eyes. "I got over it. By then we were friends. I didn't want anything so petty to get between us."

I keep moving. "Did she know anyone in Wooster? Did she ever go there? To meet anyone?"

"Wooster?" She shakes her head. "Never heard her mention it."

"We're going to need a DNA sample," Tomasetti tells her. "Prints too."

Her eyes narrow, so I add, "We need to rule you out so we don't waste anyone's time."

"Sure. Whatever." She shakes her head. "I can't believe this is happening. I can't believe she's gone."

Tomasetti taps the screen of his cell phone. "Where can we reach you if we need to get in touch?"

She rattles off a cell phone number and I punch it into my phone.

"If you go back to Cleveland, you need to keep yourself available in case we need to talk to you again," I say.

Her mouth tightens again. "I'm not going anywhere until I get some answers. How's that for guilty?"

"That'll do just fine," Tomasetti says.

CHAPTER 10

It's fully dark by the time the scene is cleared and the BCI crime scene truck pulls out. The motel manager called in a professional crew to clean the room, but they won't start until morning. According to Tomasetti, the agents retrieved a plethora of potential evidence, including DNA, fibers, blood evidence, hair, fingerprints, and footwear marks. They were able to cast a single decent tire imprint in the parking lot, ostensibly from a vehicle that had parked next to Rachael Schwartz's Lexus at some point. Everything was couriered to the police lab in London, Ohio. Fingerprint data should come back quickly. And while we won't get DNA results right away, we will likely find out soon if any of the blood is secondary—which could indicate the killer injured himself in the course of the attack. Conceivably, we could have a second set of DNA.

Tomasetti left for Cleveland to question Jared Moskowski. I'm standing at the doorway to room 9, procrastinating going inside. From where I stand, I can still discern the faint smell of blood. I can't help but think that last night at this time, Rachael Schwartz was enmeshed in the mundane of everyday life. What she would have for dinner. If she had time for a manicure. Wondering what to wear. She had a future and dreams and people who loved her. People she loved in return. Who saw fit to take all of that away?

Every light in the room burns, illuminating a still-macabre scene. As usual, the CSU left behind quite a mess. Many of the surfaces are covered with fingerprint powder. Drawers have been left open or pulled out and set on the floor. The bedsheets are gone. Bloodstains on the mattress and the single remaining pillow. Several squares have been cut out of the carpet and removed, likely to retrieve blood evidence. One of the curtains has been removed, probably for the same reason.

I think about Rachael as I enter the room. I take in the carnage and try to imagine a scene I don't want in my head. Rachael Schwartz may have been raised Amish, but she'd been English long enough to be well versed in the ways of the world. Not the kind of woman who would leave her door unlocked at night, even in a town like Painters Mill. More than likely, a knock sounded, after hours. Had she been sleeping? Surfing the internet on her cell? I look at the door, spot the peephole. Did she make use of it? Recognize the person on the other side? Or was she half asleep and simply opened the door?

I walk to the bathroom and look around. A high-tech curling iron sits on the counter. Her blow dryer. Her overnight case and handbag were transported to the lab to be gone through. Eventually, all of it will be released to her family. I leave the bathroom and cross to the bed. A small square of material has been cut out of the mattress. The hole is surrounded by blood that's soaked into the fabric. More blood on the wall, small droplets the color of red brick.

From all indications, Rachael was in bed and heard a knock at the door. She got up to answer. She greeted him. Words were exchanged.

An argument? She turned away, and he struck her from behind. Midway to the night table, she fell as her killer struck her repeatedly in a frenzied, violent attack. She made it to the night table. Scrambled across the bed. Fell to the floor on the other side. Tried to crawl to the door. But the assault kept coming. . . .

"You knew him, didn't you?" I whisper.

She'd fought her attacker. Fought for her life. I think about the position of her body. Facing the door. Arm outstretched, fingers clutching. And I suspect in the final minutes of her life, she'd known her life was going to end.

"Why did he do this to you?" I say aloud.

The only answer is the buzzing of the lamp and the strum of a hundred more unanswered questions running through my brain.

It's ten P.M. when I pull out of the gravel lot of the Willowdell Motel and head toward home. I'm beyond tired, in need of a shower and food and a few hours of sleep. With a killer on the loose and the unanswered questions coming at me like rapid fire, I don't think I'll get much in the way of shut-eye.

Why was Rachael Schwartz in Painters Mill? According to the people who knew her—Loretta Bontrager and her parents—she hadn't been back in months. No one knew she was in town. Who was she here to see? I think about the note with the scrawled address in her car. The farm where Tomasetti and I live is just south of Wooster. Too wired to sleep, I figure my time might be better spent stopping by the bar to see if anyone remembers seeing Rachael Schwartz. I drive past the township road that will take me home and continue north on Ohio 83. On the outskirts of Wooster, I pull over at Fisher Auditorium, punch the address into my GPS, and I head that way.

The Pub is located on the northwest side of town. It's a freestanding redbrick building set in a gravel lot littered with potholes and mud puddles. The no-name gas station next door is brightly lit, its green and white neon sign touting cigarettes, beer, and diesel. Farther down the street, the railroad-crossing lights flash red, the arms coming down to block traffic. It's prime time for a semirural dive bar like this one, but there are only four vehicles in the lot. I drive around to the rear. A Ford Escort is parked a few yards from the door. A blue dumpster sits at a cockeyed angle in the side lot, trash bags overflowing, a couple of cats scrounging for food.

I idle back around to the front lot and park next to an older F-150. The distant whistle of the train sounds as I head toward the front door.

There are two kinds of bars, in my mind. There's the kind where a police uniform will garner you a free cup of coffee and, if you're lucky, a burger. And then there's the kind where the sight of a cop clears the room. I know the instant I walk in that this one falls into the former group.

An old Traffic song "The Low Spark of High Heeled Boys" thrums from sleek speakers mounted on the beadboard ceiling. Two men in coveralls and caps sit at the bar, beer mugs sweating in front of them. Neither of them pays me any heed when I pass. A third man with a beard and camo jacket sits alone at the end of the bar, watching the Cavaliers trounce the Golden State Warriors on a TV mounted on the wall. Two women wearing tight jeans and equally tight shirts alternate between checking their phones and shooting pool. The bartender is a burly man in his forties, checked shirt with sleeves rolled up to his elbows, white apron tied at his waist, hair pulled into a ponytail at his nape. His eyes latch on to mine as I sidle up to the bar.

"What can I get you?" he asks.

"You have any decaf made?" I ask.

"Naw," he says. "Got a Keurig in the back, though. Makes a pretty decent cup. Cream? Sugar?"

"Black," I tell him. "Thanks."

He returns a short while later, cup and saucer in hand. "We don't get too many cops in here. They prefer the sports bar down on the south side." He tilts his head, reading the emblem on my uniform jacket. "You're a ways from home."

I pick up the coffee and sip. It's strong with a nice kick of bitter. "Good coffee."

"I like it."

I introduce myself. His name is Jack Boucher. He's owned the place for nine months. Turned his first profit last week.

"I'm working on a case." I pull the photo of Rachael Schwartz from my pocket and set it on the bar between us. "Have you seen her?"

He pulls reading glasses from his shirt pocket and squints at the photo. "She missing or something?"

"Actually, this is a murder investigation."

"Holy shit. Wow." He looks harder at the photo. "Pretty girl. Kind of classy looking." He shakes his head. "She ain't been in here that I know of. I would have remembered her."

He's still looking at the photo, so I leave it on the bar top. "Is it possible she came in when you were off?"

"I'm here seven days a week. Came in early for the lunch shift a couple times, so I could have missed her, if she came in later."

"Anyone else here I can talk to?" I ask.

"I got a gal bartends nights when I'm not here," he tells me. "Got a part-time cook, too. They both went home a couple hours ago."

"Will they be here tomorrow?"

"Dixie comes in around eleven. She's my cook. Rona, my bartender, gets here about four o'clock."

I nod. "You got a business card?"

"Yup." He snags a napkin off the bar and a pen from his breast pocket. "Right here." Grinning, he jots a number. "That's the landline. Whoever's running the place will pick up."

I take another sip of coffee. "You guys have security cameras?"

"I got one on the rear door. We were broken into a couple months ago." He shakes his head. "Damn camera's on the fritz, though."

I look around at the patrons. "Are any of these folks regulars?"

"Most of them are in here just about every night," he tells me. " 'Cept them girls playing pool. We get a regular lunch rush, too. People who work in the area mostly. You're more than welcome to talk to anyone you want."

"If you remember anything about this woman, will you give me a call?" I hand him my card.

"You know it."

I pick up the photo. "Thanks for the coffee."

"Good luck with your case, Chief Burkholder. I hope you find the cretin that done it."

CHAPTER 11

The nights tormented him. The endless hours of darkness and sleep-lessness, when the not-knowing and the fear were a cancer eating him from the inside out and he could do nothing but ponder what he now knew was inevitable. It was no longer a matter of if he would be found out, but when, by whom, and how much it would cost him. Worst of all, there wasn't a damn thing he could do to stop it.

And so tonight, like the night before and the one before that, he sat at the desk in his dimly lit office and worked through every possible scenario. He thought about everything that had happened. Everything he'd done—both past and present. Most of all he thought about what he *hadn't* done, and he wondered if it was too late to remedy any of it now.

Rachael Schwartz had destroyed a lot of lives in the short time she'd been on this earth. She was a user and a taker with a streak of nasty that ran right down the center of her back. She loved herself above all else and had no compunction about slicing the throat of anyone who crossed her. And then she'd laugh as she watched them bleed out.

How ironic that she would ruin his life after she was dead.

He hadn't spared her so much as a passing thought in over a decade. Then out of the blue came the phone call that brought all of those old mistakes rushing back. *I have proof,* she'd claimed. With a few words, she took his carefully constructed life apart, left it in pieces at his feet. After all this time, she wanted a piece of him. She wanted what she believed was rightfully hers and goddamn anyone who got in her way, including him. Especially him. She'd threatened his marriage. His career. The well-being of his children. Any semblance of a future. Probably even his freedom. She did all of it with a vicious glee and a cold proficiency the years had honed to a razor's edge.

Now she was gone. He should be relieved, her memory nothing more than a black stain on his past. But he knew this wasn't over. In fact, the nightmare was just beginning and he was right in the center of it. How many people had she confided in over the years? Who else could potentially come forward? Had she been bluffing when she bragged about having put together some kind of "insurance policy" in case something happened to her? Even dead, the rotten bitch would see to it that he paid a price for what he'd done.

He wished to God he'd never laid eyes on her.

He'd never been the type of man to sit on the sidelines and let things play out, especially when there was so much at stake. There wasn't much he could do to save himself. The time for damage control had long since passed. Soon, the wolves would be scratching at the door. It was only a matter of time before they got in and tore him to shreds.

Cursing beneath his breath, he picked up the tumbler of bourbon, swirled the ice, and he sipped. He thought about his life. How far he'd come. The things he'd accomplished. And he knew there was one thing he had going for him. The only thing that might keep the wolves at bay. Rachael Schwartz had deserved her fate—and he wasn't the only one who thought so. She had a pattern of fucking people over, using people, abusing her friendships. People like her made a lot of enemies—and he sure as hell wasn't the only one who'd benefited from her death. All he had to do was find them. Work them into the equation. At the very least, it would take some of the pressure off of him. Buy him some time. It was a starting point, anyway.

God only knew where it would go from there.

He was not going down for what he'd done. He sure as hell wasn't going down for something he *didn't* do. If that meant finding a scapegoat, then so be it. It wouldn't be the first time and it probably wouldn't be the last.

Holding that thought, he turned off the lamp, rose from the desk, and headed for the door.

CHAPTER 12

Day 2

The one thing that's always in short supply in the course of a homicide investigation is sleep. Not because there's too much to do or too many things happening at once, but because any cop worth his salt knows how crucial those first forty-eight hours are in terms of a solve. The truth of the matter is nothing happens fast when you're running against the clock. As Tomasetti is so fond of saying, "Hurry up and wait."

After leaving the bar last night, I couldn't sleep and spent the wee hours reading *AMISH NIGHTMARE: How I Escaped the Clutches of Righteousness*. I read with the goal of extracting some theory or motive or person of interest, but the tome was mostly sensationalistic bullshit. The one name that *did* rise above the rest was Amos Gingerich, the so called "bishop" of the Killbuck Amish. I don't know if the conflict that was detailed in the book is fact or fiction, but at the very least, I need to pay Gingerich a visit.

It was after three AM when I finished and, even then, I couldn't stop thinking about the case. I'm a seasoned cop; I've seen more than my share of violent crimes. The brutality of this one makes me shiver. Who hated Rachael Schwartz enough to beat her to death with such viciousness that bones were broken and her eye was dislodged from its socket? And why?

For every question answered, a dozen more emerge. One question rises above the rest. No one could tell me why she was in Painters Mill. Her parents didn't know. Loretta Bontrager didn't know. Neither did her business partner and self-proclaimed best friend.

Someone knew.

Rachael Schwartz was just thirty years old. She was a daughter. A best friend. A businesswoman. A lover. She made people laugh. Made them cry. From all indications, she made them angry, too. According to the people closest to her, she was a firebrand with a vindictive streak and thrived on making waves. Somewhere along the line, did she overstep some boundary that sent someone over the edge?

I think about my own knowledge of her. While that connection gives me some insight into her life, it's a little too close for comfort—and could lead me astray if I'm not careful. I knew her at a time in my life when I, too, was disgruntled with the Amish. I secretly admired that outspoken little tomboy. As much as I don't want to admit it, I cared for her because I understood a part of her others did not.

The mores an Amish person lives by are deeply ingrained at a young age. Close to eighty percent of Amish youths join the church after *rumspringa*. The vast majority never leave. One of the main differences between Rachael and me is that I left the fold of my own accord. Rachael Schwartz was ousted. And for the first time I realize I don't know exactly why.

It doesn't seem likely that there's an Amish connection to the murder. They are a pacifistic society, after all, and the way Rachael Schwartz was killed was incredibly violent. That said, the Amish are also human—prone to all the same weaknesses and frailties as the rest of us—so I make a mental note to find out why Rachael was excommunicated and who was involved.

The first hints of sunrise tinge the eastern sky purple as I leave the farm. I call Tomasetti as I make the turn onto Ohio 83 and head south.

"How did things go with Moskowski?" I ask.

"Cleveland PD detained him until I arrived. He claims he was home the night of the murder. Alone."

"No alibi," I murmur.

"None."

"What's your impression?"

"He's a slick son of a bitch. A player. Kept his cool with just the right amount of indignation that a bunch of dumb cops could pick him up and hold him against his will."

"How did he react to news of her death?"

"He seemed shocked. Interestingly, he didn't seem too broken up about the murder of a woman he claims to love. That said, he asked all the right questions, but then he's no dummy. He lawyered up."

"Of course he did," I mutter. "Do you know anything about the domestic she was arrested for? According to LEADS he was the RP."

"According to the report, Schwartz was highly intoxicated and slapped Moskowski in the course of an argument. He called the cops. She was arrested, spent the night in jail, but the charge was later dropped."

"Any idea what the argument was about?"

"Moskowski says she accused him of sleeping with someone else. He claims Schwartz was jealous and said it was a pattern with her." He rattles off a name I don't recognize. "The alleged other woman lives here in Cleveland, so I'm on my way to talk to her now. See if everything checks out."

"Did you find anything of interest at Schwartz's residence?" I ask.

"We got her laptop. A couple of boxes of paperwork. Some correspondence. We're going through all of it now." A thoughtful pause and then, "I did a cursory look through some of it. Interestingly, there were some letters from Amos Gingerich. Evidently, he wasn't happy with the tell-all she published."

"Did he threaten her?"

"Veiled. Talked a lot about martyrs."

I recall my conversation with Loretta Bontrager and her comments about Gingerich and *Martyrs Mirror*. "Can you send me copies of the letters?"

"I'll do it." He pauses. "One more thing that may or may not be related to any of this. It appears Rachael Schwartz and Andrea Matson lived above their means. I checked the books on the restaurant they own, and they barely make a profit. And yet they live in one of the most exclusive neighborhoods in the city."

"So where are they getting their money?"

"Still digging," he says. "Anything new on your end?"

"Spinning my wheels mostly."

"It's still early."

I smile, missing him. "Do me a favor and don't stay away too long."

"Bet on it."

The police station is usually quiet at this hour. This morning, with a homicide investigation spooling and the grapevine on fire, my entire team of officers has already arrived for the day. I walk in to find Mona standing at her desk, headset clamped over hair that's slightly wild, the switchboard ringing off the hook. Next to her, my first-shift dispatcher,

Lois, has the handset at the crook of her neck and waves a stack of pink message slips at me.

I grin at both of them. "Morning."

Both women mouth a reply, listening to their callers.

"Briefing in ten," I tell them. "Round everyone up."

Lois gives me a thumbs-up.

At the coffee station, I upend the biggest cup I can find, pour to the brim, and flip through messages. Tom Skanks, owner of the Butterhorn Bakery down the street, wants to know if there's a serial killer on the loose in Painters Mill. Town councilwoman Janine Fourman reminds me that a violent murder in Painters Mill will adversely affect tourism, not just the shops but the restaurants and B and Bs. She suggests I immediately request assistance from a larger, more proficient law enforcement agency to assure this crime gets the expertise it deserves.

I sigh as I head to my office. I'm going through my notes, struggling to read my own handwriting, when Mona appears in the doorway. "Everyone's RTG, Chief." Ready to go.

A couple of years ago, it wouldn't have been unusual to see her in a bustier and short skirt, purple streak in her hair, and still smelling of cigarette smoke from the night before. She's come a long way since those days. Though she worked through the night, she's in full uniform this morning. Hair pulled back. Minimal makeup. She looks like a cop. Unlike me, she's brimming with energy.

Feeling . . . old, I set down my cup. "You got time to sit in?"

She grins. "That's affirm."

Grabbing my notes, I round my desk, and we head toward the "war room," which is basically a storage-closet-turned-meeting-room—design compliments of Mona. I take in each member of my small police force as I stride to the half podium set up at the end of the table. Rupert "Glock" Maddox sits next to it, a spiral-bound pad and a pen on the tabletop in front of him. He's a former marine, a Little League coach, a father of three, and the first African American to grace the ranks of the department.

Next to him, Roland "Pickles" Shumaker nurses a to-go cup of coffee from LaDonna's Diner. I catch a whiff of cigarette smoke and English Leather as I pass. He may be down to working just ten hours a week—which entails crosswalk duty at the elementary school—but his uniform is creased, his hair and goatee are colored a not-so-natural hue of brown, and his trademark Lucchese boots are polished to a mirror sheen. Pickles might be an old-timer, but I've seen his file—all sixty pages of it—and I know he earned every "above the call of duty" and "risked his own life" comment, and then some. He spent years working undercover narcotics and made one of the biggest busts in the history of Holmes County.

Chuck "Skid" Skidmore sits across from Pickles looking a little rough around the edges. He's our resident jokester, and eschews early mornings, which is why he prefers second shift. I hired him shortly after becoming chief. He'd been terminated from the Ann Arbor PD for drinking on the job. But I liked him; I thought he deserved a second chance, so I hired him with the caveat that if I ever caught him drinking while on duty he would be out the door. He's never let me, or himself, down.

T.J. Banks had always been the departmental rookie—until I promoted Mona. At twenty-eight years of age, he's serious about his job, doesn't mind working graveyard, and is the first to volunteer for overtime. Baby-faced and charming, he's invariably in the process of landing a new girlfriend or breaking up with his current squeeze.

Mona sits next to T.J., looking at something he's showing her on his cell, probably some cop story that includes a generous amount of embellishment. She's not buying into it, but letting him have his moment. *Good girl,* I think, and I take my place at the half podium.

"As all of you know, thirty-year-old Rachael Schwartz was murdered in her room at the Willowdell Motel night before last. Our department is primary. BCI is assisting, as is the Holmes County Sheriff's Office. The killer or killers have not yet been apprehended or identified. That means mandatory OT until we make an arrest."

I glance down at my scrawled notes. "Doc Coblentz hasn't officially ruled on cause or manner, but this is an obvious homicide. NOK have been notified," I say, referring to "next of kin." "I don't have to tell any of you to not discuss this case with anyone. Refer any media inquiries to me."

I pass the folder containing the crime scene photos, reports, notes, and every scrap of information I've amassed so far to Glock so he can take a look and pass it on.

"From all indications, the victim was beaten to death," I tell him. "The murder weapon was not found. We're not making that public. The coroner wouldn't commit, but we're likely talking about piece of pipe or club, or some other heavy, blunt object."

I look at Skid. "I want you and T.J. to drive back out to the motel and continue our search for the murder weapon. Expand our original search area. We looked yesterday, but had to quit when it got dark. Check the ditches on either side of the road, woods, fields, walk it all the way to the highway. Check any dumpsters in the area. There's a service station down the road. If they've got security cams, get me the video."

Skid casts a half smile at T.J. "I guess we won't have to go to the gym this week," he says.

"You're welcome," I tell him, and turn my attention to Glock and

Pickles. "I want you guys to reinterview everyone who was staying at or visiting the Willowdell Motel the twenty-four hours before and after the murder. There was one person who checked out before we arrived. Find them and talk to them."

Nodding, Pickles hitches up his belt, his chest puffed out. "We're on it."

I glance at Mona. "I want you to look at Rachael Schwartz's social media accounts. I skimmed some of them last night and she's active and controversial. Twitter. Facebook. Instagram. See if she had any ongoing feuds or disagreements. Anything that catches your eye, let me know and we'll follow up."

She gives me a two-finger salute.

"Lois." I look up at my dispatcher, who's standing in the doorway, headset on, listening for incoming calls. "I want a hotline set up. Five-hundred-dollar reward for information. I emailed you a press-release draft. Give me a quick edit, if you would." I smile. "And get it out to local media. Steve Ressler at *The Advocate*. Millersburg. Wooster. Radio station down in Dover."

"Got it," she says, scribbling.

I'm not sure where the reward money will come from. I'll figure it out if and when I need it.

"Get with the technology people that handle Painters Mill's website, too. Get the hotline number on it, front and center. Our social media accounts, too."

"Yep."

I look out at my team. "We're already getting calls. Residents are anxious. Make yourselves visible around town when you can, do your best to reassure folks."

"Tell Tom Skanks free apple fritters and coffee would go a long way to keep us first responders on our toes," Skid mutters.

"Don't forget that new place," Glock adds.

"Mocha Joe's," T.J. tells them, referring to a nice little upscale coffeehouse in town.

I try not to smile, but I don't quite manage. "I'll see what I can do."

My cell phone vibrates against my hip. I glance down to see HOLMES CNTY CORONER pop up on the display. I look out at my team. "My cell is on twenty-four seven," I tell them. "Day and night. Let's go to work."

CHAPTER 13

Loretta Bontrager couldn't remember the last time she was so excited. Seeing a new baby for the first time was a happy occasion. It was one of the joys of being Amish, especially for the women. She'd known Mary Sue Miller most of her life. They'd gone to school together, played hide-and-seek in Amos Yoder's cornfield as kids, been baptized at about the same time, and were married within weeks of each other. This was Mary's fourth child. Baby Perry had been born just a few days ago and Mary was finally rested up enough to share him with the community.

Children were a gift from God. Loretta couldn't wait to cuddle him. What a joy it was to hold a new baby. Like her *mamm* always said: Children are the only treasure you can take to heaven.

Though Loretta was genuinely happy for her friend and anxious to meet the newest member of the family, the occasion was marred by the death of Rachael Schwartz. Loretta simply couldn't stop thinking about her. She hadn't been able to eat or sleep. She'd been living in a fog since it happened and that wasn't the worst of it. At night, and despite her fervent prayers at bedtime, the nightmares came for her. Dark images that left her gasping and tearful, her heart filled with grief.

Loretta had been closer to Rachael than she was to her own sister. She'd broken the rules herself to stay in touch with Rachael after she'd left. Truth be told, Loretta had always worried about her. The way she lived her life. Her lack of faith. She knew things about Rachael. Things that scared her—even now. She'd prayed for her friend's well-being. Her happiness. Most of all, she prayed for her soul.

Now that Rachael was gone, Loretta worried not only about the horror of her death and the fate of her soul, but the secrets Rachael had taken with her to her grave.

"Mamm, I bumped the *bott boi* and a piece of crust broke off the side." Potpie.

At the sound of her daughter's voice, Loretta glanced over from her driving. Even embroiled in dark thoughts she had no business thinking on such a pretty spring morning, she smiled at the sight of her sweet face. "Let me see," she said.

Fannie lifted the foil covering and pointed. Sure enough, a chunk of the lard crust had chipped off the side of one of the sausage and potato pot pies she'd made a little before five A.M.

"Looks like a little mouse sampled a piece of that crust," Loretta said.

Fannie grinned. "It wasn't me."

"Well, in that case just press it back together," Loretta told her. "No one at Mary's house will even notice."

They were in the buggy and traveling at a good clip down the township road. Around them, the pastures were astoundingly green, the trees in the woods bursting into bud, and the entire countryside was rife with birdsong. After such a long and cold winter, Loretta appreciated the gentle day.

She glanced away from her driving. A smile touched her mouth as she watched the girl press the wayward piece of crust back into place. "If we had some milk, we could glue it," Loretta told her.

She was probably taking too much food over to Mary and her family. But having a baby was a busy and exhausting time. And Loretta loved them so much. She was hoping to help with a chore or two while she was there, if Mary would allow it.

She was so enmeshed in her thoughts, Loretta didn't notice the car blocking the road until she was nearly upon it.

"Whoa!" she called to the horse.

The animal stopped so abruptly its steel shoes slid on the asphalt.

"Mamm?"

Loretta felt her daughter's questioning gaze on her as she backed the horse up a couple of steps. She watched the driver's-side door open. Her heart sank when he stepped out. She sat stone-still, the leather lines taut in her hands.

Taking his time, the man started toward them.

"Tuck that foil back around the *bott boi*," she said to Fannie, more to keep her occupied than because the potpie needed covering.

"Nice morning for a buggy ride," the *Englischer* said as he reached them.

Loretta said nothing. She could barely bring herself to look at him. Or breathe. She knew what he'd see in her eyes if she did. Fear. Knowledge. Secrets. She'd seen him around town dozens of times over the years, and she cringed every time. She knew it was wrong to have such thoughts, but she didn't like him.

She knew things about this man. Things she didn't want to know. She had no idea if he remembered her. If he knew she and Rachael had been friends. Regardless, she went out of her way to avoid him.

"Hi there, young lady," he said to Fannie.

The sight of him looking at her daughter unnerved Loretta. Before she could react, he reached into his pocket and withdrew a package of chocolate-covered peanuts. The kind you could buy at the grocery-store checkout. He extended his hand and offered it to the girl. "You like chocolate?" he asked. "These are my favorite."

Fannie nodded, her hand going up to take the candy. Quickly, Loretta snatched up the potpie, shoved it into her daughter's hands. "Take this and put it in the back seat," she said in *Deitsch*. "We don't want to lose any more of that delicious crust now, do we?"

Curious about the *Englischer,* the girl hesitated before taking the pie.

Loretta gave her a helpful little push. "Go on now. Get back there. Make sure the foil stays on that casserole, too. Hold it on your lap so it doesn't bounce around too much."

As the girl climbed into the back seat with the pie, Loretta forced her gaze to the man standing next to the buggy, trying in vain to ignore the chill lodged in her spine.

"What do you want?" she asked.

"Cute kid." He watched Fannie settle onto the back seat. "Going to be pretty when she grows up," he said. "Like you."

Loretta looked down at her hands, tried not to notice they were shaking, and loosened her grip on the leather lines.

"Kids are innocent when they're that age," he drawled. "What is she? Ten? Twelve?" When she didn't respond, he continued. "I got four at home. Two boys. Two girls. And another on the way. Boy do they keep me and my wife busy." He shrugged. "Childhood is an important time. For Amish kids, too, huh?"

She said nothing.

He continued as if he didn't expect a response. "You never want anything bad to happen to them when they're that age. Scars, you know. The girls especially. I think little girls need their moms even more than the boys, you know?"

"All children need their parents," she said, hating it that her voice was shaking, the words little more than a whisper. That he had the power to frighten her—that there wasn't anything she could do about it—disturbed her so much she could scarcely breathe.

"All I'm saying is that kids are a lot less likely to have trouble in their lives if their parents are around to raise them. You know, to guide them through their teen years and all."

Loretta didn't know what to say to that. He was talking in riddles and she wasn't sure what he meant or where the conversation was heading. All she knew was that she didn't want to talk to him. He hadn't threatened her, but the way he looked at her, the things he said, the way he said them, terrified her. She didn't want him to talk about her daughter. She didn't want Fannie exposed to him. She didn't feel safe on this back road alone with him.

She picked up the leather lines. "I have to go."

"Reason I stopped you." He leaned slightly closer. "Did you hear about what happened to your old friend?"

Loretta clucked and jiggled the lines to move the horse forward, but he grabbed the leather and held them taut so the horse remained stopped. "The one used to be Amish. The blonde. What was her name? Rachael?" He nodded. "Yeah, Rachael Schwartz. The pretty one."

She closed her eyes. She didn't want to think about Rachael or what had happened to her. She sure didn't want to discuss it with this pig of a man. "I don't want to talk about it. Not to you."

He turned his head, his eyes scanning the road behind her and in front of the buggy. She stared at his profile, seeing the muscles in his jaw work. Anger, she thought, and another layer of fear settled over her. When his eyes landed on hers, the light in them startled her.

"I heard she told some lies about me," he said. "Maybe she told you."

"I don't know what you're talking about."

"Well, in that case, why don't I bring you up to speed?" He leaned closer. "Whatever she said, it ain't true. Nothing happened. Do you understand?"

She stared at him, unable to speak, barely able to manage a jerk of her head.

"If you're smart." He lowered his voice to a hoarse whisper. "If you care about that pretty little girl in the back seat, you'll keep your goddamn mouth shut. Do you understand me?"

She swallowed, jerked her head. "I don't know anything."

"Your friend was a liar," he said. "She made things up. Ugly things that weren't true. We both know that, right? Everyone in this town knows it. Even the Amish know it, for God's sake. Whatever she told you is a damn lie. You need to forget it. Put it out of your head. You got that?"

Her heart pounded so hard she could barely hear his voice over the roar. Her throat was tight and so dry she almost couldn't get the words out. "She didn't tell me anything."

"I didn't think so." His eyes drifted to the girl in the back seat, then back to hers. "I'd hate to see something bad happen to you or, God forbid, your kid."

"Please," Loretta whispered.

Grinning, he released the lines and stepped away from the buggy. "You ladies be careful out there."

Loretta's hands were shaking so violently, she could barely snap the lines. "*Kumma druff!*" Come on now.

The horse startled and launched into a trot.

Loretta felt his eyes on her as she maneuvered the horse around his vehicle. She didn't dare look at him as she passed him, but she felt the threat.

CHAPTER 14

It's ten A.M. when I park outside the emergency room portico of Pomerene Hospital in Millersburg and take the sidewalk to the double glass doors. The volunteer at the reception desk waves as I cross to the elevator and punch the button. I return the greeting, but my smile feels grim. When the doors swish closed, I slide the tube of Blistex from my pocket and smear a dollop beneath my nose. By the time the doors open, I'm shored up and ready to face what comes next.

The reception area is nicely furnished with light blue walls, gray carpet, a pretty cherrywood desk, and a scattering of brightly patterned chairs.

"Hi, Chief Burkholder."

Carmen Anderson has worked in an administrative capacity for Doc Coblentz for several years now. She's professional, good at what she does, and cheerful despite the fact that she spends much of her day in such close proximity to the dead. This morning, she's wearing a floral wraparound dress with a red belt, black blazer, and not-quite-sensible pumps.

"Hi." I stop at her desk and sign in. "You know you're one of the best-dressed women in Painters Mill, right?"

Her smile is dazzling. "Why thank you, Chief." She chuckles. "I don't get many compliments down here."

We share a laugh as I set down the pen. "Doc in?"

"He's expecting you." She stands and motions toward the doors at the end of the hall marked MORGUE AUTHORIZED PERSONNEL.

I don't let myself think about my purpose here, focusing instead on the questions roiling in my head as I tread down the hall and push open the door. The autopsy room is straight ahead, along with the alcove where the biohazard supplies are stored for visiting officials. To my left, I see Doc Coblentz's glassed-in office. The miniblinds are open. The doctor is sitting at his cherrywood desk, a wrapper containing what looks like the remains of a fast-food breakfast on the blotter in front of him next to a to-go cup of coffee.

I've known Doc since becoming chief. He's one of five doctors in Painters Mill, and assumes the responsibilities of coroner on an as-needed basis, which isn't often. On those occasions when he *is* called upon, he tackles his duty with compassion and professionalism. His is a tough position fraught with high emotion and a drop-everything-and-get-it-done timeline. There's no room for error—and invariably some cop or lab hounding him for results. Doc's a laid-back individual with an inhuman work ethic and the curiosity of a scientist, both of which make him very good at what he does. Somehow, he manages to remain an optimist.

Setting down the coffee cup, he looks at me over the rims of his glasses. "I know you're in a hurry to get to the bottom of what happened to that young woman, so I cleared my schedule. I'm planning to do the autopsy this morning."

"Time and manner would be a big help," I tell him.

"Figured as much. I've got some preliminary observations you might find useful." Rising, he motions toward the alcove outside his office. "Shall we?"

I go to the alcove where Carmen has laid out an individually wrapped gown, disposable shoe covers, hair cap, face mask, and gloves. Doc waits in the hall while I gear up.

"You guys have any leads?" he asks.

"Not yet." I slide the covers over my shoes, tie the gown strings haphazardly, and step into the hall.

"You knew the victim?" Doc says.

I wonder how he knows that, if he heard it from someone or if I gave him some indication while we were at the scene yesterday. "Years ago." I say the words with calculated detachment, but I don't meet his gaze. I remind myself that this is not about me or my emotions. This is about Rachael Schwartz, the family that mourns her, the community that will bear the scar of her death, and the bastard who killed her.

"Tough when it hits close to home," he says.

"She was Amish," I say, keeping my answer as vague and impersonal as possible.

He makes a sound of understanding. "You make the notification?"

I nod, thinking of Rhoda and Dan, and I do my best to ignore the knot of discomfort that's tight and hard in my gut.

"A lot of people wonder how I do what I do. You know, autopsies and the like, dealing with the dead. Most are too polite to ask, but I see the questions. The truth of the matter is it's not as difficult as they think. It's not the dead who hurt. Their suffering is done."

I finally meet his gaze. "I guess we, the living, have the market cornered on that, don't we?"

His mouth pulls into a smile. "Precisely." He motions toward the double doors at the end of the hall. "Let's see what we can do to set you on track to get some justice for this young woman."

I'm aware of the buzz of the lights as I take the hall toward the doors. The only sound comes from the rustle of our protective clothing, the voice in my head telling me I'm a fool for being here when I could be knocking on doors and doing my job. But this is part of it and I've no intention of not following through. Not now. Not the next time or the next. Macabre as this pilgrimage is, it is my ritual. For better or worse, it is my introduction to the victim. I need to see her not as the girl I'd once known, but the woman whose life was cut short. It brings me one step closer to knowing her. Understanding what happened to her. It is my burden to bear. My tribute to the victim. To the family. If I'm lucky, it will bring me one step closer to getting inside the mind of a killer.

The autopsy room is too bright, the lights buzzing. Floor-to-ceiling subway tile covers the walls. Ahead, a stainless-steel gurney is draped with a sheet.

"I did a preliminary exam and went over every inch of her with a fine-tooth comb. I took samples and scrapings, took the requisite photos. Pulled blood and urine for a full tox screen. We couriered everything to the police lab in London, including the clothes she was wearing at the time of her death. This morning, my technician cleaned her up. For obvious reasons, I took a CT scan and X-rays." The doctor sighs. "I've seen a lot of injuries, a lot of deaths. Motor vehicle accidents. Farming mishaps. You name it. This woman suffered a tremendous amount of physical injury."

I resist the urge to shudder. "Says something about the killer," I say.

"That's your forte, not mine. Thank God for that." He shuffles to a clipboard hanging on the wall, flips the page, makes a note. "The victim arrived here at the morgue at four twelve P.M. Core body temperature was taken at four forty-six." He flips another page and frowns, mumbling. "Heat is lost at about one point five degrees per hour. Liver temp was seventy-seven point six." He turns to me. "My best estimation is that she died sometime between one and three A.M."

He rehangs the clipboard and crosses to me, looks at me over the tops of his bifocals. I look back, trying not to acknowledge the compassion I see in his eyes, not only for the woman lying on the gurney, but for me.

"You sure you're up to this?" he asks.

"You know I'm not going to give you a straight answer, right?"

His smile is subdued. "If it makes you feel any better, your aversion to all of this isn't necessarily a bad thing. Means you're human."

He peels away the sheet cover.

For an instant, I struggle to make sense of what I'm seeing. Too many stimuli hit my brain at once. I see white skin marred with the blue-black bruising of livor mortis. Breasts drooping to each side of a rib cage that isn't quite symmetrical. Hip bones and a flat belly with the silver pinpoint of a piercing at the navel. The dark triangle of hair at her pubis. Bare feet that are somehow undamaged. It's the pink polish on the toenails that turns me inside out and rouses the stir of outrage. And for the hundredth time I'm reminded that just a day and a half ago this young woman cared about such trivial, everyday things as a pedicure. She painted her nails and put on makeup. She went shopping and combed her hair. She laughed and breathed and touched the lives of the people around her. I take all of it in, the broken heap of what's left, and for an instant I'm frightened in some base and primal way.

A paper sheet covers the victim's head, a quarter-size stain of watery pink blood warning me that I don't want the doc to pull it away. The ends of damp blond hair stick to the stainless steel.

Then my cop's brain clicks into gear; the questions begin to boil, part habit, partly the side of me that wants to catch the sick fucker that did this to her. "Cause of death?"

"Preliminarily speaking, she likely died of nonpenetrating trauma. Of course, I won't officially rule on cause or manner until I've completed the autopsy." He shakes his head. "To be perfectly honest, Kate, the injuries are simply too numerous to quantify. Several of these injuries could have been fatal on their own. All of that said, I do have some specifics and the postmortem CT scan will help us break it down."

Reaching up, he angles the reflective overhead light. I'm aware of my heart thrumming against my ribs. The heat of the light. The hum of something unseen on the other side of the room.

Doc Coblentz pulls away the paper covering the victim's head. I see damp blond hair. The gaping red mouth of a scalp wound. A forehead that's been laid open to the bone. A cheek that's caved in. Her left eye bulges from its socket, unseeing and dull. Mouth open, tongue bulging. Front teeth missing. Her chin is simply . . . gone.

Something unpleasant jumps in my chest. I think of the little girl I used to babysit. The one that was loud and bold and challenged my authority. The one that liked to run and laugh and pick on the other kids . . .

"In looking at the CT scan," the doc begins, "I counted six impact sites on the skull alone. There are multiple cranial-bone fractures. Fracture of the occipital bone. Subdural and subarachnoid hemorrhages. The areas affected include the frontal, parietal, and temporal regions."

"Do you have any idea what the murder weapon was?" I ask.

He shakes his head. "I may be able to come up with a theory once

I'm able to look at the CT scan and take some measurements. If we're lucky, the scrapings I sent to the lab will come back with some foreign material that will tell us. Something like a flake of rust from a steel pipe. Wood splinters from a club or board. Something like that. At this point, I do not know."

I'm looking at the doc. He's staring back at me, uncertain, waiting. I force my eyes back to the victim. Calmer, I start to notice details I missed at first glance. Her right hand is purple. Her fingers twisted into unnatural shapes. The right side of her rib cage is misshapen, the ribs obviously broken.

"What about the rest of her?" I ask.

"Whoever did this struck her with indiscriminate brutality. Head. Body. Whatever he could reach. It was likely a frenzied attack." Using a swab, he indicates the swollen hand. "The middle phalanx on the right hand is fractured. Probably a defensive wound."

"She tried to protect herself," I say.

He nods. "Ulna is fractured." He shifts the swab from her forearm to her shoulder. "Clavicular fracture. Sternal fracture. Scapular fracture. Ribs four through six are fractured. There are likely internal injuries of the lateral thoracic walls and posterior thorax as well."

"Was there any indication of sexual assault?" I ask.

"There's no trauma, but as a manner of routine I took vaginal and anal swabs which will tell us if there's semen present."

I nod, trying not to look at what remains of Rachael Schwartz, but unable to look away. "Did this attack require physical strength?"

"I can't answer that definitively, but if I were to venture a guess, I would say a strong person did this. The magnitude of the force was considerable."

"Was any of this done postmortem?"

"As you know, bruising ceases once the heart stops. There are at least two locations where bones were fractured and yet there was little in the way of bruising. I would venture to say the beating continued after she was deceased, at least for a short while."

After leaving the morgue, I sit in the Explorer for several minutes, gathering the frayed edges of my composure, tucking them into some semblance of order, so I can get back to work. It's not easy. When I close my eyes, I see the horrific injuries that were done to Rachael Schwartz. The gaping wounds and broken bones. In my mind's eye, I see her as a nine-year-old Amish girl who smiled because I said something inappropriate. As a kid, Rachael wasn't quite sweet. She wasn't quite innocent. Charming, but not always genuine. If you were a parent, you were never quite sure if you wanted your own children to associate with her. But she loved life. She lived it to its fullest. Maybe with a little too much gusto—and, perhaps, at the expense of others. But she deserved the chance to live her life.

My face is hot, so I lower the window and force myself to listen to the call of a blue jay in the maple tree next to the parking lot. I focus on the breeze easing into the cab. I draw a deep breath, discern the smell of fresh-cut grass. The distant bark of a dog. After a few minutes, the jittery sensation in my stomach subsides. The darkness ebbs. My hands grow steady on the steering wheel. When I close my eyes, I recall everything I know about Rachael Schwartz not with the shock of a woman who is a little too close, but with the emotional distance of a cop determined to do her job.

Putting the Explorer in gear, I pull out of my parking spot and head toward Painters Mill.

CHAPTER 15

Summer 2008

The rager was in full swing when Loretta and Rachael arrived. Loretta had never seen so many people in one place. She sure as heck had never seen so many English cars. The pasture behind the barn had been transformed into a virtual parking lot, filled with as many cars and trucks as buggies. Two young Amish hostlers were carting around buckets and soliciting tips for watering the horses.

Levi parked his own buggy behind a pickup truck with giant tires and a big chrome tailpipe. Rachael was sitting next to Levi. Loretta was sitting on the outside seat and slid from the buggy the moment it came to a stop.

"Hold up." Reaching into the back seat, Levi tore two more beers off a six-pack and handed them to Rachael, but his eyes were on Loretta. "One for the road."

Grinning, Rachael took both cans and slid from the buggy without thanking him. "We need smokes, too, Amish boy."

Mouth pulled into an assessing half smile, he fished the pack out of his pocket, tapped out two smokes, and handed them to her. "I'll meet you back here in two hours," he said.

"Three," said Rachael.

Loretta elbowed her. "Two," she whispered.

Rachael rolled her eyes. "Two and a half."

Levi regarded them, his eyes lingering on Loretta a tad too long. "Don't be late. I gotta work tomorrow."

He secured the leather lines, then slid down from the buggy. Loretta watched as he handed a five-dollar bill to one of the hostlers. Relief slipped through her when he was finally gone.

"You're frowning."

Loretta turned to see her friend come up beside her. "I don't like him."

"Oh, Levi's all right," Rachael said. "He's just . . . finding his way, I think."

"He whips his horse too much," Loretta said, motioning toward the whip sticking out of the holder attached to the buggy. "Mamm told me the way people treat God's creatures speaks to the way they deal with people."

Two English boys, cans of Budweiser in hand, walked by. One of them, a tall boy with a scraggly beard and John Deere cap, turned and walked backward, his eyes on Rachael, and whistled.

Once they'd passed, Rachael looked at Loretta and they broke into laughter.

"*Er is schnuck,*" Rachael said. He's cute.

Feeling frumpy, Loretta looked down at her dress. "I'm not sure I fit in here."

"Hmmm." Rachael studied her clothes for a moment. "I think we can fix that."

"But Mamm will—"

"Never know."

Taking Loretta's hand, Rachael led her back to the buggy and they ducked into the shadows behind it, out of sight of the crowd. "Give me your *halsduch*," she said, referring to the capelike feature draped over her dress.

"I don't see how that's going to help," Loretta said.

Rachael held out her hand. "Trust me."

Frowning, Loretta lifted the triangular piece of cloth over her head and handed it to her friend.

Rachael tossed the *halsduch* into the buggy. "Roll up your sleeves. To your elbows." As Loretta obeyed, Rachael went to the buggy and returned with a box cutter.

"What's that for?" Loretta asked.

"Hold still or I'll cut your leg off." Kneeling, she set to work at the hem. "It's going to look great. You'll see."

Loretta closed her eyes tightly as her friend sawed at the fabric. She didn't know if she was more excited—or terrified. The one thing she did know was that she was going to let her do it despite the possibility of her *mamm* finding out.

"All done."

Loretta opened her eyes and looked down at her dress, mildly shocked by the sight of her knees. "Oh."

Rachael got to her feet, looking at her friend admiringly. "One more thing." Quickly, she removed the leather belt from the waistband of her jeans and leaned close to wrap it around her friend's waist. "There. Oh, that's nice. See?"

"I feel ridiculous."

"You have great legs. For a skinny Amish girl." Grinning, Rachael kicked off her English shoes. "Let's switch. These sandals will go great with that dress. Sneakers are fine with my jeans."

Loretta toed off her plain sneakers, then slid her feet into the sandals. This time when she looked down at her clothes, she smiled. "Almost pretty."

"Told you." Rachael gave her a big, smacking kiss on the cheek.

"My knees are knobby."

"Your knees are sexy, silly girl." Rachael snapped open her beer. "Bottoms up."

Loretta drank as fast as she could, ended up choking twice. Before she was completely finished, Rachael took her can and slung both of them into the open window of a parked car.

"Come on." Laughing, Rachael took her hand. "We've got a lot of partying to do and not much time to do it."

Hand in hand, they passed a big tent where two Amish girls had set up a table draped with a red and white cloth. The handwritten sign announced HOME-CURED HAM SANDWICH WITH CHOW-CHOW $3. A few yards down, an English man had set up beer kegs on a picnic table laden with napkins and plastic cups, and a sign that read: BEER FOR A BUCK. Just past him, an Amish boy was selling cigarettes for four dollars a pack.

Rachael rushed to the beer table. "Two beers!" she said, breathless with excitement.

The man looked from Rachael to Loretta and frowned. "How old are you?"

Loretta started to speak up, but Rachael cut her off. "We're twenty-one."

He frowned, but grabbed two plastic cups and filled them with beer. "Two bucks."

There were so many stimuli coming at her from so many directions, Loretta almost couldn't take all of it in. Generators rumbled somewhere on the periphery. Bright lights shone from a dozen or so tents and food trucks. There was the din of voices and the tinkle of laughter. The bass thump of the band in the throes of some old Lynyrd Skynyrd song.

Rachael handed Loretta a plastic glass filled with beer and then raised hers. "Let's do a toast this time," she said. "To our first rager."

Feeling grown-up and sophisticated, Loretta bumped her cup against her friend's. "And good friends."

Eyes locked, they drank. Loretta only managed half her cup. Rachael finished all of hers, licked the foam from her lips, and tossed the cup over her shoulder. "I love that song! Let's go see the band."

The closer they got to the music, the more crowded it became. Along the way, they passed a pickup truck with the tailgate down. A bearded *Englischer,* wearing denim overalls and sunglasses even though it was dark, sat on a lawn chair. The sign on the truck touted SHOTS FOR $2.

Rachael's eyes widened at the sight of it. Squealing in delight, she pulled Loretta over to it and ordered. "Two shots."

"But I'm not finished with my beer," Loretta told her.

"It's called a chaser, silly girl." She laid four dollar bills on the tailgate.

"For a bunch of Bible thumpers, you Amishers sure can put away the booze." He poured from an unlabeled bottle into two clear plastic cups. "All's I got left is moonshine."

"That'll do." Rachael watched him pour.

He thrust two cups at her. "Enjoy."

Turning her back to him, Rachael handed one of the cups to Loretta and raised her own. "Cheers!"

The two girls locked elbows and drank. There wasn't much in either cup and Loretta managed it in a single gulp. The alcohol burned all the way to her stomach.

"*Fasucha vi feiyeh!*" she said, coughing. Tastes like fire!

Rachael threw her head back and laughed. "One more."

106

Before Loretta could refuse, Rachael darted back to the truck. The surly man poured again.

"Better be careful with that," he said.

Ignoring him, Rachael handed one of the cups to Loretta.

"Are you sure about this?" Loretta asked.

"Last one," Rachael assured her.

The burn engulfed Loretta's throat with such heat that her eyes watered. This time, it migrated down to her belly, and her head began to swim.

Taking her hand, Rachael led Loretta closer to the band and into the crowd. Around her, the music pulsed like a living, breathing thing. She could feel the beat of the drums all the way to her bones. The voices seemed louder, but not quite clear. The colors around her brighter. And she wondered why the drinking of alcohol was against the rules. How could something that made you feel so good, the world around you so beautiful, be such a bad thing?

Around them, everyone was dancing and laughing. Loretta looked left and saw an English girl wearing blue jeans with only a bra, holding a bottle of beer above her head, rubbing her pelvis against an Amish boy Loretta had gone to school with. The sight embarrassed her, and yet she couldn't look away. The boy was so enthralled he didn't notice her. Probably a good thing, since she wasn't supposed to be here. The last thing she needed was someone telling her parents.

A few feet away, Rachael raised her hands over her head. Hair flying, she danced to the raucous music. Loretta thought she'd never seen her friend look so beautiful. Even one of the band members had noticed and grinned down at her from the stage as his fingers ripped across the strings of his guitar. Loretta didn't know how to dance, but the rhythm made her feel in synch with the music. She raised her hands and threw back her head and, somehow, she knew the words to the song and she belted them out. She saw the guitarist looking down at her from the stage and she smiled back at him, and in that moment, she was beautiful and desired. There were no rules holding her back, and this dusty field with its brash vendors and rowdy occupiers was the only place she ever wanted to be.

"I never want to leave!" she cried to her friend.

Rachael Schwartz threw her head back and howled.

CHAPTER 16

I'm no stranger to the intricacies of a homicide investigation. Knowing the relationships of the victim, past and present, is one of the most important factors to establish. There's no doubt in my mind that Rachael Schwartz likely knew her killer. Yet when I spoke with her parents, they claimed no knowledge of discord in her life. Not because none existed, I'm sure, but because they weren't close to her. Both Loretta Bontrager and Andy Matson indicated Rachael did, indeed, contend with a fair amount of conflict. She shared a tumultuous relationship with her lover, Jared Moskowski. According to Loretta, she may have had other lovers we've not yet identified. She'd been shunned by the Amish. While I've heard rumors, I don't know exactly why. Was it due to something specific she'd done? Or the end result of years of breaking the rules? Then, of course, there is the issue of the tell-all book. No one appreciates having their dirty laundry aired for everyone to see. How much friction was there between Rachael and the Killbuck clan?

It's late morning when I pull into the gravel two-track of Bishop

David Troyer's lane. As I drive around to the back of the house, I notice the bishop's horse is hitched to the buggy, telling me he or his wife is probably getting ready to leave. I park adjacent to a beat-up shed and take the sidewalk to the back door.

Through the window, I see the bishop in the mudroom, looking at me through the glass. He's using a walker these days. And while he seems a tad smaller in stature, his belly not quite so round, he is not diminished. His presence and those all-seeing eyes invariably make me feel like I'm fourteen years old again, and put before him for breaking some rule. I was terrified of him during my formative years. Strange as it sounds—though I'm a grown woman and a cop—a smidgen of that old fear still exists.

I push open the door and lean in. "*Guder mariye,*" I tell him. Good morning.

I've known David Troyer the entirety of my life, and he looks much the same as he did when I was a kid. A head of thick gray hair generously streaked with black, blunt cut above heavy brows. A salt-and-pepper beard that reaches nearly to his waist. As usual, he's dressed in black, but for the white shirt beneath the jacket and suspenders.

"Katie Burkholder," he says in a wet-gravel voice. No smile. Just those astute eyes digging into mine. "You are here about Rachael Schwartz?"

I nod. "Do you have a few minutes, Bishop?"

"*Kumma inseid.*" Come inside. He turns and starts toward the interior of the house.

I follow him through the mudroom and into the kitchen. I wait while he maneuvers the walker to one of four chairs and settles into it. His wife, Freda, stands at the sink, washing dishes. She looks at me over her shoulder and nods a greeting that isn't quite friendly. I do the same.

"I was on my way to see Dan and Rhoda," he tells me. "This is a dark time for them."

"I won't keep you." I take the chair across from him. "I'm trying to figure out what happened to her, Bishop. I'm wondering if you have any insights into her life. Her relationships. If she was dealing with any problems. If she had any ongoing disputes or conflicts."

His eyes settle on mine, large and rheumy behind the thick lenses of his glasses. While the years may have taken a swipe at his physical body, his intellect remains sharp, his spirituality intense.

"You know I've not seen her in years," he says.

"You knew her as a child," I say. "Growing up." I pause, hold his gaze. "You know her parents. The Amish community as a whole."

"You knew her, too, no?"

"When she was a kid."

"Then even *you* know her life was filled with conflict."

He makes the statement as if it's somehow a miracle I've figured out anything about anyone, a reference no doubt to my Englishness. I absorb the jab without reacting, keep moving. "I'm looking for details," I tell him. "Names. Circumstances."

"She disobeyed her parents at a very young age. Not once, but many times. They brought her to me dozens of times. This girl child. So full of life and with eyes for all the wrong things." The old man shrugs. "Usually a good talking-to does the trick, you know." A smile plays at the corners of his mouth. "Not so for this girl. I spoke with the *Diener,*" he says, referring to the other elected officials, the deacon and two preachers. "We did what we could. We stressed the importance of the *Ordnung.*" The unwritten rules of the church district. "We reinforced the importance of *demut,* the Christian faith, the worth of separation, and the old ways." *Demut* is *Deitsch* for "humility," a cornerstone of the Amish mindset. "Katie, young Rachael *harricht gut, awwer er foligt schlecht.*" Heard well, but obeyed poorly. "Dan and Rhoda did their best to teach her *Gelassenheit.*"

The word holds myriad meanings for the Amish. Suffering. Tranquility. Surrender. He shrugs. "Even so, there was trouble. Drinking. Gallivanting around. Lying about it. Dan came to me, asked that she be baptized early. He thought it might help. She was only seventeen. I went to the *Diener.* They agreed."

I'd heard Rachael had been baptized early, without much of an opportunity to sow a few wild oats. I'd wondered why her *rumspringa* had been cut short. Now I know.

"They thought it would fix her. We thought it was worth a try. And so the summer before she was to be baptized, the ministers took her through *die gemee nooch geh.*"

Once a young Amish person has made the decision to join the church, *die gemee nooch geh* is the period of instruction in which the ministers teach the young person *wertrational,* the values and what it means to be Amish.

"Rachael went through all the instruction. The *Diener* gave her time to turn back." He sighs. "Rachael became a member of the *Gemein.*" The community. "But she didn't make the vow with the solemnity it deserves. Six months later, she was shunned and excommunicated."

In the church district here in Painters Mill, being shunned or placed under the *bann* is usually remedied by the correction of some "bad behavior." For example, if a baptized Amish person is caught driving a car or using technology that isn't allowed—and he gets rid of the car. Excommunication, on the other hand, is usually permanent—and rare.

"Why was she excommunicated?" I ask.

The old man looks down at his hands, laces his fingers. Watching him, I realize that even after the passage of so many years he's bothered by this particular subject. Because his efforts weren't enough to save her? Or something else?

"Bishop, I'm just trying to understand what happened to her," I say quietly. "To do that, I need some insight into her history, her past."

"Are you certain you want to know, Katie?"

I look at him, taken aback by the cryptic question. "If you know something about Rachael Schwartz that might help me figure out who did that to her, I need to know about it."

Sighing, he turns his attention to his wife. "*Ich braucha zo shvetza* Chief Burkholder," he tells her. I need to speak with Chief Burkholder. "*Laynich.*" Alone.

"*Voll.*" Of course. Giving me a final look, the Amish woman sets the dish towel on the counter and leaves the room.

For a moment, the only sound is the birdsong coming in through the window above the sink. The bawling of a calf in the field.

The bishop raises his gaze to mine. "Rachael Schwartz was deviant. The type of woman to do things best saved for marriage."

"I need names."

"Some were English. The Amish . . ." He shrugs.

The hairs on the back of my neck prickle. "Was she a minor?" I ask. "Under sixteen?"

"Close to that age. I'm not sure." Another shrug. "These are things I heard."

"From whom?"

He raises his head, his eyes searching mine. "These questions . . . may be the kind that are best not answered."

"I don't have that luxury," I snap.

He's unfazed by my tone. My impatience. After a moment, he nods. "Perhaps you should ask your brother."

"Jacob?" I stare at him, aware that my face is hot, my heart beating fast and hard in my chest. "Ask him what exactly?"

"You want to know about Rachael Schwartz? Ask him."

"What does she have to do with my brother?" Defensiveness rings hard in my voice, despite my efforts to curb it.

"Jacob came to me. Years ago. For counsel."

"Counsel for wh—"

He raises his hand, slices the air, and cuts me off. "I'll not speak of it. Not now. Not ever. If you want to know, go to Jacob."

"Bishop, you can't drop something like that in my lap and then walk away without an explanation."

Grasping the rails of his walker, he pulls himself to a standing position. "I've nothing more to say to you, Kate Burkholder."

Perhaps you should ask your brother.

The bishop's words taunt me as I drive down the lane. Jacob's name is the last name I expected to hear in the same sentence as Rachael Schwartz. I simply can't get my head around the implications. Jacob and I were close as kids. I admired him. Looked up to him. Relied on him for guidance. I loved him with all my young heart. Until I was fourteen years old and a neighbor boy by the name of Daniel Lapp entered our safe and protected world and introduced me to the dark side of human nature. It wasn't my parents, but Jacob who judged me that day. It was he who blamed me. For what happened to me. For what I did about it. For the death of a man I'll never come to terms with. Our family was never the same. But it was my relationship with Jacob that was shattered. I still see him on occasion. I visit my sister-in-law and my niece and nephews. But Jacob and I rarely speak. We're strangers.

Jacob came to me. Years ago. For counsel.

I search my memory for some link between Rachael and Jacob, but there's nothing there. My brother is eleven years older than Rachael, give or take. Too much of an age gap for their paths to have crossed in terms of courting. In addition, Jacob has been married for years. Why in the name of God would he go to the bishop about Rachael Schwartz?

I'm heading in the direction of his farm when my cell phone dings. Glock's name pops up on my dash screen. I hit the ANSWER button. "Please tell me you're calling with some good news," I say without preamble.

"Try this on for size," he replies. "Lady walking her dogs found a baseball bat in the ditch off Holtzmuller Road. She thought it was odd, took a closer look, and found blood."

My interest surges. "Holtzmuller isn't too far from the Willowdell Motel. Where are you?"

"Holtzmuller and TR 13," he tells me.

"Keep the dog lady on scene. I'll be there in two minutes."

I rack the mike and cut the wheel, make a U-turn in the middle of the road. The engine groans as I crank it up to just over the speed limit. Hopefully, the bat is the break we need. At the very least, it gives me some time to figure out how to approach Jacob with questions he's probably not going to want to answer.

Holtzmuller Road crosses Township Road 13 four miles south of Painters Mill. It's a little-used stretch that's more two-track than asphalt and runs through a rural area of rolling hills and feeder creeks, pastures and fields. This afternoon, the grass and surrounding trees erupt with the color of an Irish countryside. I round a curve and spot Glock's cruiser parked on the shoulder, the overhead lights flashing. Fifty yards beyond his car, he stands in the middle of the road, talking to a woman dressed in tie-dyed yoga pants and a pink athletic bra. He had the foresight to protect the scene and set out half a dozen safety cones to block traffic. Two golden retrievers sniff around at their feet.

I roll up behind his cruiser, flip on my overheads, and start toward them.

Glock and the woman turn and watch me approach. The dogs bound over to me, tongues lolling, tails waving. I bend, run my hands over their soft coats.

"Hey, Chief." Glock and I exchange a handshake. He motions toward a single cone in the ditch twenty yards away. "Bat is over there. Hasn't been moved or touched."

Nodding, I offer my hand to the woman and introduce myself. "I hear your dogs made an interesting discovery."

"I almost didn't stop," she tells me. "But they wouldn't come when I called and they're usually so obedient." She motions in the general direction of the cone. "I stopped and walked over there for a look. I thought maybe an animal had been hit by a car and needed help. But it was a baseball bat. At first, I didn't think anything of it. But it's a perfectly fine bat, right?" She hefts a laugh. "I was going to take it home for my kids. Then I saw the blood. I remembered hearing about that woman who was killed, and it freaked me out." She pats the cell phone strapped to her hip. "So I called you guys."

"We're glad you did," I tell her. "How long ago did you find it?"

"Twenty minutes?" she says.

"Did you see anyone else out here?" I ask. "Any vehicles or buggies on the road?"

"Not a soul. That's why I run on this stretch. There's no traffic and I don't have to worry about the dogs."

I'm ever cognizant of the possibility of evidence as we speak. Tire-tread marks or footwear imprints. If we're lucky, we might be able to extract fingerprints or DNA.

"Officer Maddox will take your contact info in case we have any more questions."

"Glad to help."

While Glock takes her information, I walk toward the cone sticking out of the grass in the ditch. Avoiding the gravel shoulder, I wade through ankle-high grass. Sure enough, next to the cone—twenty feet from the road—a wooden baseball bat is tucked into the grass, hidden from sight. It's a full-size Louisville Slugger. Well used, the logo worn by time and use. Benign looking except for the copious amount of blood smeared on the business end of it.

I think about Rachael Schwartz, the damage done to her body, and I know in my gut this is no coincidence. Keeping a prudent distance from the bat, I squat, pull out my reading glasses, and lean as close as I dare. Even without magnification, I discern several long hairs, small chunks of blood and tissue, all of it smeared and dry.

Pulling out my cell phone, I call Tomasetti.

He picks up on the first ring with a growl of his name.

"I think we found the murder weapon," I tell him.

"Well, it's about damn time someone called with some good news. What do you have?"

I tell him. "I need a CSU. Can you expedite?"

"I'll have someone there inside an hour."

I give him the location. "We'll protect the scene. I haven't looked around much, but there's a gravel shoulder. Might be able to pick up tread."

"I'll make sure they have plaster," he says. "Keep me posted, will you?"

"You, too."

I'm clipping my cell back onto my belt when Glock approaches, his eyes on the bat.

"What do you think?" he asks.

"Definitely blood. If we can extract DNA or prints." I shrug. "Could be a break."

He looks around. "What are we? Three miles from the motel?"

"Thereabouts." I look around. Half a mile down the road, I see the woman and her dogs walking away. "So, if we're right and this is the murder weapon, the killer left the motel and came this way."

"Heading away from Painters Mill." Glock looks left and right. "So where the hell was he going?"

"There's not much traffic out this way. Farms mostly."

"So he might live out this way. Or he might've simply been looking for a place to ditch the bat. Grass is tall enough so that he probably figured no one would find it."

"Did you happen to notice any tire-tread marks?" I ask. "Footwear?"

"I did a cursory search when I arrived. I can take a more thorough look around if you want." He sighs. "Sure would like to find this prick."

While Glock walks the road, searching the gravel shoulder for marks, I pull out my cell and take photos of the bat. The CSU will do the same. They'll protect the blood evidence and then courier the bat to the BCI lab in London, Ohio, where any fingerprints, blood type, and DNA will be extracted. If we're lucky, there will be some identifying mark to indicate where the bat was manufactured and sold. If we can find the merchant, we might be able to find out who purchased it. DNA will take some time—a few days, depending on how busy the lab is and how hard Tomasetti can push for priority—but even if the lab can match the blood type we'll have a little more to go on, especially if any of the blood belongs to the killer.

"I got nothing, Chief."

I turn to see Glock approach. "Zero traffic out this way," he says. "He probably just stopped the car, got out, flung the bat into the grass."

I nod in agreement, but my mind has already taken me back to the situation with my brother. "I've got to drive down to Killbuck," I tell him. "Can you hang out here until the CSU arrives?"

"Yep." He cocks his head, slants me a look that's a little too

118

concerned for comfort. "Want some company? That Gingerich dude is weird as hell."

"I expect some of these people might be more apt to open up if I'm alone."

"Gotcha." He grins. "I guess I do kind of have that whole outsider vibe going on."

I smile back. "Call if you need anything."

As I leave Holtzmuller Road and head east, it isn't the thought of Amos Gingerich that claws at my brain, but a brother I haven't seen for six months, a past I'm loath to revisit, and a terrible suspicion that if I'm not careful I could sever ties I've cherished my entire life.

CHAPTER 17

A sense of nostalgia grips me as I pull into the long gravel lane of my brother's farm. I take my time as I drive toward the house, trying to remember the last time I was here. *Too long,* my conscience reminds. Last month, I missed my nephew's birthday. I have no idea what's going on in their lives.

The apple trees in the orchard on my right are in full, brilliant bloom. It seems like yesterday when Datt and my grandfather planted those trees. It never ceases to shock me to see that they're fully mature and have been bearing fruit for decades now.

The house is plain and looks exactly the same as when I was a kid. There are no flower beds or landscaping, just a small garden in the side yard with ruler-straight rows of tiny corn and tomatoes. I idle around to the rear of the house and park next to a hitching post that wasn't there last time I was here. I sit for a moment, taking all of it in, and in that instant the longing for something I can't quite identify grips me with an almost physical pain. This farm and the people who've lived here are my history. The house where I grew up. Where so much happened. The barn and outbuildings where my sister, Sarah, and Jacob and I played hide-and-seek. The fields and pasture where I ran free without a care in the world. It speaks of a time when I never questioned the wisdom of my parents or the rules set forth by the Amish leadership. This small farm with its ramshackle outbuildings and old German bank barn was my world. My family was the center of my universe, vast and unblemished. I had been painfully innocent, never lonely or alone, and my perceptions had not yet been skewed or scarred by the injustices of life.

I get out of the Explorer and take the narrow sidewalk to house. A blue jay scolds me from his perch in the cherry tree in the yard as I step onto the porch, and I'm reminded that I'm an outsider here, not only to the land, but to my own family. I'm about to knock when my sister-in-law, Irene, pushes open the screen door.

"Katie!" She does a double take, her eyes wide. "My goodness. What a nice surprise!"

Irene is pretty in a girl-next-door kind of way, with flawless skin sprinkled with freckles and clear hazel eyes. She's wearing a blue dress with a white apron that's stained with what looks like grape juice, and an organdy *kapp,* black oxfords.

"Hi." I manage a smile that doesn't feel genuine. "Is Jacob around?"

"He's in the barn, replacing a wheel on that old manure spreader. It conked out yesterday. Fourth time this spring." Frowning, she motions toward the barn. "He'll be there a while, Katie. *Kumma inseid. Witt du kaffi?*" Come inside. Would you like coffee?

Amish decorum urges me to take her up on the offer. Spend a few minutes chatting and getting caught up on things. I should ask about

121

my niece and nephews and all the things happening in their lives. I should make an effort to know her, find some common ground and put an end to the discomfort I experience every time I'm here. Of course, I don't.

"*Nay, dank,*" I say.

Had I been one of her Amish brethren, I'd likely get an argument. Or else she'd step onto the porch, take my hand, and usher me inside for a piece of pie that'll only be good one more day, or the coffee she just made. Not so for me. In all the years that I've known her, Irene has never uttered a cross word to me, but we have an understanding. She invites only because she knows I will decline. I don't know if my brother told her what happened that summer when I was fourteen, but she's never been comfortable around me and despite her best efforts, it shows.

Relief flashes in her eyes. "Next time then."

I nod. "Tell the kids hi."

"I will!" A too-bright smile. "Bye, Katie!"

The screen door slams as I start toward the barn and I shove aside a small pang of hurt. Ahead, the big sliding door stands open a couple of feet. I sidle through, give my eyes a moment to adjust to the dimly lit interior. The clank and pop of metal against metal takes me to a workshop off the main room. I enter to find my brother at the workbench, pounding a piece of steel into submission.

He's so intent on his work that he doesn't notice me. His mouth is pulled into a frown, partly from the exertion of the task, partly from what looks like frustration because the steel is refusing to bend to his will.

After a moment, as if sensing my presence, he glances up and does a quick double take. The small sledgehammer in his hand freezes in midair; then he lets go with a final, satisfying blow. *Clang!*

I put my hands on my hips, present a smile. "Are you beating that piece of steel? Or is the steel beating you?"

"Haven't decided yet."

I catch the hint of a smile in his eyes, and I wonder if he's happy to see me. I wonder if he remembers how things were between us when we were kids. How much I'd looked up to him. If he misses it. I wonder if he realizes he'd once looked at me with affection instead of the standoffishness I see today.

He sets down the hammer. "It's been a while."

"I know," I say. "Too long."

We stare at each other, sizing each other up, slipping into our respective suits of armor, putting up the defenses we need to get through this. He's too polite to ask why I'm here, but he knows me too well to assume it's for a friendly visit.

"I need to talk to you about Rachael Schwartz," I say.

Jacob is a stoic man. He's difficult to read and tends to internalize his thoughts and feelings. But I see the impact of the name. A minute quiver runs the length of his body. Suddenly, and uncharacteristically, he can't meet my gaze. Instead, he looks down at the length of steel, picks it up, puts it back down.

"I heard about what happened to her," he says.

"I didn't realize you knew her."

"I didn't, really."

"That's not what I heard."

Raising his gaze to mine, he picks up the piece of steel, turns it over, and clangs the hammer against it three times. I watch him work, wait for him to stop, to respond.

After a few minutes, he looks at the steel, gives a small nod and sets it down. "You talked to Bishop Troyer." It's a statement, not a question.

And it tells me that whatever it was that happened between him and Rachael, he told no one else.

"I'm trying to find out who did that to her, so I went to the bishop." I pause, struggling to get the words right, failing. "I was surprised to hear your name. I had no idea your paths had ever crossed." If my revealing my source causes a problem between the two men, they'll just have to work it out.

"It was a long time ago." He tosses the piece of steel into an old-fashioned slatted wood crate. "I can tell you it has no bearing on what happened to her."

"I need to make that judgment, Jacob."

Taking his time, he lifts a baton-size bolt from another box, uses pliers to pry the nut that's fused to it with rust. "I confessed."

"To what?"

He twists the pliers and the nut snaps loose. "It was a private thing." I wait.

When he raises his gaze to mine, I see anger in his eyes. "*Dich sinn mei shveshtah.*" You're my sister. "*Dich du net halda glawva.*" You do not hold the faith. "I'll not speak of it."

Irritation snaps through me, but I tamp it down. "I'm not here as your sister, Jacob. I'm here as a cop with a job to do. If something happened between you and Rachael Schwartz, you need to tell me. Right now."

"You think I did that to her?" he asks incredulously.

"No," I say, meaning it. My brother may be a lot of things, but being capable of beating a woman to death is not one of them. "But sometimes there are . . . patterns in a person's life. The more I know about Rachael Schwartz, the more likely I'll find her killer."

After a moment, he rounds the workbench, brushes past me, and goes to the door of the workshop. He glances out as if to make sure there's no one there, closes the door, and returns to the workbench. There, he sets both hands against the surface, and shakes his head.

"Rachael Schwartz was . . ." He looks around as if he's lost something, as if his surroundings will somehow help him find the right word. "*Narrisch.*" Insane.

I wait, let the silence work.

After a moment, he straightens, slides his hands into his pockets. "It happened right before she left. I was in the buggy, driving home. It was dark, nine or ten o'clock, I think. A summer storm had swept in." He shrugs. "I didn't see her. Almost ran over her. Out by the Tuscarawas Bridge. She was walking in the middle of the road, soaking wet. I knew Rhonda and Dan, so I stopped. I knew they wouldn't want their daughter walking in the dark and rain all by herself, so I asked her if she needed a ride home."

Jacob would have been twenty-eight years old and married. Rachael Schwartz left when she was seventeen.

"She got into the buggy . . . soaked to the skin and crying, shivering with cold." Shaking his head, he turns away from me, pretends to look at something on the shelf behind him. "I didn't know it at the time, but she was . . . *ksoffa.*" Intoxicated. "During the drive to her parents' farm, she . . ." He ducks his head, struggles to find the words, fails. "One minute she was sitting there, crying. The next she . . . I don't know what happened. She became *unshiklich.*" Improper.

It's the last thing I expected my brother to say. The last kind of situation I would ever suspect him of getting caught up in. "She made a pass at you?" I ask.

My brother looks at me, but doesn't hold my gaze. I see shame in his eyes. A hint of ruddiness in his cheeks. "She was . . . *iemeschwarm.*"

125

Like a swarm of bees. "It was . . . unfitting. For a girl to act that way. It was crazy."

Only then do I realize there's more to the story. Jacob won't meet my gaze. His discomfort—his shame—is tangible.

"I . . . was young. Weak. For a moment, the devil got ahold of me." He sighs. "I pushed her out of the buggy. She . . . fell down. On the road. She was . . . furious and screaming. It was as if the devil had crawled into her head. I didn't know this girl."

Grimacing, he shakes his head. "I left her there. In the rain and dark. I went home. I told no one." He sighs. "Only later did I find out she went to the bishop and told him . . . things that were not true."

"What did she tell him?" I ask.

The ruddiness in his cheeks blooms. "She told the bishop that we were of one flesh."

"Did you?"

"No." He forces his gaze to mine, his mouth pulled into a hard line. "Katie, I was married. I would not—" He cuts the sentence short, as if the final word is too forbidden to be spoken aloud. "She lied. To the bishop. To anyone who would listen. Caused many problems."

"What did the bishop do?"

"He came to me. I told him the truth." The color in his cheeks darkens and spreads. "I confessed to him. For . . . what I did. What I felt."

"He believed you?"

He gives a barely discernable nod. "He did not believe her, and rightfully so."

"Who else knows what happened?"

"No one."

I think about that a moment. "Do you know why she was upset and out walking so late and in the rain?"

"She didn't say."

126

"Do you know if there were any other incidents? With anyone else? Other men?"

"All I can tell you is that I never looked at her again. I never spoke to her. And I never, ever let myself be alone with her." He shakes his head. "A few months later, she was gone."

CHAPTER 18

The story Jacob told me about Rachael Schwartz follows me as I head south on Highway 62 toward Killbuck. I recall the passage in the book she wrote that's chillingly similar to the one Jacob just relayed. In the book, the man, whose name was not mentioned, refused to take no for an answer. He raped her in the back seat of his buggy and then threw her to the asphalt and left her. When she went to the bishop, he blamed her. None of the other Amish believed her because she was fallen. In the end, she was excommunicated.

Was that extract an embellishment of what occurred between her and Jacob? Or was there *another* incident in which she was sexually assaulted and no one believed her?

I'm not sure what to think. What to believe. About Rachael. Her motives. By sheer virtue that Jacob is my brother, I am biased. That said, as a cop—as a woman—I know there is no greater insult for a victim of sexual assault than to not be believed, to be dismissed or disparaged. But I know my brother. He's a straight shooter. He follows the rules, not because he has to, but because he subscribes to basic Amish tenets. I always believed that's one of the reasons he had such a difficult time dealing with what I did that summer.

The vast majority of Amish men are well behaved when it comes to their female counterparts. They're aware of appearances, particularly if they're married. That said, I'm not blind to the reality that Amish men are as mortal as their English counterparts. They step over the line. They behave badly. Sometimes they break the law. Am I too close—not only to my brother, but to the young Rachael Schwartz I'd once known—to see the truth?

It's afternoon when I enter the corporation limit of Killbuck. Amos Gingerich's settlement is located west of town on a county road that's riddled with potholes. The vegetation is lush and overgrown in this low-lying area. Massive trees crowd the shoulders of the road, the branches scraping the doors and roof of the Explorer.

Tomasetti made good on his promise to forward images of the letters Amos Gingerich sent Rachael Schwartz. His takeaway is spot-on. While the letters aren't overtly threatening, it's clear Gingerich wasn't happy with her. The question in my mind now is: Did he act on all the anger simmering between the lines?

Generally speaking, the Amish are pacifists and live by the canon of nonresistance. When under threat, they will not defend themselves or their property. If they have an unresolvable problem with a neighbor or town, they've been known to simply move away. In times of war, they are conscientious objectors and refuse to bear arms. I know the Amish charter by heart; I was raised with it and lived by it through my formative years. I may not agree with every aspect, but I am certain of one thing: The Amish are a good and decent society. They're hardworking, family oriented, religious, and they are good neighbors.

Amos Gingerich may have Anabaptist leanings, but I know enough about him to know he isn't Amish, and I would be wise to use extreme caution when dealing with him, especially since I opted to come alone.

Half a mile in, a wall of trees rises out of the ground and the road dead-ends. I bring the Explorer to a stop and sit there a moment, puzzled.

"Well, shit."

I'm in the process of turning around when I spot the narrow opening between two walnut trees that's shrouded with a tangle of wild raspberry bushes. The derelict remains of a mailbox slant up through hip-high bramble at a precarious angle. The number matches the address I have on file.

I pick up my police-radio mike. "I'm ten-twenty-three."

"Ten-four," comes Lois's voice. "Be careful down there, Chief."

"That's affirm."

I rack the mike and start down the lane, cringing when the branches scratch at the paint on my doors. The Explorer bumps over potholes and puddles, mud and gravel slinging into the wheel wells. I've traveled another half mile, wondering if I've made a wrong turn somewhere, when the trees fall away. The lane widens and I drive into a large clearing. A dozen or so small, clapboard buildings, the kind used for construction-site offices, form a half circle. The units are closely grouped, each with wood stairs and a porch adorned with a potted plant or lawn chair. To my left, I see a large swatch of what looks like a community garden, where two women wearing ankle-length dresses and winter bonnets hoe the soil between rows of tiny spring corn, caged tomato plants, and other, indistinguishable greens. Beyond, an old bank barn that was here long before the other structures lends a sense of character the rest of the place lacks. A couple of draft horses graze in a small pasture. In another pen, several pygmy goats stand on giant wooden spools, bleating. A black buggy—oddly adorned with an orange roof—is parked outside the barn. I take in the scene with the sense that it has been staged.

I idle across the clearing to a hitching post in front of the nearest residence and shut down the engine. The two women don't look up from their work as I get out of the Explorer, but I feel eyes on me as I make my way up the steps and cross to the door. I've barely knocked when the door cracks open several inches. I find myself looking at a woman, barely into her twenties. She's hugely pregnant and wearing a longish print dress, and a head covering that's neither Amish nor Mennonite.

Her eyes widen at the sight of my uniform. "Can I help you?" she asks.

I show her my badge. "I'm looking for Amos Gingerich," I tell her.

She blinks, her eyes darting left. "Amos?"

It's a dumb response. One designed to delay. She's not quick enough to think of a viable stall off the top of her head, and I resist the urge to roll my eyes.

"Amos Gingerich," I tell her. "I need to speak with him. Right now. Where is he?"

She visibly swallows, then raises her hand and points toward the old bank barn. Before I can say anything else, she shrinks back inside and closes the door.

"That wasn't too difficult, was it?" I mutter as I trot down the steps.

I reach the open area where my Explorer is parked and keep going at a brisk clip toward the barn. To my left lies the garden. It's a large chunk of land, an acre or so. The two women have stopped what they're doing. They lean on their hoes, watching me. I raise my hand to wave, but they don't return the gesture. I can't help but notice both women are pregnant.

The barn door stands open. I enter; the smells of cattle, horses, and freshly sawn wood lace the air. A few yards away, a man is bent over a table, working on something unseen. He's broad shouldered and

131

dressed in black. A ponytail dangles to midback. I stand there a moment, taking his measure. He's well over six feet, two-fifty, with a muscular build. The flat-brimmed straw hat speaks of Amish leanings. The ponytail curtails any such misconception.

I'm about to announce my presence when he turns. Whether he heard my approach or merely sensed my presence, I can't tell, but when his eyes land on mine he's not surprised by me or the sight of my uniform.

He's got a thin, expressive mouth. A hook nose. Salt-and-pepper beard that reaches nearly to the waistband of his trousers. If he were Amish, the beard would tell me he's married and has been for some time. With this group, I'm not so sure. Pale eyes the color of an overcast sky. Amos Gingerich. I recognize him from the photos in Rachael's book.

"Ah, the police." Good-naturedly, he presses his hand to his chest. "Am I in trouble?"

Something about him I can't quite pinpoint unsettles me in spite of his friendly tone. His accent tells me he's not originally from this area. That *Deitsch* is likely not his first language.

"That depends." I approach him, tug my badge from my pocket, and introduce myself. "Amos Gingerich?"

He nods. "What can I do for you?"

Something disingenuous peeks out at me from behind his eyes, the curl of his mouth. "I'd like to ask you a few questions," I say.

Taking his time, he sets down the sander and plucks off his leather gloves. "This is about Rachael Schwartz?"

"So you've heard."

"Word of death travels fast, especially when you're Amish."

I don't point out that his Amishness is debatable. "You knew her?"

"She came to us, here in Killbuck. Stayed for a time."

"How long ago?"

"Eleven or twelve years, I think. She'd been put under the *bann* by the bishop in Painters Mill. She was a troubled young woman." He touches his chest. "Inside, you know. She was alone. Confused. She had nowhere to go and so we took her in. We offered her refuge and counsel. A place to live. We offered her hope."

"How long did she stay?"

"Six months or so."

"That's not very long."

He shakes his head. "She was a restless soul. Searching for something she couldn't name. After a time, she realized she could not abide by our ways."

"What ways is that?"

"I don't want to disparage her. That's not our way. But she was . . . difficult."

"How so?"

He shrugs. "She was . . . disruptive. As bishop, my community comes first. When I asked her to leave, she became angry."

"Was she angry with anyone in particular?"

"Me, of course. But she also turned on some of the womenfolk. Some of the girls she lived with. Accused them of spying." He dismisses the word with a wave of his hand. "Strange things like that." He shakes his head. "She tried to come back, get into our good graces. But I wouldn't have it. A couple of years later that book came out. I was shocked by all the vicious lies. It caused problems for our small community. It seems young Rachael sold her soul for money."

I think about the rumors of polygamy, of children at risk, and the accusations that Gingerich is more cult leader than bishop. I ask anyway. "What kinds of problems?"

"Reporters started sniffing around, accosting us here or in town, asking all sorts of questions. The police came, too, as did the social people with the government, wanting to know about the children." His mouth tightens. "Our property was vandalized. People in town called us names or refused to do business with us. It was an outrage."

"What did you do?"

"What *could* we do? Like so many of our forefathers we put our fate in the hands of God and we weathered the storm."

"Did you blame Rachael Schwartz for any of it?"

"I blame intolerance," he tells me. "Ignorance."

I let it go, shift gears. "Was Rachael close with anyone in particular here in this community?"

"She was only here for a short time. I don't believe she got too close to anyone, really."

"What about you?" I ask.

He tilts his head, the spark of something I can't readily identify in his eyes. Irritation? Amusement? "What about me?"

"Were you and Rachael close?" I ask.

"No closer than any bishop and a member of his congregation."

I nod, look around, let the silence ride a moment. "So, you read her book?"

"What I could stomach."

"Then you know Rachael claimed the two of you had a relationship."

"I'm aware of that untruth." Another flash of pseudo amusement, darker this time, laced with anger. "The book was full of blasphemous lies. About me. My brethren. Written by a disgruntled and confused woman who in the end sold her soul for whatever the publisher paid her."

"You must have been angry," I say.

He gives me a pitying look, but there's an unsettling glint in his eyes.

Buried beneath all that righteousness and calm lies a cunning and indescribable menace that chills me, despite the .38 strapped to my hip.

"I hold no anger toward anyone," he tells me. "That's not our way. Rachael Schwartz *hot net der glaase.*" Didn't keep up the faith. "She made many unfounded and painful accusations. She tried to hurt those who only wanted to help. Yes, the police investigated, but then you already know that, don't you, Kate Burkholder?"

"I do."

A ghost of a smile touches his lips. "It was a painful time for all of us."

"When's the last time you had any contact with Rachael?" I ask.

"I haven't spoken to her since the day I asked her to leave."

"What about letters?" I ask.

"Ah." His mouth curls in such a way that I can't tell if it's a smile or a snarl or something in between. The one thing I do know is that it's an unpleasant mien and it's focused on me.

"You obviously know I wrote to her. Simply to ask her to stop lying about us. Leave us be in peace."

"Did it escape your mind that you also threatened her?"

"A false witness shall not be unpunished, and he that speaketh lies shall perish," he tells me. "In case you're not well versed, and I suspect you are not, that passage is from the Bible. I thought it might help her see the error of her ways. That's all."

"Where were you night before last?" I ask.

"Here, of course." He spreads his hands, encompassing the area around him.

"Can anyone substantiate that?"

"My wife. A few of the others here in our community." He recites two names.

I pull out my notebook and write them down.

When I look up, he's tilted his head, looking at me as if I'm some

135

fascinating science project. Some small animal that's about to be dissected by a kid who enjoys cutting a little too much. "I understand you're fallen, too, Chief Burkholder. Perhaps you have something to confess as well."

For an instant, I'm startled that he knows I'm formerly Amish. Quickly, I settle, reminding myself that Painters Mill isn't far from Killbuck. That gossip has wings. And that he probably knew at some point I'd drive down and talk to him.

Taking my time, I drop the notepad and pen into my pocket. "I appreciate your time," I say.

And I walk away.

CHAPTER 19

I've just entered the corporation limit of Painters Mill when my cell lights up. Seeing HOLMES CNTY CORONER on the dash display, I hit ANSWER. "Hey, Doc."

"I've completed the autopsy of Rachael Schwartz. Report is in the works, but since time is of the essence, I thought you'd want to hear my findings," he says.

"Cause and manner of death?" I ask.

"She died from multiple cranial-bone fractures, subdural and sub-arachnoid hemorrhages of the frontal, parietal, and temporal regions. Any one of those injuries could have been fatal."

"In English?" I say.

"Skull fractures." He heaves a sigh and for the first time I get the impression that this particular autopsy has exhausted him in a way that has little to do with a lack of sleep or physical stamina.

"All of it from blunt-force trauma?"

"Yes," he replies. "Manner of death is homicide," he finishes.

"Were you able to narrow down the time of death?" I ask.

"Between one and three A.M. That's as close as we're going to get, Kate."

"What about the rape kit?"

"No semen."

I think about that, once again the question of motive swirling. "Is there a preliminary report you can send me, Doc?"

"I'll email you what I have. Won't be finalized until tomorrow. I won't close out until tox comes back in a couple weeks."

I'm about to thank him when he speaks again. "Kate . . ." He makes a sound that's partly the clearing of his throat, but for the first time since I've known him, there's emotion tucked away somewhere in that sound. "That girl had seven broken bones. Internal hemorrhaging. Facial injuries. In all the years I've served in the capacity of coroner, I've never seen so much trauma as the result of a beating."

I wait, vaguely aware that I'm holding my breath. That I'm moved by his reaction, the unusualness of it, and part of me knows this moment is important. Not only for me, but for Doc Coblentz.

"I don't know if what I'm about to tell you is relevant in terms of the perpetrator or if it will be helpful to you in any way as you investigate this crime, but even after this victim was down and unable to protect herself or move, her attacker continued to strike. Those blows continued long after the victim's heart stopped beating." He pauses and I hear the hiss and flow of his breaths. "Speaking not as the coroner, but as a citizen? You need to find this guy, Kate. You need to stop him and quickly. None of us will be safe until you do."

Before I can assure him that I plan to do exactly that, the connection ends.

Rachael Schwartz was no angel, but she didn't deserve the fate that met her. No one deserves to die like that, especially at the hand of another.

. . . even after this victim was down and unable to protect herself or move, her attacker continued to strike.

The overkill indicates a high level of emotion. Intense and personal hatred. An all-consuming rage. A complete loss of control. Who hated her enough to beat her with such violence that they broke seven bones? Inside their twisted mind, what had Rachael Schwartz done to deserve it?

I'm in my office at the police station. It's after four P.M. now. Glock came in earlier for his end-of-shift reports and Skid came on board to relieve him. Lois went home for the day and my new dispatcher, Margaret, has spent the last hour cleaning and rearranging the credenza behind her workstation. I've read Doc Coblentz's preliminary autopsy report twice now. The picture that emerges is a thing of nightmares. In the early stages of the attack, Rachael Schwartz had tried to protect herself. Defensive wounds indicate she fought back; she was a fighter, after all. When those efforts proved fruitless, she tried to escape. But by then she was too injured to get away. While she was down, crawling or pulling herself along the floor, unable to defend herself, her killer stood over her and beat her to death.

I'm thinking about the baseball bat found in the ditch, in the process of reading the report for the third time, looking for details I might've overlooked, when the bell on the exterior door jangles, telling me someone has entered the station. A moment later, Tomasetti appears in the doorway of my office. He's carrying a record storage box. His laptop case strap is slung over his shoulder. He looks tired. Glad to be here. The knot in my gut loosens at the sight of him.

"You lost?" I say.

"I'm looking for Mrs. Tomasetti," he says.

I stand, ridiculously pleased by his use of the as-of-yet-unofficial title, liking the way he's looking at me, the half smile curving his mouth. "I don't think that's a done deal just yet," I tell him.

"Say the word, and we'll make it happen," he says.

"Thinking about it."

I've lost track of how many times he's proposed. Of course I plan to marry him; he's the love of my life. Even so, I haven't given him the answer he deserves. While marriage is an institution I believe in, the notion of tying that knot scares the daylights out of me. He's been a good sport about it. I'm a work in progress.

He enters my office. "Shall I close the door?"

Temptation ripples through me. I look past him, catch a glimpse of Margaret gathering the carafe and mugs from the coffee station in the hall and shake my head. "Rain check?"

"Bet on it." He sets the box on my desk, the laptop on the floor, and sinks into the visitor chair across from me.

"How was Cleveland?" I ask.

"Productive," he tells me. "Division of Police and BCI went through the house where Schwartz lived with Matson. We went over everything with a fine-tooth comb. Dusted for prints. We took her laptop to the lab. Email. Hard drive. Techs are looking at her browsing history."

"Anything interesting?" I ask.

"A couple of things stand out. According to one of her friends I talked to, Rachael was regularly intimate with two men, in addition to Moskowski."

I sit up straighter. "Did you—"

"Both have alibis for the night of the murder, but we're taking a good hard look at both of them in case this was a murder-for-hire or jealous-lover kind of thing."

Not for the first time, I'm reminded that Rachael Schwartz lived her life full bore. She was impulsive with a predilection for risky behavior and damn anyone who didn't like it.

Bending, he pulls a couple of items from the box. "You have chain

140

of custody on this." He tosses a brown envelope on my desk. "Old photos."

I open it. The photos inside are faded and stained. Poor quality. There are four of a spotted horse that means nothing. I shuffle through, come to the last photo. It's a picture of Rachael Schwartz and Loretta Bontrager when they were barely into their teens. Loretta has a kind, ordinary face mottled with freckles, and the guileless eyes of a child. Rachael was a lovely girl with a not-quite-innocent smile and eyes that, even then, were a little too direct.

He places a manila folder on my desk and slides it over to me. "This is one of the more interesting finds."

I replace the photos, open the folder, and find myself looking at copies of Schwartz's banking and financial statements. Checking account. Savings. A small investment account.

"Not much in the way of savings," I murmur as I skim. "Investment account is almost dry."

"According to her accountant, The Keyhole didn't always turn a profit. Some weeks she barely made payroll."

"She was living above her means."

Leaning forward, he reaches out and flips the page. "Checking account has been in the red several times in the last couple of years. Look at the balance now."

My eyes widen. "Almost twenty thousand dollars." I look at Tomasetti. "Any idea where the money came from?"

He runs his finger down the page and taps on a figure highlighted in yellow. I slide my reading glasses onto my nose. Sure enough, there was a deposit made two months ago in the amount of fourteen thousand dollars.

I look at Tomasetti. "That's a lot of money. Royalty payment?"

"Cash," he tells me.

"That's odd."

"It's been my experience that when people deal in cash like that, they usually have something to hide or else they don't want it traced."

"Is there any way we can figure out who it came from?" I ask.

"I'm working on getting landline records," he says. "Might take a day or two."

"Cell phone?" I ask.

"We went through the one found on scene," he tells me. "We identified every number, but they gave us nothing. According to the friend I talked to, Rachael had *two* cell phones. Only one has been accounted for."

I think of the cell phone found at the scene. I remember thinking there should have been at least one call to someone in Painters Mill. For the first time, that there wasn't such a call makes sense.

"She didn't drive down to Painters Mill to ogle the Amish," I tell him. "No one I've talked to knew she was here or even knew she was coming."

"Someone did," he says. "We both know this wasn't random."

My mind spins through possibilities. "Her killer knew about the second cell phone and took it."

"Because they'd been communicating with it."

"Burner?" I ask.

"Why would she do that?"

"Maybe she was into something she shouldn't have been into?"

"Like what?"

"I don't know." I rap my palm against the desktop.

He leans back in the chair and contemplates me. "Rachael wasn't the only one living above her means."

"Andy Matson?"

"Worth checking. At the very least, rattle her cage a little."

I smile. "Not bad for a BCI guy."

"Every now and then I get it right."

Rolling my eyes, I get to my feet. "I'll drive."

In light of her friend's unsolved murder, Andy Matson had wanted to stay in Painters Mill for a few days rather than make the drive back and forth to Cleveland, if only to "make sure these small-town Barney Fifes do their jobs." It's nothing I haven't heard before; I don't take offense. With the B and Bs booked—and the Willowdell Motel hitting a little too close to home—she's staying at Hotel Millersburg, which is half a block from the Holmes County Courthouse. She agrees to meet Tomasetti and me at a nearby coffee shop.

We find her in a booth at the rear, staring at her phone, a frothy latte and half-eaten croissant in front of her. She looks up as we approach.

"Any news?" she asks, giving us only part of her attention.

"We're following up on a few things," I say vaguely as Tomasetti and I slide into the booth opposite her.

"Like what?" she asks. "Do you have a suspect?"

I let her fidget and stew, the questions hang, while we order coffee.

When our server hustles away, I turn my attention to her. "What do you know about Rachael's finances?"

"Finances?" she echoes stupidly.

"You know," Tomasetti says. "Money. Accounts. Savings. Checking. Investments."

She blinks, looks from Tomasetti to me, as if suddenly she's not quite in such a hurry to talk.

I say her name firmly. "If you're as smart as I think you are, you'll answer the question in the next two seconds and you'll tell the truth."

Andy looks down at the cup and plate in front of her as if she's lost her appetite for both. "Why are you asking me about her finances?" she asks.

"Because we want an answer," I say evenly.

She sighs. "I guess you've realized there was something going on with her."

I say nothing. Tomasetti follows suit.

She squirms beneath our stares. "Look, the only thing I know for certain about Rachael's money situation is that she spent it like it was frickin' going out of style. I mean, she had expensive taste. In clothes. Liked to travel. She loved fancy restaurants. Nice hotels." Her brows knit. "What's odd about that is that she didn't *make* as much money as she spent. I mean, The Keyhole was doing *okay,* but there were weeks when we barely broke even. Sure, she had royalties from the book, but they were dwindling because it had been out for a couple years. She wasn't exactly rolling in the dough."

"And yet she shopped at Saks," Tomasetti says dryly. "She bought expensive art. Spent two weeks in Hawaii last year. Stuff like that."

"Did you ever ask her about it?" I ask.

"Once or twice. You know, just sort of kidding around." She shrugs. "She'd say it was from a bonus. Or for some catering gig that never seemed to materialize. Mostly, she just changed the subject or laughed it off."

Beside me, Tomasetti makes a sound of annoyance. "You can cut the bullshit. We have her financial records. We can get yours, too, if you prefer to do things that way."

Giving him a withering look, she picks up her cup, sets it down without drinking.

"Look," she says, "I loved Rachael. She was fun and alive and . . .

she was one of the most amazing people I've ever met. She just had this way about her. This . . . persuasive energy that won you over. And you guys are sitting there judging her and doing the whole assassination-of-character thing, treating her as if she was some common criminal."

She's getting herself worked up, so I give her a moment, keep my voice level. "We're not judging her," I say gently. "We're trying to find the person who murdered her."

"She wasn't perfect," she snaps. "Rachael was . . . Rachael. I loved her anyway. I accepted her. Flaws. All of it. But . . ." She struggles to find the right words. "I'm not badmouthing her, but . . . I think you both know by now that she wasn't always a good person."

"How so?" I ask.

"When she wanted something, she went for it."

Tomasetti rolls his eyes. "What the hell does that even mean?"

She looks around, as if to make sure no one is close enough to hear what she's about to say, and lowers her voice. "Look, I don't know this for a fact, but it crossed my mind that Rachael might be blackmailing someone."

"Who?" I ask.

"No clue."

Groaning, Tomasetti leans against his chair back. "Right."

"Why did you think that?" I ask.

"The money for one thing. She was always throwing it around. And she was secretive about where it came from." She lowers her voice to a whisper. "A couple weeks ago, I walked in, late, and she was on the phone, arguing with someone. I mean, they were really going at it. I heard her threaten them."

"Any idea who?" I press.

"I asked, but she just laughed and said it was this bartender she'd

145

had to fire, and he was trying to get his job back." She shakes her head. "Poor guy was in love with her, but she just . . . laughed." Her brows draw together. "I remember looking at her and thinking: She's lying."

"What's his name?" Tomasetti asks.

"Joey Knowles."

He writes down the name.

"Was the caller male or female?" I ask.

"Not sure." She gives a sheepish smile. "Rach was pretty much an equal-opportunity asshole."

"In what way did she threaten the person she was talking to?" I ask.

"I only caught the tail end of the conversation. She said something like—and I'm paraphrasing—'play your cards right and no one will ever know.' "

"Why didn't you mention this sooner?" I ask.

She looks away. "Because I don't want people thinking she was a bad person who deserved what she got. She didn't."

Tomasetti isn't buying it. "How much did she give you?" he asks.

She opens her mouth. Closes it. Blinks a dozen times. All of it accompanied by a deep flush that spreads down her throat like a sunburn. "She didn't—"

"How much?" he snaps.

"She . . . gave me the down payment for my car," she tells him. "The Audi."

"Nice of her," he says. "Did you ask her where the money came from?"

"No." She looks down at the coffee and shakes her head. "You know, the whole look-a-gift-horse-in-the-mouth thing, I guess."

"What else haven't you told us?" he asks.

She hits him with a contemptuous glare and pushes the plate away. For a moment, I think she's going to get up and leave. Instead, she looks from Tomasetti to me and heaves a sigh. "In case you haven't figured it out yet, I'm no angel either."

"We kind of got that," Tomasetti mutters.

"If there's something else we need to know," I say, "now is a good time to tell us."

"God." Andy looks down at the plate in front of her. For the span of a full minute, she says nothing. Then she sighs, curses. "I took two thousand dollars, okay? For God's sake, I found it in her office. I was . . . pissed. I mean, she owed me. I mean, for the book. Right? So I took it. And then I felt like shit. That's why I was trying to reach her. I mean, the day she died."

"You stole two thousand dollars from her?" Tomasetti asks.

"I guess I did," she says. "I mean, I would have paid it back, but . . ." She ends the sentence with a shrug. "All of this happened."

"How did you know she'd driven down to Painters Mill?" I ask.

"She left a note."

"Do you still have it?" I ask.

"Um. Gosh, I don't know. Maybe." She lifts the leather bag off the back of her chair, digs around inside. "It was just a scribbled few words. Kind of vague and snarky."

She pulls out a wadded piece of paper, smooths it out. A smile tugs at her mouth as she sets it on the tabletop and slides it over to me.

Off to PM to TCB. Dinner tomorrow @ Lola's. Booze on me!

"What's TCB?" I ask.

"Take care of business."

"Any idea what she meant by that?"

She lifts her shoulder, lets it drop. "Just that she had something to do there."

"What did you do with the two grand?" Tomasetti asks.

Her eyes skitter right. It's a subtle reaction, but enough for me to know she's thinking about lying. Instead of answering, she sets her elbows on the tabletop and rests her forehead in her hands. "I know how this is going to sound. I know what you're going to think."

"Just answer the damn question," he growls.

"I blew it, okay? Bought a few things." She raises her head, looks from Tomasetti to me. "Look, it's not like I didn't have a good reason to take it. Rachael owed me."

"She owed you money?" Tomasetti asks. "You mean for the book?"

"Last year, when Rachael was buying the house, she was short. My mom had just passed away and left me a little money." She shrugs. "I knew Rachael was good for it, so I let her borrow six grand."

"Do you have anything in writing?" I ask.

"We're not exactly write-it-down kind of people."

"When was she supposed to pay you back?" I ask.

"Months ago, but—" Her brows furrow. "Last time I asked her about it, she said she was going to pay me back soon. That she was about to come into some cash."

"How long ago was that?" I ask.

"Two weeks maybe?"

"Do you know the source of the money she was about to come into?"

"She led me to believe it had something do with the book." She looks down at the tabletop and shakes her head. "I'm not a thief. I was tired of being put off, so I took it and I went fucking shopping."

Her voice cracks with the last word and she takes a moment to compose herself. "When I calmed down, I felt awful. I spent the rest of the day trying to run her down. But when I couldn't get her on the cell, I got worried. Rachael *always* answers her cell. She's like . . . addicted

148

to it." She looks at Tomasetti. "Then I get *you* on the other end and it freaked me out. I checked motels in Painters Mill. When I got there, I found all those cop cars and I just knew . . ."

Lowering her face into her hands, she bursts into tears.

Tomasetti looks at me and frowns.

I pass her a fresh paper napkin. "Andy, do you know who she was meeting with?"

"No clue."

"Did Rachael's parents know she was coming?" I pose the question even though, according to Rhoda and Dan Schwartz, they had no idea their daughter was in town.

"I don't know." She blots at her eyes, careful not to smear her makeup. "Look, I've got nothing against the Amish. To each their own, you know? But Rachael's parents treated her like shit. Rachael tried to stay in touch with them. She missed them, wanted them in her life. All they ever did was judge her. Put her down. They disapproved of everything she did. Rachael was never good enough."

I nod, thinking about my own family and the dynamics of familial relationships. "Did Rachael stay in touch with anyone else in Painters Mill?"

"She had a friend." A wrinkle forms between her brows. "Amish."

"Male or female?" I ask.

She shakes her head. "All I remember is that Rachael had a couple of intense conversations with this so-called friend of hers and they weren't very Amish-sounding. Conversations that upset her even more than all that judgment shit coming down from her holier-than-thou parents."

CHAPTER 20

The Amish have a saying about deception. It goes something like: *Dich kann gukka an en mann kischt avvah du kann net sayna sei hatz.* You can look at a man's face, but you can't see his heart.

"What do you think?" I ask.

Tomasetti and I are sitting in the Explorer, parked outside the coffeehouse where we met with Andy Matson.

"I think if she's a liar, she's pretty good at it." He shrugs. "I don't believe she beat Rachael Schwartz to death. If she was involved, she hired someone. If she did, there will be a money trail."

I nod in agreement. "We need to look at the blackmail angle."

He grimaces. "If Rachael Schwartz knew something about someone, I don't think she'd hesitate to use it to her advantage."

"Matson may be trying to shift our interest to someone else." Even as I toss out the theory, it doesn't ring true.

His cell chirps. He pulls it from his pocket and checks the display, takes a minute to scroll. "Well, I'll be damned," he says.

"If it's not good news, I don't want to hear it."

He grins. "I just got the PDF of Schwartz's credit card activity in the thirty days before she was killed. Get this: The final transaction was at a bar in Wooster the evening before she was murdered. At seven twenty-nine P.M."

"The Pub?" I say.

He arches a brow.

"The scribbled address on the note," I remind him. "I drove up there last night. No one remembered seeing her." I think about that a moment. "How much was the charge?"

"Thirty-nine dollars and change."

Something in my chest quickens. I see the same rise of interest in Tomasetti's eyes. "It's a burger-and-fries kind of bar," I tell him. "Not the kind of place where dinner costs more than fifteen bucks, even if you have a beer."

"She wasn't alone."

"I'd venture to say she treated someone to dinner."

"In that case." He motions toward the clock on my dash, which reads 7:00 P.M. "You game for a beer?"

"Tomasetti, you're going to have to buy me something a hell of a lot stronger than beer."

The Pub was nearly vacant last time I was here. Of course, it had been late, after ten P.M. Tonight, the parking lot is chock-full of vehicles. Tomasetti and I park next to a white Dodge Ram pickup truck with the logo of a Wooster-based landscaping company emblazoned on the door.

We enter to the scream and bang of some chain-saw rock number I don't recognize. Every stool at the bar is occupied, mostly by men who look as if they've just gotten off work, wearing everything from oil-stained coveralls to shirts and ties. At the pool table in the back, three men in their twenties sip drafts in sweating mugs, shoot balls, and watch the nearest booth, where four college-age girls raise shot glasses in a toast. The bartender is female, in her fifties, with blond hair piled atop her head and a face full of artfully applied makeup. She's wearing a short black skirt with a white button-down shirt and an apron set snug against a nicely shaped body.

She nods at me and Tomasetti as we seat ourselves in a booth. In less than a minute, she's standing next to our table, order book in hand. "Hey, thanks for coming in tonight. What can I get you folks?"

I identify myself and pull out the photo of Rachael Schwartz. "I'm wondering if you've seen this woman."

She bends, pulls clunky readers off her crown, and squints at the photo. "Oh my God. That's the girl who was killed down there in Painters Mill."

I nod. "Have you seen her?"

"In here?" She shakes her head. "I don't think so. She's a pretty little thing. Unless I was crazy busy, I probably would have remembered her." She uses her pen to scratch her head. "When was she in here?"

"Night before last," I tell her. "Were you working?"

"I was." She looks at the photo again, gives another shake of her head. "Wish I could be more help. I sure don't like the idea of some monster getting away with something like that." She gives an exaggerated shiver. "But I didn't see her. We have dollar drafts that evening and this place was hopping."

Tomasetti pulls the redacted copy of Rachael Schwartz's credit card record from his pocket and shows her the charge. "Would it be possible for you to find the ticket for this charge?" he asks.

"We got computerized cash registers last summer. I bet Jack can come up with something. He's off tonight."

"I met him last time I was here," I tell her. "I'll give him a call."

Tomasetti motions in the general direction of the bar and pool tables. "Do you mind if we ask around?"

"Hey, knock your socks off." She tucks the pen and order book into the pocket of her apron. "Hope you find the bastard."

Tomasetti takes the bar. I meander to the pool table at the rear. The players are a lively group. Not too drunk—yet—and tickled to be talking to a female chief of police about a murder. I dig out the photo of Rachael Schwartz, but none of the young men remember seeing her. It doesn't take long for me to realize this second trip to The Pub is as big a waste of time as the first.

"No one who knew Rachael recalls her knowing anyone in the Wooster area." Frustration presses down on me as Tomasetti and I walk to the Explorer.

"On the other hand," he says slowly, "Wooster isn't too far to drive if you're from Painters Mill and you don't want to be seen together."

Tomasetti opens the passenger door, but doesn't get in. His eyes are narrowed on the service station and convenience store next door. The one with the green and white neon sign touting cigarettes, beer, and diesel.

We exchange a look over the top of the Explorer. "I'm not going to get my hopes up," I tell him.

"Worth a shot."

We get in. Behind the wheel, I put the vehicle in gear and idle over to the convenience store, park in front. I'm not even out of the vehicle yet when I notice the security camera tucked beneath the eve of the building. A bulging eye casting a disapproving glare in the general direction of The Pub.

I grin at Tomasetti. "Sometimes you earn your keep."

"That's what I keep telling you." He grins back and we head inside.

A lanky young woman with a pierced brow, arms covered with tats, sits on a stool behind the counter, watching a game show on TV. She eyes us suspiciously as we make our way to her.

"You the manager?" I ask.

She looks me up and down. "Who wants to know?"

Tomasetti lays his ID on the counter. "The Ohio Bureau of Criminal Investigation." He motions in the general direction of the camera. "Are your security cameras working?"

"As far as I know." She cocks her head, curious. "Something going on?"

"I need the video of that west-facing camera," he tells her. "For the day before yesterday, between noon and midnight. Can you get that for us?"

"I'll have to call the owner," she tells him.

"We'll wait."

Loretta Bontrager couldn't sleep. She hadn't slept a wink since Rachael was killed. When she was a girl, her *mamm* had chided her for *aykna bang hatz.* For being an "owner of a worried heart," and for fretting about things over which she had no control. Things that her Amish faith required her to leave to God.

Aykna bang hatz.

She couldn't stop thinking about Rachael. The closeness they'd shared as girls. The laughter and love—and secrets. The memories, both good and bad. It had been almost fourteen years since Rachael left Painters Mill. In all that time, Loretta hadn't forged another relationship that even came close to the one she'd had with Rachael. A confidante she could tell anything and not be silenced or shamed. Now, Rachael was gone. Everything they'd shared was lost. She would never again hear her voice or laughter.

Tonight, contemplating her friend's death tormented her. How she must have suffered. The terror. And pain. Dear God, she couldn't bear to think of it and yet she couldn't stop.

It was nearly midnight now, and the old farmhouse was hushed. Usually, Loretta enjoyed her evening solitude, when Ben and Fannie were safe in their beds, and she had some quiet time for reflection and prayer. Tonight, the silence was a lonely companion that made her feel as if she was the last person on earth. She should have joined her husband in bed hours ago. She'd feigned tidying up the kitchen and writing a letter to her cousin in Shipshewana, but neither of those things was the truth. She knew she wouldn't sleep and she simply couldn't bear the darkness. Not when there was already so much of it inside her. Once she laid her head down on the pillow, the images of Rachael would come to her and the dark and quiet would become intolerable.

Even now, with the sink clean and the floors mopped, the letter written and sealed, her mind whirred with images she didn't want to see, thoughts she couldn't bear to ponder. For the last two nights, desperate for peace, she'd fallen to going out to the barn. Muck boots over her socks. Her barn coat over her nightgown. Lantern in hand.

It was there, among the animals, the smells of hay and earth, that she found peace. The pygmy goats had had their babies a couple of weeks ago. The kids were tiny things, soft and warm and such a comfort to hold. The old draft mare had foaled last month, too, and the filly was a lively sprite with her *mamm*'s sense of mischief. Even the chickens roosting on the beams above the stalls calmed her nerves.

Loretta went to the goat pen first. "*Kumma do, mei lamm.*" Come here, my lamb. Bending, she leaned over the low fence to pick up the brown and white baby, her favorite. The one that melted in her arms because she enjoyed having her tummy rubbed.

She'd just lowered her cheek to the animal's muzzle when the shadow darted toward her from the darkness. Gasping, Loretta dropped the baby next to its *mamm* and stumbled back. She spun to run, but strong hands fell onto her shoulders, fingers digging in with enough force to bruise.

"Don't say a word," hissed a male voice, warm breath in her ear. "Do not make a sound. Do you understand?"

Rough hands spun her around so that she was facing him, and then he shoved her. Loretta reeled backward. Her back slammed against the wall, her head snapping hard against the wood. Simultaneously, recognition kicked, followed by a tidal wave of panic.

"You," she cried.

Lips peeled back, teeth grinding, he moved close. "Shut the hell up," he hissed.

She tried to pry his arm away, but he was too strong. All the while a thousand thoughts assailed her brain. She'd underestimated him. She'd been a fool for thinking he wouldn't come for her. She'd thought she was safe. Now, he was going to kill her.

"You lied to me," he ground out.

"No!" she squeaked.

"I heard you been talking to the cops."

"I didn't. That was before—"

He set his forearm against her throat, pressed hard enough to cut off her words. He was breathing as if he'd just run a mile. So close she could smell the stink of alcohol on his breath.

Unable to speak or breathe or even form a coherent thought, she jerked her head.

He eased some of the pressure off her throat, but he didn't release her. "What did you tell them?"

"Nothing!" she choked.

He slammed his fist against the wall inches from her head. "Don't fucking lie to me!"

The fear was like barbed wire drawn tight around her ribs. Breaths coming too fast. Chest taut. "I'm not."

"What did Schwartz tell you about that night?"

"She didn't tell me anything!" she cried.

His mouth tightened. Rage and disbelief in his eyes. Thinking about hitting her. Instead, he pulled her toward him, shook her, then slammed her back against the wall again, harder this time. Raising his hand, he jabbed his finger against her cheek hard enough to bruise skin.

"You keep your fucking mouth shut about that night. Not a word to anyone. You got me?"

She couldn't stop nodding.

He ground his teeth, looking at her as if he didn't believe her. "Nothing happened. Do you understand me? You say anything about what you *think* happened, and I'll come back. Next time, I'll kill you. I'll kill your husband. I'll kill your fucking kid. And I'll burn your goddamn house to the ground. You got that?"

"Please don't hurt them." She twisted, tried to duck away.

He clamped his hand around her throat, pressed her hard against the wall. "I'm an inch away from slitting your throat right now, you lying bitch."

She stared at him. Heart pounding. Blood raging in her veins. Terror clouding her brain. Pure evil stared back at her.

"I don't know anything," she said.

"Good. Keep it that way. Don't speak my name. Don't even think it." He lifted his hand and jabbed his finger against the side of her head. Once. Twice. Three times. "That sinking in? You got it?"

His other hand was still around her throat, crushing her windpipe, her voice box. She tried to answer, but couldn't so she nodded.

He stepped back, but didn't release her throat. She stumbled forward, set her hands on his wrist, tried to pry off his grip with her fingers, but he was too strong. He swung her around. Teeth grinding, a sound of rage gurgling in his throat, he shoved her hard.

Loretta tottered backward, struck a wood column, and went down on her backside.

Snarling a profanity, he stepped toward her, jabbed his finger at her face. "If I hear you been talking to the cops again, it's over for you."

She scrabbled back. "I won't."

"Don't make me come back," he whispered.

She didn't want to look at him, but she did. She could see his hands shaking. His finger pointing, an inch from her face. Forehead shiny and red and beaded with sweat despite the chill. Veins protruding at his temples. Spit on his lips. Breaths rushing between clenched teeth.

"Okay," she whispered.

He straightened. Shook himself as if coming out of some strange dream state. Blinking, he stepped back, looked at her as if suddenly he didn't recognize her. As if he wasn't quite sure why he was here. Abruptly, he turned and ran from the barn, disappearing into the darkness like a phantom.

CHAPTER 21

It's midnight by the time Tomasetti and I arrive back in Painters Mill. The service station owner wasn't happy at having his evening interrupted, but he met us at the station, and after a few technical issues, he provided a disk containing the security camera footage of the previous twenty-four-hour period. We're lucky, because in a matter of days, all of it would have been recorded over and lost.

I enter the station to find my newest dispatcher, Margaret, standing at the reception desk, headset clamped over brown-and-silver curls, the Painters Mill PD's policy and procedure manual open on the credenza behind her. She's updating the master file, printing everything out, and replacing the pages that have changed, something that hasn't been done since I've been chief.

"You're working late tonight," she says cheerily.

Her desk is bedecked with framed photos of grandchildren—ski vacations, summer picnics, and dogs of every shape and size. A sweating glass of iced tea and a sample-size tube of hand cream take up space next to her keyboard. Not only has she turned the reception area into her home away from home, but she runs it with a level of military discipline not before seen. My officers have learned to provide her with what she needs in a timely manner—or else receive a thorough dressing-down.

"How's the P and P manual coming along?" I ask.

"Still waiting for Jodie to email me the file with the job descriptions." She punctuates the statement with a direct look over the tops of her bifocals, brows up.

"I'll light a fire," I tell her.

I hear Tomasetti enter as I unlock the door to my office. He exchanges niceties with Margaret—a meeting of two strong personalities—and I smile as my laptop boots up. I'm sitting at my desk when he appears in the doorway.

"She runs a tight ship," he says in a low voice.

"Cross her and you'll be walking the plank."

"I've no doubt."

I slide the disk into the drive and bring up the file. Instead of taking the visitor chair across from me, he rounds my desk and comes up behind me so he'll have a better view. Using the mouse, I click PLAY. The grainy footage comes to life. The camera angle is bad; the parking lot and front entrance of The Pub are too far away for us to see much in the way of detail. The lighting is far from ideal, the angle worse. On the positive side, we have a clear line of sight without obstruction.

We're champing at the bit to discover even the most minute of clues, but finding anything useful on a twenty-four-hour run of CCTV is not a speedy process. After the first hour, Tomasetti pulls up one of the visitor chairs and settles in beside me. I roll through the footage as fast as I dare. Both of us have our necks craned, eyes squinting.

One hour turns into two. At two A.M., I turn over the mouse to him and go to reception to make coffee. I've barely finished when Tomasetti calls out. "Here we go."

I return to my office and come up behind him for a look.

He backs up the footage, clicks PLAY. It's darker now, dusk, the resolution fuzzy and disjointed. Headlights flash as a vehicle pulls into the parking lot of The Pub and parks at the side of the building. My pulse jumps when I recognize it as Rachael Schwartz's Lexus. She doesn't open the door or get out. A full minute passes with no movement. Then the female driver gets out, slams the door, leans against the car door. Though I can't see her face, I can tell by the way she moves that it's her. She's wearing dark skinny pants with a cold-shoulder top. Heels. A hat cocked at just the right angle. The outfit speaks of attitude, confidence, and style, and she has mastered all of it.

"She's talking to someone on her cell," Tomasetti murmurs.

He's put on readers at some point. Black frames. The sight warms me, makes me smile. "You look good in those cheaters, Tomasetti."

He doesn't look at me, but I see his mouth twitch. "I know."

"You're pretty full of yourself, aren't you?"

"Full of something."

We turn our attention back to the screen. Rachael is still leaning against the car, cell pressed to her ear, talking animatedly, gesturing. Smoking a cigarette now. Even though it's been years since I saw her—and she was just a kid—her mannerisms are familiar. In spite of the dim light and poor resolution, it's evident that she was a beautiful, animated woman.

"We need to find that cell phone," I murmur.

"Call records would be nice." He's looking intently at the screen. "She's not happy with whoever's on the other end."

My cop's interest stirs. Though we can't make out her expression or hear what she's saying, her body language tells us she's arguing with someone. "Looks like it."

I glance at the time in the lower corner of the screen, which indicates the footage was recorded at 6:42 P.M. According to her credit card record, she had dinner with an unknown individual and paid for it with her card, just an hour later. Is she talking to her murderer? Planning to meet him? Does the argument have anything to do with her murder?

"Who are you talking to, my girl?" I whisper.

Rachael ends the call abruptly. Shaking her head, she cuffs the roof of the car with the base of her palm, then yanks open the driver's-side door and slides inside. We watch and wait, but the car doesn't move. Anticipation hums in the air between us. Two minutes pass. Six. Tomasetti scrolls, I go to the coffee station and pour two cups. I've just set them on the desk next to my laptop when I see the flare of headlights on the screen.

"Here he comes," Tomasetti says.

The glare makes it impossible to distinguish the make or model of the vehicle, let alone the license plate number.

"Come on," Tomasetti hisses.

But the driver parks on the other side of Rachael's Lexus, so that all we can see is the roof and a portion of the hood. A dark sedan. Four-door. A male disembarks. Too dark to see his face. Average height. Muscular build. He moves with the ease of a self-assured man. Comfortable with who he is. Confident. No hesitation or uncertainty.

The door of the Lexus swings open. Rachael gets out, slams it behind her. She rounds the hood, meets the man on the other side, out of sight. The footage is too grainy to see his face or discern his expression. But even to my untrained eye, his body language speaks of tension. He's much larger than her. I recall the autopsy report. Rachael Schwartz was five feet six inches tall and weighed in at 120 pounds. This man is taller by six or eight inches and outweighs her by seventy or eighty pounds. In a physical confrontation, she wouldn't stand a chance.

They exchange words. Some gesturing. Hands on hips. The tension remains, but it's more subtle now. Two adversaries facing off, aware of appearances, indications of weakness. Some elusive element simmering beneath the surface. After a moment, the male motions toward the bar. Rachael turns and looks, then shrugs. Reluctant. He motions again. This time, she throws up her hands and they start that way.

In that instant, they face the camera dead-on.

"Show us your face, you prick." Tomasetti clicks the mouse, freezing the frame. He tries to enlarge it, but the resolution becomes too grainy. Cursing, he clicks again, moving them forward frame by frame. It doesn't help.

"Any chance you have a computer guy who can bring that into better focus?" I ask.

"We can damn well try. I know one of the computer forensic guys. I'll give him a call, see if he'll meet me first thing." He checks his watch. "Let's see if Schwartz and her pal leave together."

It takes us twenty minutes to find their departure. Sure enough, Rachael and her male counterpart walk out of The Pub an hour later. This time, we catch a glimpse of their faces. It's blurred, but something pings in my brain. Something about the male. The way he moves? The way he walks? The set of his shoulders? His clothes? What?

"Freeze it," I say abruptly.

Tomasetti clicks the mouse.

"I think there's something familiar about that guy." I reach over and usurp the mouse. Back up the footage. Play it forward. "I don't know. Something . . ."

"You've met him before?" he asks.

"I'm not sure. Maybe. Something in the way he moves. There. The way he swings his arms when he walks, the tilt of his head."

"Do you mean, see-him-at-the-grocery familiar? Or maybe you've seen him around town? Or have you met him? Arrested him?"

"I don't know." Frustration sizzling, I play it again, taking it apart frame by frame.

Tomasetti waits, dividing his attention between me and the video. I turn to him. "I need a clear shot of his face, damn it. I'm pretty sure I've seen him before. I don't know him, but I've seen him. Maybe talked to him. His mannerisms are familiar."

He reaches for my laptop, presses the button to eject the disk. "Let me get to work on this."

CHAPTER 22

I'm tired to my bones, already missing Tomasetti and nearly to the farm in Wooster when my police radio barks. "Chief, I've got a ten-fourteen." Margaret uses the police code for "prowler" and then rattles off an address that's familiar—and still fresh in my memory bank.

"Is that the Bontrager place?" I ask.

"RP is Ben Bontrager," she tells me, using the abbreviation for "reporting party." "I know you're on your way home, but since they're Amish I called you instead of Mona. Do you want me to send her since she's on duty?"

"That's okay. You did the right thing." I turn round in the parking lot of a Methodist church and head that way. "I'm ten-seven-six."

One of the things my years in law enforcement have taught me is that coincidences rarely occur, especially in the course of an investigation. I've been chief in Painters Mill for about eight years now. Aside from the selling-of-unpasteurized-milk incident, my department has never been called to the Bontrager farm. And yet just outside of twenty-four hours after the murder of Rachael Schwartz, I receive a call to report a prowler. Coincidence?

"We'll see," I murmur as I crank up my speed to just over the limit and run my overhead lights. In minutes I pull into the lane of the Bontrager farm. The house is lit with the yellow glow of lantern light. I keep my eyes open for movement as I barrel up the lane. There are no vehicles in sight. No one outside. I park behind the buggy at the rear of the house. I'm on my way around to the front when the back door swings open.

"Chief Burkholder?"

I turn to see Ben Bontrager standing on the porch, holding the door open, a lantern in hand.

"What happened?" I ask.

"There was a man. In the barn. A stranger. He threatened my wife. Roughed her up some." Looking distressed, he opens the door wider and ushers me through. "*Kumma inseid.*" Come inside.

"Is anyone hurt?" I ask as I enter.

"No."

"Where's the man?"

"He ran away."

"Did you recognize him?"

"I didn't see him." But his eyes skate away from mine. "*Deah vayk.*" This way.

I speak into my lapel mike and ask for assistance. "Mona, ten-fourteen. I'm ten-twenty-three the Bontrager farm. Ten-seven-eight."

Her voice cracks over the radio. "Ten-seven-six."

Ben and I pass through a back porch that's been enclosed and is being used as a laundry/mudroom. An old-fashioned wringer-style washer squats in the corner. A hat rack where four *kapps* and a man's straw hat are hung. A clothesline decorated with men's shirts bisects the room.

Open shelving laden with canning jars. A taxidermy deer head with twelve-point antlers stares at me from its place on the wall.

"You didn't have to come, you know."

I look toward the kitchen to see Loretta Bontrager standing in the doorway, looking at me as if I'm going to pull out my .38 and cut her down. She looks shaken and pale, her nose and eyes glowing red as if she'd been crying. Even from ten feet away I see the marks on her throat.

I cross the distance between us. "Are you hurt?" I ask. "Do you need an ambulance?"

"I'm fine." She does her best to scoff, but doesn't quite manage. The look she gives her husband is fraught with recrimination. "I told you not to call. It was nothing. I'm fine."

I point at the marks on her neck. "Who did that to you?"

Giving her husband a scornful look, she turns and walks into the kitchen.

Puzzled by her response, I follow. "Loretta, what happened?"

Ben brushes past me to stand next to his wife. He sets his hand on her shoulder, but she moves aside and it drops away. An odd mix of concern and confusion infuses his expression. I notice the trousers over his sleep shirt, telling me he'd been in bed and wakened.

Loretta sinks into a chair as if her legs aren't quite strong enough to support her. "It was nothing," she tells me. "Just . . . a man down on his luck and in need of help. That's all."

I look at Ben and raise my brows.

He meets my gaze, gives a shrug. "I woke and she wasn't in our bed. I found her in the barn, crying. I saw those marks on her neck, and she told me about the man. I thought we should tell someone." He turns his attention to his wife and his mouth tightens. "Men who are down on their luck do not leave marks like that on a woman."

When Loretta looks away from him, he adds, "*Fazayla see.*" Tell her.

The Amish woman looks down at her hands and shakes her head. "I haven't slept well since . . . what happened to Rachael. So I go to the barn sometimes to see the lambs. The babies, you know." Her mouth curves as if the thought gives her comfort. "I was holding one of the newborns when a man just . . . came out of nowhere. He grabbed me." Her eyes flick away and she lowers her head, presses her fingers against her forehead. "He . . . wanted money. I told him I didn't have any and . . . he . . ." She touches the marks at her throat. "I think he didn't believe me. He shoved me. Choked me." She shakes her head. "He'd been drinking. I could smell it on his breath. I offered to give him food, but he got angry and . . . he pushed me down and then he just . . . ran out the back."

It's not the kind of crime we have here in Painters Mill. In fact, in all the years I've been chief, I can recall only two muggings. Both times it happened in the parking lot of the Brass Rail Saloon at closing time and involved individuals who'd had too much to drink.

"Did you recognize him?" I ask. "Have you ever seen him before? Around town?"

"No." She shakes her head, but doesn't look at me. "It happened so fast. And by lantern light. I didn't get a very good look at his face."

"Did he have a weapon?"

"I don't think so."

"What did he look like?" I ask. "Was he English? Amish? White? Or black?"

"English." Her brows knit. "White." She blinks as if taking herself back to a nightmare she doesn't want to revisit. "He was just . . . average looking. Scruffy. Sandy hair. Strong, though."

"Age?"

"Maybe thirty-five? A little younger than Ben and I."

"Height? Weight?"

She looks at her husband. "Shorter than Ben. Heavier though."

The image of the man's silhouette on the CCTV video flashes unbidden in my mind's eye. "What was he wearing?" I ask.

She struggles for a moment, then shakes her head. "Blue jeans, I think. I was so shaken up I didn't really notice."

"Was he on foot?" I ask. "Did he have a vehicle?"

"I didn't see a vehicle, but he could have parked it somewhere, I guess."

"Do you have any idea where he went?" I ask. "Do you know which direction he went when he ran away?"

Another shake. "I just saw him go out the door. At the back of the barn, the underside where the pens are. Ben woke up and . . . he ran over to the neighbor's house and called 911."

Speaking into my shoulder mike, I hail Dispatch. "I need County to assist. Ten-eighty-eight." Suspicious activity. I recite the address for the Bontrager farm. "White male. Six feet. One-ninety. May be on foot."

"Roger that."

I look at Loretta, trying to isolate the source of the sense that something about this incident isn't quite right. It's not that I don't believe her. She's visibly shaken. I can plainly see the marks on her throat. The blooming bruise on her cheek. I've no doubt *someone* accosted her. But I don't believe it was some random stranger and I don't believe he was here for money. The one thing I'm relatively certain of is that I'm not getting the whole story.

That said, like much of rural America, Painters Mill has been hard hit by the opioid epidemic. It's not out of the realm of possibility that someone looking for easy money went to an Amish farm in search of cash. It's well known most Amish keep cash on hand. It's also known that they will not defend themselves or their property. Many Amish, in fact, would hand over their cash just to help someone in need.

I look at Loretta. "Do you mind if I take a look at those marks on your throat?"

Her sigh is barely discernible, but she complies, tilts her head to one side. The flesh is abraded, the outline of fingers and a thumb visible. By morning, she'll have bruises.

"You sure you don't want to get yourself checked out at the hospital?" I ask.

"I'm fine, Katie," she tells me. "Just shaken up is all. I didn't even want to call you, but Ben thought we should. I wasn't expecting anything like that to happen out in the barn of all places, especially this time of night."

"Did the man who attacked you say anything else?" I ask.

"No, he just . . . asked for money. That's all."

I nod, but that uneasy suspicion scratches at the back of my brain again. I nod, give her a moment to say more. When she doesn't, I ask, "Is there anything else you'd like to tell me?"

The couple exchange a look. Ben leans against the counter, his arms crossed at his chest, his expression closed and grim. Loretta won't make eye contact with me, instead looking down at the floor. "I think that's about it," she says.

"I'm going to take a look around." Digging into my pocket, I pull out my card and jot my cell phone number on the back. "If either of you realize there's more you need to tell me, give me a call."

I set the card on the counter and start toward the door.

CHAPTER 23

Summer 2008

Loretta didn't know how long they danced or how many songs the band played. Twice she became separated from Rachael, but found her way back. Once, she danced with an English girl with blue hair and eyes smeared with what looked like charcoal. But the girl had a nice smile and a big laugh, and Loretta thought she'd never had so much fun in her life.

But, of course, as her *mamm* liked to say, all good things must come to an end, and as she danced next to the stage, her head began to swim. Sweat broke out on the back of her neck. When she looked at the stage, it tilted left and right and then swirled around her like some out-of-control merry-go-round. Worse, she was starting to feel nauseous. She looked around for Rachael, to tell her she needed to go get some water, but her friend was dancing with an English boy. His arms were around her waist and the way he was looking at her filled Loretta with a longing she didn't quite understand. Rachael looked so happy, Loretta decided not to interrupt and headed out on her own.

By the time Loretta reached the edge of the crowd, her stomach was seesawing. She barely made it to the nearest tent before throwing up. When she was finished, she went to the booth of the guy selling water, bought a bottle, and decided to take it to the buggy and lie down.

She got lost twice on the way. By the time she reached the buggy her head was pounding. Legs jittery, she drank half the water, and then crawled into the buggy to lie down in the back. It was cooler there and almost quiet. If she could just be still for a little while, she might be able to go back and rejoin Rachael.

"*Der siffer hot zu viel geleppert.*" The drunkard had just sipped too much.

Loretta wasn't sure how long she'd dozed. A minute or two. She sat up to see Levi Yoder standing outside the buggy, looking at her.

"You okay?" he asked.

"I'm fine."

He was looking at her bare legs, so she tugged at her skirt, ran her hand over the fabric, wishing her friend hadn't cut it. "Where's Rachael?"

"I was going to ask you the same thing." He pulled out his cell phone, squinted down at it, then looked at her. "She's late."

Loretta didn't respond. Her head was still aching, but her stomach had calmed. It was just like Rachael to be late. How could she be so irresponsible? But Loretta figured it was as much her fault as her friend's.

"I reckon we're going to have to just sit here and wait for her."

He was looking at her oddly, his head tilted to one side. The kind of look a man had when he was thinking about buying a horse; he liked what he saw, but thought he might haggle a bit before making an offer.

"I'm going to go find her." Loretta started to climb out of the buggy, but Levi blocked her way.

"What's your hurry?" he drawled.

He held a can of beer in his hand. A cigarette dangled from the side of his mouth. She didn't like the way he was looking at her.

"I don't want to get into trouble," she said.

"If she doesn't show in a few minutes, I'll go look." He flicked the cigarette away.

"My parents don't know I left," she said. "I have to go." She didn't want him to know that about her; the less he knew, the better. But she couldn't think of a better excuse to get away from him.

"I'll get you home," he said. "Don't worry."

He was blocking her way out, making her feel claustrophobic and trapped.

"Bet your pal will show any moment." He set his beer on the floorboard and started to climb into the buggy.

Moving quickly, Loretta tried to slip past him. But he was faster. His hands closed around both her biceps. Lifting her, he slid her onto the back seat. "What's your hurry?"

"Let me out," she hissed.

He grinned. "I always thought you were a cute thing," he whispered.

"I have to go." Loretta had barely uttered the words when he pushed her back and came down on top of her.

"Aw, come on," he whispered. "Just a kiss."

She turned her head just in time to avoid his open mouth. She discerned the wetness of spit on her cheek. The weight of his body, crushing against hers with such force that she couldn't breathe.

"I always fancied you," he murmured.

She tried to push him away, but he was too heavy. She twisted beneath him, tried to kick, but she was pinned. Vaguely, she was aware of him reaching between them, working at the zipper of his jeans, trying to get out his thing, his other hand sliding between her legs.

Panic unfurled inside her. Her *mamm* had warned her about boys like Levi. Don't get yourself into a mess, she'd said. Of course, that was exactly what Loretta had done. It was all her fault. How could she ever have believed sneaking out was a good idea?

"Levi, stop it!" She gasped the words, squirming, trying to keep her legs together.

In the next instant he jolted as if lightning had come down from the sky to strike his back. "What the—"

Loretta looked over his shoulder, saw movement outside the door.

"Get the hell off her!"

Rachael.

Relief moved through her like an earthquake. Oxygen bursting into air-deprived lungs. Cool water on a feverish face.

Levi raised himself up off her. Loretta caught a glimpse of him pushing his thing back into his pants. A moment later, a loud *snap!* sounded behind him.

He screamed. "Yawwww! Fuck!"

"Get off her!"

Levi was climbing out of the buggy when another *crack!* sounded, like a firecracker. He lost his footing and fell to his knees in the dust.

Loretta scrambled to the door. Rachael stood a few feet away, buggy whip in hand, fury in her eyes. In that instant, Loretta knew that while Levi Yoder might be bigger and stronger, he didn't stand a chance against her friend.

"Come on!" Rachael cried. "Run!"

Loretta didn't hesitate. She scrambled from the buggy, stumbled over Levi even as he lurched to his feet. Rachael threw down the whip and they ran.

Levi hurled expletives at them as they fled into the darkness. By the time they reached the road, both girls were breathless and laughing so hard they couldn't speak.

That was the night Rachael Schwartz became Loretta's hero. She was the only person who'd ever stood up for her. The only girl who'd ever fought for her. She was the best friend Loretta had ever had and there was nothing on this earth that could ever tear them apart.

CHAPTER 24

Day 3

There is a rhythm to a small town. An ebb and flow of a community in constant motion. A certain way of doing things. Expectations to be met. There's a set dynamic among the citizens. Reputations to uphold or cut down. Rumors to be told, stories to be embellished upon or brought to an end. If you're a cop and you're not cognizant of all of those subtleties, you're not doing your job. Having lived in Painters Mill most of my life, I also know that sometimes it's those very same undercurrents that can make my job more difficult.

It was after four A.M. when I arrived home from the Bontrager place last night. Mona and I, along with a deputy from the Holmes County Sheriff's Office, searched the entire Bontrager farm from corncrib to barn to chicken house and all the way to the fence line at the back of the property. The only indication anyone had been there other than Ben and Loretta was a single muddy footprint in the pen behind the barn. I snapped a dozen photos of it, but the ground was too juicy to pick up any tread and the images aren't going to be helpful. There was no sign of a vehicle. Nothing dropped or inadvertently left behind. Because of the hour, we couldn't canvass. I left instructions with Glock to talk with the neighbors at first light. Considering the time of the attack and that most of the farms are a mile or so apart, I'm not holding my breath.

Tomasetti spent most of the night at the police lab in London, which is just west of Columbus. He crawled into bed a little before five A.M., just as I was making my way to the shower. He let me know the information technology people at BCI are working on improving the quality of the video or at least trying to come up with some decent stills. A process that will likely take a couple of days.

I arrive at the station at seven A.M. to find Margaret's Ford Taurus parked in its usual spot. A lone buggy sits next to the car. The horse—head down, rear leg cocked, snoozing—is tethered to the parking meter. If I'm not mistaken, the buggy belongs to the Bontragers. I wonder if one of them had an attack of conscience for not telling me the whole story about the intruder last night, and decided to make things right this morning.

I enter to find Margaret standing at the reception station, six P&P manuals stacked on the credenza behind her.

Ben and Loretta Bontrager sit stiffly on the sofa, looking uncomfortable and out of place. Previously, Ben was a talkative, mild-mannered man. This morning he's stone-cold silent with a fractious air. Loretta looks as if she spent the night sleepless and crying. Her face is the color of paste, dark circles beneath troubled eyes. The marks on her neck have bloomed into bruises. Their daughter sits between them, her head on her *mamm*'s shoulder, faceless doll in her lap, unaware that this isn't the kind of visit to be enjoyed.

Loretta gets to her feet when I enter, the knitting in her lap falling to the floor. I can tell by her expression this is the last place on earth she wants to be. Something has changed since I last spoke to her and the upshot isn't good.

"Good morning," I say.

"Morning, Chief." Margaret motions to the family. "Mr. and Mrs. Bontrager arrived a few minutes ago. They'd like to talk to you if you have a few minutes."

I turn my attention to the couple. "What can I do for you?"

The Amish woman stoops to pick up her knitting, nearly drops it again. She looks flustered and on edge. I can't help but notice that her hands are shaking when she tucks the spool of yarn into her sewing bag.

"I need to tell you something," she blurts. "About last night."

"All right." I motion toward my office.

Loretta looks at Margaret and offers a tremulous smile. "If you could keep an eye on Fannie for a few minutes?"

"Sure I can," Margaret says cheerfully. "I was just going to fix myself a nice cup of hot chocolate." She looks at Fannie. "Whipped cream or marshmallow, young lady?"

The Amish girl grins. "Both."

"*Heicha dei fraw.*" Obey the woman. Loretta eases her daughter toward Margaret, but her attention is already on me and what lies ahead.

At the coffee station, I pour three cups and hand both of them a cup. I unlock my office door and we go inside. I motion them to the visitor chairs and then take my own chair at my desk.

Before I can say anything, Loretta sets down her cup. "I wasn't completely honest with you last night, Chief Burkholder. I'm sorry. I should have . . . I should have . . . Ben thought I should come in as soon as possible and set things straight."

"We didn't want to get involved in all of this, Chief Burkholder," Ben adds. "But telling the truth . . . is the right thing to do, so we came."

"I'm glad you did." Interest piqued, I wait.

Loretta sits up straighter, folds her hands in her lap, looks down at her hands. "I know who came to the barn last night. I saw his face. I know him."

"Who?"

"Dane Fletcher," she tells me. "He's a police. A deputy. With the sheriff's office."

I barely hear anything past the name, over the gong of disbelief in my head. *Fletch?* I struggle to get my mind around the notion that he assaulted an Amish woman. I've known Dane Fletcher for years. He's been with the sheriff's office as long as I can remember. He's a solid guy. A husband and father. A volunteer. Little League coach. Why in the name of God would he accost an Amish woman in her barn? It simply doesn't make sense.

"Are you telling me Dane Fletcher accosted you in the barn last night, physically assaulted you, and demanded money?"

"He didn't demand money," she tells me. "What happened last night is about . . . something else."

I stare at them, first Loretta and then her husband, and I can't imagine where this is going. Is she telling the truth? Is it possible Fletcher and this woman are involved in some sort of illicit affair?

"Loretta, you need to tell me exactly what happened," I say firmly. "All of it. Don't leave anything out this time."

She looks away, fingers a frayed thread at the hem of her *halsduch*.

"*Fazayla see*," Ben snaps. *Tell her.*

I lean back in my chair, irritated that I've been misled, more than a little skeptical that I'm going to get the whole truth now.

"This deputy," Loretta begins. "He thinks I know something about him. Something he doesn't want me to talk about."

"It has to do with Rachael Schwartz," Ben cuts in, glaring at his wife. "Talk."

Loretta takes a deep breath, like a child who doesn't know how to swim contemplating a dive into a deep pool. "Fletcher did something bad to Rachael. A long time ago. When she was a teenager. She told me not to tell. Now . . ." She shrugs. "I think I need to tell you."

I nod for her to continue.

"When Rachael was seventeen years old, right before she was baptized, she got a job as a stocker at Fox Pharmacy and bought a car with the money she earned. It was an old piece of junk that didn't start half the time. But Rachael loved that car." She catches herself smiling at the memory, ducks her head, embarrassed. "Leave it to Rachael to do something like that, right?"

The Amish woman sighs. "She never 'officially' got to have her *rum-springa*. Sometimes the girls don't, you know. They sure didn't want Rachael having that kind of freedom. That didn't stop her. After she'd gone through *die gemee nooch geh* in preparation for her baptism, she was sneaking out almost every night. Drinking. Listening to music. Getting into trouble. My parents didn't like me spending too much time with her." Another smile, regretful and melancholy this time. "Maybe if I had . . ."

Her mouth tightens. "Toward the end of that summer, I didn't see her for a while, which was odd. She was always coming over in that old car. To visit with me, you know. Then she stopped coming. A couple of weeks passed. When she finally came by . . .

"She took me out to the barn." Loretta closes her eyes tightly, scrubs her hand over her face. "And she told me the most horrible story I ever heard."

CHAPTER 25

Summer 2008

Rachael Schwartz was seventeen years old the night she learned how the world worked. When she understood that getting what you wanted boiled down to how much of yourself you were willing to betray.

She'd spent the day at the county fair with Loretta and what a blast it had been. At dusk, she'd ridden the Ferris wheel with the English boy she'd met last weekend. Later, she and Loretta had bought a six-pack of beer and she'd driven out to the Tuscarawas Bridge to hang out with the usual crew, a group of both English and Amish kids, and they spent the evening swimming and drinking beer.

It had been the most wonderful day of her life. No work. No worries. No one looking over her shoulder and telling her she was going to go to hell if she didn't change her ways. She'd dropped Loretta off at ten and now Rachael was on her way home. She'd never felt so free. So *alive.* It was as if her heart couldn't contain another ounce of happiness or else it would simply burst from her chest. How could God frown upon all the things that made life so wonderful?

Most Amish girls didn't do much during their *rumspringa*. Not like the boys, anyway. Rachael had no intention of wasting what little time she had. The adults were pushing hard to get her baptized. Once that happened, she was sunk. Her parents didn't approve of her running around. They didn't approve of her friends or the choices she made. They didn't approve of the job she'd taken at the drugstore in town. But it was the car that they simply couldn't abide. Datt wouldn't even let her drive it onto the property, forcing her to park it at the end of the lane. Rachael didn't care. She wasn't going to let that keep her from doing what she wanted to do. She was finally having fun. Why did they have to go and ruin it?

No one understood. Loretta tried, but she was a good girl through and through. Unlike Rachael, who'd never quite been able to follow the rules. Just yesterday Mrs. Yoder had called her *hochmut*. Who cared if she was prideful? When you were Amish, it seemed, no one approved of anything. Did God approve? She'd been wondering about that, too. Wondering if maybe the Amish had it all wrong. Maybe she'd just find her own way. If she had to leave the fold to do so, then so be it.

Tom Petty was belting out "Breakdown," the music turned up loud enough to rattle the speakers. Rachael sang along, the windows down, the night air cool on her skin, her hair flying. How was it that she'd lived her entire life without rock and roll? And boys? And beer? Thinking about how that must seem to her Amish brethren, Rachael threw her head back and laughed out loud. She turned up the radio another notch, until the knob wouldn't go any further, and she sang along with Petty, slapping her palms on the steering wheel. She was so embroiled in the music that she didn't notice the headlights behind her until they were right on her tail. She was just a few miles from home when the red and blue lights flashed in her rearview mirror.

"Shit!"

She was still wearing her English clothes. A can of Budweiser sweating in the console. The empty one she'd finished before dropping off Loretta lay on the floor on the passenger side. She didn't think she was drunk, but she'd heard about the local cops. If they caught a whiff of alcohol on your breath, they'd make you take the sobriety test. Even if you weren't drunk, they'd haul you to jail.

Trying to remember if she had any gum, she slowed the car and pulled onto the shoulder. Quickly, she picked up the can of beer, looked around wildly, and shoved it into the opening between the console and seat, out of sight. A glance in the side-view mirror told her the cop had gotten out and was coming her way. Unfastening her seat belt, she lunged at the empty can on the floor and pushed it beneath the seat.

"Good evening."

Gasping, Rachael turned in the seat to see a young Holmes County deputy standing outside her car, bent at the hip, looking in at her. "Oh," she said. "Hi."

"Can I see your driver's license and proof of insurance please?" he asked.

He was young for a cop. Just a few years older than she was. Professional and clean shaven with buzz cut hair and the prettiest brown eyes she'd ever seen.

She dug into her bag for her driver's license, then checked the glove compartment for her insurance card and handed both to him. "Was I speeding?"

He took her license and insurance card and studied both, taking his time answering. She'd turned down the radio and with half an ear listened to the Petty song end and Nirvana start in. Hopefully, he wouldn't keep her too long.

"I clocked you going sixty-seven miles an hour," he said. "Do you know what the speed limit is?"

She searched her mind for the right answer. Tell him the truth? That she knew the speed limit, but hadn't been paying attention? Tell him she thought the speed limit was sixty-five? Maybe she could tell him she was late and rushing home so her parents wouldn't be angry with her. Or that she badly had to use the restroom.

She looked up at him, saw that he was looking back at her, waiting for an answer, and she smiled. "I guess I didn't realize I was going so fast."

"Well, you were." He smiled back and cocked his head. "Are you Dan and Rhoda's girl?"

"They're my parents."

His eyes landed on her English clothes. "If you don't mind my saying, you don't look very Amish tonight."

She laughed. She almost told him she was on *rumspringa,* which wasn't quite true, but thought it might lead to a question about her drinking. Better to play it safe. "I had to work today," she said. "Then I went to the movies with my girlfriend."

"Yeah? What did you see?"

"*Twilight.*"

"I hear that's a good one," he said.

She began to relax. For a police, he seemed like a nice guy. Laid-back. Reasonable. Hopefully, he wouldn't give her a speeding ticket.

He stepped back and looked at her car. "Never seen an Amish girl driving a car alone on a back road at one o'clock in the morning."

"I'm on my way home."

"Parents let you stay out this late?"

She laughed. "I'm kind of late."

"They wait up for you?"

"I hope not!" She laughed again and she thought maybe he liked her and had decided not to write her a ticket. All she had to do was be nice and polite. Charm him a little, the way she saw the English girls do. She was home free.

He laughed, too, then came closer and leaned in. "You been drinking tonight?"

"I don't drink." She punctuated the statement with a laugh, but she didn't miss the nervous tick at the back of her throat. "It's against the rules, you know."

"Huh." He scratched his head, looked around. "That's what I thought." Grimacing, he turned back to her and sighed. "I still have to check. You know, do my job. Would you get out of the vehicle? This won't take too long."

Rachael didn't move. She didn't want to get out. Didn't want this to go any further. But what could she do?

"But I haven't been drinking," she said. "I just . . . want to go home."

"It'll be all right." He reached for the door handle and opened it for her. "Come on, now. A quick sobriety test and then you'll be on your way. I'm sure you'll do fine."

"Oh. Well." Not knowing what else to do, Rachael got out of the vehicle. Feeling self-conscious now. Nervous because she thought he probably knew she'd lied to him. That she'd been drinking and maybe he wasn't her new best friend after all. What was she going to do if he wrote her a ticket? Or worse, took her to jail? What would she tell her parents? What if they had to bail her out of jail? How much would it cost them?

"Here's what you need to do," he said, indicating the painted line on the shoulder of the road. "Put your arms out like this." He demonstrated. "Take nine steps, one foot in front of the other, heel to toe.

185

When you reach nine steps, put your head back like this." He tilted his head back so that he was looking up at the night sky. "And touch your nose with your index finger."

Rachael took in every word, a little relieved because she thought she could do it. If she could remember all those instructions. The truth of the matter was she *had* been drinking and she wasn't exactly at the top of her game. Surely she could manage something so simple. Then she would drive straight home. Even if she got a ticket, she could pay for it herself. Her parents didn't have to know. No one had to know.

He leaned against her car and crossed his arms at his chest. It was as if he was settling in to watch a movie or something. When she hesitated, he raised his brows. "Go on," he said.

Feeling self-conscious, she walked to the painted line. She took a deep breath, stretched out her arms, and began to walk, heel to toe. Two steps in and she lost her balance, missed the line by a few inches. It was the heels, she realized. She looked back at him. "It's the shoes. May I take them off?"

He was already coming toward her, reaching for something in his belt. Alarm swirled in her gut when he pulled out what looked like handcuffs. She raised her hands, felt the tears spring in her eyes. "I can do it. It's just that these heels are—"

He reached her, set his hand on her arm, slid it down to her wrist. "I'm placing you under arrest for drunk driving."

Alarm spiraled inside her when the cuff encircled her wrist. He snugged it tight. The metal hard and cold against her wrist when it clicked into place.

"Please don't arrest me." She tried to sound calm, but panic rang in her voice.

He took her other hand, pulled it behind her, and cuffed her. "Do you have any weapons on you? Anything sharp that I should be concerned about?"

"No. Please. I didn't do anything wrong. I just want to go home."

Placing one hand at her upper arm, his other on the chain connecting the cuffs, he guided her to his car. Upon reaching the trunk, he turned her toward him, and backed her up so that her backside was against the trunk.

"I'm going to do a quick pat-down to make sure you don't have any weapons on you," he said. "Just stay calm for me, okay?"

"But I'm not drunk," she said.

"We'll get it all straightened out."

She stood stone-still while he ran his hands over her hips, squeezing the pockets, turning then inside out. He removed her pack of cigarettes, lighter, cell phone, and the twenty-dollar bill she had in her back pocket.

"Please don't arrest me," she said. "I just made a mistake. Please. I'll be in such trouble."

When he was finished searching her, he stepped back. She was leaning against the car, her hands clamped together at the small of her back. He stared at her. She stared back, aware that she was shaking, and she struggled to keep it in check.

"Looks like we got us a situation," he said.

For the first time she noticed his breathing was elevated, even though he hadn't exerted himself. Sweat beaded on his forehead and upper lip. The underarm area of his uniform shirt was wet. And for the first time, she sensed something was amiss.

"Can't you just let me go?" she whispered.

Something in his expression changed. A strange light entered his eyes. His jaw flexed, as if he were biting down on something hard. "Do you think maybe we can work something out?"

187

She blinked, not understanding the question, but the sense that something wasn't quite right burgeoned into a different kind of alarm. And for the first time it occurred to her that she was alone with a man she didn't know or trust. They were in the boondocks in the middle of the night. . . .

"Them jeans you're wearing are sure nice and tight," he whispered.

The alarm grew into something closer to panic. The urge to run swept through her. She looked around, wondering if she could make it to the field before he caught her.

"You got nice big titties for a seventeen-year-old, you know that?"

No one had ever talked to her like that. Certainly not a grown man. An adult. The terrible understanding that followed brought with it a gasp of shock that stuck in her throat like a chicken bone.

"Hold still now. You hear?" He reached for the hem of her T-shirt and pulled it up.

Instinctively, she leaned forward, hunched her shoulders forward, tried to cover herself. But he pressed her back against the vehicle, forced her to straighten so that her breasts were visible.

"Man." He didn't even look at her. Just stared at her breasts, a starving animal watching prey in the seconds before it attacked. "Man."

"You can't do that," she cried. "It's not right. You can't."

His eyes slid to hers. "Let me tell you something, Amish girl. If I take you to jail, you'll be there for at least three or four days. A DUI will cost your parents thousands of dollars. Plus a lawyer and they ain't cheap. You'll lose your driver's license. Your car. Everyone will know. All those self-righteous Bible-thumping Amish going to shun you. Is that what you want?"

"Please don't," she cried. "I promise not to do it again. Please."

"Well, listen up. If you let me put my hands on you, I'll let you go home. No ticket. No jail. We won't tell a soul. And no one will ever know." His voice had gone hoarse, his breaths coming faster.

Rachael didn't know what to think. Didn't know what to say. Did he just want to touch her? Did he want to do something else?

"I don't want to do anything," she choked.

"Then you're going to jail. You want to know what's going to happen when you get there? They're going to take your clothes. Strip-search you and they ain't very nice about it. Keep you locked up for days. Is that what you want?"

"No." Feeling trapped, she began to cry. "What do I have to do?"

"You don't have to do anything." Slowly, he turned her around so that she was facing his car. "I'll do everything."

Clamping his hand around the back of her neck, he forced her face against the trunk lid.

CHAPTER 26

Outrage boils in my gut by the time Loretta finishes her story. I tamp it down, grapple for distance. I don't trust my voice, so I say nothing. The only sound comes from the buzz of the overhead lights, the beelike hum of my computer.

Tears stream down Loretta's cheeks. She doesn't acknowledge them. Her gaze fastens to the surface of my desk, and the silence that follows is excruciating.

"Rachael told you that?" I ask.

She nods. "A couple weeks after it happened. She didn't know what to do. I think she needed someone to talk to."

Next to her, Ben sets his elbows on his knees and looks down at the floor.

"She named Dane Fletcher?" I ask.

"Yes."

I think about that a moment. "Did she tell her parents?"

"I don't think she told anyone. I mean, she was Amish. And she was out doing things she shouldn't have been doing. How could she tell anyone?"

I don't respond. Maybe because I don't want to contemplate my answer. Would Rachael's family have supported her? Would they have believed her? Or blamed her? Would her parents have gone to the police? Or would they sweep the whole, ugly incident under the rug in the hope it would go away?

"Did she seek medical help?" I ask. "Go to the doctor?"

"No." The Amish woman tightens her mouth. "She was never the same after that."

I look at her. "How so?"

"Rachael was always bold, you know." A sad smile pulls at her mouth. "The stories her *mamm* told about her when she was a little one." She turns thoughtful. "In the weeks and months after that happened to her, Rachael became even bolder. Worse, she became unkind."

I think about Dane Fletcher. The unexplained deposits into Rachael's bank account. In my mind's eye, I see the CCTV video from the gas station next to the bar in Wooster, and I realize the silhouette of the man who met with Rachael that day could very well be Fletcher's. A theory begins to take shape.

Tears shimmer in Loretta's eyes when she raises her gaze to mine. "Chief Burkholder, Rachael was barely seventeen years old. Little more than a child. Going on twenty-five, you know? She thought she could handle what happened to her. But it changed her. Changed her view of the world and not in a good way."

"Why did Fletcher show up at your place last night?" I ask.

"He knew Rachael and I grew up together. That we were friends. He must have known she told me what he did to her that night because he told me to keep my mouth shut." Her face screws up, but she fends off tears. "He threatened my family."

191

Ben raises his head. I catch a glimpse of anger in his eyes before he can tuck it away, out of sight. "In light of . . . what happened to Rachael," he says, "we thought you should know."

Loretta's eyes widen on mine. She blinks. And I realize she's arrived at the same conclusion as me. That Dane Fletcher and Rachael Schwartz met at the Willowdell Motel and something unspeakable ensued.

"*Mein Gott.*" Choking out a sound of dismay, she lowers her face into her hands.

In the backwaters of my mind, I see Rachael lying on the floor in that motel room. Her broken body and destroyed face. A beautiful young woman with her entire life ahead. A woman who was difficult and flawed and didn't always conduct herself in a way becoming to her Amish roots. But she damn well didn't deserve what happened to her.

"Do you think that policeman did this terrible thing?"

The question comes from Ben. He sits stiffly next to his wife, his expression a mosaic of horror and disbelief and a possibility he can't accept.

I don't answer. I can't for too many reasons to say, let alone the fact that a law enforcement officer has suddenly become my number-one suspect.

I divide my attention between the couple. "Do you know if Rachael has been in touch with Dane Fletcher?" I ask. "By phone or text? Do you know if they've met at any time over the years?"

They exchange a look and then Loretta shakes her head. "I've not heard of such a thing, Chief Burkholder. If they did, Rachael never mentioned it."

CHAPTER 27

I was eighteen years old the last time I saw Rachael Schwartz. The Fall Harvest Festival was a huge flea-market-type event for which the Amish traveled miles to set up booths or wagons, and sell their wares, everything from produce to livestock, from baked goods to quilts. For me, it was a day away from the farm and chores, a time to see my friends, and, of course, sample all that delicious Amish food. Every September, my *datt* loaded our old hay wagon and dragged me and my siblings, Jacob and Sarah, to the festival, where we spent the day selling pumpkins of every shape and size.

By the time I was eighteen, the festival had lost some of its luster. On that particular day, I escaped the watchful eye of my *datt* under the guise of a restroom break and I made my way to a not-so-bustling area on the periphery of the festival, far enough away from my Amish brethren to sneak a smoke. I was about to light up when a cacophony of raised voices interrupted my plans.

I should have known Rachael Schwartz would be involved. The

majority of festivalgoers were Amish, after all, and they simply did not partake in noisy public discourse.

At the edge of the gravel parking lot, next to a row of Port-a-Potties, Loretta Weaver pulled a wood crate filled with what looked like baked goods from the back of a wagon and carried it to her booth, where she'd set up a nice display. A homemade easel was bedecked with a big handwritten sign that proclaimed:

HINKELBOTTBOI (CHICKEN POTPIE)—$6.99

LATTWARRICK (APPLE BUTTER)—$4.99

FRISCHI WASCHT (FRESH SAUSAGE)—$3.69

KARSCHE BOI (CHERRY PIE)—$1.99 PER PIECE/$6.99 WHOLE PIE

A few yards away, two English girls had been working on their own booth, where they were selling cakes. A printed sign pinned to the front of their table read:

PERSONALIZED CAKES FOR BIRTHDAYS,

ANNIVERSARIES, AND OTHER SPECIAL

OCCASIONS. TAKE ONE HOME TODAY!

Evidently, a territory dispute had broken out between two groups of sellers.

"Hey you! Pilgrim girl! This is our spot."

An English girl of about fifteen wearing cut-off denim shorts and a Backstreet Boys T-shirt stood in front of her booth, hands on her hips, glaring at Loretta. Behind her, two gangly teenage boys stood next to the booth, watching, their expressions expectant and amused.

Loretta Weaver went to the English girl and offered a faltering smile.

"We're just selling for the day," she said reasonably. "Pies and such, you know. We can't leave until everything is sold."

A second English girl rounded the table to join them. This one wore a white blouse and pink shorts, a nifty summer hat cocked to one side. "Yeah, well, you're putting a crimp in our style with those pies. You're going to have to take it elsewhere."

Loretta shifted her weight from one foot to the other. "But this is my booth. I'm all set up. I think we'll be fine just where we are, don't you?"

Hat Girl rolled her eyes. "We paid a week's salary for this spot, and we were told no one next to us would be competing with our shit." She pointed toward the ocean of tables and sellers set up closer to the buildings. "You're going to have to move."

Loretta looked around as if expecting someone to come to her aid and help her defend her position. But no one was paying attention. She stood there, looking from one girl to the other, saying nothing.

"I don't think she heard you!" one of the boys called out.

"Send her a frickin' text!" the other boy added, and both of them broke into raucous laughter. "All those Amish hypocrites got phones!"

Loretta looked at the boys and swallowed. "We paid, too. We can't just move. This is our table. There's no place else to go."

The Backstreet Boys T-shirt girl pointed to the more crowded area at the front of the market. "I bet there's a table over there. Just go. You'll find something."

"But this is our assigned booth," Loretta said reasonably. "They told us to use this one. We can't just take someone else's spot."

"Oh my God, she's dense." Shaking her head, Hat Girl moved closer and got in her face. "Look, be a good little pilgrim, load up that buggy, and move your shit."

Loretta opened her mouth as if to say something, but closed it as if not certain how to respond. Instead, she looked down at the ground and shook her head. "I don't want any problems."

"Well, you got one," said the girl in the Backstreet Boys T-shirt.

Hat Girl looked at her friend and shook her head. "I've heard they were dense, but this is ridiculous."

"Maybe she needs some convincing!" one of the boys called out.

The other boy started to chant. "Catfight! Catfight!"

Even then, I was aware that people were occasionally hostile toward the Amish. It didn't happen often, but I'd seen it once or twice. I wasn't exactly a quintessential example of Amish values, but I knew right from wrong. I couldn't abide a bully. Loretta Weaver was a quiet, shy, and hardworking girl who'd been raised to be submissive and nonviolent. She hadn't been exposed to prejudice or cruelty. She was light-years out of her depth and probably didn't even realize it.

"Oh, for God's sake, are you fucking deaf!" Hat Girl strode to the Amish girl's booth. There, she paused, perused the items set on the table, and snatched up a jar of apple butter.

Loretta trailed her, fingering the hem of her apron, trying to stay calm, not quite succeeding.

Mean glinted in the girl's eyes. Holding up the jar, she unscrewed the lid, stuck her finger into the goo, and brought it to her mouth. "Oh my God. This is some good shit."

Loretta stiffened her spine, met the girl's gaze. "You have to pay for it now."

The two English girls exchanged looks and burst out laughing.

A cruel expression overtook Hat Girl's face. Her eyes slanted to the boys snickering from their place at her booth, then slid back to Loretta. "How much do I owe you?"

Loretta held out her hand. "Four dollars and ninety-nine cents."

Upending the jar, Hat Girl poured the apple butter onto Loretta's upturned palm.

"Oh my God, Britany!" The Backstreet Boys T-shirt girl gasped, then slapped her hand over her mouth to hide the bark of laughter that followed.

Loretta lowered her hand, the apple butter dripping unceremoniously to the ground at her feet. Saying nothing, not meeting the other girl's gaze, she pulled a wadded-up tissue from her dress pocket and tried to clean away the sticky apple butter.

I don't remember moving. Just the buzz of fury in my head. Tunnel vision on the girl with the hat. The mean in her eyes. In the back of my mind, I was visualizing myself punching that painted pink mouth.

I never got the chance.

I was still a few steps away when movement out of the corner of my eye snapped me from my fugue. I glanced over to see Rachael Schwartz charge Hat Girl. I barely recognized her. Her face was pulled into a mask of rage. She held a pitchfork in her hand.

I was closest to Loretta, so I grabbed her arm and pulled her out of the way. Rachael swung the pitchfork, slinging horse manure all over Hat Girl with such force that I heard each individual chunk slap against her face and clothes.

For the span of several seconds no one spoke. Hat Girl looked down at her clothes, at the green-brown smears and stains on her white blouse, her bare legs. "Ewww. *Ewww!*" A shudder moved through her. "Oh my God. *Ewww!* You *bitch!*"

Rachael had already darted back to where the horse stood for a second load of manure. Breathing hard, she held it at the ready. "Get lost or you're going to get it again," she said.

That was the day young Rachael Schwartz won my respect—and pilfered a little piece of my heart. Despite our age difference, I realized we were kindred spirits. She couldn't abide by the rules, didn't fit in. She was misunderstood. She broke molds. Worst of all, she was a fighter—a fatal flaw when you live among pacifists. As much as I didn't want to admit it, when I looked at Rachael, I saw myself. Hopelessly awkward, fatally flawed, incapable of pretense. Up until the day I left, I secretly cheered her on.

I lost track of her as she entered her teens, but I heard the stories upon my return. She liked boys a little too much. At seventeen, she got a job and bought that old junker she could never quite live down. It wasn't a first because she was Amish—it was a first because she was *female.* She drank more than her share of alcohol. Smoked cigarettes. Stayed out too late. Sometimes she didn't come home at all.

As an adult looking back, her fall from Amish grace makes me incredibly sad, and I realize something important. While my parents weren't perfect, they instilled in me a foundation that gave me the tools I needed to overcome the bad decisions I made early in my life. I didn't know Rhoda and Dan well, but I don't believe they did the same for their daughter. Because they viewed her as fallen, perhaps beyond redemption, they cut her off. That intolerance—that lack of guidance and support—set her on a path to self-destruction.

A truth that breaks my heart.

CHAPTER 28

One of the lessons life has taught me is that not everyone tells the truth. People lie for all sorts of reasons. To deflect blame. To protect themselves or others. To advance an agenda. To hurt someone or exact revenge. Or any combination of the above. Sometimes, those lies are told by omission. Sometimes with reluctance and guilt. Some people lie with unabashed glee. I've seen it all, but I'm not yet so hardened that I don't feel the occasional punch of shock.

No cop ever wants to believe one of his own is morally corrupt. That he's sullied the oath he took to protect and serve. I've known Dane Fletcher since shortly after I became chief. I always considered him a solid cop and a good person. He's a father of four with a longtime marriage to a Painters Mill elementary school teacher. We've worked several assignments together. Volunteered together. Once, he helped me nab a wayward herd of goats and we ended up laughing our asses off. I liked Fletch. I enjoyed working with him. Respected him. I've trusted him with my life. As I head north toward Millersburg, I'm having one hell of a time getting my head around the possibility that he used his position as a law enforcement officer to rape a seventeen-year-old girl. I can barely entertain the notion that he beat a young woman to death with a baseball bat.

The possibilities turn my stomach. The cop inside me wants to disprove it. But outrage and disappointments aside, I know from experience that sometimes outwardly decent people harbor a shadow side. They keep the darkness of their nature—weaknesses, perversions, addictions, immoralities—hidden from the rest of the world.

Is Dane Fletcher one of them?

Because of the sensitive nature of the accusations and the fact that he's an LEO with another agency, I can't move forward until I involve the Holmes County sheriff. I call Mike Rasmussen as I head north toward Millersburg and tell him I'm on my way to meet him. He agrees—reluctantly. He's got a golf outing with the mayor later in the day and he doesn't want to miss it. I assure him I won't take up too much of his time; I don't let on that I'm about to blow his day to smithereens.

I call Tomasetti as I reach the outskirts of Millersburg. "Where are you?" I ask.

"Where would you like me to be?" he returns evenly.

"How about the Holmes County Sheriff's Office?" I give him the highlights of my meeting with the Bontragers.

When I'm finished, he makes a sound of disgust and asks, "How well do you know Fletcher?"

I tell him. "It would be an understatement to say I'm shocked."

"Any strikes against him?"

I search my memory, realize there were a few minor incidents that never went anywhere, and I feel a churning of uneasiness in my gut.

"I think a woman filed a complaint about him several years back. If I recall there was some question about her credibility and nothing came of it."

The silence that ensues brings with it a creeping dread that climbs up the back of my neck like some slimy worm.

After a moment, he sighs. "I'll be there in ten minutes."

The Holmes County Sheriff's Office is located north of Millersburg, a few miles past Pomerene Hospital. I'm in the process of signing in with the duty deputy when Mike Rasmussen opens the door and leans out.

"Hi, Kate."

I look up from the clipboard to see the sheriff standing outside the door, grinning at me. He's out of uniform, wearing a pink polo shirt, khaki slacks, and golf shoes. "Hey, Mike."

"You want to play golf with us?" he asks. "Proceeds go to the animal shelter. Save a lot of puppies."

I can tell by the way he's looking at me that he's noticed something in my expression and it's given him pause.

"Last time I played golf with you I embarrassed myself." I cross to him and we shake hands. He opens the door wider and ushers me into the hall. Side by side, we make our way to his office.

There, he motions to the visitor chair adjacent to his desk, and he slides into the chair at his desk. Grimacing, I go to the door and close it.

"Must be bad," he says.

"And then some." I take the chair. "I think Dane Fletcher may be involved with the murder of Rachael Schwartz."

"*What?* Fletch?" He starts to laugh, realizes belatedly that I'm not kidding, and blinks hard at me. "Are you serious?"

Over the next minutes, I relay my conversation with the Bontragers.

When I'm finished, Rasmussen leans back in his chair, his arms folded at his chest, staring at me as if he'd like nothing more than to pull out his sidearm and shut me the hell up.

"If I didn't know you so well, Kate, I'd throw you out of my office."

"Yep." I sigh. "Me, too."

"Do you believe this Amish couple?" he asks.

"I believe them enough so that we need to look at it. Get to the bottom of it."

A knock sounds on the door. Cursing beneath his breath, Rasmussen gets to his feet and yanks it open. He doesn't bother greeting Tomasetti and goes back to his desk, falls into the chair.

Taking his time, Tomasetti nods at me and then takes the visitor chair next to mine. "I take it you told him."

I nod, look at Mike. "I need to talk to Fletcher." I glance at Tomasetti. "We need a warrant. I want his phone records and his banking records."

Rasmussen makes a sound of annoyance. "Based on hearsay? Based on secondhand information of something that allegedly happened almost thirteen years ago? By a woman who may or may not be telling the truth? You want to ruin a man's reputation based on that?"

"I have no intention of ruining anyone's reputation," I snap. "But I have a murder to solve."

Ignoring me, he looks at Tomasetti. "Dane Fletcher is a good cop, goddamn it. He's married with a family. Been with the department for seventeen years." He turns his rankled expression on me. "You'd better be damn sure about this before you pull him into this."

"I'm as sure as I need to be." Even as I say the words, I feel the doubt crowding that certainty.

Cursing, Rasmussen slaps his hand down on the desk.

"I don't like it either, Mike," I say. "But we have to talk to him. There's no way around it."

"I don't believe he had anything to do with that girl's murder," Rasmussen says between gritted teeth.

"At the very least, we need to talk to him about the allegation of what happened between him and Rachael Schwartz."

Rasmussen says nothing.

Tomasetti cuts in. "We looked at Rachael Schwartz's banking records. She was living above her means. Way above her means. There were several substantial cash deposits made in the last year. We're trying to find the source, but as you know it's nearly impossible to trace cash."

"So you think she was blackmailing him?" Incredulity rings hard in Rasmussen's voice. "And he murdered her?"

"That's motive. A powerful one if you consider the amount of those deposits, not to mention what word of this would do to him. We're talking professional ruination. Loss of his family. If not jail time."

"We gotta look at him," Tomasetti says.

Rasmussen receives all of it with stony silence.

I look from man to man. "I need to talk to him."

"Why don't we take a look at Fletcher's file and then see if we can ascertain where he was on the night of the murder?" Grimacing, Tomasetti looks from me to the sheriff. "I'll get things rolling on a warrant."

Rasmussen scowls at me. "I'm assuming you already know he's had a couple of complaints filed against him over the years." He looks at Tomasetti. "Nothing came of either complaint due to lack of proof. Sort of a he-said, she-said thing."

"Duly noted," Tomasetti says.

With a curse, the sheriff gets to his feet. "I'll pull his file."

Access to confidential personnel records is an extremely sensitive issue and involves many potential legal concerns. For some municipalities, it requires the involvement of a police union representative.

But due to the seriousness of the situation—in this case a homicide investigation—we've no choice but to proceed. Because both Tomasetti and I are from outside law enforcement agencies—not coworkers in the same department as Fletcher—and a warrant is in the works, we are deemed fair to look at records that we would otherwise be prohibited from viewing.

Half an hour later the three of us are sitting in a small, stuffy interview room, Dane Fletcher's personnel file open on the table in front of us. Rasmussen goes through the file page by page, passing the occasional document to Tomasetti and me.

"Fletch was off duty the night of the murder," Rasmussen tells us. "He worked first shift that day. Got off at four P.M." He flips through several pages, skimming and reading, and passes another sheet to Tomasetti. "Here's the first citizen complaint form."

Tomasetti hits the highlights aloud. "Three years ago. Female complainant. Twenty-two-year-old Lily Fredricks of Portsmouth, Ohio. Pulled her over at two A.M. for a possible OVI," he says, using the acronym for "operating a vehicle impaired." "Vehicle smelled of marijuana. Fredricks claimed Fletcher offered to let her walk if she had sex with him. She refused. Became combative. He made the arrest. Her blood alcohol was point-one-nine. She was charged with OVI and possession of marijuana." He flips the page. "She filed the complaint a few days later. The department opened an investigation, sent it to the Holmes County prosecutor's office, who declined to prosecute."

I look at Tomasetti. "We need to contact her."

He writes down the information. "Yep."

Rasmussen hands him another sheet of paper. "Second citizen complaint form."

Tomasetti reads. "Six years ago. Female complainant. Nineteen-year-old Diana Lundgren. Pulled over for speeding and possession of a controlled substance. She claims Fletcher asked her for sex in exchange for letting her walk. He detained her, kept her handcuffed. She claims he raped her outside his cruiser. Investigation ensued and she was deemed unreliable. Evidently, she's got a lengthy criminal record and a history of drug use."

I look at Mike Rasmussen. He's a good sheriff and a good cop. Like most men and women in law enforcement, he's protective of his subordinates. But he also possesses the strength of character to do the right thing even when that means taking down one of his own.

"Damn, this is a mess," he mutters.

"I want to talk to Fletcher," I say.

"The instant he asks for a union rep or a lawyer, we shut it down," Rasmussen tells me. "You got that, Kate?"

"We got it," Tomasetti puts in.

We get to our feet and head toward the door.

CHAPTER 29

Dane Fletcher owns a pretty little place just south of Millersburg. The house is a newish brick ranch that sits on a three-acre lot dotted with maples and oaks. Tomasetti and I take separate vehicles, follow Rasmussen into the gravel driveway, and park adjacent to the garage.

I meet the two men next to a lamppost where a pavestone walkway leads to the front door of the house. A tricycle lies on its side in the yard. Yellow tulips in the flower beds on either side of the door are starting to bloom. Someone in the Fletcher household has a green thumb.

Rasmussen had wanted to call Fletcher and ask him to meet us at the sheriff's office, probably to save him from any questions he'll likely get from his wife. But due to the seriousness of the allegations, Tomasetti and I thought it would be better to catch him unaware. The plan is to pick him up here and transport him to the sheriff's office so he can answer our questions in the privacy of an interview room. The only thing I know for certain at this moment is that the hours ahead are going to be difficult for everyone involved.

"I'll get him." Rasmussen has just started down the sidewalk when the door opens.

Dane Fletcher steps onto the porch. His smile falls when he sees the expression on Rasmussen's face. He looks past the sheriff, his eyes holding mine for an instant, and I see a skitter of fear whisper across his features. *He knows,* I think, and a hard pang of disappointment joins the chorus of emotions banging around inside me.

"Mike?" he says. "What is this? What's going on?"

"We need to talk to you, Dane." The sheriff reaches him and the two men shake hands.

"About what?" the deputy asks.

"Dane?"

At the sound of the female voice, I look toward the back door to see a pretty woman of about forty standing in the doorway, holding open the storm door. Her expression is more curious than worried as she presses her hand against her very pregnant belly.

"Hey, Mike," she says to the sheriff, oblivious to the undertones zinging among the rest of us.

"Hi, Jen." Rasmussen raises a hand to her. "Tulips looking good," he says conversationally. "I need to borrow the old man for a few hours. Can you spare him?"

She grins. "As long as he comes home with ice cream, we're good."

"I'll get it." Fletcher doesn't look at his wife as he says the words.

"Barbecue this weekend!" she calls out.

Rasmussen has already turned away and started toward his cruiser. No one else responds.

At the sheriff's office, I sit in the Explorer, my hands on the steering wheel, and I watch Fletcher and Sheriff Rasmussen cross the parking lot and enter the building. The sense of betrayal is a knot in my gut. At the moment, that knot is so tangled and tight that I can barely draw a breath. In my mind's eye, I see the way Fletch looked at me when he came out of the house. I'd had misgivings about the allegations against him. I thought maybe the four of us would walk into the interview room and somehow Fletch would convince us he had nothing to do with what happened to Rachael when she was seventeen—or her murder. But I saw the flash of fear and guilt etched into a face well trained to remain neutral, and the truth of that moment is so powerful I'm queasy.

I think about what he did and the anger inside me roils. Not only did he betray the badge, but he betrayed himself and everyone who loves him. His family. His friends. And every single cop who's ever considered him a brother.

A knock on the window startles me from my reverie. I glance over, see Tomasetti standing outside the Explorer. Quickly, I settle my emotions and get out, aware that his eyes are on me.

"I'd ask what you're thinking," he says, "but I'm not sure I want to know."

"You don't."

"I wouldn't want to be in Fletcher's shoes."

"You could never be in his shoes." The statement comes out harshly, but I let it stand.

Thoughtful, troubled, we start toward the building. "Those women who filed complaints against him?" I don't look at Tomasetti as I speak. "He sexually assaulted them. He abused his position. I think he sexually assaulted Rachael Schwartz. Tomasetti, for God's sake, I think he murdered her."

"She was blackmailing him," he says. "He got tired of paying."

I nod, trying to get myself into a better frame of mind for the impending interview. I don't quite manage.

"That's a powerful motive." Tomasetti shrugs.

"He had a lot to lose," I add.

There's more to say, but we've reached the building. Through the door window, I see Rasmussen and Fletcher talking to the duty deputy. Tomasetti pushes open the door and we walk inside.

Twenty minutes later, the four of us are sitting in an interview room with a beat-up table and four plastic chairs. Rasmussen and Fletcher are on one side of the table, Tomasetti and I on the other. Life and experience have given me the tools I need to keep my emotions in check. Even so, I'm barely able to look at Fletcher. I'm too angry to be sitting here, partaking in a potentially life-altering interview of a peer. But this is my case. I don't have a choice.

When the small talk ends, Fletcher sits back and makes eye contact with each of us, his final gaze landing on Rasmussen. "So are you going to tell me why I'm here or are you going to make me guess?"

Rasmussen tosses me an it's-your-show scowl and spits out my name. "Kate."

I focus on the turn of events alleged by Loretta Bontrager, and I don't pull any punches. I withhold mention of Rachael Schwartz, instead focusing on what was alleged to have happened in the barn. All the while, I watch Fletcher for a reaction.

He stares back at me, stone-faced. But he can't hide the color that climbs up his throat and creeps into his cheeks. The muscles in his jaws clamping tight and working in tandem.

When I've finished speaking, he takes a moment to make eye contact with each of us. "That did not happen," he says in a low voice. "I did not threaten her. I did not assault her. I didn't so much as *talk* to her. I don't know those people. I did not drive out to their place last night." His eyes land on mine. "And I'd like to know why the holy fuck you dragged me in here for this rash of bullshit."

"She filed a complaint against you," Rasmussen tells him.

"That's crazy." Fletcher belts out a bitter laugh. "Why the hell would I go to their farm and assault an Amish woman?"

He knows instantly the question is a mistake. I see the regret flash in his eyes. He starts to speak, but I cut in.

"Bontrager claims that Rachael Schwartz told her you pulled her over for an OVI thirteen years ago," I tell him. "She alleges Schwartz told her that you let her walk in exchange for sex. She alleges in the complaint that you knew they were friends and you assumed Rachael had told her what happened. Bontrager claims you accosted her in the barn and threatened her if she didn't keep her mouth shut."

"That's not true," he says. "She's lying."

I lean back in my chair. "Where were you last night between the hours of midnight and four A.M.?"

Fletcher chokes out a sound of exasperation. "I was home. With my wife and kids."

"All night?" Tomasetti asks.

"All night," Fletcher echoes.

"You know we're going to check," Tomasetti says.

"Stay the hell away from my wife." Fletcher's eyes flick to Rasmussen. "Are you going to let them run with this? Ruin me? My marriage? My reputation?" He shakes his head. "Mike, you're going to let them move forward with this bullshit based on accusations made by someone I don't even know? Someone I've never met? I'm telling you right now, Bontrager made the whole thing up. I wasn't anywhere near their place."

Rasmussen shrugs. "You know we've got to look at it."

Fletcher smacks his hand against the tabletop. "This is bullshit."

"Did you ever initiate a stop on Rachael Schwartz?" Tomasetti steps easily into the bad-cop role.

"You mean thirteen years ago?" Fletcher shakes his head, angry. "I don't remember. How could I?" Mouth pulled into a snarl, he looks at me. "The one thing I do know for certain is that I sure as hell didn't demand sex!"

Tomasetti doesn't give him a respite. "You have two similar citizen complaints on your record."

"So do a lot of cops," Fletcher snaps. "Those two women lied. It's on record. Nothing came of either incident. I resent it being brought up now."

For the span of a full minute no one speaks. So far, we've danced around the subject of Rachael Schwartz's murder. I can tell by the way he's looking at me that he knows there's more coming.

"So if we take a look at the tread marks we picked up at the Willowdell Motel," Tomasetti says slowly, "and footage from the game cam in the field across the road, we're not going to see you or your vehicle, right?"

He glares at Tomasetti, nostrils flaring with every elevated breath. Fury in his eyes. But I catch a glimpse of a chink in the veneer. Beneath all that anger is uncertainty—and fear. Of course, there were no viable tire-tread marks picked up at the scene. Nor is there a game cam in the field across the road. Fletcher doesn't know either of those things.

"You're not going to find shit because I've done nothing wrong." He looks at Rasmussen. "This is bullshit, Mike. I can't believe you've let this charade go this far. For God's sake I've been with the department for seventeen years and this is the thanks I get?"

"Did you ever meet Rachael Schwartz?" I ask.

"I don't think so," he says. "I don't recall."

Another silence, this one filled with unbearable tension, like a razor slicing skin.

After a moment, Tomasetti sighs. "Dane, we're looking at her banking records," he says quietly. "Yours, too."

Fletcher's Adam's apple bobs. "This is a fucking hack job."

Tomasetti stares at him, saying nothing.

"Fletch." I utter the nickname even before I realize I'm going to address him.

His eyes shift to mine.

"If you want to help yourself," I say, "tell us the truth now. You're a good enough cop to know we're going to figure it out."

"Don't patronize me, Burkholder," he snarls.

It's so quiet I can hear the whistle of quickened breaths through nose hair. The creak of a chair as someone shifts.

I look at Fletcher. He's slouched now. Head down. Elbows on the table. Hands laced at his nape, staring at the tabletop. A beaten man who knows the worst is yet to come.

Up until now, this has been an information-seeking mission. The longer we talk to Fletcher, the more apparent it becomes that this undertaking now has three levels. What happened between him and Loretta Bontrager last night. What occurred between him and Rachael Schwartz thirteen years ago. And what may or may not have happened between them the night she was murdered.

For the first time I notice the sheen of sweat on his forehead. The damp rings beneath his arms. He looks at Rasmussen. "If that's the way you're going to play this, Mike, I guess I need a lawyer."

Dane Fletcher is not under arrest. We don't have enough evidence to hold him. I have no idea how any of this is going to end. The one thing I do know is that when he walks out of this room, he will not have a badge. Whether he is put on administrative leave, suspended, or fired is up to Rasmussen and policy.

"That's your right," the sheriff tells him.

"Union rep, too."

"You got it," the sheriff tells him.

Fletcher rises, takes a moment to pull himself together, gather his composure. Eyes on his boss, he removes the Glock from his holster and lays his badge on the table.

"There you go, you sons of bitches," he says.

He turns and walks from the room.

CHAPTER 30

Day 4

Early in my career, the resolution of a case—the bringing of a bad actor to justice, the closure for the victim's family, the satisfaction that comes with the knowledge of a job well done—was one of the simple and straightforward highlights of being a cop. Now that I'm older, with a few years of experience under my belt, none of those things are quite as cut-and-dried. Rachael Schwartz is still dead, her life cut short years before her time. A colleague, a man I'd worked with for years and trusted with my life—a husband and father of four young children—will likely be spending the rest of his life in prison. And for what? Money? Lust?

It's been twenty-four hours since Tomasetti, Mike Rasmussen, and I questioned Fletcher. We let him walk because we don't have enough hard evidence to arrest him. But it's coming. We procured a search warrant and confiscated his cell phone and laptop. Banking records are in the works. I spent most of the last day combing through everything I've got so far. I'm not sure if I'm looking for something that will exonerate him—or put that last nail in his coffin so I can drive it in my-self. Do I believe he forced a seventeen-year-old Rachael Schwartz into having sex with him in exchange for letting her go? Considering the two complaints on file—and later dismissed—and the detailed state-ment from Loretta Bontrager, I do, indeed, believe he's guilty. If it's true, Fletcher is a sexual predator, a disgusting excuse for a man, and a dishonor to everyone in law enforcement. As unscrupulous as that is, I simply can't get my head around the notion of him beating Rachael Schwartz to death in that motel room.

"You look like you could use some good news."

I glance up to see Tomasetti standing at the doorway to my office, his head tilted, looking at me intently.

Despite my somber mood, I smile, liking the way he's standing there with his arms crossed, his leg cocked. "A little good news would go a long way right now."

He crosses to my desk and lowers himself into the visitor chair adja-cent to me. "The IT techs hit the jackpot on Schwartz's laptop."

I sit up straighter. "Fletcher?"

"We got him." He produces his cell and taps the screen a few times. "They found texts and emails. Deleted, but easy enough to recover."

Rising, he comes around my desk to stand beside me, sets his hand on the back of my chair. I look at the screen, find myself staring at what appears to be copied texts. The first three transmissions are from Rachael Schwartz, sent on the same day, just a few minutes apart.

What is the age of consent in the state of Ohio?

Wifey has a nice Facebook page. I didn't know she was preggers! Congrats!

Bet she'd be pissed if she found out you'd pulled over and raped a 17 year old Amish girl.

No reply.

The next day, from Schwartz:

She posted pics of you and the kids. Didn't know you guys had a pool.
Nice!
Like her accent. Where is she from? Australia? London?

I look at Tomasetti. "Fletcher's wife is from New Zealand," I tell him.
He scrolls down to the next exchange.
From Fletcher:

You call my house again and I will fucking bury you. You got that?

From Schwartz:

Don't be such a pussy. Just messing with you.

"She's taunting him," Tomasetti murmurs.

"Doing a pretty good job of it," I say, but I can't take my eyes off the
screen as he scrolls to the next exchange.

This one is from Schwartz and comes the next day at two A.M.

I see yur still a deputy with Holmes County. I wonder how Sheriff Rasmussen would feel if he nu U sodomized me in the back seat of yur cruiser?

No reply.

Bet yur sweating right now.
I'm going to call him.
330-884-5667

Recognizing the number, I look at Tomasetti. "That's Rasmussen's home number."

Fletcher doesn't reply.

Rachael Schwartz doesn't stop.

Maybe I'll just show up and tell him everything. Maybe I'll show up at your house and tell your pretty little wife what you do to little girls when you pull them over.

Finally, Fletcher responds.

You show up here and I'll put a fucking bullet in your head. You got that?

From Schwartz:

Don't be so sensitive! I'm jus kidding.
In case you're thinking about going all batshit . . . don't forget I got that insurance policy. Anything unsavory happens and presto! Out comes the proof.

"So they talked at some point," Tomasetti says.

"What proof is she referring to?" I ask.

"Be nice to know, wouldn't it?" he mutters. "I've no doubt we'll figure it out." He sighs. "There's more."

So if you can afford that pool you can afford to pay me a little something for keeping my piehole shut all these years.
How much you got saved?
How much is your marriage worth?
How much is your job worth?

No reply from Fletcher.

Tomasetti backs out of the file and goes to the next. It looks like a listing of phone numbers. "I pulled these numbers from their devices. I compared time of day with the numbers. Fletcher called her the day after those texts were sent. They talked for six minutes."

He angles the phone so I can see the next item. I find myself looking at what appears to be some kind of financial statement.

Tomasetti continues, "Two days later, Fletcher withdrew three thousand dollars from his savings account. He withdrew another two thousand from an investment account."

He thumbs through a few more screens. "The following day, Rachael Schwartz deposited five thousand bucks into her checking account."

He flicks off the phone and returns to the chair. When he looks at me his expression is sober. "There's more, Kate. Over the last six months, she's called his house a dozen times. Calls last only a minute, so they're probably hang-ups. She hounded him, posted things on Jennifer Fletcher's social media pages. I spent half the night reading some really raw and disturbing text and email exchanges. She threatened him dozens of times. She wanted money for her silence. He'd paid her up to about twelve thousand. He threatened to kill her twice."

The information settles into my gut with the power of a stomach virus. "We have motive," I say.

"The CCTV footage at the bar in Wooster?" he says. "Expert says the car that pulled in belongs to Fletcher's wife. We enlarged it, got the plate number as it was pulling into the lot. We had an expert look at the video. He says the silhouette of the male is likely Fletcher."

"They met at the bar the day she was murdered," I say.

He nods. "A few hours later, she was dead."

We stare at each other for the span of a few heartbeats and then I reach for the phone on my desk. "Let's get the arrest warrant."

CHAPTER 31

As police chief of a small town, I deal with the occasional sticky situation that requires some degree of discretion. My department is good at maintaining confidentiality when necessary, especially when it comes to protecting someone's safety. But secrets are tough to keep in a small town. When a neighbor sees a police car pull up to someone's house—even with the overhead lights off—they want to know what's going on.

I don't expect any trouble from Fletcher. He's a stable guy with four kids at home and a wife who's expecting their fifth. Still, I've dealt with enough high-stress situations to know that when Mr. Even Keel realizes his life is about to unravel, he can come unhinged.

In my rearview mirror, I see Tomasetti pull up behind me, a Holmes County deputy behind him. I get out and we meet on our way to the front door.

"You talk to Rasmussen?" he asks.

I nod. "He's on his way."

We reach the front porch. I've just pressed the doorbell when the

219

door opens. Jennifer Fletcher appears. She's wearing a yellow and white maternity dress. Huge belly. House shoes. Hair pinned atop her head. Her smile falters at the sight of us.

"What's going on?" Her voice rises a pitch with each word. "Is it Dane? What's—"

It takes me a second to realize she thinks we're here to inform her that her husband has been hurt on the job. It's a normal reaction. It's sad because he didn't fill her in on what's going on or warn her that he's in serious trouble.

"He's not hurt," I say quickly. "We need to talk to him. Is he home?"

"Oh." She sags, presses a hand against her chest. "Whew! You guys scared me for a second." Still, she knows there's something wrong. She pauses, cocks her head. "Is everything all right?"

I hear kids playing in the background. Splashing in the pool out back. A dog yapping. Laughter. The smell of popcorn wafting out. And I feel a wave of anger toward Fletcher because he had it all—and squandered it.

"We need to talk to Dane," I tell her. "Is he here?"

She blinks, worried now. Confused because she's realized this isn't a friendly visit and we're not going to go away until we get what we want. "He took Scotty to the Little League game, down at the elementary school." She glances at her watch. "They should be back any minute. Want to come in and wait?" She laughs. "Fill me in?"

Neither of us responds as we follow her into the house. Glossy wood floors. Open concept. Crisp gray paint on the walls. The kitchen is large and well used, with newish appliances. A plastic truck tossed haphazardly on the dining room floor.

Jennifer pauses at the island that separates the kitchen from the living room and turns to us. "I wish you'd tell me what's going on. You guys are starting to worry me."

I look through the window, see three kids splashing in the pool outside, oblivious to what's about to unfold, and I silently curse Dane Fletcher. How could a man who has so much—a family—children who need him—destroy it? And for what?

"Dane's in trouble," I tell her. "It's serious. We have a warrant for his arrest. That's all I can say at this point."

"What?" She pales, an odd shade of pink rising to her cheeks. "I'm going to call him." Spinning away from us, she rushes to the island, picks up her cell.

I look at Tomasetti. "I'm going to go get him." I lower my voice. "Keep an eye on them, will you?"

Argument flares in his eyes. The scowl that follows tells me he doesn't like the idea of me picking up Fletcher alone. "Take the deputy," he says.

"Okay."

"Who's on duty?" he asks.

"T.J."

"Call him, will you?"

"Yep." Taking a final look at Jennifer, I head toward the door.

I hail T.J. en route to the school and fill him in on the situation, ask him to meet me there.

The Painters Mill elementary school was built back in the 1960s at the height of the mid-century-modern phase of architecture. It's a two-story building fabricated of mud-yellow brick and mullioned windows set back from the street in a treed lot the size of a football field. A big sign stands guard in front, next to the flagpole, and proclaims: PANTHER COUNTRY!

I pull around to the rear of the building. Ahead is the baseball diamond, replete with freshly painted bleachers, overhead lights for night games. There's a small clapboard concession stand that sells soft drinks and hot dogs during games. Closer to the school is the public pool—not yet open for the season, but there's a good-size pool house and a cinder-block public restroom. A dozen or so cars are parked in the gravel lot on the south side. I idle through and spot Fletcher's Focus at the end of the row. No one inside. I park next to it and get out.

The deputy parks next to me and we meet at the rear of his cruiser. "See him?" he asks.

I shake my head, motion toward the restroom and pool house. "Want to check in there?"

"Yeah," he says, and heads that way.

It's nearly dusk now. Golden light slants down through the treetops as I make my way toward the diamond. The quiet is punctuated by the shouts and squeals of children playing baseball and the occasional bark of an overzealous mom or dad. It's an innocent scene, but when a young batter smacks out a single, I find myself thinking of the bat used to murder Rachael Schwartz.

I speak into my shoulder mike. "Ten-twenty-three," I say, letting Dispatch know I've arrived on scene. "I got eyes on our ten-fifty. T.J expedite."

"Roger that," comes T.J.'s voice, telling me he's on his way. "Ten-seven-seven ten minutes." He's ten minutes away.

My uniform draws a few stares as I approach the bleachers. I answer those stares with a wave. A dozen or so moms and dads watch their kids play. A couple of Labrador puppies wrestle in the grass behind the bleachers. No sign of Fletcher. I look toward the field, try to ascertain if his son is one of the players, catch sight of him at the shortstop position, his eyes on the batter who's just stepped up to the mound.

I stroll between the chain-link fence and the bleachers, trying to look nonchalant. One of the coaches glances my way and waves, but I can tell he's wondering why I'm here. I'm relieved he's too busy to talk.

Where the hell is Fletcher?

I reach the end of the bleachers and head toward the concession stand. A girl with a nose piercing, the tattoo of a rose on her throat, lowers a strainer of fries into a vat of boiling oil. I go to the window. "Any fries left?" I ask.

"Going to be four minutes," she says without looking at me.

"Have you seen Dane Fletcher?" I ask. "The deputy?"

The girl straightens. She looks bored. Put out by her job. Annoyed that I'm requiring her attention. "The cop?"

I nod. "You seen him?"

She raises a ring-clad hand and points toward the park across the street. "I think he went over to the park a few minutes ago."

"Thanks." I head that way.

Creekside Park has been around as long as I can remember. There's a playground replete with monkey bars and a slide. In summertime, a fountain featuring a giant catfish spurts water and beckons kids to wade or toss pennies for good luck. There's a hiking path with a footbridge that crosses a small, trickling stream that eventually feeds into Painters Creek. All six acres of it is crowded with old-growth trees that were likely here before Painters Mill became a village back in 1815.

I make my way to the trailhead, where a sign reminds me to bring water and mosquito repellent if I plan to hike. I look down at the damp earth at my feet and see the footprints. Male boots with a waffle sole. Cop's boots, I think, and I start down the path.

I've gone just a few yards when I find him. He's standing on the footbridge, leaning, his hands on the rail, looking into the forest. I stop twenty feet away. "Nice night for a softball game," I say.

He looks at me. Something not right about his eyes. "Scotty's going to be a good hitter."

"Like his dad, I guess."

He nods, keeps his hands on the rail. He's wearing khaki pants. A

223

short-sleeved shirt, untucked. The sheriff took his service revolver, but I know he owns a pistol. I wonder if said pistol is tucked into the waistband of his slacks. I wonder how close he is to the end of his rope.

He lowers his eyes to the trickling water. Not looking at anything in particular. His body language is off. He knows why I'm here.

"I saw a fox a few minutes ago," he tells me.

"They're out here." I pretend to look around. Hold my ground. Wait.

"I figured you'd show up sooner or later," he tells me.

"You know I don't have a choice," I tell him. "I'll make this as easy as possible for you, if that's any consolation."

"It's not." The laugh that follows is the harsh sound of ripping fabric. "Does Jen know?" he asks, referring to his wife.

"Not yet."

Silence descends. As thick and uncomfortable as a wet blanket on a freezing night. We listen to the spring peepers for a moment and he seems to relax, as if he's made some decision.

He steps back from the rail, reaches beneath his shirt. My heart rate jacks at the sight of the pistol. It's a semiauto H & K .45. Quickly, I slide out my sidearm, level on him, center mass.

"Dane." I say his name firmly. "Your son is playing baseball fifty yards away. You don't want to do this to him. Put down the gun."

He doesn't raise the pistol, but holds it at his side. At first, I think he's going to obey my command and toss it. But his finger is inside the guard.

"Come on," I say. "You know I'll do right by you."

He doesn't seem to hear me. Doesn't seem to care that I've got a bead on him and he has zero in the way of cover.

He turns to me, looks at me as if seeing me for the first time. "I didn't kill her," he tells me.

"No one said you did."

"Don't patronize me," he snaps. "I know how this works."

"I don't know what you want me to say to that. All I can tell you is that it isn't too late to end this. Put down the gun. Talk to me. We'll figure this out. Okay?"

He cocks his head, trying to decide if I'm bullshitting him. "It's over for me. This isn't going to go away."

"You made a mistake," I tell him.

"It's all going to come out. For God's sake, it'll destroy Jen and the kids."

"We'll deal with it. They'll get through. Come on. Toss the gun."

Every muscle in my body goes taut when he raises the pistol. But he only taps the muzzle of it against his forehead. "I pulled her over. I had sex with her. I did it. I fucked up. I . . . I don't know what happened to me that night. She was . . . just . . . there. For God's sake, it was like she *wanted* it. I'm telling you she . . . *knew* things. She was . . . and I . . . fucking lost it."

He doesn't have to say her name. I see it on his face. I bank the rise of disgust, bite back the denunciation dangling on my tongue. I'm keenly aware of the pistol in my hand, the pulse of anger in my veins. How easy it would be to put him out of his misery . . .

"Was she blackmailing you?" I ask.

He looks up at me, jerks his head. "For years."

"How much?" I ask.

"Twenty grand." He shrugs. "Maybe more. I lost track."

"Does Jen know?"

"She doesn't know anything." He shakes his head. "Schwartz was . . . crazy and . . . relentless. Said all sorts of crazy shit. Claimed she got pregnant that night. Had a kid. Said she had proof it was mine. Called it her 'insurance policy,' and she was going to wreck my life."

"She said the kid was yours?"

"There was no kid," he snaps. "She was a pathological liar. A fucking sadist. All she wanted was money. Ruining me was the icing on the cake." His smile sends a chill down my spine. "Looks like she got her way, didn't she?"

He looks down at the .45, makes a sound that's part sob, part laugh.

For an instant, I think he's going to use the gun on himself, so I try to engage him, keep him talking. "You met her at the bar in Wooster? The night she was killed?"

"I tried to reason with her. Told her I had a kid on the way. That I was out of money." He taps the muzzle of the H & K against his forehead again, so hard I hear the steel tap against his skull. "She didn't want to hear it."

I nod. "Okay."

He lowers the gun to his side. His eyes latch on to mine. "I've done some shitty things, Kate. I've raped. Lied. Cheated on my wife. But if you believe one word of what I say tonight, believe this: I did not kill Rachael Schwartz."

In the gauzy light I see the shimmer of tears in his eyes. The tremble of his mouth. The run of snot he doesn't seem to notice. A mask of hopelessness. The soul of a broken man.

"Then all you have to deal with is the assault," I tell him. "Fletch, you can do that. It's not too late." The statements aren't exactly true, but I'm free to tell him whatever I think he needs to hear in order to bring this to an end.

"Come on," I coo. "We'll figure it out. Just put down the gun."

He shakes his head. "You're a straight shooter, Kate. I always liked that about you."

"Dane—"

He cuts me off. "I'm fucking done. I used my badge to prey on that girl. She wasn't the only one. But I swear to God I didn't kill her. You

226

want the truth? You'd better keep looking." A sob escapes him. "When you find it . . . make sure my wife knows."

Finality rings in his voice, as if he's going on a trip with no plans to come back. I get a sick feeling in my gut. In the back of my mind I'm wondering where the deputy is. T.J. "Dane, your kids need you. Jen needs you."

He shakes his head. "We both know I'm going to fry for this. Everything I've ever worked for. It's gone. I got nothing left." He begins to cry. "For God's sake, I can't spend the rest of my life in prison for something I didn't do. You know what they do to cops."

Taking his time, he starts toward me. Gun at his side. Finger outside the guard.

I step back. My finger on the trigger. Pulse in the red zone. "Keep your distance," I tell him.

He keeps coming. Not in a hurry. Looking down at the pistol in his right hand.

My heart stumbles in my chest and begins to pound. "Don't do this, Dane. *Don't.*"

"I didn't kill her." His tread is steady. Gun at his side. Nearly to the edge of the footbridge. Just ten feet away from me now.

I walk backward, my pistol at the ready. Cold sweat breaks out on the back of my neck. "You need to stop right there," I tell him. "Drop the gun."

He stops, tilts his head as if I'm some puzzle he's encountered and he's not sure how to solve it.

"I'm glad it was you, Burkholder."

He looks down at the H & K in his hand, fiddles with the clip, thinking about something I can't fathom. It's like watching a wreck in slow motion. Knowing it's going to be horrific, that someone is going to die. That there isn't a damn thing you can do about it. A sense of helplessness assails me.

"Dane! No! Stop!"

Quickly and without hesitation, he raises the gun, shoves the barrel into his mouth, and pulls the trigger.

CHAPTER 32

Day 5

It's been nearly eight hours since Dane Fletcher committed suicide. The scene at the park has replayed a thousand times in my head. I've critiqued my every move, my every word, everything I did and didn't do—and yet the end result is always the same. Intellectually, I know there was nothing I could have done to stop him. I should be thankful he didn't rely on me to do his dirty work for him.

By all accounts, Dane Fletcher was a duplicitous son of a bitch, a rapist, a disgrace to the badge—to all men—and likely a murderer. Despite all of those things, there is no satisfaction that comes with the end of his life.

I spent several hours in an interview room with Sheriff Rasmussen and Tomasetti. I gave my official statement to the best of my ability, but I was exhausted and shaken. I answered dozens of questions, drank too much coffee, snapped at both men a few too many times. Because I was at the scene when Fletcher committed suicide, the Holmes County

Sheriff's Office will oversee the investigation. Normally, I'd put up some token argument. This time, I'm relieved to step aside. I'm pissed at Fletcher for using his badge to prey on women, and when he got caught, for taking the cowardly way out. What kind of man does that to his wife and children? What kind of man pulls over a seventeen-year-old Amish girl and demands sex in exchange for letting her walk away from a DUI?

It was after two A.M. when I left the sheriff's office. Tomasetti followed me home. I tossed my blood-specked uniform into the hamper and went directly to the shower and stood under the spray for ten minutes. I didn't cry or curse. I didn't close my eyes, because I knew if I did, I'd see Fletcher drop, his face destroyed, the back of his head a gaping wound.

By the time I meet Tomasetti in the kitchen, I've pulled myself together. He's already poured two fingers of scotch into a couple of tumblers. The window above the sink is open and I can hear the chorus of spring peepers from the marsh down by the pond, singing their hearts out. The simple beauty of the sound makes me feel like crying. Of course, I don't. Instead, I pick up the tumbler of whiskey and take a long drink.

Tomasetti goes to the radio on the counter and fiddles with the knob. An old Led Zeppelin tune about rambling on fills the silence around us. It's a pretty song full of memories and its own unique beauty, and suddenly I'm absurdly thankful to be here in the kitchen of our modest little farm with the man I love.

"Any word on how Fletcher's wife is doing?" I ask, already knowing the answer, hating it because it hurts.

"The chaplain stayed with her until her parents got there," he tells me. "That's all I know."

I nod, take another sip. "I didn't know him that well."

"The people who did are about to realize they really didn't."

"What kind of man does that to his wife and kids? What kind of man uses his position to rape a seventeen-year-old girl?"

"A predator. A dirty cop. A sick bastard." He shrugs. "All of the above."

Leaving his place at the counter, he crosses to the table, takes the chair across from me. He's looking at me as if he's searching for something I'm not quite ready to reveal. Or maybe I'm just tired and looking for things that aren't really there.

"So what else is bothering you?" he asks.

Over the last hours, my brain has been preoccupied with witnessing the death of a man I'd once respected. On doing my job and figuring out how it fits into the investigation at hand—the homicide of Rachael Schwartz. Now that I'm settled and thinking more clearly, I'm starting to analyze more closely the exchange between Fletch and me during those final moments.

"Fletcher admitted to pulling her over and sexually assaulting her," I say. "He admitted to preying on other women. He acknowledged that Schwartz was blackmailing him. To having paid her somewhere around twenty thousand dollars over the years. He admitted to meeting with her at the bar."

Having been present for my interview and having read my official statement, he already knows all of those things. "He knew we had him."

I nod, but I'm still mulling the conversation, the words running through my head like a script. I can't get the sound of Dane Fletcher's voice out of my head. The look in his eyes.

. . . if you believe one word of what I've said tonight, believe this: I did not kill Rachael Schwartz.

I've heard too many lies over the years to believe anything an admitted rapist would say. Fletcher lied and cheated and hurt people for years. He doesn't deserve the benefit of a doubt.

So why the hell can't I set aside his sham denial and close my damn case?

I lift the tumbler, set it down without drinking.

Tomasetti sips, looks at me over the rim of his glass. "A moment ago, you reiterated all the things Fletcher had done. The one thing you didn't mention was the murder of Rachael Schwartz."

"You're pretty astute for a BCI agent, aren't you?"

"Every now and then I get something right."

You want the truth? . . . keep looking.

I meet his gaze, hold it. "I know he was a liar. Desperate and willing to say anything. But, Tomasetti, he walked onto that trail to take his life. He had nothing to prove. Nothing to lose. Why deny the murder? Why not try to rationalize or explain why he did it?"

Tomasetti looks at me over the rim of his glass and scowls. "Fletcher had motive. He had means. And he had opportunity. Rachael Schwartz was bleeding him dry and enjoying putting him through the wringer."

I hate it that I've put myself in the position of defending an admitted dirty cop. Even so, I can't shake the sense that not all of the pieces are settling into the proper circles and squares the way they should.

"Why tell me to keep looking?" I say.

"Because he didn't give a damn about anyone, including himself," he tells me.

I know this is one of those times that no matter what I say, I'll not convince Tomasetti that the situation warrants a more thorough looking-into. To be honest, I'm not certain of it myself. But if I've learned anything over the years, it is to listen to my gut. Right now, my cop's instinct is telling me to, at the very least, keep my options open.

I swear to God I didn't kill her. You want the truth? . . . keep looking . . . make sure my wife knows.

It's as if Dane Fletcher is standing outside the window, whispering the words. The thought sends a shiver through me.

"I'm going to dig around a little," I say. "A couple days. See if there's anything else there, that we haven't looked at."

Tomasetti finishes his whiskey and sets down the glass, gives me a dubious look. "Do you need anything from me?"

"Fletcher's son plays Little League. Take the bat we found to Jennifer Fletcher," I tell him, referring to the murder weapon. "If she recognizes it, I'll close the case."

He nods, but I can tell by his expression he doesn't agree with my theory and he doesn't think my request is a very good idea. "I'll pay her a visit tomorrow."

CHAPTER 33

The final vestiges of an afternoon storm simmer in a sky the color of a bruise as I turn in to the lane of the Schwartz farm. The place looks exactly the same as the last time I was here. The same Jersey cows graze in the pasture to my right. The field across the road is still in the process of being plowed and readied for seed. Same team of horses. Same young boy behind the lines. Life goes on, as it should. As it always does.

I find the couple on the front porch. Dan is sitting in a rocking chair, legs crossed, a pipe in his mouth, a glass of iced tea sweating on the table next to him. Rhoda sits in the rocking chair next to him, the parcel of a recently started afghan in her lap. They're not happy to see me. They don't rise or greet me as I climb the steps, and they watch me as if I'm some vermin that's wandered up from the field.

"*Guder nochmiddawks,*" I say. Good afternoon.

"You come bearing bad news again, Kate Burkholder?" Dan's voice is amicable, but there's a hardness in his eyes that wasn't there before.

I take the jab in stride.

Rhoda pats her husband's hand to quiet him. "Would you like cold tea, Katie? I made a pot and if Dan drinks any more, he'll be up half the night."

"I can't stay." I take the final step onto the porch, go to the Adirondack chair across from them and I sit. "I wanted to give you an update on the investigation."

Dan picks up his tea and sips. The needles in Rhoda's hands still. With the music of birdsong all around, I tell them about Dane Fletcher and the turn of events leading up to his death.

"We heard about that policeman," Rhoda says.

"Everyone's talking about it," Dan adds.

"Such a horrible thing." She shakes her head. "We knew there was some connection to Rachael. We sure didn't know the rest of it. *Mein Gott.*" My God.

I'm loath to tell them the rest, but I know it's better for them to hear it from me rather than through the grapevine, where facts are scarce and the story grows with every telling.

Leaving out as many of the sordid details as possible, I tell them about what happened on that back road when Rachael was seventeen. Because the investigation is ongoing, I forgo speculation and anything not yet confirmed. It's not easy. But they deserve the truth even when I know it will break their hearts all over again.

"I'm sorry," I say when I've finished. "I know that was difficult to hear. But I thought you'd want to know."

Rhoda looks down at the knitting in her lap as if she doesn't quite remember why it's there. "She never told us," she whispers.

"She was baptized that summer," Ben says quietly.

"Left us in the spring," Rhoda adds. "April, I think."

I don't know what to say to any of that. I'm not big on the whole closure thing. When you lose a loved one to violence, the closing of the case does little in terms of easing the pain. As I stare into the Amish woman's eyes and see the silent scroll of agony, I curse Dane Fletcher.

"The investigation is still open, and the sheriff's office has stepped in to help, but we'll likely close it soon."

"Rachael is with God now." Dan's eyes remain glued to the floor. "At peace with the Lord."

"We've made all the notifications already," Rhoda tells me, referring to the Amish tradition of personally notifying those who will be invited to the funeral.

She raises shimmering eyes to mine. "We didn't see her much anymore. But we're going to miss her. And of course we take comfort in knowing that she's in good hands, and that one day we will join her."

"A man should not grieve overmuch," Dan says, "for that is a complaint against God."

Rhoda swipes at the tears on her cheeks. "Last time we talked, Katie, you asked me when we saw Rachael last. I realized this morning that I told you wrong. She came to see us *after* Christmas, not before, and we had such a nice visit." The chuckle that follows rings false. "I remembered because she'd been over to Loretta's that morning and mentioned the cast on little Fannie's arm."

I nod, listening more out of politeness than interest.

Rhoda uses her fingers to squeegee tears from her cheeks. "That girl. Christmas day. Broke her arm in two places. Fell off that old windmill over to the Cooper farm next door. Had to get some kind of pin put in to fix it."

Forcing a smile, she looks down at the knitting in her lap. "She's not the first girl we've known who's in love with adventure, now, is she? Should have been born a boy, that one."

The image of Fannie astride the horse and loping across the pasture plays in my mind's eye. "She must keep Loretta and Ben on their toes."

"She's a handful, with all the climbing and horses and such." She shrugs. "Poor Loretta was just beside herself. Dotes on that girl like she's newborn." Rhoda sighs, her face softening. "Anyway, that was the last time I saw my Rachael. *After* Christmas, not before. I don't know if that's even important now, but I wanted you to know."

She picks up the needles and resumes her knitting.

Something I can't put my finger on nags at me as I head toward the Bontrager farm. A kink in my gut that wasn't there before my conversation with Rhoda and Dan. I try to work it out, but nothing comes to me. I set it aside as I make the turn into the lane.

I'm on my way to the front door when voices from the side yard draw my attention. I head that way to find Loretta and Fannie painting a picnic table.

"You two look busy," I say by way of greeting.

Loretta, paintbrush in hand, looks at me over her shoulder and grins. "That's one way to put it."

"I like the teal," I tell her.

Stepping back, she puts her hands on her hips and studies the table. "I wasn't too sure at first, but I think I like it, too."

Fannie, a smaller brush in hand, peeks out at me from around the side of the table. "I picked out the color."

Despite the purpose of my visit, the sight of the girl makes me smile. She's got a smudge of paint on her chin. A perfect drop of it on her *kapp*. Someone will likely be scrubbing it with a toothbrush tonight.

I cross to her, offer her a high five. "Nice job."

A grin overtakes the girl's face. There's a space between her front teeth. A nose tinged pink from the sun. That odd sensation waggles at the back of my brain again, but I shove it aside to deal with later.

"We've got an extra paintbrush if you want to help."

I glance over to see Ben approach from the direction of the barn. He's wearing a blue work shirt with suspenders, trousers, and a straw flat-brimmed hat.

"I'll leave it to you professionals." I sober, let my gaze fall to Fannie, and then I focus on the couple. "I'm sorry to interrupt your afternoon, but I need to talk to you about Rachael Schwartz."

"Oh." Loretta tosses a look at her husband, then rounds the table and goes to her daughter. "Just look at that spot of paint on your *kapp*," she says. "Why don't you go in and take that old toothbrush to it before it dries? I'll be in to help in a few minutes."

The girl cocks her head, knowing the reason she's being sent inside has nothing to do with the paint and everything to do with our pending conversation. But she's too well behaved to balk.

"Use the laundry soap on the porch." The Amish woman takes the girl's brush and points her in the direction of the back door. "Go on now before it leaves a stain we won't be able to get out."

We watch the girl depart. When I hear the back door slam, I turn to the couple. "There's been a development in the case. I thought you'd want to know."

Ben nods. "We heard about the deputy," he says.

Since Ben and Loretta aren't family members, I give them a condensed version of the same set of facts I laid out for Dan and Rhoda Schwartz.

When I'm finished, tears shimmer in Loretta's eyes. "My *mamm* always said, good deeds have echoes. Now I know that bad deeds do, too."

I heard the adage a hundred times growing up and it's one of the few I believe in with my whole heart. "We'll probably close the case in the next few days."

"So it's over?" Ben asks.

"I think so," I tell him.

"It will be a good thing to put this behind us." The Amish man shoves his hands into his pockets. "Thank you for finding the truth, Kate Burkholder. I know the job put before you is a hard one and the Amish don't always approve. That makes it no less worthy."

I nod, a little more moved than I should be. Probably because it still matters to me what the Amish think.

Loretta and I watch him walk away. For the span of a full minute, the only sound comes from the *kuk-kuk-kuk* of a woodpecker followed by the rapid drum of its beak against a tree.

I watch as Loretta walks to the gallon pail of paint and replaces the lid. I think about my conversation with Rhoda and Dan Schwartz. The final moments I spent with Dane Fletcher. The kink in my gut that won't go away.

Claimed she got pregnant that night. Had a kid.

I pick up the hammer from the stepladder she's using as a table and hand it to her. "You spent a lot of time with Rachael that last summer she was here in Painters Mill," I say.

"I did." She taps down the lid to seal it. "It was one of the best summers of my life."

"You mentioned before that she changed. In what way?"

She sets down the hammer and straightens. "As strange as it sounds, she became even more forward. It's like she was in a rush to squeeze in every single experience she could before she became baptized." She pauses, thoughtful. "Sometimes she was mad at the world. Not too much, but more than . . . before. Rachael was strong. She didn't let what happened crush her."

"Loretta, when exactly did it happen?" I ask. "I mean, with Dane Fletcher?"

"Late summer," she tells me. "August, I think."

239

She was baptized that summer.

Left us in the spring. April, I think.

"Do you know if Rachael was ever *ime familye weg*?" I ask.

Loretta blinks, her brows knitting as if the question has caught her off-guard. "I don't think so," she says slowly. "Rachael would have told me."

"Would she have told you even if she terminated the pregnancy?"

The Amish woman looks down at the brush in her hand. "I wish I could tell you Rachael would never take the life of an unborn child." The sigh that follows is saturated with grief. "But she had a way of rationalizing things. If she did something like that, she didn't tell me. I think she'd have known I would disapprove."

Typically, at this point in an investigation, once an arrest has been made, the pressure is off and life returns to normal. I spend a few days catching up on the things I neglected over the course of the case, including sleep.

The Schwartz case has been anything but typical.

I'm in my office at the police station; it's long past time to go home and I've done little with regard to putting the case to rest. Instead, I've spent the last three hours grinding through the file, reading the dozens of reports and statements, and the like. I've been staring at paper for so long I'm no longer even sure what I'm looking for. I've scrutinized every crime scene photo and sketch. Viewed the videos. I've reread every statement, dismantled every word. Gone over the forensic reports with a fine-tooth comb. I've picked through the autopsy report so many times I'm seeing double. My neck hurts. My eyes feel like someone has tossed a handful of ground glass into them. All the while the little voice of reason sits on my shoulder, telling me I'm chasing ghosts.

Indeed.

The wall clock glares at me, reminding me that it's nine P.M. and I should have been home hours ago. Tomasetti is probably wondering where I am.

"What the hell are you doing, Burkholder?" I mutter.

I look down at my handwritten notes spread out on my desk and I frown.

. . . likely knew her killer . . .

. . . a fair amount of conflict in her life . . .

Setting my chin in my hand, I flip the page and come to my statement on the death of Dane Fletcher. Doc Coblentz ruled on the cause and manner of death. Suicide caused by a single gunshot wound to the head. According to Sheriff Rasmussen, Fletcher's wife and kids left Painters Mill to stay with her parents in Pittsburgh. Last I heard, they won't be coming back.

I skim my incident report, not wanting to revisit the moment he pulled the trigger. Instead, I focus on the section that recounts my final conversation with Fletcher.

Claimed she got pregnant that night. Had a kid.

Of all the things he told me the night he died, that's the one that stops me cold. Was Rachael Schwartz provoking him? Trying to inflame him? To what end? Make him suffer? Pay him back for what he did to her? Did Fletcher reach his limit? Follow her to that motel and proceed to bludgeon her to death?

In all likelihood, that's exactly what happened.

Even if Rachael *did* become pregnant, does it change the dynamics of the case? The answer is a resounding no.

The last thing I'll ever do is defend the likes of Dane Fletcher. What he did to a young Amish girl—and possibly others—is indefensible. He was a dirty cop. A liar. A phony. A danger to the community he'd sworn to serve and protect.

But was he a killer?

You want the truth? . . . keep looking.

Gathering the contents of the file, I stuff everything into the folder, drop it into my laptop case, and head for the door.

CHAPTER 34

I call Tomasetti from the Explorer as I back out of my parking spot in front of the station. He picks up on the first ring. "I was about to send out a search party," he says. "But I don't think anyone would have a difficult time finding you these days."

"I guess I'm officially busted," I say, keeping my voice light despite my mood. "If it's any consolation, I'm on my way home."

"The day is looking up."

In that moment, I'm unduly happy that I have him in my life, to keep me grounded. Remind me of what's important. "I was wondering if you had a chance to talk with Jennifer Fletcher," I say. "About the bat."

"I did," he tells me. "Two of their boys are in Little League. She bought two Rawlings aluminum-alloy bats in the last couple of years. They still have those bats; they still use them, and they have never owned a wood Louisville Slugger."

"Would have been nice to tie that up." I reach the edge of town and head north on US 62, toward home.

"Sometimes even the most open-and-closed cases don't tidy up the way we'd like them to." He pauses. "Wood bat like that one is common. Fletcher could have picked it up at a thrift store. Something like that."

I'm northbound on US 62, running a few miles per hour over the speed limit, headlights illuminating the blur of asphalt. Tall trees rise from a berm on my right. Left, through a veil of new-growth trees, I see the black expanse of a field.

"Not like you to get sidetracked by something like that," he says, fishing.

"This is one of those times when I don't want to be right."

"So you're still having doubts about Fletcher?"

"Yeah."

I'm just past Township Road 92 and closing in on Millersburg, fifteen minutes from home and concentrating on the call, when the steering wheel yanks hard to the right. The Explorer shudders. Something thumps hard against the undercarriage. Out of the corner of my eye I see a dark chunk fly past the passenger window. *Tire,* I think, and I stomp the brake.

"*Shit.*"

The Explorer veers left. My police training kicks in; I turn in to the skid. No room for error. An instant to react. The guardrail slams into my left front quarter panel. A tremendous *crash!* sounds as I plow through. I'm flung against my safety harness. Jerked left and right. A dozen trees thrash the windshield and hood as I careen down the hill. The windshield shatters. Dirt and glass pelt my face and chest. The Explorer nosedives. Straight down. Too fast. Too steep. I'm slung violently against my shoulder harness.

The Explorer hits a trunk the size of a telephone pole. The airbag explodes as the vehicle jumps right, then rolls to a stop. The windshield has been punched in, draped over the dash like a crystal blanket. I hear spring peepers. Cool night air pouring in. In the periphery of my disjointed thoughts, I hear Tomasetti calling my name.

"Kate! What the hell . . ."

The engine is running. Bluetooth still working. I don't know where my cell phone landed. "I'm okay," I hear myself say.

"What the hell is going on?" he shouts. "What happened?"

"Tire blew. I . . . ran off the road. I'm okay."

The Explorer sits at a steep angle, nose down, surrounded by trees. A branch the size of a fence post juts through the passenger window, two feet from my face. I'm covered with glass and dirt and mud. I'm shaking. Blood on the seat. I don't know where it came from.

In the periphery of my vision I see movement ahead and to my right. Someone in the trees. A motorist coming to help . . .

"I'm a police officer!" I unfasten my seat belt, reach for the door handle. "I'm not hurt!"

Pop! Pop! Pop! Pop!

The unmistakable sound of gunfire. Adrenaline kicks, followed by an electric zing of fear. I duck, shove open the door. It creaks, hits a tree. Simultaneously, I reach for my .38, yank it out. The door won't open enough for me to squeeze through. I'm in an awkward position. Leaning right, I look around wildly. Too dark to see. Too many trees. No sign of the gunman. In the back of my mind I wonder why a motorist would brave the incline only to take a shot . . . The answer hovers. No time to ponder.

Another *pop! Ping!*

A bullet ricochets. So close I feel the concussion on the seatback.

I raise the .38 and fire blindly. "I'm a police officer!" I scream. "Put down the weapon! Put it down!"

Two more shots ring out.

I fall against the seat, hunker down as low as I can, gripping the .38. I'm blind here. A sitting duck. I hit my radio. "Shots fired! Shots fired!" I shout out my location. "Ten-thirty-one-E! Ten-thirty-three!" Shooting in progress. Officer in trouble. Emergency.

Pop! Pop!

"Police officer!" I scream. "Drop your weapon! Drop it now! Get on the fucking ground!"

Pop! Pop! Pop!

A slug tings against steel. Another slams into the shattered slab of windshield, sending a spray of glass onto me. Vaguely, I'm aware of Tomasetti shouting through my Bluetooth. Too scared to understand the words. My police radio crackling to life as my call for help goes out.

I'm on my side. Jammed between the steering wheel and the seat. Not enough room to maneuver. I have no idea where the shooter is. I can't get to my Maglite. I raise my head. A single headlight illuminates an ocean of young trees. Ahead, a plowed field. No movement or sound.

Where the hell is the shooter?

If he were to approach from the side, I wouldn't see him until he was right on top of me. . . .

"Shit. Shit." Breaths coming like a piston in my lungs.

I swivel, reach for the passenger door handle, shove it open with my shoulder. The tree branch keeps it from opening all the way. Enough of a gap for me to slide through. Holding my weapon at the ready, I slither out. Shoulder sinking into mud. Cold penetrating my shirt.

Then I'm on my knees, exposed, heart raging, looking around. No sign of the shooter.

Relief rushes through me when I hear the distant song of a siren. I hold my position, trying not to notice that my gun is shaking, that the butt is slick against my wet palms. I can't quite catch my breath. I'm on my knees, using the passenger-side door for cover, when I see the red and blue lights flicker off the treetops.

"Sheriff's Office! Drop the weapon! Show me your hands!"

I call out and identify myself. "I don't know where the shooter is!"

I hear the crack of a police radio. The sound of breaking brush as the deputy makes his way down to me.

"Do not move!" he screams.

I see the flicker of a flashlight. My legs are shaking so violently, it takes me two tries to get to my feet. When I finally make it, I'm nauseous, so I lean against the door, shove my .38 back into my holster, and concentrate on not throwing up.

The approaching deputy blinds me with his flashlight beam as he skids down the incline.

"Painters Mill PD." I put up my hand to shield my eyes. "I haven't seen the shooter for a minute or two," I say.

"You know where he went? You get a look at him?"

"No," I say. "Male. Armed. He fired multiple times at me."

"Vehicle?"

I shake my head. "No idea."

He speaks into his shoulder mike. "Ten-thirty-five-E." Major crime alert—shooting. "Suspect at large."

He runs his flashlight over me. I see recognition in his eyes as he takes in my uniform. "You got a bloody nose." He reaches into his pocket, passes me a kerchief. "You need an ambulance, Chief?"

I take the kerchief. "No." Shaking my head in disgust, I look at the wrecked Explorer. "Might need a new car, though."

He grins. "Roger that."

It takes fifteen minutes for the wrecker to arrive. The driver is a Volkswagen-size man whose company contracts for the county. He's confident he'll be able to pull the Explorer from its muddy nest without the use of a chain saw.

"Went in through all those trees just fine so I ought to be able to pull her out the same way," he tells me as he hoists his large frame down the incline to attach the winch to the undercarriage.

I'm leaning against the hood of the deputy's cruiser when Tomasetti pulls up. Driving too fast. Braking a little too abruptly. He's out of the Tahoe in seconds and striding toward us.

"Kate." Worry resonates in his voice when he calls out. "Are you hurt?"

Tomasetti is known by most everyone at the sheriff's office. Even though we've been discreet about our relationship, my department is a small one and most of my officers have figured out we're involved. Most of them know we're living together. Even so, we do our best to maintain a certain level of professionality. Tonight, it's not easy.

I don't remember crossing to him. His body bumps against me with a little too much force. The next thing I know his arms are around me, his frame solid against me. Out of the corner of my eye I see the deputy I'd been talking to turn away, and I sink into the man I love.

"I'm betting that's the fastest trip you've ever made from the farm," I tell him.

"Record," he murmurs. "You like to keep a guy on his toes, don't you?"

I'm shaking, embarrassed because I feel as if I shouldn't be. Before I can think of an appropriate rejoinder, he pushes me to arm's length, his eyes running over me; then his gaze latches on to mine. "My radio lit up on the drive down. A *shooter*?" he says. "What happened?"

I tell him all of it, abbreviating when I can. "Initially, I thought it was a blowout. Bad tire. Whatever. The next thing I know the son of a bitch is coming down the hill and taking potshots at me."

Tomasetti is a stoic man. He can be a hard man. He's good at keeping his emotions at bay, especially when it comes to his job. I can tell by the flash of fury that this has hit too close to home. His eyes drift to the opening in the trees where the Explorer sits nose-down at the base of the incline.

"You recognize him?" he asks.

I shake my head. "Too dark."

He thinks about that a moment. "He say anything?"

"Not a word."

He nods. "I'll have the Explorer towed to impound. I'll get with the CSU and have them process it. See if our shooter left anything behind."

The next thought that occurs to me sends a shudder through me. "Tomasetti, those tires aren't very old."

His eyes narrow on mine. A dozen unspoken theories zing between us.

"This was no road-hazard situation," I tell him.

"What are you implying exactly?"

I look at him, trying not to appear paranoid or overreactive. "I think he knew I'd be coming this way. He shot out my tire. And then he came down that hill to kill me."

Tomasetti looks in the direction of the Explorer, where the wrecker is in the process of hauling it from its resting place. "You got a motive in mind?"

I look away, not wanting to say it, knowing I don't have a choice. "Maybe it has something to do with the Rachael Schwartz case."

He stares at me, searching my face. I see the wheels turning in his mind. After a moment, he nods. "I'll get another CSU out here and have them process this entire area."

CHAPTER 35

It's after midnight by the time Tomasetti and I arrive at the farm. He did his utmost to talk me into making a trip to Pomerene Hospital. Only after a paramedic with the fire department gave me a thorough field assessment did he concede. The BCI crime scene unit truck arrived on scene an hour before we left. The Ohio State Highway Patrol. It's a big deal when someone takes a shot at a cop. Every law enforcement agency in the area is on alert.

Because the scene is large and out of doors—with the complication of rough terrain—the odds of picking up some piece of evidence that will identify the shooter or his vehicle is doubtful. Our best hope lies with the discovery of forensic evidence from the firearm used. A spent cartridge from which we could conceivably pick up a fingerprint. Or a bullet or fragment from which we could recover striations. Both are possibilities, but no one is holding their breath.

I sustained a few bruises in the course of the wreck, so I took a hot shower upon arriving home. Tomasetti heated soup, and I downed a couple of preemptive ibuprofen. I planned on a good night's sleep, getting a fresh start in the morning, and hopefully finding the son of a bitch who tried to kill me. I should have known my overactive mind would throw a monkey wrench into the mix.

It's after one A.M. now. I'm at the kitchen table, my laptop open and humming. The Rachael Schwartz homicide file is spread out in untidy piles, the logic to which only I am aware. I've filled two pages of my trusty yellow legal pad with theories and conjecture, and a fair amount of chicken scratch. Whatever pinpoint of information I'm looking for continues to elude me.

The truth of the matter is that with the suicide of Dane Fletcher, the case is tied up as tidily as a case can be. Fletcher had motive, means, and opportunity. In spades. When he got caught, he took the easy way out and killed himself. Maybe Tomasetti is right. I'm wasting my time. My gut steered me wrong. It wouldn't be the first time. . . .

So who saw fit to take a shot at me earlier? And why does the thought of closing the case feel so damn wrong?

"Because I don't think he did it," I whisper. It's the first time I've said the words aloud and they sound profane in the silence of the kitchen. But as averse I am to admit it, I've drawn the conclusion that Fletcher didn't murder Rachael Schwartz. There's something else there. Something I missed.

Something.

Sighing in frustration, I page through several reports and set them aside. I come to the copies of the texts between Rachael and Fletcher, read them again.

In case you're thinking about going all batshit . . . don't forget I got that insurance policy.

That one stops me.

Fletcher's words replay in my head. *Claimed she got pregnant that night. Had a kid. Said she had proof it was mine. Called it her "insurance policy," and she was going to wreck my life.*

Then, he'd told me there was no kid. *She was a pathological liar. A fucking sadist. All she wanted was money. Ruining me was the icing on the cake.*

"So why the hell did you keep paying?" I mutter.

Did Rachael Schwartz have something else on him? Some hidden guarantee that would pay off if something happened to her?

In case you're thinking about going all batshit . . . don't forget I got that insurance policy.

"What else did you have on him?" I whisper.

A sealed envelope tucked away in some lockbox that would explain everything when found? A lawyer poised to step forward upon word of her death?

Frustrated, I set the text messages aside and continue on. My handwritten notes on my conversations with Dan and Rhoda Schwartz are paper-clipped together. I pull them apart and read, hit the passages I highlighted in yellow.

. . . she came to see us after Christmas, not before . . .

There's nothing sinister or mysterious about Rhoda changing her story simply because she remembered a detail she'd overlooked that changed the timeline of when she'd last seen her daughter.

I come to the brown envelope where I'd tucked away the old photo of Rachael Schwartz and Loretta Bontrager. They were barely into their teens. Loretta looking awkward and shy and plain. Rachael too pretty for her own good. Even at that tender age, her smile was knowing, her eyes challenging and bold.

I get that antsy sensation at the back of my neck, a sort of pseudo déjà vu that's prickly and uncomfortable. I snatch up my reading glasses, look at the photo a little more closely.

A strange sense of . . . familiarity whispers at the back of my brain. Of course, I've seen the photo before. Plus, I knew Rachael when she was that age. Neither of those things explains the quick snap of recognition.

I set down the photo. I pick it back up.

A young Rachael Schwartz stares back at me. A pretty strawberry blonde with a nose for trouble and a complete inability to follow the rules.

I straighten so abruptly I hit my knee on the underside of my desk.

The image of Fannie astride the horse and loping across the pasture plays out in my mind's eye. I don't have a photo of the girl; most Amish don't take photographs of their children—unless they're breaking the rules. But I recall the way Fannie had looked at me. The punch of shock that follows leaves me breathless.

The two look nothing alike. Rachael had light hair with blue-green eyes. Fannie is dark haired with brown eyes—like Loretta. While their physical attributes are as different as night and day, in that instant I recognize the one trait they seem to share.

Attitude.

I knew Rachael Schwartz when she was a kid. I'd secretly admired her pluck. Though she was younger than me, I'd looked at her as a kindred soul. How many times did she get herself into some situation that required help while on my watch? When she was six, I rescued her when she climbed a tree and couldn't get down. Then there was the day she rolled down the hill in that steel drum and ended up in the creek. Later,

I saw her get into a couple of fights, which goes against every Amish tenet I can think of.

Rachael was a purveyor of chaos, invariably in pursuit of some grand adventure. When she went down the slide, she didn't go feetfirst. She went headfirst, the faster the better, with no regard for safety. She pushed the envelope. Partook in activities that weren't quite safe. She wasn't a *bad* child, but she was different from the other Amish kids.

Fannie is twelve years old. Rachael left Painters Mill about twelve years ago. The timing is spot-on. I think of the parallels between Fannie Bontrager and Rachael Schwartz, and the possibilities chill me despite the sweat that's broken out on the back of my neck.

She's not the first girl we've known who's in love with adventure, now, is she? Should have been born a boy, that one.

Rhoda Schwartz's words reverberate in my head.

Sick with something akin to dread, I dig through the papers in front of me, pull my incident report from the night Dane Fletcher took his life, and read.

Claimed she got pregnant that night. Had a kid.

What if Rachael Schwartz *hadn't* been lying—at least about that part of it? What if she *had* gotten pregnant the night Fletcher assaulted her? I'd assumed he paid the blackmail money because she threatened to go public with the assault. What if the blackmail was about something else? A child born out of an act of violence?

The questions don't stop there. In fact, the most excruciating questions have yet to be posed. Is it possible Fannie Bontrager is Rachael's child?

In case you're thinking about going all batshit . . . don't forget I got that insurance policy. Anything unsavory happens and presto! Out comes the proof.

I think about Fannie, riding the horse as well or better than any boy, breaking her arm in a fall off a windmill. A pattern of similar behaviors.

She's not the first girl we've known who's in love with adventure . . .

It's not a cohesive theory. Far from it. There's too much conjecture. Too many loose ends, none of which ever quite meet. Most importantly, and never far from mind, is the fact that an innocent child lies at the heart of it. Parents and grandparents are involved, their lives and reputations hang in the balance.

"What did you do?" I whisper, not quite sure who I'm addressing.

How does all of this affect my case? If my suspicions are correct, how much does Ben Bontrager know? And how is it that Loretta and Ben Bontrager raised the girl as their own with no questions asked? I don't dare put into words the thoughts crowding into my brain.

Movement at the door yanks a gasp from my throat. Tomasetti stands in the kitchen doorway, arms crossed at his chest, hair mussed, frowning.

"You've been busy," he says.

I look down at the papers and reports and notes strewn about the table and floor. I'm aware of how I must look. Exhausted. Fixated. "Dane Fletcher didn't kill Rachael Schwartz."

"Why am I not surprised to hear you say that?" Despite the frustration evident on his face, his voice is kind.

"I could use a sounding board," I tell him.

"I'll make coffee."

A few minutes later, he's sitting across from me, nursing a cup of dark roast, looking at me over the rim. "All right, Chief," he says. "Hit me with your best shot."

I lay out my theory, holes and all, struggling with every word because I'm not sure of any of it.

"Rachael Schwartz and Fannie Bontrager don't share any physical characteristics," I say. "They do, however, share a psychological trait that could be even more important."

"Like what?" he asks.

"A predilection for reckless behavior. For breaking the rules, the norms set forth by the adults in their lives."

"I think the official term for that is 'being a kid,' " he says.

I'm talking too fast, stumbling over the words because I'm attempting to explain something I'm not well versed on. "There's a difference." I take a breath, slow down, and tell him about some of the behaviors I witnessed in Rachael Schwartz when she was a kid.

"You're asserting that behavior carried over to adulthood." He's listening now, but skepticism rings hard in his voice.

"What if this . . . propensity for thrill seeking is hereditary?" I ask. "Fannie Bontrager displays some of the same tendencies." I tell him about her riding the horse with such utter confidence. The broken arm.

"You believe Fannie Bontrager is Rachael Schwartz's daughter?" he asks.

"I think Rachael Schwartz got pregnant the night Fletcher assaulted her. She wasn't prepared to raise a child. Didn't want a baby. Especially *that* baby. Loretta on the other hand had just gotten married. I remember hearing the birth of her first child was a little too close to her wedding day."

"How old is the girl?"

"Twelve."

The silence that follows breaks beneath its own weight. "So if Fletcher didn't murder Rachael Schwartz, who did?" he asks after a moment.

He knows where I'm going with this. He wants me to say it. I hate it that it's so damn difficult. Doubt sits on my shoulder, stabbing me with its steely little knife. "What if Rachael Schwartz had a change of heart?" I say. "What if she came back to Painters Mill, not only to extort money from Fletcher, but to see her daughter? What if she wanted more? More than Loretta and Ben were willing to grant?"

Tomasetti holds his silence for a full minute. I see the wheels of thought spinning in his eyes. He doesn't like this any more than I do, but he knows it's something we cannot ignore.

"Even if the girl is the biological child of Rachael Schwartz, it doesn't prove Loretta Bontrager committed murder. We can't place her in that room. We can't tie her to the bat."

"It gives her motive," I say.

"Maybe." But he frowns. "What about Ben Bontrager? Do you think he's involved?"

"I don't know. He has to know that Fannie isn't their biological child. Whether he knows Fannie is Rachael Schwartz's child . . ." I let the words trail when the image of Rachael Schwartz's broken body flashes in my mind's eye. "That said, the level of violence . . . the strength required to do that kind of damage . . . maybe."

"It's flimsy."

"I know."

"Any human being capable of doing what was done to Rachael Schwartz needs to be taken off the street," he says.

I nod. "DNA would be a good place to start."

"No judge in his right mind is going to sign off on a warrant."

"I can get something."

He scoffs at the notion. "You know surreptitious sampling isn't admissible."

"It doesn't need to be. But at least we would know. It would change the way we look at the case." I think about that a moment. "Who we look at."

"If you're wrong?"

"I drop everything, leave it as it is, and close the case," I tell him.

He scowls at me. "If you're right, you're going to have to prove your case."

"I'm aware."

"At the moment, you've got nothing."

Except that kernel of suspicion that's been nibbling away at my gut from the start. "For now, I'm going to do some research, see what I can find." I shrug. "The rest . . . I'll cross that bridge when I come to it."

CHAPTER 36

Day 6

It's just after eight A.M. when I walk out of the Butterhorn Bakery in downtown Painters Mill, a baker's dozen of still-warm doughnuts tucked into a paper bag. I didn't sleep last night after my conversation with Tomasetti and the ensuing research marathon. I couldn't turn off my brain. Couldn't stop thinking about Rachael Schwartz and Fannie Bontrager and all the ugly implications of a theory I'm still not sure of.

I wasn't surprised to discover several academic studies on "sensation seeking in children." One of the articles I read used phrases like "novelty seeking" and "desire to engage in activities involving speed or risk" and "behavioral difficulties." A second study used the term "heritable trait," and I had my answer.

I don't like the idea of obtaining a DNA sample without a warrant. It's not illegal in the state of Ohio, but as Tomasetti pointed out, even if I'm able to prove that Fannie Bontrager is Rachael Schwartz's daughter,

I can't use the information as evidence. The one thing it will do is establish a motive for Ben and Loretta Bontrager, and set me on track to take a hard look at them.

The warm cinnamon aroma of the doughnuts fills the interior of my rental car as I make the turn onto the township road and idle past the Bontrager farm. I look for garbage cans at the end of the lane, but like most Amish, the Bontragers burn their trash. No help whatsoever in terms of my gaining a DNA sample.

Half a mile down the road, I make a U-turn and pull onto the shoulder. I don't expect any problems with Ben or Loretta, but it's always prudent to let a fellow officer know where you are no matter how benign the assignment.

I call my on-duty officer, Skid. "Where are you?" I ask.

"I just stopped Ron Zelinski's kid," he tells me. "Caught him doing ninety out on Township Road 89. Claims he was late for school."

That particular stretch is smooth, flat, and wide, which makes it a favorite spot for all sorts of illicit driving activities, everything from street racing to car surfing. Two years ago, a sixteen-year-old was thrown from a pickup truck and sustained a serious head injury.

"Now he really *is* going to be late," I say. "Don't cut him any slack."

"Wouldn't dream of it. Kid's a shit."

Like his dad, I think, but I don't say it. "Look, I'm about to swing by the Bontrager place. I shouldn't be there more than twenty minutes or so. I'll call you when I finish up."

A beat of silence and then, "Something going on, Chief?"

"Fishing expedition, mostly." Because I'm not sure of any of my suspicions—because I'm dealing with the welfare of a minor child and the reputation of a well-thought-of family—I keep it vague. "I need to talk to them about the Schwartz case. There are a couple of things that don't add up. I'm not sure I got the whole story from them."

"You want me to meet you out there?" he asks. "I can tie this up in two minutes."

"With their being Amish, I think they'll be more apt to speak openly if I'm alone. I don't expect things to go south—I just want you to know where I am."

"If I don't hear from you in twenty, I'll call out the posse."

"Roger that."

I pull onto the road and make the turn into the Bontrager lane. The horse I'd seen Fannie riding a few days ago grazes in the field to my right. I continue on past the house and park in the gravel area between the house and barn. The reek of manure drifts on the breeze as I take the sidewalk to the front porch. I've barely knocked when the door swings open.

"Katie! Hello!" Loretta motions me in. "*Kumma inseid.*" Come inside.

"I won't take up too much of your time." I hold up the bag of doughnuts. "I come bearing gifts."

"Oh, how nice." She smiles. "The Butterhorn Bakery. Fannie's favorite." She laughs and touches her backside with her hand. "Mine, too, as if you can't tell. What brings you to our neck of the woods this morning?"

"I'm about to close the case and I wanted to tie up a couple of loose ends."

Her expression turns thoughtful. "This has been a dark time for all of us. I'm glad it's over. I reckon you are, too." She glances over her shoulder toward the kitchen. "I've got bone broth on the stove. We can sit in the kitchen if you'd like."

I follow her through the living room, to a big typically Amish kitchen. Cabinets painted robin's-egg blue. Formica countertops. The cast-iron woodstove throws off a little too much heat. A kerosene-powered refrigerator vibrates in the corner. Ahead, a doorway leads to the mudroom. There, I see the coat tree, laden with *kapp*s and a man's flat-brimmed hat.

"Bone broth smells good." I set the bag of doughnuts on the table and pull out the three paper plates and napkins I brought with me.

"It's my *mamm*'s recipe. An old one." At the stove, she stirs the broth and replaces the lid. Mild surprise registers in her eyes when she sees that I've set out plates and napkins. "Well then, while Ben's in the barn, maybe the three of us will just sneak a few of these doughnuts.

"Fannie!" she calls out, and then to me, "*Kaffi?*"

"*Dank.*" Using a napkin, I set doughnuts on the plates.

Fannie appears in the doorway. She's wearing a green dress. White *kapp*. Gray sneakers. I'm surprised to see the pediatric sling that secures her left arm in place across her chest.

"Hi, Chief Burkholder," she says with a smile.

"That's a nice-looking sling you're wearing," I say to the girl. "What happened?"

Loretta pours coffee from a percolator, looks at us over her shoulder. "Snuck out of the house to ride that horse last night is what happened." She clucks her mouth. "Going too fast, I imagine. Fell off down by the creek. Broke her clavicle." She carries two cups to the table, sets one in front of me. "We knew she was going to get hurt sooner or later."

I look at Fannie. "You weren't speeding, were you?"

A not-so-guilty grin. "The rein broke and I couldn't stop him."

"*Sitz dich anne un havva faasnachtkuche.*" Sit yourself down and have a doughnut.

The girl pulls out a chair next to me and sits. Despite her injury, she goes directly for the doughnut and bites into it with relish.

At the counter, Loretta pours milk into her coffee. "You'll be lucky if your *datt* doesn't sell that horse."

"He's a good horse," Fannie defends.

Knowing I don't have much time, I smile at Fannie and touch the side of my mouth with my finger, indicating to her she's got a speck of doughnut on her lip.

"Oh." She scrubs the napkin across her mouth and raises her brows.

"Let me." I take her napkin, blot in a place where I'll likely get spit. "There you go."

The girl grins, takes the napkin, and for an instant I can't look away.

Rachael Schwartz had strawberry-blond hair, eyes the color of a tropical sea, and a face so pretty it hurt to look at her because the world somehow never seemed to measure up. Fannie is brown haired and brown eyed. She's plain, her face unremarkable. Except for that dazzle of light in her eyes . . .

"Katie?"

Loretta hands me a cup of coffee. She's looking at me oddly. Fannie, too, and I realize one of them said something I didn't hear.

"*Dank.*"

"Are you feeling all right?" Loretta asks.

"Just a little sleep deprived," I tell her.

"Well, now that this horrible mess is over, maybe you can get some rest," the Amish woman tells me.

I glance toward the doorway to the mudroom, where the coat tree holding the *kapp*s stares back at me. Most Amish women have at least two. One for every day and one for worship. From where I'm sitting, I can see that one of the *kapp*s has a tiny bow at the back. A shadowy spot of teal paint on top. Fannie's *kapp*. The one she wears every day that's waiting to be washed—and likely laden with DNA. If I can't get Fannie's napkin into a baggie without being seen, I might be able to pocket the *kapp*.

"All right, my girl." Loretta brings her hands together. "Why don't

264

you run next door and see if Mrs. Yoder wants some of this nice broth, so Katie and I can talk."

"Can I have another doughnut?" The girl rises, scoots her chair back to the table.

I look at the napkin on her plate. The one I used to blot her mouth. I'm aware of the baggie in my jacket pocket.

"She eats like her *datt.*" Loretta shakes her head. "Go on now. Tell Mrs. Yoder I got plenty."

I rise to gather the paper plates.

At the doorway, Fannie looks at me and smiles. "Bye, Katie."

I grin, look at her over my shoulder. "Stay out of trouble."

Aware that Loretta is at the stove, replacing the lid on the Dutch oven, I snatch up the girl's napkin. Keeping my back to Loretta, I flick out the baggie, tuck the napkin into it.

"Oh, I can take care of the throwaways, Katie. You just sit and enjoy your *kaffi.*"

"No problem," I say easily. "I've got it."

I'm sealing the baggie when I hear the creak of a floorboard. I look up to see Ben Bontrager standing in the doorway of the mudroom, looking at me.

"What was it you wanted to talk about?"

I hear Loretta's voice behind me. The tap of her spoon against the Dutch oven where the bone brother simmers. I can't stop looking at Ben. I don't know how long he's been there. If he saw what I did. If he understands what he saw.

"I mainly just wanted to bring the doughnuts." As nonchalantly as I can manage, I shove the baggie into my jacket pocket.

I meet Ben's stare, force a smile. "If you like doughnuts, you're in luck."

"I like them just fine."

He steps into the kitchen. He's been working. Leather gloves in his left hand. A shovel in his right hand. Mud on his boots. Bits of hay stuck to his trousers.

"Now just look at all that mud you've tracked in," Loretta says.

Ben says nothing. Continues to stare at me. The hairs prickle at my nape. I'm aware of my police radio clipped to my shirt. My .38 pressing against my hip. "I've got to get back to work," I say.

The blow comes from behind. A *clang!* of steel above my ear. The force snaps my head sideways. A lightning strike of pain as my scalp splits open. Before I even realize I'm going to fall, my knees hit the floor.

I shake myself, glance right, see Loretta swing the cast-iron lid lifter. I block the blow with my forearm. The steel zings against bone. Another explosion of pain. The length of cast iron clatters to the floor between us.

I yank out the .38, bring it up. "Do not move! Get your hands up!"

I get one foot under me, lurch to my feet when another blow smashes against the back of my head. My vision narrows and dims. I swivel, catch a glimpse of Ben. Shovel at the ready. Lips peeled back. Teeth clenched.

I fire twice, the sound deafening in the confines of the kitchen. My timing is off, my balance skewed. I sway right. The shovel goes up again.

"Drop it!" I shout.

The steel spade crashes against my crown with the force of a freight train. Consciousness spirals down, water being sucked into a drain. The lights flicker. Then my cheek slams against the floor and the darkness welcomes me in.

CHAPTER 37

Spring 2009

For the first time in her life, Rachael Schwartz mourned the loss of her faith. Tonight, the darkest of nights, she needed the comfort of knowing she wasn't going to die alone and in agony, and that she wasn't the last person left on earth.

She should have been prepared. She'd known this moment would come. She and Loretta had discussed it. For months now, they'd planned everything down to the last detail. But Rachael had been in denial. She'd spent weeks ignoring the changes, hiding the weight gain and the swelling of her breasts. Not only from her parents, but from herself. She'd denied the cold, hard truth of what had happened.

Of course, Fate didn't give a good damn if she was ready or not.

Pain screamed through her body. The power of it took her breath, frightened her. It shook her physically, emotionally. Rachael was no stranger to pain. She'd broken her arm when she was nine. Last year, she'd had her wisdom teeth pulled by the English dentist. This was like nothing she'd ever experienced.

Rachael hadn't told anyone. Not even her *mamm*. No one in the Amish community knew she was *ime familye weg*. She'd known they would judge her harshly. And so she'd weathered this storm alone.

The pains had started after supper. At first, Rachael thought it was indigestion. By midnight she was pacing and upset and she knew it wasn't going to go away. If she didn't leave soon, everyone would know; her life would be over. And so after her parents went to bed, she'd sneaked from the house. She cut through the cornfield, fighting her way through mud, panting like an animal, bending and clutching her belly with every wave of pain. She called Loretta from the phone shack and asked her to meet her at the bridge, like they'd planned. By the time Rachael got there, she was hysterical and crying and certain this would be her last night on earth.

Relief swamped her at the sight of her friend's buggy.

"Rachael!" Loretta rushed toward her. "What's wrong?"

"It's time," she cried.

Loretta reached her, set her hand on her back. "You're going to be all right. Come on. Let's go."

She choked out a sob as another cramp ripped through her middle. She staggered right, leaned against the beam. A warm flood gushed between her legs, soaking her underthings and shoes. Horrified, Rachael looked down, watched it run down her legs, and splash onto the ground at her feet.

She knew what it was; she'd read about all the things that would happen. But to see it was an out-of-body experience.

"I don't want to do this!" she cried.

"It's okay," Loretta said. "It's normal. But we don't have much time."

Loretta put her arm around her. Rachael closed her eyes and let her friend guide her to the buggy. For the first time in hours, she didn't feel alone. Still, she sobbed while her friend climbed onto the driver's bench. She lost herself to the pain as they drove, the horse's shod hooves clanking against the asphalt.

The Willowdell Motel was a trashy old place that had been sitting on an unsightly slice of land for as long as Rachael could remember. For weeks now, she'd debated where she would go. She'd thought about the abandoned Hemmelgarn place down by Dogleg Road. The old barn out on Township Road 1442. At one point, she'd even considered going to the midwife in Coshocton. In the end, she'd decided on the motel, where there was a bed and towels and a shower.

Lying in the back seat of the buggy, Rachael rode out another cramp while Loretta went inside and paid for a room. Rachael had given the money to her a week ago, after she'd made the decision to do it here.

"Room 9."

Rachael looked up from her misery and watched her friend climb into the buggy. "Park in the back," she said. "Where no one can see the buggy. Hurry."

The room was furnished with a single bed draped with a blue coverlet. A window covered with ill-fitting curtains squatted over a metal air conditioner that blew air reeking of mildew and rattled like a train. While Loretta tethered the horse, Rachael went inside, dropped her overnight bag on the chair next to the bed, and went to the bathroom.

Fear and a terrible sense of disbelief roiled inside her as she stripped off her clothes. Bare feet on a broken tile floor. A smear of blood on her leg. A bright red drop of it on the tile next to her toes. Fear pulsing in a body that was no longer hers. A body she didn't recognize or understand. Pain so frightening she could do nothing but sob as she stepped into the tub. She soaped up, not caring that her hair got wet. Twice she went to her knees. Not to pray, but to ease the pain.

Still damp, she crawled into the bed, pulled the sheet and coverlet over her. She barely noticed when Loretta came in. But she saw the uncertainty on her friend's face as she took the chair next to the bed. "I brought Tylenol."

Rachael knew it wouldn't help. Nothing would help. She didn't even care at this point. "Give them to me. Hurry."

Quickly, Loretta went to the bathroom and filled a plastic glass with tap water. Next to the bed, she tapped out four acetaminophen tablets and handed them to her.

Rachael snatched them up, tossed all four into her mouth, and swallowed them with a gulp of water. She'd never been prone to tears; not like some girls. She was tougher than that. But at some point, she'd begun to cry again. The helpless, whimpering sobs of a dying animal.

"I don't think I can do this," she cried.

"Yes, you can. Women do it all the time."

Agony ripped at her insides, turning her inside out. Nausea seesawed in her gut and for a moment she thought she might throw up. "I have to . . ." Rachael bit down on the word, grinding her teeth. "Use the bathroom."

"No, you don't," Loretta said. "It's just the baby telling you he's ready to come into the world."

Rachael fisted the sheets, turning left and right, trying to find a position that would ease the pain. Angry now because nothing helped. "I don't know how to do this! I don't—" A wail squeezed from her throat. "I have to . . ."

"Shhh! Quiet!"

Rachael squeezed her eyes closed, brought the pillow to her face and screamed. "It hurts!"

Straightening, Loretta rushed to the bathroom and returned with two face cloths. A damp one, which she placed on Rachael's forehead.

A dry one, which she rolled up and handed it to her. "Bite down on this when the pain is too much," she whispered.

Rachael grabbed her friend's hand, squeezed it hard. Before she could say anything, the pain gripped her. Writhing, she fumbled with the cloth, jammed it into her mouth, and bit down as hard as she could. She rode the wave that way, biting down so hard she thought she might shatter her teeth.

The urge to push overrode her fear that she would mess the bed. She bore down hard, felt her insides cramp and tear. She screamed into the towel, pulled it hard against her lower molars. Body wet with sweat. Hair still damp from her shower.

This time, the cramp didn't subside. It came and came and came until she couldn't breathe. Thought she would pass out. Or die. She bore down again, grunting, the ugly sounds of a mindless beast. She opened her legs, spread them wide, not caring about modesty or the sheets or anything else. All she knew was that she wanted this thing out of her. She wanted the pain to stop. She wanted to be done with it.

She pushed against the pressure with all of her might. At some point, she looked at her friend, saw her pale face suffused with horror and fascination. Before she could speak or think, another riot of pain ripped through her.

She grabbed her knees, pulled them to her shoulders. She wanted to sit up, but couldn't. Another cramp rolled through her, movement in her abdomen. Pressure low and building. An elongated scream tore from her throat as she pushed. She bore down hard, unable to catch her breath, and the room spun. She closed her eyes, sucked in a breath, held it as she tried desperately to force it from her body.

A tearing sensation between her legs. Lessening pressure, like bowels breaking free.

"I see the top of his head!" Squealing, Loretta took her hand. "It's coming out! Go ahead and push!"

Lying on her back, she gripped both knees, curling upward with the effort. Sounds she didn't recognize tearing from her throat. Everything else falling away.

Loretta moved to the foot of the bed. Bent over her, looking at her. "Keep going!" she said. "Push. You can do it. Push!"

Rachael closed her eyes and bore down. The sensation of tearing. The knowledge that her body would never be the same.

"Oh! Oh! It's a girl!"

Rachael caught a glimpse of her friend's face. Eyes wide and excited and filled with awe.

"She's out," Loretta said. "I've got her."

Rachael fell back into the pillows. Breaths rushing. Body slicked with perspiration. The sheets around her damp with it.

"There's a cord."

Loretta set the baby in a ratty towel. A tiny body slicked with fluids. An instant later, Rachael heard a cry, like a kitten's mewl. The sensation of the cord still within her.

She looked away. "Cut it," she said, and for the first time since the first pang of labor, she thought about what came next.

"I brought Mamm's shears." Loretta cut the cord, capturing the blood with a face cloth. "There."

She then swaddled the baby tightly in the towel, rolling her from side to side and tucking in the edges. "That's how the midwife does it," she said. "Tight, like this, so she doesn't scratch herself with those little fingernails."

Loretta got to her feet and looked at Rachael, her expression uncertain, questioning. "Do you want to hold her?"

Rachael didn't look at her friend; she didn't look at the baby. She shook her head.

"Oh, but she's so cute. Just look at her." Smiling, Loretta looked down at the baby, running her finger over the little cheek. "Such a precious thing. Her lips are like a satin bow."

When Rachael said nothing, she added, "This child is a gift from God. No matter how she came to be, this little angel is—"

Rachael cut her off. "You're not having second thoughts, are you?"

A moment of hesitation and then, "Of course not. It's just that . . . you're exhausted and overwhelmed. Maybe *you're* the one having second thoughts. I wouldn't blame you, especially after what you've been through."

"I don't want her," Rachael said. "I don't want to be a mother. You know that."

Loretta looked down at the baby, tears glittering. "Are you sure?"

Rachael studied her friend, wondering how she could be so happy— so *good*—when life dished out such terrible things. Having children and a family are a key part of being Amish. Children are welcomed with joy and considered "a heritage of the Lord." She wondered what was wrong with her. Why didn't she want her own baby?

"You and Ben have been married for what? Seven months now?" Rachael asked. "And yet God hasn't seen fit to bless you with a child."

"These things take time," Loretta said. "God will not be rushed."

"It's a sign, Loretta. It means everything we talked about is the right thing to do."

Loretta looked up, met her gaze, her expression serene. "But how . . ."

"Ben still thinks you're *ime familye weg*?" Rachael asked.

Loretta nodded. "Mamm, too. Everyone does. I made that pillow, you know. I've been wearing it under my dress for weeks now." She looked down at the baby, but not before Rachael discerned the hint of shame in her eyes.

"So we go through with our plan," Rachael said. "Just like we talked about."

"What if it doesn't work?" Loretta whispered. "What if someone finds out?"

"No one is going to find out," Rachael assured her. "All we have to do is stay calm and stick to our plan."

Looking down at the newborn in her arms, Loretta blinked back tears. "I love her already."

"See? You're a natural," Rachael said, watching, relieved. "You'll see. Everything will work out. Ben is going to be so happy. Your *mamm* and *datt*. You, too."

Loretta's brows knit. "It sounded so . . . easy when we talked about it. I mean, before. Now that the baby is here, how do I explain—"

"I got it all worked out." Rachael tapped her temple with her index finger. "I thought of every last detail. Every question. Here's what we're going to do."

And she began to talk.

CHAPTER 38

"Hello? Anyone home?" Skid knocked on the door hard enough to rattle the glass.

No one came.

He'd tried the front door, the back door, and the side door off the porch by the garden, all to no avail.

Puzzled, he hit his shoulder mike and hailed the chief. "I'm ten-twenty-three," he said. "What's your twenty?"

Radio silence hissed, same as it had the first time he'd tried to reach her, ten minutes ago.

He took the steps to the sidewalk and started toward his cruiser, which was parked in the gravel area between the house and barn. He'd been looking forward to a quiet shift. A breakfast burrito from LaDonna's Diner. Coffee from that new café on Main. He'd especially been looking forward to using the men's room somewhere.

Where the hell was Burkholder?

Cursing beneath his breath, he hailed Dispatch. "Mona?"

"What up?"

He grinned at the sound of her voice—which he liked a little too much these days—and he was glad there was no one around to see him. She was filling in for Lois today, which meant she'd be there when he ended his shift. "Any idea where the chief is?"

"Last I heard she was headed out to the Bontrager place."

"That's what I thought." He looked around. "She's not here."

"That's weird." A beat of silence. "Did you try her cell?"

"I'll try again. Over and out." Skid pulled his cell from his pocket, hit the speed dial for Kate. Four rings and then voicemail. "Well, shit."

Puzzled, he walked to his cruiser, opened the door to get in, and then closed it. Fingers of something that felt vaguely like concern pressed into the back of his neck. One of the things he liked most about the chief was that she was reliable and always available. Day or night.

"So unless you're in the damn shower," he muttered, "you ought to be picking up the phone."

Had she run into some problem on her way here? Or was there something else going on?

Leaning against the hood of his cruiser, he checked his phone again and looked around, wrinkled his nose at the waft of manure coming from the barn. Damn, he hated dairy operations. They were all mud and stink and he'd had enough of both to last him a lifetime. He was reaching for the car door handle when he noticed the barn's sliding door standing open about a foot. Wondering if there was someone inside who hadn't seen or heard him, he started that way.

He reached the barn, pushed the door open another foot, and peeked inside. "Hello?" he called out. "Police department! Anyone here?"

The interior smelled of cattle and sour milk, the stink made worse by the manure pit out back. He entered, his eyes adjusting to the murky light. A dozen or so stanchions ahead. Milking apparatus that didn't look too clean. A big generator that smelled of kerosene and sludge. To his right were the stairs to the hayloft above. Skid glanced left. Everything inside him ground to a halt at the sight of the vehicle parked halfway down the aisle. It was a newish Toyota Camry. Red. If he wasn't mistaken, that was the rental car the chief was driving.

Senses on alert, he strode to the vehicle, set his hand against the hood, found it warm to the touch. Did she have some mechanical problem after she'd arrived? Dead battery and no jump? If that was the case, why was the vehicle parked in the barn?

He spoke into his radio. "I'm ten-twenty-three out at the Bontrager place. Mona, I got a vehicle out here. I'm pretty sure it's the chief's. Can you ten-twenty-eight?" He read the license plate number to her. "She been in contact?"

"Negative."

Skid looked around. No one in sight. Not even a damn cow. He was reaching for the Camry's door handle when he spotted a smear on the window. Not dirt or mud. Pulling out his mini Maglite, he leaned close for a better look. Blood.

"Shit."

"What's going on?"

"I got blood." He yanked open the door. His heart did a slow roll at the sight of the .38 revolver on the seat. Her clip-on mike. "Get County out here. Ten-thirty-nine." Lights and siren. "I'm going to take a look around."

CHAPTER 39

Consciousness returns with the ebb and flow of a gentle tide. Warm water lapping against sand and then rushing back out to sea. I'm aware of movement and light and the vicious pound of pain in my head. Something coarse scraping my cheek. The smells of old wood and dust and moldy feed. Nausea bubbles like hot grease in my stomach. Bile in my mouth.

I spit, realize I've been slobbering. I try to lift my hand to wipe my mouth, but I can't move my arms. I have no idea where I am. All I know is that I'm in a bad way. Confusion is a bottomless pit. But the muscle memory of fear hovers just out of reach, coiled tight and ready to spring.

Get up, a little voice whispers. *Get up.*

I open my eyes. I see a mound of loose hay a foot from my face. I'm lying on my side, my face against weathered wood. I'm being jostled, bumped and rocked back and forth. I hear the jingle of a harness. The clip-clop of shod hooves.

I raise my head, look around. My vision blurs, so I blink it away, try to focus. Pain roils in my head. The jostling triggers another rise of nausea. I spit, set my head back down, close my eyes.

Get up, Kate. Get up! Hurry!

The memory of the events that brought me to this moment rushes back. Adrenaline jets into my muscles, making them twitch. The fear that follows sends me bolt upright. I'm in the back bed of a hay wagon. Two horses pulling it along a dirt road. There's an open field to my left. Thick woods on the right. I see blood on the wood where I'd been lying. My hands are bound behind my back. Ben Bontrager sits in the driver seat, leather lines in his hands, looking at me over his shoulder. Blank expression. Mouth set. Loretta sits next to him, staring straight ahead.

"Ben, what the hell are you doing?" I grind out the words as I test the binding at my wrists. Wire, I realize, tight enough to cut off my circulation.

"Stay where you are." He turns back to his driving. "We're almost there."

"Ben, you can't do this." I work at the wire, twisting and tugging as I speak. "I'm a cop. There's an officer on the way."

The Amish man ignores me, jiggles the lines, continues on.

I take in my surroundings, try to get my bearings. Nothing is familiar. I have no idea how far we've traveled or how long I was unconscious. We're not on a public road. No sign of the farmhouse. My best guess is that we're somewhere in the back of his property.

I glance down at my right hip. My .38 is gone. My radio and shoulder mike are gone. Shit. *Shit.*

"Ben." I say his name firmly, as if I still have any say in a matter that has spiraled out of control. "Stop the horses. Untie me. Right now. Before this goes too far."

No response. No indication that he even heard me.

"Where's my gun?" I ask. "My radio. For God's sake, people are looking for me. Cops."

Nothing.

"Turn around and look at me," I snap, adding authority to my voice that's ridiculous at this point.

Loretta looks over her shoulder at me. Her face impassive.

"Take me back to the house," I tell her. "So we can talk about this. Get things worked out."

No one responds.

I try another tack. "Where are you taking me?"

The couple exchanges a look, but they don't answer, they don't look at me.

I shift, try to get my legs under me. I'm unsteady, but manage to get to one knee. I'm about to rise when, without warning, Ben swings around. He lifts the buggy whip and brings the thick handle end of it down on my shoulder. "Stay there," he warns.

I duck and turn away. The second blow strikes my back. The lash of pain roils my temper. "Cut it out," I hiss.

He offers up a third blow. A glance off my right cheekbone. I grit my teeth, take it. Nothing else I can do.

"*Mer sott em sei eegne net verlosse,*" the Amish man snaps. One should not abandon one's own. "You did, Kate Burkholder. You left the Amish way. You abandoned God. He no longer sees you as one of us."

I stare at him, wondering if he's got my .38 on him. "God loves all of His children," I hear myself say. "Amish. English. It doesn't matter to Him."

"*Huahrah.*" Whoremonger. Making a sound of disgust, he turns away and goes back to his driving.

I lean against the side of the wagon, the wood rasping my back. Desperation presses down. I'm unarmed and incapacitated, in the middle of nowhere, with a man who will likely do me harm. I remind myself that Skid is probably wondering where I am. It's only a matter of time before he comes looking. My feet aren't bound, which means I can run if I get the chance. If I can reach the woods, I might be able to elude them until backup arrives.

I stare at their backs a moment before speaking. "What about Fannie?" I ask. "Have you thought about what this will do to her?"

Loretta turns to me. No longer is she the mouselike woman with the dish towel tossed over her shoulder and her eyes cast down. Now, she is a mother whose child is under threat, willing to do whatever it takes to protect what is hers.

"You are *veesht*," she hisses. Wicked. "Your heart is filled with *lushtahrei*." Immorality. "You are not *Amisch*. You were never Amish." She raps the heel of her hand against her chest. "Not inside. Not here, where it counts."

"This isn't about me," I tell her. "It's about Fannie."

"Leave her out of this," Loretta spits.

My mind races for some way to reach her, land upon some point that will help me negotiate my way out of this or at least defuse the situation until help arrives.

"I know what happened," I tell her. "I know it wasn't your fault."

Neither of them engage, so I keep going. "I think Rachael became *ime familye weg* the night Dane Fletcher assaulted her. I think she hid it from her family. From everyone. She had the baby. An innocent little girl. Only she didn't want it, did she?"

The Amish woman stares straight ahead. "Be quiet, Katie."

I keep pushing. "I know what she did. I know what you did. I'm not blaming either of you."

"*Leeyah.*" Liar. She turns to me, eyes flaring. "You know nothing. Backslider. Who are you to judge? We will not let you take her."

In the minutes I've been talking, I've worked at the wires wrapped around my wrists, bending and flexing, but the steel holds fast. At some point, I've cut my skin. I feel a dribble of blood making its way across my knuckles.

"No one's going to take her from you." I say the words with a gentleness that belies the situation. "There may be some legal issues, but there's no reason why you can't legally adopt Fannie and continue to raise her as your own."

It's not true, of course. This couple has committed multiple felonies. They will be prosecuted and, if convicted, probably spend time behind bars.

"All you have to do," I say, "is untie me. We go back to the house and come up with a plan. I know we can work it out."

The Amish woman slants a questioning look at her husband. For the first time, she appears uncertain. She wants the words to be true. She wants the problem of me to go away. Most of all, she wants Fannie.

"I think it's too late," she whispers.

"Do the right thing," I coax. "The police will be here any moment. Whatever you have planned isn't going to work."

Ben casts a warning look at his wife. "*Sell is nix as baeffzes.*" That is nothing but trifling talk. "No one is coming. Don't listen to her."

I look around. The woods are about fifty yards away. The field to my left looks fallow. There's no cover, not a single tree or fence. I have no idea what they have planned or where they're taking me. They're not going to let me go. If I'm going to get away, now is the time.

Never taking my eyes from the couple, I set my heels against the wood bed. The jingle of the harnesses, the wagon bumping and rocking over the rough road, cover the noise I make as I scooch my feet closer to the side of the wagon. Using the side for balance, I get to my knees. The horses are trotting, but the pace is slow enough for me to jump without getting hurt.

Eyes on the backs of my captors, I get to my feet, set my right foot atop the side. Out of the corner of my eye I see Ben's head swivel. I jump, land on my feet, and hit the ground running.

"*Ivvah-nemma!*" Take over.

Ben Bontrager's voice rings out. No time to look. I keep going, sprint toward the tree line fifty yards away. I hear Loretta shout, but I don't comprehend the words. I train my eyes on the woods ahead. Old-growth forest, thick with bramble.

"*Shtobba!*" Stop!

Ben's voice, scant yards behind me. I pour on the speed, too fast. Praying I don't trip. My balance off because I can't use my hands.

There's a ditch at the edge of the woods. Too wide to hurdle. I plunge into a foot of muddy water, muscle through, charge up the other side. Then I'm in the trees, zigzagging between trunks as wide as a man's shoulders. I hear the sound of breaking brush behind me. Another jet of adrenaline hits my muscles. A branch comes out of nowhere, punches my cheek, opens the skin. I duck, ignoring the pain, keep running.

"Skid! *Skid!*" I know there's no one around. I call out anyway. "Police Department! Help! *Help me!*"

I know Bontrager is going to catch me. It's inevitable. He's faster, not hampered by bound hands. Still, it's a shock when his fingers clamp around my arm. One moment I'm running full out, the next I'm being yanked backward with so much force that my feet leave the ground. I land on my backside and roll. I'm scrambling to my feet when Bontrager puts his boot on my back.

"Get off me," I snarl.

He looks down at me, breaths labored. Sweat beaded on his forehead.

I see stress etched into his every feature, and I know the fear of losing the child he's raised from birth has sent him over the edge. Looking into his eyes, I see something else, even more unexpected. The regret of a man who knows he's about to make a mistake that cannot be undone.

"Please don't do this," I say.

"*Greeyah ruff.*" Get up. There's no rage or high passion in his voice— just the steel resolve of a man who expects complete submission.

"I'm not going anywhere with you," I say.

Bending, he hauls me to my feet and shoves me toward the wagon. "*Gay.*" Go.

When I don't move fast enough, he shoves me in the direction of the wagon. "Keep walking."

We leave the cover of trees. I listen for a distant siren. The rumble of an engine. Where the hell is Skid?

Ahead, I see Loretta standing near the wagon, looking around, her hands on her hips. "*Dumla,*" she says. Hurry.

I slow, stalling, but Ben shoves me again.

Only then do I recognize where we are. We've left the Bontrager property and entered adjacent land upon which a two-room Amish school once stood. I attended school here. A few years ago, a tornado leveled the structure. The only thing left is the decrepit foundation and stone chimney. Beyond, there's a gravel two-track that continues on for another half mile or so, eventually opening onto County Road 60.

Why the hell have they brought me here?

"Bring her." The Amish woman strides past the foundation to an area overrun with high grass and the spindly stalks of last year's weeds.

"Walk." Ben shoves my shoulder again.

I have no idea what they have planned or hope to accomplish. What are my options? Appeal to reason? Their Amish mores? Threaten

284

them with the consequences of their actions? Losing custody of their daughter?

Loretta stops next to the stump of a long-dead tree. I've been here before, I realize. The school outhouse once stood on this very spot. The only thing left is the pit, where the refuse was stored and removed.

Uneasiness quivers in my gut at the sight of the pit. It's about five feet deep with crumbling cinder-block walls choked with roots and tangled with weeds. A huge pile of freshly excavated dirt is next to the pit. Someone has recently taken a shovel to it, cleared out most of the debris and earth.

"This is not the way we wanted to do this," Loretta whispers.

"Don't do anything stupid," I say. "It'll only make things worse for you. For Fannie."

"You should have let things lie." Ben says the words as if he didn't hear me. "You've left us no choice. Whatever happens here today is between you and God."

I'd been working under the assumption that I'd be able to talk them out of whatever crazy scheme they'd hatched. For the first time it occurs to me they didn't bring me here to convince me of their cause. I'm in danger. The ripple of fear that follows is so powerful that the ground trembles beneath my feet.

"I know what we are about to do is a sin against God," Ben says. "That we will go to hell for it. But I will not let them take Fannie."

My heart begins to pound. If I were to be pushed into the pit, I'm pretty sure I could eventually climb out, even with my wrists bound. In the back of my mind, I wonder if he's going to pull out the .38 and kill me and then push all that dirt into the pit. . . .

"You have brought the wrath of the Lord down upon yourself," Loretta says. "You are *eevil.*" Evil. "You are a threat. Not only to us and our daughter's life. But everything that is decent and good—"

I launch myself toward the trees. Ben lunges so quickly, I don't have time to brace. He shoves me with so much force that I fly sideways and plummet into the pit. I hit the ground so hard that the breath is knocked from my lungs.

I roll, spit dirt, try to suck in a breath of air. I struggle to my knees, look up in time to see the shovel. I duck, avoid the blow, but it's so close I feel the puff of air against my face.

Holding the shovel like a bat, Ben swings again. Purpose etched into his features. Lips drawn back. I lunge sideways, but I'm not fast enough. The blade grazes the top of my head with enough force to open the skin. I feel the warm trickle of blood.

"Don't do this!" I shout. "Think of Fannie! She needs you!"

Staying low, watching for the shovel, I look around for a way out. A place where the wall isn't vertical. A foothold, a broken cinder block or root or jut of rebar. The pit is about five feet square, the muddy floor littered with dead vegetation and loose dirt.

Ben jabs the shovel at me again. I'm far enough below him that I'm able to get out of the way and he misses again. I stumble to the opposite side of the pit, spot the jut of root. I rush to it, step up on it, press my shoulder against the wall to keep my balance. If I can find another foothold, I might be able to wriggle high enough to escape. . . .

The shovel strikes the side of my head with so much force that I'm knocked off my perch. I hear the *tink!* of the blade strike my skull. The zing of pain down the side of my face. Then I'm falling into space and the darkness swallows me whole.

CHAPTER 40

Skid was well versed in all the ins and outs of police procedure. He'd had it drilled into his head since his first day at the academy a life-time ago. He figured his finding the chief's abandoned vehicle and .38 qualified as just cause to enter the premises sans a warrant. He didn't bother knocking. It took him just a few minutes to ascertain there was no one in the house. He even went into the basement and attic. All to no avail.

"House is clear," he said into his shoulder mike. "You got an ETA on County?"

"They're ten-seven-six."

"Put out a BOLO for Ben and/or Loretta Bontrager's buggy." The request didn't feel right, because he'd seen a buggy in the barn. Did Amish people have more than one?

"Roger that."

"Something's wonky here, Mona," he said. "I'm going to look around."

"Pickles is ten-seven-six."

287

"Ten-four."

Skid left the house, jogged to the gravel area between the house and barn. There was a rusted steel gate next to the barn and a muddy two-track that ran toward the back of the property. He got into the cruiser, idled to the gate, and got out. Sure enough, marks in the dirt told him someone had recently opened the gate. On the other side were fresh horse tracks and the ruts of tires. He pushed open the gate. Back in the cruiser, he drove through.

At the top of the hill, he hailed Pickles. "What's your twenty, old man?"

"I'm two minutes out."

"I'm headed to the rear of the Bontrager property. Do you know if you can get in through the back? There a gate back there?"

"I think there's an old two-track down where that old schoolhouse used to be. You want me to meet you back there?"

Skid didn't know about the old schoolhouse. In fact, he wasn't counting on much help from Pickles. The guy might've been a good cop back in the day, but he was almost eighty now and sneaking a smoke every chance he got.

"That's affirm. Keep your eyes open, old man," he said. "I'm pretty sure someone's come back this way."

I don't remember falling or striking the ground. The next thing I become aware of is the press of damp earth against my cheek. Pain above my ear. The smell of dirt and decaying organic matter. I can't move my arms. . . .

I open my eyes to find myself staring at a wall of dirt and concrete block, dangling roots, and nondescript vegetation. I'm prone, the ground cold and wet beneath me. Raising my head, I look up to see Ben Bontrager slide a shovel into a pile of loose dirt.

It's a surreal scene. So strange that for a moment, I wonder if I blink, it'll go away. A shovelful of earth clatters onto my back. I try to sit up, but I'm tied to something heavy. I twist my head, smell the creosote an instant before I recognize the railroad tie.

A hot flare of panic courses through me as the hopelessness of the situation hits home. A railroad tie weighs about two hundred pounds; there's no way I can move it. I'm lying in the base of a deep pit and from all indications Ben Bontrager is planning to bury me alive.

"Loretta!" I look around for the Amish woman. "Don't do this!"

She looks down at me, then walks away without speaking, leaving my line of vision.

"*Help me!*" I work at the wires binding my wrists, no longer noticing the pain. My feet aren't bound, so I use the strength in my legs to try and disengage myself from the railroad tie. I dig my toes into the dirt. I grunt and scramble, like an animal snared in a trap. All to no avail.

A torrent of earth rains down. It goes into my hair. Down my collar, into my eyes. I look up to see Ben upend a wheelbarrow. "Stop!" I scream.

Blinking dirt from my eyes, I see Loretta come up beside him, pushing a second wheelbarrow. Ben usurps the handles and upends it.

Dirt and small stones come down atop me. It gets into my mouth. This time, there's so much, I feel the weight of it on my back.

I struggle mindlessly against the bonds, twisting. Back and forth. Back and forth. I kick my legs, throwing off the dirt. I buck against the railroad tie, clods rolling off me. Another wheelbarrow full of dirt plummets. I suck in dust and begin to cough. Panic smolders inside me, but I tamp it down, knowing it will do nothing but hinder my efforts.

Abruptly, I go still. I take a deep breath, release it slowly. I close my eyes. Grapple for a calm that isn't there. I hear the rattle of the wheelbarrow. The hiss of the shovel penetrating earth. I focus on the wires at my wrists. Try to pinpoint the weak point. I go at it again. Ignoring the steel slicing my flesh.

I remind myself Skid is on his way. He's a good cop; he'll find me. Eyes closed, I take a deep breath and scream at the top of my lungs. "Skid! I'm here! Help me! Help!"

My cries echo against the walls of the pit. I quash another wave of panic. A payload of earth hits my back, the weight pressing me down. I kick my legs, twist to rid myself of it. But the railroad tie locks me down tight. The dirt stays, and I can't help but wonder: How long before my face is covered? How long until I can't breathe? How long until I'm completely buried and even if someone comes, they won't find me?

Another volley of dirt pours down, strikes my face. It goes into my left ear. My eyes. My nose. Grit in my mouth.

Dear God.

I lift my head. Spit mud. "Skid!"

The wire on my wrists snaps. I twist my head around, look up to see Ben Bontrager. His back is to me. Loretta is nowhere in sight. I twist my hands and the remaining wire falls away.

I lie still. Facedown. Listening. My mind racing. Even with my hands free, if I try to climb out, one of them will bludgeon me and force me back down. I don't have much time. In the periphery of my vision, I see Ben move away, leaving my line of sight. No sign of Loretta, but I hear her speaking to him.

I jump to my feet, look around wildly. For a foothold. A weapon. Anything I can use. A three-foot length of rebar lies on the ground. I snatch it up, spot the jut of a broken cinder block. Heart pounding, I set my boot on the cinder block and heave myself up.

I hear the whoosh of air before I see the shovel. I glance left, see Ben swing it like a nine iron. But his angle is bad. I flatten myself against the earthen wall, feel the gust against the back of my head. I throw my leg over the top of the pit, scramble out. I roll, get to my knees, swing the rebar with all my might. Steel clangs against his shin with such force that I nearly lose my grip.

A howl tears from his throat. He drops the shovel. Goes down on one knee. Face contorted. But his eyes are on me. Enraged and filled with intent as he rises.

I scramble to my feet, kick his shovel away. Gripping the rebar with both hands, I swing it with all my might. The steel clocks him across the chest. He dances sideways, bends, snatches up the shovel, comes at me.

"Drop it! Do it now!"

Skid.

I swivel, catch sight of my officer rushing toward us, weapon drawn, moving fast.

Ben Bontrager swings the shovel at me. I pivot, reel backward. Trip on a clod of dirt. Lose my balance. I land on my backside.

The shovel arcs 180 degrees. A heavy hitter smacking in a home run, inches above my head.

"Drop it!" Skid screams. "Get your hands up! Now!"

A dozen things happen at once. I see Loretta rush Skid from behind, shovel raised over her head. "Behind you!" I shout.

Skid spins, fires once as the shovel comes down on his shoulder. The Amish woman drops. The shovel clatters to the ground. Cursing, Skid lowers his weapon, goes to his knees, injured.

Ben Bontrager charges Skid. Shovel at the ready. Footfalls heavy and pounding. A roar pouring from his mouth.

"Get on the ground! Show me your hands!" Pickles lumbers toward us. Ten yards away. An old man's run. But his weapon is trained and steady on Bontrager. Authority rings in his voice. "Do not move or I will put you down! Do you understand me? Get the hell down!"

For a moment, I think Bontrager isn't going to comply. That he's going to force Pickles to fire his weapon. But the Amish man's stride falters. A couple of feet from his wife, he stops. He looks down at her. The shovel clatters to the ground. He goes to his knees and raises both hands.

Pickles goes to him, works the handcuffs from the compartment on his belt. "Get down. On your face." He sets his knee on the Amish man's back. "Do not move."

Bontrager doesn't resist. Doesn't seem to care as Pickles snaps the cuffs onto his wrists and pats him down. The Amish man never takes his eyes off his wife.

I get to my feet. My legs are still shaking as I cross to where Loretta lies. I'm aware of Skid standing a few feet away, speaking into his shoulder mike, requesting an ambulance. Of Pickles standing over Ben Bontrager.

I kneel next to her. She's lying on her side, one arm stretched over her head, the other bent with her hand pressed against her abdomen. I can see the rise and fall of her chest. Her eyes open and blinking.

"You're going to be all right," I tell her.

Wincing, she shifts, rolls onto her back. "He shot me."

"I know," I say. "Be still. An ambulance is on the way."

Her hand falls away from her abdomen as if she no longer has the strength to keep it there. I see a hole the size of my thumb in the fabric of her dress, just below her rib cage. Blood runs from the wound, soaking the fabric and pooling on the ground.

"Here you go, Chief."

I look up to see Skid approach, his first aid kit in hand. He sets it on the ground, then passes me a sterile pack of gauze and a pair of disposable gloves.

"You okay?" I ask him.

"Didn't need that rotator cuff anyway." But he manages a half smile.

Snapping on the gloves, I turn my attention back to the injured woman. I open the gauze and press it firmly over the wound.

Loretta squeezes her eyes closed against the pain. "It was me," she whispers.

Blood soaks quickly through the gauze. I look up at Skid. He nods, letting me know he's listening, and he hands me a fresh wad. Saying nothing, I press it to the wound.

"Rachael," the Amish woman says. "She asked me to meet her at the motel. She'd been calling. I knew what she wanted."

"Fannie?" I ask.

"She said she wanted to know her daughter. I didn't believe her. Not for a moment. Rachael might've been curious, but she had no use for a twelve-year-old girl. Not with the kind of lifestyle she led. All she cared about was the money."

"What money?" I ask.

"I paid her four thousand dollars. To stay away from us. Away from Painters Mill. It wasn't enough. I knew it would never be enough. So I stopped her. To protect Fannie."

"How did you stop her?" I ask.

Her face screws up, in pain from the gunshot wound—or anguish because of what she did. I don't know. "I remember getting Fannie's bat out of the buggy. I was just going to scare her, you know. Tell her to take the money. To go away and never come back."

Loretta begins to cry. "She was actually happy to see me. Can you imagine? And then I just . . . I don't know what happened. I was so angry. I hit her and then she was on the floor. The bat was in my hand. It was as if the devil took over my body. He made me do ungodly things."

Skid hands me another wad of gauze and I put it to use. "How much does Ben know?" I ask.

"He didn't know any of it. Just that Fannie was adopted. He never questioned me. It all came out the night that deputy attacked me in the barn. I told him everything."

I hear the wail of sirens. I'm aware of Pickles and Skid standing next to us. The bark and hiss of their radios. Most of all, I'm aware of the blood soaking the gauze, oozing between my fingers at an alarming rate, and the growing pool beneath her.

"I was always the good one," she whispers.

"Loretta, stay with me," I say. "Stay with me."

The Amish woman fades to unconsciousness.

CHAPTER 41

There is comfort in what is familiar. An inner calm that comes with ritual and routine. We find reprieve from turmoil when we partake in the things we know. The heart finds solace in the company of those we love. I'm lucky to have all of those elements in my life, especially the people I love.

I'm sitting on a gurney in the emergency room of Pomerene Hospital, wondering where the doctor has gone, debating whether I should make my getaway while the getting away is good. The side of my head is numb where two nasty lacerations were cleaned and closed. I've been X-rayed, injected, and CT-scanned. Hopefully I'll get a clean bill of health and be on my way soon. I've no intention of spending the night.

I'm wearing a hospital gown with a paper sheet covering my legs, which are bruised and smeared with mud. Someone tucked my trousers, shirt, and boots into a bag and placed them on a shelf. I can see the caked mud from where I'm sitting.

Through all the tests and good humor, I haven't been able to stop thinking about the case. About Rachael Schwartz. About Loretta and Ben Bontrager. And, of course, Fannie.

I understand why they did what they did. To protect the child they'd loved since birth and raised as their own. Rachael Schwartz threatened to destroy all of it. After she was gone, I became a threat. What I can't reconcile is that these two people were willing to commit multiple violent crimes—including murder—to protect their secrets. What they did goes against the very foundation of what it means to be Amish. How could they possibly believe that God would forgive them their sins and they would be welcomed into heaven? Were the stakes so high that they convinced themselves the risk of hell was worth the gain?

Ben Bontrager was booked into the Holmes County jail. Loretta was taken by ambulance to Pomerene Hospital. Last I heard, Fannie was picked up by Children Services shortly after. The girl faces a great deal of upheaval in the coming hours and days and weeks. Likely, she'll be placed with a foster family initially, and then probably with her biological grandparents Rhoda and Dan Schwartz. I don't know how she'll fare. The one thing I do know is that the Amish community will step in to help with the transition and support her.

"Someone said there's a dirty cop back here."

I look up to see Glock shove aside the privacy curtain and pause upon seeing me.

"Dude, we're not supposed to be back here." Behind him, Skid glances over his shoulder as if expecting some stout nurse to stop them and escort them out.

Next to him, Pickles and Mona struggle to see past the curtain.

"You decent, Chief?" Mona asks.

Despite the headache pulsing above my left ear, I find myself grinning. "Decent enough."

I'm embarrassed because I'm pretty sure my smile is lopsided. Not only did the doc numb my scalp before applying a the staples, but they gave me some pain medication that's a little stronger than I expected.

When the men hesitate, Mona pushes her way past them and thrusts out a pretty bouquet of flowers she probably bought at the hospital gift shop. "How're you feeling?" she asks.

"I'm fine." Ignoring the thickness of my tongue, I watch my other three officers crowd in behind her, the men feeling awkward, trying not to show it.

"Nice mohawk, anyway," Skid says.

Mona elbows him. "Dude."

He shoots her a what-did-I-do look.

All of it for my benefit, which I appreciate more than they can know.

"Any word on Loretta Bontrager's condition?" I ask.

"They airlifted her to Cleveland Clinic in Akron," Glock tells me. "No word on her condition, but they think she's going to pull through."

No one looks at Skid, including me. We're following that unwritten script. The one that tells us to give him some space, and a little time to shore up before you talk about it. Even if your suspect is going to be all right, having to fire your weapon at another human being is a traumatic experience that takes a toll.

Mona hefts the flowers and looks around for a place to put the vase.

Glock taps the side of his head with his index finger. "How's the head?" he asks me.

"The proud recipient of nine staples," I say, deadpan.

"That's pretty impressive." He looks at Skid. "You just got your departmental record beat."

He shakes his head, whistles. "Guess I'm going to have to up my game."

I turn my attention to Pickles. The old man is frowning at Mona, who's set the flowers atop a shelf that's too small and likely used for medical supplies.

"I owe you a big thank-you, Pickles," I tell him. "Situation would have turned out a lot differently if you hadn't gotten there when you did."

The old man raises his gaze to mine. He's a surly guy. He doesn't like the fact that he's getting old. That he can't move as fast as he once did. That he's past putting in long hours and being in the thick of things.

"Just doing my job, Chief." He can't quite meet my gaze. And in that moment, I see how much my recognizing him before his peers means to him.

Glock grins. "Don't let that go to your head, old man."

Skid follows suit. "Can't run worth a damn," he says good-naturedly.

Pickles huffs a laugh, but not before I see the flash of emotion in his eyes.

The curtain whooshes aside. All of us look that way, guilty because too many visitors have crowded into an otherwise quiet ER. Tomasetti stands there a moment, looking from person to person, and then offering me a look that's part smile, part scowl.

"Evidently, I'm late for the party," he says.

Glock clears his throat. Pickles brushes at a nonexistent speck of lint on his uniform. Skid looks down at his cell phone. Mona fiddles with the vase of flowers.

"I'll see if I can get a status on Loretta Bontrager," Glock says.

Nodding at Tomasetti, Mona makes a beeline for the still-open curtain. "Glad you're okay," she says.

"See you around, Chief." Skid offers a mock salute.

I look past Tomasetti to see Glock holding the curtain open and the rest of my team file out.

I smile at Tomasetti. "Took you long enough to get here."

He stares back. "Can't leave you alone for more than a few hours, can I?"

"Once again you underestimate my ability to get myself into trouble."

"Apparently, you are correct."

He crosses the distance between us in two strides, his eyes intense and steady on mine. Upon reaching me, he leans close and presses a kiss to my temple. "You scared the hell out of me," he whispers.

I close my eyes, overcome by his presence, his closeness, the sight and smell of him, the feel of his lips against my skin. "Not the first time," I whisper.

"Probably not the last."

His arms go around me. He pulls me tight against him. I feel the warmth of his face against mine. His hand against the back of my head. "I heard you had a close call."

"Too close," I say. "If it wasn't for Pickles and Skid . . ."

He shushes me with a kiss, then pulls away, runs his knuckles down the side of my face. "I heard about Pickles," he said. "Not bad for an old guy."

"You old guys are so underappreciated." My smile feels tremulous on my lips. "Any news on Fannie Bontrager?"

He grimaces and I'm reminded this man I love was the father of two girls who were about Fannie's age when they were killed. "Children Services picked her up. Foster parents will probably keep her for a day or two, until they can figure out the family situation."

I think about Rhoda and Dan Schwartz. Already mourning the loss of a daughter. A granddaughter they didn't know existed about to enter their lives. "The Amish believe children are a gift from God," I tell him.

"Most of us believe that," he tells me.

I nod. "If there's any good news to come out of this, it is that Fannie has family here in Painters Mill."

"Do you think they'll—"

"Yes," I say. "They will. They're Amish."

"I guess that just about says it all," he murmurs.

I motion toward my clothes on the shelf. "What do you say we get out of here before the nurse comes back and tries to cart me out in a wheelchair?"

He grins. "I think that's the best idea I've heard all week."

CHAPTER 42

Life is a river that never stops flowing. You can dam it, you can harness its power, you can poison it, but you can't stop it. A river never ends. It changes course and cuts through the land. It floods and damages and kills. It can be weakened by drought. But it never stops. It is the fundamental giver of life.

It's been two weeks since Loretta and Ben Bontrager tried to murder me in the field where the old Amish schoolhouse used to stand. My cuts and bruises are healed for the most part. The nightmares have dwindled. Tomasetti and I don't talk about it, but he always lets me know he's there for me if I need to.

This afternoon, I'm on duty and covering for Glock, who had an appointment with his wife, LaShonda. He hasn't made the announcement yet, but I'm pretty sure they're expecting their fourth child. That river of life, I think. It's a beautiful thing that fills me with hope for the future.

I'm idling down Folkerth Road, watching a team of horses pull a plow through river-bottom soil, when Lois's voice snaps over my radio.

"Chief, ten-twenty-nine."

A 10-29 is a general code my department uses for any type of juvenile situation and usually entails the Tuscarawas Bridge and a can of spray paint. "What's the twenty on that?"

"I just took a call from Rhoda Schwartz," she tells me. "Seems their granddaughter is missing."

A thread of worry whispers through me at the mention of Fannie. I'm not surprised. "Any idea how long she's been gone?"

"She thinks maybe a couple of hours. She called from the phone shack. She and her husband are out in the buggy looking."

"I'm ten-seven-six," I say, letting her know I'm on my way to the Schwartz farm.

I hang a U-turn in the middle of the road and head that way. I haven't seen or spoken to Fannie since the day Loretta and Ben Bontrager accosted me at their farm. But I've spent quite a bit of time thinking about her. Twelve is a difficult age for a girl, whether you're Amish or English. That's usually about the time you leave childhood behind and take that first tentative step—or misstep—into adulthood. There are a lot of unknowns, a lot of fears, none of which are easy to talk about. Add the kind of upheaval Fannie has been through to the mix, and it's a time that can become emotionally chaotic.

I'm passing by the Bontrager farm, which stands vacant now, and nearly to the greenbelt at the edge of the pasture when in the periphery of my vision I spot the horse and rider. I know immediately the rider is Fannie. I brake hard, hang another U-turn, and head that way.

If the girl notices me, she doesn't show it. The horse is galloping in the ditch alongside the road at a speed that would give any parent a panic attack. The girl leans forward, reins in one hand, a tuft of mane in the other, keeping perfect time with the animal's stride. I stop the Explorer a hundred or so yards ahead of her, so I'm visible to both horse and rider.

I pick up my radio. "I've got eyes on our ten-twenty-nine."

"Roger that."

I get out, walk around to the front, and lean against the hood. I watch her ride, a little awed because she's good, a little sad because at some point she probably won't be allowed to continue. A few yards away from where I stand, she straightens slightly, tugs gently on the reins.

"Whoa," she says quietly.

The animal slows to a trot and then to a walk; its steel shoes crunch against the gravel on the shoulder as it walks up to me. Ten feet away, she stops the animal. It's the same horse she was riding the day I met her. His nostrils are flared. There's a bit of lather on his flanks and where the saddle blanket rests on his shoulder.

"He's beautiful," I say.

She's not happy to see me. "You arrested my *mamm* and *datt*," she says.

"I don't blame you for being angry." I pretend to study the horse, but I'm cognizant of the girl, too. She's been crying. There's a smudge of dirt on her left cheek, and her tears left a trail.

I go to the animal, run my hand over its forehead, along its neck. She's braided the mane, securing the ends with rubber bands. I find myself thinking about Rachael Schwartz and that long-ago day when I found her sitting on that rocky shoal in Painters Creek, grinning like an imp, her face aglow with the aftereffects of adrenaline—and the eternal question of nurture versus nature stirs.

"I know professional horse trainers who can't ride like that," I tell her.

Her gaze jerks to mine, untrusting of the compliment, too angry with me to accept it. She doesn't quite know how to reject it, so I simply let the statement stand.

"I guess they sent you to pick me up," she mutters after a moment.

"They love you. They worry." I shrug. "Might've helped if you'd let them know where you were going."

"Like they'd give me permission," she huffs.

I don't know how much they've told her about Rachael Schwartz or the Bontragers. I don't know how much she's heard via the grapevine. I don't even know whether to call the Schwartzes her grandparents. Does she know that Rachael Schwartz was her mother? Does she know Loretta Bontrager took her mother's life?

"They don't like me to ride," she tells me. "They're probably going to sell him."

"Maybe you can come up with some kind of compromise."

"It's because I'm a girl." She speaks over me. I almost smile, because Rachael used to do exactly the same thing. "Amish girls don't ride."

I nod, pretend I don't notice when she swipes angrily at the tears that have begun to fall. "It's not fair," she spits.

This is where I have to bite my tongue. The truth of the matter is the Amish *are* a patriarchal society. Sometimes the boys and men are allowed to do things the women and girls are not. What some people fail to recognize is that while those roles are defined and separate, they're also equally important.

"You're right," I tell her. "Sometimes life isn't fair. It's a hard lesson, but we do the best we can. And we try not to worry the people who love us."

Fannie rolls her eyes at my philosophy, sniffs.

The clatter of shod hooves draws our attention. I look past Fannie to see a horse and buggy coming down the road at a fast clip. Dan Schwartz stands abruptly, cranes his head, and speeds toward us. A few yards away from where I'm parked, he stops the horse. I watch as Rhoda climbs down from the buggy and rushes toward us, the remnants of worry etched into her features.

"Fannie." The Amish woman reaches us, presses her hand to her chest. "Hi, Katie."

"She was exercising the horse," I say in *Deitsch*.

I feel Fannie's eyes on me, but I don't look at her. "*Sell is en goodah,*" I say, referring to the horse. That is a good one.

Neither Dan nor Rhoda was born yesterday. They know their granddaughter was out here, riding like the wind. Even so, I suspect both of them have learned something important in the wake of Rachael's death. Something that feels a little bit like . . . forbearance.

Nodding, Rhoda steps forward, runs her hand over the animal's sweaty shoulder. "He's young," she says. "Looks strong, too."

"He's too strong," Dan grumbles from his place in the buggy. "Pushes too hard. Shies in traffic."

"He's the fastest trotter in all of Painters Mill," Fannie tells him.

Dan grunts. "We've already got a buggy horse."

"Nellie's getting old, Dan." Rhoda touches the braids with her fingertips. "Got a nice mane on him and just look at that pink nose."

Knowing he's being played, but sensing this is an important moment, Dan leaves the buggy and crosses to the horse in question. He smooths his hand over the animal's rump, frowning dubiously.

"Needs work," he mutters.

"Good buggy horse costs a pretty penny," Rhoda counters.

I shrug. "If you find someone to work with him, he might just surprise you."

Fannie clears her throat and climbs down from the horse. "I can do it," she says quietly. "Train him, I mean. Turn him into a better horse."

"Riding a horse . . ." Frowning at his wife, Dan shoves his hands into the pockets of his trousers. "Is no place for a girl."

Rhoda waves off the comment. "*En bisli gevva un namma is net en shlecht ding, eh?*" A little give-and-take is not a bad thing, eh?

I look at Fannie. "I think that's called compromise," I say to her. When the girl says nothing, I add, "It takes two."

Dan looks at his granddaughter over the rim of his glasses. "You think you can do this thing?"

"*Ja.*" She says the word a little too quickly.

"You have to stop running him," the Amish man tells her. "Train him to be calm and steady so he's safe on the road."

"I can do it," she says.

Rhoda looks at me. "Thank you for finding her for us, Kate Burkholder."

I nod, then turn my attention to Fannie, and I wait until the girl meets my gaze. "*Vann du broviahra hatt genunk, du finna vassannahshtah mechta sei faloahra,*" I say. When you try hard enough, you find what otherwise might be lost.

I hope the girl understands that the phrase encompasses more than one meaning. That one is more complex than the other, and yet both are equally important.

CHAPTER 43

A spring storm hovers on the western horizon when I pull into the gravel lane of the farm I share with Tomasetti. It's dusk and I can just make out the occasional flicker of lightning within the roiling clouds. I roll down the window, breathe in the fragrant air, humid and rich with the smell of growing things and life. For the first time in days, I notice the new foliage on the trees that grow alongside the driveway. The grass in the pasture is an ocean of green, made even greener by the slant of sun beaming through the thunderheads.

I park behind Tomasetti's Tahoe, grab my laptop case, and start toward the house. I'm midway to the back door when I hear the *clang!* of a hammer against something solid. I round the corner and a few yards away, down the hill about halfway to the pond, Tomasetti stands next to a stone firepit that wasn't there when I left this morning. Yellow and orange flames dance a couple of feet into the air, illuminating the circle of meticulously placed stone and the sight of a man I suddenly can't wait to touch.

"You've been busy," I call out as I make my way down the incline.

He turns. My heart stutters in my chest when his eyes sweep over me. His expression warms as he takes my measure. "If you want someone to stay out of trouble," he says, "give them a job."

I break into a run, drop my laptop case on the bench seat, and go to him. Holding his gaze, I put my arms around his neck, and fall against him, set my face against his shoulder.

"If I'd known building a firepit would get me that kind of reaction," he says, "I'd have done it a long time ago."

Laughing, I pull back, give him a playful punch on the arm.

"What do you think?" he asks.

"I think the chief of police is incredibly glad she has a certain BCI guy to come home to."

"Well, in that case . . ." Tilting his head, he looks at me, a little puzzled but pleased nonetheless, and presses a kiss to my mouth.

I try not to be moved, but I am, on too many levels to sort through at the moment. "You smell like woodsmoke," I tell him.

Without speaking, he eases me to arm's length and looks at me closely. "Everything all right, Chief?"

I choke out a laugh, but I can't hide the note of melancholy in its depths. "Fannie Bontrager took off without telling her grandparents."

"Ah." He runs both hands down my arms. "You find her?"

"At the Bontrager place. On her horse."

He motions toward the bench seat constructed of old wood from the barn. I sit, look out across the land where the red-winged blackbirds swoop over the pond to the weeping willow at the water's edge. The last of the spring peepers sing their final song. Before long, summer will arrive. Another chapter, different, but just as beloved.

Tomasetti sits next to me. "I take it that's not a good thing?"

"Fannie's not going to stay Amish," I tell him.

"In case you need a reminder, Kate, *you* left the fold and everything turned out all right." He takes my hand, squeezes it gently.

I know what I want to say. What I *need* to say. What I feel in my heart. But to put it into words is no easy feat. "Rachael Schwartz was no-holds-barred, fearless to a fault, and traveling at a hundred miles an hour." Loretta Bontrager's description of her floats through my mind and I mumble it, realizing that of all the terms I could use to describe Rachael, that one is the one that best captures the essence of her. "*Frei geisht.*" Free spirit.

"Fannie is exactly like her," I tell him. "She's being raised by the same parents who raised Rachael. The Schwartzes didn't give Rachael the tools she needed to . . ." I almost say the one word I don't want to say: "survive."

He looks into the fire, thoughtful. "That doesn't mean Fannie is bound for the same fate as her mother."

"The kid's got a nose for trouble, just like her mom."

Thunder rumbles in the distance. The sun has sunk behind the clouds. The birds have gone silent. The tempo of the bullfrogs from the pond strikes a crescendo.

"Fannie Bontrager has a couple of things going for her that Rachael Schwartz didn't," he tells me. "The people raising her have learned a thing or two about life since they raised their daughter." He looks at me. "And Fannie has a good-hearted chief of police to keep an eye on her over the next few years."

The wind has picked up, sending the flames into a frenzy. The first fat drops of rain splat against the stone, sizzle when they hit the glowing coals.

"You know, Tomasetti, if you ever decide to leave BCI, you could probably make it as a shrink."

"Or a bartender."

"Same thing, right?"

We grin at each other and, hand in hand, hightail it through the rain toward the house.

ACKNOWLEDGMENTS

As is the case with every book, I've many talented and dedicated people to thank at Minotaur Books—for their expertise and hard work, their willingness to go above and beyond, their belief in me and the story, and, most of all, for the friendship. My editor, Charles Spicer. My agent, Nancy Yost. Jennifer Enderlin. Andrew Martin. Sally Richardson. Sarah Melnyk. Sarah Grill. Kerry Nordling. Paul Hochman. Allison Ziegler. Kelley Ragland. David Baldeosingh Rotstein. Marta Fleming. Martin Quinn. Joseph Brosnan. Lisa Davis. A heartfelt thank you to all!

ANTOINE FRÉDÉRIC OZANAM

ANTOINE FRÉDÉRIC OZANAM

RAYMOND L. SICKINGER

University of Notre Dame Press

Notre Dame, Indiana

University of Notre Dame Press
Notre Dame, Indiana 46556
undpress.nd.edu

Published in the United States of America

Library of Congress Cataloging-in-Publication Data
Names: Sickinger, Raymond L., 1949– author.
Title: Antoine Frédéric Ozanam / Raymond L. Sickinger.
Description: Notre Dame : University of Notre Dame Press, 2017. | Includes
bibliographical references and index.
Identifiers: LCCN 2016058502 (print) | LCCN 2017008978 (ebook) | ISBN
9780268101428 (hardcover : alk. paper) | ISBN 0268101426 (hardcover :
alk. paper) | ISBN 9780268101442 (pdf) | ISBN 9780268101459 (epub)
Subjects: LCSH: Ozanam, Frédéric, 1813-1853. | Catholics—France—Biography. |
Society of St. Vincent de Paul—History.
Classification: LCC BX4705.O8 S53 2017 (print) | LCC BX4705.O8 (ebook) |
DDC 282.092 [B] — dc23
LC record available at https://lccn.loc.gov/2016058502

This book is dedicated to the memory of my parents,
Gerhard and Cecile Sickinger, whose deep love for one another,
for family, for friends, and for all people
is a constant source of inspiration and strength.

CONTENTS

_____

LIST OF ILLUSTRATIONS

Illustrations are located between Parts I and II, following page 172. Unless otherwise indicated, photos are reproduced by permission of the museum Souvenir Ozanam/Council General International (CGI), Society of St. Vincent de Paul (SSVP).

PREFACE

The mural shown on the cover of this book, painted by Sieger Köder, illustrates the lifelong commitment of Antoine Frédéric Ozanam to serving the needs of those in poverty.[1] Köder attempted to depict Ozanam's awareness that the Catholic Church of his day had failed to protect or secure the rights and dignity of the poor and marginalized. The dark windows of Paris's Notre Dame Cathedral in the painting evoke this failure. Lacking the support of the Church, many desperate people had turned away from religion and found refuge in ideologies such as socialism. At the center of the painting, in a busy street among poor and working-class citizens of Paris, is Ozanam, speaking from his Sorbonne podium. The collegiate motto of the Sorbonne is emblazoned on the podium: *vivere socialiter, et collegialiter, et moraliter, et scholariter* (to live as a member of society, a colleague, a moral being, and a scholar).

Ozanam believed that the Gospels contained the true principles of liberty, equality, and fraternity that had been promised in the French Revolution. In both his teachings and his writings he called on the Catholic Church to embrace the worker class—a class often thought of as a new wave of barbarians in civilized society. Although Ozanam stands behind his podium in Köder's mural, his hands and body extend outward in solidarity with those in need. He put his words into practice. In the background of the mural is Christ, filled with compassion for those who suffer. Father Köder's painting captures Ozanam and his times and offers some insight into the reasons why Ozanam founded the Society of St. Vincent de Paul.

1. For details on the German priest and painter Sieger Köder (1925–2015), see an obituary by Gemma Simmonds, "Sieger Köder RIP," *Independent Catholic News,* February 11, 2015. http://www.indcatholicnews.com/. For another treatment of his mural on Ozanam and more information on Köder, see http://vinformation.famvin .org/prayers-reflections-novenas/frederic-ozanam-mural-tribute-to-german-priest -painter-sieger-koder/.

I remember the first time I heard of the Society of St. Vincent de Paul. I was a teenager who had just lost his grandfather. To me, he was simply "pépère," a wonderful French Canadian patriarch whose family was the most important thing in his life. As the family greeted the numerous guests who attended his wake, it quickly became apparent that many of them had been helped by the Society, and especially by my pépère, who had been a member most of his life. The stories that I heard about him and the Society intrigued me, and when I was invited some years later to an information night about the Society, I attended. At that meeting I first heard the name of Antoine Frédéric Ozanam, the principal founder of the Society. As a young university professor, I was inspired by the example of Ozanam. I was drawn to him as a moth to a flame. From that moment, it was as if he and I became friends. It has been a friendship developed over more than twenty-five years. Although Ozanam would be the first to admit his weaknesses, he was determined to overcome them. His overriding desire was to anticipate and to help fulfill the will of God in his life. Ozanam understood that the road to sanctification is one that is neither straight nor smooth. But it is a road worth traveling if one wishes to "lead a better life." For Ozanam, "to live better and to do a little good" was not only an aspiration but a vision for a better world.

ACKNOWLEDGMENTS

I am deeply grateful for all the assistance I have received, enabling me to complete this manuscript. First, I thank DePaul University's Vincentian Studies Institute for a generous research grant of $15,000 to support my work. In particular, I thank Rev. Edward R. Udovic, C.M., Senior Executive for University Mission at DePaul, and Nathan Michaud, director of Publications at the Vincentian Studies Institute, for their support and advice both before and after receiving the grant. Their kindness is genuinely appreciated. I am also thankful for their willingness to allow me to reuse material from articles I had written for the journal *Vincentian Heritage*.

I thank Providence College for a sabbatical leave, which gave me the necessary time to finish my research, and for its support of my research with a generous Committee on Aid to Faculty Research grant. This grant not only allowed me to purchase some of Ozanam's letters but also enabled me to travel to Paris for my research. In particular, I thank Kris A. Monahan, director of Sponsored Research and Programs at Providence College, whose help in applying for a research grant from DePaul and in administering the funds once it was awarded was invaluable.

I am deeply grateful to the University of Notre Dame Press for agreeing to publish my manuscript and for its ongoing support and guidance in preparing the work for publication.

I am also deeply grateful to the staff of the International Office of the Society of St. Vincent de Paul in Paris, France. Their kindness and hospitality to me and to my wife were extraordinary. They were instrumental in locating certain necessary documents. I appreciate their willingness to allow me to use photographs that I took in the museum Souvenir Ozanam. In particular, I owe a deep debt of gratitude to Amin de Tarrazi of the Paris Council and former international president of the Society of St. Vincent de Paul. A wonderful person and a genuine Vincentian,

Monsieur Tarrazi graciously guided me through the museum, where I spent several hours looking at artifacts of Ozanam's life.

I thank the Association of the Miraculous Medal (www.amm.org) for permission to include an image of a painting of Ozanam that was produced for the association by artist Gary Schumer. I am equally thankful for permission from St. Vincent's Parish in Graz, Austria, to use the mural of Ozanam by Sieger Köder as a cover image.

I thank both Sister Kieran Kneaves, Daughters of Charity, and Ralph Middlecamp, executive director of the Council of Madison, Wisconsin, for leading an informative and inspiring Vincentian Heritage tour of Paris, which acquainted me with the most important sites for Ozanam's life and gave me a better understanding of the Paris of Ozanam's milieu. I also thank Ralph Middlecamp for sharing with me some of his own original research, as well as artwork and photographs of Ozanam and his times. His insights were extremely helpful.

I recognize and thank Gene Smith, former national president of the Society of St. Vincent de Paul in the United States. He was the first to suggest that I write a biography of Ozanam, and he constantly encouraged me to do so.

Last and most of all, I deeply acknowledge my dear wife, Patricia Sickinger, for her patience, understanding, and loving support, without which this manuscript would never have been possible. She has been, and continues to be, my own "Amélie Soulacroix."

Introduction

When Antoine Frédéric Ozanam was born in the spring of 1813, France was still ostensibly the most powerful nation on the continent of Europe. Although the French army had been decimated by the failed 1812 invasion of Russia, the Emperor Napoleon continued to fight the allies arrayed against France and to threaten all of Europe and Great Britain. He suffered another humiliating defeat at the Battle of Leipzig in October 1813. Within the next two years, the Bourbons, who had been ousted from the throne in 1789, were back in power. Strained by over twenty-five years of revolutionary politics and incessant warfare, France in the early nineteenth century was disillusioned by defeat and devoid of a clear sense of destiny.

Revolution and warfare were just two of France's manifold problems. France was plagued by grave political, economic, and social disorders. The economic and social changes caused by the transition from a predominantly rural and agricultural society to an urban and industrialized one threatened to disrupt French society, and the problems were all too often ineffectively addressed, or else ignored, by governmental authorities. The authorities of the Catholic Church, which was recovering from the serious and often deadly challenges to established religion that had begun with the Revolution in 1789, and who often favored conservative social and political solutions, were no more successful in either understanding or responding to the desperation of the common working people. Some groups of intellectuals, such as the followers of the utopian social theorist Henri de Saint-Simon, began to suggest ways to improve the condition of the poor by forming ideal societies of laborers. They were often severe critics of both the government and the institutional Catholic Church.

Ozanam's short life spanned a tumultuous period of French political and social history. He witnessed two major political upheavals in France before 1850—the overthrow of the Bourbon dynasty in the 1830 July Revolution that brought Louis-Philippe to power, and the end of Louis-Philippe's "bourgeois monarchy" during the Revolutions of 1848. With respect to social thought, at the early age of eighteen, in 1831, he openly criticized Saint-Simon's teachings in a published document. He argued that Saint-Simon's utopian ideas offered those living in poverty a false hope for, and an equally false path toward, a better life. Two years later, in 1833, while Ozanam was a student in Paris, certain young followers of Saint-Simon dared him to practice what he preached. In response to their taunt, Ozanam and several like-minded students formed a group that they called the conference of charity. Starting with only seven members, its numbers soared to more than one hundred by 1834. By 1835, the conference of charity had its own official "Rule" and a new official name: the Society of St. Vincent de Paul. Today, the Society is active in approximately 150 countries around the world and is still growing. During his lifetime Ozanam gradually became committed to the principles of Christian democracy and favored a French republic that supported the poor, not just the rich. At the time of his death in 1853, however, France was once again an empire ruled by a Napoleon, with the coronation of Louis-Napoléon as Napoleon III in 1852.

Ozanam led an interesting life in a turbulent period of French history, and it is his life that this book will explore. This biography of Ozanam is also intended to fill a gap. Although there are a number of fine, recent studies about Ozanam produced in France, most have not been translated into English and are not, therefore, readily accessible to English-speaking readers. There are also histories written in English, but they are, for the most part, out-of-date or incomplete. Many of the older works provide essential information but do not cite sources or adequately identify the references for their evidence. In many cases, they do not meet modern scholarly standards. To date, there are no comprehensive, recent biographies of Ozanam in English. Some of the newer studies are helpful but are often intended primarily for a local or limited popular audience.

This biography is not a straightforward chronological account of Ozanam's life. In the first part, I explore the various roles he filled in his forty years on earth—as son, sibling, student, member of and inspiration for the Society of St. Vincent de Paul, scholar, spouse, and spokesperson for the common people. In the second part, I examine the lessons he learned in his life that can be shared by those who study his thought and work for insights. Among those lessons are the importance of friendship, the meaning and significance of solidarity, the nature of spirituality and the desire for sanctification, the role and purpose of suffering, the nature and importance of servant leadership, and the seeds of systemic thinking and systemic change planted in his lifetime, to be harvested in a later era. At the end of Part II, I review his living and enduring legacy. Although Ozanam feared that he would not have a fruitful career, his legacy remains a powerful testimony to his greatness.

PART I

———

OZANAM'S LIFE

CHAPTER 1

Son and Sibling

On April 23, 1813, Antoine Frédéric Ozanam was born in Milan, the capital of Lombardy in the Italian peninsula. That peninsula has long been associated with Dante and St. Francis of Assisi, both of whom Ozanam later eloquently celebrated in his scholarly work. French victories over Austria had brought Milan into the French fold. After Emperor Napoleon Bonaparte's final defeat, however, Milan was returned to Austria in 1815. Ozanam's father had "no taste to live under the new regime of the Lombard-Venetian Kingdom." The family found their way back to Lyon, France, from which both his parents originated.[1] According to Ozanam's friend Léonce Curnier, at the time the young Frédéric (as he was called by many of his family and friends) was "barely able to get out of the cradle."[2] In fact, when the family sailed from Milan to Marseilles on October 31, 1816, Frédéric was "a toddler of 3 years and a half, too young to keep his hometown memories precise."[3] Once the family settled in Lyon, "the home of his mother could thus count him among its most illustrious children because it [was] in Lyon that he received the first education of the domestic hearth, which truly engenders in us the moral life."[4] Curnier has remarked that Ozanam was the product of two places: "Ozanam felt this double origin. Italy and France had both left their mark, as if two fairies had made him a gift each by rocking him in their arms."[5] He has been joined in that view by Père Lacordaire: "Frederic Ozanam . . . had in him the influence of two skies and two sanctuaries. Lyon had anointed him with a serious piety; Milan, something of a brighter flame. The city of St. Ambrose and of St. Irenaeus had joined, to baptize him, the graces of their traditions."[6] Whatever the truth of these descriptions, a curious mixture of seriousness and burning zeal would remain hallmarks of Ozanam's character throughout his life.

Ozanam did not return to Milan until seventeen years later, when he journeyed to Italy with his parents in 1833 to visit relatives. This trip fed his growing interest in literature and history, especially the history and literature of the Middle Ages. His mother stayed with her sister in Florence while Monsieur Ozanam trekked toward the north and center of Italy with his two older sons, Frédéric and Alphonse.[7] The young Charles most likely was left at home in the care of Marie Cruziat, the trusted household servant. Alphonse described the effect on his younger sibling of the visit to Milan: "Our brother . . . was then 20 years of age. His soul was full to overflowing of ardent enthusiasm. He saw the street, *San Pietro a L'Orto*, where he had been born; the Church, *Santa Maria de' servi*, where he had been baptized. Kneeling at the holy font he renewed his baptismal vows and thanked God for having made him His child."[8] But it was not only Milan that impressed the young scholar. Bologna with its rich medieval past, Rome with its rich Christian heritage and its invaluable manuscripts, and, most of all, Florence, where every corner provided an encounter with the great poet Dante, left an indelible mark on the impressionable Frédéric. As Alphonse suggests, the trip profoundly influenced his brother's life, teaching, and scholarship.[9]

Lyon, the city that Ozanam would always call home, exercised an equally important sway on the young boy. Known as the city of bridges, Lyon is located at the convergence of the Rhône and Saône rivers. Long a bastion of Christianity, its citizens had a particular devotion to the Blessed Mother. Many made the pilgrimage to the shrine of Notre Dame de Fourvières, located on a height above the city, where it had existed since the second century. Lyon sparked in Frédéric a fire of devotion to the Virgin Mary that would last throughout his life. His devotion later inspired him to suggest her as the patroness of the Society of St. Vincent de Paul.[10] There is also no doubt that he "was in love with this city . . . with its high narrow streets, its embankments, its hills, its 'slopes,' its panoramas, its noise (the clatter of the [silk] looms, the stamping of the horses pulling the countless heavy cargoes of silk bundles), and its active and industrious population."[11] As late as 1843 he recalled in a letter to Dominique Meynis his deep attachment to Lyon, by the very "roots of the heart." In that same letter Frédéric wrote, "since I was called to my perilous Parisian functions, each year I went to put them under the patronage of Notre-Dame de Fourvières, to which I have been devoted since childhood."[12] A journalist in the early twentieth century asserted that Lyon "has always been one of the centers where spiritual life and Christian thought exist in all their intensity. . . . The soul of the natives of Lyon is deeply religious and accompanied by a remarkably practical and cool spirit and a bold enterprising character."[13] Ozanam, proud of his origins in Lyon, exhibited much of this Lyonnais soul in his lifetime.

THE OZANAM FAMILY: HIS FATHER

The Ozanam family was not only proud of its Lyonnais origins but also traced its heritage back to Roman times. According to family lore, a distant ancestor of Frédéric's father was a praetor in the thirty-eighth Roman Legion, named Jeremiah Hozannam. Entering Gaul with the conquering Julius Caesar, Hozannam was rewarded with a share of the conquered lands north of Lyon, known later as the village of Boulignieus. The land was covered with woods and swamps, but, despite these obstacles, Jeremiah reclaimed it for use. He founded a small Jewish colony, which prospered. Long after Jeremiah's death, in the seventh century, the Hozannam family was baptized. According to the family account, an ancestor named Samuel Hozannam had offered shelter to St. Didier after the saint had denounced the reigning queen for her wickedness.[14] St. Didier, grateful for his kindness and hospitality, baptized Samuel and his people, bringing them into the Christian fold. From that point in the detailed family genealogical record, Christian names such as Matthias, John, and Peter appear. It was not until Frédéric's grandfather, Benedict, decided to drop one letter "n" and the letter "h" from the family name that the spelling "Ozanam" became the permanent family designation.[15]

Frédéric's father, Jean-Antoine-François Ozanam, belonged neither to the traditional aristocracy nor to the upper middle class. He was also not from the working class or the Lyon merchant class, to which his wife's family belonged. One historian places him in a category he calls "bourgeoisie with talent" (*bourgeoisie à talent*), suggesting that he was bourgeois but probably better off than the average Lyonnaise bourgeoisie.[16] Frédéric's father would certainly add luster to the Ozanam family name.

As a young boy, Frédéric delighted in his father's stories about his military service. The father regaled his sons with the true story of how he had rescued his own father from death at the hands of the Committee of Public Safety during the infamous Reign of Terror of the French Revolution. A soldier in the regiment of the Berchiny Hussars,[17] Jean-Antoine risked his life by leaving his regiment to try to retrieve his father from the clutches of the Terrorists. As he mounted his horse, he promised his mother that all would be well, though he knew in his heart that the situation was desperate. Along with some companions from his regiment, he dashed to Bourg, where the Committee of Public Safety was in session. There, he discovered that his father was imprisoned on the charge of treason, which meant certain death in the tempestuous days of the Terror. Jean-Antoine drew his weapons and demanded his father's immediate release. The Terrorists, intimidated by this unexpected chain of events, yielded to his request. As quickly as they had arrived, Jean-Antoine and his associates fled the vicinity of Bourg with their prize. Fortunately for them, their absence from the regiment was never noticed. When the Reign of Terror came to an end soon afterward, the threat of any action against either Jean-Antoine or his father was removed.[18] As one biographer remarks, "Is it any wonder that hero worship was mixed with the love and regard of young Frederick Ozanam for his father? The boy's lively imagination enabled him to relish to the full all the true stories of the hussar's dash and daring, to see him in the brave Berchiny uniform and live again for himself the battles in which this father of his had shown such valor as to gain the approving notice of his commander and earn rapid promotion."[19] Jean-Antoine's army career came to an honorable end in 1798, when he retired from military service at the age of twenty-five with the rank of captain.[20]

From their father, Frédéric and his siblings inherited valuable traits and learned precious lessons. A person of staunch character, Jean-Antoine had tried several professions before becoming a practicing doctor of medicine, during his residence in Italy. He earned his medical degree from the University of Pavia. His determination and resolve are witnessed by the fact that every three months for two years he traveled on foot the difficult nineteen-mile route from Milan to Pavia in order to obtain his degree because he could not afford the stagecoach fare.[21] The medical profession would be more than a job for Doctor Ozanam; it was a calling, a kind of priesthood, for which he eventually sacrificed his life. Remuneration was never the first thing on his mind in treating his patients. His reputation grew not only as a practitioner and medical scholar but also as a cultural scholar.[22] His eldest son, Alphonse, attested to his father's temperament: "My father was an extremely strong character, but a great heart, tender, compassionate and very sensitive, full of courage, honor and dedication."[23] He placed a premium on "righteousness and . . . rigor in social morality: traits that we will meet again in Frederic."[24] According to Ozanam's biographer Marcel Vincent, Jean-Antoine "never relinquished either his spirit of enterprise or . . . his anti-conformity, qualities that his children will be indebted to him more from heredity than from education."[25] Jean-Antoine indeed did not bend easily to authority. His anti-conformity extended even to matters religious. Historian Gérard Cholvy indicates that he was an independent thinker. Jean-Antoine disliked the Jesuits in particular, and he feared that the further the Catholic Church moved away from its primitive roots and precepts, the more isolated from the authentic spirit of Christianity it would become.[26] He was also concerned by clergy who seemed opposed to the ideas of the progress of the human spirit and enlightenment.[27] According to Cholvy, Jean-Antoine was "a friend of truth" and would defend it vigorously.[28]

Enlightenment of the mind through education was a cherished treasure in the Ozanam household, and, despite his busy professional schedule, Frédéric's father took an active interest in his children's learning. While living in Milan, the doctor had been responsible for the schooling of his children, which "included Latin, French, Italian and mathematics."[29] He expected high standards of his brood and regularly checked their homework assignments. As Frédéric later remembered of his father, "He loved Science, Art, and work. He inspired us with a taste for the beautiful and sublime."[30] These latter tastes found an especially receptive home in Frédéric. But Jean-Antoine also knew how to make learning a pleasure, showing his children that all of life was a learning experience to be intimately embraced. The family enjoyed "long runs in the countryside, often four or five leagues, to fortify our health and harden us from fatigue." The father used these excursions as teaching moments: to spark informative conversation, to hunt and identify butterflies, or to catch caterpillars in glass jars so that the children could observe and care for them, learn about the plants upon which they feed, witness their metamorphosis into cocoons, and then behold their emergence as butterflies.[31] Doctor Ozanam was an advocate of the classical ideal of a sound mind and body. He not only brought his clan on runs but also taught his children how to swim in the nearby river waters.[32] Cholvy notes that a certain penchant for Jean-Jacques Rousseau can be detected in his pedagogical principles, because Rousseau favored an experiential education for children and the freedom to explore.[33]

Doctor Ozanam's influence extended into matters religious as well. His children witnessed his participation in the processions and devotions of the Confraternity of the Most Blessed Sacrament; they knew that he not only prayed with and for his patients but often sent for the priest when death was near for the person in his charge.[34] Frédéric was quick to point out that throughout adversity, his father always kept "the faith, a noble character and a strong sense of justice, a tireless charity for the poor."[35] His older brother Alphonse added to this image of a man of faith the following memories: "My father was sincerely religious and he had a living faith: every night there was family prayer with his wife, his children, and our good Marie [Marie Cruziat, the family's faithful domestic servant]. Often even a devotional reading followed prayer!"[36] Léonce Curnier's biography of Frédéric Ozanam offers a marvelous summary of this extraordinary father's character:

> A learned and skillful physician, he joined together the most extensive knowledge, the strongest education, admirable charity; his profession was for him a true ministry of charity. No one knew better than the good doctor the way to the home of the poor person. He did not confine himself to merely giving him the alms of his care, he gave him besides . . . the alms of his heart, seeking to console him, addressing him with

pious encouragements, for in this unfortunate person crushed under the weight of suffering, he saw a brother and one of the best friends of his God.... He turned the thought of the patient to the supreme physician, and he prayed with him at the foot of his bed. He constantly acquitted his mission with dedication, a selflessness to which religion alone has the secret; he was to die in the exercise of a ministry so nobly understood.[37]

In their own ways, the lives of the doctor's two sons would testify to both the quality and integrity of their father's life. Both sons, however, would also have to face the strong convictions of their father, who mapped out careers for them that were not in full accord with their wishes.

THE OZANAM FAMILY: HIS MOTHER

Frédéric's mother was Marie Nantas, the daughter of a Lyon silk merchant. She married Jean-Antoine in 1800, when she was barely nineteen and he was twenty-seven.[38] After settling with him in Paris and enjoying an initially successful and prosperous life together, she eventually followed her husband to Milan. One explanation for the move to Milan revolves around an imprudent decision made by Jean-Antoine to help a needy relative, a decision that left the family near bankruptcy and proved an embarrassment.[39] Another explanation is based on political exigencies, including the war with England and the Continental blockade, which closed off some favorable trading opportunities for the Ozanam family.[40] An ever loyal wife, Marie again supported her husband's decision to relocate from Milan to Lyon in 1816, after Milan was returned to Austria.[41]

Marie had her own stories about the French Revolution, which rivaled those of Jean-Antoine. Hers were tales not of heroic exploits but of affliction and suffering. In May 1793, Lyon rebelled against the Jacobin revolutionary government centered in Paris. The Committee of Public Safety, the governing body led by Maximilien Robespierre in Paris, ordered the siege of Lyon.[42] During the siege, Marie Nantas and her sisters crouched in cellars while her father, a captain in charge of the city's fortifications, worked tirelessly to safeguard his beloved home. Her brother, Jean-Baptiste, who was barely nineteen, was put to death at Bouttreaux. The painful memory of his passing remained with her throughout her life. Not only did she lose her brother, she was also separated from her parents when they were imprisoned for their resistance. She remembered how she feared that she would never again see them alive.[43] The beseiged city fell in October 1793 and was dealt with brutally; the conquerors meant for no one to "escape from . . . just vengeance."[44] Whether or not the vengeance was just can be debated, but that it was ruthless is without question. The Reign of Terror fed on such violence. In the words of R. R. Palmer, during the Terror, "Suspects poured into the prisons, and the guillotines fell more frequently on out-stretched necks. The more the deaths mounted, the more enemies the executioners had to fear. The more severe the government became the more opposition it aroused, and the only answer to opposition seemed to be an increase of severity."[45] Lyon felt the full wrath of the Terror. Less than one year after the rebellion began, "almost two thousand persons had been put to death at Lyons, more than a tenth of all those sentenced by revolutionary courts for all France during the whole period of the Terror. Of the victims at Lyons 64 percent came from the middle and upper classes. For France outside Lyons the figure for these classes was only 28 percent."[46] The Lyonnaise bourgeoisie paid a heavy price for their opposition.

Miraculously, Marie's parents were spared and the family were gradually reunited. For a time they found refuge and relief from the Terror in Switzerland. There, Marie received her first Holy Communion in a church used by Protestants and Catholics alike. When peace was finally declared, the Nantas family returned to their beloved Lyon, only to discover that their property had been confiscated and was irrecover-able. The family was no longer prosperous. Her early experiences taught Marie how to bear up under hardship and how to face poverty with fortitude. These lessons were not only valuable to her but were also con-veyed to her children.[47] The hardships she faced during the Terror also may have contributed to her "gentle melancholy," a trait exhibited later by her son Frédéric.[48]

As important as the influence of the father is on a family, the mother often has the most profound and lasting impact on her children. Fré-déric's mother was no exception. A woman of great intelligence, Marie could both write and speak well, had some talent for drawing, valued good literature, and loved music. According to Baunard, "No family feast was complete without a joyful song from that delightful mother."[49] She shared her musical talents with her husband, who was adept at playing a number of instruments and who loved to hear the strains of music whenever he was home after his long medical rounds.[50] Marie also had the greatest influence on her children's religious development. As Frédéric recounted in 1831, he cherished "this Catholicism that I was once taught by the mouth of a great mother . . . and which nourishes so often my mind and my heart with its memories and the most beautiful hopes: Catholicism with all its grandeur, with all its delights!"[51] Léonce Curnier asserts that Frédéric "found God with her and he never lost him."[52] She especially deepened all of her sons' faith by her own word and example.[53] Under her patient guidance, her children were taught their prayers and especially the importance and meaning of the Catholic mass.[54] She exercised a solid moral influence with a gentle manner that made her "the best obeyed and the most beloved of mothers."[55] Like Frédéric's father, his mother also had a compassionate and charitable heart for those living in poverty. Madame Ozanam was one of "The Watchers," an association of women who took turns sitting at the bedside of those who were poor and sick. Often she and her husband would cross paths on their respective missions of care. From both his mother and father Frédéric received "the example of twenty years of . . . devoted charity before his eyes."[56] It was a powerful lesson indeed. Their examples bore fruit later on in the charitable work of the conference of charity that became the Society of St. Vincent de Paul.

Frédéric's mother and father created a warm, loving household for their children. Members of the family all had their pet nicknames. Marie referred to her husband as "Oza," most often preceding it with *Cher* or *Pauvre*. She in turn was "Madame Oza." Frédéric's sister Élisabeth was assigned the shortened version "Élisa," and his older brother, Alphonse, became simply "Alph." Frédéric was referred to by his father as "Fred," but his mother affectionately dubbed him "Déric."[57] Even the household servant, Marie Cruziat, had her nickname, "Guigui."[58] Throughout his early life one of Frédéric's greatest joys was to return home for special occasions and celebrations.[59] In his biography of Ozanam, Schimberg offers the following assessment of the parents' powerful impact on Frédéric's character: "The complex character of Frederick Ozanam reflected his father's energy, dogged perseverance, serenity, and even gaiety . . . in the face of hardships and struggles; love of books and all intellectual pursuits, devotion to duty, eagerness to help and willingness to follow up sympathy with action. It reflected, too, his mother's gracious and gentle personality, her love of beauty in nature and in art, her conscientious attitude toward life, which was regarded as a rather serious matter. From her he inherited a heart full of tenderness and an inclination to diffidence and melancholy."[60] Theirs would be a lasting influence on their son.

THE FIFTH CHILD: FRÉDÉRIC

Frédéric was the fifth child to whom Marie gave birth. Because of the plague in Milan at the time, his baptism was postponed for a few weeks, until May 13, when it was held in the Church of Santa Maria dei Servi.[61] The baby Frédéric had only two surviving siblings at the time— Alphonse and Élisabeth. Two other children had already died at a very tender age. Unfortunately, the family faced the tragic loss of their children numerous times. Only four of the fourteen children born to Marie and Jean-Antoine reached early adulthood—Alphonse, Élisabeth, Frédéric, and Charles, and only the three male children survived past the age of twenty.[62] Élisabeth lived to the age of nineteen, Frédéric to the age of forty, and Charles and Alphonse to the ages, respectively, of sixty-six and eighty-four.[63] The early deaths of so many children meant perpetual sorrow in the household. Carrying fourteen children would be a heavy physical burden for most women, but it was especially burdensome for Marie, whose health was described as "delicate."[64]

Fortunately for the Ozanams, their faith counseled them that death was not only the end of life but the beginning of a new one. This comforting belief fortified the family in their losses and their sorrows. Frédéric clearly understood this: "On how many occasions have I not seen my parents in tears; when heaven had left them but three children out of fourteen! But how often, too, have not those three survivors, in adversity and in trial, counted on the assistance of those brothers and sisters whom they had among the angels! . . . Happy is the home that can count one half its members in Heaven, to help the rest along the narrow way which leads there!"[65] When writing this passage, Frédéric must certainly have recalled that he nearly died at the age of six.[66] In June 1819 Frédéric became seriously ill, and "death was on his lips." The illness was most likely typhoid fever, which often proved fatal. Doctor Ozanam consulted with other physicians. The situation looked bleak, and they counseled the family to prepare for the worst. For two weeks Frédéric was delirious and in agony. It is little wonder that his mother turned to prayer, asking Saint Francis Regis for his intercession on behalf of her son and placing a relic of the saint around his neck. In his delirium, Frédéric suddenly requested a drink of beer, which he normally found repugnant. Stunned by the request, the parents brought him the beer. Shortly thereafter he began to show signs of revival, and the illness finally subsided.[67]

Although he made a complete recovery, Frédéric's convalescence was slow. His father began to instruct him in Latin during this period, both to occupy him and to excite his mind. Later, the young Frédéric was convinced that the beer was the cure: "I had a serious illness, which brought me so near death that everybody said I was saved by a miracle; not that I wanted kind care: my dear father and mother hardly left my bedside for fifteen days and nights. I was on the point of expiring when suddenly I asked for some beer. I had always disliked beer, but it saved me."[68] His parents attributed his recovery to the power of intercessory prayer.[69] In spite of his recovery, however, Frédéric's health remained problematic throughout his life. He had "a delicate constitution" since birth.[70] For several months after his birth, his face was covered with a milky crust and his eyes were closed. As an infant, he also contracted whooping cough twice, nearly dying in both instances.[71]

In spite of his persistent ill health, Frédéric never became a bookworm. He loved games and the outdoors, where he "was very appreciative of the beauties of nature."[72] Nor was he always submissive to others. He had a willful side too, like most young boys. When playing games he could be a sore loser. Although he insisted on fair play, when he lost or was wrong he would refuse to admit it to his playmates, stamping his feet and yelling that he "would rather die than say it."[73] Ozanam later admitted his faults: "I studied Latin, and in studying it I acquired malice. Truly I have never been as bad, I believe, as I was at eight. Nevertheless a good father, mother and brother went on with my schooling. At that time I had no friends besides my family. I became bad tempered, arrogant and disobedient. I was punished, and grew obstinate under it. . . . I would write letters to Mama to plead for me. And then there began to run through my head all kinds of wicked ideas that I tried in vain to resist."[74]

THE DEATH OF ÉLISABETH AND THE HELP OF GUIGUI

Perhaps one of the main reasons Frédéric, who was so "very good and docile" at an earlier age, began to act out when around the age of eight was not his Latin instruction but rather the death of his only sister, Élisabeth. Frédéric recalled the love and attention of his "beloved sister, who taught me together with my mother, and their lessons were so good, so well presented, so well tempered to my childish mind that I found real pleasure in them."[75] Élisabeth died in November 1820 after a severe illness. Stricken with a sudden headache and fever, she complained of pain in her ears, neck, and eyes. Doctor Ozanam examined her and found her pulse rapid and her breathing labored. When she showed little improvement by the next morning, the doctor sent for colleagues, who counseled him that she might have contracted meningitis.[76] Her suffering first began on the nineteenth of November and ended on the twenty-ninth. The medicinal treatments proved ineffective. She was only nineteen years old.[77] The grieving father provided this beautiful testimony to his daughter's goodness: "This child, endowed with rare virtue, of great piety, kind, nice, full of knowledge and talents for languages and drawing, was the friend and the companion of her mother, the joy and the consolation of her unfortunate father, loved by her two brothers and esteemed by all who knew her. Gay and cheerful in our home, loving little the world and its pleasures, she was all for God and her family. Our desolation has been at its peak, and, if there is any consolation for us, it is to see her constantly before our eyes, placed in the blissful dwelling where we will rejoin her when it pleases God to receive us."[78]

Frédéric was devastated. As one of his biographers remarks, "For more than two years he was to wage an inward struggle between wanting to please his parents, even if apparently only to keep faith with Élisa, and wanting to withdraw into the private world of his own thoughts."[79] He eventually adjusted to her loss, but he would never forget the influence of his dear sister. Later in his life he wrote the following lines in the manner of a dedication in the preface of his book *La civilisation au cinquième siècle*: "In the midst of a century of skepticism, God gave me the grace to be born in the faith. As a child, he put me on the knees of a Christian father and a saintly mother; he gave me as the first teacher an intelligent sister, pious as the angels that she went to rejoin."[80]

The household servant Marie Cruziat, fondly referred to by all the family as "Guigui," watched out for Frédéric once Élisa was gone, even carrying food to his room whenever he was ill or was being punished for misbehavior.[81] Cruziat, who was forty-five at the time of Frédéric's birth, lived to be eighty-nine, dying in 1857.[82] She served the Ozanam family for seventy-two years as "a model, unique perhaps, of fidelity, devotion, and constancy."[83] Frédéric "benefited from the warmth" of her presence in his life.[84] As a young village girl, the feisty Marie Cruziat had fended off a wolf attack on livestock with only her shoe as a weapon. In her service to the Ozanam family, she rose every morning at six a.m. in the summer and at seven a.m. in the winter. Her cooking was excellent; she was economical, scrupulously watching out for the household budget. Although faithful, however, she was not without her faults. She was prone to grumbling and occasionally using coarse language, both of which drove Frédéric's mother to distraction.[85]

With Guigui's help, Frédéric managed to survive the trauma of his sister's passing, but he still remained *le petit dernier* (the last little one) in his family for the next four years, until December 1824, when Charles was born.[86] Frédéric was actually glad to be rid of the attention that is normally lavished on the youngest child: "The new baby had become a welcome centre of attention."[87] Although his little brother could sometimes annoy him,[88] nevertheless, throughout his lifetime Frédéric remained a caring and devoted brother to his new sibling, whom he affectionately referred to as "my Charlot."[89]

APPEARANCE AND CHARACTER

Frédéric Ozanam did not grow up to be one of those handsome, dashing young men whose attractive features, impressive physique, and elegant style immediately command the attention of others. One of the best likenesses of the young Frédéric is the pencil sketch of Louis Janmot, a close childhood friend.[90] He was of average build and "of medium height."[91] The only reference point we have for his height is a comment from Frédéric to his mother in 1832. Describing some of the young men who traveled with him to participate in a Corpus Christi procession in Nanterre, he wrote that "most sport moustaches, and five or six reach to five feet eight inches."[92] This was considered fairly tall for his day.[93] In 1848, the average height for French soldiers was listed as between sixty-three to sixty-five inches.[94] Frédéric was therefore probably in the same range. He reportedly shared "the pallor of the Lyons people."[95] With "chestnut hair, large nose, and grey eyes," he had at first glance "a rather wild look" about him or a "strange appearance," because his hair was often long and disheveled.[96] His eyes were weak; he was nearsighted, causing him to sometimes appear perplexed or embarrassed. And indeed he was prone to embarrassment in certain situations.[97] Often there was "awkwardness in his first words. His speech, at the beginning, seemed to suffer from some sort of physical shyness; it was difficult, slow."[98] Although Ozanam was precocious, his mind was often "anxious and indecisive."[99] Yet "he had a face that preserved an expression of sweetness," while his "eyes flashed fire."[100] On second glance, according to his brother Charles, one could not remain "indifferent to this expression of softness and goodness, transmitted from the heart."[101] He had a compelling smile "of very spiritual fineness"[102] and enjoyed laughter, puns, and happy moments with his friends.[103]

Frédéric would have been the first to confess that he had an extremely nervous temperament that occasionally "made him very irritable and . . . impatient." However, "all his life, . . . he fought with courage this evil inclination."[104] He continuously worked on exercising patience and would readily apologize to any person whom he thought he had offended by a sharp word.[105] Scrupulous to a fault and severe with himself, yet he was very tolerant of others.[106] In 1830, the seventeen-year-old Frédéric confided in a letter to a classmate and close friend both his bad and his good points in an honest self-assessment:

> I believe that I have always a good enough heart, cherish my friends, am habitually compassionate toward the poor, grateful to those who are good to me, and never hold a grudge. That is what I was; this is what I am. I tell

you everything without prejudice, the bad and the good. As for the bad, I reduce it to four predominant faults: pride, impatience, weakness, and an extreme meticulousness. Pride and everything in its train: love of praise, difficulty in seeing my faults, sometimes a bit of arrogance. Impatience, only toward my little brother, who often riles me. When I speak of weakness, I mean human respect, little firmness in holding to a resolution, etc., and scrupulosity, extreme meticulousness, I mean regarding spiritual matters and exactness in composition. Add to these faults that of despising the neighbor a little too easily and you have my bad side.

As to the good in me, it is this: a heart which I think not perverse, an intention ordinarily excellent, but which often fails in certain circumstances, and a desire to do well which dominates me overall. I think I possess the two qualities which make a good Frenchman, patriotism and loyalty. I love my country very much and have ever abhorred duplicity. . . . I think I am grateful and am certain I keep secrets well. For the rest I am devoted to religion without being very pious, which is why I can sometimes be or appear intolerant. I swear that I love to work, but I let myself be distracted easily. To sum up, I think I could become either a very wicked or a very virtuous man. I hope I have now chosen the latter and will be all my life at least a good Frenchman, a good friend, and a good Christian. There is your man: I have told all; I have opened my heart to you; you know me thoroughly.[107]

His letter offers a glimpse into the mind and heart of Ozanam and demonstrates the thoughtful introspection that was one of his hallmarks. In his biography of Ozanam, Schimberg offers this assessment of Frédéric's character: "He was not without temptations to stubborn willfulness and to pride. There were and would continue to be contradictions in his soul, tendencies in conflict with one another. The sublime height of spiritual greatness to which he finally attained was won only by the most strenuous kind of climbing, begun early in life."[108]

THE DEATHS OF PARENTS

As a faithful and loving son, Frédéric Ozanam often worried about his parents' health and welfare. He knew that as they grew older, the

charitable work in which they engaged often placed them in dangerous conditions. On April 11, 1837, Frédéric wrote to his mother that "it
is upsetting to learn that Papa is traveling the streets at night, in the
lingering sleet which is so dangerous."[109] He most likely feared that his
father might suffer a serious injury from a fall on ice or in the dark of
night. Both parents had promised not to climb the unsafe stairwells
to the garrets of those living in poverty; both were unfaithful to this
promise.[110] His father had survived the terrible cholera epidemic of
1832 even while aiding afflicted patients[111] and was in excellent health,
despite his tiring duties and his worries.[112] The only infirmity from
which he occasionally suffered was lightheadedness, which may have
played a role in his eventual demise.[113] On May 12, 1837, a month after
Frédéric had fretted to his mother about his father traveling at night,
the sixty-three-year-old Jean-Antoine made a fatal miscalculation. In
the dark of night he mistook a staircase leading to a cellar for the one
that would lead up to the invalid he intended to visit. Losing his balance, he had a terrible fall and suffered a severe blow to his head. He
survived for only a few hours after the deadly accident, time enough to
receive the consolation of the last rites.[114] His death came as a complete
surprise to his family.

At the time, Frédéric was studying in Paris. With no railway and no
telegraph, it took him at least three days to discover the full extent of
the tragedy.[115] Frédéric had little choice but to take charge. His brother
Charles was too young to do so. His older brother, Alphonse, who had
chosen the priesthood over a career in medicine against the father's
wishes, "was taken up with his 'missions.'" The young, inexperienced,
and grieving Frédéric had to carry the "burden of settling his father's
affairs, of becoming master of his house. . . . It was a dreary and doleful
necessity."[116] Moreover, he had the added concern of his mother's health
and state of mind.[117] One of his friends, Léonce Curnier, sensed that
Frédéric would be distraught by his father's untimely demise. He sent
sincere condolences and received a reply from Frédéric that exhibited
"all the sensitivity of his heart and all the maturity of his judgement."[118]
Frédéric wrote to Léonce that although his friend's letter "has been the
first, it was no less sweeter than the others."[119] For Frédéric, the death of
his father was "most overwhelming. It . . . leaves behind it a sort of terror."[120] He poignantly described his deepest fears:

As a young child, accustomed to live in the shadow of another, if he is left for an hour alone in a house, penetrated with the feeling of his own weakness, is frightened and begins to weep, so, when one has lived so peacefully in the shadow of a paternal authority, of a visible providence in which he trusted for all things, in seeing it all at once disappear, in finding himself alone, charged with an unaccustomed responsibility in the midst of this bad world, he experiences one of the most grievous troubles which have been prepared since the commencement of the world to chastise fallen man. It is true that my mother is still here to encourage me with her presence and bless me with her hands; but cast down, suffering, desolating me by the uneasiness her health gives me. It is true that I have excellent brothers; but however good those are with whom we are surrounded, they cannot supply the absence of those who protected us. Myself, above all, of an irresolute and fearful tempera-ment, I need not only to have better men than myself about me, but to have them also above me. I need intermediaries between my littleness and the immensity of God; and now I am like him who, living in a stormy region, under the shelter of a large roof in which he had put his confidence, should see it rudely blown away, and should be left forlorn under the infinite vault of the heavens.[121]

One can sense in this letter the palpable anguish of Ozanam. He con-tinued his litany of worry to Léonce: "I do not know if I make you com-prehend my principal kind of affliction; add to it the spectacle of the affliction of my family, the rapidity of the blow which has struck us, the affairs of a succession importunately mingled with the sadness of a mourning, and many things too long to say."[122]

There was, however, a significant consolation, to which he clung. "For the rest, we feel a great consolation in thinking that the piety of my father, strengthened during these last years by a more frequent use of the sacraments, the virtues, the labours, the griefs, the perils of his life, have rendered easy to him the access to the celestial dwelling place; and that soon, if we are good, we shall find him again at the eternal rendezvous, where death shall not be."[123] Frédéric closed with a final request of Léonce: "What would it serve me, my dear friend, to tell you of my griefs, if I could only sadden you by my recitals? And what a cruel pleasure it would be to make for friendship a community of troubles!

But when we pour these troubles into a heart loving and religious at one time, we draw forth from it a prayer, and this prayer rises agreeable towards heaven, which hears it always. It is, then, before God that I desire that you would remember my misfortunes, and the needs of my entire family."[124] This letter to Léonce Curnier is at one and the same time a frank admission of Frédéric's deepest anxieties and a powerful testimony to his deep faith, which had been nourished by the example of both his father and his mother.

In a letter of May 20, Frédéric informed Emmanuel Bailly, the president of the Society of St. Vincent de Paul, of his father's passing: "My poor father is dead. But I am writing to you to let you know that the liveliness of his faith, the piety he showed in a special way so very recently, the religious consolations he received, give us reason to hope strongly for the welfare of his soul if the many prayers go up to God in whom he ever hoped."[125] He then made a passionate request for prayers: "Those prayers, I write to ask you for them. My father knew from its beginning and loved our Society of Saint Vincent de Paul. He rejoiced to see his son called as one of the first to take part in it. He often encouraged [me] by his advice and example [despite] my inexperience in good works. He himself always welcomed and assisted the poor, whose unanimous sympathy is today one of our comforts."[126] With the deaths of both his father and André-Marie Ampère, who had supported him in his early student days in Paris, Frédéric placed himself in Bailly's guiding hands: "Adieu, Monsieur. After my poor father who raised me so tenderly, God gave me two persons to take his place at Paris at an age and during a stay filled with dangers: M. Ampère and you. Of the three, only you remain. Allow me, then, to transfer to you, as much as I can, all the unbounded confidence and unreserved and sometimes indiscreet affection I had for them."[127]

With support from his friends and family, Frédéric proved equal to the tests that faced him. He decided to remain in Lyon for the time being to put the family affairs in order and to compensate for the loss of their father's income. He implored Bailly to continue to send writing assignments his way, for which he would receive some necessary income.[128] He also engaged in tutoring students for the sake of additional income, as well as performing the legal duties in which he was employed at that time. Perhaps he remembered that his father had once tutored students in Milan to make ends meet.[129] But as one biographer astutely observes, "the trial was more severe than it had been for the father, less sensitive, less introspective, physically more robust and buoyed up by a more optimistic nature [than his son]."[130]

Frédéric had described his father's death as "most overwhelming," but for him, "the death of a mother is most heartrending for her sons."[131] Within two years of their father's untimely death, the three sons also experienced the loss of their mother. Frédéric had grown accustomed to unburdening his soul to his mother: "I am a good enough child, but not at all a *man of merit* (as you would say), and I have a deal of self-love, but no esteem for myself whatever. I am not certain whether I am right or wrong to write you all this, but, good mother, I have too much need to unburden my heart."[132] He trusted her: "Please believe, . . . good mother, . . . that . . . I find many things to recount to you, a wealth of ideas to confide in you, a wealth of affection to confide to your heart."[133] He was often concerned about her health; she was never as robust as her spouse. In an 1836 letter he inquired: "How is that dear health? Is it stronger? Does it promise me a joyous arrival?"[134] In the letter of April 11, 1837, quoted above, a month before his father's death, Frédéric also expressed genuine concern about his mother's well-being: "Take care of that health which is not your own, but beloved to your children; do not expose it to the intemperance of this bad season; please, do not tire yourself."[135] His concerns were justified.

The summer of 1839 was a difficult one for Madame Ozanam, whose suffering, both physical and mental, was intensified by the extreme summer heat.[136] Her health fluctuated throughout the summer. In August, around the feast of the Assumption, the three brothers feared for the worst. For a brief period there was some hope of her recovery, but this hope was crushed. She passed away on October 14, 1839, joining her beloved Oza.[137] According to Alphonse, "the death of our mother plunged Ozanam [Frédéric] into an inexpressible anguish."[138] In late December Frédéric recounted for his friend François Lallier the last moments of his mother:

She hung on almost three days, calm, serene, murmuring prayers or answering by some words of ineffable maternal goodness to our caresses and attentions. Finally came the fatal night: I was the one watching by her. Weeping, I would suggest to this poor mother acts of faith, hope, and charity, which she had made me lisp once when I was very small. After about an hour new symptoms alarmed me. I called my older brother, who was sleeping in the next room. Charles heard us, and got up. The servants came running. All of us knelt around the bed. Alphonse said the heart-breaking prayers to which we replied with sobs. Every help which religion holds in reserve for this solemn hour, absolution, indulgences, were bestowed once more. The remembrance of a blameless life, and the good works which perhaps too many and too tiring had hastened its end, three sons preserved in the faith in the middle of so outrageous a time, and brought together there by an almost providential coincidence, and then, finally, the hopes already upon us of happy immortality—all these circumstances seemed joined to sweeten the horror and brighten the darkness of death. Neither convulsions nor agony, but a sleep which left her face almost smiling, a light breath which began to abate: an instant came when it was stifled.[139]

Frédéric felt bereft: "we were left orphans."[140] And then he shared with his true friend his most intimate sentiments about her death:

How to describe the desolation then and the tears streaming down, and yet the inexpressible, the ineffable interior peace we enjoyed, and how a new happiness seized upon us in spite of ourselves, and not only us, but the dearest members of the family; then that immense crowd at the funeral, and the tears of the poor, the prayers spontaneously offered up on all sides without waiting for us to ask for them, and finally, to come back to you, the loving ardor of friendship which was undoubtedly amazed at finding us so calm in our grief. Happy the man to whom God gives a holy mother! This dear memory has not left us. Even in my real solitude in the midst of the lassitude which often ravages my soul, the thought of this august scene comes to remind me, to raise me up again. Considering how short life is, how little distant undoubtedly will be the reunion of those separated by death, I feel the temptations to self-love and the evil instincts of the flesh vanish away. All my desired courage for one thing only: to die like my mother![141]

Only fourteen years later, he would indeed find the courage he needed to face death like his cherished mother.

Before his mother's passing, Ozanam had successfully passed his examinations for the title of Doctor of Literature, but he had decided to accept a position as professor of commercial law instead of the more tempting offer of a position of chair of philosophy in Orléans. The primary reason for his decision at the time was his mother's health. He did not want to leave her in Lyon "for ten months every year, at the risk of a similar shock to that which happened on the 12th [of] May, 1837."[142] As he explained to Lallier, he never regretted this decision: "How I experience now the truth of your words, and how happy I am not to have deserted that bed of suffering and benediction to run after the doubtful promises of a university promotion! When, at the price of that negligible sacrifice, I could only have bought the favor of spending some months longer with my mother, to find myself at this final night I have been already paid too much. I had such regret at not being able to close the eyes of my poor unfortunate father! May they now be reunited in a common happiness, as they were here below in common works and troubles!"[143]

FRÉDÉRIC AND HIS BROTHERS

Even before his parents' passing, Frédéric was close to his two brothers, especially Alphonse. In 1836, three years after the family visit to Italy, Frédéric and Alphonse had enjoyed each other's company on a journey through Switzerland. Alphonse had "wanted to hike in Switzerland" as a necessary distraction from his "laborious occupations," and Frédéric "was his natural companion."[144] Frédéric even referred to Alphonse in his correspondence as "my guardian angel."[145] In numerous letters, Frédéric was also solicitous of his younger brother Charles's well-being, showing deep concern for "that little gentleman."[146] After the deaths of both parents, however, the three "orphans"—Frédéric, Alphonse, and Charles—became "welded together,"[147] like the three musketeers of Dumas's imagination, a close-knit band trusting in each other's support and devotion. If Frédéric complained of his brothers, the complaints were about not being able to see them frequently.[148] His affection for his spouse after his marriage in 1841 in no way diminished his affection for his brothers.[149] On March 28, 1842, for example, he reaffirmed their fraternal connection: "In praying for all [at the Easter ceremonies at Notre Dame], I could not forget my good brothers. I asked for you that wisdom which reinforces judgment, that strength which sustains the will amid the thunderstorms of adolescence. I have asked that you may preserve that piety with which you are endowed, so that you may know your vocation and will not fail in the courage to follow it, nor the consolations to embellish it. . . . I begged that fraternal union, symbol of and prelude to the celestial company of the saints, flourish among us."[150]

In the same correspondence, he was quick to applaud the academic success of his now seventeen-year-old brother Charles, offering him both encouragement and praise: "It was not without a lively pleasure that we learned of your placing second. . . . If you continue in this way, nothing prevents your having a share of the prizes at the end of the year. But it is especially proof of intellectual development. . . . You should be very grateful to the excellent M. Noirot, whose solicitude has made the introduction to philosophy easier for you. . . . His teaching is a great boon; I have daily proof of his influence over my early years."[151] He even rewarded Charles for his accomplishment with a small sum of money: "Do not despise a 20-sous piece from a poor professor, Alphonse will give it to you."[152] Frédéric anticipated the day when "better circumstances will have brought us together. . . . I look forward to it eagerly: your being here will enliven our exile; and Amélie, who loves you very much, will be delighted to see one of her four brothers again."[153] His heartfelt letter to Charles concluded with the following request: "I will write to Alphonse in a few days; give him a fond hug for me and tell him what a painful privation it has been for me not to be able to visit him at Easter, like last year."[154] The following excerpt from another letter to Charles in 1842 provides an intimate insight into the loving relationship of the two:

> To-day [sic] is Sunday. We are in a little palace with a garden on the edge of the Luxembourg, whose green alleys form a delightful prospect from our windows. . . . I remember that Alphonse must by this [time] have left Lyons, that you are alone, and that consequently a little brotherly visit will not come amiss to you. And this reminds me, my dear boy, that we must strengthen our mind and our heart not to be afraid of solitude and not to give way to those temptations to melancholy which

are sure to assail us in it. You will soon be eighteen; at this age I had to leave all—or in those days we had all to leave—and to come away here, where I had not, like you, a brother and many friends. Instead of that I had a lonely room, books that had no memories for me, strange faces everywhere around me.

For you, whatever God's will may be, wheresoever your vocation may lead you, you will find a brother who will be a guide and a support to you; you will find the way prepared for you, a circle of friends, many less dangers awaiting you. You are in one of those periods of life when all the faculties take a rapid development; we feel ourselves growing and maturing. If I were near you, I would try and be of use to you; I would perhaps help to clear away your doubts, to direct your reading. It is a great pleasure to philosophize. Only yesterday I spent more than an hour and a half discussing the ideas of Plato with a friend. If you wrote to me fully on certain difficult points, I would try and answer them by long and full explanations; but you will do better to talk them over with your fellow-students, some of whom have great ability and experience.[155]

Most of all, Frédéric wanted his family to remain close together. His wishes were finally fulfilled in 1844, when Charles resided with him and his wife Amélie in Paris and Alphonse lived in a Marist community "five minutes away" from their home. Charles eventually followed in his father's footsteps by becoming a doctor and a supporter of homeopathic medicine. Charles, Frédéric, and Amélie were also joined by Marie Cruziat (Guigui), "who has never been happier than among her sweet *children*."[156] This scene of domestic happiness delighted Frédéric: "Amélie manages her increased household marvelously, and in her sweet company, that knowing and lively kindness, that Christian union under the eye of God, I have found the only kind of good fortune which does not dry up."[157] Throughout his short lifetime, Frédéric, a faithful son and a devoted sibling, held precious the sacred bonds of family.

CHAPTER 2

———

Student

Frédéric's playground as a young boy was the clos Willermoz, an abandoned convent on the slopes of the Croix-Rousse. It proved to be "a wonderful land of adventures" for Ozanam and his playmates,[1] whom he later referred to collectively as "les chevaliers du clos Willermoz."[2] Many of the names of the Lyonnais "chevaliers du clos Willermoz" would later appear on the list of the first hundred members of the Society of St. Vincent de Paul.[3] In this "secret garden of imagination," only a short distance from Frédéric's home at rue Pizay no. 5, he and his friends fought imaginary battles, launched military parades, and played Blind Man's Bluff. The pleasures of childhood were sweet.[4] Early life for Frédéric was filled with "games of the body and the spirit" and with "hot confidences between friends."[5] Yet he was also aware of other children less fortunate in the streets of Lyon; he knew that he was blessed to be born into his loving and supportive home.[6]

Along with games and play, the young Frédéric also experienced the pleasures and the value of learning. At the tender age of seven, he began the study of Latin with his father, an excellent Latinist. Until he entered the collège royal of Lyon as a young student at the age of nine and a half, his father and his elder brother, Alphonse, continued to give Frédéric his first lessons.[7] Like most parents, Frédéric Ozanam's father and mother wanted their children to succeed in life. They believed that education was instrumental to that success. Monsieur Ozanam planned for Alphonse to be a doctor like himself and pictured his son Frédéric in the role of a barrister.

A parent's plans, however, do not always come to fruition. Alphonse announced to his father that he wished to enter the priesthood. In fact, the archbishop of Lyon hoped to increase vocations by encouraging young men like Alphonse to consider the life of a priest. Although Monsieur Ozanam was not adamantly opposed to his son's choice, he believed that Alphonse was still too immature to enter the seminary. He counseled his son to study medicine first in Lyon before studying for the priesthood. Again, Alphonse opposed his father by deciding to study medicine in Paris rather than Lyon. The family was naturally concerned about his welfare away from home. Some of those fears were relieved by the presence of the Abbé J. B. Marduel, who had recently moved from the church of Saint-Nizier in Lyon to the church of Saint-Roch in Paris. He could keep an eye on Alphonse. This priest would eventually become the confessor of both Alphonse and Frédéric throughout their lives and may have already been a mentor of sorts to Alphonse in Lyon.[8]

The departure of Alphonse for Paris in November 1821 was especially disconcerting for the young Frédéric, who had become close to his elder brother after the death of his sister Élisabeth one year earlier, in November 1820. As Marcel Vincent relates, "Madame Ozanam was then in the sixth month of waiting for her fourteenth child, Alphonse having left, there would be with her only her little Déric."[9] Frédéric would not see Alphonse again for nearly ten months.[10] Entering the collège royal in the fall of 1822 proved to be a beneficial experience for the lonely and distraught Frédéric.

THE COLLÈGE ROYAL

The collège royal of Lyon was a "sad and unsightly building" located a short distance from the Ozanam home on the rue Pizay.[11] But Frédéric never disparaged it. For him it was not "a silo of austerity, sadness, and boredom," as it was for some of his contemporaries.[12] Although a bit willful and stubborn when he entered the collège, Frédéric admitted that his school days eventually transformed him, making him "modest, good, docile, and unfortunately also a little [too] scrupulous."[13] They also made him "more hardworking," although he readily confessed that he was still prone to impatience and pride.[14] He consciously worked to overcome the latter two traits throughout his life. Frédéric also had a quick and ready mind. When he eventually entered formal schooling, he soon "astonished his masters."[15]

Two teachers at the collège had a profound impact on Frédéric's development. One was Urbain Legeay, who was thirty-three years of age at the time Frédéric entered the collège.[16] Legeay was a "veteran classicist of the old school."[17] He encouraged Frédéric to produce his best and to work hard in all of his studies.[18] The young Ozanam favorably impressed Legeay, who preserved and actually published some of Frédéric's Latin verses after 1853. According to O'Meara, "The range of his juvenile muse was wide and ambitious, judging from the specimens preserved by M. Legeay. There were airy flights with the skylark, mystic communing with the moon and the stars, an adieu of Marie Antoinette to the Princess Elizabeth, written in stately Virgilian hexameters, hymns on sacred subjects, tender canticles to the Madonna."[19] Legeay acknowledged that he "was often astounded at the strength and elevation of these young flights. . . . His analyses of sacred and ancient history were quite surprising. The subjects where he shone most were those which gave scope for religious and patriotic sentiments."[20]

The other teacher was Abbé Joseph Mathias Noirot, who taught philosophy using the Socratic method.[21] According to the great French scientist André-Marie Ampère, "All those who studied under this cherished master agree that he had a particular gift for directing and developing each one in his vocation. . . . When he saw a young rhetorician arrive at his class of philosophy, puffed out with recent success, and . . . full of importance . . . , the Christian Socrates began by bringing the young rhetorician gently to recognize the fact that he knew nothing; and then, when he had crushed him under the weight of his own weakness, he raised him up, and set to work to point out to him what he could really do. The influence of this able master decided the course of Ozanam's mind."[22]

Although Frédéric made his first Holy Communion once he turned thirteen, on April 23, 1826, nevertheless he was plagued by a crisis of faith when he turned fourteen, a crisis through which Noirot skillfully guided him. In Frédéric's own words, "I must go into some detail about a painful period of my life. . . . From hearing about unbelievers and unbelief, I asked myself why I believed. I doubted . . . and although I wanted to believe and resisted doubt, I read every book where religion was proven and not one of them satisfied me completely. I would believe for a month or two on the authority of certain reasoning: an objection would leap into my mind, and I would doubt again. Oh! How I suffered, for I wanted to be religious. . . . My faith was not firm, and meanwhile I preferred to believe without reason than to doubt."[23]

The philosopher-priest Abbé Noirot helped the young Ozanam steer a course through the turbulent seas of youth and of his doubts. He taught him to confront ideas that challenged the principles and values that he had learned in the sheltered and comfortable environment of his home. From him Frédéric learned how to navigate such challenges without necessarily abandoning his familial values and principles. In 1851 he recalled this troubled period of his life and the powerful impact of Noirot: "I have known the extreme horror of these doubts that plague the heart during the day, and that encounter the night on a bedside wet with tears. The uncertainty of my eternal destiny would not let me rest. I attached myself with despair to the sacred dogmas, and I thought I felt them break under my hand. It was then that the teaching of a philosopher priest saved me. He put my thoughts in order and light; I thought now with an assured faith, and received a rare benefit; I promised God to devote my life to the service of the truth that gave me peace."[24]

The Abbé Noirot knew that Frédéric was the youngest of his 130 pupils and was a sensitive boy.[25] After Ozanam's death in 1853, he recalled him fondly and provides us with a portrait of the young Frédéric at the age of approximately seventeen. "He was cheerful, even gay," and he "loved a joke dearly, and was sure to be in the midst of any fun going, for there was never a boy more popular with other boys."[26] Noirot also paid high tribute to his virtues, talents, and intelligence: "He was an elect soul . . . he was marvelously endowed by nature, both in mind and heart; his industry was incredible; he worked all day without intermission, and a part of the night; he was devoted, ardent, and singularly modest; . . . he was most affectionate and sympathetic; I don't believe Frederic was capable of inspiring or harboring an antipathy; he was, however, very fiery, and had often vehement bursts of indignation, but not against individuals; I never knew him angry or embittered against any one; he was simply inaccessible to hatred, except against falsehood or wrong-doing."[27]

Despite his initial crisis of faith, Ozanam later fondly recalled to his mother his days at the collège royal: "Sometime there are happy memories. . . . The initial delights of study, the uncertainties, explorations, the healthy and stimulating philosophy of the Abbé Noiret [sic], and . . . many friendships begun on the benches at school, which still endure. And all the games we played, from Noah's Ark and the tin soldiers to our sentimental rambles and our serious parties at chess. Afterward . . . life at home, your caresses and spoiling, your gentle words while I worked at the table beside you . . . ; the counsels and, sometimes, the good-natured growls of Papa, my long walks with him and his stories which used to give me so much pleasure."[28] At the end of 1829, when he was sixteen, Ozanam's collège experience came to an end with the successful achievement of his *baccalauréat* (school-leaving certificate), and he received the *bachelier ès lettres* (bachelor of letters).[29] This baccalauréat was necessary for the study of both law and medicine.[30]

LEGAL APPRENTICESHIP

On leaving the collège, Frédéric embarked on a two-year apprenticeship until he left Lyon to study law in Paris. A Lyon attorney, Jean Baptiste Coulet, employed him as a junior clerk. His apprenticeship was unpleasant at best. He was expected to "copy dull legal documents, full of stilted phrases, circumlocutions, evasions, and technicalities."[31] Only his love of literature enabled him to persevere. He would walk to Coulet's office reading a book. Often he was so deeply engrossed in what he was reading or in a thought provoked by his book that he would bump into people in the street.[32] He devoured books on history, literature, science, philosophy, and the arts[33] and "lightened the intervals by studying English, German, Hebrew, and even Sanscrit [sic]; in after-office-hours he also read enormously."[34] Frédéric never challenged his father's plans for him to study law, but the law was never his ideal career. He was simply not cut from that bolt of cloth. He chafed under its demands. Frédéric inherited from his father a deep respect for reason and the value of science, but he also inherited from his mother an affinity for the arts and letters. He found it difficult to ignore the siren's call of literature. Although he would not oppose his father as his brother Alphonse had done, nevertheless he remained unfulfilled in a legal career and unhappy until he could pursue his love—the study of literature. Once he had completed the doctorate in law (1836), in fact, he embarked immediately on the pursuit of a doctoral degree in letters.

While serving at Monsieur Coulet's office, Ozanam learned to stand up for what he thought was right. In one instance he encountered some rather rough and crude individuals. He took their bravado for just so long and "then, losing patience and filled with indignation, he boldly broke in upon their conversation, scorned their ill-timed jests, exposed their ignorance, made them ashamed of their subjects of conversation and silenced them."[35] His willingness to speak up with such strength actually won him the respect of the young men he had dressed down.[36] A similar experience was related by his friend Léonce Curnier. Both had enrolled in a drawing class in Lyon at the end of 1830. Curnier remembered: "We were at drawing class, sitting beside one another, surrounded by dissolute young men. It pained us to have to listen to them; but, overwhelmed by numbers, we maintained silence looking from one to another." The men in question disparaged religion and poked fun at the saints. It was more than Frédéric could endure. Eventually, as Curnier relates, "matters came to such a pass that we both cried out in protest. Ozanam stood up. I seem now to see that countenance and hear that voice, of which I had hitherto only known the modesty and gentleness. He grew animated, became indignant, commanded and imposed silence. In a firm but restrained tone he proclaimed his Catholic Faith, without, at the same time, uttering one word that could hurt the feelings of those misguided young men. These were silenced."[37] Curnier also witnessed one of Ozanam's traits that he carefully tried to control throughout his life—his temper. From his mother, Frédéric inherited a nervous temperament. As mentioned in chapter 1, he could be anxious and irritable. Indeed, those who knew him well could recognize his growing impatience in one of his gestures. He would push back any of his hair that had fallen on his forehead with the fingers of his right hand, and his eyes would be bright with emotion. If he believed that he had truly offended someone in one of his occasional outbursts, however, he was also quick to apologize and ask forgiveness.[38]

The friendship of Curnier and Frédéric lasted throughout their lifetimes. In his biography of the young Ozanam, written later in his life, Curnier remarked on the significance of their friendship during these years before Frédéric left for Paris: "My daily contact with Frederick Ozanam constituted the whole charm of my stay in Lyons. We often had delightful walks together on the charming banks of the Saône, the beauty of which threw him into poetical ecstasy. A picturesque site, a landscape with an infinite horizon, a river with a graceful sinuous course would ever entrance him. The fields and the woods, the verdure and the flowers held for him ineffable delight, which evoked expressions of thanks and homage to the Creator. . . . On each occasion, as if hanging on his lips, I felt drawn upward by him on those mystic flights, and my soul endeavoured to soar with his."[39] Curnier continued: "With us both the isle of Barbe, that enchanting oasis of verdure, so dear to the inhabitants of Lyons, was a favourite spot. Ozanam would point out to me with veneration the remains of an old Abbey of the 7th century, or he would make me climb with him the steep rocks, from the summit of which, it is said, Charlemagne beheld his army file past, in that heroic age of Faith which was to live again in the writings of my young companion."[40]

He also recalled Ozanam's deep devotion to the Blessed Mother: "Notre Dame de Fourvière held for him a charm other than the splendid panorama which unfolded itself from the mountain. It was for him a place of prayer. He had a great devotion to the Mother of God, whose modest shrine bore on its walls many evidences of miracles obtained through her intercession." Ozanam "knew the history of this holy place intimately, called up before my eyes the notable visitors of former times: Thomas à Beckett, Innocent IV, Louis XI, Anne of Austria, Louis XIII, and, in our days, Pius VII, on his return from the coronation of Napoleon."[41]

Curnier valued Ozanam's friendship, one that had a profound and lasting impact on his own life: "When God, in His infinite mercy, gave me Ozanam for a friend, I was young, left to myself, far from home, in a great city where many dangers surrounded me. At the first breath of that general scepticism which was characteristic of the time, I felt the faith which I had had at the knees of my mother totter, and the only force which I could oppose to the seduction of the passions weaken. Ozanam crossed my path to arrest me at the edge of the precipice. I afterwards walked with a firm and steady step in the path traced out for me by his example.... It was the destiny of Frederick Ozanam to preserve, or to win back from the demon of unbelief many young men of his own time. I am perhaps the first who was thus saved from ruin."[42] It is apparent that Ozanam's faith had been strengthened since his days of questioning when he was fourteen. Indeed, in January 1831 he indicated his desire to "seek in the ruins of the ancient world the cornerstone on which to build the new."[43] That cornerstone would be "the perpetuity, the Catholicism of religious ideas, the truth, the excellence, the beauty of Christianity."[44] The young Ozanam began to envision establishing "on an indisputable scientific basis an historical apologetic." This was a lifetime task he hoped to undertake with the help of his cousin Ernest Falconnet.[45] He knew it would require much learning on his part, including the study of perhaps a dozen languages. At the age of eighteen, Ozanam began to picture himself as one called to defend and champion his Catholic faith in the pursuit of truth. He soon discovered an opportunity to assume that role.

CRITIQUE OF SAINT-SIMON

In the spring of 1831 certain ardent young followers of Claude Henri de Rouvroy, Comte de Saint-Simon, arrived in Lyon. Saint-Simon was a social reformer who espoused the doctrine of progress by applying science and technology to social problems. His was a "gospel of productivity," which he combined with a call for universal brotherhood. His ideal society was a "hierarchical society of unequals, guided by an elite of engineers and entrepreneurs," in which all classes "would collaborate for the common welfare."[46] Saint-Simon saw little value in traditional religion. In fact, he openly challenged the social conscience of the pope: "You must not content yourself with preaching to the faithful of all classes that the poor are the beloved children of God, but you must frankly and energetically employ all the power and all the resources acquired by the Church militant to bring about a speedy improvement

in the moral and physical condition of the most numerous class."[47]
Although Saint-Simon died in 1825, his disciples tried to "organize a
semireligious communal sect" that was based on his thought but went
well beyond Saint-Simon's original intentions.[48] These young disciples
wore "bizarre, blue-stoled costumes," while preaching the legacy of their
founder.[49] They selected Lyon for their campaign because silk workers,
frustrated with the changes of a burgeoning industrial economy, were a
receptive audience for their ideas.[50]

At the age of barely eighteen, Ozanam criticized Saint-Simon's
teachings in a published document. His treatise on Saint-Simon was
divided into three parts. The first was an examination of Saint-Simon's
historical critique.[51] According to Ozanam, Saint-Simon claimed that
"the world needed a new source of revelation to build again on the ruins
of the civilization generated by the Catholic religion."[52] He presented
the essential points of the socialist reformer's argument and then sys-
tematically addressed them with appropriate historical evidence that
countered Saint-Simon's contentions. He concluded the first part by
emphatically maintaining: "Let it no longer be said that the Catholic
religion has no knowledge of the needs of mankind. Christianity knows
its needs. Christianity anticipated those needs and provided for them. It
treasured the sciences, the arts and industry. It went further by sanctify-
ing them and making them acceptable to the Creator."[53]

The second part was an examination of Saint-Simon's dogmatic and
organic system.[54] For Ozanam, Saint-Simon's secular religion was merely
an ideal conception, not a proven fact like Christianity.[55] Saint-Simon,
according to Ozanam, believed that he had discovered the "definitive
law of perfection. This law was epitomized in that truly complete religion which embraced all relations between men and renewed the face
of the world, a religion which will bring peace, justice, and love on earth
forever and ever."[56] In this scheme of things, "God is not the God of
material fetishism, nor the pure-spirited God of Christians."[57] Instead
God is "the sum of all existences . . . God . . . is the soul of the world, and
one could say the world is his body, its co-eternal form, and therefore
increate [uncreated]."[58] Within Saint-Simon's socialist worldview, the
system of private property would eventually cease, and woman would
be emancipated. Ozanam took issue with both of these latter claims.
He argued strongly for the value and benefit of property to individuals,

families, and society and further argued that Christianity had "raised womankind to her greatest dignity" by making her "man's companion, not his slave," as Saint-Simon had claimed.[59] Saint-Simon's system, according to Ozanam, "consists of a series of fragmented, misconceived ideas held by a few men scattered throughout the ages, which today's magnificent and generous philosophy has successfully dismissed."[60] The third part contained Ozanam's concluding remarks.[61] Saint-Simon's so-called "revelation is a falsehood, its novelty deception; and finally, its application, if ever contemplated, would be disastrous." Furthermore, "it would destroy knowledge and morality. It would be contrary to its own principles of progress, for it would drive mankind back a long way from where it stands today. On the other hand, Christianity proclaims its catholic nature and its universality, and therefore it must span all ages, places and needs of human kind."[62]

First published in the journal *Précurseur* and then published in an expanded form, Ozanam's critique was noticed by influential French intellectuals, including Lamennais, Lamartine, and Châteaubriand.[63] Alphonse Marie Louis de Prat de Lamartine, a well-known writer, romantic poet, and an active politician, wrote to Frédéric in August 1831: "I have just received and read with pleasure your work, which you have done me the honour to send me. When I consider your age, I am astonished and filled with admiration for your genius. Please accept my best thanks. I am proud to think that a thought of mine, merely expressed, should have inspired you to write such a beautiful critique. Believe rather that the thought was not mine but yours; mine has been but the spark which fired your soul. Your first effort guarantees one more combatant in the crusade of moral and religious philosophy against gross and material reaction."[64]

The journal *L'Avenir* (The Future) published a favorable review of Ozanam's piece.[65] In the same month that the review appeared, Châteaubriand, the famed defender of the Catholic Church, penned the following words to a friend: "I have glanced over the little work of M. Ozanam. I had already read something of it in the *Précurseur*. The work is excellently conceived and the closing passage is arresting. I am only sorry that the author should have squandered his time and talent in refuting what was not worthy of his attention. We all know Saint-Simon. He is, to say the least, a madman. Surely an extraordinary Christ! Please convey my best thanks to M. Ozanam."[66] The praise did not signify that this early work by Ozanam was perfect. It contained turns of phrase that a more seasoned writer might avoid. Yet it was a first work that held great promise for the future of this young student. Perhaps Jean-Jacques Ampère, the son of the famed scientist and a person who later became a dear friend of Ozanam, stated the case best: "I find in that work the germ of qualities which developed late[r] in Ozanam: a keen, though still immature, taste for knowledge drawn from widely different sources; enthusiasm, loftiness of thought, great moderation in dealing with persons; above all, settled convictions, and a sincere and courageous sense of duty, which drove this young David alone to combat, armed with a sling and five polished stones taken from the bed of the stream."[67] Labor historian Parker Moon maintains that "Ozanam's entire life might be regarded as a reply to Saint-Simon's challenge, and not a wholly unconscious reply."[68] Frédéric would have concurred. In September 1831, he explained that the "reason why I like this work is, that in it I have planted the seed of what [must] occupy [our] life."[69]

PARIS

Shortly after the appearance of Ozanam's critique of Saint-Simon, his father felt it was time for him to leave his apprenticeship and to engage in serious legal studies. Frédéric's older brother, Alphonse, had now realized his dream. Ordained a priest on February 25, 1831, Alphonse was appointed chaplain of the Charity Hospital in Lyon, residing close to his family.[70] In his family diary, Monsieur Ozanam expressed his dream for his next youngest son: "I desire to make Frederick a Barrister, or preferably a member of the Magistracy or a Judge in the Royal Court of Justice. He has refined, pure and noble sentiments: he will make an upright and enlightened judge. I venture to hope that he will be our consolation in our old age. . . . ; he will go to read law at Paris or Dijon."[71] Paris was the choice. Frédéric continued to feel the intense pressure of pursuing a career that was far from his personal dream.

Between early November 1831, when he arrived in Paris, and late August 1836, when he received his law degree, Frédéric Ozanam was a university student at the Sorbonne in the famous Latin Quarter. He was one of thousands of young men who journeyed each year to Paris, the "capitol of learning," as the famed writer Honoré de Balzac chose to describe it.[72] The attraction of Paris can be attributed to its esteemed universities, whose renown was based upon "the diversity of disciplines taught there, as well as by the richness of their libraries."[73] Yet living in Paris was not easy for many, including Frédéric. When he first arrived he resided in a *pension* near the Jardin des Plantes, a neighborhood that was relatively inexpensive but also distant from the university. Frédéric felt isolated and alone. He wrote to his mother that Paris was "a capital of selfishness, and a whirlwind of passions and human errors." Moreover, the company he found at the first location was far from the best. In his opinion there were women of questionable behavior boarding there.[74] He confided to his father that there was a great deal of scandalous conversation going on as well.[75] His cousin Ernest Falconnet received word from him that "Paris displeases me, because there is no life, no faith, no love; it is like a vast corpse, to which I am tied—all young and living—of which the coldness freezes me, and of which the corruption kills me. It is truly . . . [a] moral desert."[76]

Fortunately, Frédéric found a guardian in André-Marie Ampère, a relative of Ozanam's father,[77] a mathematical expert, and a French physician who himself was Lyonnais.[78] Frédéric received a "most cordial welcome" upon making a courtesy visit to Ampère, who offered him room and board at the same price he was already paying.[79] Ampère took a fatherly interest in Frédéric. He regularly conversed with him, sharing his ideas on scientific subjects. Frédéric benefited greatly from these interchanges, developing a genuine understanding of and an appreciation for scientific knowledge.[80] As O'Meara, one of Ozanam's biographers, contends, "Science proved a valuable helpmate to him; he owed to it, probably, in great measure his sheer inability to treat any subject superficially. He loved it, too, for its own sake, because it opened out to him resources in every part of nature, revealing secrets which literature cannot discover, but only describe; because it furnished him with contrasts and comparisons of endless variety and beauty, and was unconsciously educating him to be deep, philosophical, and harmonious as a writer."[81] Most importantly, Frédéric found in this "patriarch of mathematicians" a model of simple but genuine faith, as illustrated in one incident. Frédéric often visited Saint-Étienne-du-Mont, a church located close to the school of law. On one such occasion his eyes fell upon the figure of Ampère, who was kneeling and praying fervently.[82] The scene had an immediate and powerful impact upon the young Ozanam. Here was a man of science who was not afraid to display his faith. It was a lesson he would never forget.

With the transfer from his former *pension* to his new living quarters at Ampère's home, Frédéric also had new opportunities. According to O'Meara, he now made "contact with the most distinguished men of science and letters of the day; they all seem to have treated the modest young student with a kindness . . . which charmed him."[83] His exchanges with such eminent minds benefited Ozanam immensely. His circle of ideas expanded; he encountered topics unknown to him.[84] Among the famous people whom Frédéric met in Paris was François-René, vicomte de Châteaubriand, the author of the celebrated defense of the Catholic faith, *Génie du christianisme* (*The Genius of Christianity*). Frédéric was provided with a letter of introduction, but at first he hesitated to visit such an important figure. He finally gathered the courage in early 1832. Châteaubriand received him graciously, and soon they entered into lively discussion. Finally, the great author inquired whether Frédéric had attended any of the theaters. At first Ozanam hesitated to answer because he had made a solemn promise to his mother before he left home that he would never set foot inside a theater. When he finally answered the question frankly, Châteaubriand's face lit up. He embraced Frédéric, while imploring him never to break that promise. Indeed, he told his young visitor that he would gain little by attending the theater and probably would lose much. In the future, when others pressed him on this issue, Frédéric would boldly pronounce that Monsieur Châteaubriand had personally advised him not to do so and he had solemnly promised him that he would not.[85]

CLASSES, CONFRONTATIONS, AND CONFERENCES

In his classes at the Sorbonne, Frédéric often encountered anti-religious sentiment. As Jean-Claude Caron points out, "Contemporary accounts agree that the majority of the bourgeois youth in colleges, lycees, and universities were hostile to the Church as an institution and indifferent to Catholicism as a religion."[86] Many professors shared this outlook.

Frédéric eventually worked up enough courage to challenge some of his teachers. He wrote his cousin Ernest, "I have found young people here of strong conviction and full of generosity. . . . Every time a rationalist professor raises his voice against revelation, Catholic voices are raised in response. There are many of us joined to this end. I have already twice taken part in this noble work by addressing written objections to these gentlemen. But we have especially succeeded in M. Saint-Marc Girardin's history course. . . . Our replies read publicly have produced the greatest result, both on the professor, who has all but retracted, and on the audience, which applauded."[87]

Frédéric was encouraged by the belief that his actions and those of others like him demonstrated to "student youth that it is possible to be Catholic and have common sense, to love religion and liberty, and finally to draw it [i.e., student youth] out of indifference to religion and get it used to grave and serious discussions."[88] In March 1832 he described another incident, which he referred to as "a more serious battle." A philosopher and rationalist, Théodore Jouffroy, "took the liberty of attacking revelation, even the very possibility of revelation."[89] The incident provoked a challenge that Frédéric again described in a letter to his cousin: "A Catholic, a young man, addressed some observations to him in writing, and the philosopher promised to reply. He waited for fifteen days, [undoubtedly] in order to prepare his [weapons], and at the end of that time, without reading the letter, analyzed it to suit himself and tried to refute it. The Catholic, seeing that he was poorly understood, presented the professor with a second letter, which he paid no attention to; he only made mention of it and continued his defamatory attacks, asserting that Catholicism repudiated science and liberty." Ozanam and others then "enunciated our true beliefs. It was hastily endorsed with 15 signatures and addressed to M. Jouffroy. This time he could not dispense himself from reading it. The numerous audience, composed of more than 200 people, listened with respect to our profession. In vain the philosopher strove to respond, and confounded himself with excuses, assuring that he had not wished to attack Christianity in particular, that he had a high veneration for it, that he would be careful not to offend beliefs in the future."[90]

Frédéric fully comprehended the inadequacy of the professor's explanations. He described how Jouffroy floundered as he tried "to solve by the forces of reason alone the problem of human destiny: each day contradictions, absurdities, involuntary admissions escaped him." Under attack from his students, he eventually "dared to affirm that it was unjust for there to be afflicted good men and affluent villains in this world." And finally, Jouffroy "confessed that intellectual needs were immense and that science, far from meeting them, only succeeded in making the whole dimension plain and leading man to despair by show-ing the impossibility of arriving at perfection." He admitted that "natu-ral satisfactions did not suffice our spirit and that after having exhausted them he experienced a great emptiness and found himself relentlessly driven to look for supernatural illuminations. He finally acknowledged that reason could not attain a high degree of development so as to become the basis of our moral conduct."[91] For the young Ozanam, this incident taught a valuable lesson: "Courage, then, for our adversaries are weak; courage, for the teachers of unbelief can be confounded by the least of our country vicars. Courage, for God's work is operative, it is operative in the hands even of youth: perhaps even our own."[92]

The conferences (public lectures) offered by the Abbé Philippe Olympe Gerbet at the request of students provided much comfort to Ozanam and other Christian youth. Gerbet was a friend of Lamennais, the controversial French priest who attempted to combine political liberalism with Roman Catholicism. In February 1832 Frédéric wrote: "Every fifteen days M. Gerbet gives a lecture on the philosophy of his-tory. Never have our ears been attuned to a story more sublime, a doc-trine more profound. He has given so far only three sessions, and the hall is full, full of famous men and eager youngsters. The Lammenaisian system [sic] expounded by him is . . . an immortal alliance of faith and science, charity and industry, power and liberty. Applied to history, it sheds light on it and reveals the destinies of the future. No charlatanism here, a weak voice, clumsy gestures, good, simple, quiet delivery, but by the end of his discourse his heart is on fire, his figure radiant, the light of fire on his forehead, prophecy in his mouth."[93] By January 1833 Frédéric was also actively engaged in the intellectual meetings called the confer-ence of law and the conference of history, and was regularly attending gatherings at the home of the Comte de Montalembert, a journalist, poli-tician, and defender of liberal Catholicism. Frédéric sincerely wanted to prepare himself to be a "legal consultant, man of letters, and social man."[94] In order to accomplish this he thought that he must have knowledge of the "law, the moral sciences, and . . . the world looked at from the Christian point of view."[95] What precisely took place at the conference of law, held twice a week? Frédéric gives us the following glimpse: "Controversial questions are argued. Two lawyers assist in each discussion, and a third has the function of public minister. The others judge both the basis of the cause and the merit of the arguments. Reading is not allowed; generally one improvises, especially in reply to questions. There are some very spiritual young men who acquit themselves in an admirable manner. I have already spoken twice."[96]

The conference of history was different. Its forty members met every Saturday and, unlike the conference of law, it was "open to everything: history, philosophy, literature. . . . Every opinion finds an open door, and as a result there is very lively and well-intentioned rivalry. For, if one strives to do well, it is not to seek applause and praise, but to give more solid proofs for the cause one has championed." Ozanam explained that "after each effort has been presented, it is submitted to a committee, which criticizes it, discusses it, and names a reporter who is its voice before the conference. Nothing escapes the severity of its censure; serious probing takes place, and criticism, which is at times very malicious. Finally, a higher committee is established in order to give impetus to the whole conference, to indicate ways of perfection, to make detailed reports, and to unify the results of the common effort."[97] These gatherings brought needed companionship and intellectual stimulation. It was out of this conference of history that the first "conference of charity"—the origin of the Society of St. Vincent de Paul—was formed in April 1833.

The evenings at Montalembert's home were highlights for Ozanam. Montalembert sponsored "evening gatherings for young people every Sunday."[98] At these weekly events, "there is much conversation and good-natured summing up by bands of four or five." And they were filled with "a perfume of Catholicism and brotherhood. M. Montalembert has an angelic appearance and a very instructive conversation. The points of doctrine on which Rome has asked for silence are not brought up; the wisest discretion reigns in that regard. But literature, history, the interests of the poor, and the progress of civilization are introduced. One is renewed, the heart is stirred up and lifts itself on high with a sweet satisfaction, a pure pleasure, a soul mistress of itself, resolutions and courage for the future."[99] On one visit, intrigued by the conversation and chatter, Frédéric stayed until midnight: "A great deal was said about the actual misery of the people and somber presages for the future drawn from it. For the rest, very little was said of politics and a great deal about knowledge. The young men are numerous, and M. Montalembert does the honors with a marvelous grace. He speaks very well and knows a number of things."[100] Such experiences and debates shaped the mind and the character of Ozanam as he pondered the course of his future life.

RELUCTANT LEADER AND BARRISTER, 1834

In the spring of 1833 Frédéric left the Ampères to live in the rue des Grès, where other Lyonnais students were located. He established a network of friends that included not only other students but also his father's relatives and clergy from Lyon.[101] According to Jean-Claude Caron, Frédéric was "a moralist, worried as much about the moral divergences of his friends as their political divergences. . . . He eagerly, tactfully, and firmly assumed the role of spiritual advisor whenever he felt a friend was straying from the principles of Christian morality; he purposely adopted a sermonizing tone in these instances."[102] Certainly there is much truth in this description, but Caron paints a rather somber portrait of the young Frédéric. It fails to see another side of him, one that explains why so many young men were attracted to Ozanam and found in him an ideal friend. In one instance Frédéric invited a group to a soirée at his apartment on the rue des Grès. Because he possessed only three chairs, the invitation included a request to "bring your own chair." Down the street came a procession of young men, each sporting a chair on his head. There was much laughter and joking among the cortége of friends on the way and much teasing when they arrived. The guests enjoyed good company, fine conversation, and genuine hospitality, which included syrups and little cakes. As they left with their chairs perched again on their heads, they provided an amusing sight to others in the streets. One of those in attendance put it best: "But oh! How we did enjoy ourselves . . . we nearly died of laughter, and between times there was such earnest, enthusiastic talk on so many deep subjects. I don't believe young men know how to amuse themselves or laugh nowadays, as we used to do; they want so much money for everything; we used to be jolly on nothing at all."[103]

Simple pleasures and mutual delight in the company of friends were the key to enjoyment, for Frédéric. He eschewed the debauched behavior for which university students were notorious, but he thoroughly enjoyed other social diversions: "I vary my enjoyments: in the beautiful days of September there were trips to the country, the pilgrimages of adventure, the happy strolls, the friendly conversations prolonged until the moon comes up, the sun, the greenery, the [harvest] . . . , the autumn with all its treasures. . . . Other times I would make only a passing visit to the countryside and return to close the evening with carefree comrades. . . . Last week especially was monumental in the gastronomic history of my life. Every day, except All Saints, I had invitations, and today again and tomorrow. . . . In a word, were I not to find excellent company, I would be ashamed of myself, so plunged am I in good cheer and debauchery."[104] Frédéric had a serious and even preachy side, as Caron depicts, but to balance this, he also possessed a genuinely friendly, social side.

By early 1834 he was recognized as a leader among Catholic students. But he remained a reluctant leader: "Because God and education have endowed me with a certain tact, a certain appreciation of ideas, a certain breadth of tolerance, they wish to make me a sort of leader of Catholic youth in this country. Numerous young people full of merit accord me an esteem of which I feel myself very unworthy, and men of mature years have approached me. I must be at the head of all endeavors, and whenever there is something difficult to be done it must be I who bears the burden. Impossible to have a meeting, a conference on law or literature unless I chair it. Five or six groups of journals ask me for articles."[105] What caused him the most concern, however, was that he was being distracted from his study of law and the plans his father had made for him. Still, those concerns did not prevent him from actively engaging in a dialogue with Hyacinthe-Louis de Quèlen, the archbishop of Paris. In 1833 Frédéric and two other students had visited the archbishop with a petition signed by one hundred students. They sought permission for a Lenten series of sermons at Notre Dame Cathedral to combat the anti-Christian mood of the day.[106] Quèlen listened but did not act.[107]

Ozanam persisted. In 1834 he returned to Archbishop Quèlen with a petition signed by two hundred students. The petition stated: "Therefore, your Grace, we had desired someone, who without losing time in refuting arguments that are today out of date, would display Christianity in all of its grandeur, and in harmony with the aspirations and necessities of man and society."[108] On this occasion Ozanam was joined by his friends François Lallier and Paul Lamache, two of the original seven members who formed the first conference of charity in April 1833. The three young men respectfully suggested the popular priest Jean-Baptiste Henri Lacordaire as a possible candidate for the speaker, although his name was not mentioned in the petition. This time the archbishop responded favorably to the petition, but not to the proposed speaker. Instead he opened a Lenten series of sermons by seven men of his choosing. The series proved to be a dismal failure. None of the choices of speakers excited the young students.[109] Instead, the young men flocked to the lectures given by Père Lacordaire at the chapel of Stanislaus college.[110]

Finally, in 1835, Archbishop Quèlen relented and invited Lacordaire to speak. The Lenten sermons of Lacordaire that year were so popular that Notre Dame Cathedral was packed to capacity with both Catholics and non-Catholics. The series became an annual event, which continues to the present day. According to one biographer, "Lacordaire was apparently able to capture his listeners by his enthusiasm and his personality. He possessed the intangible quality of all great orators, the charismatic gift of personal magnetism."[111] These presentations were not merely a defense of the Church or Christianity, but rather were lectures "presented in an open, public manner" with "an attractive presentation of [Christianity's] truths."[112] Ozanam was ecstatic: "The great gathering of young Catholic and non-Catholic people was at Notre Dame." In attendance were "nearly six thousand men, without counting women."[113] The presentations centered on "the Church, its necessity, its infallibility, its formation, its history," and "they all were excellent."[114] According to him, the only weakness in Lacordaire's presentations was that they were too few in number.[115] Approaching Archbishop Quèlen had been a challenge for the normally shy Ozanam. As he entered the archbishop's quarters, he later recalled, he had trembled.[116] But the effort had been worthwhile.

In the summer of 1834 Ozanam came to the end of his initial law studies. He described facing a tough law examination to his cousin: "I am taken up with material for the fourth examination, which is very extensive and gives me no leisure. I am writing in haste. It is one o'clock in the morning."[117] He successfully completed the Bachelor of Arts in law, and by August he returned to Lyon, where he had been called to the bar. His degree had brought him the title of barrister.[118] But was it enough? In May 1834, he indicated to his mother that it probably was not: "I feel that my duty is to fill some place, but I cannot see where it is. . . . And then, even if I saw my place clearly marked out, I want the necessary energy to fill it; you know this is the constant burden of my complaint— irresolution and frailty. . . . I cannot forget that this year my education will be finished, and that in the month of August I may be a barrister if I wish—I, a barrister! After all, it is no great thing, a barrister."[119] He consulted his older brother, who suggested that he should perhaps pursue law and literature at the same time. By the middle of November Frédéric was back in Paris at the Sorbonne. He had decided to pursue the doctorate in law and study literature as well. For the next two years he settled into a small room that he shared with Auguste Le Taillandier, one of the original seven members of the conference of charity.[120]

COMPLETION OF THE LAW
AND LETTERS DEGREES, 1835–39

Once again in Paris, Ozanam promised his mother to concentrate on his studies; he would not become distracted with other matters: "I must express to you . . . my fixed desire at all times to do anything in my power to fulfill my duty. Before I return to you this year, I shall sit for my examination of Doctor of Laws. I hope to pass with Honours. If I may not do something in addition to that; if I may not devote myself as much as I should wish to other more congenial studies; if I may not have *two strings to my bow*; if I am to use only the strong G string and neglect the brilliant and harmonious E string, I shall be resigned." He told her: "I shall suffer as a consequence; I shall be deprived of a source of pleasure to which I looked forward. But at least I shall not have been found wanting in my duty."[121]

Ozanam's promise was sincere, but he was unable to keep it. He did not pass the doctoral examination with high honors, as he had hoped. In April 1835 he wrote to his parents: "God be praised, provided that Papa will be happy. I confess that I am afraid of him, but this poor father has nevertheless given me his word not to scold me, and really, he would be wrong, for I worked hard and passed not too badly and then he knows well that I try to satisfy him, and he must bear in mind my willingness. Well, my dear parents, I am counting on your favorable reception. Really, I love you very much, but I am too much afraid of you. Your son who leaves in two hours and who will embrace you in three days."[122] In this letter he also listed numerous health problems and the severe difficulty of the exam as reasons for failing to achieve something more positive.[123] Were these simply excuses, or was the health issue a portent of things to come?

Frédéric's father was a strong man, forever vigilant in asking for a regular accounting of his son's expenses ever since Frédéric first arrived as a student in Paris. In May 1832, Frédéric had written home: "Those sixty francs will not grow moldy in my purse. I have already given 5 francs to the laundress, 42 sous for candles that I owed etc. I will inevitably need two pairs of pants: one from 14 to 18 francs for the fine days and the other from 6 to 10 francs for the working days. For my gray pants with which I made the trip are almost worn out especially in the backside."[124] His father often complained of his son's spending but inevitably submitted to most of his requests.[125] Frédéric also helped raise funds for his expenses by writing articles for the *Revue européene* and *l'Université catholique.*[126]

His father had promised Frédéric to pay for two more years of study for the doctorate in law, but he again expected a full accounting.[127] Frédéric reported on expenses in February 1835: "I forgot to tell you that in so much as my new clothes make me handsome, my old clothes are in bad condition. For 8 francs, I had some mending done and still more trouble. The cloth is worn, ruined. I am very much afraid that this summer I will be obliged to wear the blue suit every day in order to go out. The black suit No. 2 already shows its teeth. As for the frock-coat, the sleeves and the elbows are full of holes."[128] Again in May 1835 he declared: "I examined the account, and I found that it was indeed 150 francs that I had taken. In fact, in the month of April I had to pay: 1) a matriculation fee of 15 francs; 2) my trimester rent of 35 francs and 18 francs for Dufieux = 68 francs, which left 82 francs for my month. When

I had written to Papa that I would take 140 francs, I had not thought of the matriculation fee. . . . My private little finances scarcely go far enough. I spent 8 francs for a hat, 6 francs 50 for shoes, 15 francs for my frock-coat (for my part), 65 francs for my B.A. exam [*examen licence ès-lettres*] which equals 95 francs. I will be made very short of cash if I have to buy pants and socks at my own expense."[129] Frédéric knew that his father had gone to considerable expense to cover both his initial education and his return to Paris, and he felt guilty about his failed promise of high honors.

Although he made no mention of the fact in his letters, Frédéric eventually added a top hat to his wardrobe of clothes, a feature that led his biographer James Patrick Derum to entitle his book *Apostle in a Top Hat*.[130] According to Derum, "The top hat was the customary headgear of young gentlemen, and of older gentlemen, too. It was the sign of the upper classes in an era of formality in dress and manners—but on Frederic's head in his adult years it was to be seen more frequently in the tenements of the poor than in the mansions of the powerful."[131] Historically, Derum is only in part correct. Introduced in the early nineteenth century, the top hat was actually sported by "men of all classes, for all occasions, at any time of day."[132]

With the passage of his examination, Frédéric turned to the completion of his theses for the law degree. This was achieved within the next year. On April 30, 1836, he defended his two theses, one on Roman law and one on French law, and was officially awarded his doctoral degree. As Baunard points out, "few students in those days went as far as the Degree of Doctor, which alone conferred the privilege of lecturing advanced classes in a Faculty."[133] According to O'Meara, however, "He could not divest himself of the feeling that . . . he was betraying his true calling; that Literature, not Law, was the mistress who claimed his first allegiance, and who would best requite his services. Reason, interest, the wishes of his family, all pleaded in favor of the bar, but he himself was conscious of an insurmountable repugnance to the profession."[134]

Ozanam's misgivings about a career in law were made clear to his friend François Lallier in November 1836: "The moment of choosing a destiny for oneself is a solemn moment, and everything solemn is sad. I suffer from this lack of vocation which makes me see the dust and stones of all my life's paths as well as the flowers on each. In particular, the one I am closest to now, that of the bar, seems less enchanting to me. I have chatted with some businessmen. I have seen the troubles to which you must resign yourself in order to obtain employment, and the other troubles that go with the employment. It is customary to say that lawyers are the most independent of men; they are at least as much slaves as others, for there are two kinds of tyrants equally insupportable: the procedural officers in the beginning, and the clientele later." He still felt pangs of guilt about his parents' sacrifices for him: "I am still making myself unhappy at the sight of my father, who needs rest, and my mother, who needs more careful attention, being obliged to live still by work and economy because of me, when I could have relieved them of supporting me and left them to enjoy the rights of old age sooner if I had chosen a profession at the same time more comfortable to my tastes."[135]

Despite the guilt, Frédéric could not ignore the desire to pursue literature. Within a few days of the letter to Lallier on his misgivings, he informed another friend, Louis Janmot, that he wanted the doctoral degree in letters to increase his future options: "You ask me what I am going to do, and I scarcely know myself. I have finished my fifth year of law and have received the doctorate; now here I am settled in Lyon where I am content. But there is no career for me here beyond the bar, and believing it too difficult for me, I am trying to prepare for another which, suits me better: I mean teaching. It is possible that Chairs of Law or Letters will be established here, and I will try to be ready." He further disclosed that he was busy on his thesis for the doctorate in letters, but he confessed that there was not enough time to complete it at the moment. He would have to travel back to Paris for some weeks. His thesis was to be on "the Philosophy of Dante," and his excitement about the topic was evident: "This has led me to a long study of the poet whom I admire more and more. I am also studying his times, and am compelled to delve a bit into some of the obscure questions encountered there, and I cannot help but admire the action of the popes of the Middle Ages. . . . Happy are those whose life can be consecrated to the research of truth, good, and beauty and whom the vulgar thought of monetary usefulness does not importune!"[136] Between the fall of 1836 and the end of 1838, Ozanam's life remained unsettled.

In May 1837 Frédéric's father died from an accidental fall, as described in the previous chapter. Because his brother Alphonse was in the priesthood and his brother Charles was still young, all of the burdens formerly carried by Monsieur Ozanam fell on Frédéric's shoulders. It was a great weight for him to bear. His most intimate thoughts and anxieties were revealed to his dear friend Lallier: "Alongside these matters which touch so closely the interests of eternity, how little and miserable temporal interests seem, and how much it costs to be occupied with them! The whole administration of our little fortune unhappily devolves on me, and my inexperience makes the burden all the heavier.... Every day still unsettled bills must be pursued before the justice of the peace, tenants disposed to decamp must be watched, bondings must be renewed ... Added to that, an old octogenarian took the notion to die and bequeath us a sum capable of making us rich, but under conditions capable of embroiling us with half the town."[137]

Although Ozanam had both the talent and the ability for practicing law, the legal profession continued to hold little attraction for him. The following lines penned to Lallier make his deepest concerns about the law crystal clear: "I have pleaded about a dozen times this year.... The troubles of pleading are not unattractive to me, but payment does not come easy, and the relationships with officialdom are so disagreeable, humiliating, and unjust, that I cannot submit to them. *Justice is the last moral haven, the last sanctuary of contemporary society; to see it surrounded with corruption is for me reason for indignation each instant renewed* [my emphasis]. That sort of life irritates me too much, and I almost always return from court deeply disturbed. I can no longer resign myself to behold the evil which is allowed to go on." He now felt trapped by the necessity of taking care of his mother and his younger brother: "Nevertheless, I am far from wanting to give up a profession which real circumstances have made more than ever a necessity. I am even obliged to supplement the slowness of its results by seeking resources elsewhere.... I will teach law to three young men whose ecus I hope to see and who consider themselves lords too great to sit upon school benches. That does not limit the horizon of my future: it is larger, but rather stormy."[138] He was caught in an inescapable dilemma.

Ozanam hoped for the establishment of a chair of commercial law at the Academy of Lyon. In 1838 the municipal council voted in favor of establishing a chair of commercial law and intended to nominate three candidates. Ozanam had "already taken numerous steps to make sure of a place on this list."[139] He again shared his intimate thoughts with Lallier in April 1838, as he awaited word of the position:

> This whole affair is for me a question of vocation: I am waiting for the solution with respect, and I hope to accept it calmly, whatever it may be. It is nonetheless true that a considerable temporal interest is involved, for I am experiencing like you the anxieties of the *Res angusta domi* and, what is worse, this anxiety is not borne by myself alone, but extends to my little brother and mother, whose needs increase in the measure that her health grows weaker. And I who, after so many sacrifices made by my father for my education, ought to be able to take his place today and become the support of my family, I am on the contrary more of a charge than ever. A law lesson which I give every day is the surest of my incomes. Clients give me great leisure. With the exception of two criminal cases which resulted in more noise than money, two suits that I have been able to initiate, one that I pleaded in business court last week, a rather considerable debt on which I got a settlement in a suit between merchants, and finally a certain amount of free consultations, there is all the business the worthy law profession has given me for five months, a profession where a goodly fortune is made in the end, if you do not die of hunger in the beginning.[140]

But as always he was honest; he admitted that the law profession still disturbed his sense of integrity and provided little intellectual nourishment: "I cannot get used to the atmosphere of chicanery; the discussions of pecuniary interests bore me; it is not a matter of a good cause or mutual wrongs; nor of legal argument or of failing to cover up certain weak points. There exist customs of hyberbole and reticence of which the most respected members of the bar are the exemplars, and to which one must submit.... It is expected that 200 for damages be sought when fifty are hoped for, that the client surely has reason for his allegations, and that his adversary is a fool. Make your presentation in the most rational terms, and you will be considered to have made concessions . . . ; colleagues reproach you; the client pretends to be betrayed."[141] He knew that he could teach law and could even find thinking about the philosophy of law interesting, but he was ill disposed toward the practice of law. It appeared to violate everything he held dear.

As 1839 arrived, life seemed to brighten for Ozanam. His thesis on Dante had been successfully completed by April 1838; it would become one of his most famous and respected works. On January 7, 1839, he was awarded his coveted degree—Doctor of Letters. Shortly after, he received the much anticipated news that he was to be appointed to the chair of commercial law at the Academy of Lyon.[142] By the time he began his first lectures in December 1839, however, this happiness had been dimmed by the death of his beloved mother in the fall of 1839. For a time he was devastated. It was another event requiring him to trust in divine providence, just as he trusted that divine providence had guided him on the long and sometimes arduous journey from his early days at the collège royal to the completion of his doctoral studies.

No longer a matriculating student, Ozanam nevertheless remained an engaged learner for the rest of his life. By 1839 he had already published several significant scholarly works, including *Deux chanceliers d'Angleterre* (*Two Chancellors of England*), *Du protestantisme dans ses rapports avec la liberté* (Protestantism in Its Relation to Freedom), and *Dante et la philosophie catholique au treizième siècle* (*Dante and Catholic Philosophy in the Thirteenth Century*).[143] He had been admired as a student; he would soon be admired as both a scholar and a teacher. As he now became Professor Ozanam, his thoughts most likely returned for consolation to his student days. They held fond memories for him, especially the memory of the conference of charity and the formation of the Society of St. Vincent de Paul in 1833. For him, that too had been created by an act of God's providence.

CHAPTER 3

The Society of St. Vincent de Paul

On Tuesday, April 23, 1833, at eight o'clock in the evening, a group of seven men met for the first time in the office of the newspaper *Tribune catholique*, located at 18 rue du Petit Bourbon-Saint-Sulpice.[1] One of their number, Auguste Le Taillandier, had suggested earlier to his friend Frédéric Ozanam that the members of the conference of history needed to move from simply talking to taking practical action through charitable works. Le Taillandier, a quiet and reserved young man, was a regular participant in the meetings called the conference of history, along with Ozanam. But unlike Ozanam, he rarely spoke out on issues.[2] His suggestion was warmly embraced by Ozanam, who had recently been frustrated by the taunts and challenges of socialists in a meeting of the conference of history. As their first act of charity, Ozanam and Le Taillandier brought some wood to a man living in poverty. Shortly afterward, Ozanam shared the idea of charitable action with their mutual friends Paul Lamache and François Lallier. Within a few days, the idea germinated; it began to spark genuine interest and excitement. For advice on how to proceed, the four friends approached a person they trusted, Joseph Emmanuel Bailly, who not only welcomed them to use the offices of his newspaper but also joined them in their endeavor.[3]

On the advice of Ozanam, two others were invited to the April 23 inaugural meeting: Jules Devaux, a medical student, and Félix Clavé, a recent convert from the socialist doctrines of Saint-Simon.[4] The purpose of this initial meeting of seven, primarily young, Catholic men was not only to talk about charity but also to do charitable works. The new *conférence de charité* would develop, organize, and grow in size over the course of the next two years. Joseph H. Fichter, S.J., refers to it as "a resuscitation of the *Conférences* of that outstanding Apostle of Charity of the seventeenth century [Saint Vincent de Paul]. . . . The group's meetings, too, were called 'Conférences' in imitation of the Saint's usage in that they should confer with each other for their mutual aid, and should confer upon the recipients of their charity the benefit of their personal attention."[5] The Society of St. Vincent de Paul finds its origin in this first humble meeting, which grew out of the conference of history mentioned in chapter 2.

On April 23, Frédéric Ozanam also celebrated his twentieth birthday. The youngest member of the initial group was François Lallier, at the age of nineteen, and the oldest was Joseph Emmanuel Bailly, at thirty-nine.[6] It was Ozanam who brought the request for guidance to Bailly,[7] affectionately referred to by the younger men as "le Père."[8] Bailly was not only helpful to them but also necessary to their success: he had valuable experience to share. As a former member of the Société des Bonnes Études (Society of Good Studies), he had "encountered students anxious to combine their academic efforts with religious formation." As a former member of the Société des Bonnes Oeuvres (Society of Good Works), he had visited the sick in hospitals. Both of these societies were part of the Congregation of the Blessed Virgin, a lay religious order founded in 1801. Entering the Congregation's ranks in the spring of 1820 (he was its 776th member), Bailly soon became one of its leaders. In fact, the Society of Good Studies and the Society of Good Works eventually merged, with Bailly managing them from a building he owned on the Place de l'Estrapade in 1828. Groups such as this, however, were repressed after the fall of the Bourbon Restoration monarchy in 1830. The new government feared that they might become pockets of potential sedition, especially because young students often joined their ranks.

In response to the closings of these societies, Bailly had established the conference of history, which attracted talented students such as Ozanam and his friends.[9] Unlike the earlier organizations just mentioned that limited members to "a certain class of young Catholics of a particular shade of political thought," this conference of history "was open to every mind desirous of instruction, to every shade and difference of contemporary thought," all of which Frédéric Ozanam counted on winning over.[10] To support passionate students such as Frédéric, Bailly also opened his newspaper office as a gathering place, providing a wide selection of newspapers there for the students to read in order to keep up with current events. Lively discussion dominated the atmosphere in Bailly's office. Bailly himself was often an active and ardent participant. For some years Bailly also ran a boarding house (*pension*) to which many young students were attracted. He was not an absentee landlord but rather was genuinely concerned about the well-being, both physical and moral, of his charges. In 1825, six years before Frédéric arrived in Paris as a student, Bailly purchased a larger building located at 11 Place de l'Estrapade. In addition to boarding rooms, it sported both a dining area and meeting space. Bailly's home was next door at 13 Place de l'Estrapade.[11] Bailly had much to offer the budding group of young charity workers.

Although the conference of charity was very similar to the Société des Bonnes Oeuvres,[12] there were important differences. First, the latter group had approved a regulation that "bound its members to aid one another in their worldly careers."[13] There would be no such provision for the conference of charity or the Society of St. Vincent de Paul that grew out of it. Second, there was greater clerical influence in the Société des Bonnes Oeuvres compared to the conference of charity, and then the Society, because the Congregation of the Blessed Virgin required that its director always be "a priest and authorized by ecclesiastical superiors."[14] The Society of St. Vincent de Paul was a lay organization with lay leadership from its beginning. As the historian Gérard Cholvy states: "The Society of Saint Vincent de Paul was founded by lay people, was run by them, and did not involve the Church."[15] It was, however, the clerical characteristic of the Société des Bonnes Oeuvres that at first led Bailly to send the eager younger men to the pastor of Saint-Étienne-du-Mont for advice on the kinds of works that it would be appropriate for them to do. The pastor suggested teaching catechism to children living in poverty, a suggestion that moved neither the minds nor the hearts of the young disciples of charity. Ozanam may have already been familiar with the idea of visiting those living in poverty in their homes from a work entitled *Le Visiteur du Pauvre*, written in 1820 by le baron Joseph-Marie de Gérando, a Lyonnais. In this work, de Gérando sought to harmonize public beneficence and private charity. To achieve this end, he counseled that those in need must be befriended by people speaking the same language as the poor, building their trust, and capable of forming a deep friendship that supplied more than merely material aid. This was very different from the common practice of providing aid, in which the poor came to the homes of the wealthy on fixed days to receive some kind of assistance. The young friends had discussed the new approach, which was similar to the spontaneous visit initially made by Frédéric and Auguste. They then broached the idea with Bailly, who was very sympathetic to it. In fact, Bailly's wife had been visiting poor homes on behalf of the Daughters of Charity but had confided to her husband that it was work better left to young men. Bailly took her recommendation to heart.[16]

On that night of April 23, the group of seven discussed how they would conduct visits and how they would know who was in need. Jules Devaux was charged with obtaining a list of those who required help from Sister Rosalie Rendu, a Daughter of Charity in the Mouffetard District.[17] Jules may have been chosen because, as some evidence indicates, he had already done work for Sister Rosalie before the initial gathering.[18] It is no surprise that Bailly would have suggested Sister Rosalie, because his wife had been helping her and because his brother was a Lazarist priest.[19] Bailly's family also had a deep devotion to Saint Vincent de Paul, and he was, therefore, well acquainted with the Vincentian Family and its spirituality.[20] The group was not disappointed. Sister Rosalie warmly received Jules Devaux. As to the question of resources, a secret collection was held, and "one collection at the end of each Tuesday meeting would be receipts from the articles submitted to *La Tribune*."[21] Jules Devaux carried a hat behind his back for the collection; he became the first treasurer.[22] In an 1834 letter to his friend Léonce Curnier, who later founded a new conference at Nîmes, Ozanam listed the kinds of resources available to them at the start: "Our resources are the following: first, from collections, we make among ourselves each Tuesday; second, from the alms of certain charitable persons who wish to assist thus in our works; third, from cleaning out our wardrobe."[23] The seven members were now ready to enter the streets of Paris to begin their mission.

THE FIRST REPORT, 1834

By April 30, 1833, a week after the first meeting, the young students set off on their visits with addresses, *bons de vivres* (food vouchers), and bread in hand. According to Lacordaire, "While the innovators were exhausting themselves in theories that were to change the world, [these young men] in more modest fashion began climbing the stairs to the hidden wretchedness of the district. In the flower of youth, barely past their schooldays, we see them entering the meanest hovels to reveal the vision of charity to these unknown dwellers in the land of pain."[24] At each meeting they would render an account of their experiences in the hope of becoming better at their work. Although there was some discussion in favor of remaining the same size, they decided to admit new members. By August the initial group had added eight new members, bringing the total to fifteen.[25] One of the eight new members was Gustave Colas de La Noue (1812–38), who was most likely the eighth member to join the conference, at its third or fourth meeting. As a participant in the conference of history, La Noue was a friend of François Lallier and also known to Ozanam and some of the other members. La Noue delivered the first official recorded report of the conference, on Friday, June 27, 1834. The report, which incorrectly has been attributed solely to La Noue, was actually the result of a commission appointed ten days earlier. Besides La Noue, the commission included Jules Devaux and Frédéric Ozanam. In fact, Frédéric made many annotations and corrections to the draft report, which in the end greatly reflected his ideas.[26] The official report provides an interesting look at both Frédéric's thoughts and at an organization that was barely a year old on that June day.

The report clearly stated what had been learned to date: "We understand very well that charity must be done in secret, that the work must be unobtrusive. Here we are not strangers to one another; what we have done has been accomplished with the cooperation of one another. The principal end of our association is to do everything with one heart and one soul, of a sort that we recount to one another the different services we have delivered not to be adulated but to give advice and mutual encouragement, to give better service."[27] The report also revealed that the young members thought of themselves as auxiliaries of the Daughters of Charity: "We must, in order to continue, lean on an arm that is already strong and mature. We have made ourselves auxiliaries of the Daughters of Charity. It is from them that we have asked assistance. It is from them that we have learned to recognize the misery of the poor."[28]

Saint Vincent de Paul had never organized a group of men to do charitable work. One scholar has suggested that perhaps he did not do so because there was already such a group in his day, organized in 1630 by a layman named Henry de Levis, Duke of Ventadour. Henry de Levis brought together seven men and founded the Company of the Blessed Sacrament. Interestingly, de Levis called the meetings of the group "conferences." This Company was a secret organization formed to "work not only for the relief of the poor, the sick, the prisoners, the afflicted of every description, but also for the conversion of heretics and the propagation of the faith; it was to exert itself in preventing scandals, godlessness, blasphemy, in forestalling all evils and remedying them, promoting general and particular good, and was expected to take a hand in every difficult, hard and neglected work of relief." Lasting some thirty-five years, the organization died out, and little was known about it until research in the early twentieth century.[29] It is highly unlikely, however, that any of the original seven members of the conference of charity had ever heard of this organization, given its high degree of secrecy and the distance of two centuries. The superficial similarity should not be surprising: "That there is between the two institutions an undeniable family likeness is not to be wondered at, since both are the offspring of the same spirit of Catholic faith and zeal moving kindred souls to cope with analogous social ills."[30] What Frédéric and his friends were undertaking, as men, in contrast, was a remarkable innovation in the world of nineteenth-century charitable work. In particular, they offered an alternative to the model of men prevalent in the nineteenth century that emphasized qualities of honor, aggressiveness, and religious indifference. Instead they offered a model based on sensitivity and religious practice that was in large part countercultural.[31]

According to the June report, much had been accomplished through visits to those living in poverty, including a quiet evangelization:

> At present you have all acquired the experience of one of the best rendered Charities and one that produces the best results, above all, in these times when help is generally dispensed with such culpable indifference. . . . It is by our taking care of their body that the poor will permit us one day to read into their soul. . . . As Vincent taught us, the poor are hungry, so we must first give them bread in order to dispose them to receive the Gospel. By observing the preceding maxim, we have experienced consolation more than once. It is in distributing bread to the poor that many of you have succeeded in having those who until then remained deaf to the Word, listen to the Christian message. By giving clothes, others of you have given children moral instruction, the clothing of the heart. It is thus that others among you were able to approach the beds of the dying in order to speak to them about another life, much happier than the one on earth. More than once we have had the sweet satisfaction of rescuing, in favor of religion, hearts whose union had until then been divided between state and church. Therefore it is in entering the homes of the poor that we were first permitted to soothe the wounds of their bodies and then those of their souls, that we delivered bread and clothing before books which are the bread and clothing of knowledge.[32]

In addition, according to the report, the conference of charity had now risen from seven to seventy members and had been able to collect "approximately 1400 [francs for our treasury]." This amount, the report noted, was the "same amount of revenue which sufficed for St. Vincent to support the foundling home at its beginning." The members were then reminded "that we have chosen this great saint as our Patron and it is not solely his virtues which we ought to model, but his works as well and the manner in which he understood his works. Charity does not consist so much in the distributing of bread as in the manner it is distributed."[33]

The report then extolled the significance of charity for its members: "It is with charity that we will rally together men and situations; it is through charity that humanity one day will be as precious as one's own brother. It is charity which in the future will arise above the debris of human law and be the sole and unique law of the world. So let us continue to do charity if we want to fulfill our mission."[34] It also included a cogent warning about the sharp division between rich and poor: "Gentlemen, humanity is divided into . . . the class of the rich and the class of the poor. . . . The day when the rich and the poor help each other will be the day of general peace: a day of rest for all mankind. We who are rich, gentlemen, let us hasten with all our power this great epoch. When the poor want to shake our hand, do not refuse to respond by extending our own. Approach him so that he will feel welcome. . . . Let us recall that the angel of God struck the powerful of Egypt and saved the poor and afflicted Israelites."

The conclusion of the report contained a final exhortation: "Let us continue without fanfare the work of charity, because charity is as beautiful as it is salutary. It is a flower which fills the desert with perfume and which fades and dries up at midday. Charity is a fresh and limpid stream which runs through mud and slime as it crosses the city. Charity, gentlemen, is mother and virgin together. Let us continue to be charitable among ourselves and continue to love our brothers and sisters who are poor, because as all of you know, gentlemen, in exchange for our love they will give us their prayers[, and you all know, Messieurs, that blessings from the poor are blessings from God]."[35] Many of the ideas in this first report are ones that appear in Ozanam's correspondence both before and after this June meeting, suggesting that his role on this commission to draft the report was a decisive one.

TOWARD THE SOCIETY OF ST. VINCENT DE PAUL, 1834–35

The first important decision made in 1834 and noted in the June report was the selection of Saint Vincent de Paul as the official patron of the conference. At the suggestion of one of its newer members, Jean-Léon Le Prévost, the conference of charity had been placed under the patronage of Saint Vincent de Paul in February 1834.[36] Le Prévost was not a college student and, at age thirty, was somewhat older than most of the other members. He had met Frédéric Ozanam and his friends in a small restaurant located near the church of Saint-Sulpice, where they often took lunch. He was soon invited to join the conference.[37] Although Le Prévost suggested Saint Vincent as patron, it was Frédéric who became particularly passionate about fidelity to this patron saint. He insisted that Saint Vincent always remain "a model one must strive to imitate, . . . a heart in which one's own heart is enkindled," because by "appropriating the thoughts and virtues of the saint" the Society could "escape from the personal imperfections of its members, that it can make itself useful in the Church and give reason for its existence."[38] At that same February meeting, Frédéric also petitioned the members to place themselves under the protection of the Blessed Virgin Mary, recommending that they choose one of her feasts to honor her. The members approved; the Feast of the Immaculate Conception (December 8) was selected as the appropriate time of remembrance. Both the suggestion of Le Prévost and that of Ozanam were the first two proposals adopted unanimously.[39] With the selection of Saint Vincent as its patron, the conference of charity soon became known as the Society of St. Vincent de Paul. The Rule for the new society, adopted in 1835, commented on this development: "Our little association for a time bore the name of *Conference of Charity of St. Vincent de Paul*, because this was the name under which it was commenced. . . . Having become numerous, and being obliged to divide into sections—moreover, many of us desiring to meet together in other towns, where we were to reside thenceforth, the name of *Conference* has continued to be applied to each of those sections, all of which are comprised under the common denomination of the *Society of St. Vincent de Paul*."[40] The last sentence of this passage from the Rule actually identified the second important decision made by the conference of charity—the decision "to divide into sections."

The decision "to divide into sections" was not an easy one. Ozanam raised the prospect of such a division in November 1834 to Emmanuel Bailly, who was then serving as the first president of the conference: "But do you not think that our charitable society itself in order to survive ought to make changes, and the spirit of intimacy on which it is built and the daily growth it should have can only be achieved by breaking it up into groups which would have a common center and from time to time general assemblies?" Ozanam was quick to add this message of deference: "I am very rash to propose my young man's ideas to you who have a long experience in charity and who are so radically acquainted with our needs and those of the poor."[41] The conference had become too large (one hundred members) for its current meeting location, and the meetings had gradually degenerated into noisy affairs often incapable of handling the business of the day.[42] At the meeting on December 16, 1834, Ozanam raised the issue of division that he had mentioned to Bailly in November. He did not take his proposal lightly but thought it was for the betterment of the conference's work. His proposal may have even been supported by Sister Rosalie Rendu.[43] He recommended dividing into three sections or "conferences" that would maintain a close link to each other. According to one of the other members present in December, this proposal "raised such a violent storm ... that M. Bailly, the President, instead of appearing to doze, as was his practice on such occasions, at once adjourned the discussion for a week, and appointed a sub-committee of three members from each side to examine and report on the proposal."[44] At the meeting on December 23, "M. Bailly remained the impartial judge, but it was sufficiently clear that the proposition did not find favor with him." Even some of the first members were torn. Lallier favored the proposition, but Le Taillandier did not.[45] The meeting of the 23rd was as stormy as that of the 16th; it ended in adjournment without a resolution of the question. On December 31 the issue was again revisited, but again no final decision was reached. One account claimed that Frédéric rose to embrace the leader of the opposition and that all present parted as friends, wishing blessings for the New Year.[46] It took Bailly more than six weeks to reach a final decision. Two conferences, one at Saint-Sulpice and the other at Saint-Étienne-du-Mont, were created and soon joined by a third. A general meeting held at least once each month helped to maintain unity.[47] The name "conference" was retained for each of these sections, located at parishes, but they were grouped together and known as the Society of St. Vincent de Paul.

THE RULE: PURPOSE AND VIRTUES, 1835

By the end of 1835 the practices and procedures that had been developed over the course of two years were written down in the first Rule of the Society. The writing of the first Rule has been generally attributed to Emmanuel Bailly and François Lallier. Some scholars have put forward strong claims that Frédéric Ozanam was also involved in its drafting and had an important influence on its content.[48] Given his close friendship with Lallier, it is likely that he had significant input. The Rule was not written until 1835 because it was "necessary that it [the Society] should be well established—that it should know what Heaven required of it— that it should judge what it can do by what it already has done, before framing its rules and prescribing its duties."[49] This practice of embodying what was already proven to work is in the best tradition of Saint Vincent de Paul and Saint Louise de Marillac.[50]

The Rule set forth the Society's five purposes. Its primary purpose was "to sustain its members, by mutual example, in the practice of Christian life." Its secondary purpose was "to visit the poor at their dwellings, to carry them succor in kind, to afford them, also, religious consolations." "The elementary and Christian instruction of poor children, whether free or imprisoned," was its third purpose. The fourth and fifth purposes, respectively, were "to distribute moral and religious books ... [and] to be willing to undertake any other sort of charitable work to which ... resources may be adequate, and which will not oppose the chief end of the Society." Growth in holiness, especially, but not only, in service to those in poverty, was its ultimate and overarching goal.[51] Consequently, the Rule encouraged members to be virtuous. In particular, it encouraged the practice of certain essential virtues. The first was self-denial or self-sacrifice: "By *self-denial* we should understand the surrendering of our own opinion. . . . The man who is in love with his own ideas will disdain the opinion of others. . . . We should . . . willingly acquiesce in the judgment of others, and should not feel annoyed if our own propositions be not accepted. . . . Our mutual goodwill should proceed from the heart. . . . We should . . . avoid all spirit of contention with the poor, and we must not consider ourselves offended if they should not yield implicitly to our advice; we must not attempt to make them receive it as from authority and by command."[52]

The second virtue was Christian prudence: "Among the poor, there are some who have the happiness to be good Christians; others are careless, and some, perhaps, impious. We ought not to repulse them . . . , remembering that Jesus Christ recommended His disciples to unite the wisdom of the serpent to the simplicity of the dove. Bounty opens the heart to confidence, and it is by charitable gifts that we prepare the way for spiritual benefits. St. Vincent de Paul often recommended not to try the latter until the former had been freely bestowed."[53] Christian prudence also suggested that the members be cautious when visiting those of the opposite sex: "Now the poor are of either sex. As the *Society of Charity* is chiefly composed of young men, they should never forget that their mission is not to such of the other sex as are young, lest they should meet with their own destruction, whilst desiring to promote the salvation of others; moreover, it is necessary to shun even the appearance of evil, and all which might scandalize the weak."[54] Christian prudence further required that politics be left at the door of the meeting room. Politics and political wrangling had no part in the structure of conference life: "The spirit of charity, together with Christian prudence, will further induce us to banish political discussions forever from our meetings, general as well as ordinary. St. Vincent de Paul would not allow his ecclesiastics even to converse upon those differences which arm princes against each other, or upon the motives of rivalry which estrange nations. With more reason, those who wish to be of one mind, and to exercise a ministry of charity, should abstain from being inflamed by political leanings which array parties in opposition. . . . Our Society is all charity: politics is wholly foreign to it."[55]

The third virtue was "Love of our neighbor, and zeal for the salvation of souls": "This is the very essence of the *Conference of Charity*. He who is not animated by this twofold sentiment . . . should not become a member. We must never murmur at the labors, the fatigues, nor even at the repulses to which the exercise of charity may subject us. We expose ourselves to all these things, in associating for the service of our neighbor. Neither should we regret the pecuniary sacrifices that we may make to our work, esteeming ourselves happy in offering something to Jesus Christ in the persons of the poor, and in being able to carry some relief to His suffering members."[56]

The fourth virtue was meekness or humility. Christ, the divine model, and the patron, Saint Vincent de Paul, both gave witness to the importance of being meek and humble: "We should be kind and obliging to one another, and we should be equally so to the poor whom we visit. We can have no power over the mind, except through meekness. . . . The spirit of humility and meekness is more particularly necessary in giving advice, and in exhorting others to fly from evil and to practice virtue. Without gentleness, zeal for the salvation of souls is a ship without sails."[57]

The fifth and last in this list of virtues was the spirit of brotherly love:

> It is the *spirit of brotherly love* which will insure our *Society of Charity* becoming beneficial to its members and edifying to others. Faithful to the maxims of our divine Master and His beloved disciple, let us love one another. We should love one another now and ever, far and near, from one Conference to another, from town to town, from clime to clime. This love will render us able to bear with one another's failings. We shall never give credence to an evil report of a brother but with sorrow; and when we cannot reject the evidence of facts, even then, . . . in a spirit of charity, and with all the earnestness of sincere friendship, we will ourselves counsel our falling, or fallen brother, or cause advice to be conveyed to him; We will endeavor to strengthen him in virtue, or raise him from his fall. If any member of the Conference should become ill, his brethren will visit him, will tend him, if it be necessary, will assuage the irksomeness of his convalescence; if his malady be dangerous, they should take the utmost care that he receive the Sacraments. In a word, the troubles and the joys of each of us shall be shared by all, in accordance with the advice of the apostle, who tells us to weep with those who weep, and rejoice with those who rejoice.[58]

With the phrase "the troubles and the joys of each of us shall be shared by all," the Rule sought to establish a unity among members that would be a genuine "model of Christian friendship."

All five of these virtues not only reinforced the bonds of friendship but also ensured that the dignity of each person—the person serving and the person served alike—was respected.[59] The Rule was clear: "Our love of our neighbor, then, should be without respect of persons. The title of the poor to our commiseration is their poverty itself. We are not to inquire whether they belong to any party, or sect, in particular. Jesus Christ came to redeem and save all men, the Greeks as well as Jews, barbarians as well as Romans. We will not discriminate more than did He, between those whom suffering and misery have visited."[60] In the words of Frédéric's wife, Amélie, her husband took to heart these virtues and admonitions:

"Frédéric loved the poor so much because in them he honored our Lord. This thought did not leave him and if charity was a great enjoyment for his heart, its goal has always been the propagation of the faith. The last winter that he spent in Paris, he was already very ill and my prayers could not prevent him from going weekly to . . . a lost and very ungodly old man. . . . Frédéric remained sometimes three quarters of an hour to one hour on his feet, exposed to all the winds, in the middle of the cries of market routes to educate, to persuade this man who was extremely bad. He was an old Septembrist jacobin, a terrorist who kept hating and blaspheming."[61] With great love and patience Frédéric persisted for two years. His efforts and prayers finally worked. The old man was persuaded by Frédéric "to forgive and to make his Easter communion which he did in very good feelings." When the old man died, "he died well."[62]

The basic unit of the Society remained the conference: "When several members of the Society are found in any locality, they meet to encourage each other in the practice of virtue. This meeting is called a *Conference*, the name originally given to the Society itself."[63] The primary work of the conference was defined as visiting those living in poverty, but the Rule emphasized that "no work of charity should be regarded as foreign to the Society."[64] When several conferences were established in the same town, "each takes the name of the parish where its members meet, and the several Conferences are united by a *Particular Council*, which takes the name of the town itself."[65] Both the conference and the Particular Council were to be administered by a president, spiritual director, vice-president, secretary, and treasurer.[66] The Particular Council was composed of these officers, as well as the presidents, spiritual directors, and vice-presidents of all conferences and special works. It was "charged with those works and important measures which interest all the conferences of the town" and maintained a common fund "to meet the expenses of the special works of the town, and to sustain the poorer Conferences."[67]

All of the conferences of the Society were to be "united by a Council-General,"[68] which was "composed of a President, Vice-President, Secretary, Treasurer, and of several Councillors," and the Council-General was to be the "bond" that "maintains the unity of the Society."[69] It administered a general fund intended to support the progress of the Society. Funds were raised through donations, collections at general meetings, and contributions from conferences and councils.[70] The president-general of the Council-General both called and presided over general meetings and any special meetings. Four annual general meetings were identified in the Rule: the Feast of the Immaculate Conception of Mary on December 8, the first Sunday of Lent, the Sunday of the Good Shepherd (the fourth Sunday of Easter), which recalled the translation or solemn transfer of the relics of Saint Vincent, and July 19, which was formerly the feast of Saint Vincent de Paul.[71] At the general meetings, the member conferences were expected to report on the progress of the Society in their areas as well as the work of the Society in alleviating poverty.[72]

As regards membership of the conferences, the Rule specified the following: "*This Society of Charity* is composed of active members, and of others who cannot devote themselves to the works in which it is engaged. The members of this latter class assist the former by their efforts and by their influence: by their offerings and their prayers they supply the absence of that actual co-operation which they are necessitated to forego."[73] Four levels of membership were recognized in the Rule and by the Council-General: active, corresponding, honorary, and subscribing.[74] Active members were engaged directly in the meetings and work of the conference. Honorary members did not attend the regular conference meetings but were invited to other meetings, while subscribing members were regular benefactors who contributed to the Society. Corresponding members were members who moved to a new location where the Society of St. Vincent de Paul did not have a presence. According to the Rule, such a person "does not thereby cease to belong to the Society;—he becomes a *corresponding member*; he puts himself in communication with the Conference or Conferences of the town of the diocese nearest to his residence, and corresponds with the Secretary of the Council or of the Conference of that town." If there is no conference in the diocese, then "he corresponds with the Secretary-General. He receives every year a report on the works of the Society, and maintains with it a communion both of prayers and good works, by doing whatever works of charity he can, and by advancing the interests of the Society whenever he has an opportunity." Interestingly, it was Frédéric Ozanam who was most responsible for creating this category of membership.[75] It certainly met the needs of a young itinerant student population.

GROWTH AND COMPOSITION OF THE SOCIETY

With the Rule in place by the end of 1835, the Society was poised to prosper. On July 23, 1836, Frédéric wrote to his mother and testified to the great work that was already being done. At the general meeting on July 19, it was reported that "the Society consists of about 200 members visiting 300 poor families, and distributing each year a little more than 4,000 francs in domestic assistance, in the four corners of Paris."[76] But there was much more: "We maintain a house of apprenticeship for printing where we lodge, feed, and instruct ten poor children, nearly all orphans. We pay two charitable persons a wage equal to a half-pension. . . . They learn printing . . . and some of our members give them lessons in Scripture, calculus, sacred history. . . . There are even two more advanced who understand a little Latin, which is necessary now in order to be admitted . . . in the better printing houses of Paris. They have to look after them a fine man and wife without children who are delighted with their adopted family . . . we give them lodging and a little indemnity of money besides."[77] He confessed to his mother that at first he had worried because they "had only 180 francs." But according to him, "Providence has provided. I am now very much convinced that to do works of charity, it is never necessary to worry about pecuniary resources, they always come."[78] Fréderic himself was the most energetic in fostering extension of the membership, recruiting thirty-three members during the first three years.[79] By the fall of 1837 he confided in his best friend and the secretary-general of the Society, François Lallier, that "our little Society of St. Vincent de Paul has grown large enough to be considered a providential fact."[80] By the end of 1848, there were approximately 9,000 active members and 388 conferences, of which 282 were in France.[81] At Ozanam's death in 1853, the Society was expending over one million francs on assistance to those in poverty.[82] As the amount of aid increased, so too did the Society, not only in total number of members and conferences but also in geographic location. By April 1855, twenty-two years after its inception, the Society had received papal recognition, had a presence in at least fifteen countries, and numbered over 2,800 conferences, including thirty conferences formed in the United States,[83] nineteen in Mexico, and thirty-five in Canada. It had a presence in Asia and Africa as well.[84] The historian Matthieu Brejon de

Lavergnée describes the period between 1840 and 1860 as one of "formidable expansion." In fact, much of that expansion occurred under the presidency of Adolphe Baudon, who has sometimes been referred to as the "second founder."[85]

In 1836 Frédéric addressed the nature of the membership in another letter to his mother: "The government and ecclesiastical authority have been informed of the existence of our little society and have shown a great deal of satisfaction with it. We have among our colleagues a peer of France, nobles, distinguished artists, a musician who, every month, travels all of London for his concerts, employees of the ministries, former Saint-Simonians, many lawyers, physicians, students, small merchants and even shop salesmen. The only two things they have in common are youth and good intentions."[86] Brejon de Lavergnée, who has studied the composition of the Society from its founding through the late nineteenth century, adds vital detail to Ozanam's remarks about membership. According to Brejon de Lavergnée, 60 percent of the members were *bourgeoisie* (middle class), which is "without surprise. The Society is an urban association born in the midst of the schools."[87] The next largest group were members of the *noblesse* (nobility). Approximately 21 percent of the Society came from its ranks. The *petite bourgeoisie* constituted 10 percent of the Society's members, and the *milieux populaires* (working class) were 9 percent.[88] Many of the young members came from fervent families with pious mothers, had large families once they married, and brought the Society to their new places of residence after they had completed their studies and left Paris.[89] As Brejon de Lavergnée remarks: "There is no doubt that, in a century of feminization of Catholicism, the confreres have formed a small male religious elite."[90] Moreover, many of the members who joined the Society as students entered into important professional and political occupations when they left school, "allowing them to work more widely on poverty."[91] This was precisely the vision of regeneration that Ozanam had entertained in 1834: "The earth has grown cold. It is for us Catholics to revive the vital beat to restore it, it is for us to begin over again the great work of regeneration."[92] In 1841 he wrote: "How can there not be given some hope to such a strength of association, exerted mainly in the large cities, in every law school, in every enlightened home, upon a generation called to fill a variety of offices and influential posts? . . . Eight years . . .

[have raised] our number from eight to two thousand, [and] . . . several of us without the help of intrigue and favor already move in the highest levels of society; . . . on all sides we invade the bar, medicine, the courts, the professorships; . . . a single one of our conferences is composed of nearly a third of the École Normale and the brightest students of the École Polytechique."[93]

OZANAM AND THE LAY NATURE OF THE SOCIETY

For Ozanam, all members of the Society should faithfully serve the needy. He practiced what he preached. He was extremely conscientious about personally serving those in need and visiting the homes of those living in poverty. He wrote to his wife, Amélie, about his experiences on one such home visit in 1842: "The sore that the wife had on her arm required another operation whose consequences prevent her from carrying her little children. They remain sitting all day long in their sad courtyard, without any exercise, and their limbs are not developing, even though the weather is so beautiful and the season so salutary . . . the very ill father is also obliged to sweep. . . . With that, provisions are extravagantly dear. . . . [Another family] have their two youngest children in danger. Their oldest daughter does all that she can to help her mother."[94] His heart broke for the suffering of these people: "What pain to see this poor maternal love in grip with the impossibility of doing what would be needed to save her family! And after that, we complain; we would like to give ourselves the joys of life! My sweet friend, allow me, before leaving, to give them something for your feast day; I will take that from the gift, already very modest, that I am reserving for you."[95] Amélie knew only too well her husband's compassion: "He was busy for a long time with a noble and excellent young man, very miserable because of his conversion, and as it was impossible to find him a position, he feared that in the end, the necessity of receiving continuous aid would humble the noble character of this young man. Then he pretended to place him in an administrative office; there he was given work and a salary, but it was M. Ozanam who was paying." Because this young man thought he was earning a living, he "regained courage; he is now in a very respectable career thanks to Frédéric's attentions, but he has always been unaware of his generosity."[96] According to Amélie, Frédéric was immensely forgiving; he believed that he did not have the right to judge others. She related this moving episode:

> He had aided an Italian for a long time by making him do translations for which he had no need. Believing himself to be sure of his integrity, he found him a position as a master of supervision and discipline. But shortly afterwards, [the man] was dismissed under the most serious accusations. This man remained without resources, and one day, driven by misery, he came to ask for some aid. Frederic, indignant, reproached him for his infamous conduct and sent him away without giving anything to him. But he quickly repented for his harshness, saying that one should never push a man to despair, that one did not have the right to refuse a slice of bread, even to the vilest scoundrel, and that finally, he would need, one day, that God would not be as harsh to him as he had just been to this man. Not being able to hold himself back any longer, he takes his hat and runs with all his might to the Luxembourg Garden where he catches up with this man and gives him what he needed.[97]

According to his wife, Frédéric could not be happy when others were suffering. On New Year's day in 1852, Frédéric was saddened by the news that a couple whom he had served were forced to sell their chest of drawers. According to Amélie, "it was the last of their former comforts. . . . [The wife] . . . had had the chest of drawers since her marriage and . . . she no longer knew where to keep her scanty clothes and those of her children. He told me that he wanted to give these poor people a joyous surprise in returning this chest of drawers to them as their New Year's gift." Amélie in turn advised him that "the 25 francs that it would cost would be better used in giving little by little to them in order that the husband might rest because he was threatened with an attack on account of too much work. He said that this was true, and he went on his rounds of official visits. When he returned, he was very sad, scarcely looking at the toys which crowded the parlor and not wanting to touch the candies that his little Marie offered to him."[98] She inquired about "the reason for his sadness; he said to me that he thought about the poor, that a slight part of the money that we had spent to amuse his daughter would have been enough to cause true happiness. And as

I begged him to pursue his first thought, he left immediately, taking a porter with him . . . to get this chest of drawers and to have it taken to those poor people; he then returned to the house very cheerful."[99] Not only in words but also in actions, Ozanam was a model of the kind of Christian compassion and love that was at the heart of the Society of St. Vincent de Paul.

Ozanam believed firmly in the "apostleship of the laity."[100] He fully understood, to borrow from Pope Paul VI's 1965 document on this concept, that the laity "exercise the apostolate in fact by their activity directed to the evangelization and sanctification of men and to the penetrating and perfecting of the temporal order through the spirit of the Gospel. In this way, their temporal activity openly bears witness to Christ and promotes the salvation of men. Since the laity, in accordance with their state of life, live in the midst of the world and its concerns, they are called by God to exercise their apostolate in the world like leaven, with the ardor of the spirit of Christ."[101] In a February 1835 letter to his friend Léonce Curnier, who was then establishing a conference in Nîmes, Ozanam expressed in powerful and emotional language this concept of the apostolate of the laity:

Are we not, like the Christians of the first centuries, thrown into the midst of a corrupt civilization, of a collapsing society? Are we not as relegated to the catacombs in obscurity and beneath the contempt of those who consider themselves great and wise? Cast your eyes on the world around us. Are the rich and the favored much better than those who replied to St. Paul: "We will hear you another time?" And are the poor and the populace better instructed and are they better off than those to whom the apostles preached? The savants have compared the state of the slaves of antiquity with the condition of our workers and proletariat and have found these latter to have more to complain of, after eighteen centuries of Christianity. Then, for a like evil, a like remedy. The earth has grown cold. It is for us Catholics to revive the vital beat to restore it, it is for us to begin over again the great work of regeneration, if necessary to bring back the era of the martyrs. For to be a martyr is possible for every Christian, to be a martyr is to give his life for God and his brothers, to give his life in sacrifice, whether the sacrifice be consumed in an instant like a holocaust, or be accomplished slowly and smoke night and day like perfume on the altar. To be a martyr is to give back to heaven all that one has received: his money, his blood, his whole soul. This offering is in our hands; we can make this sacrifice. It is up to us to choose to which altar it pleases us to bring it, to what divinity we will consecrate our youth and the time following, in what temple we will assemble: at the foot of the idol of egoism, or in the sanctuary of God and humanity.[102]

In the same letter, Ozanam used the story of the Good Samaritan to highlight the necessary role of a layperson in addressing the needs of those living in desperation and leading them back to the faith. "Humanity of our days seems comparable to the traveler of whom the Gospel speaks: it also . . . has been attacked by the cutthroats and robbers of thought, by wicked men who have robbed it of what it possessed: the treasure of faith and love, and they have left it naked and wounded and lying by the side of the road. Priests and levites have passed by, and this time, since they were true priests and levites, they have approached suffering themselves and wished to heal it. But in its delirium, it did not recognize them and repulsed them."

He continued with his insight into our own human frailty: "In our turn, weak Samaritans, worldly and people of little faith that we are, let us dare nonetheless to approach this great sick one. Perhaps it will not be frightened of us. Let us try to probe its wounds and pour in oil, soothing its ear with words of consolation and peace; then, when its eyes are opened, we will place it in the hands of those whom God has constituted as the guardians and doctors of souls, who are also, in a way, our innkeepers in our pilgrimage here below, so as to give our errant and famished spirits the holy word for nourishment and the hope of a better world for a shield."[103] Ozanam was convinced he was called to this "sublime vocation God has given us."[104] This letter to Curnier remains one of the most eloquent expressions of the layperson's call to ministry in the world and dramatically reveals the depth of Ozanam's faith.

In October 1835 he again wrote to Curnier, expressing a similar vision: "We are still only in our apprenticeship in the art of charity. Let us hope that one day we will become able and assiduous workers. Then, in different circumstances where Providence will have placed us, we will strive to be like those born more blessed and more virtuous around us;

then, when you will share your successes with us, we will reply with ours, and from every spot in France there will arise a harmonious concept of faith and love to the praise of God."[105] Years later, in an 1846 letter to Lallier, Ozanam expressed the following thoughts about this ministry: "Catholics have this happiness: that our cause wills to be served at the same time in different ways, that adapt themselves to the diversity of characters and minds; it requires men of war and men of peace, the crusade of controversy and the proselytism of charity. I admire those who fight gloriously in the breach, but I cannot help preferring for my friends and myself the other ministry, which, if less brilliant, is also less dangerous."[106] By the 1840s the Society of St. Vincent de Paul itself embraced this idea of an apostolate where "the laity participate in the priesthood of priests."[107] In fact, some of the members, including Ozanam, became actively involved with the work of the Catholic Church's Society for the Propagation of the Faith, which looked to advance the Catholic faith around the world. Indeed, Ozanam referred to this work as "the peaceful crusade of the nineteenth century."[108]

Although respectful of church authority, Ozanam was prepared to defend the lay nature and leadership of the Society. In Lyon he first encountered significant challenges to the Society's lay character. He wrote to Lallier about his concerns: "For some time we have been holding frequent meetings . . . to put an end to several serious discussions which have arisen on the part the clergy should play in our affairs. Some are already complaining of invaders, while others still accuse them of indifference and coldness. We have a right wing which would like to live in the shadow of the biretta, and a left wing which is still living according to the *Paroles d'un croyant*.[109] Outside both is your servant who, as you know, is rather centrist, finds himself greatly embarrassed, and calls on the help of your prayers."[110] Ten days later Ozanam again wrote to Lallier, who was secretary-general of the Society, with a report and recommendations. As the president of the Society in Lyon, Ozanam informed the secretary-general of two concerns. The first was a laxity in observing religious celebrations. Some members wanted to "stimulate piety and the spirit of Christian brotherhood" in order to "preserve our conferences from degenerating to welfare bureaus."[111] The second was raised by other members who "were alarmed at certain acts of ecclesiastical protection, which seemed to them outside encroachments, and which could assimilate the Society into certain religious congregations, undoubtedly praiseworthy in themselves, but absolutely different in their end."[112]

Ozanam then offered a solution that would address both concerns by "drawing up unified measures capable of giving our work a character at once profoundly Christian and absolutely lay."[113] Five recommendations followed in his report. The first was that "from the time of the next general assembly, the active chairmanship of the meeting should be exercised not by the pastor of Saint-Pierre but by the president of the Society. . . . A place will be looked for within the two parishes of Saint-Pierre and Saint-Francois to avoid the inconvenience of meeting in a sacristy." The second was that presidents of conferences would still have their proceedings approved by the clergy and would remind their members frequently "that the end of the Society is especially to rekindle and refresh in the youth the spirit of Catholicism, that fidelity to meetings, and union of intention and prayer are indispensible [*sic*] to this end, and that visiting the poor should be the means and not the end of our association." The third was that a request be made to extend to all the members of the Society the benefit of the indulgences from Rome now enjoyed only by the members in Paris. The fourth asked for a modification of the language of the Rule concerning "ecclesiastical superiors": "The paragraph that deals with the deference owed ecclesiastical superiors, contains the following words: 'They will accept with an *absolute docility the direction* that the superiors *will judge proper* to give them.' Once we had received from the president general a clear interpretation, discussion was terminated on the sense which should be given it. But, since these words seem to *exaggerate* the thought they ought to present, the Council of Paris is asked to modify them in a next edition."

The fifth and final recommendation was that the "Council of Paris . . . meet more often and . . . enter into a more active correspondence with the provincial conferences, so as to prevent isolation and extreme individuality in some, and to rekindle languishing zeal in others." The recommendations ended with an acknowledgment that the conferences of Lyon understood "that their strength is in union and that the entire uniqueness of their work is precisely in its universality."[114] Frédéric continued to foster both the spiritual life and lay character of the Society. One year later (1839), in correspondence asking Joseph Arthaud to be president of the conferences in Lyon, he insisted that the Society must "never wish to be either a grouping or a school or an association, unless it be profoundly Catholic without ceasing to be lay." He believed that Arthaud was the right person to ensure the integrity of the Society in Lyon. He further shared with Arthaud his hopes that this lay apostolate could bring a true renewal: "The work of St. Vincent de Paul is growing in importance without stop and . . . a magnificent mission has been given it, that it alone, by the multitude and status of its adherents, by its stable existence in so many diverse ways, and by its abnegation of all philosophical and political interest, can rally youth to the right paths, bring a new spirit little by little to the upper classes and the most influential actions, resist the secret associations which are menacing the civilization of our country, and perhaps in the end save France."[115]

THE CONTROVERSY OVER THE FOUNDATION OF THE SOCIETY

The first Rule of the Society cautioned its lay members that "we must ever avoid giving to our undertaking the name of any particular member, whatever may have been his individual services, or of the places in which we assemble, for fear we may accustom ourselves to look upon it as the work of man. Christian works belong to God alone, the sole Author of all good."[116] Although the first members did not attribute the founding to one person, the question of a founder or founders eventually arose. In part, Ozanam raised the issue by his remarks when Emmanuel Bailly stepped down as president-general in 1844. Self-effacing by nature, Ozanam attributed the foundation to Bailly, referring to Bailly as the *fondateur* (founder).[117] As Marcel Vincent argues, Emmanuel Bailly had been chosen as the first president because "of his age, his authority, and the trust of the young friends," and he played the role of "spiritual animator, of *lay chaplain*"—a role for which he had been well prepared by his work with youth.[118] Of all people, Ozanam appreciated this role that Bailly fulfilled.

A heated controversy, however, began less than three years after Ozanam's death, when Père Lacordaire in an article referred to Ozanam as the "Saint Peter" of the group.[119] His remarks were taken as attributing the role of founder to Ozanam, although Lacordaire never in fact made that claim. Certainly, his remarks implied that Ozanam was the first among the founders, just as Saint Peter was the first among the apostles.[120] But the daily paper *L'Univers*, with its vitriolic editor, Louis Veuillot, jumped on the issue.[121] Veuillot had a running feud with Ozanam since 1843. Ozanam had made the following public statement in a lecture to the Catholic Circle in the presence of the archbishop of Paris: "One must not . . . compromise the saintliness of the cause through the violence of means. . . . It is not a question of humiliating unbelievers but of convincing them." Founded in 1843, the Catholic Circle was a gathering of prominent Catholic intellectual laymen sponsored by the archbishop of Paris. Although Ozanam did not specifically name Veuillot, he thereby called into question Veuillot's methods. Veuillot became a severe critic of Ozanam and especially of Ozanam's work at, and his articles published in, the newspaper *L'Ère nouvelle* in 1848 (discussed in chapter 6). He even accused Ozanam then, and again in 1850, of being too moderate and a deserter from the Catholic cause. Given this background, it is not surprising that Veuillot refused to stand by quietly while Ozanam was praised. Instead he made the case for Bailly as sole founder.[122] Bailly had written the lines in the Rule that instructed members never to attribute the foundation to any one person. He was thus caught in a bit of a bind, but he did not publicly deny Veuillot's assertions. Perhaps Bailly needed a sense of pride and accomplishment; he had experienced serious personal and financial setbacks in the years leading up to this controversy. As Léonce Celier points out, "Having arrived at the end of his service, impoverished, divested of all his enterprises, having resigned his presidency, and witness of the failure of all that he had wanted to do, except the Society of Saint Vincent de Paul, it is quite natural that he [Bailly] delighted in the success of it and was consoled by the thought of the role he had played in it. He would not have expressed this more or less confused feeling, but, the question having been raised outside of him, one could not expect him to publicly obliterate a comforting page from his life."[123]

The controversy continued when a number of Ozanam's Lyonnais friends, members of the Society, published a statement in the press contradicting Veuillot.[124] The intensity of the debate became worrisome for the Council-General of the Society. A special meeting intended to end the dissension was held on February 25, 1856, at which Bailly was present. At that gathering Bailly "denied, in guarded terms, all claims to the title of founder, while expressing the opinion that it was necessary to let the dispute dwindle away by itself without publishing anything on the issue."[125] Unfortunately, Bailly's advice was not followed. A notice was placed in the next "Bulletin" of the Society upholding the idea of a collective founding, but also including the remarks of Ozanam from 1844 that attributed the founding to Bailly.[126] This notice only threw oil on the fire of controversy. Ozanam's Lyonnais friends and supporters made a joint declaration in the *Lyon Gazette* on March 25, 1856: "If it is true that the Society of St. Vincent de Paul has been jointly founded by many, it is none the less true that *Frederick Ozanam* had a *preponderating and decisive* part in that foundation. It was he who shared with M. Le Taillandier the idea of an Association, whose members would join the practice of charitable works to faith: it was he who carried by his *initiative* the majority of the members to adopt that act of devotedness to the poor." It was signed "on the 20th March by Messieurs F. Alday, J. Arthaud, C. Biétrix, A. Bouchacourt, Chaurand, J. Freney, J. Janmot, A. Lacour, L. Lacuria, P. de la Perrière, E. Rieussec, all members of the *first Conference* in Paris in the Parish of St. Etienne-du-Mont." The names of Airne Bouvier in Bourg and Henri Pessonneaux in Paris were added on March 20 and 21.[127]

Before Bailly could be convinced to make a public statement, the situation was further complicated by the unexpected interference of Bailly's children. Bailly's son Vincent de Paul, "who later became one of the prides of the Congregation of the Assumptionists, expressed his indignation with a youthful violence in a letter which has been preserved. This letter accuses Ozanam's friends of an attempt of blackmail."[128] As Ralph Middlecamp notes in his article on the founders, "After the hardships Emmanuel [Bailly] had experienced, it is not surprising that his sons, especially Vincent de Paul, would adamantly defend their father's claim to the honor of founder. It is a controversy that continued to haunt the Society—especially in Paris, where both Ozanam and Bailly were well-known—even after the latter's death. These two friends were noted for their humility, and we could expect that they would have preferred to avoid this controversy."[129] Some twenty-four years after this controversy, as the "Golden Anniversary" of the Society approached, the surviving members of the first conference shared their thoughts on the origins of the Society of St. Vincent de Paul. Frédéric Ozanam's name was mentioned numerous times throughout the remembrances and his role was highlighted, but the title of founder was not attached to him, most likely to avoid any further controversy.[130] In 1883 Paul Lamache, one of the original seven members, wrote the following: "It was Ozanam who first spoke to me of that Conference; that he was its soul as he had been of the Conference of Literature . . . ; a very big share of the recognition is owed to the venerable . . . [Monsieur] Bailly, and without him, without his experience and help, the formation of the first conference would perhaps have stayed at the stage of generous desires; but *certainly* without Ozanam, this first conference would never have been born."[131]

In 1913, when the Society celebrated its hundredth anniversary, the important role of Frédéric Ozanam was more clearly defined: "The Society of Saint Vincent de Paul had . . . seven founders: the six students and Bailly, but Ozanam is the principal one because he is the one who best understood the intention and worked the most actively to realize it."[132] Indeed, of all the members, Ozanam had "the most profound concept of charity."[133] The controversy was finally laid to rest. Bailly and the other five members were rightly recognized for their roles in the founding, and Ozanam also received his rightful recognition as the principal founder and, most importantly, the Society's "radiant source of inspiration."[134] As the historian Charles Mercier astutely commented, "From the first seven members, it is Ozanam who progressively commands attention as the one who symbolizes the foundation. The commencement of valuing one founding member, and the omission of the others is on the whole a classic phenomenon of a collective memory. . . . Remembering Frédéric Ozanam as founder gives a new dynamism to the Society of Saint Vincent de Paul as it proves the success of the Centenary."[135] For family and friends of Ozanam, the recognition was "an assurance that his memory will not be forgotten."[136]

The controversy over the founding was an unfortunate incident in the long history of the Society. Despite the rancor, the Society is a lasting tribute to the bold commitment of the original seven members who founded the first conference of charity and to the exemplary vision and leadership of Frédéric Ozanam, who inspired the fledgling Society of St. Vincent de Paul to respond faithfully and efficaciously to the call of both charity and justice. Ozanam understood best that despite the various differences among conferences, "like divergent spokes touching the same center, so our varied efforts tending toward divers ends come together in one and the same charitable mind and proceed from the same principle."[137] For him, the "Little Society" had the power to transform the world: "the power of association is great because it is the power of love."[138] His entire life was a testimony to this belief.

CHAPTER 4

Husband and Father

On June 23, 1841, at the church of Saint-Nizier in Lyon, Antoine Frédéric Ozanam wed Marie-Joséphine-Amélie Soulacroix. Ozanam's older
brother Alphonse was "at the altar . . . raising his priestly hands, and
at his feet, his young brother, making the responses to the liturgi-
cal prayers."[1] Frédéric was already twenty-eight years old, and Amélie
was nearly twenty.[2] Frédéric's marriage surprised some of his friends
because he had been averse to marriage. On that day in June, however, it
was apparent that he was happy. He may have married to overcome the
loneliness he experienced after his parents' deaths, he may have married
because he needed emotional support, and he may even have married
because he had watched so many of his friends enter into married life,
but once he wed Amélie Soulacroix he discovered the power of conjugal
love. He found a true partner who made him a better man, who brought
out all of his best traits, and to whom he became deeply devoted. In loving Amélie he came to understand fully the meaning of the scriptural
passage about two becoming one.

VIEWS ON WOMEN AND MARRIAGE, 1834–38

One of the earliest references to marriage in Ozanam's correspondence comes in a response to his friend Léonce Curnier's impending nuptial day. Ozanam wrote: "The great action you are contemplating at present will only serve to redouble your zeal and your strength. 'When two or three are gathered together in my name,' says the Savior, 'there am I in the midst of them.' It is in that divine name that you will prepare to unite yourself to a wise and pious wife: the promise will be accomplished in you both. In giving your love to someone who will be justifiably dear, you will not withdraw it from the poor and miserable whom you loved first."[3] In this last line Frédéric gave voice to a question that he was struggling to answer: Will marriage distract one too much from the ultimate purpose for which one's life is destined by God? In his next words, he waxed eloquent on the topic of married love, a topic on which he had no direct experience at this point: "Love possesses something of the divine nature, which gives itself without diminishing, which shares itself without division, which multiplies itself, which is present in many places at once, and whose intensity is increased in the measure that it gains in extension. In your wife you will first love God, whose admirable and precious work she is, and then humanity, that race of Adam whose pure and lovable daughter she is." Then Frédéric, so often plagued by loneliness and isolation in his student days, described for Léonce the pleasures of such a partnership. His words suggest to the reader that he himself might have begun to feel the need for such pleasures and that he had also begun to long for them, despite any protestations to the contrary: "You will draw comfort from her tenderness on bad days, you will find courage in her example in perilous times, you will be her guardian angel, she will be yours. You will then no longer experience the weaknesses, discouragements and terrors which have seized upon you at certain times of your life: for you will no longer be alone. . . . The alliance you are about to contract will be an immortal alliance: what God joins together, what He has insisted no man separate, He will not Himself separate, and in heaven He will invest with the same glory those who here below were companions in the same exile."[4]

As if awakening from a dream, Frédéric immediately recognized his lack of credentials to speak on this subject: "But I babble a tongue I do not yet know, I speak of things not yet revealed to me. Imagination has developed early in me, sensibility is very tardy; but if my age be that of passions, I am just beginning to feel their stirrings. My poor head has already suffered greatly, but my heart has not yet known any affections but that of blood and friendship."[5] Yet he hinted that these stirrings had unsettled his mind, causing him to think about his future: "Nevertheless, it seems to me that I sometimes experience the early symptoms of a new order of sentiment, and I am afraid. I feel in myself a great emptiness which neither friendship nor study fill. I do not know who will come to fill it: will it be God? Will it be another creature?"[6] He even identified the characteristics of his own ideal spouse: "I pray that she will bring with her what is needed of temporal advantages and exterior charms so that she will leave no place for any regret; but I pray especially that she will come with a fine soul, that she brings great virtue, that she is a great deal better than I am, that she lifts me up and not drags me down, that she be courageous, because I am often timid, that she be fervent, because I am often lukewarm in the things of God, that finally she be compassionate, so that I need not blush in her presence for my inferiority. There are my desires, my dreams; but, as I have told you, nothing is more hidden than my own future."[7] His search would last another six years until in 1841 he discovered his ideal spouse.

At the age of twenty-two, Frédéric was still caught up in his studies and unwilling to reach a final decision on marriage. In fact, he frankly admitted that he was not inclined, like Curnier, "to light the candles at the altar of hymen." Instead he prepared to brace himself against any temptation to wed: "To fortify myself against such a fate, and to inoculate myself against such a contagion, to steep myself in the love of solitude and liberty, I have just concluded a pilgrimage with my brother to the monks of the Grand Chartreuse."[8] After the unexpected death of his father in 1837, thoughts of his future again took hold of him, but the prospect of marriage still remained unattractive: "I envy the lot of those who devote themselves entirely to God and humanity. And on the other hand, the question of marriage presents itself frequently to my mind; and it never departs without leaving behind unbelievable repugnances. I am weaker than many others, and the wanderings of my imagination have the power of leading my heart far astray. Nevertheless I feel that there is a virile virginity which is not without honor and grace, and there seems to me a kind of abdication and opprobrium in the conjugal union." At this stage in his life, Frédéric's view of women was less than flattering: "It could be that there is some unjust disrespect for women [in my thoughts]. . . . While the Blessed Virgin and my mother . . . bring me to pardon the daughters of Eve many things, I admit that . . . I do not understand them. Their sensitivity is sometimes admirable, but their intelligence is of a light and despairing inconsequence. Have you ever seen conversation more capriciously interrupted, less logical than theirs? And to bind oneself to an association without reserve and without end, with a human, mortal, infirm and miserable creature, however perfect she be! It is this perpetuity of the bond, especially, which is a thing of terror for me."[9]

Ozanam was not impervious to the attractions of the opposite sex. Although he wrote Curnier that his "heart has not yet known any affections but that of blood and friendship," there are certainly intimations in some of Ozanam's letters, especially those to his close friend François Lallier, that, like most young men, Ozanam struggled with an awakening sexuality. The historian Gérard Cholvy points to references in the correspondence such as "falls that a miserable desire does not always prevent," and "this perpetual battle in the lower part" as evidence of this.[10] In 1834 Ozanam shared with Lallier intimate concerns that he has had "the misfortune of fully understanding these painful combats" and that "his conscience had to suffer terrible storms."[11] These comments and pieces of evidence, according to Cholvy, offer important insights into Frédéric's struggle between the choice to lead a life of chastity, perhaps as a priest, or to enter into married life with a suitable spouse.[12] A letter to his friend Auguste Le Taillandier on August 19, 1838, provides further insight into his reluctance to marry. In it he congratulated Le Taillandier on his recent marriage: "I have known for a month as coming, of the great solemnity which you tell me is over, and which marks a new era in your life. Your youth was too meritorious not to close with a happy event which itself is about to serve as the point of departure for still better days." He then wrote: "I do not feel for you those fears that cast a bit of melancholy into the hearts of friends present at nuptial feasts. There is often apprehension that the new cares of father of the family will make him forget the remembrances of being a co-disciple; it is obvious that his door will always be open, but there is fear that there is little place left in his thoughts. Yours are too magnanimous, dear friend, for a like calamity to befall us! You have no need to reassure me of it."[13] In these last lines Ozanam clearly expressed his ongoing fear that marriage and the duties of both husband and father could be a distraction from the commitment to the Society of St. Vincent de Paul and the circle of friends devoted to its mission. It was a fear that he shared for himself as well as others.

PRIESTHOOD OR MARRIAGE, 1839–41

After the death of his mother in the fall of 1839, Frédéric's indecision intensified. He confided at Christmas to François Lallier: "My perplexity is very great: already they are speaking to me on all sides about marriage. I do not yet know my own mind sufficiently to come to a solution. Give me your advice: you know the responsibilities and the consolations of the state, you know my character."[14] He was torn between entering the priesthood, particularly the Dominican Order, or married life.[15] Lallier offered him the following advice: "The courage to live alone in chastity? That's the question. If you have this courage, choose the holy career of a priest, doctor, missionary, preacher, pilgrim of science and faith."[16] He continued with a warning: "But the purity of body ought to be entire . . . chastity is both a punishment and a reward. . . . Do you feel the strength to overcome the unruly desires of the body? If you have any doubt yourself, Marriage is desirable."[17]

Frédéric was being spoken to "on all sides about marriage" because his friends sensed his desperate loneliness and "sympathised with his isolation, which, indeed, showed itself plaintively in all his correspondence. He was obviously lonely and bored by the side of his own hearth."[18] To his cousin Henri Pessonneaux, he complained in 1840: "In the measure that the generation which preceded us and protected us . . . is falling away and leaving us, newly come to manhood, face to face with the enemy, we need to close our ranks, and seeing ourselves vigorously guarding one another, we shall attack head-on the obstacles and perils of life with the greatest courage. And that is so strongly felt in the difficult days in which we find ourselves that the ordinary attachments of marriage and fatherhood no longer suffice rather generous souls, and going out from the domestic sanctuary where they come together to relax and pray, they continue to search in associations of another kind the strength to do battle."[19] Ozanam certainly thought of himself as one of these "generous souls." As late as the summer of 1840 he was still cautioning Lallier that he never intended to marry: "I rejoice even more in total freedom, freedom sometimes troublesome, in the sense that one is exposed to the matrimonial speculations of others and finds himself compromised without being aware by the most embarrassing advances."[20]

There is no doubt that Ozanam was a tough nut to crack on the subject of matrimony. But crack he would. The person who knew how to do it was none other than Abbé Noirot, his former philosophy teacher in the collège royal. When Ozanam sought his advice, Noirot did not hesitate to recommend marriage. The Abbé knew all too well Ozanam's sensitive nature; priesthood would never offer him the kind of emotional support he required. Noirot had also identified a potential prospect— Marie-Joséphine-Amélie Soulacroix, the daughter of the rector of the Academy of Lyon, Monsieur Jean-Baptiste Soulacroix. But he was careful not to frighten Ozanam away. Noirot was subtle; he arranged for a chance meeting.[21] Ozanam had contact with Monsieur Soulacroix, who was his immediate superior at the academy, where Ozanam held his chair of commercial law.[22] On one visit to the Soulacroix home, Noirot accompanied Ozanam and seized the opportunity to introduce him to Madame Soulacroix, who was in the drawing-room. As he entered the room, Frédéric noticed a young woman, Amélie Soulacroix, attentively caring for her paralyzed brother, Théophile. Mesmerized by this picture of a loving sister displaying great tenderness, Frédéric was hopelessly smitten. He could not take his eyes off Amélie.[23] Noirot's instincts had been correct. Amélie had all of the traits necessary to captivate this elusive young man. She was educated well by her father and was a superb musician, yet had also been instructed by her mother in those things necessary to make a home both dignified and charming.[24] From the moment he encountered her, Frédéric found every excuse and opportunity to visit the Soulacroix home in the hope of catching another glimpse of Amélie.[25] He had once been determined never to fall into the trap of marriage, but when he did fall, he fell hard and fell willingly.

Noirot left little to chance. He actually broached the possibility of a union of the two young people with Monsieur Soulacroix. He found a receptive ear. Soulacroix admired Ozanam and had already helped to advance his career in Lyon. He had even recently raised Ozanam's salary.[26] He and his family assumed that if they married, the couple would reside in Lyon. There was even an opportunity for Ozanam to combine the chair of foreign literature with that of commercial law. Through his prospective father-in-law's influence, he was offered the additional position at Lyon. The combined income of the two positions would ensure an annual amount of 15,000 francs for the young couple. It meant security.[27]

Circumstances, however, had changed. An enticing opportunity to teach at the Sorbonne was a temptation too great for Frédéric to resist. Earlier in 1840 he had been encouraged by the Minister of Education, Victor Cousin, to enter a special competition for a newly established chair of foreign literature at the Sorbonne. Cousin desperately wanted the competition to be "brilliant." Frédéric had less than five months to prepare, but he agreed to accept the challenge. When the day of the competition arrived, in the fall of 1840, Ozanam faced seven other professors, all of whom had distinct advantages over him.[28] As Ozanam wrote his friend Lallier, "When the dreaded day came, [we were placed] under lock and key in a hall of the Sorbonne, with eight hours before us, for a Latin dissertation."[29] The assigned topic was the reasons why the progress of tragedy in Roman literature was halted. The next day the competitors faced another eight hours of writing, this time in French, on the historical merit of the *oraisons funèbres* (funeral orations) of the French bishop and theologian Jacques-Bénigne Bossuet. These written arguments were followed by three days of oral examinations in the form of lectures on Greek, Latin, and French texts. There was also to be one full day assigned to oral examination lectures on English, Italian, German, and Spanish literature. If this burden of preparation were not enough, the eight competing professors drew thesis subjects for a final round of oral presentations. Ozanam's pick was one of the most difficult: the topic of the Latin and Greek Scholiasts.[30] His presentation of two hours on this subject was considered to be of such an excellent quality that he took the first prize. Normally the winner would have been called at a later date to take the position for which he had competed. Ozanam's successful performance, however, brought him an early invitation from a distinguished professor of foreign literature, Monsieur Fauriel, "to supply for him [take over his class] at the opening of the forthcoming term."[31] This was not a permanent teaching position, but it was an opportunity.

His success in the competition led Frédéric to think twice about the chair of foreign literature at Lyon that was now his for the asking. He was pressed by his friend Jean-Jacques Ampère to make a quick decision.[32] As he often had done in the past, Frédéric wrote to Lallier in October 1840: "Heavy sacrifices have to be made, cruel partings to be endured, business and family complications to be solved, all that is more than enough to terrify one of ordinary energy. It is fortunate that the appreciation of my weakness makes me lift my eyes to Him who strengthens. Up to the present I asked for light to know His will; I ask now for the courage to do it."[33] He understood that he was undertaking a "new and perilous career."[34] Moreover, he had to secure the approval of the Soulacroix family. Abbé Noirot had been negotiating the terms of a marriage agreement since the summer; now it was up to Frédéric to seal the arrangement.[35] Ozanam visited his future father-in-law and made his case. Paris would hold opportunities he could not have in Lyon, such as rapid advancement, close connections to famous scholars and thinkers, the best libraries, and the finest students.[36] No doubt the work of the Society of St. Vincent de Paul also featured in his decision. Soulacroix decided to leave the final decision to his daughter. Frédéric explained to Amélie that he would have to abandon the mission in life he had dreamed of fulfilling if he stayed in Lyon. He concluded by asking for her trust. She placed her hands in his and declared that he had her complete confidence.[37] The die was now cast.

According to Frédéric's older brother, Abbé Ozanam, "When the Abbé Noirot communicated to my brother the assent of his principal [Monsieur Soulacroix] to the consideration of marriage, Frederick could not believe it, so far below that choice did he regard himself, so stunned was he by his good fortune."[38] Frédéric rejoiced, for "the woman of his dreams was to be his prize."[39] On November 24, 1840, the families met to celebrate and formalize the engagement.[40] Monsieur Soulacroix "took the hands of the engaged couple and with overflowing heart, held them to his own, as if to knit those bonds which the Church was to consecrate later."[41] The Abbé Ozanam quickly perceived the goodness of Amélie. She was well suited for his brother: "*Amélie* was the name of the one who made Frédéric happy. A name whose sweetness responded admirably to the fineness and delicacy of her features as to the friendliness of her character. An even more harmonious name in our ears because she was also now like one of our aunts who would become something for us of a second mother since we were orphans."[42] Frédéric had found a new home and family and soon "transferred his affection to his parents-in-law," referring to them as "my mother" and "my father."[43] He readily embraced Amélie's two brothers, Théophile and Charles, as his own. His brother Alphonse was correct about his happiness. His good fortune was also shared with his friends: "You will find me tenderly in love; but I don't hide it from myself, even though I cannot prevent myself from laughing about it sometimes; I thought my heart was made more of stone."[44] To his friend Lallier, he referred to his new fiancée as his "guardian angel to console my solitude."[45] Amélie Soulacroix had indeed melted the heart of this once solitary bachelor.

THE SEPARATION OF THE BETROTHED COUPLE, JANUARY–JUNE 1841

Because of his decision to accept the position in Paris, Frédéric began teaching in January, resulting in a fairly long separation for the two lovers before their June wedding. Both recognized that correspondence, though imperfect, was their only means to connect during Ozanam's absence. Later Amélie referred to their correspondence as "blessed" because it enabled them to know one another better.[46] In her letters to Frédéric, she was not afraid to share her thoughts and fears: "I was thinking about the day when I will be there, before God and you at my side . . . we will say Yes and that will be for always, forever! These words seem to me still a little scary, but when I reread your letters, your last especially, I am reassured because you promise me to make me happy, you assure me of your affection that will always endure."[47] Frédéric indeed would continue to assure her of his love. He corresponded regularly with Amélie because he found in it both the consolation he needed and a confirmation of the traits he had hoped to find in a wife. For him she exhibited "a serene faith because it is enlightened, a purity whose visible reflection is grace, a charity which can see no evil, merciful to poverty, suffering, even (am I right?) to the pangs of exile. These are in a word the admirable traits of moral character I see taking form more each day, emerging little by little from the cloud of mystery and modesty with which a young girl's life constantly veils itself. The more the beloved figure comes near bathed in clearer light the happier I am with the choice Providence has made for me." Her goodness also prodded Frédéric to search his own soul: "At the same time, I feel less worthy, am envious of the virtues which are still great strangers to me, but I console myself with the thought that they will be an example and safeguard for me, a merit in which I shall share."[48] His loneliness and his pain while separated from her are evident in his letters:

> Exhausted with fatigue, I could not rest because one does not rest upon himself. The child puts his head on his mother's knees; the sister washes the dirt from her young brother's face; the wife may seem to support her hand on her husband's arm, but that hand which he presses to him supports his heart. We have the external power but it is you who provide the secret energy from within. There is a slot which you alone can fill, and when you fail to fill it there ensues weakness and injury; and I experience in a regular way the fitness of this aphorism grown trite in the conversational language of sentiment. I bear the scar of a pain which will not go away. Melancholy overcomes me, and when I measure the five months remaining against the slow passing of the last forty days, I fear I shall not be able to hold out to the end. Every distraction importunes me, no conversation pleases me, unless I can clothe it with the remembrance of you. The piano under strange fingers annoys me. . . . But when the lines signed by you arrive in their soft envelope, then this delicious vision once more haunts my solitude. I see you again not with all the attraction of reality but under the idealized forms of sweetness, intelligence, and simplicity which ravish me.[49]

At the end of this letter, written on January 24, 1841, he opened up his heart to Amélie: "Frankly it is quite natural for me—a poor young man so isolated from the world, ever in rather bleak surroundings, stranger for the most part to the joys of life—to be deeply moved when the will of Providence introduces me to a pious young girl, loving and pure, joining high character to the culture of the mind, and [trimmed] with that external splendor which never fails to attract attention; . . . [and] when she herself gives her consent and, scorning the homage the world could render her, prefers to come and to embellish in adopting it, my solitary and toilsome destiny."[50]

In correspondence to Amélie six days later, Frédéric described a picture of their wedded life: "I will reflect then that this time next year my return from the Sorbonne will be happier, that another's voice will greet my steps at the door, another's hand will squeeze mine by the fireside. And then . . . I will not set myself to toiling over some business letter, but take the necessary ease for a complete unburdening; I will slip away from problems, distractions, outside worries, in order to be more natural, truer, in a word more *myself*, because I will be more yours."[51] He lovingly confided his desire to become closer to her: "You make me happy. I will be even more so if on your side you wish to exercise a little more the rights which are yours: to ask me questions, to scold me when needed, to form me in advance for the sweet duties I will take upon myself in the near future, to allow me a glimpse of the job's requirements—presumptious [sic] requirements for my part, but you will make them easy—the job of procuring happiness. Well! you will not take offense at my occasional frankness in expressing my feelings, nor at the vividness of my words when I speak of my respectful but always deep tenderness."[52] Amélie's humor and wit also helped the anxious Frédéric cope with the anxieties of preparing and delivering new lectures at the Sorbonne.[53] With each passing letter during these months of separation, the closeness of the couple was fostered, while their understanding of each other was enhanced.

By early February some of the formality began to diminish, and Frédéric became more poetic: "When Noah was shut up in his ark in that frightening solitude the deluge had made around him, the dove came on occasion with the olive branch which promised him deliverance. As for me, in my Parisian desert, in my Sorbonne ark where I find myself in the midst of animals of every species (I do not refer to my colleagues), your letters are the green branch of hope. Only, why must they come alone and the beautiful dove herself not bring them! Ah! if some day she comes to sit upon my hand, as on the hand of the patriarch, I will do as he did, I will draw her inside quickly lest she fly away, and the window will be opened no more."[54] He was enamored with her mementos that she had recently given him: "The little ring whose red cornelian comes loose in my hand, the medallion which I wear over my heart, the letters pressed between leaves of velour and satin in the center of the desk on which I write; the beloved name Amelie which rises so often on my lips while a vanishing image passes across my memory, these are so many cords which bind and at the same time support me. I am happy and proud to wear them."[55] And he was immune to the good-natured teasing of some of his colleagues, picturing himself in a chivalric metaphor as her devoted medieval knight: "I love the vowed title of fiancé with which my friends laughingly greet me: your knight joyously dons your colors when he descends to the lists. If a prayer or two rise before the altar of the Blessed Virgin of Lyon on Saturday, here the cherished ringlet, the lock of hair, is gazed on, and then kissed: that brings luck. It is true that in the course of a lecture if certain words of feeling issue from me with some heat, I see some well-known faces in the audience assume a malicious expression and neighbors give one another the elbow. But they are not the less pleased for it and the waggishness of the compliments they make me is not offensive."[56]

At the end of this February letter, Frédéric painted an imaginative picture of life after their June wedding: "It fastens you to my arm in delightful walks on summer evenings. It takes you to the shore of Swiss lakes, to Venetian gondolas, around that lovely Florence which is indeed like a jewel in a basket of flowers, to Rome amid the ruins, to Naples and the length of bright Mediterranean coasts. Then a little later, Paris and the joyous care of our own establishment, the modest happiness of a young household, the little circle of chosen friends, and the sweeter hours still of intimacy, and those long winter evenings too short for our conversations."[57] The tone of this letter suggests that barriers of formality had begun to break apart; the two had begun to form a lasting bond of intimacy and trust.

Frédéric loved to listen to the songs Amélie skillfully played on the piano. In fact, he asked her not to play a certain favorite ballad for anyone but him when he left Lyon for Paris. In late February she wrote that she had honored his request. She had refused to play the ballad for another young man because it was exclusively reserved for her fiancé's ears. Her thoughtful action pleased the ever sensitive Frédéric and inspired him to write back: "That graceful name of Amelie seems to be this latest time more charming than ever: you have surrounded it for me with a very lovely setting, that title of fiancée which suits it better than a tiara does a duchess. It is different with my name, which has special need of a companion to pardon its awkwardness and gravity."[58] He closed by signing himself: "Your fiancé who loves you very much."[59] Although he loved her music, unfortunately Frédéric was not an accomplished dancer. When later in May Amélie raised the prospect of dancing at the impending wedding, he humorously confessed his complete ineptitude: "To the number of [my] exterior imperfections you could add the complete ineptitude of the individual concerned for dance steps, nor are they themselves subject to improvement. . . . I cannot oblige you by returning a passable dancer. But, . . . if dancing must inaugurate things, I am equally ridiculous whether I dance badly or not at all. My humility is not equal to resigning itself to ridicule on such a solemn occasion nor would you yourself wish it. Besides, however proper the protocol, . . . my older brother would be rather out of place, my younger brother could take no part (he is no cleverer than I). . . . There, I admit a calamity."[60] For all the accomplishments of the Ozanam family, apparently dancing was not one of them.

In April 1841 Frédéric returned on Palm Sunday to Lyon for twelve days.[61] He reveled in the time spent with Amélie, but the visit passed too quickly. He found himself once again exiled in Paris until June 21. Of course, he penned a moving letter to his fiancée:

Can you believe that only a week has passed since the day of parting, since the moment when on your threshold I still held your hand, since I threw myself into that fatal carriage, looking back time and again at the walls of Lyon from which I have exiled myself for two months? Can you believe that seven more dragging weeks must pass before the blessed hour which will unite me to you? I dare hope that you have some pain in thinking of it; as for me, I do not know how to reconcile myself. *Mon Dieu!* What must purgatory be, what suffering, after having seen the Eternal Beauty face to face, to be separated from it for ages, if absence brings so much bitterness to the affections here below! To have gazed upon you so for some days, to have been able to sit beside you, to look into your eyes, to read your smile, to hear that sweet tongue whose accents are like rose-dew to the dryness of my soul, to exchange all my thoughts with yours in silence. . . . And then, after so much joy, to have left it at one stroke, to have allowed myself to be carried far away from you, and to find myself once more in my loneliness, in this desert of aridity and boredom assigned to me, and to wait thus through the whole springtime when nature does not wait to bedeck herself with flowers, when the heart no longer waits for anything in order to love. . . . Thus, while preparing my lecture just now, I came upon the story of a poor banished knight: he sends his beloved a symbolic present of honeysuckle blossoms wrapped in a branch of hazel; these verses, too charming not to repeat to you, and which I have modernized a bit, are inscribed there. They are by a woman of the twelfth century, Marie de France.[62]

In May the couple began to exchange correspondence more often. Amélie believed that her fiancé needed the additional attention. She was correct in her assessment. The more frequent correspondence lifted Frédéric's spirits and soothed his melancholy nature: "For while I was indicating last Tuesday that this weekly correspondence would be from now on at too long an interval, when I was begging you to shorten it, you were . . . preparing a very sweet surprise for me for Wednesday. At first the unexpected letter raised that feeling of uneasiness you know as characteristic of me. But when I had torn open the envelope and . . . had read those charming pages all perfumed with sweet and affection-ate things, I sighed with pleasure and the grateful kiss was pressed more tenderly than ever on the consoling paper. If then the consciousness of a good act is not without charm for you, if my desires are not indiscreet, repeat what you have done."[63] He recalled pressing her hand in his at Easter: "Ah! when I pressed your hand in mine, it seemed that nothing could again rob me of it; yet behold now my lips only too happy to brush the page your fingers folded. . . . But another day will come when I shall be allowed to see you again, and on that day it will be your heart that I shall press to mine and then we shall see whether there is any power in the world strong enough to tear you away!"[64]

In that same letter he honestly recounted to her his weaknesses:

A tender love of God, an active good will toward men, a right and unbending conscience in regard to oneself, these are the elements of a truly Christian life, and you shall not be slow to learn all that is want-ing to me in this three-fold regard. Side by side with a usually lively sensibility, you will find a despairing coldness toward holy things, with mild inclinations toward impatience, general aptitudes for good imparted by education, and yet comprised of inertia and idleness, resolutions reduced to no more than wishes, and each morning's proposals dissipating each evening. And then the vanity, weak point of people like me, the constant preoccupation with self, apparently justified by the demands of advancement and fortune, but in whose shadow hides the universal root of evil, egoism.[65]

With a humorous bit of self-mockery, Frédéric admitted to her that his long letters filled with "my plethora of words" clearly proved that "taciturnity" was not one of his faults.[66] Amélie was destined to be his "guardian angel," the one who would steadfastly guide him toward being a better and more virtuous person. He firmly believed that she was sent to be "the guide and companion of my future years." As he confessed, he now fully understood the "words spoken to the young Tobias in sacred scripture: 'Hold back no longer: for she has been destined for you for all Eternity; she will walk in the same paths with you, and the merciful Lord will save you by means of each other.... And ... from that moment Tobias loved her, and his soul felt itself drawn to her with an infinite power.'" He concluded with this simple admission: "The end of this story is also the end of mine."[67] Ozanam sincerely hoped "to arrive at that union of souls which is the marvelous work of love, to draw ever nearer each day by mutual imitation of whatever is good, to bind closer together by reciprocal devotion two wills that are now but one, to lose and find oneself in each other, and to do it so well that only God could distinguish and recognize them, but without ever separating them!"[68] His hope would not be in vain. The two became "one" long before the wedding in June. Amélie was the first to use the term "us" when writing to Frédéric in February: "When you have some worries, some sorrows, come to me to confide them. Abandon the me and make me share all in order to be able to say: 'Us.'"[69] Frédéric gave eloquent voice to his acceptance of this request in March:

Yes, there is a happiness which is neither in fortune nor in the noise of the world, a quiet, sweet and deep happiness which comes from the union of souls and that the outside storms would not be able to trouble.

God keeps it for those whom he loves best. I know it, but I thank you for having said it; I thank you for having believed it; I thank you for having enough faith in me to believe that without these vulgar means of wealth and pleasure, I would have the power to make you happy. Be blessed for this confidence and for having shown it to me; this selfish solitude does not suit the needs of my character; I need the moral circle of family, the feeling of "Us." You are good and charitable to allow it, and you will be taken on your word. From now on, we will say "us": there will no longer be any isolation, and it will no longer be the simple presence of the remembrance of one in the thought of the other; this will be the already complete mingling of two destinies, and there where the steps of a single person faltered, two people will stand firm.[70]

His desire to be close to Amélie caused him to become frantic when he accidentally lost the locket of her hair that she had given to him. He called it his "talisman." Frédéric begged her forgiveness, seeking another ringlet to replace the one he lost. He teasingly wrote: "I would imagine myself in the attitude of my last confession: kneeling before you, head hanging, my hands in yours, your repentant knight, gracious suzeraine, would humbly confess his misdeed."[71] Amélie in turn teased him, feigning anger but readily acquiescing to his request: "But you *play acted* at anger so well, with so much grace and gaiety that from the first lines I ceased to believe in your resentment. . . . You made a fair semblance of wishing to be implored. I knew you too well, knew you to be too soft-hearted and easy to have supposed that you could long keep up an assumed role and prolong my already overlong suffering. And you ask me whether I am happy, whether I still love you? And how could I not love so affectionate a playfulness, so sweet a sensibility? . . . Above all, how not thrill with joy and pride while musing that so many merits and charms have been brought together by nature, and cultivated by education, only to belong so soon to me?"[72] He promised her in return for the ringlet to send his coat of arms which she had requested, remarking that it "will soon be yours and with it I will give you something worthier I have to offer you, the name it serves. Oh! be assured that it is a fine name and was my mother's and grandmother's. It is the name those good and respectable ladies bore who prayed from the beautiful Book of Hours given into your hands today. It is a name which the angels of heaven have often repeated with praise, which here below numberless children have repeated with love. The poor hold it in benediction still."[73]

In a letter shortly before the wedding, Frédéric offered to Amélie what he thought was best in him: "I do not come to offer you the pleasure of an amicable dealing, or the prestige of a brilliant fortune, or fame, or rest, or anything of that which attracts the greatest number of people. And yet, I am still counting that my so humble offering will be well received, for it is what the Divine Majesty receives from us, what it prefers, the only thing that it asks, the only thing that deserves to be offered to you: I come to offer you the will of a man, a just and loyal will, the will to be good so that you will be happy."[74] In turn Amélie recalled the Canticle of Canticles in her last letter to Frédéric before the marriage: "Come along, come without fear, I believe at times that I hear you arrive and my heart beats so strong that it seems it will explode."[75] Both she and he would never be disappointed in each other.

WEDDING, HONEYMOON, AND MARRIED LIFE, 1841–43

At eight o'clock in the morning on Wednesday June 23, 1841, a day during which "the rain fell in torrents,"[76] Frédéric knelt at the altar of the church of Saint-Nizier in Lyon next to Amélie, "a white-veiled young girl" who was "pious as an angel, and . . . as tender and affectionate as a loving friend."[77] During the ceremony, perhaps he reflected back on the words he had written to Auguste Le Taillandier some three years earlier: "It seems to me that the pomp of a wedding, so sad and insignificant for the common run of men, ought to be, when it joins two young Christian souls, a kind of triumph where virtue, victorious over the passions and troubles of youth, receives as reward the sweetest happiness here below. Love outside Christianity is an idol and therefore a demon: within Christianity it cleanses itself, and its baptismal name is charity; it sanctifies those it unites. The family . . . should be the image of the Church: the husband and father holds the place of Christ. . . . this magnificent model of marriage."[78] Present at the ceremony were both of his brothers, his remaining family members, and many of his friends and comrades.[79] Amélie's family, including her brothers Théophile and Charles, also attended the ceremony.[80] The only person who did not seem to approve of the marriage was Père Lacordaire, who was disappointed that Ozanam had decided against entering the Dominican Order. In a later interview with Pope Pius IX, Lacordaire informed the pope that Ozanam had fallen into the trap of marriage. With a quick wit, Pius IX put Lacordaire in his place by replying that he was unaware that Christ had instituted six sacraments and a trap.[81]

Many of the members of the Society of St. Vincent de Paul were present at the nuptial celebration. Unfortunately, both Emmanuel Bailly and François Lallier were unable to attend. Frédéric wrote to Lallier five days later: "O my dear Lallier! you, the companion of my toils and weariness, you, the consoler of my evil days, why were you not there? I would have asked you to place your signature to the commemorative deed of this great *fête*. I would have presented you to the charming bride who has been given to me, and she would have greeted you with that smile of hers that enchants every one."[82] But Frédéric was far too joyful to be disappointed in Lallier's absence or in the torrents of rain that fell: "I do not count the days or hours. Time does not exist for me. What matters the future? Happiness in the present is eternity. I understand what heaven means."[83] He informed Lallier that his soul was finally calm and serene where before it had been so unsettled and so prone to suffering and self-doubt. Moreover, he asked his friend to help him always to be "good and grateful."[84] Lallier understood completely. This loyal friend, who had shared in most of Frédéric's sorrows and uncertainties, most likely smiled now while reading his dear friend's letter filled with such joy.

The Ozanams honeymooned in Italy, visiting Naples, Sicily, and Rome. Frédéric's correspondence with his family reveals the excitement the couple experienced in seeing the monuments of Greek and Roman antiquity. But the highlight of their first marital adventure was the pilgrimage to Rome, where they had a special audience with the current pope, Gregory XVI. The pope received them warmly.[85] Frédéric wrote to his cousin Henri Pessonneaux: "Yesterday we had the honor of being received by the Pope. His Holiness deigned to admit us to an audience devoid of all protocol; it was not the rather awesome majesty of the tiara, but the simplicity and sweetness of a father. During the fifteen-minute conversation he spoke to me of France with singularly moving kindness, and of my studies with all the learning and presence of mind of a scholar speaking in his special field. I received his blessing for myself, my family, and the

Society of St. Vincent de Paul which he knows and loves."[86] To Amélie's parents, whom he now referred to as "my dear parents," he sent the following remarks about his new wife: "This trip, by testing Amélie's ways, patience, sweetness, and devotions so greatly, is demonstrating to me how much she is capable of. But, even more, you could not believe what she does for me by her presence in other circumstances, what more gracious hospitality I especially encounter when she is with me, how she interests and captivates from the very first."[87] The honeymoon had also offered the opportunity for the couple "to kneel at the tomb of the holy apostles and pray together before the simple stone which covers the remains of St. Peter," and it provided Frédéric with more essential knowledge for his work: "What the trip to Sicily was for the understanding of antiquity, the stay in Rome was even more for the understanding of Christianity."[88] The two finally reached Marseille at the end of November 1841. After visiting with family in Lyon, they arrived in Paris by December 1841 to begin their new life together.[89] They at first settled in a small place on the rue Grenelle-Saint-Germain. But because the heat in the summer was intolerable there, they accepted the kind offer of Monsieur Bailly to rent an apartment in the rue de Fleurus with a lovely view of the Luxembourg Gardens.[90]

Frédéric knew that his wife missed her family in Lyon. On their first Easter together, March 27, 1842, Amélie awoke to a surprise: "Sunday morning, I got up very sad; I was alone; Fred had left early in the morning to attend the end of the retreat. But judge my pleasant surprise when in entering the parlor, I found on the table, surrounded by flowers, a beautiful prayer-book in shagreen, and on the first page some delightful verses of my dear Frédéric. This attention touched me very much."[91] The verses were as follows:

> When I see you pray, on your knees next to me,
> On your lips love, in your blue eyes faith,
> And that your pious heart overflows drop by drop
> Like a too full vase, – I know God is listening to you.
>
> It seems to me that then among your blond hairs
> Escape, badly hidden, luminous rays:
> That a mist of incense plays around you:
> And that an invisible wing has caressed my cheek.

And I finally understand that a brotherly angel
Was given to me from above, like to Tobias
To prevent me, during the journey of life,
From cursing the earth or forgetting heaven.[92]

It was not the first nor would it be the last sign of Frédéric's devotion to Amélie. She remembered affectionately, for example, that during the twelve years they were married he never forgot to give her flowers on the twenty-third of every month, the date of their marriage.[93]

Amélie came to know Frédéric and his simple tastes well: "The small details of material life, well-being, arrangements, comfort, were perfectly indifferent to him. But what touched on the delicacies of the spirit, on the delicacies of feelings, the poetry of life, were of an infinite price. He was indifferent to being badly dressed and badly furnished; a bouquet of flowers on his desk delighted him; a beautiful engraving enraptured him. He could not be consoled if one had forgotten the smallest family birthday."[94] According to Amélie, her "Fred," as she affectionately called him, "was extremely sober, and most often, he did not know what he was eating. And yet it was very important to him that on Sundays, the days of the major Church holy days, and the days of small family reunions, there were some extra foods on the table that he was pleased to order or to buy himself."[95] Perhaps because he had always been held accountable for expenses by his father, Frédéric "loathed foolish expenses and luxury. But he knew never to deprive himself of a trip to visit a beautiful place and a beautiful monument nor resist having flowers."[96] Amélie was not complaining. She felt blessed that her husband always showed her the utmost goodness and kindness. In her opinion, God had bestowed on them a special grace.[97]

Both Amélie and Frédéric hoped to become parents and raise a large family. Unfortunately, this was not to be. Between 1842 and 1843 Amélie experienced two miscarriages, and she spent considerable time recovering with her parents in Lyon. After her first miscarriage, in the summer of 1842, she was slow to return from her visit. During this visit she sat for the marble bust of her that was sculpted by Charles Soulacroix, her artist brother. Her parents, especially her mother, were highly protective of her. Frédéric again felt the pangs of separation he had experienced before his marriage: "How painful it was for me to be separated from you, Amélie. With what deep bonds God unites our hearts!" He wrote to her: "When I saw the carriage that bore you away disappear, I ran to St. Germain L'Auxerrois, to pour out my feelings. I remained for 20 minutes drowned in sorrow and I shed many tears."[98] Frédéric passionately added: "My sweet little companion, I never lose sight of you. . . . I feel the caresses of your fingers so often kissed!"[99] He grew impatient to have his wife back home in Paris; this impatience led to some turbulence in the Ozanam household. However, both spouses were quick to forgive and to forget any perceived wrongs.[100] In October 1843, as Frédéric anticipated Amélie's return during her second absence from him, he penned the following heartfelt thoughts: "I am aware of all you are capable of, because you have shown me what your heart is endowed with, and I believe that you are capable of growing each day in merit and grace before God and men. Even the saints could be better since the Creator alone enjoys infinite perfection. But as I have known you, as I have loved you, as I see you, there is already more than enough for my pride and happiness. . . . I would not try to hold you back, my angel, because you draw me with you and so lead me to heaven."[101] He admitted frankly that he had been thinking too much of himself during these separations and promised to be better:

See how I was stricken two years ago in what was dearest to me, and after having settled everything for my happiness in this world, it so happened that it was disturbed in an unforeseen and terrible way by the illnesses [miscarriages] you have borne in a Christian manner. I ought to regard the trials which are sent me as expiation for my faults, and as a proof to test my fidelity. In thus turning in on myself and questioning these two years passed in the state of marriage, I find that I have ill-used their benefits and graces. A spouse has been given me to be for me an image of the goodness of God and make me better by the charming power she exercises over me. Instead of loving in her Him who gave her to me, it is myself I have sought in her, it is myself I have wished to have adored in her heart, it is myself alone I have wished to be allowed in her thoughts, and this miserable egoism, not understanding itself to be at the caprice of its impatience, has been the cause of all my anxieties. Of all these annoying preoccupations, the black humors which are taking root and growing, the longings for Lyon, the distaste for men and things, that fear of failing in my career, and those cowardly apprehensions that it was too much for me. Were I to abandon myself to such any longer, I should little by little be discouraged in my vocation, preferring the security of a position to the generous struggle of work, and would fall into the shameful habits of softness and self-interest that I have so often reproached in the men of our days. In the same way that I have weakened myself by these useless solicitudes and vain imaginings, I have made my work harder and prayer less fervent. I lost what . . . [instead] I ought to be acquiring: energy and activity. You . . . have nothing to reproach yourself with, O my well-beloved, and on the contrary it is to you that I owe, after God, the resolution I now take to change and no longer sadden with my weaknesses your young years which I have promised to adorn. . . . I come to beg you to pardon my faults and the annoyances they have given you: I come to ask again for your trust, your esteem, and that love which never fails me: I will make better use of it. . . . You are in love with everything great; you will sustain me, assist me, be the ray of light ever there in my thoughts.[102]

The depth of Ozanam's love and need for his wife is unmistakable in the closing remarks of this 1843 letter: "Your voice, your glance, your smile, even those melodies you are adept at choosing for me on your piano, all of these will spur me on to good and turn back the clouds I would not know how to chase by myself. . . . Come, then, my well-beloved, my dove, my angel, come into my arms, against my heart, come bringing me yours so pure and generous: come and God bless you that after two years we love each other a thousand times more than on the first day!"[103] Over time Amélie also came to dislike being separated from her husband as much as her husband disliked being separated from her.[104] It was a testimony to their growing intimacy and love.

"A SMALL ANGEL IN MY HOME": THE BIRTH OF MARIE, 1845

In 1844 prospects began to brighten for the Ozanams, when Frédéric attained the chair of foreign literature at the Sorbonne. Not only were his brothers and Guigui with him in Paris by this time,[105] but in April

1845 Monsieur Soulacroix, bringing his family, also arrived in Paris to take up a new position. The Soulacroixs found a home on the rue de Vaugirard. Amélie's family was now much closer to her.[106] But the greatest joy in 1845 was the arrival of the Ozanams' only child, Marie. Frédéric embraced fatherhood willingly and with gratitude; he penned the following note to his dear friend Lallier: "God has made me a father. . . . I am already so happy! I will be more so when I will have a small angel in my home."[107] He excitedly wrote again to Lallier on the same day: "The little angel for whom we were waiting arrived sooner than we had expected, this morning at 5 o'clock, after three hours of pains ended by a successful delivery. Up until now, the mother and the child are in good health. I would like to give God as much gratitude as He has given me happiness. Here I am, the father of a pretty little girl, well-formed and who can await her true godfather in forty-eight hours."[108] The baptism was an important event; Frédéric did not want his child to be without "the grace of holy baptism" for very long after her birth.[109] Marie was baptized on Saturday, July 26, 1845, in the church of Saint-Sulpice. It was a true family celebration. At this time the Ozanams resided at 7 rue Garancière, just behind the church and still near the Luxembourg Gardens, where Amélie and Frédéric frequently took walks.[110]

Ozanam knew what a blessing and a responsibility a young child could be: "These little children that we think we are educating are precisely those who complete our own upbringing and give us many more lessons than they receive. When I see this poor little angel, so pure and so beautiful, there I find, so to speak, the most visible mark of the Creator. It seems to me that the house is very blessed by the presence of a soul who has not yet sinned."[111] He believed that his beloved mother, who had died in 1839, had in some way interceded with God to send this little child in order to continue her guidance of his life and his soul toward goodness.[112] Perhaps because he remembered poignantly the untimely deaths of many siblings, Frédéric would constantly be attentive to Marie's health. Yet he was not afraid to bring both Marie and Amélie on a journey through Italy in 1846–47. In fact, he bragged that his "Nini," as Marie was affectionately nicknamed, had called out "Pâpa! Pâpa!" to greet the pope, just like "a little Italian," as he passed by. It was one of the twenty or so words in her small vocabulary.[113] Ozanam also both fretted about and rejoiced in her educational achievements.[114] A doting father, he composed the following poem to his "little Marie" on July 5, 1849, when she was four years old:

> When the Dear Lord made you, little earthly angel,
> To wipe the tears in your mother's eyes
> I asked for you all the precious gifts
> That the Holy Spirit lavishes on the heavenly angels.
> For you I asked their eternal graces,
> Their purity, their faith, all, except their wings,
> Lest one day the wish come to you
> To return there above without us and to vanish.
>
> That is why you do not have the two airy wings
> That your brothers the Cherubims bear in heaven:
> They who would shield your brow from the intense heat of the sun,
> Or, beating the air with a similar movement,
> Would cause you to breathe, refreshed and delighted,
> The salutary gust of a sweet breeze.
> Now your head, like a poor flower
> Bends and uncomfortably bears the weight of the heat.
> The fan, a necessary ornament of hot days,
> Plays the role of the wing which you lack.
> Let the soft zephyr which has escaped from its bond
> Give to my beloved angel the pure air of Paradise![115]

With the birth of Marie, the Ozanams became not just a loving couple but a loving family.

Historians and other readers often regard Ozanam primarily as a serious and scholarly individual, but in his correspondence with his family there are glimpses of another side to him. An example is the following playful story of his excursion to Reims and the comedy of errors that ensued, as related to his wife:

> At the Chateau-Thierry station, the timetable grants a ten-minute stop. All the travelers hurry toward the dining room, and I don't know what demon pushes me there. Not that you had not provided me with enough provisions that I scrupulously consumed, but as chocolate does

not quench thirst, my discomfort compelled me to allow myself to buy little cherry tarts which were quite appetizing, at the small price of 15 centimes. Like a man who had the Gobert Award and who thinks that everything is permitted him, I thus take one of your delightful provisions and I eat it and think of you, in the hope that at the same time you are doing as much. Then, espying some good-looking apricots, for two sous, I put my hand on one of the ripest: the traitor escapes me, carrying in its path several of its colleagues, and all together like an avalanche, they fall from their shelf on the sideboard where they upset a large glass sugar bowl, placed there for my sins. The utensil falls and breaks; at the noise, the owner rushes over and finds that his sugar bowl was a Greek vase of higher value, in cut glass; the pair, he said, has cost him at least 15 francs. I clearly saw that the only Greek in this was my man. But what? The train was leaving, the justice of the peace lived too far away to reconcile us, and hurried to compromise, I had to be very happy to get out of it for one hundred sous. I then got in the carriage again, quite confused for *having paid one hundred and three sous for my cherry tart* [my emphasis]. . . . Finally . . . we arrived in Reims at 6:15, not too bruised, and my whole person, except the heart, in a better state than I would have hoped. On our disembarkment, we were led to a fleecer who claims to be the inkeeper of the "Lion d'Or," and all that he has of the lion are the claws. This honest man made me pay, in my capacity as president of the commission, two and a half francs for my room, service included, and for four francs apiece, he served us the paltriest dinner that ever appeared on a lawyer's table. If all the products of Reims are like his fatty meat, I foresee ill for its bachelors. But fortunately, the windows open; we see the Cathedral; we see nothing more than the admirable Cathedral, its porch as rich as that of Amiens, its towers rival those of Paris.[116]

At the end of this humorous tale he inquired teasingly: "Is little Marie well? Did she buy a bouquet for her Mama? Was it pretty? Did it smell good? I thank her very much for her sugared almonds that I found and which were a nice surprise. Tell her that her Papa kisses her and blesses her. He will say a 'Hail Mary' for her tonight; she will give it back to him tomorrow." Not surprisingly he concluded with "Adieu mes anges (Farewell my Angels)."[117] Frédéric's home life had finally brought him a comfort and a confidence that put him at ease. His home and his family had become the sources of his strength.

One of the greatest agonies endured by Ozanam as he faced an early death was the knowledge that he would not see his beloved daughter grow into womanhood. She was only eight years old in 1853, when he died. In the marriage of her parents, however, Marie had a wonderful model on which to base her own marriage to Laurent Laporte thirteen years later, on July 16, 1866. Her parents saw marriage not as a social arrangement but as a genuine vocation.[118] Frédéric may have feared marriage in his youth, but in his marriage to Amélie he "discovered that these three forms of love, eros, philia, and agape enrich each other."[119] He discovered "philia," the love of friendship, in the relationships he began as a young man in Lyon and Paris; he discovered agape, sharing and self-sacrifice, in the charity of the Society of St. Vincent de Paul; and he discovered eros in his love for Amélie.[120] These three forms of love merged in their married life, and their conjugal love grew and matured because it ultimately became focused on the other, "the loving gift of self."[121] From an early point in their relationship Amélie and Frédéric had promised each other to speak only of "us." They lived up to that solemn promise. On August 23, 1853, just two weeks before his death, and suffering from great physical pain, Frédéric still managed to find and pick a beautiful branch of myrtle at the seaside to give to his Amélie because it was the monthly anniversary of the date of their wedding.[122] Amélie in turn uncomplainingly cared for her invalid husband to his dying day. The two had become as one.

CHAPTER 5

Scholar

The Ozanams were a "family of two glorious traditions: sturdy Catholicism and wide, competent scholarship."[1] Gifted with a brilliant mind, Frédéric Ozanam would be both the beneficiary and the benefactor of these two traditions. He began writing at an early age, appearing to delight in the realm of thought and commentary. In 1831 his critique of the socialist Saint-Simon appeared in the journal *Précurseur* and then was published in an expanded form. As discussed in chapter 2, noted French writers immediately recognized Ozanam's potential as a scholar.[2] And as early as 1832, Ozanam proposed engaging in a massive historical study of the ancient origins of religion that would require knowledge of numerous fields and perhaps as many as twelve languages in order to read original sources.[3] The intention of this study, as quoted earlier, was to demonstrate "the perpetuity, the Catholicism of religious ideas, the truth, the excellence, the beauty of Christianity."[4] Although such a project was nearly impossible, especially given Ozanam's short lifetime, nevertheless he remained faithful to the essential purpose. He came close to learning the twelve languages he had identified. Besides his native French and ancient Sanskrit, he "was at home in the romance tongues, as well as German and English and classical Latin, Greek and Hebrew."[5] He obviously had genius; once he became a university professor, "his genius flourished in the fame of his courses and the intensity and originality of his literary criticisms and expositions."[6] By the age of twenty-six, Ozanam had already published a number of scholarly works, including *Deux chanceliers d'Angleterre* (*Two Chancellors of England*), *Du protestantisme dans ses rapports avec la liberté* (Protestantism in Its Relation to Freedom), and *Dante et la philosophie catholique au treizième siècle* (*Dante and Catholic Philosophy in the Thirteenth Century*).[7] His death at the age of forty prematurely halted a remarkably productive and valuable scholarly career.

DEUX CHANCELIERS D'ANGLETERRE

Shortly before Ozanam officially received his doctorate in law and before completing work on his doctorate in literature, he completed *Deux chanceliers d'Angleterre* (*Two Chancellors of England*). He wrote it over the holidays in 1835 while he was at home in Lyon. In 1836 it appeared in the *Revue Européenne* before being published in final book form. Baunard refers to it as his "first great work," one that "shows the prentice-hand of an eloquent scholar . . . [and] the work of a powerful apologist."[8] *Deux chanceliers* compared and contrasted two famous English chancellors—Francis Bacon and Thomas à Becket, Archbishop of Canterbury: "The two men I evoke represent two principles, the Rationalist and the Christian, reason elevated to the highest degree, faith put to the hardest test. I wish to test which of the two principles is most fruitful for the common weal. I wish to measure a Great Man and a Saint in order to find out in which of the two human nature reaches its capacity and is crowned with the greatest glory."[9] Ozanam anticipated the initial criticism of his study: "The parallel is not invidious. I have not chosen the least among the world's sages. In Bacon philosophy has done what she could. Nor have I sought the foremost among Catholic sages. There are in the Church heads crowned with brighter aureoles than that of St. Thomas. Neither is the parallel arbitrary. St. Thomas and Bacon have both borne the seals of the same State. They trod the same earth. In the time of the first, that land bore the title of Island of Saints. In the time of the second, it preferred the title of land of freedom of thought. . . . We are about to see whether this was a change for the better."[10]

For Ozanam, Bacon was gifted with a "magnificent genius" and was also "a profoundly religious man."[11] His weakness, however, was revealed in his claim that the theories and method of science could be applied not only to the material world but also to the moral sphere. Ozanam offered this telling critique:

> If humanity has a certain sacred mission to fulfil here below, it must know it at every hour of its existence; it must know itself; its origin and its end, the laws of life and the hopes of death; it must know all these things without effort and without uncertainty, under the penalty of remaining inactive and of losing in worldly controversy the time which was given it to march to its immortal destiny. That is why, when deep obscurity surrounded fallen man, two beacon lights remained to him and formed the luminous column which was to guide him in his life. These two lights came from God; one shone from within and was called conscience; the other shone without and was called tradition. All the mortal sciences are but the reflection of these two lifesaving beacons, the development of these two primary gifts. Their point of departure is not then in the observation of facts but in the knowledge of principles, for would it not be folly to seek in transient phenomena, succeeding one another rapidly in the midst of time and space, the immutable secrets of the Infinite and the Eternal? They begin with an Act of Faith and repulse methodical doubt as a usurpation and a falsehood.[12]

The acceptance and interpretation of Bacon's ideas meant that sensation became "the principle of all knowledge, and as sensation only bears witness to the phenomena of the visible world, this school of thought ceased to believe in invisible things, that is to say, in God and in immortality."[13] Ozanam acknowledged that Bacon himself may not have intended this development. But these were the ultimate consequences of his philosophical ideas. Ozanam was not oblivious to Bacon's positive contributions: "The chief service of Bacon is first of all to . . . have given the final blow to the decaying empire of Aristotle and to have revealed the true destiny of sciences. Secondly he made it clear that nature everywhere bursts through the formulas in which reason wished to imprison her and that she can be subdued only on condition of knowing her. Finally he prepared the way for and gave example of conscientious and fertile research."[14]

Ozanam was also critical of Bacon's apparently Machiavellian approach to politics. He offered as one example of many this quote from Bacon: "Dissimulation is the epitome of wisdom; it is like a live hedge protecting the designs of skilful men; it is a kind of intellectual modesty covering the nakedness of our thoughts. He who never dissimulates deceives none the less, for, the majority of men being accustomed to falsehood, nothing surprises them and puts them on the wrong track like the truth. Magnanimity is only a poetical virtue. Flattery is always excusable."[15] Bacon's career provided evidence that he practiced what he preached.[16] Accused of graft and corruption, Bacon eventually fell from power and influence and "died in solitude in 1626 at the age of sixty-six years."[17]

Turning next to Thomas à Becket, "one of those glorious figures who appear in the Middle Ages, supporting on their heads the religious edifice," Ozanam purported "to explain the principles which he defended" and "to see if the thought which led him to martyrdom was personal, conceived in a day of pride, or if it was the product of the eleven centuries of Christianity which preceded him."[18] After examining closely the quarrel between Thomas and King Henry II over the state's control of the Catholic Church and the king's attempted usurpation of church authority, eventually leading to the death of Thomas, Ozanam wrote the following: "When two men in the Middle Ages submitted their quarrel to the judgment of God they fought it out in an enclosed area. It was perhaps an old remnant of paganism, of the worship of nature, which, by giving a mysterious portent to every physical phenomenon and divinizing brute force, submitted all things to a law of terror. Thomas's quarrel had ended in a sort of combat in which virtue came to grips with evil. Evil had conquered by the sword. According to the barbarous ideas of the time, Thomas, no longer living, stood condemned."[19]

But the story does not end on that note. Ozanam proceeded to assert eloquently the integrity and courage of this second chancellor: "But there is another law, a law of love, by which right is freed from the deed, which recognises an invisible justice, which does not stand still before the silence of death, and which hears the voice of spilt blood. Before this law he triumphs who has most loved; he who has loved to the death is called a martyr."[20] For Ozanam, who was himself prepared to be a martyr, martyrdom was "crowned with a triple glory." It consisted of three essential acts: "Firstly, an act of moral independence: the soul abandons the flesh. . . . Secondly, an act of charity: martyrdom is the witness that a man bears, not to his own beliefs but those of his brothers, believing as he does and by which he confirms in them what is of all things the most precious and most fragile, namely, faith. Nothing confirms the faith like the testimony of a man of worth and nothing gives greater value to this affirmation than the seal of death. Finally, and most important of all, martyrdom is a sacrifice, a sacrifice offered to God, Who in return gives victory and peace."[21] According to Ozanam, "This is how Thomas was justified at the hour he fell massacred at the foot of the altar."[22]

The issue separating the two chancellors thus revolved around a choice between egoism and charity: "Egoism and charity are two rival powers which from the beginning have disputed the possession of the world. Egoism is produced in societies under two forms which are very dear to it, despotism and anarchy. Charity, in the Church, opposes liberty to despotism, and to anarchy, authority."[23] Ozanam concluded: "They are not, then, two men who stand before us but two types, the philosopher and the saint, and . . . one allowed himself to be degraded in spite of so much genius and . . . the other preserved inviolate the sheen of his virtue. Humanly speaking, both were equal. On the side of the victorious one, therefore, there must have been something of the Divine."[24] His essay ended with this thoughtful admonition: "Rationalism made one, Catholicism the other; it is for you to decide to which of these two powers you will deliver your soul."[25]

DU PROTESTANTISME DANS SES RAPPORTS AVEC LA LIBERTÉ

Deux chanceliers was Ozanam's first major historical work. It was followed by *Du protestantisme dans ses rapports avec la liberté* (Protestantism in Its Relation to Freedom) in 1838 and *Dante et la philosophie catholique au treizième siècle* (*Dante and Catholic Philosophy in the Thirteenth Century*) in 1839. In the former work, which first appeared in the journal *L'Univers*, Ozanam intended to demonstrate that Catholicism, the true form of Christianity, not Protestantism, was the authentic source of liberty and political freedom. He was challenging both scholarly and popular assumptions. Christianity had opposed the false philosophies of Ancient Rome. It had weathered persecution and supported authentic liberty by ending what he called the "double usurpation of error and doubt." As a result, it contributed to the creation of a more just empire built on a solid foundation of faith.[26] The Catholic Church was instrumental in attacking servitude of all kinds, and inevitably, he concluded, it was the Church that supported political liberty throughout much of its history.[27] Protestantism gave rise to radical movements that "[consecrate] the material power of the number." It also supported the development of an absolutism that "divinized unity." Both, according to Ozanam, "are only forms of the same materialism, a necessary destroyer of public liberty."[28] As Baunard points out, for Ozanam, "Protestantism in fact, and from its very nature, played its part in the oppression and tyranny over conscience, wherever the independence of the Catholic faith did not defend it. [His] article appeared at the moment when the imprisonment of the Archbishop of Cologne caused a flutter not only on the banks of the Rhine, but in every political centre in Europe."[29]

Although he disagreed with Protestants, Ozanam never stooped to harsh polemic or vilification. He was tolerant of differences of opinion. According to Jean-Jacques Ampère, "Toleration, in Ozanam, was not to be confused with weakness. He had a breadth of view which enabled him to appreciate differences, even in opponents. He had an intimate knowledge of men. His gentle and discreet patience always succeeded in disarming their prejudices. His conduct was a touching imitation of that of Our Lord, who never broke the bent twig nor extinguished the smouldering lamp."[30]

DANTE ET LA PHILOSOPHIE CATHOLIQUE AU TREIZIÈME SIÈCLE

Dante et la philosophie catholique au treizième siècle (*Dante and Catholic Philosophy in the Thirteenth Century*) resulted from Ozanam's thesis for the doctorate in literature, which he received in 1839. During his visit to Italy with his family in 1833, Frédéric was struck by the presence of

Dante in a painting by the great artist Raphael. In the beginning of the introduction to his study, he vividly recalled the scene and raised the central question of the book:

> When the pilgrimage to Rome, so often dreamed of, is finally realized, and the traveller, impelled by a pious curiosity, has ascended the great staircase of the Vatican, and has surveyed the wonders of every age and of every country gathered together under favor of the hospitality of that magnificent residence, he reaches a spot that may fitly be called the sanctuary of Christian art, the *Stanze* of Raphael. The artist, in a series of historical and symbolic frescos, has there depicted the glories and the benefactions of the Catholic faith. Among those frescos is one on which the eye rests most lovingly, both by reason of the beauty of the subject and the felicity of the execution. The Holy Eucharist is there represented on an altar lifted up between heaven and earth; heaven opens, and amid its splendor permits us to see the Divine Trinity, the angels, and the saints; the earth beneath is crowned by a numerous assemblage of pontiffs and doctors of the Church. In one of the groups composing the assemblage, the spectator distinguishes a figure remarkable by the originality of its character, its head encircled, not by a tiara or a mitre, but by a wreath of laurel. The countenance is noble and austere, nowise unworthy of such company. A momentary glance into the memory brings to mind Dante Alighieri. The question then naturally rises, by what right has the portrait of such a man been introduced among those of the venerated witnesses of the faith, and that by an artist accustomed to the scrupulous observance of liturgical traditions, under the eyes of the popes, in the very citadel of orthodoxy?[31]

As a young and talented scholar, Ozanam was well aware that some Catholics questioned both Dante's worth as a poet and his orthodoxy. Certain critics even suggested that Dante had contributed to the coming of the Protestant Reformation.[32] Ozanam rejected those claims, maintaining that Dante's words were interpreted incorrectly: "Sundry passages in his poem, ingeniously contorted, seemed . . . to contain derisive allusions to the most sacred mysteries of the Catholic liturgy."[33]

After a thorough examination of the subject, Ozanam concluded definitively: "The orthodoxy of Dante, sufficiently established by the proofs that have been adduced, seems to us still more plainly evidenced from the entire course of the work undertaken by us and now drawing to a close. We find it to be a dominant truth, the resultant of all our researches and inductions."[34] He continued: "When studying the circumstances environing the poet, we found that he was born . . . on the latest verge of the heroic days of the Middle Ages when Catholic philosophy had reached its apogee, and in a country illumined by its purest rays. Amid these salutary influences, and through the vicissitudes of a life filled with misfortunes, with moral emotions and profound studies, the whole concourse of which must have tended to develop within him the religious sentiment, we have beheld him conceive a magnificent work, the plan of which, borrowed from the methods of legendary poetry, was intended to embrace both the most sublime mysteries of faith and the loftiest conceptions of science."[35] For him, Dante "belongs above all to the two great schools, the mystic and the dogmatic, of the thirteenth century, of which he docilely accepts not only the essential dogmas, but also the accessory ideas, often even the favorite expressions."[36] Ozanam rejected the description of Dante as "the Homer of Christian times" because, "while honoring his genius, [it] wrongs his religion." The poet Dante knew how "to lift man up and cause him to ascend toward the Divinity. It is through this quality, through the purity and the immaterial character of his symbolism, as also through the limitless breadth of his conception, that he has left far beneath him poets ancient and recent."[37] In the final analysis, Ozanam likened Dante to St. Thomas Aquinas: "the Divine Comedy is the literary and philosophic *Summa* of the Middle Ages, and . . . Dante is the St. Thomas of poetry."[38] In Ozanam's opinion, Raphael had appropriately placed Dante in his painting together with the "venerated witnesses of the faith."

OZANAM'S "GERMANS"

On January 7, 1839, Ozanam was awarded the degree of doctor of letters. Shortly after this, as discussed earlier, he received the much anticipated news that he was to be appointed to the chair of commercial law at Lyon.[39] Moreover, after a brilliant performance in an 1840 academic competition, he was offered a position teaching at the Sorbonne with a future prospect of permanent employment. At the age of twenty-seven, Ozanam already had a reputation for erudition: "Ozanam has seemed to the judges [of the competition] to merit first rank, less by his classical knowledge—doubtless extensive but equaled perhaps by others—than by his broad and firm manner of conceiving an author or a subject; by the breadth of his comments and plans; by his bold and just views; and by a language which allies originality with reason and imagination with gravity. He seems to be eminently suited for a public professorship. He was the only candidate to give proof of a grammatical and literary study of the four foreign languages listed on the program, Italian, Spanish, German, and English."[40]

He began his lectures in January 1841, some six months before his marriage to Amélie Soulacroix. His task was to lecture on two types of foreign literature; the first was Italian literature, especially Dante, and "the other Teutonic, dealing with the dawn of literature in Germany."[41] Conscientious by nature, Ozanam journeyed throughout Germany to research the topic carefully and to appreciate fully the milieu of the literature he was about to teach.[42] Commencing in 1842, he was expected to deliver a specialized course on German literature, including the *Niebelungen Lied*, often referred to as "the *Iliad* of the Germanic nations."[43]

Certain German scholars, such as Hegel, Goethe, David Friedrich Strauss, Christian Lassen, and Georg Gottfried Gervinus, had proposed that the essence of German genius and character was rooted in its pagan heritage, and that Christianity had been an enormous obstacle to Germanic progress.[44] This thesis naturally caught Ozanam's attention. In a letter to François Lallier, he explained the intent of the research he had been conducting, in particular at Sainte-Genèvieve Library: "I am showing that Germany owes its genius and civilization almost entirely to the Christian education which was given it; that its grandeur was in proportion to its union with Christianity; that it has power, light, and poetry only by fraternal communication with the other European nations; that for her as for all, there is not, there cannot be, true destinies except by oneness with Rome, depository of all the temporal traditions of humanity as well as the eternal designs of Providence."[45] He sought Lallier's advice on his thesis: "There seems to me some utility in ... making them see that by themselves they were only barbarians; how, through bishops and monks, by the Roman faith, by the Roman language, by Roman law, they entered into the procession of the religious, scientific, and political heritage of modern peoples, and how in repudiating it they will return little by little to barbarism. An introduction which precedes and the conclusions which will follow the history of the literature of chivalry, principal topic of my book, will bear witness to this idea. Do you think such a work could be really valuable?"[46]

The rest of the letter includes an interesting description of Ozanam's research and writing methods:

> I am working on the Introduction at present. My former lessons have been of little help in this section whose importance I perceived only latterly: that caused me to make extensive research. The Germans under the Romans, the military structures, the municipal organization, and the schools. The original preaching of Christianity before the invasion of the barbarians. The activity of the church in the face of, and following, the invasion. The development of the state: on one side the empire, on the other the towns. Finally the preservation and propagation of letters, the interrupted teaching of the languages and arts of antiquity, the admirable works which made of the monasteries of Fulda and Saint-Gall the schools of Germany. In the absence of general treatments I had to research particular histories, the lives of the saints, and the chronicles of the towns. I seem to have discovered unknown and decisive facts which will establish the perpetuity of the scholarly tradition in an era accustomed to being branded with the name of barbarian. . . . I am going to try editing all this, about two hundred and fifty pages, and publishing some of it in the review, in order to stimulate good advice. A book in a short time is not a small matter, especially for me who compose slowly and risk taking a great deal of trouble for little result. I do not hesitate, therefore, to recommend what I have begun to your good and fraternal prayers.[47]

This proved to be a fruitful line of research, resulting in several significant publications: the essays "De l'établissement du christianisme en Allemagne" (August 1843) and "Études sur les peoples germanique avant le Christianisme" (January 1846), and Ozanam's book *Les Germains avant le christianisme* (July 1847).[48]

THE FRANCISCAN POETS

In 1846 Ozanam turned again to Italian literature, focusing his attention on the Franciscan poets. Apparently Ozanam became intrigued by Saint Francis of Assisi after hearing Père Lacordaire speak about the "man mad with love."[49] His journey to Italy for health reasons in 1846–47 furnished him with an opportunity not only to find "some clusters of poetry" but also to do some "original research and scientific criticism."[50] Spending much of his time "rummaging through the libraries of Italy," he later was able to publish the volumes entitled *Documents inédits pour server à l'histoire littéraire de l'Italie* and *Les poètes franciscains en Italie au treizième siècle.*[51]

Ozanam argued in *Poètes franciscains* that Saint Francis's literary education "was accomplished less by classical studies, to which he devoted little time, than by the French language, which was already esteemed in Italy as the most melodious of all and as the preserver of the traditions of chivalry which softened the uncouthness of the Middle Ages. . . . He made the neighboring woods resound with French canticles."[52] Francis "gained inspiration from French poetry, he found in it sentiments of courtesy and generosity which took root in his heart."[53] Like a true medieval knight, Francis devoted himself to the chivalric service of a lady—Lady Poverty: "O my most sweet Lord Jesus Christ, have pity on me and on my Lady Poverty, for I burn with love of her, and without her I cannot rest."[54] Francis and his compatriots not only raised the awareness of poverty but also gave those living in poverty a renewed sense of importance.[55] Ozanam discussed several Franciscan poets besides Saint Francis in his work. The most significant was Jacopone de Todi,[56] whom he referred to as "an Italian predecessor of Dante, who lived to be the most popular and the most inspired of the poets of the Franciscan Order."[57] By including Jacopone in this study, Ozanam was "the first in France" to call attention to this poet, "to whom is attributed with a fair degree of probability our *Stabat Mater.*"[58] More important, Jacopone's "Italian poems in the form of dialogue, such as the Passion, and the Debate between Justice and Mercy, exercised an undeniable influence upon the origin and development of Miracle-plays and Mysteries."[59] As Baunard comments, "What made Jacopone de Todi a poet and a great poet was love and grief, and therein lay his attraction for Ozanam."[60]

Ozanam saw an authentic connection between his beloved Dante and his equally beloved Saint Francis: "Dante stands nearer than one would suppose to the religious and literary school of the disciples of St. Francis. Not that he ought to be reckoned . . . among the Franciscan writers, but because he exhausted all the wealth of his genius in celebrating the penitent of Assisi." Moreover, "It was . . . from the lessons of St. Bonaventura that he [Dante] borrowed the purest lights of his mystic theology, and, above all, when the great man died, laden with [both] the admiration and the ingratitude of his contemporaries, he wished to be buried in the habit of the Third Order, and in the Church of St. Francis."[61] Like Dante, Ozanam, too, knew the benefits of Franciscan life.[62] His *Poètes franciscains* proved to be "the most popular of his works."[63] Jean-Jacques Ampère called this work "a masterpiece of refinement and grace. I insist on the word grace . . . because it remained a characteristic of an imagination which an austere life and laborious study had not blunted."[64] It is fair to say that Ozanam's work helped to spark the popularity of Franciscan studies.[65]

TOWARD THE HISTORY OF THE FIFTH CENTURY

By early 1848, Ozanam had conceived of a study that would bring together "his Germans" and his work on Dante. He outlined his scheme to his friend Théophile Foisset in January 1848: "My [work] on Dante and on the early Germans are the cornerstones of a work which I have already partially done in my public lectures, and which I should like to take up again and complete. It would be a literary history of Barbarian Times, a history of Letters, and therefore a history of civilisation from the decadence of Rome and the earliest dawn of the genius of Christianity down to the close of the 13th century. I should make that the matter of my lectures for ten years, if necessary, and if God spared my life. My lectures, which could be taken down in shorthand, would form the first draft of a volume which I would revise and issue at the close of each year."[66] Recognizing his own limitations, he confessed to Foisset that this approach would be kinder to his health. But he was enthusiastic about the project: "The subject would be an admirable one, because it would result in revealing to modern society the long and laborious course of education carried out by the Church. I should commence with an introductory volume in which I would attempt to show the intellectual state of the world at the advent of Christianity; how much the Church salvaged of the heritage of antiquity, and by what means it preserved that legacy; then the origin of Christian Art and of Christian Knowledge, from the times of the catacombs and the First Fathers of the Church. Every excursion which I made in Italy last year was directed to that end."[67] With vision and imagination, Ozanam sketched the basic narrative of his proposed project: "A description of the barbarian world would follow much the same lines as in my work on the Early Germans: then their entry into the Catholic fold: the prodigious labours of such men as, Boetius, Isidore de Seville, Bede, St. Boniface, who rested neither night nor day, but carried the torch of learning from one end of the invaded Empire to the other, penetrated into inaccessible places, and passed on the torch from hand to hand down to Charlemagne. It would be necessary to study the constructive work of that great man and to show that literature, which had not perished before his time, was not extinguished afterwards."[68]

The great story would by no means end there: "I should then show all that was great in England in the time of Alfred, in Germany under the Othos: I should come to Gregory VII and the Crusades. I should then have the three most glorious centuries of the Middle Ages to deal with: theologians like St. Anselm, St. Bernard, Peter Lombard, Albert the Great, St. Thomas, St. Bonaventure: legislators of Church and State, Gregory VII, Alexander III, Innocent III and Innocent IV, Frederick II, St. Louis, Alphonsus X: the quarrel of the priesthood and the Empire: the Communes, Italian Republics: chroniclers and historians: Universities and the Knowledge of Law." And he would "have to deal with Romance, poetry, the common patrimony of all Europe; and incidentally all epic tradition peculiar to each people, which are the foundations of national literatures. I should see modern languages in the making, and my work would close with the *Divine Comedy*, that most sublime monument, the culmination and the glory of the period."[69] At this point in the letter to Foisset, it was as if Ozanam caught his breath, took stock of his own limitations, and finally realized the magnitude of what he was proposing to accomplish: "That is, my dear friend, what a man is prepared to undertake who barely missed dying eighteen months ago, who has not yet quite recovered, who has to look after himself in a dozen different ways, and who, as you know, is both irresolute and weak."[70] But his faith and his hope were far from shattered: "But I am counting on God's goodness if He will grant me health; on my course of lectures which will carry on my plan, on the compass to which it will be necessary to reduce so many questions for an educated public, anyone of which would occupy several lives. I count somewhat on eight years uninterrupted preparation for lectures, wherein I have endeavoured to collect and fix the results of my research, having first submitted them to the critical opinion of kind friends."[71]

This enormous scholarly labor would be entitled *History of Civilization in the Times of the Barbarians.* In fact, Ozanam's Germanic studies had already commenced this grand scheme. *Les Germains avant le christianisme* was published in 1847, and *La civilisation chrétienne chez les francs* was published two years later. In 1849 the French Academy recognized the value of these works by awarding Ozanam the prestigious Gobert Prize.[72] Unfortunately, Ozanam had only five more years to pursue his grand project before his untimely death, and there were many distractions from the project in the years 1848–49.

In the "Avant-Propos" (author's preface) to his most famous work, *La civilization au cinquième siècle* (*History of Civilization in the Fifth Century*), published posthumously, Ozanam again defined his desire to write the monumental study he had proposed to Foisset: "I propose to write the literary history of the Middle Age, from the fifth to the end of the thirteenth century, the time of Dante, before whom I pause as the worthiest representative of that great epoch. But in the history of literature my principal study will be the civilization of which it is the flower, and in that civilization I shall glance especially at the handiwork of Christianity. The whole idea, therefore, of my book will be to show how Christianity availed to evoke from the ruins of Rome, and the hordes encamped thereupon, a new society which was capable of holding truth, doing good, and finding the true idea of beauty."[73] Ozanam entered into these realms of historical study and interpretation partly in response to the view of Gibbon: "While in the first flush of youth, the historian Gibbon visited Eternal Rome. As he was wandering on the Capitol, pondering over the vanished glories of the past, the silence was suddenly broken by the sound of a religious chant, and he beheld a long procession of Franciscans emerging from the Basilica of Ara Coeli—treading with their sandaled feet the path along which so many triumphal conquerors had passed. He was filled with indignation and forthwith planned to write 'The Decline and Fall of the Roman Empire' in vindication of classical antiquity thus outraged by Christian barbarism." The heart and mind of Ozanam were moved by a far different view: "I too have watched the friars of Ara Coeli walking over the stones of the Capitol. I saw in this sight the symbol of victory of love over force, and resolved to write of the progress of mankind during that epoch in which the English historian saw nothing but decadence."[74]

The intended book was to be a compilation of his meticulously researched and prepared lectures. He fascinated his students with his vision and especially inspired them when he came to the Franks: "With them began in the 5th century a new era of civilization, in the course of which Christianity poured forth its treasures of knowledge, charity, virtue, and grace."[75] Each of Ozanam's lectures delineated "some benefit—In the first place *Christian Law* illuminating that world which it could have destroyed, but which it preferred to reform . . . : *Literature* finding its way gradually into the Church . . . : *Theology* confounding the fables of paganism and the subtleties of heresy with the indestructible permanence of its dogma: *Christian Philosophy*, uniting . . . the sublime speculations of Plato with the truths of Revealed Religion: the *Papacy* staying the torrent of invasion with its authority: *Monasticism*, training educators, benefactors, apostles and models for new races: *Christian Morality* mindful of the slave, the poor, the worker, the woman . . . : *Eloquence, History, Poetry, Art*, regenerated."[76] According to Baunard, "Each lecture was to be a chapter in a volume which would be more eloquent even than the lecture."[77]

Ozanam's lectures of 1848–49, taken down by a stenographer and eventually revised, were transformed into the two volumes that became known as *La civilization au cinquième siècle*.[78] At the end of volume 1, Ozanam boldly defined the civilizing mission of the Catholic Church throughout Western history: "It is upon this great and potent system of Christian metaphysics that, from the fifth century down to our own times, the totality of modern civilization has hinged. . . . Metaphysics, the idea of God, form the point whereupon the whole heaven of our thought, of our nature, of our education, all society, the entirety of the Christian organism, is suspended. So, as long as no one has shaken that point, nor laid violent hands on that Divine idea, there need be no fear for our civilization."[79] In volume 2, he continued on his journey of thought. Of particular interest in this volume is his treatment of Christian manners, which focused on the dignity of the human person and respect for women. It was the Church, for Ozanam, that emancipated the classes, emphasized the dignity of labor, and raised the dignity of women in a way that antiquity had never accomplished.[80] He devoted an entire chapter to "the women of Christendom" (*Les femmes chrétiennes*), emphasizing their importance and achievements especially, but not only, in the arts.[81]

Not surprisingly, Ozanam focused on the subject of poverty. He stressed that "the poor were not only respected by, but also necessary to, Christendom."[82] The poor will always be with us not because destitution is something that God ordains, but rather because "poverty must always exist in voluntary if not compulsory form, the reason of the institutions in which every member abnegates his own possessions, and vows himself to [poverty]; and so poverty has taken its proper rank in the divine economy, and become the mainspring of Christian society. Yet this was not enough, and want must also be succoured and consoled."[83] Ancient Rome had a system of public almsgiving, but for Rome, "almsgiving was not the duty of the individual but the right of all. But Christianity inverted the rule, and in its economy charity was not the right of any person, but the duty of the whole community. Benevolence became a sacred duty."[84] At the conclusion of volume 2, Ozanam offered these reflections: "While the ancient barrier of Roman civilization was falling stone by stone, the Christian rampart was being formed behind which society might find another entrenchment. . . . The invasion of the barbarians was without doubt the mightiest and most terrible revolution that has ever occurred; and yet we see the infinite care with which Providence softened the blow in some respects, and broke the fall of the ancient world. Let us also trust that our own epoch will not be more unfortunate; that if our old fortress is fated to fall, new and solid defenses will be raised to protect us; and [that finally] the civilization which has cost so much to God and to man will never perish."[85]

Regrettably, Ozanam did not live long enough to see the fruits of his own labors in the publication of this two-volume history.

THE HISTORICAL THOUGHT OF OZANAM

The field of history in the early nineteenth century was intimately connected with the field of literature. Not until the end of the nineteenth century would history become a professional discipline based on rigorous, scientific research methods. By modern standards, Frédéric Ozanam falls short. He was too credulous of the legends of the Middle Ages. Yet to judge him only in light of modern historical standards is to lose sight of his remarkable achievements and to fail to realize that he stood head and shoulders above many other scholars of his day in terms of the quality and integrity of his research. As one of his biographers, Sister Emmanuel Renner, O.S.B., has commented, "He firmly believed that only harm would result from an historian's attempt to color the facts by doubtful witnesses and premature conclusions. . . . In short, he approached his study of history in a spirit of intellectual open-mindedness."[86] In particular, Ozanam failed to succumb to the temptation of total admiration for and idealization of the Middle Ages that plagued the judgments of numerous other scholars of his time. He contended that in dealing with the Middle Ages, a historian must certainly appreciate "the majesty of the cathedrals and the heroism of the crusades," but, at the same time, the historian must not overlook "the horrors of perpetual war, the harshness of feudal institutions, the scandal of those kings. . . . It is necessary to see the evil."[87] He did not, however, agree with the eighteenth-century French writer Voltaire that the Middle Ages were an abyss and that there were "isolated golden ages." Rather, he thought that "there was a continuous tradition of learning which grew with the efforts of each succeeding generation. At times this fount of learning was increased considerably by men of genius, but in most ages it was enlarged only by a very laborious process."[88] As a historian, he likewise recognized the need to study the history of the Church not as a separate story but rather as an intimate part of history, and he fully comprehended the necessity of studying European history rather than simply the history of individual nations.[89]

As a Christian apologist, Ozanam interpreted history as a working out of the plan of divine providence: "Christian historians . . . sought not only secondary causes to explain events of the past but also first causes, the spiritual causes which rule the world and which manifest the whole order of the divine economy."[90] For him, "Divine Providence and human liberty [are] . . . the two great powers whose combined operation explains history," and these powers "sometimes act in unison that the work of the ages may be prosecuted with increased vigor, and the face of all things renewed."[91] Not content to merely recite political facts and military events, Ozanam wished to "discuss intellectual history in such a manner as to depict the revolutions of the human mind."[92] He would not, however, compromise truth and accuracy. According to Ozanam, there were three important features of any good historical narrative: "chronology which gives facts . . . ; legend which produces life, color, and movement in history; and philosophy which gives it a coherent explanation."[93] He was critical of the famous Jules Michelet's historical work, because Michelet's literary abilities often clouded the history he wrote and provided a less than accurate portrait.[94] Michelet shared in the same weakness as the historians of antiquity who "reduced history to a kind of poetry which fed national pride."[95]

Renner, in her study of Ozanam's historical thought, argues: "According to Ozanam history is an impartial and complete account of nations. Although passion, sensitivity, and imagination can profitably accompany the account, it must never dominate it. The historian must point out deeds which have been verified even if they are not inspiring in themselves. It is particularly important for the historian to restrict himself to the disciplined historical method when tracing the history of institutions, ideas, and science."[96] Ozanam believed, however, that religious beliefs and personal values had a place in scholarship: "I do not know of any man of feeling or courage . . . who would be willing to uphold a manner of writing which had no conviction dominating it. I never aspire to this sad independence of which the chief characteristic is to believe nothing and love nothing."[97] In the final analysis, two things are required of the historian, according to Ozanam: "First, that his conviction is free and intelligent. . . . Second, that the desire to justify a belief does not tempt to misrepresent the facts, to be satisfied with dubious evidence and premature consequences."[98]

Frédéric Ozanam deserves the title of historian; his contributions to the field were significant and valuable: "At a time when most scholars saw only a degeneration of the Latin language resulting finally in the Romance languages, Ozanam realized that there existed a unique Christian Latin which began to develop in the first centuries of the Christian era. Besides contributing to the descriptive study of the art of the catacombs, he also helped to restore an appreciation for medieval art in general. In his study of the civilization of the fifth century Ozanam gave evidence of a good understanding of the development of early Christian poetry and prose."[99] His role as a historian has sometimes been ignored because of his work with social reform. But Ozanam was really "a pioneer in these studies. . . . [and] manifested real ability to penetrate into the spirit of the Middle Ages and point out their great contribution to Western civilization. His thorough understanding of the Catholic Church gave him a valuable insight into medieval society and enabled him, without ignoring the imperfections of the time, to portray the essential influence of Christianity on medieval language, literature, and art."[100]

OZANAM AND OTHER SCHOLARS

Students of Ozanam's scholarly works have sometimes compared and contrasted his thoughts with those of other scholars who lived both during his lifetime and after it. Like Ozanam, the famous philosopher George Wilhelm Friedrich Hegel (1770–1831), for example, believed in the progress of freedom in the world: "The History of the world is none other than the progress of the consciousness of freedom."[101] But Ozanam's thought was profoundly different from Hegel's. In a letter of April 9, 1838, to François Lallier, he clearly stated his position on Hegel, among others: "In which of the two camps lies liberty? In the one where all the traditions of Joseph II [ruler of Austria], Louis XIV, and Henry VIII are joined with the rationalism of Kant, Hegel, and Goethe under the cloak of Frederick William [Frederick William III, king of Prussia]? Or in the one where behind Gregory XVI reappear the great figures of Pius VII, Innocent XI, Innocent IV, and Gregory VII with the faith of St. Ambrose, St. John Chrysostom, and St. Thomas? For us Frenchmen, slave to words, a great thing has been accomplished: the separation of the two great worlds which seem inseparable, the throne and the altar."[102] Some four years later Ozanam revisited the topic of Hegel with Lallier. He asserted that Hegel believed in "the dream of native-born civilization, which without Latin contact would have developed with an unexampled splendor, and . . . of a future which shall be magnificent if its strength is renewed in an unmixed Teutonism." He intended to refute such ideas.[103] On the issue of democracy and the positive role of the Catholic Church, Ozanam and Hegel certainly parted company. Unlike Ozanam, Hegel regarded the Catholic Church as a serious obstacle to the development of science.[104] Indeed, he associated Catholicism with governments that were based on "the bondage of the spirit." It was not the agent to lead humans to true freedom, which is only recognized in the state.[105] Moreover, Hegel was highly critical of the vow of poverty, which "muddled up into a contradiction of assigning merit to whoso-ever gives away goods to the poor." He favored "the precept of action to acquire goods through one's own intelligence and industry."[106]

For Ozanam, history was "a constant struggle between truth and error."[107] For Hegel, the spectacle of history involved a dialectical struggle between two competing theses, resulting in a new synthesis, which then would be challenged by another opposing thesis, and so on in a march of progress. Ozanam, however, subscribed to the view that "civilization periodically declines and then goes through a regenerating process." He referred to this process as palingenesis. As he wrote in September 1831, "If, then, it is true that society is to undergo a transformation at the end of revolutions which it experiences, we must acknowledge that the elements of this definitive synthesis are to be found in the past."[108] Palin-genesis implied that history was a process akin to "the flower containing innumerable seeds which will succeed it; in this manner, the present which comes from the past contains the future."[109] Ozanam's concept of progress, then, was fundamentally different from that of Hegel. In that historical process, both Ozanam and Hegel recognized the contribu-tions of great people. Hegel spoke of "world historical individuals" who are "devoted to the One Aim, regardless of all else. It is even possible that such men may treat other great, even sacred interests, inconsider-ately; conduct which is indeed obnoxious to moral reprehension. But so mighty a form must trample down many an innocent flower—crush to pieces many an object in its path."[110] Ozanam's concept of "great persons" in history was founded upon individuals who "were considered to be servants of Providence, and in this position they were able to render tremendous service to civilization."[111] They served "to sum up the past with all the power of an original way of thinking, and transcend the present by preparing the future."[112] It is little wonder that Ozanam found nothing to embrace and much to confront in the thought of Hegel.

There are similarities in the backgrounds of both Ozanam and the Danish philosopher Søren Kierkegaard. Both were born in the spring of 1813, and both died at an early age (Ozanam in 1853; Kierkegaard in 1855), both hoped to renew Christianity, both suffered from bouts of melancholy, and both objected to the thought of Hegel. Both also developed an idea of three key stages in human life, or three possible stages of self-actualization. For Kierkegaard, these are the aesthetic stage, in which the self concentrates primarily on personal pleasure; the ethical stage, concentrated on ethical principles; and the religious stage. In the second stage an individual looks for direction in life and becomes aware of responsibility and commitment. The final stage represents an individual encounter with and commitment to God.[113] Ozanam wrote to his friend Lallier in 1837: "I believe . . . that there are three kinds of ways of life from which one must choose: the external life which is dissipated in material pleasures, and which belongs to pagans and the lowest class of humanity . . . ; the internal and reflective life which concentrates on the consideration of the soul's infirmities and needs, but which is sterile and void if one stops there, like the philosophers of antiquity and some weak minds of our day; the higher and Christian life, which draws us out of ourselves to lead us to God, where we find the point of departure for all of our thoughts, the point of comparison for all our thoughts and actions." He asked Lallier to join him in supporting each other in the movement toward the third stage.[114] Although these two sets of stages have certain features in common, they also differ significantly. The very request that Ozanam made of Lallier would never have resonated with Kierkegaard, because faith for Kierkegaard was the lonely act of an individual. Moreover, for Kierkegaard, subjective truth, or how one believes, was always more important than objective truth or what is believed.[115] Ozanam would not accept that position; for him there were universal truths to be discovered and known. Finally, Kierkegaard had genuine concerns for the common man and understood the biblical admonition to "love one's neighbor,"[116] but he was not a genuine supporter of the masses or "the public," and he had a unique conception of democracy in its relationship to Christianity.[117] And as Gérard Cholvy notes, Kierke-gaard ultimately lacked "the quiet faith of Ozanam."[118]

As in the case of Ozanam, some scholars have emphasized both the "Catholicity, as well as the democratic nature" of Alexis de Tocqueville's thought. According to Tocqueville, another contemporary of Ozanam, "It is a mistake . . . to regard the Catholic religion as a natural enemy of democracy." He further stated that "of the various Christian doctrines, Catholicism seems to me, on the contrary, among those most favorable to equality of conditions."[119] Tocqueville had a compassion, much like Ozanam, that led him to champion "the causes of slave emancipation, colonial administration, and prison reform."[120] The two men had close friends in common, including Jean-Jacques Ampère and Père Lacor-daire, but they never met each other.[121] In a letter that Tocqueville wrote in 1853 to Jean-Jacques Ampère after reading Ampère's article on Oza-nam, he professed that he sincerely regretted never having known Oza-nam, and that the recent article had only served to intensify that regret.[122]

Ozanam also most likely never made the acquaintance of John Henry Newman, the famous convert to Catholicism, but he was com-pared favorably to Newman in an article published in the *New York Times* in 1878:

> The whole career of Ozanam, and the early beginnings of the move-ment which has so greatly assisted to resubdue France to-day [*sic*] to the Catholic faith, correspond with singular points of coincidence to the Tractarian movement which John Keble and Dr. Newman inaugurated for a similar purpose in 1833 in the Church of England. In each coun-try the established Church was in a state of apathy; abuses had become ingrained; religious discipline was in abeyance; younger men panted for the freer and better life of the earlier days; the efforts to change the reli-gious tone were seemingly fitful, hap-hazard [*sic*] movements, entirely disproportionate to the ends in view; but what Newman did in England Ozanam did in France by means different in details, and yet similar in general bearing; they both attempted to revive the old faith; they were the inspiring leaders to men who had special gifts to be employed; they had the rare faculty of intellectual attractiveness joined to the like

rare gift of conspicuous sincerity, and in spite of points in which the two careers are widely apart, they were permitted to succeed in what they specially aimed at—the revival of Christianity in their respective nations, and the vast enlargement of the practical applications of Christianity to social life.[123]

Ozanam would have been flattered by the comparison, and he certainly rejoiced that Newman had converted to Catholicism. He penned these words in 1851: "Each day counts new conversions, and the example of these two great souls, Newman and Maning [sic] continues to loosen the more religious hearts of the anglican clergy. Nothing is more moving."[124]

In an article in *Vincentian Heritage*, Thomas O'Brien makes a strong case for similarities between Ozanam and the twentieth-century American theologian John Courtney Murray. O'Brien argues that Murray employed a kind of historical argument similar to that of Ozanam "in order to affect a similar kind of liberal reconciliation between the Catholic tradition and the American political experiment."[125] Both men attempted "to demonstrate that the Catholic tradition was not essentially hostile to liberalism, or even to the notion of the separation of Church and State. Both argued that the Church had mistakenly tied itself to an 'invalid' monarchical conception of governance, and that it needed to free itself from this fateful alliance in order to regain credence in the eyes of the people."[126] According to O'Brien, "Ozanam's advocacy for the development of doctrine was subtle. . . . However, by suggesting that the Church's alliance to medieval royal structures was merely an historical expedience, and that the Church should rethink its position in relation to modern political, economic, and social sensibilities, Ozanam was challenging the doctrine of the confessional state. . . . His claim that the Church should embrace the modern concept of the separation of Church and State was tantamount to claiming that longstanding doctrines of the Church, even ones carrying the highest authority, were open to debate and change. This, of course, was not something the Church of his era was prepared to acknowledge."[127]

Unlike Ozanam, Murray eventually faced a more receptive climate; he made "his doctrinal development arguments based on an analysis of Leo XIII's *Rerum Novarum*." He encountered serious opposition, yet "he was asked to draft the Declaration on Religious Liberty at the Second

Vatican Council. The idea that Church doctrine develops over time became mainstreamed implicitly in that moment, and although there is no direct evidence that Murray studied Ozanam's work extensively, [the latter], nevertheless, paved the way for the kind of historical hermeneutic employed by Murray to ground his argument for religious liberty."[128] Frédéric Ozanam may have failed "to reconcile leaders of his Catholic faith tradition with revolutionary representatives espousing liberal democratic principles," but he "did leave future social Catholics with the important legacy of his historical hermeneutic—the conviction that historical context can influence Church teaching, and the simple yet subversive understanding that Church teaching develops over time."[129]

FREEDOM OF EDUCATION

One of the most contentious issues Ozanam faced in his lifetime as a scholar was that of "freedom of education" or "liberty of teaching," as opposed to the monopoly of the secular state university system in France, which was a *cause célèbre* with Catholic intellectuals. French Catholic intellectuals resented the fact that the secular state controlled higher education. They hoped that freedom of education would allow for the formation of Catholic institutions of higher education. As early as 1834, Ozanam had protested against university student opposition to the "establishment of Louvain in Belgium as a Catholic and free institution of learning."[130] Fully aware of the fact that he and other students were attending a secular university, Ozanam nevertheless spoke out: "We are first and above all sons of the Church; without ingratitude to our own *alma mater*, we to-day [*sic*] envy our Belgian brothers the happiness of receiving from one and the same hand the bread of scientific knowledge and the bread of the Sacred Word; they have not to divide their instructions into two parts, one of error and one of truth." He hoped that France, too, would have Catholic universities in the future.[131] Debate on the issue intensified in 1843 when the famous Catholic writer Charles Forbes de Montalembert published his *Du devoir des Catholiques dans la question de la liberté d'enseignement* (On the Duty of Catholics concerning the Question of Liberty of Education) in the *Correspondant*. Montalembert mentioned Ozanam as one of "a small number of upright men, who have what is greater than talent, faith. Christians like . . . M. Ozanam, protest by the publicity of their Christianity and the solidity of their knowledge, against the scandals of their colleagues in their lectures."[132]

At the time Ozanam had not as yet been appointed to a permanent post at the Sorbonne. He was conscious of the delicate situation in which he was placed, but he refused to compromise his principles. Théophile Foisset, actively engaged in the work of the journal, warned Ozanam that his name was included in Montalembert's article and asked whether or not it should be removed. Ozanam responded: "There is certainly a dubious honor in being singled out as an exception to an offensive rule. But it is an honor, and it would be cowardly to cause the allusion to be suppressed."[133] He did, however, clarify a few points in the article that were in error: "It is not true that in the University there is only a *small number* of exceptions; the archbishop of Lyon's letter said yesterday that they are *numerous*, and I am proof that Catholics are in the university, as nearly everywhere in a public capacity, a considerable minority." Neither was it true that Ozanam protested "against the teaching of . . . colleagues . . . of the Sorbonne." Those professors "belonging to the Collège de France have nothing in common with us," claimed Ozanam.[134] He and other like-minded colleagues in the Sorbonne had "proudly professed our faith and refuted contrary systems, striving to fulfill our vocation as professors in a Christian manner and to serve God in serving wholesome teaching."[135] In fact, Ozanam suggested that there were only two professors who were particularly vocal in their opposition to Christianity, Edgar Quinet and Jules Michelet, both of whom "were growing in popularity in the College of France by the side of the Sorbonne."[136] However, "we have not sought to make a division in the Faculty of Paris that does not exist, to effect two camps and give battle, and I believe that it is very important for the good of the young people that such be not the case, that our lectures not be looked upon by our colleagues as provocations demanding a reply and that, if some are strangers to the faith, they not be made into enemies."[137]

Unfortunately, Ozanam was accused of being too lenient. One of his most vocal critics was Louis Veuillot of *L'Univers*, who referred to Ozanam as a "deserter of the Catholic cause."[138] The charge was not only unjust but also hurtful. Ozanam's response nevertheless was filled with compassion: "I am sometimes charged with excessive gentleness towards unbelievers. When one has passed, as I have, through the crucible of doubt, it would indeed be cruelty and ingratitude to be harsh to those whom God has not yet vouchsafed to give the priceless gift of faith."[139] Despite his stance and the publicity, Ozanam succeeded Professor Fauriel as the Chair of Foreign Literature at the Sorbonne in 1844. He was honored with the Legion of Honor in 1846. He achieved both of these honors without any hint of compromise or cowardice.

Ozanam had little concern about protecting his own academic position when defending his principles, including freedom of teaching. One of his colleagues, Professor Lenormant, a convert to Christianity, had beome the subject of taunts and reprisals by certain hostile students. Lenormant was ridiculed as the "convert of the Sorbonne" by Michelet and Quinet of the Collège de France. Their provocation of anti-Christian students was fully intended to discredit Lenormant. Ozanam lent his support to Lenormant by attending his classes, and when the hostile comments and hisses began, Ozanam, filled with indignation, "leaped up beside the lecturer and stood for a moment surveying the tumult with proud defiance." He then "adjured them in the name of liberty, which they so loudly invoked, to respect liberty in others, and to allow every man the freedom of his conscience." The tumult came to an end; the students listened courteously to the rest of the lecture. Unfortunately, the government fell prey to pressure and canceled Lenormant's course the following day. Ozanam remained undaunted. When one student scratched out the words "foreign literature" on the door to Ozanam's lecture hall and wrote instead "theology," he waited to the very end of his lecture, which was never interrupted, and then with firm voice delivered the following statement: "I have not the *honor* to be a theologian, gentlemen, but I have the happiness to believe, and the ambition to place my whole soul with all my might at the service of truth." The hall erupted with cheers.[140]

The Dominican priest Père Lacordaire penned an accurate assessment of Ozanam's dilemma on this issue: "By the position in which God had placed him, Ozanam was the most awkwardly-situated of us all. Ardent Catholic as he was, firm supporter of social liberty, and above all of liberty of conscience, . . . he could not . . . refuse to recognize that he belonged to the body which by law held the monopoly of teaching. Was he to break with this body which had received him so young and heaped honours upon him? Was he to remain a member of it while taking an active and necessarily conspicuous part in the war being waged against it? In the first case Ozanam would be obliged to resign his Chair. Could that course be recommended to him? In the second he would be inviting dismissal. Could that course be recommended either?"[141] Ozanam made his way through this maze of pitfalls without abandoning his principles. As Lacordaire reported, "Ozanam kept his Chair; that was his post in Truth's critical hour. He did not expressly attack the body to which he belonged; his duty as a colleague and his debt of gratitude forbade it. But his solidarity remained entire and unbroken with those of us who were wholeheartedly behind the sacred cause of freedom of education."[142]

In 1850 the Falloux Law attempted a solution to this burning issue. In effect, the law allowed the Catholic Church to operate schools, but the state retained supervision rights. On this law both Ozanam and Lacordaire remained silent. It included features affecting the university that Ozanam did not favor.[143] Louis Veuillot was also unhappy with the law, for it maintained the right of university surveillance of education.[144] Ozanam ultimately loved the university life and believed that Catholics could gain much from it and bring much to it. As Cholvy remarks: "His dearest wish was the largest presence of devout Catholics in the University, a university where different opinions are expressed."[145]

THE SCHOLAR AS TEACHER

In the early nineteenth century most scholarship was intimately linked to teaching and the classroom. Frédéric Ozanam was no exception; he was first and foremost a teacher. And he became a gifted one. It was never easy for him to stand in a large lecture hall facing an intimidating crowd. As he came to the rostrum to lecture he was noticeably nervous: "He was pale almost to ghastliness; his dark eye[s] wandered over the heads of his audience, as if dreading to encounter a direct glance; his utterance was labored, his whole manner constrained."[146] But once he began speaking, a transformation occurred: "His eyes kindled, and met responsive glances boldly; his action, always simple, grew animated and expressive; his voice rang out in full and thrilling tones, until the audience, wrought to sympathy with the rising flame, caught fire at it and broke out into short but irrepressible bursts of applause. The victory once gained, the orator held it to the end, rising to loftier flights as he proceeded, and keeping his hearers captive to the close."[147] This scene played out time and time again.

His friend Jean-Jacques Ampère, whose rejection of the Chair of Foreign Literature (discussed in chapter 7) opened the way for Ozanam's appointment in 1844, recounted the diligence in Ozanam's preparation and delivery, but also the toll it took upon him over time: "Those who have not heard Professor Ozanam, do not know the personality of his genius. First, laborious preparation, dogged research, and a vast accumulation of knowledge; then, brilliant delivery in beautiful language which carried the audience with it; such was the course of his lectures. He prepared his lectures like a Benedictine, and delivered them like an orator: a double task in which a highly-strung constitution was used up and ultimately consumed."[148] His father-in-law, Monsieur Soulacroix, was actually alarmed by the excessive fatigue often induced by Ozanam's intense preparation and lecturing style.[149] But Ozanam was devoted to his students at the Sorbonne and at Stanislaus College, where he taught three classes to seniors each week to enhance his meager salary until he received the Chair of Foreign Literature in 1844. In his first year at Stanislaus College, Ozanam was able to achieve what no one had accomplished before him; his students in his class of rhetoric did well in the general competitions, receiving several firsts.[150] When Ozanam made the difficult decision to leave his post at Stanislaus because of the permanent appointment at the Sorbonne, his students were devastated, and one was charged with the task of writing to him on behalf of the group: "We cannot adequately express to you the surprise and grief with which we learned for the first time yesterday of the misfortune which has befallen us. Those who have been with you for a few months only, those who passed a year at your lectures and who looked forward to passing a second, those whom other courses have claimed after Rhetoric, have all equally been affected. I have been charged with the sad duty of communicating to you that general sense of grief. . . . In any case, . . . we shall never forget the many acts of kindness which you have showered on us. Deign to accept our sincere gratitude, and pardon this indiscretion for the sake of the love and affection which is hereby conveyed to you by *all the students of Stanislaus College*."[151]

Except for the days on which his lectures were scheduled, Ozanam reserved from eight to ten o'clock each morning for his students, who lined up to speak to him. With great patience and wisdom, he listened to their concerns and offered advice.[152] As Kathleen O'Meara writes: "no matter how tired he was, they were never dismissed; he welcomed their noisy company, with its eager talk, its comments and questions, as if it were the most refreshing rest."[153] He was especially patient with students who struggled, as long as they made a serious effort to succeed. His compassion was not reserved only for those living in poverty. He often inspired his students to achieve more than they had ever dreamed possible,[154] and both his example and his faith led some of his students to regain their faith.[155] His popularity increased, but not at the expense of high standards. Ozanam had the reputation of being a fair but intense examiner for the degrees of "baccalauréat, de licence, de doctorat."[156] When a student failed, he explained carefully and painstakingly the reasons why and the ways to improve. It was a task that demanded much of his time and placed great strains on his health.[157] In the heat of August, when most examinations occurred, it was often difficult "sitting for eight or ten hours a day at that blessed green table."[158]

There is little doubt that Ozanam "loved the young, and had the secret of gaining their fullest confidence."[159] His students in general were devoted to him, frequently following him after class across the Luxembourg Gardens and peppering him with questions as he returned to his home on the rue de Fleurus.[160] They remembered him with great affection. One of his students, who later became a professor of philosophy at the Sorbonne, wrote the following:

> I remember . . . the first day that we came into the class-room. The first impression was one of curiosity . . . Ozanam was neither handsome, elegant, or graceful. His appearance was common-place, his manner awkward and embarrassed. Extreme short-sightedness and a tangled mass of hair completed a rather strange ensemble. A spirit of malice in the class was however rapidly replaced by a feeling of sympathy. It was impossible to remain long insensible to an expression of kindliness coming direct from the heart through a face which, if somewhat heavy, was yet not without distinction. Then, a smile of beautiful refinement, and at moments, a flashing intelligence transformed the face, as if it had been

illumined by a ray of light from the soul. He unbent willingly with a gaiety, with a laugh so boyish and so natural, a wit so charming and so well turned, that it was a delight to find him in one of those happy moments when he let himself go. We tempted him on; he refrained, taking refuge in the severity of duty and the seriousness of instruction. He unbent occasionally. Then you should hear him! What youth in that spirit so mature in knowledge! What refinement and frankness! Refinement and frankness: that constituted the charm of nature which had preserved simplicity of heart with the most complete refinement of mind.[161]

Even Ernest Renan, who, as a scholar, would deny the divinity of Christ and cause much scandal in the early 1860s,[162] remembered his teacher Ozanam with great affection: "I never leave one of his lectures without feeling strengthened, more determined to do something great, more full of courage and hope as regards the future. . . . Ozanam's course of lectures are a continual defence of everything which is most worthy of our admiration. . . . Ozanam, how fond of him we were! What a fine soul!"[163] This is a powerful testimony to Ozanam as a teacher. Ozanam, too, in the last year of his life, remembered his teaching days at the Sorbonne with genuine fondness for his students: "Oh, poor Sorbonne, how many times have I returned in spirit to your dark walls, to your cold but studious courtyard, in your smoky classrooms, only to see them filled with happy young persons. Dear friend, after the infinite consolations that a Catholic finds at the foot of the altars, after the joys of family life, I know of no greater happiness than to speak to young people who have intelligence and a good heart."[164] Teaching remained a most cherished privilege and a sacred ministry for this humble scholar.

In his lifetime, Ozanam, the scholar, believed that he could achieve an alliance of science and faith: "With never the need to dissimulate or water down my convictions, I have always met with a sympathetic hearing from the young people in my courses at the Sorbonne. . . . I continue to strive . . . for that alliance of science and faith, of the Church and freedom, which I hope to see emerge from the storms of the 19th century."[165] If he was demanding of his students, he was no less demanding of himself. Both his research and his teaching were serious matters and sacred trusts. He could give no less than his entire self to these enterprises. Modern readers might think he was blind to the improper actions of

Catholic princes and rulers, but he was not. Rather, he saw his purpose as defending Christianity against the sometimes unjust and biased misrepresentations to which it had been subjected since the onset of the Enlightenment in the eighteenth century, a purpose he had defined very early in his life. As his friend Jean-Jacques Ampère remarked: "What Ozanam placed above everything on earth, what enabled him to undertake extraordinary research, to produce scientific works, to speak with rare eloquence, to establish many associations of good works, what distinguishes all his actions and words with an ineffaceable seal was his great Catholic Faith, the dominating influence of his life."[166] Ozanam's life provided a convincing demonstration that to be a good Catholic and to be a good scholar were fully compatible pursuits.

CHAPTER 6

———

Spokesperson for the People

When Frédéric Ozanam's family left Milan and returned to Lyon in 1816, France was again under the rule of the Bourbon dynasty in the person of King Louis XVIII. His Restoration government had proved unpopular and was readily toppled by Napoleon when the former emperor escaped from captivity on Elba in March 1815. The coalition of countries that opposed Napoleon returned Louis to power after their victory at Waterloo on June 18, 1815.[1] Unfortunately, the Bourbons were slow learners. At first unwilling to bend to the former revolutionaries, Louis XVIII had granted a charter in 1814 that provided for a constitutional monarchy, including a bicameral legislature (the Chamber of Peers and the Chamber of Deputies, who were elected). Suffrage was limited to males over twenty-five years of age who paid taxes in the amount of at least 300 francs.[2] This meant that among a total population of 29 million, less than 90,000 men were eligible to vote. Of those eligible to vote, less than 15,000 had the right to stand for election as deputies. This was a far cry from the idea of universal suffrage that had been a catchword of the more radical days of the French Revolution.[3] Louis XVIII insisted that he was the king by God's grace. Any freedoms, such as freedom of speech, press, assembly, and religion, were at best vaguely outlined in the Charter of 1814, and the "Charter provided for their control" in case any citizen "abused" them. In effect, "personal freedom . . . was subject to the whims of the Ministry of Police."[4] A preamble was actually inserted in the charter, clearly indicating that these freedoms were a gift from the king; they were not to be misconstrued as the people's fundamental rights.[5] According to one historian, "The Restoration government remained an uneasy hybrid of liberal and counter-revolutionary principles."[6]

Despite these tensions, the reign of Louis XVIII after Waterloo (1816–24) proved to be rather tranquil. This was not the case under his immediate successor.[7] The death of Louis XVIII in 1824 brought his brother to the throne as King Charles X. During the period of exile in the revolutionary years, Charles had become "intransigent and devoted to Catholicism."[8] When he came to power he was spoiling for a fight: "He was sixty-seven years old, a legitimist to the core[,] and willingly undertook divisive measures that his elder brother had avoided."[9] He scorned the charter as an objectionable restraint on his rightful power.[10] Under Charles, the French government was especially ill-prepared to deal with the social and economic conditions that France faced in the early nineteenth century. Tensions mounted between 1824 and 1830. A number of bourgeois intellectuals, many of whom were professors or journalists, became increasingly critical of the government and vocal in their protests. Despite strict censorship attempts, the press engaged in the highly charged political debate, adding fuel to the fire of indignation and discontent. Parisian students and artisan workers were intensely interested in the political scene; both groups formed secret societies and secured arms in the event of a conflict. There were riots in 1827, and it was merely a matter of time before events would erupt and barricades be erected.[11] During the month of July, Charles X announced a set of ordinances that curbed the freedom of the press, dissolved the chamber of elected deputies, and restricted the suffrage to only 25,000 men. His action was perhaps legal, but it was viewed as tantamount to a coup d'état by many Parisians. On July 27, 1830, workers, petite bourgeoisie, and university students erected and manned barricades. Completely shocked by and unprepared for this resistance, Charles X abdicated. He fled France, never to return.[12]

Eugene Delacroix depicted the events of July 1830 in his famous painting *Liberty Leading the People*. As noted by one historian, "*Liberty Leading the People* . . . dramatically captures the ambiguity of the events that toppled the Bourbon Restoration in July 1830."[13] It may have been workers, petite bourgeoisie, and students who staged the overthrow, but others determined who would actually rule France.[14] The fighters in the painting include a well-dressed bourgeois man wearing a top hat. Liberal deputies and journalists, most of them prominent members of the bourgeoisie, assumed control of the revolution before it could take a more radical course.[15] They looked to a person as their next king who would willingly accept the constitution and parliamentary rule. That person was Louis-Philippe, the duc d'Orléans. He was the leader of a younger branch of the Bourbon family and had served with the revolutionary army. During the Terror he left France for safer quarters, returning when the Bourbons were restored to power. He had led a relatively quiet existence until 1830. The leader of the liberal group, Adolphe Thiers, proclaimed that Louis-Philippe was the ideal citizen king. The popular but elderly General Lafayette was convinced to throw his support to the candidate.[16] On August 9, 1830, Louis-Philippe became, not King of France, but "King of the French."[17] The king's power now derived from *le peuple* (the people), not from *le Dieu* (God). Indeed, Catholicism was no longer to be the religion of the state; it was to be recognized as the "religion professed by most Frenchmen." This wording "probably derived from Guizot's Protestantism and the mild anticlericalism of most liberals."[18] The white-colored banner of the House of Bourbon brought back during the Restoration was again removed. Replacing it was the tricolor, the new national flag.[19]

FACTIONS DURING THE REIGN OF LOUIS-PHILIPPE

Many factions, both from the right and the left, were disenchanted with the choice of Louis-Philippe. One of these factions included avid royalists who viewed his claim as illegitimate and saw him as little better than a traitor.[20] The new *Charte* (Charter) to which he agreed favored the wealthy bourgeoisie. Although the electorate was increased to 166,000 in 1831, activists who favored a more authentic republic and who had hoped for universal suffrage were genuinely frustrated and believed that they had been betrayed. They posed a significant threat to the new king.[21] The government countered by encouraging people to get rich ("*Enrichissez-vous*")[22] as the only viable way to augment the ranks of voters. By 1847, eligible voters reached the 240,000 mark, a sure sign that wealth was increasing for some, but still a far cry from universal suffrage.[23] Catholics were also distressed by the lack of security afforded by the government. Popular anger was sometimes directed at the Catholic Church, not because it was associated with Louis-Philippe but because it was associated in people's minds with the now defeated Bourbons. In Paris, rioters sacked the palace of the archbishop in February 1831. The government showed little enthusiasm for protecting the Church and its property; anticlericalism and anticlerical protests became a hallmark of the period.[24]

Some prominent French Catholics seized the moment to promote a more liberal agenda. One of the most famous was Felicité de Lamennais, a writer whose ideas had inspired both Ozanam and his father. Lamennais had originally advocated a close relationship between the Catholic Church and the state. During the 1820s, however, he became disenchanted with the reality of the union of throne and altar. He concluded that the Restoration rulers were toying with the Catholic Church, using it for their own selfish purposes. By the time of the 1830 revolution, Lamennais was convinced that throne and altar should be separate. His ideas attracted a number of young enthusiasts. He established the journal *L'Avenir* (The Future) to spread his ideas. Articles published in *L'Avenir* formed the basis of what has been termed "liberal Catholicism" and encouraged greater involvement by the Catholic Church in the social and economic problems of the day. Both *L'Avenir* and Lamennais found disfavor with the French clergy.[25] His doctrines were officially rebuked in the 1832 papal encyclical *Mirari vos.*[26] Unlike most of his followers, however, Lamennais refused to bend to the strictures of the Catholic Church. His *Paroles d'un croyant* (Remarks of a Believer) appeared in 1834, denouncing all civil and ecclesiastical authority; it was condemned by the pope. In it Lamennais predicted the fall of existing governments, followed by the triumphant victory of democracy inspired by Christian ideals.[27]

The common people were another dissatisfied faction. They had manned the barricades in 1830, but not necessarily because they favored

Louis-Philippe. His policies over the next eighteen years increasingly alienated them from his regime.[28] Workers and artisans were particularly dismayed. The historian Roger Magraw argues that "militancy in the proletarian sector was . . . at best embryonic. The French working class was born in the workshops, not the factory, among artisans whose immediate experience in the July Monarchy were reflected through values lodged deep in their culture-norms, profoundly antagonistic to the ethos of the capitalist emphasis on profit maximization." According to Magraw, "Radicalization of the artisanate occurred most spectacularly in Lyon, where the silk industry, which produced one-third of the value of French exports, employed 50,000 in a city population of 180,000."[29] The Lyon silk workers objected to the introduction of machines and procedures that threatened their jobs and way of life. In 1831 there was an uprising of silk workers in Lyon, Frédéric's home town. According to reports, their slogan was "Live Working or Die Fighting," a phrase that illuminates both the intensity of feelings and the depth of dissension. The government had tried to guarantee a minimum price favorable to the silk workers, but local merchants objected. The government caved in to the wealthy interest group. The result was a strike by the silk workers. Troops then had to reconquer the city, but they could never repress the discontent.[30]

When the revolt broke out, Frédéric was not in Lyon. He had just arrived in Paris to attend school. His father, however, witnessed and wrote about the events in *L'Histoire de Lyon pendant le journées des 21, 22 et 23 novembre 1831*.[31] Although he was a proponent of humane measures in dealing with the revolt, nevertheless, Frédéric's father believed that "authority cannot and should not intervene in the regulation of private interests; that it is impossible to impose conditions on industry, daughter of liberty; and that competition and particular interests alone suffice to regulate the role that labor should play in the economy of textile production."[32] His words reflected nineteenth-century liberal economic principles,[33] some of which his son Frédéric would later call into question. The discontent of the Lyon silk workers continued to fester. It resurfaced more forcefully in 1834 during an eight-day strike that resulted in arrests and a six-day assault to crush the revolt. Nearly three hundred silk workers were killed.[34] Lyon became "the symbol for a new working-class threat, its risings compared to St. Domingo slave revolts by terrified Orleanist bourgeois."[35]

LES BARBARES AND THE BOURGEOISIE

Saint-Marc Girardin, a journalist who had witnessed the Lyon strike, commented that the disturbance was "a rising of the poor against the rich, the workers against the manufacturers, not in order to obtain political rights, but to get an increase in wages. It was only a strike in the form of an insurrection."[36] Once in Paris he quickly composed an article with the title "Les Barbares" for *Le Journal des Débats* in early December 1831.[37] In it he compared the workers not to the slaves of the French colonies but rather to the tribes that threatened the late Roman Empire: "The barbarians who threaten society are not in the Caucasus or on the steppes of Tartary; they are in the suburbs of our industrial towns. These barbarians should not be insulted; alas, they deserve pity rather than blame. They suffer; they are crushed by poverty. How should they not seek better conditions of life?"[38] Saint-Marc Girardin claimed that the term *barbare* was not one of censure, but he warned against permitting the masses to join the National Guard or to participate in elections.[39] He argued further that the only way to counter this threat was to make sure workers could gain an interest in a stable society by acquiring money and land, essentially the same prescription recommended by Louis-Philippe's government.[40] With the appearance of his article, the term *barbare* came into popular usage. Many liberals viewed it as a term of opprobrium, but Frédéric Ozanam later used it with a new and positive twist.[41]

In 1831 Louis-Philippe's government had responded to growing fears of social disorder with stricter measures of repression, including an April law banning public demonstrations. In 1832 supporters of a more open and free republic used the funeral of the popular General Lamarque to stage an insurrection. Its only result was a bitter and bloody siege,[42] which was immortalized in Victor Hugo's *Les Misérables*. Three years later, in 1835, a failed assassination attempt on the king resulted in the "September Laws," which increased the control of the government over the press and made the process of obtaining convictions for political agitation less difficult.[43] Louis-Philippe survived the opposition of various discontented factions by following a strategy of self-preservation; he effectively played one group against another. But his government was corrupt, and this corruption eventually undermined any hope for truly responsible or responsive rule.[44]

The years after 1830 witnessed the beginnings of significant industrialization in France and its attendant social changes. France certainly did not rival Great Britain's rapid industrial development. For example, in 1845 France imported only 60,000 tons of raw cotton for its textile mills, compared to Britain's imports of 276,000 tons. Between 1842 and 1845, however, France enjoyed an industrial surge from railroad construction, a form of transportation that was revolutionizing many countries. Interestingly, Ozanam lamented some of the negative consequences of the new rail system and shared his thoughts in an 1843 letter with his wife, Amélie: "One can imagine nothing more bizarre than the procedures by which one succeeds in placing a carriage on the rails; I will not succeed in explaining it to you other than in person. Also, there is nothing more savage or more worthy of a barbaric century than these railroads which do not respect any of the most beautiful things, valleys, mountains, streams, and which fill everything, penetrate everything, which go straight ahead and which are always black so that this beautiful countryside from Rouen to Paris becomes very monotonous and the most grayish thing in the world."[45] Despite Ozanam's reservations, the railroad was there to stay, although railroad construction slowed during an economic depression in 1846 and 1847. It would be 1850 before the economic benefits of railroad production were realized.[46]

To many French citizens, Louis-Philippe's regime was a new "bourgeois monarchy" that brought great economic growth. Although land ownership remained the chief source of wealth in France, groups such as bankers, industrialists, lawyers, magistrates, and top government officials, all part of the rising bourgeoisie, benefited from the times.[47] The most prosperous bourgeoisie invested in land and then adopted the lifestyle of aristocrats. They became the *haute bourgeoisie* (the high middle class), in contrast to the petite bourgeoisie. Between these two groups of the middle class was sandwiched another large and diverse layer of bourgeoisie, composed of lawyers, doctors, notaries, professors, journalists, businessmen, and even some rural landowners.[48] Paris was most affected by the increase in the bourgeois class. Older *hotels* formerly occupied by a single aristocratic family were "now subdivided into apartments for the increasingly numerous bourgeois who filled them with a clutter of furniture and decorative objects."[49]

The growth of the middle class came hand in hand with increased urbanization. Although most French at the beginning of the nineteenth century made their living through agriculture, farming areas during the reign of Louis-Philippe suffered a decrease in population. Young people left rural areas to find their fortune in the cities.[50] Paris was the leader. Its population doubled between 1800 and 1850, to over one million people. Many who came to Paris seeking success unfortunately found only squalor.[51] In 1825 "poor housing, sewerage, and overcrowding made the Parisian death rate 40 per cent above the national average."[52] Louis-René Villermé, who wrote about the conditions of French textile workers in 1840, detailed the horrendous conditions of the growing urban slums: "A single, bad straw mattress for the whole family, a small stove which serves for cooking and for heating, a crate or large box masquerading as a cupboard, a table, two or three chairs, a bench, some dishes—these make up the normal furnishings of the rooms of workers."[53] What a contrast this was to the cluttered homes of the bourgeoisie. Cholera outbreaks were a real and ever-present threat. Violence and crime were further consequences of these squalid living conditions. Property owners feared what they referred to as the "dangerous classes." They pressured the government to repress any threat rather than seek remedies to address such conditions humanely.[54] In fact, some of the middle class were adamant that those living in poverty and those who lacked education should be excluded from participation in public life.[55] One of the few pieces of legislation for social reform appeared only in 1841, when a law limiting child labor attested to a growing concern about the welfare of children. It was the "French state's first intervention in the workplace."[56] It was also not a particularly successful one. The historian Gordon Wright paints a bleak image of the conditions of the French working class, Saint-Marc Girardin's *barbares*:

> If Karl Marx had written *Das Kapital* in the Bibliothèque Nationale rather than in the British Museum, he might have buttressed his argument with French examples just as appalling as those which he drew from official British surveys. In those cities where the factory system was emerging, a working day of fifteen hours or even more was normal during the Bourbon and Orleanist epochs. Wages rarely sufficed to keep a family alive, even if both parents and children worked; a supplement

from private charity was common. In the Lille area in 1828 two-thirds of the workers were carried on some kind of relief roll. Only a minority of workers could expect to eat meat more than once or twice a year. From 30 to 50 per cent of a working family's budget went for the purchase of bread; it was quite literally the staff of life. Contemporary descriptions of housing conditions in the slums of Lille or Nantes are almost beyond belief. At Mulhouse about 1830 the average life expectancy for children of the bourgeoisie was thirty-one years; for children of weavers, less than four years. In Louis-Philippe's reign nine-tenths of the army draftees from industrial areas had to be rejected for physical deficiencies. Alcoholism and promiscuity were common; in one representative year, one-third of all births in Paris were illegitimate. Illiteracy among the workers was almost universal. Price and wage studies for the period 1814–48 are undependable, but real wages almost certainly fell during the Bourbon era and barely held their own under Louis-Philippe. Until the 1840's at least, population growth far outstripped economic growth, and the workers of both city and countryside suffered the consequences.[57]

Since 1791 French workers had been forbidden to organize by the Chapelier Law, but the laboring classes in France became more conscious of themselves as a group between 1815 and 1848. They learned how to circumvent the system. Workers formed legal mutual aid societies, which provided help to workers who were sick and unemployed or who needed to cover funeral expenses. These societies expanded in number between 1830 and 1848. Here, workers could clandestinely gather to consider action such as a strike. Several periodicals for workers also appeared. Lyon had the *Echo de la Fabrique*, while Paris boasted *L'Atelier*, beginning in 1840.[58] Angry workers employed the threat of *sabotage*, a word derived from the wooden clog called a *sabot* that was worn by peasant workers and sometimes used by them to jam machinery.[59] In 1840 strikers held out the hope that "perhaps our forceful acts will open people's eyes to the traitors who made such pretty promises after the Revolution of 1830 and never kept one."[60] The new target of radical language was the growing "financial aristocracy," not the noble class.[61] Unfortunately, the lot of workers only worsened between 1846 and 1848, when the economy was depressed due to a serious potato and grain shortage, which exacerbated the desperation of urban centers.[62]

The discontent and disillusionment with the government of Louis-Philippe came to a climax in the year 1848. Alexis de Tocqueville, the famous French writer on American democracy, had warned the Chamber of Deputies early in 1848: "We are lulling ourselves to sleep over an active volcano."[63] He was correct. The volcano erupted in February 1848 and spread to other countries in Europe facing similar problems (the famous revolutions of 1848). The most significant opposition in France came not from the working classes but from members of those groups and classes that most resented being excluded from the political mainstream, including Catholics, aristocratic landowners, students, and, most important, the bourgeoisie, many of whom still could not vote.[64] The government of Louis-Philippe, the so-called "bourgeois monarch," was quickly overthrown, but the process of forming a new government and determining who was to be included was not so easy.

OZANAM'S POLITICAL VIEWS:
MONARCHY TO DEMOCRACY

Living through these turbulent times, Frédéric Ozanam was absolutely clear that a deep knowledge of the course of history had eventually led him "to the conclusion that in the nature of mankind democracy is the final stage in the development of political progress, and that God leads the world in that direction."[65] In 1848 he firmly maintained: "I still believe in the possibility of Christian democracy; I don't believe in anything else in political matters."[66] Ozanam's views on democracy had evolved over time; his mature political views were formed only gradually, after significant study, experience, and deep reflection. He was at first a royalist. After the revolution of 1830 that deposed the Bourbons and installed Louis-Philippe, the young Frédéric wrote to his Lyonnais friend Auguste Materne that he had just heard news of the overthrow of Charles X. He was bursting with indignation. Proclaiming that he was and always would be "a faithful subject of the legitimate King Charles X," Frédéric referred to the usurpers as "criminals" and denounced their illegal actions.[67] Just before Christmas in 1831 he informed his mother that the new king was "generally detested."[68] Moreover, he told her that as a young student in Paris he was occasionally harassed by the National

Guard, who thought that all students were troublemakers.[69] In 1832 Frédéric (only eighteen years old) again shared with his cousin Ernest Falconnet his support of the idea of monarchy: "I do not believe that French society has yet come of age. . . . I believe its character to be such that it needs a monarchical regime to direct it in its wanderings and the heredity of the throne to maintain stability in its progress and unity in its diversity. . . . The king is then for me the symbol of national destinies, the old French idea presiding over the development of society, the representation of the people par excellence. On his forehead shines the glories of France ancient and modern."[70]

Two years later, in 1834—the fourth year of Louis-Philippe's reign, the year of the Lyon silk workers' second revolt, and a little more than a year since the first conference of charity was begun—Ozanam had further refined his thoughts. The twenty-one-year-old Frédéric confided to Falconnet that although he had not yet completely abandoned his support of monarchy as a form of government, he had serious reservations: "I am without contradiction for the old royalism in every respect even if it is a glorious invalid, but I do not insist on it because, with its wooden leg, it cannot march in step with the new generations."[71] His views were undergoing a significant change: "I declare neither for nor against any government combination, but accept them as instruments for making man happier and better. If you want a formula, here it is: I believe in authority as a means, in liberty as a means, and in love as the end."[72]

His position was that there were two types of monarchical government, inspired by two diametrically opposed principles: "There is either the exploitation of everyone for the good of a single person, the monarchy of Nero, a monarchy I abhor. Or there is the sacrifice of a single person for the good of all, the monarchy of Saint Louis, which I revere with love."[73] Ozanam, however, did not discuss only monarchy; he also noted other possible forms of government based upon either of these two different principles: "There is either the exploitation of all for the good of the few, the republic of Athens and that of the Terror, and such a republic I condemn. Or there is the sacrifice of a few for the good of all, the Christian republic of the primitive Church at Jerusalem. . . . Humanity cannot attain a higher state."[74] Frédéric firmly believed that the two great powers behind history were divine providence and human liberty[75] and that the Church's mission was to regenerate civilization.[76] For Ozanam,

"Egoism and charity are two rival powers which from the beginning have disputed the possession of the world. Egoism is produced under two forms which are very dear to it, despotism and anarchy. Charity, in the Church, opposes liberty to despotism, and to anarchy, authority."[77]

By 1838 Frédéric was able to refer to the separation of church and state, or "throne and altar," as a "great thing" for Frenchmen.[78] And by 1845 he had arrived at the point where he could assert in his work on Dante that "monarchical authority . . . has its limitations. The social order exists only in the interest of the human race: they who obey the law were not created for the good pleasure of the lawgiver: on the contrary, the lawgiver was made for their needs. It is an incontestable axiom that the monarch is to be considered the servant of all."[79] He counseled François Lallier in that same year that he did not want Catholics to form a separate political party; rather, he wanted a Catholic France that was open to reform and regeneration. "I would not want a Catholic party, because then there would no longer be a nation which would be Catholic. . . . I prefer that God spread his gifts with diversity and that there will be daring men, even if one should find them rash; that there be prudent ones, even if they should be accused of indifference."[80] Although Ozanam had condemned the abuses of the Reign of Terror in France (1793–95), increasingly he distinguished the Terror and its excesses from authentic democracy. Consequently, he developed a genuine appreciation for the value and the necessity of democratic reform, especially if France hoped to be resurrected, like a phoenix, from the ashes of the French Revolution. According to the Catholic Church historian Thomas Bokenkotter, Ozanam began to interpret the French Revolution "as humanity's cry for greater freedom, and . . . he tried to move the Church to hear that cry and join the struggle."[81]

What transformed his thinking in such a radical way? In addition to his studies, research, and reading, his experience of service to others in the Society of St. Vincent de Paul and his deep reflection on that experience had the greatest impact on him. This service gradually led him to embrace the idea of a democracy that was responsive to the Christian principles of personal dignity, freedom, and the common good. As the historian Gérard Cholvy has noted: "Although the Conference of Charity (1833) initially arose from a desire to unite faith students from the provinces who had come to Paris, the gradual discovery . . . of the 'social issue,' that is, poverty born of industrialization, owed much to the visits they made to the tenements of the poor."[82] It took Ozanam time to understand fully the serious desperation that leads to violence. As a young student, he was horrified by one of the first scenes of violence he witnessed while away from home. After this incident, which was sparked by a cholera epidemic in Paris (1832), he wrote to his mother: "Last Sunday I saw revolutionary rabble. *Never* was there seen so frightful a *mob*. . . . It was a great pity to see this race of accursed men of whom the tallest was not 5 feet, with weak and ugly bodies, pale faces, sunken eyes with shifty glances, and the women who followed crying like the furies, nothing more hideous than those women!"[83] Again, in 1834, he wrote in a letter to Falconnet that "opposition is useful and admissible, but not insurrection; active obedience, passive resistance."[84]

Ozanam returned to this topic in an 1837 letter, lamenting that "Alas! We see each day the schism started . . . become deeper: there are no longer political opinions dividing men, they are less opinions than interests, here the camp of riches, there the camp of the poor. . . . Between the two, an irreconcilable hatred, rumblings of a coming war which will be a war of extermination." According to Ozanam, the interposition of Christians between the two camps would provide the "only means of salvation." The members of the Society of St. Vincent de Paul could travel "from one side to the other doing good, obtaining many alms from the rich and much resignation from the poor, . . . getting them used to looking upon one another as brothers, infusing them with a bit of mutual charity." He genuinely hoped for the day when "the two camps will rise up and destroy the barriers of prejudice, throw away their angry weapons, and march to meet each other, not to battle, but to mingle, embrace, and become one sheepfold under one shepherd."[85] This kind of reconciliation could never be achieved by political agendas or political gatherings; Ozanam clearly understood that only a transformation of the human person and of society would lead to true liberty, equality, and fraternity.

As he came to know those living in poverty in Paris through charitable community service in the Society of St. Vincent de Paul, his opinion of them changed and the cause of their physical appearance became apparent. He would always abhor insurrection, but his abhorrence was no longer because of the unruly and unsightly mob. Instead

he understood that insurrection's violence was born of profound desperation and that it served no purpose other than to harden hearts
and minds. Indeed, it is significant that the language Ozanam chose to
describe the situations he confronted moves away from the assumption
that physical beauty was the primary indicator of moral or social integrity, a prejudice that was shared by many in Ozanam's day: "In these foul
cellars and garrets, . . . we have often come upon the loveliest domestic
virtues, on a refinement and intelligence that one does not always meet
under gilded ceilings."[86]

Ozanam recognized that some people living in poverty were prone
"to sloth and vice," but he saw these qualities more as a consequence
than as a cause of poverty. He cautioned that "there is no room for that
ready excuse of the hardhearted, that the poor are wretched by their
own fault."[87] The social historian Katherine Lynch provides an excellent
assessment of Ozanam's view: "His belief that poverty among workers
was exacerbated by their tendency to debauchery, gambling, and other
vices was not a new one. Even within the highly spiritualized view
of the poor among noble Catholic activists of Counter-Reformation
France, there had been room for this belief and for ambivalence about
the poor themselves. However, Ozanam's point was to emphasize the
societal and systemic [my emphasis] rather than the accidental or individual causes of poverty and, furthermore, to implicate the behavior
and mores of both worker and bourgeois in the class estrangement of
industrial capitalist society."[88]

Ozanam's visits as a friend to those living in poverty enhanced his
appreciation of the essential dignity and nobility of the common person.
In his own words he described one such epiphany: "Among these inhabitants of the Faubourgs, whom it is the custom to represent as a people
devoid of all faith, there are very few who have not a cross at the head of
their bed." He noted the following with compassion: "a poor cooper, of
past seventy years of age, tiring his infirm arms to get bread for the child
of a son who had died in the flower of his age; a deaf and dumb boy of
twelve, whose education has been carried on by the self-devotion of his
poor relatives. . . . We shall never forget one poor room, of irreproach-
able cleanliness, where a mother, clothed in the threadbare costume of
her native place, Auvergne, was working with her four daughters, modest young girls . . . ; but the faith which these honest people had brought

with them from their native mountains illuminated their lives."[89] Meeting face to face those living in poverty dispelled any false notions and foolish stereotypes about them. Ozanam became convinced that both his country and his church had to support the common people.

1848

In 1848, the year of revolutions across Europe, Ozanam published one of his most famous, and perhaps most controversial, writings. It was a call to embrace the cause of the masses. During his travels in Italy in 1846–47, he had been impressed by the example of the new pope, Pius IX, who was instituting several liberal reforms in the Papal States. Recalling the current use of the word *barbare* that had been coined by Saint-Marc Girardin in 1831, Ozanam used the term, but he used it "with the tone of a Christian who rejoices at their conversion."[90] He elaborated his message in an article published in *Le Correspondant* entitled "Les dangers de Rome et ses espérances." The article appeared on February 10, just two weeks before the fall of Louis-Philippe and the beginning of the 1848 revolution in Paris.[91] The workers were the new barbarians of the current century, Ozanam argued, and, like the barbarians in Roman times, they needed to be embraced and converted: "Let us sacrifice our prejudices and turn to democracy, this proletariat, which knows us not. Let us go after it not only with our preaching but with our benefits, and let us help it not only with our alms but with our efforts to obtain for it institutions which will set it free and make it better. Let us follow Pius IX and go over to the barbarians [Suivons Pie IX et passons aux barbares!]."[92] Unlike others, Ozanam employed the barbarian metaphor in support of workers, not as a rebuke.[93] A storm of criticism ensued. Ozanam sought to explain himself. He countered objections by stating that his article was intended to make the plea that "instead of espousing the interests of a doctrinaire ministry, of a fearful peerage, or of an egotistical bourgeoisie, we take care of the people who have too many needs and not enough rights and who justly demand a more complete role in public affairs, guarantees for work and against misery."[94] He was stunned but not deterred by the opposition: "It is in the people that I see enough remnants of faith and morality to save a society in which the upper classes are lost."[95]

Ozanam was critical of those who continued to ignore the cries of those living in poverty. On March 6, 1848, he wrote to his brother Alphonse and poured out his feelings to one he so trusted: "Behind the political revolution [of 1848], there is a social revolution. . . . Behind the Republic . . . there are issues which interest the people and for which they fought: issues of work, leisure and salary. One must not think he can escape these problems."[96] He wrote to Alphonse again nine days later: "If a greater number of Christians, and especially clergymen, had looked after the workers for ten years, we would be more sure of the future."[97] Using strong words of admonishment in April 1848, Ozanam again confided in Alphonse. He wished the Catholic Church would "take care of the workers like the rich people; it is from now on the only way to salvation for the Church of France. The priests must give up their little bourgeois parishes, flocks of elite people in the middle of an immense population which they do not know."[98] He then asked his priestly brother for his prayers because he had been asked to stand as a candidate from Lyon in the upcoming elections, and he knew the risks involved.[99]

Although Ozanam was not interested in a political career, he was approached to stand for election as a representative in the new assembly to be formed following the revolution that unseated Louis-Philippe in 1848. Out of a sense of civic duty he agreed to offer his name as a candidate. He proudly and publicly claimed that he had "the passionate love of my country, the enthusiasm of common interests," and that he longed for "the alliance of Christianity and freedom."[100] Ozanam was not elected, but he left a clear record of his mature political and social beliefs, nurtured by both his studies and his experiences of social service from 1833 to 1848.[101] In a public statement issued on April 15 to the constituents of the department of the Rhône, he declared that liberty, equality, and fraternity—the catchwords of the French Revolution—signaled the "temporal advent of the Gospel." The French Revolution of 1789 had been bloody and violent precisely because it had forgotten its religious heritage, a Christian heritage that could and should embrace the people in a loving way.

In the case of liberty, Ozanam declared: "I want the sovereignty of the people. And, as the people are made up of the universality of free men, I want above all else the sanction of the natural rights of man and of family. In the constitution one must put, above the uncertainty of parliamentary majorities, freedom of people, freedom of speech, of teaching, of associations and of religions. Power must not, entrusted to the instability of parties, ever be able to suspend individual freedom, to intrigue in questions of conscience or to silence the press."[102] In the case of equality, he affirmed: "I want a republican constitution without a return to royalties which are henceforth impossible. I want it with equality for all, therefore with universal suffrage for the National Assembly.... I ... reject all thoughts of a federate republic [a federation of largely independent states]. But, at the same time, I reject an excessive centralization which would still enlarge Paris to the detriment of the departments, the cities to the detriment of the country, and which would bring back inequality among those whom the law makes equal."[103] Considering how limited the suffrage had been since 1815, his call for universal suffrage was a bold one.

Finally, in the case of fraternity, he proclaimed:

I want fraternity with all of its consequences. I will defend the principle of property. But without touching this foundation of all civil order, one can introduce a system of progressive tax which would lessen the consumption taxes: one can replace the concession rights and insure a cheaper life. I will also support the rights to work; the independent work of the laborer, of the artisan, of the merchant who remains the master of his work and salary; the associations of workers among themselves, or of workers and contractors who voluntarily join together their work and their capital, finally the works of public service undertaken by the State and offering a home to laborers who are out of work or resources. I will forward with all my efforts the measures of justice and foresight which will alleviate the sufferings of the people. In my opinion, all these means are not too much in order to resolve this formidable question of work, the most pressing question of the present time.[104]

At the end of his public statement, Ozanam argued that "fraternity does not know boundaries" and expressed his sincere hope that France would have both the courage and the will to help deliver "nations suppressed by an unjust conquest, and which restore themselves while renouncing foreign domination."[105] One biographer of Ozanam, Thomas Auge, has argued that Ozanam's "advocacy of democracy places this moderate, gentle, scholarly man among the radicals of nineteenth-century French Catholics."[106] Whether Ozanam fully recognized the radical nature of his views is perhaps open to debate, but that he was firmly convinced by 1848 that church and state should be separate, that democracy was the best future form of government for France, and that the church must embrace the masses is beyond any doubt.[107]

Ozanam was willing to stand for election in 1848 and would soon discuss political issues in the newspaper *L'Ère nouvelle* (The New Era), but he did so not as a member or a leader of the Society of St. Vincent de Paul but as a concerned Catholic citizen. Ozanam had two clear positions on politics and political issues with respect to the Society. First, although he wanted all of its members to be civically responsible and civically engaged and regarded this engagement as a sacred duty, he thought that the Society itself should neither become embroiled in politics nor favor one political party over another. From its inception the Society was intended to be "an association of *mutual encouragement* for young Catholic people where one finds friendship, support, and example; . . . But the strongest tie, the principle of true friendship, is charity, . . . and good works are the food of charity."[108] The first Rule of the Society in 1835 was clear that politics and political wrangling had no place in the conference meeting.[109] The president-general of the Society, Jules Gossin, circulated his thoughts on politics to the members in 1844: "We shall continue our work and exclude therefrom everything which savors of politics. . . . On . . . that day on which one word of politics will be heard amongst us, on that day will . . . the Society of St. Vincent de Paul be destroyed."[110] A remark by Ozanam in 1839 indicates that he would have concurred with Gossin: "In the middle of the philosophical and political schools which divide spirits and that disturb hearts, may the society of which we are part become a great school where the vexing questions of this world will not agitate, where those who struggled once will meet to get to know and love one another, where one will learn that one thing, but something intelligible, acceptable, accommodating to all, a beautifully simple thing and yet infinite, eternal as God from which it comes, namely: charity!"[111]

In the Rule of the Society to this day, members are advised that the Society "does not identify with any political party and always adopts a non-violent approach." While recognizing that there is much good that can come from the political vocation of members who "bring Christian values to political matters" and while encouraging them to be good and active citizens, the Rule clearly states: "Those members who hold political offices will be asked, always with charity, not to hold any mission of representation in the Society during their term of political office."[112] Despite the caution about political connections, however, the Society, its leaders, and its members have always been encouraged to seek social justice, engaging openly in advocacy for those who otherwise have no voice. Article 7 of the Rule speaks to this latter issue. The Society wants to identify the unjust structures that cause need: "It is, therefore, committed to identifying the root causes of poverty and to contributing to their elimination." Its members "envision a more just society in which the rights, responsibilities and development of all people are promoted." Ultimately, the Society of St. Vincent de Paul "helps the poor and disadvantaged speak for themselves. When they cannot, the Society must speak on behalf of those ignored."[113] Ozanam's career provides ample evidence that he took seriously this role of speaking for the voiceless.

Ozanam was also convinced that the most pressing questions of his day were social, not political, in nature. "The problem that divides men in our day is no longer a problem of political structure; it is a social problem; it has to do with what is preferred, the spirit of self-interest or the spirit of sacrifice, whether society will be only a great exploitation to the profit of the strongest or a consecration of each individual for the good of all and especially for the protection of the weak." He had witnessed firsthand that there "are a great many men who have too much and who wish to have more; there are a great many others who do not have enough, who have nothing, and who are willing to take if someone gives to them." He observed that "between these two classes of men, a confrontation is coming, and this menacing confrontation will be terrible: on the one side, the power of gold, on the other the power of despair. We must cast ourselves between these two enemy armies, if not to prevent, at least to deaden the shock."[114] According to the historian Jay Corrin, a statement such as this "displays Ozanam's prescient sociological analysis as well as his faith in charity." Corrin argues that although Ozanam could never have embraced the ideas of Marx or of any of the nineteenth-century socialists, yet at least ten years before Marx's *Communist Manifesto* (1848), he had already "recognized that divisions between men were linked to economic disparities and warned of class warfare unless social programs were initiated to mitigate such inequities."[115]

Ozanam's growing faith in democracy led him to write articles on political and social matters in the newspaper *L'Ère nouvelle*.[116] He saw this work as a type of civic duty. He intended to speak out boldly in order to influence minds and persuade people to support democratic reforms. According to Christine Morel, Ozanam believed that it was a Catholic's duty in general to participate in public affairs and in the life of politics; this was the reason for his participation in the newspaper, along with the urgent need of the moment for action.[117] The prospectus for that publication (March 1, 1848) was signed by Ozanam. He, L'Abbé Maret, and Père Lacordaire were the three people most responsible for founding it.[118] *L'Ère nouvelle*'s express purpose was to "reconcile religion and the democratic Republic, to demand from the Republic liberty of education, liberty of association, amelioration of the condition of the working men." It also called for the protection of "all peoples who have lost their nationality by unjust conquests which time cannot rectify, and those other peoples which . . . aspire to achieve their own political and moral emancipation."[119]

The historian Claude Bressolette maintains that *L'Ère nouvelle* focused on five essential points. First, the February Revolution of 1848 was more than just another revolution. It signaled the beginning of a merciful plan to help the laboring class reclaim their rights. Second, Christianity would help to establish the true meaning of the three democratic maxims of liberty, equality, and fraternity in the temporal order. Third, the Republic was not a misfortune, but something to defend in order to preserve democracy. Fourth, the French people must reject the republican doctrines of 1793 concerning the supremacy of the state. Those doctrines looked toward establishing an earthly paradise but actually attacked liberty by undermining the rights of private property and of work. Fifth, the Republic that was to be promoted should be respectful of all freedoms, be resolved to maintain equal rights, be indefatigable in pursuing the ideal of the brotherhood for some five million workers and twenty-seven million farmers, and be committed as a sacred duty to the question of work, which must be studied to help solve the social problem.[120] Carol Harrison suggests that "*L'Ère nouvelle* was in some senses the heir to *L'Avenir*," because "Lacordaire's participation made that lineage clear."[121] *L'Avenir*, however, had "argued that representative government was not necessarily incompatible with Christianity," while *L'Ère nouvelle* "insisted that democracy was intrinsically Christian"[122]—an important distinction. In view of this, *L'Ère nouvelle* has justifiably been referred to as "the leading voice of Christian democracy and an important stage in the history of the Catholic press in the nineteenth century and in the history of Catholicism."[123]

When the first issue appeared in April, there were approximately 1,000 subscribers, but 20,000 copies were being printed by June.[124] During its short tenure (from April 15, 1848, to April 2, 1849), Ozanam wrote sixty-five articles for *L'Ère nouvelle*. Twenty-three of his articles developed the ideas he had announced in his manifesto to the electors of the department of the Rhône.[125] His last article appeared on January 11, 1849.[126] One of his earliest articles bore the title "Les deux républiques" (issue no. 9, April 23, 1848).[127] In it Ozanam contrasted the kind of republic that *L'Ère nouvelle* did not support with the kind that it promoted. The wrong kind of democracy was one that allowed the tyranny of the majority. As Ozanam proclaimed, popular sovereignty was "the most imposing temporal manifestation of the sovereignty of God."[128] He continued: "The end therefore of all society is not to establish the power of the greatest number, but to protect the liberty of all."[129] He eagerly anticipated a democratic society in which all persons were protected equally and that was especially sensitive to the needs of those who were the lowest or the most threatened.[130] In his view, "Only Christianity contains this unexampled society which condemned all the oppressions, all the inequalities, all the hostilities of the old world."[131]

From its start, conservative critics claimed that *L'Ère nouvelle* was merely a revival of *L'Avenir*, the liberal journal associated with Lamennais, whose ideas had been condemned by the pope.[132] Those criticisms particularly worried Lacordaire. He was not a convinced supporter of democracy, but rather he favored a constitutional monarchy.[133] In February 1848 he admitted: "I did not agree with Ozanam's views. I did not wish to treat the question of democracy theoretically, but confined myself to accepting the *fait accompli*, and drawing from it as much advantage as possible for religion and society."[134] Some of the critics of *L'Ère nouvelle* even raised the specter of socialism. One of Ozanam's Lyon friends, Alexandre Dufieux, wrote to him with concerns about these criticisms, which he had read in Louis Veuillot's *L'Univers*.[135] As Gordon Wright points out: "In 1842 . . . Louis Veuillot took over the editorship of the Paris daily *L'Univers* and established himself over the next forty years as one of the most powerful figures in modern French religious history. . . . He was the bitterest enemy of the liberals and the compromisers. Intolerant of error, a master of whipping up emotions, he . . . possessed remarkable journalistic talent and a flair for speaking the language of the people; he has been called one of the most influential journalists of all time."[136]

Ozanam and his colleagues at *L'Ère nouvelle* did not escape Veuillot's vigilant notice. Indeed, Ozanam once remarked that Veuillot was determined "not to win back unbelievers, but to arouse the passions of believers."[137] In contrast to Veuillot, Ozanam's style of writing was more kindly and restrained.[138] In a letter of response to Dufieux of May 1848, Ozanam clarified that he and his colleagues at *L'Ère nouvelle* were not socialists; they did not espouse the overthrow of society. Instead, they wanted "a free, progressive Christian reform of it." In addition, he voiced this warning: "We believe that one would be strangely mistaken if he supposed the movement of 1848 must only result in a question of public right. One cannot avoid the social issues; precisely because they are formidable, God does not want us to turn them aside. We must lay a bold hand on the sore of pauperism. . . . I am afraid that if property does not know how to freely strip itself, it will be sooner or later violently compromised."[139] In June 1848 Ozanam's warning would prove to be prophetic, when worker violence broke out during the so-called June Days uprising, from June 23 to June 26.

French workers had at first been hopeful when revolution broke out in early 1848. According to Gordon Wright, the Revolution of 1848 "seemed destined for a time to reverse the order of precedence and to make France the world's model for social advance. The working day in Parisian factories was reduced to ten hours; several large producers' cooperatives were organized with state aid; a government commission to study labor problems was set up, with two hundred employers and two hundred workers as members and the socialist Louis Blanc as chairman." There was also "much talk of guaranteeing the right to work and of adding a minister of labor to the cabinet. But by the end of the year the proposals had been abandoned and the reforms repealed. The vanished mirage of a new utopian era left the workers more bitter and frustrated than ever."[140]

The workers and artisans of Paris soon realized that the democratic republic they had hoped to create in February was not to include their voices. The result was a massive insurrection of workers in June 1848. As the historian Jeremy Popkin comments: "Arrest statistics show that the rebels were a cross-section of the city's poorer classes. Some came from the lower reaches of the petty bourgeoisie, some were skilled artisans whose trades were feeling the pressure of industrial competition, some were factory workers, and some were casual laborers or unemployed. Engravings from the period emphasize the fact that women fought alongside the men. Altogether, 50,000 may have taken an active part in the struggle."[141] The new government responded much as Louis-Philippe had done. With the aid of the army it reconquered the city of Paris in a brutal fashion. Nearly 3,000 people were killed and 15,000 arrested, many of whom were sent to Algerian prison camps.[142]

Ozanam was intimately involved in these events. Out of a desire to do his civic duty and as a matter of conscience, he had become a member of the National Guard and patrolled near the areas of the barricades. He wrote his brother Alphonse: "My company was stationed nearly all the time at the corner of the Rue Garancière and the Rue Palatine; later at the corner of the Rue Madame and the Rue de Fleurus. There were excursions and alarms. . . . But thank God, we did not fire a cartridge. My conscience was easy and I should not have recoiled from any danger. However, I am free to admit that it is a terrible moment when a man bids what he believes to be his last farewell to his wife and child."[143] During the course of the uprising, he and two companions visited the archbishop of Paris, Monseigneur Denis-Auguste Affre.[144] In their audience with him, they respectfully suggested that by intervening, the archbishop could possibly end the rebellion. Having considered this option before their visit, Archbishop Affre was convinced that he should act decisively in the hope of halting the bloodshed. Once he received from the commander of the government forces both permission to try and a promise of pardon for the rebels, Affre began his brave journey toward the barricades. Both sides ceased fire. There was a silence as several of the rebels came forward to speak with the archbishop. Then a single shot rang out, probably not from the defenders of the barricades, and

Monseigneur Affre suffered a mortal wound. His death, however, was not completely in vain. The fighting did cease. But for a long time afterward, Ozanam agonized over this incident, fearing that he was partly responsible for the archbishop's untimely death.[145]

Ozanam did not condone the violence, but he fully understood the reasons behind it. He addressed the June violence in *L'Ère nouvelle* between 28 June and 8 July in three articles devoted to the topic.[146] The first was entitled "Les coupables et les égarés" (The Guilty and the Misled; no. 72, June 28, 1848), the second "Où étaient les ouvriers de Paris pendant le combat?" (Where Were the Workers of Paris during the Conflict?; no. 74, June 30, 1848), and the third "Aux insurgés désarmés" (To the Disarmed Insurgents; no. 82, July 8, 1848).[147] The first made the argument that many of those involved in the June Days were in fact misled by some of their leaders, who were the ones most culpable for swaying these vulnerable people. Because their misery forced some workers to join the barricades, Ozanam argued that the Assembly's task must now be to attack pauperism and address the question of work, a question essential to the health of any Christian civilization.[148] The second made the case that many workers did not actually join in the insurrection, but rather refused to allow a handful of seditious usurpers to claim the name of the people.[149] The third article begged workers to denounce those who had deceived them into armed insurrection and who had deceived them for a long time about their true destiny. Workers had been led to believe that there should be neither suffering nor sacrifice in life, according to Ozanam. For him it came down to a choice between selfishness and exploitation, on the one side, and devotion and sacrifice, on the other. At the same time, Ozanam advocated that the condition of the working people could and must be relieved by measures such as voluntary associations of workers and masters, as well as the agricultural colonies in France and Algeria. These things, and not violent uprisings, could effectively reduce the progress of pauperism and strengthen labor.[150]

In addressing the workers, Ozanam spoke of the need for sacrifice, and earlier in his life he had counseled "much resignation from the poor."[151] The word "resignation" needs to be clarified, or else Ozanam might be perceived as someone counseling the poor to know their place and to accept their lot in life. That would be a complete misreading of his position. A word rich in meaning, "resignation" for Ozanam should be understood in three ways. First, it signifies forbearance. Ozanam wanted those in need with genuine grievances to refrain from resorting to violence to try to better their prospects. Second, he wanted those in need to comprehend that in an actual pitched battle with the rich, the prospect of ultimate defeat loomed large, and, therefore, he hoped that the poor would refuse to follow this doomed and dangerous course of action. There was much evidence to suggest that he was correct in his assessment. Third, for Ozanam, resignation implies a giving up of oneself to God, trusting in divine providence to reveal the best way to resolve the present crisis. He did not think that those who were desperate should simply resign themselves to their lot in life. Instead he was convinced that God hears the cry of the poor and will respond, by moving good people to act out of genuine charity and justice to their neighbor, like the Good Samaritan of the Gospel.[152] The Society of St. Vincent de Paul was proof of that conviction. Ultimately, Ozanam wanted to remove from the rich any excuse to inflict more violence upon the poor and "to make equality as operative as possible among men; to make voluntary community replace imposition and brute force; to make charity accomplish what justice alone cannot do."[153] He genuinely thanked God for placing him and his fellow Vincentians "by Providence on neutral ground between the two belligerents, to have paths and minds open to both."[154]

WRITINGS, MAY–OCTOBER 1848

The greatest number of Ozanam's articles in *L'Ère nouvelle* appeared between May and October 1848.[155] They "give evidence of certain themes common with all social catholic thinkers: a taste for works and charitable accomplishments, the conviction that a spiritual conversion must proceed social improvements, and the certainty that education, at all ages of life, allows the destiny of people to improve."[156] Ozanam had a minimal background in economics, although he had taught commercial law in Lyon. His legal training and his intellectual background in history were the bases upon which he approached the social question.[157] He hoped to bring questions of morality into the subject of economic relations between human beings.[158] Ozanam's position was clear: serious social problems such as poverty generally develop when any individual pursues only her or his interests or the interests of a small group (*égoïsme*) to the detriment of the common good. Yet he never entertained the simple notion that poverty would be eradicated only by fulfilling individual material needs. In his view, poverty destroys the very soul of people who need to know, and to believe, that they have value as human beings and that they can genuinely contribute in positive ways to their community. They need food for the soul as much as they need food for the body. In many cases, it is not the bread or the clothes that are given, but the hand extended in true friendship as an equal, not as a superior, that is the most vital part of an act of charity.

For Ozanam, the regeneration of society was to be accomplished first and foremost by forming a true community and building just, caring relationships between the different social classes who ultimately shared the same goals for society: peace, order, and happiness. He believed that his Catholic faith had much to offer on this subject to those who might be willing to listen and engage in dialogue. In particular, he developed these ideas in such articles as "Aux gens de bien" (To People of Good Will; no. 151, September 16, 1848), "Les causes de la misère" (The Causes of the Present Misery; no. 180, October 8, 1848), and "De l'assistance qui humilie et de celle qui honore" (Concerning Assistance Which Humiliates and That Which Honors; no. 187, October 22, 1848).[159] As of October 1848, Ozanam announced that columns in *L'Ère nouvelle* were to be reserved especially for the question of "charitable economy" in order to bring greater knowledge to the service of the suffering. He pronounced, "We will open the investigation of charity." According to Bressolette, "Like a doctor it was necessary to examine the sickness in its sources, for example housing of workers, cleanliness of manufacturing concerns, education as important for preparing for the future."[160] Ozanam hoped that as the "old world showed the love that Christians had for one another, the new world will render the proof of the love that Christians will have for it."[161]

Some of the principles most dear to Frédéric Ozanam and evident in his articles for *L'Ère nouvelle* were the sovereignty of the people as a temporal manifestation of the sovereignty of God, the need for collaboration among social classes, the protection and elevation of the working class, the efficacy of voluntary associations, and the necessary, but limited, intervention of the government.[162] He also addressed issues such as divorce and socialism, both of which he saw as counterproductive to the values of a democracy. His interest in the subject of divorce was sparked by legislation approving civil divorce proposed in May 1848. Adolphe Crémieux, the minister of justice, had supported civil divorce for some time, and the subject became an important topic of debate. Although the proposed law received little political support, nevertheless, Ozanam devoted three articles to the subject in June. Unlike Louis de Bonald, who made a political argument against divorce in 1801, Ozanam's argument was based on social rather than political grounds. For Bonald, both marriage and the state were hierarchical in nature. Consequently, divorce was equivalent to democracy in a family context: "divorce gave women the unwarranted capacity to challenge their husbands' authority," just as democracy gave an unwarranted capacity for people to challenge the state's authority.[163] Ozanam instead argued that divorce weakened democracy because it favored "the interests of the strong (men) over against those of the weak (women and children)."[164] As Carol Harrison points out, "For Bonald, divorce produced an abusive egalitarianism; it gave the weak an unnatural leverage against the strong. For Ozanam, divorce encouraged an equally abusive authoritarianism, giving men license to indulge their appetites and to use their greater strength against their wives and children."[165]

Ozanam's argument against divorce resulted from his conception of marriage, described in detail in his chapter on Christian women in his book *La civilisation au cinquième siècle*:

In marriage there is not only a contract, there is, above all, a sacrifice, a twofold sacrifice. The woman sacrifices that which God has given her, and which is irreparable, that which was the object of her mother's anxious care—her fresh, young beauty, often her health, and that faculty of loving which women have but once. The man, in his turn, sacrifices the liberty of his youth, those incomparable years which never return, that power of devoting himself to her he loves, which is only to be found at the outset of his life, and that effort of a first love to secure to her a proud and happy lot. This is what a man can do but once, between the ages of twenty and thirty. . . . This is why I say that Christian marriage is a double sacrifice. It is two cups; one filled with virtue, purity, innocence; the other with an untainted love, self-devotion, the immortal consecration of the man to her . . . who was unknown to him yesterday, and with whom today he is content to spend the remainder of his life; and these two cups must both be full to the brim, in order that the union may be holy, and that heaven may bless it.[166]

For him, marriage was the first time when a man comprehended the importance of society because he voluntarily relinquished his autonomy: "The moment in which a man gives away his heart is also the moment when he controls his destiny."[167] It is in the family formed by marriage that one learns to abandon egoism, to embrace sacrifice, and to work toward the good of all.[168] Marriage, then, is not intended to be a short-term proposition. According to his argument, ultimately divorce is favored, not by the people, but rather by those who hate religion more than they love liberty.[169] For Ozanam, the proper role of democracy "is to rebuild from the bottom, it will begin with the family." Authentic democracy should never tear the family apart.[170]

Socialism was another societal peril, in his opinion. In fact, Ozanam referred to it as "the greatest philosophical and political peril of the present age."[171] Because it was based on a material view of reality, socialism provided an incomplete answer and a false hope to the masses. Socialism, according to Ozanam, did not present a new set of doctrines but rather ideas that had been around since antiquity and that had proven to be inadequate. It promised the perfectibility of humanity without supplying a solid formula for achieving it.[172] France had been plagued too long by the desolating maxims of selfishness and indifference.[173] For Ozanam, only Christianity was "capable of realizing the ideal of fraternity without immolating liberty."[174]

It is no surprise that Pius IX and the "Italian question" also appeared as an important topic in *L'Ère nouvelle*. Twenty-nine of Ozanam's articles were devoted to this issue.[175] Elected pope in June 1846, Cardinal Mastai-Ferretti took the name Pius IX (*Pio Nono*). He brought great hopes for reform. One of his first acts as head of the Papal States was to grant a general amnesty to political exiles and prisoners. He also granted a constitution. However, he did not want to become embroiled in a conflict with Catholic Austria to remove its influence in Italy, as some liberal extremists urged him to do. Ever since his visit to Italy in

1846–47, Ozanam had invested his hopes in Pius IX; he never lost faith in Pius's papacy. Unfortunately, the revolution of 1848 in Italy went far beyond Pius IX's intentions for liberal reform. The pontiff's prime minister was assassinated. Extremists in Rome revolted and proclaimed the establishment of a republic, and leadership in the movement for Italian liberation and unification devolved to Rome and Venice. The "Italian question" took center stage. Forced to flee his lands, Pope Pius IX became increasingly disillusioned with liberal reforms.[176] Ozanam's last article in January 1849 was a final plea to the French people to continue to support the future efforts of Pius IX.[177] But when Pius IX was returned to the Papal States in 1850 with the aid of French troops, he was not the same man he was before 1848.[178] Ozanam saw one of his cherished dreams fade. As Schimberg states: "It was a bitter disappointment to his thoroughly Catholic heart and to his democratic idealism."[179]

In the sequel of the violent June Days of 1848, the French Assembly looked to a strong government to keep the lower classes in their place. It therefore designed a constitution with a strong executive. The elected president would have extensive powers but could serve for only one four-year term. The deputies of the Assembly retained universal suffrage in the constitution less from principle than from a fear of further disturbance if this concession from the February revolution were revoked.[180] In the ensuing election in December 1848, surprisingly, Louis-Napoléon Bonaparte, the nephew of the former emperor Napoleon I, won the election for president, most likely because of his name and because "he was identified neither with radicalism nor with repression."[181]

As the end of his presidential term approached in 1852, Bonaparte scrambled to change the constitution. When his attempts failed, he turned to a coup d'état. On December 2, 1851, the anniversary of one of his uncle's greatest military victories (at Austerlitz), Bonaparte posted a proclamation that condemned the deputies of the Assembly for incompetence, promised a new constitution that would restore the universal suffrage limited in 1850 (universal suffrage had been curtailed by an election law of May 31, 1850, designed to reduce the influence of the "vile multitude"), and deliberately invoked the memories of his uncle's First Empire. Although faced with opposition, Louis-Napoléon succeeded in repressing any threat of insurgence.[182] In 1852 he took advantage of various political divisions and opportunities to be recognized, not as president, but as emperor. On November 20, 1852, a plebiscite was held, and 7,800,000 Frenchmen voted "yes" to the restoration of the hereditary Napoleonic empire. Out of respect for the deceased son of Napoleon I, Louis-Napoléon Bonaparte took the title of Emperor Napoleon III.[183] France had come full circle.

Ozanam never completely lost hope in democracy, although his spirit was profoundly saddened by the setbacks of democratic reform and the failure of the dreams of 1848. On April 9, 1851, he offered these sober reflections to Alexandre Dufieux: "I believe more than ever in the life of the Republic. I believe it especially for the sake of religion and for the salvation of the Church of France, which would be severely compromised if events gave power to a party ready to repeat all the mistakes of the Restoration."[184] He ended his thoughts on a positive note: "Ah! My dear friend, what a troublous, but what an instructive time it is, through which we are passing! We may perish, but we must not regret having lived in it. Let us learn from it. Let us learn, first of all, to defend our belief without hating our adversaries, to appreciate those who do not think as we do, to recognize that there are Christians in every camp, and that God can be served now as always! Let us complain less of our times and more of ourselves. Let us not be discouraged, let us be better."[185]

In both his speeches and his writings, Ozanam consistently and eloquently promoted and defended the principles of liberty, equality, and fraternity that signaled for him the temporal advent of the gospel. He bravely spoke out for all those whose own voices were silenced by poverty, by fear, or by repression. Few would disagree that in his lifetime, Frédéric Ozanam had become an authentic spokesperson for the people.

Frédéric Ozanam's certificate of First Communion. Souvenir Ozanam/CGI, SSVP.

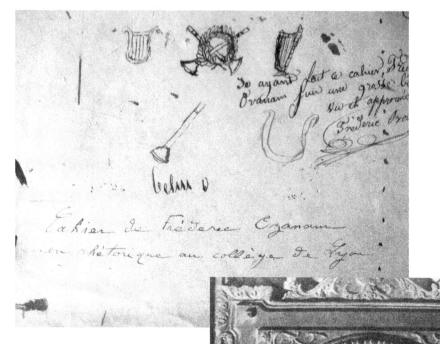

Frédéric Ozanam's notebook from the collège royal of Lyon. Souvenir Ozanam/CGI, SSVP.

Abbé Joseph Mathias Noirot, who had a lasting impact on Frédéric. Souvenir Ozanam/CGI, SSVP.

The young Frédéric Ozanam. Souvenir Ozanam/CGI, SSVP.

Ozanam's Law Degree. Souvenir Ozanam/CGI, SSVP.

Ozanam's Letters Degree. Souvenir Ozanam/CGI, SSVP.

Père Lacordaire preaching in Notre Dame Cathedral. A man in the front row, middle, with a top hat resting on his knee may be Ozanam, who was responsible for starting the Lenten series of sermons and after whom it is still named. By permission of Bibliothèque nationale de France.

The First Conference of Charity. Artist unknown. By permission of the Maison Mère of the Congregation of the Mission, 95 rue de Sèvres, Paris.

Ozanam at the age of thirty-five, by Charles Soulacroix. Souvenir Ozanam/ CGI, SSVP.

Amélie and Marie. Souvenir Ozanam/ CGI, SSVP.

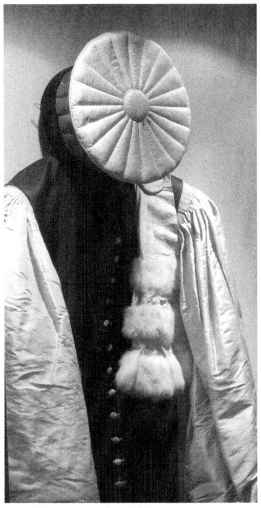

Amélie Soulacroix Ozanam at the age of thirty-five. Souvenir Ozanam/CGI, SSVP.

Ozanam's academic robes, worn at the Sorbonne.
Souvenir Ozanam/CGI, SSVP.

Tomb of Frédéric Ozanam at Saint-Joseph-des-Carmes. Author's photo.

Amélie Soulacroix Ozanam in later life. Souvenir Ozanam/CGI, SSVP.

Soulacroix family grave in Montparnasse Cemetery. Author's photo.

FAMILLES
SOULACROIX
OZANAM-LAPORTE

ICI REPOSENT
EN ATTENDANT LE JOUR DE LA RÉSURRECTION

JN JN ET THÉOPHILE
SOULACROIX,
DÉCÉDÉ
LE 9 MARS 1847
À L'ÂGE DE 23 ANS,

ZÉLIE MAGAGNOS
VEUVE SOULACROIX,
NÉE À NORFOLK
LE 10 AOÛT 1798,
DÉCÉDÉE À PARIS LE VENDREDI
SAINT 7 AVRIL 1882,

JEAN JOSEPH SOULACROIX,
Rⁿⁿ MR CHEF DE DIVISION
AU MRE DE L'Sⁿ Pⁿⁿⁿ,
DÉCÉDÉ LE 23 JUILLET 1848
À L'ÂGE DE 57 ANS.

AMÉLIE SOULACROIX,
VEUVE DE FRÉDÉRIC OZANAM
DÉCÉDÉE À ECULLY (RHÔNE)
LE 26 SEPTEMBRE 1894
À L'ÂGE DE 74 ANS.

Frédéric Ozanam, in his Sorbonne academic robes, visiting a poor family at their home. Painting by Gary Schumer. Two students, carrying a book and basket of food, accompany Ozanam. In the distant background are Sister Rosalie Rendu in the white wings of the Daughters of Charity and a man in a top hat, representing Emmanuel Bailly. By permission of Association of the Miraculous Medal (www.amm.org).

PART II

———

OZANAM'S LESSONS AND LEGACY

CHAPTER 7

———

Friendship

In his biography of Ozanam, Albert Paul Schimberg asserts that Ozanam "had a genius for friendship, which was for him a communion of spirits, a meeting of minds."[1] Perhaps that is why Schimberg entitled his work *The Great Friend*. Of the many attributes that could be bestowed on him, Frédéric most likely would have cherished this one in particular. He truly valued his friends and regarded friendship as a genuine gift from God.

Even at the young age of seventeen, Frédéric displayed both a need for and a deep attachment to friends. One of his early friends was Auguste Materne, a young man whose father was a businessman in Lyon. In 1832 Materne entered the École Normale. He had a fairly undistinguished career compared to that of Ozanam.[2] Frédéric wrote some twenty-four letters to Materne between September 12, 1829, and August 6, 1832. For the young Ozanam this was a "difficult time" in his life, full of the doubts and anxieties that vex many adolescents.[3] On September 12, 1829, Ozanam responded to Materne's criticisms of his article "On the Trafficking of Negroes," which had been published in the review *L'Abeille française.*[4] "I have clearly pointed out, as you admit, the intellectual and moral slavery joined to bodily slavery; . . . I even added that Christianity, freeing people from intellectual slavery and moral slavery and giving them liberty of the children of God, ought also to free them from bodily slavery." He admitted, however, that his argument might be misinterpreted by some and thanked Auguste for the "good advice of a good friend," teasing him in the process that his friend's letter digressed too much. He humorously admonished him: "Get to the matter, lawyer."[5] He later sent Auguste a poem concerning a recent political incident in Algeria. Auguste expressed serious reservations about the poem's contents. Frédéric replied in May 1830: "How could you wonder whether I would accuse you of indifference to our country? Oh how well I know you, and know well that if our minds do not always agree on some political matters, both our hearts at least beat together for our *belle France.*"[6] He closed the letter with a plea: "Do not be angry with me, my dear friend, for having spoken frankly and for not taking your advice at once. . . . Let us dare to contradict each other sometimes: truth and concord will end up by banishing strife. Let us open our hearts and discuss things with wisdom. Our friendship will only become firmer."[7] Even at this young age Frédéric displayed a keen sense that true friendship is not based upon always thinking alike. Friends should be able to differ in opinion and still remain friends; he sought an honest exchange of ideas and ideals that would be of mutual benefit. As his correspondence with Auguste Materne demonstrates, he believed friends should know each other well, share their deepest fears and hopes, and contribute to each other's improvement.

In June 1830, a month later, Frédéric confided in Auguste, pouring out all of his doubts and listing the weaknesses that plagued him. He concluded with the statement: "I have opened my heart to you; you know me thoroughly. You now know whether you want to continue our friendship, break it off or deepen it. Whatever happens, I will always love you, always wish to remain and become ever more your friend."[8] When he received Materne's reply a few days later, Frédéric rejoiced: "What good your letter, which I have just received, has done me. How happy I am! If you knew what it cost me to write my last letter. *Dieu!* I said to myself, if he should find me unworthy of his friendship!" Frédéric also included the following petition: "Oh! Dear friend, . . . Let us flatter each other no longer, but tell each other the truth. Good advice often, sometimes criticism, but always the criticism of friends. . . . Let us promise each other never to be offended over mutual advice. Let us ask it as a right and receive it as a benefit."[9] It was wise advice from one so young. As Marcel Vincent contends in his biography of the young Ozanam, his correspondence with Materne represents the revealing of "precious secrets" and also documents a critical period in Ozanam's development.[10]

ANDRÉ-MARIE AMPÈRE AND EARLY PARISIAN FRIENDS

The importance of friendship struck a particularly resonant chord in Ozanam when he arrived in Paris to study law in November 1831, at the age of eighteen. He encountered a city to which many parents, especially Catholic ones, were reluctant to send their sons for study. Paris was reputed to be "the recognized centre of disturbance and disorder, the hearth from which the spark flew to set fire abroad."[11] It was known for atheism and secular temptations. Nevertheless, the city provided the best opportunities for a liberal education.[12] Overcome by his "immense solitude" and perhaps also a little frightened, Frédéric longed for friends once he arrived but despaired of finding any worthy ones. The first boardinghouse or *pension* in which he lived provided few opportunities for friendships, and some of his former friends from Lyon were situated in a distant part of the city.[13]

Fortunately, as discussed in chapter 2, Frédéric was quickly befriended by André-Marie Ampère, a relative of Ozanam's father[14] and a mathematical expert and physician of Lyonnais origin.[15] Shortly after Frédéric's courtesy call, as he informed his parents in a letter, the "untidy old savant"[16] offered him room and board, professing that "your tastes and sentiments are compatible with mine, and I would enjoy having an opportunity to chat with you." Ampère further promised, "You will get to know my son who is very much involved with German literature, and his library will be at your disposal. You are simple, so are we. My sister-in-law, daughter, and son dine with me, and would be good company for you." At the end of his letter Frédéric, like the typical student, begged his father for some extra money. But his reason for asking is telling: "I would be very obliged if you could give me a little allotment each month for my recreation, as you did in Lyon; I have a great need to distract myself. It is very hard, being alone."[17] With the transfer from his former *pension* to his new living quarters in Ampère's home, however, came new opportunities to meet others, including distinguished men of science and letters.[18] His friendship with the Ampère family lasted through his lifetime and was the beginning of his own circle of famous friends.

Frédéric remained with the Ampères until the spring of 1833, when he rented a room in the rue des Grès at the same location as other Lyonnais students. He "quickly fell in with other members of the Lyonnais colony living in Paris," including his father's relatives and Lyonnais clergy as well as students.[19] In March he wrote to his mother: "I have . . . a circle of friends who gather every day in worthwhile enterprises and whom I love as brothers, from the old childhood companion, good Henri; to Lallier, that excellent young man; Lamache the soul of an artist; and practically a knight, Cherruel, the converted Saint-Simonian. . . . What delightful hours we have spent together speaking of country, family, religion, science, literature, legislation. . . . What satisfaction to be with sometimes about thirty young men at the famous M. Cornbalot's sermon, or the evening gatherings at M. de Montalembert's."[20]

Lallier, Lamache, and Cherruel would all become members of the Society of St. Vincent de Paul after its early beginnings in 1833.[21] These friends, he wrote his mother in the same letter, treated one another "as supports and mutual guides."[22] After their intellectual gatherings, he and his friends journeyed home "five or six with arms interlocked, loving one another in life and death, and promising to carry back each to his own province some portion of that sacred fire they share."[23] He asked his mother, rhetorically: "Is that not time well employed? Is it not delightful?" He then confided to her why good friends were so vital to him: "I have a great need for others. I am so little able to be self-sufficient that if I had unworthy friends they could do with me whatever they wished, and I am forever following others, much more than anyone follows me. . . . I must have communication and contacts. Indeed, it is impossible for me to do passable work without having talked about it and discussed it with someone."[24] In letter to Lallier five years later, he expressed a similar sentiment: "I sit alone, knowing no more disagreeable company than myself, and closet myself with a magazine or a book.

I appreciate now by its privation the whole value of the spoken word, how much more it cultivates thought than the dead letter of the greatest writers. I need conversation."[25]

ERNEST FALCONNET

Numerous letters to Ernest Falconnet are to be found in Frédéric's voluminous correspondence. Born in 1815, Falconnet was a "distant cousin of Ozanam" who would have an interesting legal career.[26] The mutual trust between the two young men is evident. Ozanam readily shared his concerns, and Falconnet in turn confessed his own doubts, joys, and sorrows.[27] In one of his letters to this cousin, in March 1833, Frédéric not only detailed his experiences as a student at the Sorbonne but also counseled, and even reprimanded, his younger relative: "The rather cold style of some of your letters hurt (not irritated) me. Your love of pleasure especially worried me, but your last two letters amply repaired the damage so far as the first point is concerned. The second no longer alarms me as much since I have confidence in God in your virtue." He ended his admonitions with important assurances: "The future is before us, gray as the ocean, but immense like it. Hardy marines, we sail in the same vessel and steer together. Before us religion, bright star given us to follow, before us the glorious wake of great countrymen and coreligionists; behind us our young brothers, more timid companions who await example. Yes, Heaven has not given us the same blood, the same heart, the same thought and even the same age in vain. . . . Perhaps someday it will happen that some graces will be bestowed on us and we will be greeted as good men in the assembly of the wise." Frédéric then offered a final prescription for both of them: "More seriousness for you, more ardor and energy for me, for both of us the lessons of our fathers, the example of our mothers, and the benevolence of heaven."[28]

In reference to issues of health raised by Falconnet in another piece of correspondence, Ozanam implored him in an 1834 letter to "protect your chest, speak little, take milk and other sedatives, and avoid carefully every excess of work and pleasure especially late hours." He knowingly added: "I am sure that your too many dances . . . and too great literary activity have contributed to making you so ill." There is, however, more to health and well-being than these prescriptions: "Write and reflect, try to acquire a serious manner. . . . Try to acquire that calm and serenity of soul which makes great men of science, saints in faith, and good constitutions in hygiene. Health, says Plato, is the harmony between all the power of soul and body."

He further cautioned his cousin that he should have "a little circle of friends; join especially with good comrades instead of the world's social gatherings. Some hours spent together before the fire in familiar conversation with open heart does more good and gives more repose than an entire week of parties. . . . You know the world is a pyre of fire which wears down young lives, do not give it yours." He offered this caveat: "I do not . . . want to assume the air of giving a lesson. We are co-disciples, we are brothers. . . . If I have spoken so, it is simply to say what is in my heart. . . . Please do the same for me and tell me at this renewal of the year what reforms you would like to see in my character, work, and moral direction."[29] In the same letter he did not shy away from sharing with Ernest his own concern that he harbored an "uncertitude about a vocation."[30] "Practice what you preach" was a central part of Ozanam's code of conduct with his friends.

When their lives eventually took different directions, the bonds of friendship between Frédéric and Ernest were strained but remained intact. After Falconnet suffered the loss of his dear father in 1851, Ozanam did not hesitate to write and to comfort his friend. He called to mind many fond memories they had shared, humbly requesting that they "pick up the links of the chain connecting us to one another and with those whom we have lost."[31] He gently counseled him that there is "only one consolation for such sorrow, it is that God has taken what He had given. In taking them to Himself, He compels us too to take the road to Heaven."[32] He praised their mothers for having shared their faith with their sons; they had taught both Frédéric and Ernest how "to believe, to hope, and to love." By doing so they had constructed for them a holy "staircase by which we should climb up to them again after we had lost them."[33] Ozanam then made this final point and a promise: "Forgive me, then, dear friend, if I do not find all the words which I have desired for so great a misfortune, but rely on my tender devotion."[34] The correspondence with Ernest Falconnet witnesses to Ozanam's genuine and continuing desire not only to inform his friends about events in his life and his maturing thoughts, but also to support, encourage, and advise them and to receive, in return, their advice and direction.

LOUIS JANMOT

Ozanam's many friendships included a close relationship with the painter Louis Janmot, who had known him since childhood, when they made their First Communion together.[35] Janmot produced a famous sketch of the twenty-year-old Ozanam in 1833, as well as the one in 1852 that portrayed a Frédéric worn and weak at the age of thirty-nine, only fifteen months before his death.[36] It was Janmot to whom Ozanam wrote exuberantly in November 1836 of Saint Francis of Assisi, "the fool of Love," sharing with Janmot from the heart his view that "the problem that divides men in our day is no longer a problem of political structure; it is a social problem."[37] Janmot was one of the most attentive friends at his bedside when he fell ill in Paris in 1852. In a letter of October 1852, Ozanam expressed how Janmot's goodness moved him: "I shall never forget the friendly anxiety with which you came each day of my illness to feel my pulse and to shake my hand with the grip of an old school comrade, and a fellow First Communicant. My wife and relatives are indebted to you for the portrait of one whom they all love. . . . Farewell, my dear friend, may the guardian angel of great inspirations guide your brush! You are so good that you deserve to be happy."[38]

THE FRIENDSHIP OF THE SOCIETY
OF ST. VINCENT DE PAUL

The first conference of charity, from which the Society of St. Vincent de Paul quickly developed, was formed in April 1833 on Ozanam's twentieth birthday. There could be no closer circle of friends than the one Ozanam found in the Society of St. Vincent de Paul. Friendship was one of the paramount reasons for forming the Society, and it continued to be one of its most treasured values. Indeed, Ozanam voiced these very ideas to Léonce Curnier in a letter of March 1837. Curnier, who had provided assistance at one of the early meetings of the conference of charity, in June 1833, was the son of a silk manufacturer in Nîmes.[39] Ozanam befriended him in Lyon and corresponded with him throughout his own short life.[40] Curnier, as mentioned earlier, also formed a conference of charity in Nîmes after being inspired by Ozanam.[41] He later served in public office and wrote numerous historical works, including a biography of Ozanam. Born in November 1813, the same year as Ozanam, Curnier died in Paris in June 1894 at the age of eighty.[42] Frédéric wrote Léonce in his March 1837 letter that friendship is "a harmony between souls, it cannot subsist in a prolonged absence, unless it is given from time to time certain signs of good accord, and these signs can be two-fold: words and actions." The act of writing letters to friends confirms their importance, while convincing them that they are not forgotten. Kind words help to alleviate anxieties, and ultimately, both parties benefit.

Although it is a cliché, actions do speak louder than words. According to Ozanam, "nothing creates intimacy between two men [more] than to eat together, travel together, and work together; but if purely human acts have this power, moral acts have it even more, and if two or three come together to do good, their union will be perfect." He knew, after all, that Jesus Christ had assured everyone that if two or three were gathered in his name he would be present in their midst. Ozanam then proceeded to confirm that it is for this very reason "that in Paris we wished to found our little Society of St. Vincent de Paul, and it is also for this reason perhaps that heaven has seen fit to bless it."[43] As secretary-general of the Society, François Lallier reinforced Ozanam's statements in a circular letter in the same month and year: "You know that one thing especially supports and strengthens us in this world—it is the thought of having near us friends on whom we can rely for advice and example.... You have indeed felt the power of such a Christian relationship, when you adopted our prayers and mode of proceeding.... You have, therefore, become our brothers in order to share and make us sharers in Christian intimacy. We shall all profit ... by this precious advantage derived from our faith."[44] In his biography of Ozanam, Léonce Curnier reflected back on the friendship of the Society and gave a final eloquent voice to the powerful role it played in the lives of many young men like himself: "How mothers have blessed the Society of Saint Vincent de Paul from the bottom of their hearts because it exercised an influence on their sons and aided them to triumph in a struggle at the age of ardent passions! Of all the benefits of so admirable an organization, this one [friendship] was certainly not the less great from a moral point of view or from a religious point of view."[45] Ozanam firmly believed that friendship was a vital and necessary part of the Society. Clearly, he was not alone in this opinion.

Both Ozanam and Lallier were quick to add to their list of friends the people in poverty whom they visited as members of the Society of St. Vincent de Paul. When visiting those in need, Ozanam "came as an equal, not as an official or superior. . . . He felt . . . that he was under a compliment to those who admitted him into what was their domestic sanctuary," however foul or cramped their accommodations. These were friends, and Ozanam was quick to remind his colleagues that "those who know the road to the poor man's house . . . never knock at his door without a sentiment of respect."[46] As one biographer, Edward O'Connor, comments, "It was not as a relief-officer that he came but as a friend."[47] Lallier wholeheartedly subscribed to this view. In his circular letter of 1837, he instructed the members of the Society: "We tell the poor that . . . we hope to be able to afford them some assistance," and, especially if they are not afraid of a religious group, then "a friendship is soon formed."[48] He further counseled the members that they should never be considered by those in poverty simply "as relieving officers coming from the workhouse, and calling every week to deal out regular doles, but rather as friends and advisers to be applied to in the hard and painful emergencies of life."[49] For both Ozanam and Lallier, help would become honorable "because it may become mutual."[50]

FRANÇOIS LALLIER

One of Ozanam's deepest friendships was with François Lallier, who "was, and always continued to be, the strong religious spirit to whom the friend unbosomed his weakness and his tenderness."[51] Theirs was "a great friendship."[52] While still residing in Lyon, Ozanam hoped to bring Lallier there in order to be close to him, and he lovingly chided his friend for not being a Lyonnais: "That is all that is wanting in you."[53] In an 1838 letter to Lallier, Ozanam described the crucial importance to him of their early student friendships and his lasting memories of them.

Those friendships formed under the auspices of faith and charity, in a double confraternity of religious discussion and benevolent works, far from languishing as the result of prolonged absence, look inward and focus in some way; they feed on remembrance, and you know that remembrance embellishes everything, idealizes reality, purifies images, and more willingly preserves sweet impressions than painful emotions. Besides, all those humble scenes of our student life, when they come back to me in the half-light of the past, have an ineffable charm for me. . . . All that, dear friend, serves me as the base of a tableau of my thoughts; all that casts a soft light and a rather sorrowful one on my present life, which loses a great deal by comparison. I think I really understand how history becomes poetry for the human mind and why people guard their traditions with such filial attachment. I have in these things, if you please, my golden age, my fabled time. . . . But truer, more serious, striking deeper roots not only in the imagination but to the bottom of the heart are the affections formed during this period of life. . . . Each day I acquire new confidence, when some letter of yours arrives, some article of Lamache's in a magazine, some news of Le Taillandier, Pessonneaux or others like them; it makes me forget all the anxieties of the present time, and were it not ridiculous to use the expression at twenty-four, I would say, it makes me young again.[54]

The two friends exchanged visits in 1837, 1839, and 1840. In 1840 Ozanam traveled to Sens, where Lallier resided. On his return he spoke of this trip to several of their friends in the Society of St. Vincent de Paul. Ozanam teased Lallier that their mutual friends all began to picture Lallier's young son as "already clothed with the . . . gravity" of his father, and they laughed together about that incongruous image.[55]

Yet the friends did much more than tease or confide in one another. They shared both joys and sorrows. When Lallier lost his young daughter Julie in 1844, Ozanam was quick to send his sincerest condolences in "a consoling letter wet with tears."[56] He opened with this touching phrase: "My dear friend, God visits those most whom He loves best." He praised Lallier for the deep faith and trust in God he exhibited throughout this ordeal: "My dear friend, it is of faith that, Christian families, marriage, paternity, all those sacred ties exist in order to people Heaven. You had already one saint in Paradise, your mother; you will now have an angel in your daughter. Between them they will keep your place for you. If you find that you have too long to wait to join them, remember that thirty years will soon pass; you and I know what that means."[57] His deep compassion for Lallier's loss may have brought back memories of the loss of his own beloved sister, Élisa. One year before, in 1843, he had rejoiced with Lallier on the birth of his second child: "I congratulate you upon your second paternity. . . . I am glad to know that your children are well. How God blesses those two little angels He has placed under your roof; it is already the first blessing and a rare one today to have a father like you."[58] Now he shared in the deep sorrow caused by his friend's sudden loss.

In 1845, Ozanam greeted Lallier with his own joyful news, the birth of his daughter Marie. He asked Lallier to be godfather.[59] In August he described to Lallier how delighted he was to return home after a long day to his loving wife Amélie, cradling their cherished daughter in her arms.[60] At the end of the correspondence Ozanam begged his dear friend to pray for his goddaughter as well as her father and mother, proclaiming that now "there is a sacred bond that unites us before God and before man."[61] Gratitude for Lallier's "good wishes and prayers for our little angel" is openly expressed in a letter in December. Ozanam assured Lallier that "she owes you in some measure her wings, for terrestrial angels have none other than those of Faith and Love, which are conferred on them in the Sacrament of Baptism. . . . Your name is one of the first which shall be formed on her lips as soon as she will begin to pray."[62]

Lallier received more from his friend than simply letters. The Ozanams welcomed into their home Lallier's son, who lived in Paris at the Poiloup Pension. He became one of the family. There is a reference to him in an Easter Week letter in 1852: "To-day [sic], Wednesday in Easter Week, we have your Henri with us after a long Lenten captivity. He is growing in mind and body, is always gentle and does not scorn to take part in the games of our little daughter. We are about to take them with us to the Champs-Élysées. The weather is glorious and if we succeed in locating Punch and Judy, the children will have touched the pinnacle of earthly happiness."[63] As Baunard notes, "there are eighty such letters to Lallier, in which the human and the divine are blended harmoniously."[64] The correspondence between Ozanam and his dear friend

François Lallier provides us with a rich tapestry of profound friendship woven over a lifetime of intimate sharing.

JEAN-JACQUES AMPÈRE

Although the elder Ampère died on June 10, 1836, Ozanam maintained a lifetime friendship with his son, Jean-Jacques Ampère, a "French Litterateur and historian."[65] Born in 1800, Jean-Jacques Ampère was Ozanam's senior by thirteen years, yet there were great similarities between the two men. Both valued friendship highly, had sensitive dispositions and a deep awareness of the beauty of nature, shared a taste for literature, and loved and spoke different languages. Both also longed to travel.[66] What began as a relationship of mentor (Jean-Jacques Ampère) and protégé (Ozanam) changed over the years into a deep brotherly relationship.[67] From the start, Ozanam's academic career was of great interest to Ampère. In Ozanam's early critique of Saint-Simonian socialism, Ampère discovered, as quoted earlier, "the germ of qualities which developed later in Ozanam: a keen, though still immature, taste for knowledge drawn from widely different sources; enthusiasm, loftiness of thought, great moderation in dealing with persons." Ampère was convinced that this early essay of Ozanam "was the preface to the book at which he was to labor even to his last day."[68]

Ampère's interest in Ozanam and their friendship continued to grow. In February 1840, Frédéric wrote to Jean-Jacques about the success of his lectures on commercial law in Lyon, indicating, however, that he hoped to replace Edgar Quinet, who held the Chair of Foreign Literature but who was leaving Lyon for Paris. Ozanam confided that "they [other faculty who were anti-Catholic] have canvassed against me. My political views, my religious convictions have been quoted against me." But he insisted that he would never compromise his principles. It is possible that Ampère brought this letter to the attention of the Minister of Education, for he replied with this assurance: "You can count on me. When you will be able to return [from Paris] you will find me."[69]

In 1844 Ampère lived up to such assurances. When the position of Chair of Foreign Literature at the Sorbonne, a plum appointment, was first offered to him, Ampère immediately refused to accept it. He was aware of the importance for his friend of a less precarious academic position, especially now that Ozanam was married and living in Paris rather than Lyon. But he went far beyond this initial act. Contending that Ozanam was the preferred candidate, he used "all of the weight of his influence" and "all of the warmth of his friendship" to achieve the final goal. He was successful; Ozanam obtained the position and was eternally grateful. He wrote to Jean-Jacques with sincere appreciation: "I knew well from experience that one needed friends in adversity, but I did not know that one stood in such need of them in prosperity." He further insisted that his friend "should derive pleasure from what you have done, you who, next to God, are the author of all my prosperity, you who received me into the house of your saintly and distinguished father, who placed my feet first on the road, who guided me from trial to trial, step by step, to this professorial Chair, in which I am now sitting, because the only one worthy of the position was not willing to occupy it."[70]

A powerful link had now been forged between the two. In fact, they were working on similar studies, yet they enjoyed the sharing of their ideas. As Ampère good-humoredly teased his friend, they never would be in direct competition, for "I have taken from you the men of Letters and the men of state; but make your mind easy, I have left you the missionaries and the saints."[71] When Ozanam rented a country house in Sceaux, not far from Paris, in 1851, his friend visited him on a regular schedule. Ampère divided his time during the summer of 1851 between Frédéric and his other friend, Alexis de Tocqueville, the famous French writer on American democracy, who lived in Montreuil near Versailles.[72] Surprisingly, it appears that de Tocqueville and Ozanam neither met nor corresponded.[73] At Sceaux the two friends discussed literary matters as well as Ozanam's recent writings.[74] Jean-Jacques later convinced his friend to travel to England because, as Ozanam related, "the Professor of Foreign Literature would fail in his obligations, if he did not seize the opportunity of a cheap trip to the country of Shakespeare."[75] Ozanam acquiesced, and Ampère accompanied the Ozanams on the journey. Ozanam, in fact, was shocked by the poverty that he encountered and that his faith caused him to confront during his visit to England. In many respects their friendship became a "brotherhood."[76]

In her biography of Ozanam, O'Meara claims: "The two *savants* presented as perfect a type of manly friendship as any we can recall. . . .

They had no secrets from one another; there was only one point in which their union was not perfect; but it was an essential one, and Ozanam could never refer to it without a pang."[77] Ozanam was aware that the younger Ampère "lacked the glowing faith of his great father, and seemed unable to swim out of the dangerous currents to the serene shore of certainty, as Ozanam had in his youth."[78] Moreover, "in Ozanam's circle of friends, Jean-Jacques Ampère in effect held a place apart, being the only close friend to not share his religious convictions."[79] Ampère was not openly hostile to Christianity, but he was reluctant to approach closer to faith. He was deeply influenced by the skepticism of his day, which he shared with many of his other friends. Yet the emptiness and restlessness that he felt as a result of his skepticism made him want to believe, and his studies provided him with little relief from the cacophony of his everyday life.

When Ampère decided to leave Europe to travel to America, Frédéric seized the opportunity to write tenderly to him and sensitively broach the subject of their underlying disagreement: "Are you astonished, my dear friend, at the sadness which I feel at your departure? I could not tell you verbally wherein the cause of it lies, because I did not wish that you should be obliged to answer me. If I am writing to you now it is because, if the outpouring of my heart is indiscreet, the seas that are bearing you to America will obliterate all recollection of the indiscretion. . . . My dear friend, you suffer much fatigue which is not without danger to your health; please excuse my uneasiness. You are seeking out new interests to occupy your mind, and you are making a tour of the world for that purpose. Yet there exists one sovereign interest, one Good capable of attracting and of filling your great heart." Ozanam then expressed his deepest concern: "I fear, my dear friend, I fear, perhaps unjustly, that you do not think enough of that? You are a Christian at heart, by the blood of your incomparable father; you discharge all the duties of Christianity to men; must they not also be discharged towards God? Must we not serve Him, must we not live in continuous communication with Him? Would you not find infinite consolation in such a service? Would you not find the security of eternity?"[80]

Ozanam had previously avoided this subject, but now the urgency of the moment and the demands of friendship compelled him to speak further. He suggested to Jean-Jacques that he had given Frédéric "reason to think more than once that such sentiments were not strangers to your heart."[81] Ampère's extensive research and work, according to Ozanam, have "brought you into contact with so many distinguished Christians; you have known so many eminent men who closed their lives in Christian peace. Such examples invite you, but the difficulties of belief hold you back."[82] With deference to his famous friend, Ozanam elucidated why he had never mentioned these concerns before: "I have never ventured to talk over such matters with you, because you have infinitely more knowledge and wisdom than I." Having attempted to stir his friend's conscience, Ozanam proposed the following argument for his thoughtful consideration: "Let me . . . say that there are but two schools. Philosophy and Religion. Philosophy has its inspirations. It knows, but does not love, God. It has never caused a single one of those loving tears to fall, which come to the eyes of a Catholic in Holy Communion, Whose incomparable sweetness and consolation is worth the sacrifice of life. . . . You would find in it [communion] the interior evidence before which all doubts flee. Faith is an act of virtue and therefore an act of the will. We must will to believe, we must surrender our soul, and then God gives light superabundantly."[83]

The letter ended with this fervent petition: "Ah! my dear friend, if you should fall ill some day in an American city without a friend at your bedside, remember that there is not a spot of any importance in the United States, to which the love of Jesus Christ has not drawn the steps of a priest, to console the Catholic traveller."[84] Ozanam feared that he might offend. On the contrary, Ampère was deeply moved. He posted this response: "My very dear and good friend. I do not wish to lose a minute in thanking you for your letter. Offend me? You would not be my friend if you had felt otherwise; in any case I would have known that you felt so, even if you had not written. Forgive me if I do not answer your arguments. Believe, that the sight of Catholic orthodoxy in a mind like yours is for me a sermon more eloquent than any speech." He added a postscript, which read: "I came across the little cripple yesterday at Waterloo Bridge and I gave him something *from us four.*"[85]

The two men continued to exchange correspondence. Through Ampère's letters, Ozanam learned much about American writers such as the poet Longfellow.[86] Ozanam's unease about his friend, however, would not be relieved. He employed all of his wit and logic to convince his friend to return home. But unfortunately they were never able to meet face to face again.[87] After Ozanam's death, Ampère honored his friend by writing the preface to his collected works, attesting to the world that with "very tender interest" he had always followed the career of "this young friend, this young brother."[88] Ozanam would have been pleased that Ampère continued the search for truth for the remainder of his life: "I persevere in the search for truth in good faith. Nobody desires to have it more sincerely than I, and I offer up this prayer each night to God, 'Enlighten me.'"[89]

HENRI DOMINIQUE LACORDAIRE

Henri Dominique Lacordaire, the brilliant Dominican preacher and friend of Ozanam, once described Frédéric as "that type of Christian, as ancient as his religion, as modern as his time."[90] His regard for Ozanam was exceedingly high: "Seeing him on his way to lecture at the Sorbonne one would have taken him for a student. His bearing was unchanged, his gaze ... kindly and gentle. ... Often he read as he went, but not with such intense application as to miss the friendly greetings that he received and returned with even deeper marks of respect. During the twenty years I knew him I have seen him troubled, indignant. But never once have I witnessed in him the slightest shadow of haughtiness or affectation, and that is a sure sign of a soul that is master of its fate and has its gaze fixed constantly on God."[91] The fact that Ozanam treasured friendships was readily apparent to Lacordaire, who noted that, for Ozanam, "friendship was not a fleeting sentiment that passed with youth." No obstacle, neither "the passing of years, nor his marriage, nor fame could suppress the need he had of loving his fellowmen." His effect on others, especially younger men, was especially noteworthy. As Lacordaire attested, "I have had touching proof of the affection he could inspire."[92] The Lenten series of lectures at Notre Dame Cathedral in the 1830s, discussed in chapter 2, first brought Ozanam and Lacordaire into contact. Lacordaire remembered Ozanam as a young man who "came as the advance-guard of the youthful throng soon to surround my pulpit."[93] That would be only the first of many encounters.

In 1839 Lacordaire, a diocesan priest since 1833, decided to enter the Order of Preachers. Ozanam wrote to him not only to congratulate him but also to earn the title of friend.[94] After referring to the Society of St. Vincent de Paul, which "sees its ranks growing in surprising fashion," and Lacordaire's influence on the spread of faith, Ozanam confided that he required Lacordaire's prayers to discern whether he should enter the priesthood: "It is this interior malaise from which I have long been suffering that I recommend to your charitable prayers; for, if God indeed wishes to call me to Himself, I see no finer militia in which to serve Him than the one you are sworn to." Ozanam concluded by asking for advice on where to find a copy of the Rule followed by the "Friars Preachers," professing that "you will thus obligate once again one who already owes you so much."[95]

Ozanam did not choose to enter the priesthood, but his connection to Lacordaire continued throughout the rest of his life. Both collaborated in writing for *L'Ère nouvelle* in 1848, although, as mentioned in the previous chapter, Ozanam was the stronger supporter of democracy.[96] Three years later, in 1851, Père Lacordaire trusted Ozanam sufficiently to seek his friend's advice about his preaching. At first Ozanam balked at the request and then declined. He later regretted his initial reply: "My dear Reverend Father, you asked me a question this morning as a friend, and I answered it as a stranger, as one whom you would not allow to tell the truth. . . . I am too much attached to you, and too warm an admirer of your preaching, not to repeat observations which I have heard made." He then proceeded as a true friend to list certain defects to be corrected: "The fondness for strange words, the startling nature of some comparisons, the too frequent use of profane allusions in a sacred subject, a touch of the old Romanticism, a little carelessness in the printed text of sermons which are destined to be immortal." Lacordaire sincerely thanked Ozanam for his honest appraisal.[97]

Lacordaire, as Ozanam's close friend, wrote the following after Ozanam's death in 1853 as a fitting epitaph: "Dear Frederic Ozanam! None of us will fill the gap you have left. Not one of us will carry away from men's hearts what you have taken from ours. You were the leader in virtue. . . . The poor prayed for you, and stole your soul away from us. . . . You were for twenty years the purest if not the most powerful object of our gaze. . . . You were the teacher of many, the consolation of us all."[98] As a young man, Ozanam had once written: "I hope I . . . will be all my life at least a good Frenchman, a good friend, and a good Christian."[99] Lacordaire attests that Ozanam's hope had been fulfilled.

FRIENDSHIP TOWARD OTHERS

Besides the many close, and often famous, friends whom Ozanam cherished, many others came to know this essential feature of Ozanam's character. His students were treated with kindness and respect but always with a view to their growth and development. According to Schimberg, "Ozanam . . . won the attachment of his students. . . . He was always at their disposal, none ever felt abashed in asking his help or counsel. This was a part of his . . . apostolate of friendliness, a part of his giving of self to others, as in the work of the Vincentian society."[100] He spent extra time with students who were plagued by the difficulty of a subject or endowed with less talent than some of their classmates.[101] In one example of his generosity as a teacher, a Carmelite student, hoping to discuss his thesis, arrived at Ozanam's home just before dinner was ready to be served. Although he was called to dinner several times and the student rose to leave, Ozanam insisted that the student remain. The young man, who later became bishop of Versailles, fondly recalled the incident: "I have experienced courtesy from many. But with him it was pure Christian charity. I was quite unknown to him. I would not see him again, yet he treated me as a friend and a brother."[102]

Another example of his warmth may be found in Ozanam's letter to Alexandre Ferriny-Jérusalemy, a letter that has been referred to as "the perfection of kindness."[103] Jérusalemy, who had converted to Christianity from Judaism, had suffered much for his change of faith. In a letter in 1853 Ozanam consoled and uplifted him: "Ah, my dear friend, when one has the happiness of being a Christian, it is a great honor to be born a Jew and to feel oneself the lineal descendant of the patriarchs and the prophets, whose words are so beautiful that the Church finds nothing better to put into the mouths of her children."[104] He wrote to Jérusalemy that the Psalms of David never left his own hands "during the long weeks of lassitude" caused by his deteriorating health. Ozanam referred to the fact that he and his brother Charles, with whom Jérusalemy was acquainted, were of Jewish descent, creating "another bond of union between us."[105] As Frédéric reassured him, "You ought, therefore, to understand why we brothers have a deep interest in all that concerns you. I believe that Charles will have introduced you into a Conference of the Society of St. Vincent de Paul. It does me good to know that we are linked together by that bond. Do not weary of loving, nor of praying, my dear Jérusalemy, for one who is yours wholeheartedly."[106] He sought to dispel Jérusalemy's feeling of solitude with a statement of solidarity.

In the words of biographer Christine Franconnet, Ozanam "accorded a great importance to friendship," and the "goodwill shown toward his friends" should not be underestimated.[107] According to Baunard, "It can be readily understood how admirably such a mind, character, and heart were formed for friendship. A whole chapter could be devoted to Ozanam's numerous friends. They were family, literary, academic, political, home, Parisian, and foreign. All his friendships were, in a sense, religious; that characteristic is the key to them all."[108] Ozanam fully comprehended that "to lift up a soul there is need of another soul; this attraction is called love; in the language of philosophy, it is known as friendship, and in that of Christianity, charity."[109] For him, love, friendship, and charity were one and the same, all deeply rooted in God's infinite mercy, unending wisdom, and bountiful providence. No wonder that he "poured out his heart in letters to his friends, was happy when they were happy, shared their disappointments and griefs, let them share his joys and sorrows, gave them counsel and asked for theirs. . . . His friendship was an apostolate."[110]

CHAPTER 8

Spirituality and Sanctification

Ozanam, as earlier chapters have made clear, was brought up in a household of deep abiding faith and was highly sensitive to the development of his own spiritual life. He learned from his parents that God was both benevolent and just. He also learned from them that strength and support would come from God in times of loss and pain. After suffering through a brief but painfully unsettling religious crisis in his youth, he never again wavered in his faith. He trusted in God's providence for him, his family, his friends, and his world. His spiritual life, then, became an essential part of his pilgrimage on earth. Each day he faithfully read from scripture, his source of both inspiration and comfort. Whether he traveled or worked at his desk, a cross was his constant companion. Because his life was centered on his faith, the most cherished events were deeply spiritual moments, when he experienced in a profound way the presence of a loving God—events such as his First Communion, the conference meetings of the Society, the Lenten series of Père Lacordaire, his wedding to his beloved Amélie, the baptism of his cherished daughter Marie, and his audience with

Pius IX. In every respect, his life was a spiritual journey toward the good, the beautiful, and the true.

At the age of twenty-one, Ozanam wrote of his worship and prayer life in a letter to his cousin Ernest Falconnet: "I . . . believe worship to be the expression of faith, the symbol of hope, the earthly result of the love of God. For that reason I practice it as much as I can and according to the best habits given me from childhood, and find in prayer and the sacraments the needed sustenance for my moral life amid temptations of a consuming imagination and fantasizing world."[1] Prayer and the sacraments were vital to him in meeting the challenges and obstacles to his spiritual development. According to historian Ronald Ramson, "he received the sacrament of confession and communion frequently, which was unusual for that time in the French Church."[2] In a letter to another friend, Ozanam wrote that he experienced "the inexpressible sweetness of Holy Communion" and that "in the transport which it causes, there is a power for conviction which would enable me to embrace the Cross and defy unbelief, should all the world have abjured Christ."[3] Interestingly, he rarely used the name Jesus Christ; out of respect, he preferred *Notre-Seigneur* or *Sauveur*.[4]

His wife, Amélie, attested to the fact that prayer and scripture reading (what he called his "daily bread") were an intimate part of his daily routine: "I never saw him wake up or fall asleep without making the sign of the cross and praying. In the morning he read the bible, in Greek, on which he meditated about half an hour. In the last years of his life, he went to Mass every day for his support and consolation. He never did anything serious without praying. Before leaving for his course, he always got on his knees to ask God for the grace of saying nothing which would attract public praise to himself but of only speaking for the Glory of God and the service of the truth."[5] Reading from the *Imitation of Christ*, which has justly been called the "bedside book of generations of Catholics," was a regular part of his evenings.[6] His days were spent in putting into action what he had earlier read. As he wrote Falconnet in 1834, "Yet religious ideas can have no value if they have no practical and positive value. Religion is meant less for thinking than for action and, if it teaches how to live, it is in order to teach how to die."[7]

Ozanam was fortunate in having two people especially to guide him on his journey toward holiness. One was Amélie, who became an essential support in his life, enabling him to develop his fullest potential as a scholar and as a Christian. Frédéric referred to her as his "guide and companion," and, like Tobias in the scripture, he recognized that she was destined for him for all eternity: "She will walk in the same paths with you, and the merciful lord will save you by means of each other." Like Tobias, he felt his soul "drawn to her with infinite power."[8] The other was Abbé J. B. Marduel, who was Ozanam's spiritual director for most of his life. Marduel had moved from the church of Saint-Nizier in Lyon to the church of Saint-Roch in Paris. This priest became the confessor of both Frédéric and his brother Alphonse throughout their lives, and of Amélie as well.[9]

Frédéric's brother Alphonse attested to the powerful impact of this priest on his younger brother: "Under his direction, this well-beloved brother, notwithstanding his many occupations, found plenty of time each day for meditation and prayer." In Marduel's "school of gentle piety," Frédéric was able "to triumph in the interior spiritual struggle for truth and virtue."[10] He confessed to his mother in 1834 that Père Marduel was "the only intimate spiritual advisor that I have, the only one who, in kindness and wisdom, can take the place of father and mother."[11] While awaiting his wedding day in 1841, Frédéric confided to Amélie that Père Marduel, "the good old priest," "is trying to calm my impatient mood . . . and assures me with a patriarchal smile and the experience of seventy-nine years."[12] When he and Amélie were separated for a time in 1842 because of her first miscarriage, he felt lost while she was at her parents' home. Marduel advised him to visit the Chapel of Saint Vincent de Paul, where Ozanam felt spiritually reunited with his dear spouse.[13]

Ozanam wrote in a letter to Amélie after his visit, "This morning, my good Amélie, I went to find the confessor of every trouble, the friend of the afflicted [Saint Vincent de Paul]. The remains of the blessed patron were exposed in their crystal *chasse*. This simple and humble priest was surrounded with all the homage of the Church and of that double family of missionaries and sisters who carry his benefactions to the utmost limits of the world and the last degree of misery."[14] Ozanam then "had the good fortune to receive Communion. And there in the bosom of Him whose arms are wide enough to encompass all distances, I found you again. I felt your soul like a white dove beside mine, and I offered your purity, your sweetness, your simplicity, and all those things God loves in return for my pride, impatience, and perverse imaginations. I renewed the resolution to become better."[15] His letter is a tribute to the importance of both Père Marduel and Amélie in Frédéric's spiritual development. It is likewise a powerful piece of evidence demonstrating the devotion to Saint Vincent de Paul that became a regular part of Ozanam's spirituality.

In the words of Ramson, "Frédéric Ozanam heard the call of holiness; he knew that call and the challenge to grow in the divine life which he had received when he was baptized. He pursued holiness first as a single male, then as a married man and father of a family. Frederic understood that unity with Christ Jesus depended on his willingness and readiness to choose Him at progressively deeper levels whether it be daily or during each stage of his existence. Frédéric was a man of exceptional piety throughout his entire life."[16] In his journey toward holiness, he desired most to live a life of moral perfection, with "a true and inflexible conscience."[17]

DIVINE PROVIDENCE

Crucial to Ozanam's spiritual journey was his growing understanding of and trust in divine providence. In a letter to Emmanuel Bailly of October 22, 1836, he wrote: "Beyond doubt Providence does not need us for the execution of its merciful designs, but we, we need it and it promises us its assistance only on the condition of our efforts. . . . Carry on the work begun and work for its propagation and consolidation."[18] In the same spirit Ozanam counseled his dear friend François Lallier: "Our little Society of St. Vincent de Paul has grown large enough to be considered a providential fact, and it is not without reason that you occupy a place of importance in it. Do not fail it. As secretary general, you are, after M. Bailly, the Society's soul. . . . See, then, the great responsibilities imposed on you."[19] For Ozanam, cooperation with the purposes of divine providence was crucial to the ultimate success of a Christian.

One of the most beautiful passages written by Ozanam on the role of God's providence in his life is contained in a letter to Amélie in 1843: "Then, three years ago, when the success of my teaching was uncertain, I did not falter, I did not listen to dictates of self-interest: I sought in my career knowledge only. I believe that it was God who thus inspired me, and made me act with a confidence that was foreign to my weak character. Then Providence led you into my path, and I offered you the sharing of a life poor, . . . but sanctified, ennobled by the cultivation of all that is beautiful: I offered you solitude far from all belonging to you, but with the tenderness of a heart which had never belonged to anyone but you."[20] His trust in divine providence was not unlike that of Saint Vincent de Paul, who wrote: "Grace has its moments. Let us abandon ourselves to the Providence of God and be very careful not to run ahead of it . . . and let us put our feet only on the paths Providence has marked out for us." According to Vincent de Paul, "A consolation Our Lord gives me . . . to believe that by the grace of God, we have always tried to follow and not to anticipate Providence which knows how to conduct all things so wisely to the end Our Lord destines for them."[21]

In his spiritual life, Frédéric embraced a "Vincentian concept of Divine Providence." Ramson offers this explanation: "[Although] it may well be running the risk of being too simplistic, . . . the Vincentian concept of Divine Providence can be summarized in several key phrases: 'We must will what Divine Providence wills. Grace has its moments. Let us abandon ourselves to Providence. Do not run ahead of Providence. Do not run behind Providence. Follow Providence on the path it leads without desiring to know its length or windings.' "[22]

THE BLESSED VIRGIN MARY

It was no surprise to his friends that Frédéric Ozanam proposed honoring the Blessed Virgin Mary as the patroness of the Society of St. Vincent de Paul in February 1834. He already nurtured a strong devotion to the Blessed Mother, as described in earlier chapters. Frédéric was only nineteen in 1832 when the first two thousand medals were struck according to the specifications of Catherine Labouré, who had been visited by the Blessed Mother in 1830 and who had been charged by Mary to have a medal struck in her honor.[23] The year 1832 also witnessed a terrible cholera epidemic in Paris. Although the medal was officially called the "Medal of the Immaculate Conception," healing miracles were immediately attributed to it, and soon it was most commonly known as the "Miraculous Medal."[24] There is a strong possibility that Ozanam was wearing one of the original medals when he and his friends met to form the first conference of charity in April 1833.[25] He was also fascinated by the story of the Jewish convert Marie Alphonse Ratisbonne, who embraced the Catholic faith in 1842 supposedly because of the influence of the medal.[26] Ozanam helped to distribute accounts of that conversion.[27]

Ozanam's devotion to the Blessed Mother was also revealed in the choice of his daughter's name, Marie. The Ozanams chose the name both to honor Frédéric's mother and to pay homage to the Blessed Mother, the "powerful patroness" who, in their opinion, was responsible for "this happy birth."[28] Marie's loving father died when she was only eight years old, on September 8, 1853, the feast of the nativity of the Blessed Virgin Mary. Given his lifelong devotion to Mary, it was fitting that he breathed his last on this Marian feast day.

FEASTS AND HOLY DAYS

Along with the private side of Ozanam's spiritual life, he relished the feasts and holy days of the Christian year. He enjoyed these communal celebrations to the fullest. In 1833, on the Feast of the Epiphany, he wrote to Ernest Falconnet: "It is Saturday evening, midnight is about to strike, a new day will begin, a great and solemn day, the anniversary of the first homage rendered by the pagan world to infant Christianity. There is something of beautiful awesomeness in this legend of the three magi representing three human races at the crib of the Savior, something venerable in the family feast which consecrates joy. . . . It is always a good occasion for drawing closer relatives and friends to open their hearts."[29] In the same year, he and his friends left Paris on the Feast of Corpus Christi to participate in the religious procession held at Nanterre.[30] It was a grand spectacle, in which some thirty students processed: "The procession was large and full of elegant simplicity, all the houses close together, the paths strewn with flowers, and there was a faith, a piety difficult to describe, good elderly people who had not been able to follow the procession were waiting at the crossing. It was principally in front of their homes that the street-altars were set up. The ceremony lasted close to two hours. . . . Afterward we attended the high Mass, where the crowd flowed to outside the doors of the Church."[31]

Easter (*le saint jour de Pâques*) was always one of his favorite holy days. As he wrote on Easter of 1842, "Today is too beautiful not to spend with my family. Even this morning at Notre Dame I was not alone. . . . It would be especially impossible to see anything more beautiful than the congregation: on leaving, the crowd streamed out of the three doors and covered the plaza. The great basilica with its black façade and majestic towers revealing the illuminated nave through its portal represented so to speak the sacred edifice of the faith whose mysteries are also imposing and grave outwardly but conceal an interior of infinite charity. . . . After Communion, which, given by two priests, took an hour, a magnificent *Te Deum* filled the vaults, and we broke up deeply moved."[32] On Christmas day in the same year, he and Amélie attended Notre Dame at nine o'clock in the morning. They had already attended midnight mass at the Abbey-au-Bois, located on the rue de Sèvres. On the evening of the twenty-fifth, they also went to hear a sermon at Saint-Sulpice. Finally, after the solemnities were over, they partook of a dinner of goose stew.[33]

For Frédéric, all of the feasts and holy days, including the Assumption (August 15, which was also Amélie's birthday), the Feast of All Saints (November 1), the Feast of the Immaculate Conception (December 8), and even the Feast of All Souls (November 2), were special events to be commemorated and cherished as opportunities to renew one's spiritual life and commitment to the faith. They likewise provided an ideal opportunity to share one's faith with family and friends.

SPIRITUAL SETBACKS

Although Ozanam was strong in his faith, at times he experienced setbacks and questioned himself. For example, he wrote to his friend Léonce Curnier in 1835: "If you knew how weak I am! . . . How I pass from ambitious presumption to discouragement and inaction! What vanity of thought, what puniness of works! What daily abuse of divine graces! What infidelity to generous inspirations! What loss of precious time! . . . Providence has embraced me with such great solicitude, it has provided me so handsomely with the benefits of education, it has lavished on me such good parents, wise teachers, exemplary friends, that often I am led to reflect that it wishes from me something more than common virtue; and meanwhile . . . my soul is like a sterile shore which the waves of heaven overflow without fertilizing."[34] He expressed similar concerns to his friend Alexandre Dufieux in the same year: "And I, wretched plant, I have not unfolded my petals to the divine breathing; I have not driven my roots into the good soil; I have become dried up and withered. I recognized God's gift; I felt the living waters bathe my lips and I opened them not. I remained a passive creature, I wrapped myself up in a cowardly inertia. I am incapable of willing or of acting, and I feel accumulating on my head the crushing responsibility of favours that I daily ignore."[35] He confessed that from time to time, "piety seems to me a yoke, prayer a lip-habit, Christian practices the last branch to which I cling to save myself from falling into the abyss, but the fruit of which I cannot gather," but he then assured Dufieux that he had found renewed strength in the reception of Christ in the Eucharist: "Yesterday I had the great happiness of receiving Him, Who is the strength of the weak and the Doctor of souls."[36]

From such setbacks, Ozanam emerged with a stronger faith and a greater sense of purpose. He also discovered that an authentic spiritual journey is not a straight course, but rather is filled with many twists and turns along the way: "Yes, we are unprofitable servants, but we are servants, and wages are given according to the quality of work we are doing in the vineyard of the Lord in the portion assigned to us. Yes, life is despicable if we consider it according to how we use it, but not if we . . . consider it as the most perfect work of the Creator, as the sacred vestments with which the Savior has willed to clothe himself: life then is worthy of reverence and love. Let us pray for each other, dear good friend. . . . Let us go in simplicity where merciful Providence leads us, content to see the stone on which we should step without wanting to discover all at once and completely the windings of the road."[37]

THE SOCIETY OF ST. VINCENT DE PAUL

Ozanam cherished the Society of St. Vincent de Paul and its experiences of service to those in need as a means to achieve greater holiness. For him, the person in poverty was "the messenger of God to us, sent to prove our justice and charity."[38] Through the Society and its community, his own faith was reinforced. As he confided to his fiancée, Amélie, in 1841, "In the morning a pious throng crowded around the altar where this glorious Apostle of Charity [Vincent de Paul] reposes in his silver *chasse*. There were deputations from the twenty-five Paris conferences, young people with whom some illustrious old men mingled in fraternal equality.... At the same hour, thirty other conferences established in the farthest removed sections of the country celebrated the same solemnity. How can there not be given some hope to such a strength of association.... Can we not believe without too much madness that divine Providence calls us to the moral rehabilitation of our country[?]"[39] In 1843 Frédéric wrote to his younger brother, Charles, also a member of the Society of St. Vincent de Paul, of the great fortune they had in the Society: "Let us thank divine Providence ... for having brought us both to enter this young and growing family which may be destined to regenerate France by preparing for all the liberal professions, science, art, politics, a recruitment of Christians. Whatever is said about it, souls are returning to the faith; it grows slowly like things that last, and will continue on to the end so long as we do not compromise it by our weakness or imprudence."[40] Before his death in 1853, Ozanam confessed: "This dear Society [of St. Vincent de Paul] is also my family. It is, after God, what kept me in the faith, when I had lost my good and pious parents. I love it, and I hold it in the deepest part of my heart."[41]

Although Ozanam was open to the various and less orthodox spiritual traditions of the Catholic Church,[42] although he was sometimes critical of the Catholic leaders who failed to respond to the genuine needs of those in poverty and who catered to the rich, and although he had an appreciation for ancient religions such as Buddhism and was fascinated by how they compared to Christianity,[43] nevertheless, he remained a staunch supporter of the fundamental truths of the Catholic faith throughout his life. That is one of the reasons why he took over the editing of the annals of the Society for the Propagation of the Faith, which had been started in Lyon in 1822. He remained with this project until 1848.[44] He served as the liaison between the Paris and Lyon councils of the Society for the Propagation of the Faith and was delegated to have an audience with Queen Marie-Amélie on behalf of this Society in order to obtain royal recognition and support for its mission and work.[45]

Ozanam sincerely hoped that Catholicism would find many converts in his nineteenth-century world.

As Ramson notes, the spirituality of Frédéric Ozanam was "that of the person in the pew who burns with the desire to love God and neighbor and who, also, wants to put into practice that love." He was a man "of prayer and action, each supporting and fostering the other." The spirituality of Frederic Ozanam was "the spirituality of humility, simplicity, mortification, meekness and zeal for souls." It was "that of the Good Samaritan, the person who ardently practices the spiritual and corporal works of mercy," and of "the spirituality of St. Vincent de Paul, who believes and recognizes that it is truly Jesus in that person of the poor before him. For Frederic, the poor person was the Risen Jesus; for Frederic, the poor person was the sacred image of the God whom he did not see." The spirituality of Ozanam was "the spirituality of compassion without judgement."[46]

Ozanam would have balked at the idea that he was a saint. However, he lived a life of genuine piety and holiness that exhibited full trust in and cooperation with divine providence. He walked a lifelong spiritual journey toward holiness, a journey that can justly be called that of "a strong Christian witness, a virtuous man, a saint."[47]

CHAPTER 9

Solidarity

Ozanam and Catholic Social Teaching

Solidarity, an important principle in Catholic social teaching, is fundamentally "a firm and persevering determination to commit oneself to the common good; that is to say, to the good of all and of each individual, because we are all really responsible for all."[1] Solidarity is achieved within society only "when its members recognize one another as persons."[2] According to Meghan J. Clark, "In order to cultivate solidarity, one's approach must be both personal and institutional. It must involve charity, justice, and organization."[3]

Frédéric Ozanam may never have used the term *solidarité*, but he fully comprehended the meaning of the concept, and he spent much of his short life pursuing an authentic solidarity that would bring the different social classes toward greater mutual understanding and cooperation. For him, charity and justice were intimate partners in the process of creating solidarity; both were required to renew the world of his day, which was filled with strife and suffering. Charity and justice in turn became deeply embedded in the organization of the Society of St. Vincent de Paul. In the opinion of some thinkers, Ozanam was "both a pioneer and a prophet for modern Catholic social thought,"[4] in which solidarity is a key governing principle.

CHARITY AND JUSTICE

Ozanam valued charity, once comparing it to "a tender mother who keeps her eyes fixed on the infant she carries at her breast, who no longer thinks of herself, and who forgets her beauty for her love."[5] He wrote to his friend Léonce Curnier, "Oh, yes, my friend, the faith, the charity of the first centuries! It is not too much for our century."[6] He clearly saw the need for charity and for lay leadership in charitable outreach. And it was his fervent hope that the Society of St. Vincent de Paul would be the means to achieve this vision.

One special model for Frédéric, as we have seen, was Saint Vincent de Paul, who eloquently counseled that the poor were really the masters, the reflections of the sacred image of God.[7] Another was Saint Francis of Assisi. This "fool of love" exhibited an "immense charity" that "embraced God, humanity, nature."[8] In Ozanam's words, when Saint Francis had reflected that "God was made poor in order to live on earth, that the majority of poor, and that nature itself in the midst of its magnificences is poor, since it is subject to death, he himself wished to be poor; it belongs to love to assimilate the things loved into himself."[9] Ozanam chose these two saints to guide him and his work. Charity, thus, was more than the simple act of almsgiving for Frédéric; it was "love which moves beyond emotion, it is lived, practiced, a virtue, and . . . ultimately friendship with God."[10]

Ozanam also fully appreciated the role of justice in society. As a young man practicing law, he was outraged by the corruption that he observed in the legal system, as described in chapter 2. He acknowledged that there was an intimate and necessary connection between justice and charity. He voiced this view in comments to Emmanuel Bailly, the president of the Society of St. Vincent de Paul, in 1836: "Let us work to increase and multiply, to become better, more tender and stronger; . . . the disorder in society becomes more and more apparent;

the social problems, the conflict between poverty and riches, between self-interest which wants to take and self-interest which wants to keep, succeeds political problems. And the confrontation between these two self-interests, the poor who have the force of numbers and the rich that of silver, will be terrible if charity does not interpose, become a mediator, if Christians do not dominate with all the force of love."[11]

He expressed a similar idea to François Lallier a short time later: "Our duty to ourselves as Christians is to throw ourselves between these two irreconcilable enemies."[12] As discussed in chapter 6, he genuinely believed that there was only one viable solution to relieve the tensions between rich and poor: "In the name of charity Christians must interpose themselves between the two camps . . . getting them used to looking upon one another as brothers, infusing them with a bit of mutual charity; and this charity paralyzing, stifling self-interest of both sides, lessening the antipathies day by day."[13]

Justice required the assistance of charity, but charity in turn required the pursuit of justice. According to Ozanam, "Public Charity must intervene in crises. But Charity is the Samaritan who pours oil on the wounds of the attacked traveler.—It is for Justice to prevent the attacks."[14] The relationship was one of mutual necessity, with charity "widening the focus of justice to include God and groups of people previously passed over."[15] For Frédéric, "Love becomes the principle of progress in social institutions. The order of society rests on two virtues: justice and charity. But justice presupposes a lot of love already, because it is necessary to love man a great deal in order to respect his right which limits our right and his freedom that hinders our freedom. But justice has limits; charity knows none."[16]

To the critics of charity, he had this reply: "Yes, no doubt charity does put the poor man under an obligation, and for some people the ideal world is a world where nobody would be under an obligation to anybody, where each would have the proud satisfaction of feeling himself unbeholden to all. . . . That is what they call the coming of justice in the place of charity; as if the whole economy of Providence did not consist in a reciprocity of obligations which are never paid off; as if a son was not the eternal debtor of his father, a father of his children, a citizen of his country."[17] In an imperfect world, Ozanam knew that there could be no justice without its companion, charity.

DIGNITY OF THE HUMAN PERSON
AND RESPECT FOR HUMAN LIFE

William J. Byron, former president of Catholic University of America, and Robert P. Maloney, C.M., former superior general of the Congregation of the Mission, have each written about ten foundational principles in Catholic social teaching.[18] Both have emphatically suggested that one can only understand Catholic social teaching by examining closely the lives and thoughts of people who embodied its principles. Frédéric Ozanam is clearly a candidate for such an examination. By advocating a more charitable and just world in his writings, by founding the Society of St. Vincent de Paul, and by cultivating authentic solidarity, he not only anticipated but also fully embodied the ten foundational principles of Catholic social teaching as identified by Byron and Maloney.

The first principle of Catholic social teaching is the principle of the dignity of the human person, and the second is respect for human life. According to the United States Catholic Conference of Bishops, "Every human being is created in the image of God and redeemed by Jesus Christ, and therefore is invaluable and worthy of respect as a member of the human family."[19] For Byron and Maloney, "This is the bedrock principle of Catholic social teaching. Every person—regardless of race, sex, age, national origin, religion, sexual orientation, employment or economic status, health, intelligence, achievement or any other differentiating characteristic—is worthy of respect. It is not what you do or what you have that gives you a claim on respect: it is simply being human that establishes your dignity."[20] Although individuals have dignity, "individualism has no place in Catholic social thought. The principle of human dignity gives the human person a claim on membership in a community, the human family."[21]

In an 1836 letter to his friend Louis Janmot, Ozanam wrote about these principles and reflected that the dignity of the person was rooted in Christ: "Both men and the poor we see with the eyes of the flesh; they are there and we can put finger and hand in their wounds and the scars of the crown of thorns visible on their foreheads; at this point incredulity no longer has place and we should fall at their feet and say with the Apostle, *Tu est Dominus et Deus meus.* You are our masters, and we will be your servants. You are for us the sacred images of that God whom we do not see, and not knowing how to love Him otherwise shall we not love Him in your persons?"[22] In serving those in need, Ozanam was invariably concerned about treating them with the utmost respect:

> Help is humiliating when it appeals to men from below, taking heed of their material wants only, paying no attention but to those of the flesh, to the cry of hunger and cold, to what excites pity, to what one succors even in the beasts. It humiliates when there is no reciprocity. . . . But it honors when it appeals to him from above, when it occupies itself with his soul, his religious, moral, and political education, with all that emancipates him from his passions and from a portion of his wants, with those things that make him free, and may make him great. Help honors when to the bread that nourishes it adds the visit that consoles . . . ; when it treats the poor man with respect, not only as an equal but as a superior, since he is suffering what perhaps we are incapable of suffering; since he is the messenger of God to us, sent to prove our justice and charity, and to save us by our works. Help then becomes honorable because it may become mutual.[23]

And, as earlier chapters have shown, in visiting the poor Ozanam often detected qualities that filled him with admiration. For him, everyone, "from the moment of conception to natural death, has inherent dignity and a right to life consistent with that dignity."[24]

In the Catholic tradition, the sacredness of human life must be a "part of any moral vision for a just and good society."[25] Ozanam's visits to those in poverty made him painfully aware of the large number of people leading a life of degradation. The following passage resulted, not from his literary imagination, but from his own experience:

> In Paris alone the number of individuals out of work amounts to *two hundred and sixty-seven thousand*. They get assistance, it is true, and this fact lulls your conscience and your alarms to sleep; but those who have the privilege of distributing the public help . . . go . . . to the twelfth arrondissement, one of the strongholds of insurrection, and out of about ninety thousand inhabitants they find eight thousand families inscribed on the list of the benevolent fund, twenty-one thousand nine hundred and ninety-two who receive extra help, making a total of some

seventy thousand individuals who are living on the precarious bread of alms. Half of this district, all the Montagne Ste. Geneviève, and all the neighborhood of the Gobelins, is composed of narrow, crooked streets, where the sun never penetrates, where a carriage could not venture without risk, and where a man in a coat never passes without making a sensation, and attracting to the doorsteps groups of naked children and women in rags. On either side of a filthy sewer rise houses five stories high, many of which shelter fifty families. Low, damp, and noxious rooms are let out at one franc and a half a week when they have a fireplace, and one franc and a quarter when they have not. No paper, often not a single piece of furniture, hides the nakedness of the walls. In a house of the Rue des Lyonnais we ourselves saw ten married couples without even a bed. One family lived in the depths of a cellar, with nothing but a handful of straw on the earthen floor, and a rope fastened from wall to wall, from which the poor creatures hung their bread in a rag to keep it out of the reach of rats. In the next room a woman had lost three children from consumption, and she pointed in despair to three others who awaited the same fate.[26]

The social injustices that he witnessed deeply angered Ozanam, and he tirelessly labored to achieve a decent life for every person from birth to death.

ASSOCIATION AND PARTICIPATION

The next two principles of Catholic social teaching are based on the values of association and participation: "Our tradition proclaims that the person is not only sacred but also social. How we organize our society—in economics and politics, in law and policy—directly affects human dignity and the capacity of individuals to grow in community."[27] The focus is "the family; family stability must always be protected and never undermined. By association with others—in families and in other social institutions that foster growth, protect dignity and promote the common good—human persons achieve their fulfillment."[28] Moreover, people "have a right and a duty to participate in society, seeking together the common good and well-being of all, especially the poor and vulnerable.

Our Church teaches that the role of government and other institutions is to protect human life and human dignity and promote the common good."[29] No person should be "shut out from participating in those institutions that are necessary for human fulfillment."[30]

Ozanam, as earlier chapters have richly demonstrated, prized family. He himself was a devoted son, husband, and father; he was formed by and he flourished through the bonds of family. He frequently witnessed the importance of family bonds and support in his service to others through the Society. In his political thought, he also maintained that a true democracy must begin with and must strengthen the family unit.

According to the Catholic tradition, "responsible citizenship is a virtue, and participation in political life is a moral obligation."[31] Indeed, "it is necessary that all participate, each according to his position and role, in promoting the common good. This obligation is inherent in the dignity of the human person."[32] As we have seen, Ozanam participated actively in public life, serving in the National Guard and running for elective office in 1848.[33] He believed that all people should be allowed a more active role in the political process. As quoted earlier, he firmly maintained in the face of criticism that "we [must] take care of the people . . . who justly demand a more complete role in public affairs, guarantees for work and against misery."[34] Furthermore, he was convinced that the "social order exists only in the interest of the human race: they who obey the law were not created for the good pleasure of the lawgiver: on the contrary, the lawgiver was made for their needs."[35] It is no wonder, then, that he raised a call to embrace the proletariat in 1848 and to "obtain for it institutions which will set it free and make it better."[36] He was also convinced by that time that church and state should be separate, and that democracy was the answer for the future.[37] These were radical positions for a Catholic of the times and were not embraced by the Church. The principles of association and participation also have important implications for labor. Work is not only a way to earn a living but also "a form of continuing participation in God's creation. If the dignity of work is to be protected, then the basic rights of workers must be respected—the right to productive work, to decent and fair wages, to organize and join unions, to private property, and to economic initiative."[38] Ozanam's public statement of his platform for political office in 1848, as we saw in chapter 6, boldly supported the rights to work, to receive adequate earnings for one's work, to form labor associations, and to receive public support if lacking employment and resources.

His defense of workers in 1848 was not a new idea for him. In his lectures on commercial law between 1839 and 1840, Ozanam had spoken forcefully about the dignity of work and the rights of workers. For him, Christianity raised the worker up by emphasizing the dignity of work, whether it be by the efforts of the mind or by the sweat of the brow.[39] All work has its necessary price: "Wages are the price of work . . . all toil deserves wages." Those wages are related to the value of goods produced and, therefore, should be proportional to profit. There should be no exploitation of the worker by the employer. As Ozanam pointed out, unfortunately, the rate of actual wage (*le taux reel du salaire*) a worker receives often is less than the rate of authentic wages (*taux du salaire naturel*). A truly just wage would allow for the worker to meet his normal living expenses, provide a sum for education, especially for children, and still leave a sufficient amount for retirement, a sacred estate.[40]

For the good of society, according to Ozanam, there must be an impartial reconciliation of the interests of employer and employees. This will only be accomplished by abandoning the two extremes of complete government control of the economy and unrestricted laissez-faire (or extreme individualism, in Ozanam's terminology). Government should intervene only in extraordinary cases: "Never has Christianity consented to that enforced Communism which seizes upon the human person at his birth, thrusts him into the national school and the national workshops, makes him nothing more than a soldier, without any will of his own, in the industrial army, a wheel without intelligence in the machine of the State."[41]

He also argued that the "old [i.e., individualistic] school of economics knew no greater social danger than insufficient production; no other welfare than to urge and multiply it by an unlimited competition; no other law of labor than personal interest: the interest of the most insatiable masters."[42] However, socialism was not the answer because "the school of modern Socialism traced all evil to a vicious distribution, and believed it could save society by suppressing competition, by making of the organization of labor a prison which would feed its prisoners; by urging the people to exchange their liberty for the certainty of bread and the promise of pleasure."[43] For him, both "systems, of which one made the destiny of

man to consist in production, the other in enjoyment, lead by two different ways into the same materialism."[44] To achieve genuine reform the two
principles of authority and liberty had to be reconciled.

Ozanam minced no words: "Between the individualism of the last
century and the Socialism of the present, Christianity alone has foreseen
the only possible solution of the formidable question which we are now
facing, and alone has arrived at the point to which the more intelligent
minds return to-day [*sic*], after their wide circuit, when they insist upon
association, but voluntary association."[45] When employers exploit their
workers by treating them like machines, he argued, they inevitably ruin the
health of their employees, degrade them both morally and intellectually,
and destroy family life.[46] Workers must be allowed to form associations or
unions (*Association des travailleurs*) that will give them leverage in bar-
gaining for just wages. Such associations of workers will enable workers
to receive better compensation. As a consequence, workers will increase
their productivity and value their work more. In fact, each laborer will
become "attached to his work as to something that is his own, industry
will advance in perfection, and that demoralization which we make at the
same time a reproach and a necessity for the proletarian will cease with
the prospect of his going forth one day from his state of helotism."[47]

Leo XIII's encyclical *Rerum Novarum*, the foundational work on
Catholic social teaching and the rights of workers, would not appear
until 1891, nearly thirty-eight years after Ozanam's death. As David
Gregory points out, the silence of the Church on workers' rights was
deafening for most of the nineteenth century.[48] But Ozanam's voice
spoke out loudly on their behalf. Some of his ideas would eventually
find their way into that famous encyclical, especially because Giuseppe
Toniolo, a dedicated member of the Society of St. Vincent de Paul, a professor of political economy, and "the leading Italian authority on Catholic social teaching[,] . . . was consulted for technical assistance by Pope
Leo XIII as he drafted *Rerum Novarum*."[49]

THE OPTION FOR THE POOR AND VULNERABLE

A fifth principle of Catholic social teaching is the preferential protection
for, or "preferential option for," the poor and vulnerable.[50] "In a society

marred by deepening divisions between rich and poor, our [Catholic] tradition recalls the story of the last judgment (Mt. 25:31–46) and instructs us to put the needs of the poor and vulnerable first."[51] There is a reason for putting the needs of those most vulnerable first. As Byron and Maloney point out, "The common good—the good of society as a whole—requires it. The opposite of rich and powerful is poor and powerless. If the good of all, the common good, is to prevail, preferential protection must move toward those affected adversely by the absence of power and the presence of privation. Otherwise the balance needed to keep society in one piece will be broken to the detriment of the whole."[52]

The poor and the vulnerable were consistently placed first by Ozanam. In 1848, as quoted in chapter 6, he advised his brother Alphonse, himself a priest, that "priests must give up their little bourgeois parishes, flocks of elite people in the middle of an immense population which they do not know."[53] In the same year, he wrote in the newspaper *L'Ère nouvelle* about a particular lesson he had learned in service to others: "God did not make the poor ... God forbid that we should calumniate the poor whom the Gospel blesses, or render the suffering classes responsible for their misery, thus pandering to the hardness of those bad hearts that fancy themselves exonerated from helping the poor man when they have proved his wrong-doing."[54] Nor did he glamorize destitution: "And let no one say that in treating poverty as a priesthood we aim at perpetuating it; the same authority which tells us that we shall always have the poor amongst us is the same that commands us to do all we can that there may cease to be any."[55]

SOLIDARITY

The sixth principle is solidarity: "Catholic social teaching proclaims that we are our brothers' and sisters' keepers, wherever they live. We are one human family.... Learning to practice the virtue of solidarity means learning that 'loving our neighbor' has global dimensions in an interdependent world."[56] As Byron and Maloney point out, "The principle of solidarity functions as a moral category that leads to choices that will promote and protect the common good."[57] David Gregory has remarked that Ozanam's "theory of work was rooted in the classic Catholic conception of the common good."[58] Ozanam believed that serious social problems such as poverty generally develop when any individual pursues only his or her interests or the interests of a small group to the detriment of the common good. But perhaps Ozanam's greatest contribution to solidarity was his vision of "a network of charity." He aspired "to encircle the world in a network of charity." His aspiration appears in a letter from Léonce Curnier on November 3, 1834, in which Curnier mentioned how inspired he was by Ozanam's vision of a "network of Charity" for France.[59] The Society of St. Vincent de Paul was the chief means to achieve this goal, and as the Society developed, Ozanam readily and naturally expanded his vision of a network of charity well beyond the confines of France. He "anticipated the theme of solidarity in bringing together people of different classes who were artificially alienated from one another by sinful social and economic structures, and giving them the opportunity of experiencing their genuine and deep filial bonds under their common divine parent."[60] By the time he spoke to the Society's conference in Florence (January 1853), Ozanam had witnessed his dream of a network of charity and justice become a reality: "God has made our work His and wanted it to spread throughout the world by filling it with blessings."[61] The Society ultimately became a worldwide organization because of a genuine shared vision of charity and justice, a vision founded upon the belief that all were ultimately responsible for all, the fundamental essence of solidarity.

STEWARDSHIP: CARE FOR GOD'S CREATION

The seventh principle involves stewardship: "The Catholic tradition insists that we show our respect for the Creator by our stewardship of creation."[62] The good steward "is a manager, not an owner" and is called to be morally responsible "for the protection of the environment—croplands, grasslands, woodlands, air, water, minerals and other natural deposits."[63]

Ozanam's writings provide ample evidence of his love of and respect for creation, as well as his belief that Christianity taught these values: "God is not only the great legislator, the great geometrician, he is also the great artist.... He decreed that the world ... [the] work of his hands should be good, he also decreed that it should be beautiful."[64] For

Frédéric, "Christianity, so often accused of trampling Nature under foot, has alone taught man to respect her, to love her truly, by making apparent the divine plan which upholds her, illumines and sanctifies her."[65] He saw nature as sacramental: "The mountains are all divine. They bear the imprint of the Hand that formed them. But what shall I say of the sea . . . ? Its grandeur strikes us at once; but we must contemplate it a long time ere recognizing that other ingredient of beauty which it possesses— grace."[66] He was saddened by scenes of the modern industrial world that brutalized both men and nature: "I visited Saint-Etienne where I saw industry in all the apparel of its most laborious works, and carried away a sad impression, considering to what horrible toil millions of men apply themselves to put bread between their teeth, and procure opulent well-being for a small number of the fortunate; and how the intelligence must be brutalized and the heart hardened in the midst of those machines and the immense deployment of material force."[67]

In 1851 Ozanam visited London to view the international exhibition at the Crystal Palace in Hyde Park, celebrating modern industry and civilization.[68] He was deeply troubled by his sight of the same kind of poverty that Friedrich Engels had also witnessed and addressed in his *The Condition of the Working Class in England* (1845). Ozanam's visit caused him to pause and reflect on the idea of material progress: "I am quite disenchanted by the monotonous uniformity in which material civilization threatens to envelop the whole world. . . . God made the earth with an endless variety that was pleasant to the eyes; industry threatens to cover it with a uniformity that will engender disgust and weariness. For my part, after beholding this epitome of human power at the end of nearly sixty centuries, I said to myself, 'What! Can man do no more than this? . . . And I went out and was glad to see the greensward of the Park, the groups of noble trees with the sheep grazing under the shade, and all those things that industry has not made."[69] As impressive a structure as the Crystal Palace of the Great London Exhibition was, it nevertheless represented a testimony to the avarice, egoism, and materialism that plagued modern society, according to Frédéric.[70] For him, good stewardship of God's creation required caring for nature and all living things because they ultimately are made sacred by the Divine; the good steward of the Bible not only cared for his Master's goods, he returned them in better condition than he received them.

For Byron and Maloney, "stewardship responsibilities also look toward our use of our personal talents, our attention to personal health and our use of personal property."[71] Again, Ozanam was alert to these demands of good stewardship. Although his health was problematic, he cared for his body as a gift from God.[72] He used his talents as a teacher and writer to work toward a better world. In his characteristically humble manner, he wrote: "If I can do anything however small, it is in my University chair or perhaps in the seclusion of my library, in extracting from [Christian] Philosophy and from History [of Christian times] thoughts which I can put before young men, before troubled and vacillating minds, in order to steady, to encourage, to rally them together, in the confusion of the present and the terrible uncertainty of the future."[73] He was a firm defender of the right of private property, but he urged a system of progressive taxation to reduce the burden on the poor caused by the taxes on consumption of basic goods. In addition, he was personally generous with his own property. As his wife recounted: "Frédéric always dedicated a tenth of his expenditures to the poor, sometimes he gave far more to the sixth; often he gave with a great heart and a generous way. Alms were not a duty for him, but a great happiness."[74]

EQUALITY, SUBSIDIARITY, AND THE COMMON GOOD

Equality, subsidiarity, and the common good are, respectively, the eighth, ninth, and tenth principles:[75] "Equality of all persons comes from their essential dignity. . . . While differences in talents are a part of God's plan, social and cultural discrimination in fundamental rights . . . is not compatible with God's design."[76] Nor should governments intervene unnecessarily in the lives of citizens. Instead they should follow the principles of subsidiarity and the common good, which concern "the responsibilities and limits of government, and the essential roles of voluntary associations."[77]

Subsidiarity establishes "a proper limit on government by insisting that no higher level of organization should perform any function that can be handled efficiently and effectively at a lower level of organization by human persons who, individually or in groups, are closer to the problems and closer to the ground."[78] While subsidiarity is based on a genuine concern for rights and responsibilities, it also seeks to uphold the common good, which is "understood as the social conditions that allow people to reach their full human potential and to realize their human dignity." The social conditions referred to presume that every person is respected, that the "social well-being and development of the group" has high priority, and that "peace and security" are maintained.[79]

In his lifetime, Ozanam clearly acknowledged that all are equal in the sight of God and believed in full political equality, urging universal suffrage and fundamental human rights. He thought that government had a legitimate role in providing help in times of crisis, but he never favored government actions that interfered unnecessarily and arbitrarily in people's lives or restricted their rights.[80] He forcefully rejected any kind of centralization that could diminish these rights and increase inequality. For Ozanam, it was selfishness that ultimately obstructed the path toward the common good. All people should be equal in their rights, but all had the attendant responsibility to put aside personal interests and seek the common good.

His devotion to those living in poverty is incontestable, as shown in earlier chapters; it was reinforced by his numerous visits to those in need as a member of the Society of St. Vincent de Paul. According to Thomas O'Brien, "Ozanam was one of the earliest of the nineteenth-century Catholic Action reformers who claimed that Christian discipleship demanded direct involvement in the critical issues facing French society. . . . Service to the poorest of the poor was, for Ozanam, the clearest and most compelling sign of Christ's presence in the life of the Church. . . . It was the kind of service that required direct immersion . . . in the lives of the poor and suffering."[81] As Ozanam exhorted the members of the conference of Florence, Italy, in 1853, "Let us help our neighbor as Jesus Christ did and let us put our faith under the protection of charity."[82]

OZANAM AND CATHOLIC SOCIAL THOUGHT

In his first social encyclical, *Caritas in Veritate*, Pope Benedict XVI posited an intimate link between the two Christian virtues of justice and charity. Its opening lines make this abundantly clear: "Charity in truth, to which Jesus Christ bore witness by his earthly life and especially by his death and resurrection, is the principal driving force behind the authentic development of every person and of all humanity. Love—*caritas*—is an extraordinary force which leads people to opt for courageous and generous engagement in the field of justice and peace."[83] Pope Benedict continues: "If we love others with charity, then first of all we are just towards them. Not only is justice not extraneous to charity, not only is it not an alternative or parallel path to charity: justice is inseparable from charity, and intrinsic to it."[84] As regards the common good, "To desire the *common good* and strive towards it *is a requirement of justice and charity*. . . . The more we strive to secure a common good corresponding to the real needs of our neighbours, the more effectively we love them."[85] These lines of Pope Benedict closely correlate with the thought of Ozanam, who fully understood this profound and complex relationship. His was "a model of cultivating solidarity through justice and charity as integral to the life of Christian discipleship."[86] This model is steeped in the Vincentian tradition.

Ozanam would also have found a genuine friend in the person of Pope Francis I. Ozanam understood the power of love (charity) and the need for solidarity in a way that is voiced eloquently by the current pope. In the words of Pope Francis: "Therefore we see that love is not simply social assistance and not in the least social assistance to reassure consciences. No, that is not love, that is business, those are transactions. Love is free. Charity, love is life choice, it is a way of being, a way of life, it is a path of humility and of solidarity. There is no other way for this love: to be humble and in solidarity with others. . . . [Solidarity] requires you to look at another and give yourself to another with love. . . . It is a way of being and a way of life that comes from love and from God's heart."[87] In a meeting with workers, the pope stated emphatically: "It is a form of suffering, the shortage of work. . . . [It] leads you . . . to feel that you are deprived of dignity! Where there is no work there is no dignity! . . . [I]t is the result of a global decision, of an economic system which leads to this tragedy; an economic system centered on an idol called 'money.'"[88] Both statements could have been uttered by Frédéric Ozanam; both reflect Ozanam's passion for authentic solidarity and his genuine concern for the suffering of workers, which was all too often caused by the unbridled greed of others.

As many have maintained, Frédéric Ozanam was a forerunner of modern Catholic social thought. In their work *The Church and Labor*, John Ryan and Joseph Husslein, S.J., claim that Ozanam's views on "the leading economic issues of our day have far more than a mere historic interest. They bring us face to face with the great Catholic social principles and demonstrate the continuity of Catholic teaching. . . . His doctrines themselves are not new to us; they perfectly agree in substance with the teaching of our Catholic economists."[89] In his lifetime, Frédéric Ozanam "distinguished himself as an articulate defender of the Church . . . that reached out to the people, seeking bonds of solidarity and embracing the rule of all by all."[90] He envisioned a world in which all would be responsible for all, building upon a structure of authentic solidarity created by the interplay of the Christian virtues of justice and charity. But he was not merely a visionary; he lived and practiced what he preached.

CHAPTER 10

Servant Leadership

The ideal of the good servant was eloquently articulated by Frédéric Ozanam: "Pressed by this commandment to do unto others the good he wants for himself, and wanting an infinite good, the one who loves . . . will never find he has done enough . . . until he has spent his life in sacrifice and dies saying: 'I am an unprofitable servant.'"[1] It is this ideal, infused with the Christian notion of selflessness, to which Ozanam aspired. His primary model was Jesus Christ, but his notion of servanthood also closely resembles ideas that have been expressed in twentieth-century terms by Robert K. Greenleaf.[2] Greenleaf argued that the "servant-leader *is* servant first."[3] He or she is committed to ensuring "that other people's highest priority needs are being served."[4] Three fundamental questions determine whether someone is an authentic servant leader, according to Greenleaf: "Do those served grow as persons? Do they, *while being served*, become healthier, wiser, freer, more autonomous, more likely themselves to become servants? *And*, what is the effect on the least privileged in society; will they benefit, or, at least, not be further deprived?"[5] Ozanam was clearly a servant first. Under his leadership in the Society of St. Vincent de Paul, those who were served by the Society grew as persons; they became healthier, wiser, freer, and more autonomous, and the least privileged of them benefitted by becoming the focal point of attention. Servant leader concepts, therefore, are closely related to the life and work of Frédéric Ozanam, himself an authentic servant leader.

JESUS AND SAINT VINCENT DE PAUL AS MODELS

Ozanam's goal was to help "our neighbor, *as did Jesus Christ* [my emphasis], and put our faith under the protection of charity,"[6] a goal he reaffirmed in an address to the conference of Florence in 1853. His focus on Christ is pertinent because the essential message of Jesus was leadership as service and not as power: "In the kingdoms of the world the standard of greatness is power. In the Kingdom of Jesus the standard is that of service. . . . True greatness, therefore, lies not in power, but in one's capacity to minister to another."[7] The most powerful image of this new approach to leadership is Jesus' washing of the Apostles' feet. It was a dramatic gesture to emphasize his point. Moreover, Jesus never intended to be the only servant leader but rather encouraged everyone to follow his example. Ozanam embraced as his own this message and example of Jesus. This model was further reinforced by the selection of Saint Vincent de Paul as the patron of the fledgling conference of charity. Ozanam made the connection very quickly: "A patron . . . is a model one must strive to imitate, as he [Vincent de Paul] himself *imitated the model of Christ* [my emphasis]. He is a life to be carried on, a heart in which one's own heart is enkindled, an intelligence from which the light would be sought; he is a model on earth and a protector in heaven."[8]

Saint Vincent himself has been identified by J. P. Murphy as an authentic servant leader.[9] To Vincent, who saw the face of Christ in those he served, "the liberty and dignity of the person helped must be respected with the greatest sensitivity. The aid contributed should be organized in such a way that beneficiaries are gradually freed from their dependence on others and become self-supporting."[10] Vincent de Paul "realized that followers are incomplete creations and the only way to accomplish anything through them was to serve them."[11] As

Murphy contends, "Vincent was the servant leader of his day. He was a disturber and an awakener. He planted his vision firmly in the mind of his followers."[12] Ozanam was one of those followers, and the seeds of Saint Vincent's lessons, as well as the gospel of Jesus Christ, fell on fertile ground.

DEVELOPMENT AS A SERVANT LEADER

Following Greenleaf's concept of servant leadership—a leadership based on service rather than power—Larry Spears has identified ten fundamental characteristics of an authentic servant leader.[13] Frédéric Ozanam's life and work may be measured against these. The first is the capacity to listen: "Only the true natural servant automatically responds to any problem by listening *first*."[14] Ozanam rarely spoke first at conference meetings or other gatherings. As Kathleen O'Meara remarks: "He would remain an entire evening listening to the conversation going on around him without ever volunteering a remark unless it was directly elicited; but if any one appealed to him he answered willingly. . . . Nor did the silence, which he was sure to command the moment he began to talk, intimidate, but the contrary: it stimulated and encouraged him."[15] He was always respectful of the opinions of others, even when holding an opposing view.[16] However, the servant leader also "seeks to identify the will of a group and helps to clarify that will. He or she listens receptively to what is being said and unsaid. Listening also encompasses hearing one's own inner voice. Listening, coupled with periods of reflection, is essential to the growth and well-being of the servant leader."[17] Ozanam consistently exhibited a deep concern for the will of the group. This concern and respect were especially evident, for example, when the first conference of charity was divided into sections because the original group had grown too large for efficient action (see chapter 3). Although tensions were high over the proposed division, Ozanam, who favored it, was sensitive to the position of those who opposed the change. Ultimately, after much discussion, a peaceful resolution was achieved. As Shaun McCarty comments, "Ozanam's leadership among his brother Vincentians advocated great openness, flexibility, and a diversity kept in unity by sharing the same mission and spirit."[18]

Reflection, listening to his own inner voice, was another of Ozanam's fundamental traits. His letters are replete with examples. To mention only one, his disappointment after the failure of the Revolutions of 1848–49 and the lost hopes of democratic reform was profound (see chapter 6), yet he ended an 1851 letter with the words, "Let us learn from it. . . . Let us not be discouraged, let us be better."[19] Despite grave setbacks, Ozanam could still identify the good and to continue to hope for change.

A second characteristic is empathy: "The servant leader strives to understand and empathize with others. People need to be accepted and recognized for their special and unique spirits."[20] Ozanam's wife, Amélie, related the following story of her husband's capacity for empathy: "A poor woman whose husband Frederic had aided in his last moments said to me: 'Mr. Ozanam was so good, so kind; for him, everyone was the same, poor or rich; he made you enter his study and sit in his armchairs.'"[21] Ozanam's care and love for those less fortunate than himself were revealed to Amélie on numerous occasions, both in person and through his heartfelt descriptions of visits to sufferers in his letters to her. No wonder Amélie described her husband in the following manner: "He was very charitable and very sympathetic with the poor, patient listening to them, strict with facts and indulgent with people."[22]

A third characteristic is spiritual and emotional healing: "The healing of relationships is a powerful force for transformation and integration. One of the great strengths of servant leadership is the potential for healing one's self and one's relationship to others. Many people have broken spirits and have suffered from a variety of emotional hurts. Although this is a part of being human, servant leaders recognize that they have an opportunity to help make whole those with whom they come in contact."[23] Ozanam valued loving relationships, as we have seen over and over in previous chapters. He believed that most of what human beings call "evil" results from broken relationships with one another and also with God. For him, healing relationships between the social and economic classes were the only answer to the great social ills and divisions of the day.

A fourth trait is awareness: "General awareness, and especially self-awareness, strengthens the servant-leader. Awareness helps one in understanding issues involving ethics, power, and values. It lends itself to being able to view most situations from a more integrated, holistic position."[24] From an early point in his career, Frédéric was deeply aware of the issues at stake and of his own fortunate situation, and weakness:

> I want to thank God for having made me be born in one of these positions on the edge of poverty and convenience which is accustomed to privations without completely ignoring pleasure, where one cannot be lulled by the satiating of all desires, but where one is neither distracted by the continual solicitation of need. God knows, with the natural weakness of my character, what dangers the indolence of wealthy circumstances or the baseness of the poor classes would have been to me. I also feel that this humble post of mine puts me at the level of better serving my fellow-men. For if the question which today troubles the world around us is neither a question of people nor a question of political forms, but a social question, if it is a struggle of those who have nothing and those who have too much, if it is a violent clash of opulence and poverty which causes the earth to tremble beneath our feet, our Christian duty is to intervene between these irreconcilable enemies.[25]

He was also aware that the task he and others faced was daunting: "Charity must never look to the past, but always to the future, because the number of its past good works is still very small, and because the present and future miseries that it must alleviate are infinite."[26]

A fifth characteristic of servant leaders "is reliance on persuasion, rather than on one's positional authority, in making decisions within an organization. The servant leader seeks to convince others, rather than coerce compliance. This particular element offers one of the clearest distinctions between the traditional authoritarian model and that of servant leadership. The servant leader is effective at building consensus within groups."[27] Persuasion came naturally to Ozanam, as we have seen. He admitted to himself that he was less "a man of action," at least in some senses, than many others; he "was not born for the tribune [sic] or the public square."[28] In the words of Craig B. Mousin, "Ozanam believed in non-violent means of using persuasion—using all 'honest weapons'—through speaking, writing, and recruiting others to side with the working poor."[29] In particular, during the Revolution of 1848 Ozanam wrote for the journal *L'Ère nouvelle* precisely to persuade people and to influence public opinion: "Whether we want to or not, we have gone over to the common working people. . . . We are trying not to abandon ourselves, we are not emigrating. We are resolved to be involved in everything that is going around us, and we will use all honest weapons."[30] But he later added that he and his fellow writers were not to be feared as socialists; they did not favor the violent "overthrow of the society." Instead they hoped for peaceful, progressive reform. Powerful words poured from his pen; in the words of Mousin, "Outside of the academy, Ozanam . . . exercised his writing skills as a journalist to provide an alternative voice to the status quo and persuade those with power to move France and the Church toward democracy."[31] But he steadfastly opposed the use of force of any kind.

A sixth characteristic is conceptualization: "Servant leaders seek to nurture their abilities to dream great dreams. The ability to look at a problem or an organization from a conceptualizing perspective means that one must think beyond day-to-day realities. . . . Servant leaders are called to seek a delicate balance between conceptual thinking and a day-to-day operational approach."[32] As discussed in the previous chapter, of all the early members of the Society of St. Vincent de Paul, Ozanam stood out in imagining a "network of charity and justice" that went far beyond the confines of a local or even national organization. His brother, the abbé Alphonse Ozanam, described this vision of his: "As soon as Ozanam saw the finger of God in the rapid growth of the work, he comprehended that the small charitable association, of which he had at first thought, might perhaps begin to realize the design which he had long meditated: the reconciliation of those who have not enough with those who have too much, by means of charitable works."[33] Because of his dream he encouraged and delighted in the establishment of conferences in places other than Paris or France. As he wrote to Father Tommaso Pendola: "I was filled with joy to see the good seed germinate and thrive in this land of Tuscany. . . . We [now also] have conferences in Quebec and in Mexico. We are in Jerusalem. We have the same assurance of one conference in paradise, because more than one thousand of ours, since we have existed for twenty years, have taken the way of a better life."[34]

A seventh characteristic is foresight: "The ability to foresee the likely outcome of a situation is hard to define, but easier to identify. One knows foresight when one experiences it. Foresight is a characteristic that enables the servant leader to understand the lessons from the past, the realities of the present, and the likely consequence of a decision for the future."[35] As a scholar by profession, Ozanam was deeply conscious of the past and its importance. As a member of the Society of St. Vincent de Paul, he constantly confronted the painful realities of poverty in his visits to those in need. But as a person of foresight, he combined his knowledge of the past and his experiences of the present in order to anticipate future consequences. This is the kind of thinking behind his views on the regeneration of society after periodic declines (see chapter 5). His foresight enabled him to identify the potential class conflict that he saw developing daily. Anticipating elements of Marx's *Communist Manifesto* (1848), Ozanam was already fully aware of the class divisions created and fostered by economic disparities; he expected that there would be class warfare if these disparities and resulting inequities were not seriously addressed.[36]

An eighth characteristic is stewardship. Stewardship involves being entrusted with something for the sake of another. According to Greenleaf, all institutions should be "in trust for the greater good of society."[37] This sense of stewardship was evident in the first report of the Society of St. Vincent de Paul, which Ozanam had a hand in preparing (see chapter 3): its principal end was to serve together "with one heart and soul."[38] Ozanam encouraged his colleagues in the same manner to become better, to combat human misery and narrow self-interest, and to seek the common good. In the biblical sense of stewardship, the good steward not only protects what is entrusted to him but returns it improved to the master. Ozanam shared this biblical sense of stewardship, regarding those in need as "his masters," in the tradition of Saint Vincent de Paul.[39]

A ninth characteristic is a commitment to the growth of people: "Servant leaders believe that people have an intrinsic value beyond their tangible contributions as workers. As such, the servant leader is deeply committed to the growth of each and every individual within his or her organization. The servant leader recognizes the tremendous responsibility to do everything in his or her power to nurture the personal and professional growth of employees and colleagues."[40] This characteristic directly addresses the first two of the three questions posed by Greenleaf, as described above: "Do those served grow as persons? Do they, *while being served,* become healthier, wiser, freer, more autonomous, more likely themselves to become servants?"[41] As we have seen, Oza-nam was a primary catalyst for the growth of the Society of St. Vincent de Paul and its members. He constantly wrote letters of encouragement and advice to Society members, urging them to be their very best. As he wrote his friend Léonce Curnier, "There must be frequent commu-nications which provide us a laudable example for good and render us a common joy in the success of each one."[42] He fully embraced the Rule of the Society, created in 1835, which advised this common joy and mutual love and support among members.

Ozanam, moreover, was devoted not only to the growth of the Soci-ety's members but also to helping those living in poverty reach their greatest potential. His words and actions as a member and principal founder of the Society of St. Vincent de Paul serve as the answer to Greenleaf's third question: "What is the effect on the least privileged in society; will they benefit, or, at least, not be further deprived?"[43] As Oza-nam informed his students at the Sorbonne: "You have always known me to be passionately in favour of liberty, in favour of the legitimate tri-umphs of the people, in favour of reforms which elevate, and in favour of those dogmas of equality and fraternity which are but the introduc-tion of the Gospel into the temporal domain."[44]

A tenth and last characteristic identified by Spears is that of build-ing community: "The servant leader senses that much has been lost in recent human history as a result of the shift from local communities to large institutions as the primary shaper of human lives. This awareness causes the servant leader to seek to identify some means for building community among those who work within a given institution. Servant leadership suggests that true community can be created among those who work in . . . institutions."[45] Greenleaf argued: "All that is needed to rebuild community as a viable life form for large numbers of people is for enough servant-leaders to show the way, not by mass movements, but by each servant-leader demonstrating his or her unlimited liability for a quite specific community-related group."[46] Ozanam expressed early on his commitment to the great work of "regenerating French society."[47] In 1841 he further articulated that vision to his fiancée, Amélie Sou-lacroix. To her he described "a community of faith and works erasing little by little the old divisions of political parties and preparing for a not-too-distant future a new generation which would carry into science, the arts, and industry, into administration, the judiciary, the bar, the unanimous resolve to make it a moral country, and to become better themselves in order to make others happier."[48] He clearly discerned that authentic regeneration would result only from a dramatic change in the hearts and minds of Frenchmen, not simply from some external program of action. By forming genuine bonds of "friendship, support, and example,"[49] a remarkable transformation could be achieved. Those living in poverty were not to be kept on the fringe. They were included in the bonds of friendship: "But the strongest tie, the principle of true friendship, is charity, and charity could not exist in the hearts of many without sweetening itself from the outside. It is a fire that dies without being fed, and good works are the food of charity . . . and if we assemble under the roof of the poor, it is at least equally for them as for ourselves, so as to become progressively better friends."[50]

Today, the International Rule of the Society emphasizes the importance of servant leadership: "Following Christ's example, the Presidents at all levels of the Society endeavor to be servant leaders. They provide an encouraging atmosphere in which the talents, capacities and spiritual charism of the members are identified, developed and put to the service of the poor and the Society of Saint Vincent de Paul."[51] Ozanam, however, pictured himself as a servant but not as a successful leader. He was his own harshest critic; as quoted earlier, "Yes, we are unprofitable servants, but we are servants. . . . Yes, life is despicable if we consider it according to how we use it, but not if we recognize how we could use it, if we consider it as the most perfect work of the Creator."[52] He thought it a matter of simple humility to take this view.[53]

Vincent de Paul and Robert Greenleaf each would have understood such a view: "For Greenleaf acceptance is receiving what is offered, with approbation, satisfaction, or acquiescence. Vincent might call that humility."[54] But Ozanam also clearly understood the meaning of the ideal of servant leadership. When the first president-general of the Society, Emmanuel Bailly, decided to leave the position in 1844, Ozanam was largely responsible for defining the necessary qualities for holding that office. In a circular letter of June 1844, he portrayed that person as one who should have "great piety, in order to be an example to all, and perhaps still greater affability in order not to discourage others by too rigid virtues; he must have the habit of devotion, the spirit of true fraternity, the experience of good works." Zeal and prudence were equally essential, coupled with an ability "to maintain the Society in the paths of simplicity and prudent liberty." In his final analysis, the president's character "must attract confidence and respect, while his gentle familiarity renders him the friend of the younger members in the numerous family united around him."[55]

Frédéric Ozanam may have had reservations about his own leadership; others did not. On January 12, 1954, Pope Pius XII opened the cause of Ozanam for sainthood and assigned to him the official title of "Servant of God."[56] Whenever Ozanam entered the homes of those in need, he invariably introduced himself by saying: "I am your servant."[57] The following words of Vincent de Paul could very well be those of Ozanam: "It is most beneficial to strive unceasingly after perfection so that all our actions may be pleasing to God, and so that we may be made worthy to render assistance to others."[58] Ozanam was indeed a servant first—and a leader.

CHAPTER 11

Systemic Thinking and Systemic Change

A number of biographies document the story of the young Frédéric Ozanam's assistance to a beleaguered Parisian woman with five children in the spring of 1833.[1] She was in desperate need. When her husband drank to excess—which was often—he became terribly abusive to both her and the children. He wasted nearly all of her hard-earned wages on drink. He left his children to suffer not only from hunger but also from neglect. She was at her wits' end when Ozanam first visited her. After providing her with necessary material assistance, he probed more deeply into the details of her situation. As a young law student, he hoped to understand her legal options in order to advise her about courses of action. Fortunately, he discovered that she was never officially married and was therefore legally free to leave this oppressive household.

To assure her of her freedom to leave, he obtained an official decision from the procureur du roi stating this fact. When he first informed the woman of this result, Ozanam intimated that she should leave the premises to live elsewhere in Paris with her children. But soon afterward he realized that the anger of the foiled husband, particularly once he learned of the potential loss of drinking income, put them in danger. Concerned for the family's safety, Ozanam first suggested a legal procedure to force the man to quit Paris. He took the time, however, to listen carefully to the woman's counsel, and, based on her recommendation, he instead sought a legal order that would prevent the husband from leaving Paris. The woman and her children could now safely live with her mother in Brittany. A collection was taken up by Ozanam and his friends for her travel expenses. When she departed from Paris with her youngest children, the two eldest boys, eleven and twelve years of age, were apprenticed with Monsieur Bailly's printing establishment and cared for at the Bailly house. Frédéric had succeeded in working for and with this woman to make the journey out of poverty.[2] In his lifetime, he would never have heard of the modern phrases "systemic change" or "systemic thinking." Yet the story above illustrates a compelling point: he was committed to helping people escape poverty and achieve a sustainable way of life. Sustainability is a key element in changing the situations that entrap people in poverty.

Thinking about the world as a complex interrelated system rather than as a simple mechanism has been fundamental to modern science, but the actual phrase "systemic change" has most often been applied to the field of education. The term has gradually expanded into other areas, especially the study of poverty and its root causes. It has been attributed by some to Peter M. Senge, who identified systemic thinking as the "fifth discipline"[3] and inspired the phrase "systemic change." According to Senge, "Vision without systems thinking ends up painting lovely pictures of the future with no deep understanding of the forces that must be mastered to move from here to there. . . . Without systems thinking the seed of vision falls on harsh soil."[4]

At the same time, Senge argues that "systems thinking also needs the disciplines of building shared vision, mental models, team learning, and personal mastery to realize its potential. Building a shared vision fosters a commitment to the long term. Mental models focus on the openness needed to unearth shortcomings in our present ways of seeing the world. Team learning develops the skills of groups of people to look for the larger picture that lies beyond individual perspectives." He insists, however, that "personal mastery fosters the personal motivation to continually learn how our actions affect our world. Without personal mastery, people are so steeped in the reactive mindset ('someone/something else is creating my problems') that they are deeply threatened by the systems perspective."[5] For Senge, the fifth discipline, systems thinking, "integrates the disciplines," fusing them into a coherent body of theory and practice. In the final analysis, he is emphatic that "a shift of mind," or a change in attitudes, is absolutely crucial to genuine change.[6]

In 2006 the Superior General of the Congregation of the Mission, the Reverend Gregory Gay, C.M., responded to the growing interest in systemic change that began with Senge's work and formed a commission for the promotion of systemic change. The commission's expressed mandate was "to help bring about systemic change through the apostolates of the members of the Vincentian Family, especially those ministering to the oppressed poor." The commission placed particular emphasis on "self-help and self-sustaining programs," so that those living in poverty might be "active participants in the planning and realization of the projects envisioned."[7] Reverend Gay's call was for all members of the Vincentian Family—that is, all groups and organizations formed by or inspired by Saint Vincent de Paul, including the Society of St. Vincent de Paul—to engage in strategies that would help end poverty through systemic change and to remain faithful to Vincentian virtues and values in the process.

According to the definition developed and adopted by the leadership of the international Vincentian Family, systemic change refers to aid that moves "beyond providing food, clothing and shelter to alleviate immediate needs, and enables people themselves to engage in the identification of the root causes of their poverty and to create strategies to change those structures which keep them in poverty." Just as Senge had intimated, the Vincentian Family also embraced a belief that systemic change "requires changing attitudes that have caused the problems."[8] In the case of the Parisian mother trapped in an abusive marriage, Ozanam was seeking a systemic change: his aid was not limited to satisfying immediate needs. He identified a situation that, if left unchanged, would perpetuate a family's poverty. Acting on this knowledge, he informed the mother of options and, more importantly, listened carefully to her wise advice, consequently engaging her directly in strategies that could change her dire situation. Attitudes, including Ozanam's, were also changed in the process. This is only one example; but throughout his short lifetime, there is considerable evidence that Ozanam consistently engaged in what might be called systemic thinking. He developed a clear vision for a more charitable and just world, understood the forces that needed to be mastered to achieve that vision, inspired people to participate in that process, attempted to address the political, social, and economic problems that were obstacles in the path of success, and tirelessly worked to change the attitudes of and toward those living in poverty. He, then, has much to offer Vincentians, as well as others, in their effort both to understand and to achieve systemic thinking and systemic change.

The Vincentian publication *Seeds of Hope: Stories of Systemic Change* identifies four distinct types of strategies: mission-oriented strategies; person-oriented strategies; task-oriented strategies; and strategies for co-responsibility, networking, and political action.[9] Within these four groups are twenty specific strategies that are considered "seeds" for genuine systemic change. Both Senge's analysis and the twenty strategies in *Seeds of Hope* provide a useful framework for appreciating the contributions of Ozanam. In light of the Vincentian Family aim to foster systemic change, Ozanam is especially relevant; his thought and work illustrate both the ideas and the ideals related to systemic change, as well as possible strategies to achieve it. Much like the twenty strategies, Ozanam's contributions may also be considered "seeds" of systemic change and systemic thinking.

"REGENERATION OF SOCIETY"

As a young man, Ozanam identified a crisis in France that would shape his life. After years of revolution and with the onset of industrialization, France faced a difficult future. The prospects for resolving its religious, social, political, and economic problems were daunting. But Ozanam believed that genuine change in society could occur, as it had in the past, if there was a profound change in the minds and hearts of his countrymen. Regeneration was his first cherished vision; the Society of St. Vincent de Paul that he helped to organize was one of the essential efforts to realize this regeneration. Its youthful character was a genuine benefit, and he saw it "situated at the schools' gates, that is, at the wellsprings of the new generation, that generation destined one day to occupy positions where influence is exercised, can give such happy stimulation to our poor French society, and through France, to the whole world."[10] He readily acknowledged to his fiancée that his dreams for the Society and for social reform were "ambitious dreams," but also admitted that they consoled him and brought him closer to her.[11] He confessed that every day he witnessed his vision of regeneration becoming a reality. According to *Seeds of Hope*, systemic change strategies should establish "structural and institutional models, where communities can identify their resources and needs, make informed decisions, and exchange information,"[12] as well as "construct a shared vision . . . toward change."[13] Ozanam constructed his own vision based on a perceived need for "regeneration" and the model of an association dedicated to reviving France morally, spiritually, politically, economically, and socially.

Senge warned that although a vision is important because it fosters long-term commitment, it can prove fruitless if one does not understand the forces that must be mastered.[14] The Vincentian Family also cautions that when dealing with those living in poverty, systemic change strategies should always "start with a serious analysis of the local reality, flowing from concrete data, and tailor all projects to this reality."[15] Ozanam anticipated these concerns. Because he was an exemplary scholar of his times, one might expect that he would have believed that poverty could best be grasped deductively, by applying a grand theory on how society is constructed and functions. But Ozanam understood the serious limitations and implications of such an approach, one that many socialists of his day employed. Baunard, the translator of much of Ozanam's correspondence, has argued that Ozanam knew that "all social theories from Plato to Muncer and John Leyden, have only resulted in visionary Utopias, disorder and violence."[16]

Instead, Ozanam embraced an inductive approach based on experience as the only viable way toward a thorough understanding of the complexity of poverty: "The knowledge of social well-being and reform is to be learned, not from books, nor from the public platform, but in climbing the stairs to the poor's man garret, sitting by his bedside, feeling the same cold that pierces him, sharing the secret of his lonely heart and troubled mind. When the conditions of the poor have been examined, in school, at work, in hospital, in the city, in the country . . . it is then and then only, that we know the elements of that formidable problem, that we begin to grasp it and may hope to solve it."[17] Ozanam's vision of the complete "regeneration of society," then, has a connection to systemic change strategies and thinking. It is his first contribution, or the first seed.

"LET US GO TO THE POOR"

When challenged in a meeting of the early conference of history to identify what he and his friends were doing for those in need, Ozanam spontaneously responded: "We must do what is most agreeable to God. Therefore, we must do what Our Lord Jesus Christ did when preaching the Gospel. Let us go to the Poor."[18] As described in chapter 3, the initial group that formed for this purpose at first simply called itself the conference of charity and consisted of Auguste Le Taillandier, Paul Lamache, François Lallier, Jules Devaux, Félix Clavé, Frédéric Ozanam, and Joseph Emmanuel Bailly. In the words of the Society's *International Rule*, Bailly became "the first President General of the flourishing Society" and Ozanam became its "radiant source of inspiration."[19] Like the systemic change strategies in the modern-day *Seeds of Hope*, Ozanam and his friends designed "projects, creative approaches, policies and guidelines that flow from . . . Christian and Vincentian values and mission." The purpose of their activities was exactly what *Seeds of Hope* now emphasizes: to "evangelize while maintaining a profound respect for local culture, thus enculturating Christian and Vincentian charism and values in that culture."[20]

With the guidance and mentoring of Sister Rosalie Rendu, a member of the Vincentian Daughters of Charity, the young Frédéric and his companions not only began to live out the Christian imperative to bring succor to those in need but also became imbued with the Vincentian charism. According to Armand de Melun, her collaborator and biographer, Sister Rosalie "recommended to them patience, which never considers time spent listening to a poor person as wasted, since this person already takes comfort in the good will that we demonstrate by attending to the recitation of his sufferings; understanding, more inclined to pity than to condemn faults that a good upbringing did not ward off; and finally, politeness, so sweet to a person who has never experienced anything but disdain and contempt."[21] She further admonished her young

Vincentians to "love those who are poor.... The world says, 'It's their fault. They are cowardly ... ignorant ... vicious ... lazy. It is with such words that we dispense ourselves from the very strict obligation of charity. Hate the sin but love the poor persons [who commit it]. If we had suffered as they have, if we had spent our childhood deprived of all Christian inspiration, we would be far from their equal."[22] Her words took seed and rooted deeply in Frédéric Ozanam. His own recognition that egoism or selfishness had to be overcome in order to live the Christian imperative is also a good example of what Senge terms "personal mastery."[23] Ozanam was fully aware of how human behavior, including his own, affected others and the world.

In his advocacy of Christian and Vincentian values, Ozanam thought of himself as an evangelizer through commitment to action and example. The projects, approaches, and policies that flowed from the young Society were genuinely inspired by Christian and Vincentian values. In a July 1836 letter, for example, Ozanam recounted to his mother some of the works with which he and his companions in charity were engaged, including supporting the care and apprenticeships of poor children and the fact that "several of our colleagues have been charged by the president of the Civil Tribunal with visiting children detained at the request of their parents."[24] Again, in April 1837, he proudly reported to her that "a lottery was drawn which realized three thousand and six francs for our adopted children."[25] Saint Vincent de Paul himself had also made use of such a lottery to raise funds for orphans.[26] In a letter to his intended, Amélie Soulacroix, dated February 1841, Ozanam enthusiastically proclaimed that "1500 families here in Paris alone have been helped, the daily bread brought under the needy roof, wood assured for many a dismal home. Besides twenty boys educated for free in a paternal household, a truly large number supervised, protected, and encouraged, apprenticed in reliable shops, brought together each Sunday for divine service, corrupt fathers have been brought back to an ordered and frugal life."[27]

In December 1837 the Society in Lyon set up a ministry to soldiers. To counteract "the perverse temptations of idleness" and the "evil temptations of a great city," the members established a special work, a library of books for the soldiers. As Ozanam faithfully reported to the General

Assembly of the Society held in Paris, "we have distributed a large number of leaflets to inform the soldiers of our existence. During the last five months 268 soldiers have attended and have chosen reading matter, according to their taste and their intelligence."[28] The list of the Society's deeds inspired by Christian faith and Vincentian values could easily be expanded. It is no wonder that Ozanam wrote Lallier with conviction in 1837, as quoted in chapter 3, that "our little Society of St. Vincent de Paul has grown large enough to be considered a providential fact."[29] The second seed is contained in Ozanam's advice to his colleagues: "Let us go to the poor."

"THE POOR ARE OUR MASTERS"

The third seed is represented in Ozanam's belief that the poor are "our lords and masters," a belief deeply grounded in the words of Saint Vincent de Paul, who first uttered them,[30] and who served as an inspiration to Frédéric and his young companions. According to *Seeds of Hope*, systemic change strategies are predicated on a deep respect for the dignity of the human person. One must "listen carefully and seek to understand the needs and aspirations of the poor, creating an atmosphere of respect and mutual confidence and fostering self-esteem among the people." And one must "involve the poor themselves."[31]

Ozanam's genuine love for persons living in poverty inspired him to become a true friend of those he visited, and he was always ready to work with them and defend their interests. The personal visit to the home, as advocated by the Society of St. Vincent de Paul, was intended to empower the person in poverty and to provide insights into the person's genuine needs. Initially, in his visits, Ozanam would listen attentively; then he would attempt to engage the person in the journey out of poverty. To borrow Senge's words on mental models, quoted above, Ozanam demonstrated a genuine openness necessary to unearth the shortcomings in how he saw the world, particularly the world of those living in poverty. As the French Dominican priest Lacordaire fondly remembered, "His [Ozanam's] manner towards the poor was one of the warmest and most kindly respect. If they came to visit him, he made them sit in his arm-chairs like distinguished guests. When he went to their homes, after giving his time, his conversation and his money, he never failed to take off his hat and say with the gracious bow that was customary with him: 'I am your servant.'"[32]

SPIRITUALITY, FRIENDSHIP, AND SERVICE

The three essential elements of the Society of St. Vincent de Paul, from its beginnings in 1833, have been spirituality, friendship, and service. These elements are fundamental to the formation of members. Vincentian systemic change strategies insist on the necessity to "educate, train and offer spiritual formation to all participants in the project." For success, one must "promote learning processes in which the members of the group . . . speak with one another about their successes and failures, share their insights and talents, and work toward forming effective multiplying agents and visionary leaders in the local community, servant-leaders inspired by St. Vincent de Paul."[33] From its inception the Society's early members, and most of all Ozanam, recognized and valued the development of conference members through this trinity of essential elements: "Let us work to increase and multiply, to become better, more tender and stronger."[34] Along with this, they were devoted to the example of their patron saint. As Ozanam wrote his close friend François Lallier in 1838, "We are now reading . . . *the Life of St. Vincent de Paul*, so as to better imbue ourselves with his examples and traditions."[35]

Although the official name of the organization became the Society of St. Vincent de Paul, the conference remained "the primary basic unit" of the group,[36] reflecting the original nature of the first conference of charity as a forum for the discussion of ideas, exchange of information, and a reflection upon what is learned both in study and through visits to those living in poverty. And although the evidence is far from conclusive,[37] it is possible that members of the first conference were taught the practice of theological reflection by Sister Rosalie Rendu.[38] After making their visits to the poor and needy, the members may have gathered in her parlor to recount their actions, reflect on their service, and receive both advice and support.[39] Whether or not Sister Rosalie instructed the first members in reflection, certainly, reflection became an essential feature of conference life in the Society.[40]

Ozanam remained at the forefront of instructing and encouraging members of the Society to improve their lives, and to help others improve their lives as well. In April 1838 he counseled members to meet often because coming together "more frequently we love each other more. The more numerous our meetings in the name of Him Who promised to be in the midst of those who should come together in His name, the more clearly do we seem to realize the fulfilment of His promise."[41] Conscious of the potential power the visit had to transform both the visitor and the visited, Ozanam begged members to examine their consciences: "We must bring light into this semi-darkness, warm up this chill; edification, rather than conversion, is the chief necessity. . . . But how to make saints, when one lacks sanctity? How preach to the unfortunate resignation and courage which one does not possess? How rebuke them for failings present in oneself? There, gentlemen, is the main difficulty of our position; that is why we are so often overcome by confusion of heart and remain silent in the presence of families we visit who, if they are our equals in weakness, are often our superiors in virtue." He reminded them that it "is such a time that we acknowledge, in the words of St. Vincent de Paul, 'that the poor . . . are our lords and masters, and that we are hardly worthy of rendering to them our petty services.'"[42] Moreover, Ozanam's vision of the world determined that a person living in poverty was not a useless person, because in suffering the person "is serving God and consequently serving society just as someone who is praying." This person fulfils "a ministry of expiation, a sacrifice from which we benefit."[43]

Robert P. Maloney observes that "forming people for leadership roles is fundamental for bringing about long-lasting change. But experience teaches that a vertical style of leadership is rarely effective in systemic change projects. Servant leaders are needed, men and women who listen, help the group to formulate projects, involve it in implementing them, and engage it in evaluating and re-structuring them."[44] Ozanam was such a leader, as discussed in the previous chapter. His style was the opposite of what we call "vertical." Shaun McCarty has remarked that "Ozanam's leadership among his brother Vincentians advocated great openness, flexibility, and diversity kept in unity by sharing the same mission and spirit."[45] Ozanam may have thought of himself as a weak Samaritan,[46] but others saw him as an authentic leader.[47] The very qualities listed not only describe an ideal leader but are also intimately connected to the fundamental Vincentian principles of spirituality, friendship, and service.

Senge has argued that systemic thinking requires mental models to help identify shortcomings and team learning that develops the skill to see the big picture. The three essential elements of the Society serve as a perfect mental model by which to gauge and overcome shortcomings. They also serve as the key to the group's ongoing learning and formation. Ozanam's fourth seed, then, consists of these three elements.

"HUMBLE SIMPLICITY"

Ozanam used the cogent expression "humble simplicity" in a letter to his fiancée, Amélie Soulacroix, dated May 1, 1841: "Only one thing could hinder and destroy us: the adulteration of our primitive spirit, the pharisaism that sounds the trumpet before it, the exclusive self-esteem which belittles any power other than that of the elite, excessive customs and structure resulting in languor and relaxation or rather verbose philanthropy more eager to talk than to act, or again bureaucracies which impede our march by multiplying our machinery. And especially to forget the *humble simplicity* [my emphasis] which has presided over our coming together from the beginning."[48] This expression adheres to the intent of Vincentian systemic change strategy, namely, to start "modestly, delegating tasks and responsibilities, and providing quality services respectful of human dignity."

Simplicity, with its emphasis on openness, honesty, and modesty, was also one of the hallmarks of Saint Vincent de Paul: "Jesus, the Lord, expects us to have the simplicity of a dove. This means giving a straightforward opinion about things in the way we honestly see them, without needless reservations. It also means doing things without any double-dealing or manipulation, our intention being focused solely on God. Each of us, then, should take care to behave always in this spirit of simplicity, remembering that God likes to deal with the simple, and that he conceals the secrets of heaven from the wise and prudent of this world and reveals them to little ones."[49] An essential feature of Vincentian pragmatism has always been "practical, concrete, and effective services . . . underpinned by the absolute belief that each person is made in the image and likeness of God and is a temple of the Holy Spirit. . . . All projects for the poor start modestly and grow into being." And even today, the Rule guiding the Society of St. Vincent de Paul clearly identifies "simplicity—frankness, integrity, genuineness" as one of its essential virtues.[50] When Emmanuel Bailly stepped down in 1844, he was praised for his fidelity to the traditions of humble simplicity, which he had helped to establish.[51]

Ozanam was fully aware of the need for both an affective and an effective organization. To his friend Lallier, secretary-general of the Society under Bailly's presidency, Ozanam thoughtfully advised the following: "It is your duty, by age and office in the Society of St. Vincent de Paul, to reanimate it from time to time by new inspirations which, without harm to its primitive spirit, foresee the dangers of too monotonous a uniformity." He further cautioned Lallier: "Let us be careful not to straighten ourselves with customs too hidebound, within bounds impassable in number or density. Why cannot the conferences of Saint-Étienne and Saint-Sulpice go beyond fifty members? Why cannot the Society here get larger than forty members? Think about it."[52]

Vincentian systemic change strategies attempt to "systematize, institutionalize and evaluate the project and its procedures, describing measurable indicators and results."[53] In this spirit, Ozanam was faithful to the accurate reporting and honest evaluation of the Society's works, its accomplishments as well as its failures. There can be little doubt that he rejoiced in the growth of the Society and its works. Yet he also maintained an important perspective on the process of growth, informing his fellow Vincentians that they should not only share "statistical statements crammed with enumerations of our successes," useful as such reports might be, but must also personally "exchange ideas, our inspirations . . . sometimes our fears, and always our hopes."[54] Advising his friends to think of another kind of balance sheet, he exhorted them "to enquire not so much whether our numbers have increased but rather if our unity has grown; not so much whether our works are more numerous but if they are better; to report, indeed, what aid we have given to our poor, but far rather what tears we have dried and how many Christians we have brought back to the fold."[55] Humble simplicity fostered each member's motivation to think deeply about how his actions were affecting the world—"personal mastery," in the words of Senge—and may be called Ozanam's fifth seed.

THE RULE

A fundamental assumption in Vincentian systemic change strategy is that any project or undertaking should be "self-sustaining by guaranteeing that it will have the human and economic resources needed for it to last."[56] The Rule of the Society was intended to provide guidance for long-term sustainability. As already discussed in chapter 3, the young Society produced a Rule to govern its members' actions, and there is little doubt that Ozanam influenced its content. According to Edward O'Connor, moreover, "We shall not err in attributing to Frederick himself the conclusion of the Rule, with all its warmth of feeling." The words to which O'Connor refers are: "Together or separated, near or far, let us love one another; let us love and serve the poor. Let us love this little Society which has made us known to one another, which has placed us on the path of a more charitable and more Christian life. Much evil is being done, said a holy priest, let us do some little good. Oh! How glad we shall be that we did not leave empty the years of our youth."[57]

The Rule that resulted in December 1835 came two years after the founding of the Society and after many of its practices were in place. As Bailly wrote, "Now we have only to embody . . . in Regulations, usages already followed and cherished; and this is a guarantee that Our Rule will be well received by all and not forgotten."[58] Its primary aim, however, was "Christian piety," a growing in holiness by service to those in need. Consequently, members were encouraged to be virtuous and in particular to practice the virtues, as described in chapter 3, of "self-sacrifice; Christian prudence; an efficacious love for one's neighbor; zeal for the salvation of souls; gentleness of heart and humility in words; and especially fraternal spirit."[59] In its own way, the Rule provided members with the mental model to see the world differently and encouraged team learning in order to recognize "the larger picture that lies beyond individual perspectives."[60]

The Rule today is fundamentally the same as it was in the nineteenth century. It emphasizes the importance of reflection upon service experiences as an essential part of the development and growth of its members. Members, known as Vincentians, grow in holiness and lead better lives by visiting the poor, "whose faith and courage often teach Vincentians how to live." By reflecting and meditating on their experiences, Vincentians arrive at "internal spiritual knowledge of themselves, others and the goodness of God" and transform "their concern into action and their compassion into practical love."[61] Ozanam is an excellent example of this kind of reflection and transformation: "How often has it not happened that being weighed down by some interior trouble, uneasy as to my poor state of health, I entered the home of the poor confided to my care. There, face to face with so many miserable poor who had so much more to complain of, I felt better able to bear sorrow, and I gave thanks to that unhappy one, the contemplation of whose sorrows had consoled and fortified me! How could I avoid henceforward loving him more."[62] With the Rule in place, the Society continued to flourish and grow. Ozanam's sixth seed is embedded in the Rule.

CIRCULAR LETTERS AND LETTERS OF REPORT

Seeds of Hope counsels that systemic change strategies should foster transparency "by inviting participation in preparing budgets and in commenting on financial reports." There must be "careful controls over money management," and those participating must fully "support and respect the mechanisms for promoting solidarity that exist among the community members."[63] Both the circular letters and other letters of report that were the practice within the fledgling Society of St. Vincent de Paul constitute a primary example of promoting transparency and solidarity.

From the first beginnings of the Society, as we have seen, Ozanam insisted that regular communication among the members was essential. The president should circulate letters on a regular basis that not only provided facts or described key events but also addressed key concerns and necessary changes. In addition, each local conference of the Society should make regular reports. For example, Emmanuel Bailly received a report from Ozanam in July 1838 listing the membership and the monies of the Society in Lyon, in which Ozanam took great care to provide accurate figures as well as a description of the works the Lyon members had accomplished. Numerous examples of the same kinds of reports not only bring to light the work of the Society but also provide evidence of its good stewardship. Ozanam admonished his friend Lallier in 1837, for instance, to "attend particular assemblies frequently; see the presidents from time to time; take part in the meetings of the administrative council; prod sometimes the excessive tranquility of the president general; do not neglect correspondence with the provincial conferences." He further counseled: "If you think as I do, when a conference fails to write by a designated date, you should write to it yourself a little in advance of the next date, to ask it to be more faithful in communicating. No longer allow the circular letters to be delayed too long. The one you sent me two months ago was very good and responded to an urgent need; visiting families is not as easy as it seems; instructions in this regard are extremely useful, and it would be good to repeat them."[64]

Senge has advised that mental models focus on "the openness needed to unearth shortcomings in our present ways of seeing the world."[65] The early Society's circular letters and letters of report, like mental models, provided that openness for Ozanam and the other members to identify significant shortcomings as well as celebrate successes. Using a cogent organic image, Ozanam once described these letters as "brotherly communications" that "are like the circulation which keeps life in the Society."[66] They were also in the best tradition of Saint Vincent de Paul, who valued honest communication. Indeed, the circular letters and letters of report were, and still are, the Society's lifeblood, bringing rich nourishment to both the transparency and solidarity of the Society. In them we discover Ozanam's seventh seed.

HEARING HUMANITY'S CRY FOR FREEDOM

According to William Hartenbach, C.M., it "can safely be said that he [Ozanam] involved himself in activities which were directed toward 'systemic social change,'" because Ozanam "was active in politics and was part of a group of Catholic intellectuals who were committed to the democratic ideal."[67] Indeed, those committed to Vincentian systemic change strategies, in the words of *Seeds of Hope*, "promote engagement in political processes, through civic education of individuals and communities." They "struggle to transform unjust situations and to have a positive impact, through political action, on public policy and laws." Such persons often "have a prophetic attitude"; they "announce, denounce, and, by networking with others, engage in actions that exert pressure for bringing about change."[68]

An acute appreciation of history led Ozanam to conclude, as discussed in depth in chapter 6, "that in the nature of mankind democracy is the final stage in the development of political progress, and that God leads the world in that direction."[69] As we have seen, he advocated reform, not the overthrow of society, and he tried to influence public opinion through his writings as well as one attempt at running for public office. But despite his peaceful approach, he passionately advocated that it "was time to demonstrate that the proletarian cause can be pleaded, the uplifting of the suffering poor be engaged in, and the abolition of pauperism pursued."[70] His words were indeed bold and prophetic. He called out not only to his countrymen but also to "all in the Vincentian tradition to find new ways to seek the temporal Gospel principles of liberty, equality, and fraternity to revitalize democracy, and with it, encourage the flourishing of humanity."[71] Most important, he focused on changing people's attitudes, which is essential to effecting systemic change according to both the Vincentian Family and Senge. In hearing humanity's cry for freedom, and in writing in L'Ère nouvelle to champion democracy, support basic human rights, and address the root causes of poverty, Ozanam planted his eighth seed of systemic change.

"HELP THAT HONORS"

Vincentian systemic change strategies "consider poverty not just as the inevitable result of circumstances, but as the product of unjust situations that can be changed, and focus on actions that will break the cycle of poverty." They require "a holistic vision, addressing a series of basic human needs—individual and social, spiritual and physical, especially jobs, health care, housing, education, spiritual growth—with an integral approach toward prevention and sustainable development."[72]

In an article for *L'Ère nouvelle*,[73] Ozanam distinguished between help that humiliates and help that honors. He proposed a holistic approach that offers more than simply providing for the material needs of the human person. He was painfully aware that poverty was a complex phenomenon, and that the poor were not to blame for their condition. As we have seen, he was an ardent advocate of education, worker associations, and other practices that would give those in need a hand up instead of just a handout.[74] In line with Senge's beliefs, Ozanam proved open to change, looked for the larger picture, and continually learned and shared what he learned.

Ozanam embraced the Christian ideal of detachment from material goods, an ideal reinforced by his scholarly study of and writing about the Middle Ages, especially about Saint Francis of Assisi. He clearly understood, however, that severe poverty or destitution—the absence of essential material, physical, and spiritual needs—was neither to be glamorized nor condoned. He was acquainted with the vicious cycle of poverty that entraps people, and his aim was to break it. For him, love was an essential part of change and was the solution to both alleviating and eliminating poverty. His ninth seed is found in the understanding and promotion of help that honors.

"WORLD-WIDE NETWORK OF CHARITY"

The tenth and final seed Ozanam offers, as discussed in chapter 9, is his vision of a "world-wide network of charity," with which he aspired "to encircle the world." According to Vincentian systemic change strategies, one must "construct a shared vision" as well as work to "promote social co-responsibility and networking, sensitizing society at all levels . . . about changing the unjust conditions that affect the lives of the poor."[75] Ozanam is an exemplar of someone who followed these goals. Throughout his life he was tireless in his efforts to expand the Society. In his speech at the Society's conference in Florence in 1853, he recounted the taunts of young socialists who claimed to have the answer to the future. But he countered that they were no longer effective; their voices were silent. Instead, through its reliance on love, its trust in providence, and its message of truth, the Society of St. Vincent de Paul had prospered and expanded globally:

It is especially comforting to think that in the midst of this quick increase our society has lost nothing of its primitive spirit. Let me remind you what this spirit is for your fraternal attention.—Our main goal was not just to help the poor. . . . Our goal was to keep us firm in the Catholic faith and to spread it among others by means of charity. We also wanted to advance a response to anyone who would ask in the words of the Psalmist: *Ubi est Deus eorum*? Where is their God? There was very little religion in Paris, and young people, even Christians, dared hardly go to church because they were pointed at, that is to say they simulated piety for positions. Today it is no longer so, and, thank God, we can say that young men, older and more educated, are also the most religious. I am convinced that this is due in large part to our Society and, to this point of view, we can say that she glorified God in her works.[76]

The transformation of individuals, and thereby the transformation of the society in which they lived, was the express intention of this network of charity and justice. It was the answer to Ozanam's initial vision of a regeneration of society. There is no doubt that he believed that the Catholic Church held out hope for both social and spiritual salvation; he wished for the Church to flourish because it held out the promise of progress. Indeed, he argued: "We must . . . restore the doctrine of progress by Christianity as a comfort in these troubled days."[77] But he was neither a single-minded nor a close-minded missionary. For him, service to others was to be based solely upon need, not creed. In one famous reported case, a Protestant congregation had provided a substantial amount of money to Ozanam and his conference for assistance to those in poverty. Other members of his conference suggested that the sum should first be used to help Catholics. In an impassioned speech, Ozanam informed his companions that if they were to do this, then they would not be worthy of the confidence of the donors. He refused to be a party to such a dishonorable action. Throughout his life he was also willing to work with secular agencies who took notice of the Society's work, such as the Bureau of Public Assistance, which worked with Sister Rosalie and the Daughters of Charity with whom she served.[78]

Senge would likely say that Ozanam's vision was realized because he had a "deep understanding of the forces that must be mastered to move from here to there," and because he was able to integrate the disciplines of building shared vision, mental models, team learning, and personal mastery.[79] In other words, Ozanam engaged in systemic thinking. It was based on a vision of love that would inspire many long beyond Ozanam's short life span.

As a final note, it is appropriate to point out that the genuinely transformative character of the Society of St. Vincent de Paul, for which Ozanam was an inspiration, itself has often been overlooked as an agent of systemic change. *Seeds of Hope* enumerates five criteria for systemic change projects.[80] If we examine all five, it quickly becomes evident that at least in its early history the Society fulfilled, or came decidedly close to fulfilling, each of these criteria.

The first criterion is long-range social impact: the project "helps to change the overall life-situation of those who benefit from it." The Society of St. Vincent de Paul helped to address the multiple needs of many individuals, thereby improving their lives. The letters of report mentioned earlier provide ample evidence that those aided by the Society often found their way to a better, or more sustainable, way of life. The Rule today stresses that the Society is "committed to identifying the root causes of poverty and to contributing to their elimination."[81] The second criterion is sustainability: "The project helps create the social structures that are needed for a permanent change in the lives of the poor, like employment, education, housing, the availability of clean water and sufficient food, ongoing local leadership, etc." Especially through its Rule, the Society ensured its own sustainability to the present day. Its members provided not only help in satisfying immediate needs, but also opportunities for appropriate food supplies, apprenticeships, and other forms of employment, as well as education. Many of these activities eventually became the organized "special works" of the Society.[82] No work of charity was foreign to the Society.[83]

The third criterion is replicability: "The project can be adapted to solve similar problems in other places. The philosophy or spirituality that grounds the project, the strategies it employs and the techniques that it uses can be applied in a variety of circumstances." The fourth criterion is scope: "The project actually has spread beyond its initial context and has been used successfully in other settings in the country where it began, or internationally, either by those who initiated it, or by others who have adapted elements of it." The early Society meets both criteria; it expanded quickly not only in France but elsewhere, and its principles and strategies were easily transferable to other countries and other needs. In 1855, two years after Ozanam's death, the Society had a presence in approximately thirty-five countries.[84] It currently exists in more than 150 countries throughout the world. The fifth and final criterion is innovation: "The project has brought about significant social change by transforming traditional practice. Transformation has been achieved through the development of a pattern-changing idea and its successful implementation."[85] The Society was actually countercultural in its day,[86] aspiring both to resist and to change the systems of thought and practice that were part of French social, economic, political, and religious life.

It would be disingenuous to claim that Frédéric Ozanam was knowingly engaged in systemic change initiatives; the phrase "systemic change" was not in the vocabulary of his day. However, if Ozanam's thought, work, and strategies are compared to the Vincentian definition of systemic change and to the criteria and strategies for creating systemic change recommended in *Seeds of Hope*, remarkable similarities and significant correlations are evident. Likewise, if Peter Senge's five disciplines are applied to Ozanam's thought, work, and strategies, significant correspondences and resonances are apparent. Senge claims that a "learning organization is a place where people are continually discovering how they create their reality. And how they can change it."[87] Ozanam diligently worked to make the Society of St. Vincent de Paul such a learning organization. It would be equally disingenuous, then, to fail to recognize that Ozanam was attuned to the realities and need for fundamental change in the religious, political, economic, and social systems of his day, and that he sometimes thought systemically, planting seeds which grew into genuine hope for those living in poverty. As *Seeds of Hope* proclaims: "Hope is a tiny seed that contains the germ of life. When watered, it sprouts and generates sturdy plants, beautiful flowers, fruit bushes and trees."[88] In thought and through his works, Frédéric Ozanam brought such hope to a despairing world. As Pope Pius X said of him: "The mustard seed sown by Ozanam in 1833 is today a mighty tree."[89]

CHAPTER 12

Suffering

Frédéric Ozanam was no stranger to suffering. As a young boy he nearly succumbed to a severe fever, and his health remained problematic throughout his short life. His correspondence with friends and family provides ample evidence that his health was a constant concern, that he was not as strong as he wanted to be, and that his nervous temperament exacerbated some of his health issues. Ozanam's heavy burden of personal and professional responsibilities also weighed him down and contributed to his fragile health. He confided to his mother-in-law, Madame Soulacroix, at Easter 1849: "When the head is worn out with work, and the heart is by controversy and disappointment, one leaves the petty rivalry of men and contact with wicked passions to aspire to the peace of these holy days."[1] Beyond his own health concerns, he regularly encountered the suffering experienced by people living in poverty through his personal visits to their homes, and he felt the anguish of witnessing their struggles. And he knew all too well the suffering caused by the death of loved ones. Eleven of his siblings died before reaching the age of twenty-one. His beloved parents died far too early in his life.

Most people confront the challenges and the consequences of suffering at some point in their lives. Ozanam knew suffering as an intimate companion throughout his life, and it contributed to his development as a person. Suffering framed the picture of how he lived, worked, thought, and grew in his faith. Like the ancient Greek playwrights, he learned that through suffering comes wisdom, and as a Christian he learned that suffering plays a necessary role in God's eternal plan and in one's journey toward sanctification.

ILLNESS

Ozanam's health, according to historian Ronald Ramson, was "delicate or fragile as evidenced throughout his life: the typhoid fever scare, whooping cough (twice), and susceptibility to colds, respiratory ailments, pleurisy, and finally Bright's disease."[2] Although he was every bit a workaholic and was accustomed to bouts of illness, nevertheless he attempted to guard his health, especially after his marriage. The medical profession was a part of his family tradition, after all; his younger brother Charles became a physician like his father, receiving his medical degree in late December 1849. The Ozanams walked, spent time traveling, visited health spas, loved the ocean air, and welcomed medical advice.[3] In the long run, however, such efforts were in vain. Ozanam's health improved from time to time, but ultimately it followed a course of consistent decline. Besides stomach problems, headaches, palpitations of the heart—many of which were brought on by his intense and nervous disposition—persistent sore throats were among his chief complaints.[4] In May 1841, for example, he confided to his fiancée, Amélie: "In the course of the evening . . . a raging sore throat assailed me. The general weakness which accompanied it and the remedies necessary to fight it absorbed the greatest part of these past days."[5] Although he was assured by the doctor of a speedy recovery from this attack, in less than two weeks he experienced a "severe attack of the flu." The sore throat returned with a vengeance, and "its consequences lasted three weeks."[6] This malady, of course, disrupted his classes, causing him much anxiety.[7] He soon confessed to a friend that the sore throat had again "recurred in strength." He lamented: "The larynx is less affected than the pharynx, but the latter has a particularly sore spot which goes quite deep on the left side. Headaches and perhaps some fever accompany the pain which, moreover, is more intense when I swallow. Speech greatly fatigues me."[8] By June 1841 he admitted to another friend that his sore throat continued to persist and referred to it as "stubborn."[9] It seems likely that he suffered from severe strep throat. In this lay the possible seeds of the illness that would eventually ruin his health. Bright's disease, also referred to as glomerulonephritis, "can arise from streptococcal infections such as strep throat."[10] Ozanam eventually succumbed to this disease that attacked his kidneys.[11]

MASTERING SUFFERING

Frédéric had been stunned by one of his first encounters with death in late 1833. He wrote to his parents at the end of December that a young student had died: "His cries in his delirium could be heard in my room . . . the image of the poor sick patient haunted us. . . . Last night he was terrible to look at, terrible to listen to. . . . I had never before seen someone die."[12] After this distressing event he confessed to his cousin, Ernest Falconnet, that he was thinking about "God and Death." He admitted that "if religion teaches us how to live, it is to prepare us for death."[13] With the death of his father four years later (1837) and his fears for his mother's health (she would die two years later, in 1839), he was beset with a depressing sorrow. He experienced a dark night of the soul. Confiding his deepest thoughts to his good friend François Lallier in October 1837, he pondered his situation and poured out his soul: "You see that life does not seem strewn with roses to me. . . . I will tell you, so that nothing is hidden from you, that even blacker thoughts come sometimes, and because of a rather violent stomach disorder which has lasted for the past two days, last night I thought I was dying and recommended my soul to God. For a little more than a week now prolonged brooding on my interior and exterior misfortunes has so upset my mind that I am incapable of thinking and acting. My head is on fire, every sense is flooded with depressing thoughts, and the most depressing of all, perhaps, even thought of my real state (of soul)." He added that he had sought and received advice from a priest: "The excess of evil brings me to have recourse to the doctor ... who holds the secret of moral infirmity and the disposition of the balm of divine grace. But, after I have exposed, with a vehemence which is uncommon for me in these cases, my sadness and the subjects of my sadness to this charitable man whom I call father, what do you think he replied to me? He replied in the words of the Apostle: *Gaudete in Domino semper* [Rejoice in the Lord always]. Is that not, now, strange advice?"[14]

The priest's advice, as he wrote Lallier, at first unsettled him. Ozanam had been looking for a sympathetic ear: "Behold a poor man about to suffer the greatest misfortune in the spiritual order, that of offending God, and the greatest misfortune in the natural order, that of finding himself an orphan. He has an old and sick mother. . . . He sees himself separated by absence or death from many friends to whom he was tenderly attached. . . . Even more, he is in every anguish of undecided destiny. . . . If he withdraws into himself to flee the unnerving spectacles without, he discovers that he is full of weaknesses, imperfections and faults. . . . And then he is told, not to resign himself, not to console himself, but to rejoice: *Gaudete semper!*" In a passionate outburst, Frédéric protested that "it takes all the audacity, all the pious insolence of Christianity to speak like that." But then he recovered himself, adding: "Nevertheless, Christianity has reason."[15]

The bold words of the priest soon took hold of Ozanam's heart; he reflected deeply on their wisdom in a memorable passage worth quoting in its entirety:

> Sadness has its dangers ... There are, in my view, two kinds of pride: the one grosser and an easy trap for people, that is, satisfaction with oneself, the other more subtle, more easily insinuated without being noticed, more reasonable, hiding itself amid the displeasure one takes in his own miseries, displeasure which, if it does not turn to contrition, turns to contempt. We are desolated because we cannot be self-sufficient, our conscience is a witness making us our own accusers, we are angry at being of such little moment, because we have inherited some of the first culpable esteem of our first father, and we want to be gods. In this state, we reproach ourselves for the imperfections which depend least on our will, we would rather despise than condemn ourselves. We willingly blame the Creator for not having endowed us more

advantageously, we are almost jealous of the talents and virtues of others. Thus love grows weak and self-love hides beneath this trumped-up austerity of our regrets. We are displeased with ourselves so violently only because we love ourselves too much. And, in fact, note how much pleasure one takes in melancholy: first, because in default of merits one would like to discover in oneself in order to admire them, one is happy at least in entertaining regret at not having them. It is a sentiment of honorable mien, a kind of justice, almost a virtue. And then, it is easier to dream than to act; tears cost us less than sweat; and it is sweat that the inexorable sentence demands of us. It could then be the beginning of wisdom to make man probe himself anew, and indeed the ancient pagan wisdom knew that precept; but if one does not wish the man so probed to die of shame and discouragement, a ray from on high must be allowed into the prism.[16]

In this process of deep self-reflection in his letter, Ozanam gradually came to the conclusion that divine grace and love are absolutely necessary in the struggle to overcome one's pride and dispel one's suffering: "Something which is not human is needed, which, nonetheless, comes to visit man in the solitude of his heart, and makes him go out to do: that something is charity, it is that alone which changes remorse to penitence, which waters sorrow and causes it to flower in good resolutions, it is that which effects confidence and courage, for it dissolves that view of ourselves which shames us in the sight of God, . . . who enlightens us with His light, and strengthens us with His strength. *In those high regions, everything changes in aspect and, looked at in the economy of the divine wishes, the most desolating events are explained, justified, and reveal a comforting sign* [my emphasis]." Ozanam's thought had come full circle, as he returned to the priest's original admonition: "Thus those evils before and behind which we suffered recently no longer affect anything but our sensibility, the lowest floor of our soul; its highest part raises itself above; the best preoccupations dwell there; a joy, grave but true, surrounds it; and the prodigy is accomplished, the precept of the Apostle realized; *Gaudete semper,* because God Himself is the cause of this joy unknown to nature: *Gaudete in Domino.*"[17]

After unburdening his thoughts and his very soul to Lallier, Frédéric closed the letter by exhorting his friend: "Let us make ourselves strong, for the malady of the age is weakness. Let us consider that we have lived probably more than a third of our existence by the benefit of others, and must live the remainder for the good of others. Let us do such good as is offered without ever drawing back through false humility."[18] This 1837 letter provides a crucial insight into Ozanam's understanding and acceptance of suffering. Like the ancient Greeks, he found wisdom through suffering, but he also found his deepest understanding and consolation in the grace and love of God that called him into service to others. He would continue to rejoice in that epiphany until his death.

MARTYRDOM

As a member of the Society of St. Vincent de Paul, Ozanam was often faced with the following question: To what degree must we love Jesus Christ in the person of the poor? His answer was "to the point of self-sacrifice, to that point of the sublime proof of love."[19] As he wrote to his friend Léonce Curnier in 1835, "to be a martyr is possible for every Christian, to be a martyr is to give his life for God and his brothers, to give his life in sacrifice, whether the sacrifice be consumed in an instant like a holocaust, or be accomplished slowly."[20] As Ramson has noted, Saint Vincent de Paul had a similar view of martyrdom: "May it please God, Fathers and Brothers, that all those who wish to join the Company enter it with the thought of martyrdom in mind with the desire to suffer martyrdom in it and to devote themselves entirely to the service of God. . . . Is there anything more reasonable than to give ourselves to Him who has so generously given Himself for us all such as we are?"[21] As we have seen, for Ozanam, both Saint Vincent de Paul and Saint Francis of Assisi were worthy models: "Alas, if, in the Middle Ages, sick society was not able to be healed except by the immense effusion of love shown in a special way by St. Francis of Assisi, if much later new sorrows cried out to the soothing hands of . . . St. Vincent de Paul, how much charity, devotion and patience do we not need at present to heal the sufferings of these poor people, poorer than ever, because they have rejected the nourishment of the soul at the same time the bread of the body was lacking to them."[22]

The root meaning of the word martyr is "witness." In an essay on the nature of service, Keith Morton interviewed a Dominican priest who offered the following insight about the connection of witness and service: "The essential nature of service is witness . . . involving oneself in activities benefiting others and, if necessary, laying down one's life; challenging structures that are not life-giving. Service always means an encounter with powers out there: confronting conditions that make service necessary in the first place."[23] Frédéric Ozanam not only would have understood these words but also would have wholeheartedly endorsed this view of "service as witness." As a "weak Samaritan," Ozanam was willing to consume his life in service for others and to God. In many respects, he did so. His fragile health was taxed to the limit until it was consumed by the fire of his love for God and neighbor: "Frederic's dream was to be an apostle and martyr. In a sense, he realized that dream in his short life of loving service to humankind, although, in humility, he would never have admitted it."[24]

DECLINING HEALTH

The years 1848–49 were years of intense activity. During 1849, Ozanam fell prey to severe fatigue, back pain, and periodic hemorrhages.[25] He expressed his anxiety to Dr. Joseph Arthaud, a physician in Lyon, in an 1849 letter: "I am demoralized; give me a fresh heart. Tell me if I can start work again, and to what extent. Tell me, must I behave like a man who can still count a little on his strength in the future, or must I tighten the sails and think of nothing more but providing for my loved ones, like the father of a family threatened with premature disability?" Ozanam had already begun to assume the worst. In fact, he concluded his letter with a heartfelt petition: "Pray for me so that if God does not wish me to serve him by working, I resign myself to serving him by suffering."[26] If there was still some hope in the years up to 1850, they were soon dispelled. By 1851 his health was definitely on a downward spiral: "My state of health renders many duties and pleasures impossible; but I admire the dispensation of Providence, which will not permit us to acclimatize ourselves here below. I had done everything to make life comfortable. . . . God does not will that I should take root in that happiness. He leaves me the joys of the heart, [but] he sends me the pains of the body; I bless Him for my lot. But I am praying Him not to prolong the trial."[27] He further expressed his concerns about his diminishing strength in February 1852: "I am the least well in the home, and yet I can, not without fatigue, almost deliver my lectures. I thank God for such favours and am resigned to the suffering which He sends with them. One of my greatest griefs is that, having studied deeply, I believe I have some ideas, without the strength to reproduce them."[28]

Fréderic's deteriorating health eventually forced him to leave his teaching post. Against the advice of family, friends, and doctors, he had returned to his duties at the Sorbonne in early 1852. Cautious of his health, he tried to avoid over-exertion: "I am careful to incur less fatigue in speaking. I do not seek to be impassioned when there is no emotion. I remain seated, and the audience does not object. . . . But the young men are mostly quiet and studious."[29] His careful efforts were fruitless. By Easter of 1852 he was bedridden. Reluctantly, he requested that his lectures be postponed. The reaction of some students was unfortunately less than compassionate; they accused him of self-indulgence. He was cut to the quick by this accusation. Against Amélie's impassioned pleas, he rose, dressed, and made his way to the Sorbonne. With considerable effort he entered the lecture hall to thunderous applause from the embarrassed students and spoke to them as follows: "Gentlemen, our age is charged with selfishness, and professors are stated to be affected with the general complaint. Yet, it is here that we wear out our health, and use up our strength. I do not complain, our life is yours; we owe it to you to our last breath, and you shall have it. As for me, if I die, it will be in your service." The eloquent words continued to flow, and he delivered a masterful lecture. It was his farewell address, filled with all of the power and passion for which he had become famous as a professor. Afterward, he returned home and collapsed on his bed, thoroughly spent.[30]

From that day in 1852 until his death in 1853, Ozanam continued to fight the ravages of his illness; he held out a slim hope that he might be healed, but he also resigned himself to what he saw as God's will. He wrote to his friend Lallier: "The worst is the emptiness in which I am forced to live. . . . When I reach the end of the day, having done nothing, this idleness weighs on me like a kind of remorse; it seems I do not deserve the bread which I eat, nor the bed on which I lie. Besides when my imagination finds my head empty, it settles in like its mistress and, completely at ease, pounds it with blackness. I am far less troubled by my current ills and with their likely consequences and even the fear of death does not affect me as much as the cruel want in which I might leave my family." He confessed to his friend: "Thinking about the Faith is not powerful enough to snatch me from those temptations. I certainly do not say that religion may have no power even over my wretched heart: it keeps me from despair, giving me a few rays of light every day and often prevents me from giving free reign [*sic*] to my bouts of sadness."[31]

The example of Théophile Soulacroix, Amélie's young invalid brother, helped to bolster his resolve to bear up under pain. Théophile had inspired Ozanam by his ability to endure hardship and physical suffering before his early death on March 9, 1847. The two became close friends; Ozanam actually involved Amélie's brother in his own Germanic studies because Théophile had a fine mind and knew German.[32] Whereas Théophile played the role of student to Ozanam's teacher, the memory of Théophile now took on the role of teacher for Ozanam in his last days. His example instructed Ozanam about the transformative role of suffering in the process of sanctification. Ozanam was deeply moved by the young invalid, who had displayed great resignation, enormous courage, and a simple and sublime virtue before his death.[33] In a letter to his in-laws, Ozanam referred to Théophile's death as a martyrdom and confessed that Théophile's life had provided for him a model not only for living but also for dying.[34] At Easter in 1847, Prosper Dugas, one of Ozanam's dear friends, received correspondence that contained the following beautiful reflection on Théophile: "Our beloved brother, who had lived the life of a martyr, had died a saint: at the age of twenty-three years he departed from the earth, not with resignation, but with a totally divine joy."[35] Now, some five years later, Frédéric found himself facing death, like his dear brother-in-law. He would pray to Théophile for support during his own ordeal because he firmly believed that Théophile was now a part of the communion of saints.

The Ozanams embarked on several journeys in Ozanam's last years, which they desperately hoped would allow his health to improve. The travels also provided him with opportunities for research and distraction. An account of his travels in Spain, for instance, occupied him and gave him purpose. His *Un pèlerinage au pays du Cid* (*A Pilgrimage to the Land of the Cid*) as well as his *La civilization au cinquième siècle* (*History of Civilization in the Fifth Century*) would be published posthumously. He was not a man who took rest easily, however. As he traveled, he visited conferences of the Society of St. Vincent de Paul, inspiring the members with his words. One of his last services to the Society was performed in Italy, where the Ozanams decided to winter because of the climate. The conferences of Florence, Pisa, and Livorno were languishing because the Grand Duke of Tuscany thought they might be secretly subversive. Because of his reputation as a Dante scholar, Ozanam received an invitation for an audience with the Grand Duchess. Despite the fact that he was in bed with a fever, he leaped at the opportunity. He refused to listen to Amélie's pleas. Later she remarked that "when he wanted something, his will was irresistible." During the audience he charmed the Duchess, finding the right words to convince her of the Society's benefits and integrity. Because of his efforts the Society in Florence, Pisa, and Livorno obtained official recognition.[36] As the feast of Saint Vincent de Paul approached, Ozanam even managed to write an official report on the conferences in Tuscany to the Council General.[37]

Approximately nine months before his death, Ozanam made a pilgrimage to Notre Dame de Buglose. He could not resist the temptation to visit the nearby birthplace of his beloved patron, Saint Vincent de Paul: "I owed a visit to the birthplace of this beloved patron, who preserved my youth from so many dangers, and who spread such unexpected blessings on our humble conferences. . . . We saw there the old oak under which Saint Vincent, the little shepherd, took refuge while tending his sheep. This beautiful tree is only attached to the ground by the bark of a trunk destroyed by the years. But its branches are magnificent. . . . I clearly saw the image of the foundations of Saint Vincent de Paul, which seem to be attached to the ground by nothing human, and which, however, triumph over the centuries and grow in revolutions."[38] He promised his friend Alexandre Dufieux to send him "a leaf from the blessed tree: it will dry in the book where you will place it, but charity will never dry up in your heart. . . . The Saint is venerated in the Church of Buglosse [sic] . . . It is there that tomorrow morning I hope to receive communion and pay a part of the debt towards those who have prayed for me."[39] A few days later he informed his brother Charles: "The priest of Saint Vincent de Paul was waiting for us on the road with a servant with a ladder and a scythe; he had him cut, before our eyes, a branch of the venerable oak that I am going to send to the Council General. But at the same time, Amélie gathered leaves, small branches and acorns about which she intends to tell you. Little Marie was very delighted to see some sheep on the moor which had to be the great-great-grandchildren of those the Saint tended."[40] This excursion caused him much joy; he was briefly distracted from his waning health.

By April 1853 the Ozanams were situated in Pisa. Amélie watched over Frédéric, witnessing his struggle with the eyes of deep faith: "God apparently wants to purify him even before he takes him. The more his body is weakened by his suffering, the more beautiful his soul grows and develops. Never was his heart warmer; never was his spirit livelier. Not a word of complaint!"[41] She lovingly imposed upon him a daily regimen that would not overwhelm his weakened body; he in turn lovingly referred to her as his guardian angel. He would arise at nine in the morning, eat his breakfast close to the fire because of the cold dampness,[42] attend mass at eleven if he was strong enough to walk, spend some time reading in the local library, write a letter or two, instruct his daughter Marie, eat dinner again by fireside, and then retire for the evening after a little reading.[43] By now Ozanam realized fully the enemy he was combatting. On April 3, 1853, in a letter to Dr. Salvat Franchisteguy, he referred to his illness as "néphrite albumineuse" (albuminous nephritis), and by April 30, in a letter to his brother Alphonse, he referred to it as "la maladie de Bréglet [sic]" (Bright's disease).[44] To Dr. Franchisteguy he wrote that he knew his state of health was serious, but that he would not despair. He wanted to abandon himself with love to the will of God: "I will what you will, when you will, in whatever way you will, because you will." The words are from a prayer in *The Imitation of Christ* by Thomas à Kempis. The work was dear to Ozanam, and he fondly remembered reading it in the early days of the first conference of charity.[45] He had nothing but praise for his dear wife Amélie: "You can have no idea of the resources she . . . has discovered in her heart, not only to relieve but to cheer me; with what ingenious, patient, indefatigable tenderness she surrounds my life, guessing, anticipating every wish . . . divine providence, while trying us, does not abandon us. God treats us mercifully; and if there are days of despondency, there are moments too of exquisite enjoyment between my wife and child."[46]

OZANAM'S DEATH

On April 23, 1853, Frédéric Ozanam celebrated his fortieth birthday. He would not live to see his forty-first. Sensing that his end was near, he composed his last will and testament. Not surprisingly, he began it in the form of a prayer: "In the Name of the Father, Son and Holy Ghost, Amen. This day, the 23rd of April, 1853, on completing my 40th year, in great physical sickness but sound in mind, I express here in a few words my last wishes, intending to set forth more fully when I shall have more strength." He then poured out his last thoughts and wishes: "I commit my soul to Jesus Christ my Saviour, while being frightened at my sins, but trusting in his infinite mercy. I die in the Holy, Catholic, Apostolic and Roman Catholic Church. I have known the difficulties of belief of the present age, but my whole life has convinced me that there is neither rest for the mind nor peace for the heart save in the Church and in obedience to her authority. If I set any value on my research, it is that it gives me the right to entreat all whom I love, to remain faithful to the religion in which I found light and peace. My supreme prayer for my family, my wife, my child, and grandchildren, is that they will persevere in the Faith." He then bid farewell to his wife, "my dear Amelie, who has been the joy and the charm of my life, and whose tender care has softened all my pain for more than a year. I thank her, I bless her, I await her in heaven. There, and only there, can I give her such love as she deserves." His last will and testament closed with an impassioned plea to be forgiven for any wrongs he had committed and to be remembered fondly and forever in prayers.[47]

Perhaps the greatest source of grief for Ozanam was the thought that he would never witness his beloved Marie's growth into adulthood. As Madeleine des Rivières describes Marie, "she was the prettiest flower in the gardens of Versailles. A round face, encircled by beautiful blond braids, big gentle eyes, a small body, slightly plump and chubby, bright and very much alive. This was Marie. . . . Picture her in a crinoline dress, tapered lace panties, and tiny white buttoned booties, and you have the little girl whom Frederic loved to take for a walk every evening after supper."[48] In those last days he must have thought about how he had cradled his daughter in his arms, or how she had "knelt all by herself (she was only eighteen months old at the time) and joined her hands together with a look of veneration" when they met Pope Pius IX.[49] Perhaps he recalled how his brothers affectionately nicknamed her "Nini"[50] or how she "was so thrilled with illuminations . . . and equally thrilled with music" at Christmas mass.[51] To alleviate his illness or to help him forget about it, Marie would often jump into his arms, warmly embracing her loving father.[52] She was his precious jewel, and, like a precious jewel, he made careful provision to guard and protect his daughter: "I give to my child the benediction of the patriarchs, in the Name of the Father and of the Son and of the Holy Ghost. I am sad that I cannot labour longer at the dear task of her education, but I entrust her absolutely to her virtuous and well-loved mother."[53]

Ozanam named Léon Cornudet, with whom he had a "very special friendship" and whom he referred to as "one of my best friends,"[54] to watch over and protect Marie after his death. (Marie's godfather, François Lallier, might have been chosen, but he did not live nearby the Ozanams.) Frédéric and Léon had worked closely together in 1844 as joint vice-presidents of the Society of St. Vincent de Paul. Cornudet proved faithful to his charge until Marie's marriage to Laurent Laporte in 1866. After Ozanam's death, Amélie and Marie were frequent dinner guests at the home of Cornudet and his beloved wife, Eudoxie. Their daughter Elisabeth acted as Marie's tutor. She also later gave personal testimony during the canonization process for Frédéric Ozanam.[55]

On his birthday in April, as on every day, Ozanam opened his Bible to a passage of scripture to meditate. His eyes fell on the Canticle of Ezechias (Isa. 38:10–20).[56] A portion of the poignant reflection that he composed on this passage from Isaiah follows:

> It's the beginning of the Canticle of Ezechias: I don't know if God will permit me to carry it through to the end. I know that today I have reached my fortieth year, more than half of a life. I know that I have a young and beloved wife, and enchanting child, excellent brothers, a second mother, many friends, an honorable career; my research has in fact reached the point that it could serve as the basis of a book of which I have dreamed for a long time. Yet here I am struck down by a serious and persistent illness which is all the more dangerous for the fact that it is probably underlain by total exhaustion. Must I then leave all these goods that you yourself have given me, my God? Lord, will you not be content with only a part of the sacrifice? Which of my disordered affections must I sacrifice to you?

Would you not accept the holocaust of my literary pride, of my academic ambitions, or even of my research plans in which perhaps was contained more pride than zeal for the truth? If I sold half of my books in order to give the proceeds to the poor, and limited myself to carrying out the duties of my state of life, or if I devoted the rest of my life to visiting the poor, and educating trainees and soldiers, would you be satisfied, Lord? Would you allow me the pleasure of living through to old age with my wife and completing the education of my child? Perhaps, my God, that is not your will at all. You don't accept these self-interested offerings, you reject my holocausts and sacrifices! It is written at the beginning of the book that I must do your will and I have said: Here I am, Lord. I am answering your call and I have no reason to complain. You have given me forty years of life. . . . If I go back over in your presence the years I have lived with bitterness, I see it is because of the sins with which I soiled them. Yet when I consider the graces with which you have enriched them, I again go over these years in your presence with gratitude, Lord. When you chain me to my bed for what is left of my life there will not be enough time to thank you for all the time I have lived. Ah! If these pages are the last that I am to write, may they be a hymn to your goodness.[57]

God, he claimed, had bestowed upon him "the courage, the resignation, the peace of soul and its inexpressible consolations which accompany your real presence." His poignant reflection concluded with a sincere expression of gratitude to the God who had provided him with caring and nurturing parents, one of God's greatest gifts.[58] He had indeed resigned himself to his death. As Gérard Cholvy remarks, "Since Marx and Nietzsche, resignation is not good press and many Christians feel embarrassed when it comes up. But resignation is 'the very foundation of Christianity,' Ozanam wrote to Lallier."[59]

Ozanam's reflections on scripture had been essential on his spiritual journey toward the acceptance of both his suffering and his death: "I should be inconsolable for my weakness if I did not find in the Psalms those cries of sorrow which David sends forth to God, and which God at last answers by granting him pardon and peace. . . . During many weeks of extreme languor the Psalms have never been out of my hands. I was never wearied of reading over and over those sublime lamentations, those flights of hope, those supplications of full love which answer to all the wants and all the miseries of human nature."[60] Later, Amélie collected the scriptural passages that her husband had read and cherished. She organized them in a publication entitled *Le Livre des malades* (produced in English with the various titles *The Bible for the Sick*, *Companion of the Sick*, and *The Book of the Sick*) under four parts: "The Foundations of Faith and Hope," "The Sick in the Old Testament," "Counsels—Sentiments of Piety—Prayers," and "The Sick in the New Testament." She hoped this collection would bring others the consolation and peace her husband had enjoyed: "These passages were selected by a Christian who, during sickness, found in the Holy Scripture strength to suffer with patience, steadfastness always to wish with love and submission [to] the will of God, and courage to give his life when it was required of him."[61]

Despite his resignation, Ozanam still entertained visitors. He never willingly turned someone away. Amélie recounted one such incident:

> While we were in San Jacopo at the end of May, 1853, a young seminarian who had attended Frédéric's course in Paris came to find him and to beg him to make a Novena to regain his health. But Fred refused, saying, "He wanted the will of God and nothing else, that he prayed to submit himself entirely to it, but that he no longer wanted to ask for his recovery not knowing if it would be for the good or the evil of his soul." And yet the good and ardent young man repeatedly insisted, "he [Ozanam] was too necessary to religion, that God would not let him perish because he needed him." At these words Fred could not contain himself, and he broke out with a natural impetuosity, saying that God had need of no person and him even less than any other, he who was so unworthy to serve. If God had need of men he would not have let Donso Cortes die in a moment when Spain had so great a need of eminent minds for its regeneration, nor Lady Fielding who expired at Naples, when she seemed so necessary to English Catholics, she who employed part of her vast fortune to build churches, that all of us were unworthy servants, and finally it was a profanity to say that God had need of him.

According to Amélie, the young man was terribly disconcerted by Ozanam's unexpected outburst. But almost as quickly as he had replied, Ozanam regretted distressing the young man. He feared that he might have "offended him by not showing enough faith in the power of prayers." Not only did he apologize to his visitor, he also agreed to make the Novena. Only then did Ozanam feel he had treated the young man fairly. Two months later, as Amélie recounted, "when Fred was near death, this same young man was so sorry that he offered to God his life in exchange for that of my poor loved one for the good it could do in this world."[62] The young man's name was Bartoloměï. He was a Creole and became a priest, choosing "to spend his life and his great fortune in the education of the Negroes of St. Thomas."[63]

Originally the Ozanams had traveled to Pisa for the sake of a dry climate. Unfortunately, they encountered nearly fifty days of rain, which exacerbated Frédéric's condition.[64] As the months progressed, his pain increased. Incessant sharp pains in his kidneys, swollen, purplish-blue legs, and a sensitive lumbar region plagued him.[65] From May to June, the family located in San Jacopo near Livorno on the Mediterranean. The sea air briefly energized Ozanam. His fondest memory of this period was the recognition of his work by the Franciscan Order, which led to his election to the Florentine academy De La Crusca.[66] Just before moving yet again, Frédéric and Amélie celebrated their twelfth wedding anniversary, on June 23, 1853. While looking at the white sails on the nearby sea, Frédéric composed the following verses for his dear wife:

> Stranded on a distant rock our little barque awaits the saving tide to bring it into port. The Madonna, to whom the vessel is dedicated, seems deaf to our appeals and the Infant Jesus slumbers!
>
> It is twelve years to-day [sic] since we set out on our voyage full of hope: garlands decorated thy head. To bless the voyage, a little fair-haired angel soon appeared at the stern.
>
> Since then the heavens have grown dark and the storms have blown our little skiff hither and thither by night and day. But neither the trials of the tempest nor the hardships of the climate could extinguish our love.
>
> Dearest companion of the exile whom God allotted to me, I have no further tear in your sweet care. Already the merciful eyes of the Virgin Mother are turning to us: the Infant Jesus will soon awaken.
>
> Drawn by His hand into a calm sea we shall reach at length the shore where our longing, loving friends are waiting to receive us.[67]

It would be their last wedding anniversary. Amélie fondly recalled sitting on the balcony in San Jacopo with her husband as the sun set over the nearby port.[68]

Between July and August the doctors recommended a move to Antignano, where "the best society in Florence, Pisa, Sienna, and Leghorn [Livorno] spent those months."[69] It would be his last abode in Italy. Until the end of July, Frédéric found the strength to walk to mass in the morning and to the sea in the evening, although each walk exhausted him. He often thought of earlier times, when he was a young man in Lyon. As he remarked in one letter: "I have had to learn how to cut out a good part of the things that bind man to earth, and I have lived a wanderer looking for health. . . . I am sure that you would refuse to pity me if you saw the charming slopes where I inhale the Mediterranean breezes, with my small, well-beloved family. . . . Yet . . . I would give all the splendor of these Italian skies, all the perfumes of this exotic vegetation, all the magic of this beautiful language . . . to be able to visit my humble home, to see the streamlet in my own street, the staircase of my own third storey, the books in my own library, and still more to shake the hands of my own friends in Lyons."[70] Two local members of the Society of St. Vincent de Paul became attached to Ozanam; their devotion included supplying him with his favorite flowers and with ice to relieve the pain in his kidneys. The two Bevilacqua brothers had located the ice, which they then carefully cut, covered with sawdust in a wooden box, and carried on foot or carted to the Ozanam residence.[71] By the feast of the Assumption, August 15, 1853, Frédéric was barely able to walk to mass. It was the last time he would attend. In his characteristic manner, he remarked to his family: "It may be my last walk in this world, and I desire that it shall be to pay a visit to my God, and His Blessed Mother."[72]

By early August his brother Charles had joined him, and his brother Alphonse arrived by the middle of August. With their arrival, Frédéric anticipated that his end was near.[73] Both brothers feared he could not last much longer. A return to France seemed the best course. That return home began on the last day of August. Several days before their departure, Frédéric begged his wife to bring him his will, for he wanted to make some changes. He had already added a provision that, after his death, the following special prayer was to be placed alongside a picture of angels welcoming the deceased into paradise. The prayer and the picture, which was based on a work by Fra Angelico, were a gift intended to console his beloved wife: "Those angels were awaiting at the moment of departure from this earth the faithful who had been entrusted to their fostering care. You, my guardian angel, will remain on earth; your prayers will open Heaven to me. You will remain for yet a little while, to guide the footsteps of the darling child who was our joy. Teach her to think of me, endow her with your virtues. We shall meet again in the abode of love, and under the eyes of the good God Himself we shall love one another with a love that will know no end."[74] He now added a codicil that would require an autopsy after his death. The doctors had remained divided about whether his condition was a disease of the chest (tuberculosis) or one of the kidneys. Fearful for the health of his spouse and especially for his child if the first diagnosis were correct, Frédéric wanted his wife to have certain knowledge of the cause of his death. He could not be dissuaded. The autopsy later confirmed a disease of the kidneys (Bright's disease). It at least removed from Amélie's mind the fear that Marie might have contracted tuberculosis or any other transmissible disease from her father.[75]

As he left Antignano to embark on the journey home, Ozanam remarked that he was thankful to God for the sufferings and afflictions he had endured in the past months because they served as a just expiation for his sins. He then embraced Amélie and thanked her profusely for all of the wonderful consolations she had brought him in his time of trial.[76] They sailed out of Livorno on the steamer *Industry*, which docked in Marseille on September 2, 1853.[77] They were met by the rest of the family, who had traveled to Marseille. Frédéric greeted his mother-in-law warmly and placed Amélie in her watchful care. "Now," he said, "God will do with me what He wills."[78]

Ozanam's final day came in Marseille, on the feast day celebrating the nativity of the Blessed Virgin Mary, September 8, 1853.[79] He received the last rites. Amélie wanted him to be alert for this sacrament: "I always asked God for the price of such a sacrifice that Frederic, my beloved husband, was ready to appear before him, supported by all the help, all the graces which may be acquired on earth, and I could not bear the thought that he would receive the last rites without his knowledge." With love she gently guided his hand to complete the sign of the cross.[80] In the evening his breathing grew labored and irregular. He opened his eyes, raised his arms in supplication, and cried out: "My God, My God, have pity on me!" His brother Alphonse recognized that they were the same words of Christ on the cross.[81] The family present fell to their knees and prayed. At 7:50 in the evening, Frédéric sighed deeply, then stopped breathing. His brother Alphonse poignantly commented, "Our excellent brother was no more! . . . The Virgin Mary, to solemnly celebrate the day of her blessed birth, had wanted one of her more cherished children to enter into eternal glory."[82] Frédéric had lived for only forty years.[83] There would be no more suffering for him.

After a mass for the repose of his soul was celebrated in Marseille, Frédéric's body was transported to Lyon. A second funeral mass was celebrated in Saint-Pierre, the church where he had made his First Communion. Friends and family in Lyon begged Amélie to bury her husband in Lyon, but she refused for a number of reasons, one of which was the obstacle she encountered to having his body interred in a church.[84] The body was then brought to Paris, where a third, full requiem mass was offered at the Church of Saint-Sulpice on September 15, 1853.[85] The coffin remained at Saint-Sulpice until Amélie found a suitable location for interment. Family members encouraged Amélie to bury his remains in Montparnasse Cemetery, but she had other plans for her beloved husband. She arranged for burial at the Church of Saint-Joseph-des-Carmes with the help of members of the Dominican Order who staffed the church. The Dominican provincial, the Reverend Henri Lacordaire, who had collaborated with Ozanam on *L'Ère nouvelle* in 1848, was in residence there. Permission to remove the body from Saint-Sulpice was obtained, and the Dominican community provided a final resting place in a lower crypt near the remains of 114 priests massacred during the French Revolution in September 1792. Frédéric's tomb was located beneath the Chapel of the Guardian Angels, where Amélie had once had a premonition that her husband would find his final resting place.[86] As Raphaëlle Chevalier-Montrariol has remarked, was it her "caprice? stubbornness? or wishful thinking implemented with tenacity?"[87] Amélie's persistence had fulfilled her wishes, and yet Amélie was prevented from entering the crypt by the rules of the Dominican Order. She was only allowed to peek through a small grate to see her husband's last resting place. In 1855, however, she received special permission from Pope Pius IX to enter the crypt by the garden. From that moment, the

Dominican fathers were treated to the daily sight of Amélie and Marie, their arms laden with flowers, crossing the interior courtyard.[88]

Shortly before his death, Frédéric had written to Father Tommaso Pendola encouraging him to form a conference of charity in Siena. He stressed the importance of understanding suffering: "You have amongst your children many who are rich. . . . [H]ow strengthening for those soft young hearts, to show them the poor, to show them Jesus Christ, not in pictures painted by great masters or on altars resplendent with gold and light, but to show them Jesus Christ and His wounds in the persons of the poor! . . . These young seigneurs ought to know what hunger and thirst and the destitution of a naked garret mean. They ought to see fellow-creatures in misery and distress—sick children, little ones crying with hunger. They ought to see them that they may love them. Either the spectacle would make their hearts beat with awakened pulses or they are a lost generation."[89] By the end of his life, Frédéric Ozanam had acquired the wisdom that suffering offers: through it, one can grow spiritually and achieve greater sanctification. As the *Bible for the Sick* relates, Frédéric "had to undergo all the trials of a lingering disease . . . ; he stood the vain hopes of apparent cures and the discouragement of relapses, each more serious than the last; he knew how to live wavering between life and death, by turns grateful or resigned. He saw himself forced to live away from home, deprived of the dearest occupations of his life, far from those he loved, overwhelmed each day with new infirmities, forspent [*sic*] with suffering and weakness, without a murmur from his lips. . . . To his first turmoil of spirit, succeeded calm, and peace of heart, the sweetest gift of God to man, was the anticipated reward of his complete sacrifice."[90]

CHAPTER 13

An Enduring Legacy

If Ozanam had been asked about his legacy for the future, he might have responded with his words in an 1850 letter to his friend Alexandre Dufieux:

> If God has granted me a certain enthusiasm for work, I have never seen this grace as a glittering gift of genius. Undoubtedly, in the lower rank which is my place, I wished to dedicate my life to the service of the faith, but all the while considering myself as the useless servant, the worker of the last hour whom the master of the vineyard accepts only through charity. It seemed to me that my days were well filled if, in spite of my scant merit, I was able to keep gathered around my rostrum many young people, and to build up for my listeners the principles of Christian learning, and make them respect all that they despised: the Church, the papacy, monks. I should have liked to gather these same thoughts into books more durable than my lessons, and all my wishes would have been more than satisfied if a few errant souls found in these teachings a reason to abjure their prejudices, to clear up their doubts and to return

with God's help to Catholic truth. That is what I aimed to do for the last ten years without seeking a more ambitious destiny, but also without my having the misfortune to abandon the combat.[1]

He was humble about his achievements. After his burial in 1853, however, there were numerous tributes to Ozanam's character and his contributions. François Guizot, for example, who had served in the government of Louis-Philippe and who now seemed to forget the disagreements he once had with Ozanam, spoke in his praise at a special meeting of the French Academy: "[Ozanam was] the model of the Christian man of Letters, the ardent lover of Science, and the steady champion of Faith, who was patient and meek in long and fatal suffering, who was snatched away from the purest joys of life, but who was already *ripe for Heaven* as well as for glory."[2] Pope John Paul II, in his homily on the occasion of Frédéric's beatification in 1997, added another dimension to Guizot's remarks: "Frédéric Ozanam believed in love, the love of God for every individual. He felt himself called to love, giving the example of a great love for God and others. . . . Blessed Frédéric Ozanam, apostle of charity, exemplary spouse and father, grand figure of the Catholic laity of the nineteenth century, . . . played an important role in the intellectual movement of his time. A student, and then an eminent professor at Lyon and later at Paris, at the Sorbonne, he aimed above all at seeking and communicating the truth in serenity and respect for the convictions of those who did not share his own."[3] Love infused his actions, adding luster to a life well lived. A legacy is not only something that is handed down, but it is also something that should be cherished, preserved, and emulated. Although Frédéric Ozanam's early death "left a legacy of unfinished work,"[4] nevertheless, it is one worthy of closer examination.

PROFESSIONAL LEGACY

In his professional life, the love of truth was paramount for Frédéric. His standards for research and teaching, as discussed in chapter 5, were impeccable. As he once told his students, "I have the happiness to believe, and the ambition to place my whole soul with all my might at the service of truth."[5] Although a Sorbonne professor and intellectual, he favored higher education for all those entering jobs and professions in industry and commerce so that "industry would receive formally the consecration of Science" and become "ennobled by a public alliance with higher intellectual discipline."[6] As a beloved and trusted teacher, he was a perfect model of intellectual engagement for young people, as historian Gérard Cholvy puts it.[7] His students recognized in him "the sacred fire" and remarked that he possessed "such an air of interior conviction ... that without the appearance of doing so, he convinces and moves you."[8]

Ozanam's historical research "demonstrated a sense of historical criticism which he developed largely through self-education."[9] He applied rigid standards to verify the materials he employed in his arguments, and it is fair to say that he set new standards of research for the field. His contributions to the study of Dante and his recognition of "a unique Christian Latin which began to develop in the first centuries of the Christian Era" were among his most significant scholarly achievements.[10] Baunard's study of Ozanam nearly a century ago raises a question about the objectivity of Ozanam's treatment of Dante: "Ozanam discovered in the proud Florentine patriot an advocate and a prophet of the coming democracy. But did he not in that, rather express his own personal inclinations and convictions?"[11] It is certainly true that Ozanam felt an affinity with Dante. Craig Mousin suggests that "Ozanam viewed Dante as a pioneer of his own choices during destructive times."[12] According to Mousin, Ozanam understood Dante as one who was wedded to reason and faith, like himself. Dante's use of poetry "to persuade, as a political tool," was akin to Ozanam's "own rhetoric and persuasive skills influencing the public debate." Both men were also born with more privileges than many of their contemporaries, but both urged the cause of the masses after witnessing the vast divisions between the poor and the wealthy.[13] One of Ozanam's descriptions of Dante could equally well be applied to himself: "He did not wander, an irresolute deserter, between the two rival camps; he set up his tent on independent ground, not that he might repose in an indifferent neutrality, but that he might fight out the fight alone, with all the strength of his own individual genius."[14] Mousin argues that "Ozanam saw himself, like Dante, not as an irresolute deserter ignoring both sides, but called by his Christian duty as a 'beneficent deserter' charged with doing good and bringing benefit to both sides in eliminating the great divide between the poor and rich."[15] Both men lost friends and discovered new enemies because of their actions. Both men embraced "democratic doctrines," even though neither Dante nor Ozanam embraced a purely modern secular democracy that was purged of faith.[16] Despite raising the question of objectivity, Baunard nevertheless insisted that "no one has contributed more to rescue Dante from . . . oblivion."[17] There is some validity to his claim.

Ozanam, importantly, viewed late antiquity not as decadent but as a time when Christianity became the savior of ancient culture: "In response to some German scholars at the Sorbonne, he tried to demonstrate that a rejection of Roman and Christian heritage would lead to a return to barbarism. . . . As professor of foreign literature at the Sorbonne, . . . Ozanam believed that the genius of Rome needed to be passed on, and that it would serve as a cultural meeting place. . . . Ozanam was among those who defended the legacy of Greek and Roman culture."[18] He also had "the conviction and the courage to make Christianity relevant for his own time and culture."[19] As historian Léonce Celier pointed out, throughout Ozanam's writings "the sincerity of his words is evident."[20]

PUBLIC LEGACY

Ozanam's social thought is one of his most enduring public contributions. His recognition of the common good, the rights of workers, the need to engage the common person in political decisions, the danger to society of the great division between classes, and his holistic approach to the needs of each person laid the foundation for much of the later Catholic social tradition. Historian Joseph Fichter maintains that Ozanam was not ahead of his times in his social thought—other people expressed similar ideas in the nineteenth century and earlier.[21] Historian Edward O'Connor points out that socialists and other secular critics of his day claimed that Ozanam failed to attack poverty itself, focusing instead only on helping individuals in poverty.[22] These kinds of criticisms, however, are misleading. As Gordon Wright argues, "Ozanam was the fountainhead of the durable current called 'social Catholicism' in the nineteenth-century France. Although conservative in spirit, it refused to be satisfied with the mere practice of charity but insisted on seeking the reasons for poverty and on working toward greater social justice."[23] Ozanam worked to relieve the distress of individuals, but he was also convinced that poverty could be addressed only by understanding it in all its dimensions and confronting its causes. One had to experience first what those living in poverty suffered, listening intently to their stories in order to grasp the complexity of poverty. Moreover, Ozanam recognized that those living in poverty needed not only material aid but spiritual aid. Their very souls had become desolate. Without some attention to their inner needs, their true humanity and their dignity could never be restored. Once poverty was understood in its many dimensions, a potential solution could then be identified. As Sean McCarty maintains, "For Ozanam, the real school for those who would serve the poor was personal involvement in the lives of those served through visiting them where they lived and struggled. It meant for him not just bringing material aid, but deeper attention to the needs of the spirit."[24] This approach was fundamentally different from other reformers who tried to apply grand theories without reference to individuals.

In addition to the importance of personally confronting the realities of poverty, Ozanam discerned that social and political attitudes had to change. As Fichter remarks, "There would have to be a revolutionary change in the attitude of officials toward such questions as wages, industrial expansion, and economic concentration."[25] The rich must recognize others as human beings with aspirations for a better quality of life. The poor must recognize themselves as valuable human beings, and not turn to violence as their only means of improvement. Only through changing attitudes could authentic systemic change—the regeneration of society—be accomplished.

According to Ozanam, regeneration of society or "social change" occurs not simply by rehabilitating the needy, but rather by rehabilitating the society that has become unresponsive to the needs of its people and by opening up opportunities for those excluded from dialogue to enter into an inclusive community open to all voices in a democratic process. His view of democracy is founded upon the essential dignity of the human person, but it does not emphasize individualism to the exclusion of community. Ozanam clearly recognized that many problems perceived to be political are fundamentally social in nature, representing a breakdown in genuine community. His answer required changing society, by building just, caring, and tolerant relationships.

Importantly, Ozanam was one of the first prominent Catholic laymen to comprehend that Christianity and democracy were not necessarily incompatible and to advocate democratic decision-making processes on social and religious grounds. Democracy to him was the temporal advent of the gospel. Eugène Duthoit has argued that Ozanam was the leader of a crusade not only to ameliorate suffering but to achieve social progress.[26] In their work *The Church and Labor*, John Ryan and Joseph Husslein draw a careful distinction: "The doctrines of Ozanam . . . on social and industrial questions were at once original and traditional. They were original in the sense that they had not been enunciated by any previous Catholic authority." Ozanam had before him "no papal encyclical as a guide and inspiration." The moral judgments that he "uttered on contemporary industrial practices and on current proposals of reform, many of the moral principles . . . [he] enunciated for the abolition of industrial evils, and most of the economic proposals for betterment that . . . [he] defended, had never been expressed by a Pope, nor indeed by any important Catholic." Yet, they argue, his ideas are in "complete harmony with the traditional doctrines of the Fathers and the theologians."[27] According to Craig Mousin, "Ozanam continues to call all in the Vincentian tradition to find new ways to seek the temporal Gospel principles of liberty, equality, and fraternity to revitalize democracy, and with it, encourage the flourishing of humanity."[28]

Ozanam's social thought influenced other thinkers beyond his time. His ideas are closely related to those of Dorothy Day, and his influence on Day and the Catholic Worker Movement is especially noteworthy. In her 1939 book, *House of Hospitality*, Day commented: "I have been reading a lot of Ozanam lately." Day found Ozanam's thoughts and actions compelling. She and fellow Catholic social activist Peter Maurin firmly believed "that the work is more important than the talking and writing about the work. It has always been through the performance of the works of mercy that love is expressed, that people are converted, that the masses are reached."[29] Citing several significant passages taken directly from Ozanam's writings, Day concluded that "in season and out of season, he [Ozanam] pleaded for 'the annihilation of the political spirit in the interests of the social spirit.' "[30] Ozanam's influence on the Catholic Worker Movement also extends beyond Day's comments in her 1939 book. Peter Maurin, for example, was profoundly influenced by the thought of the twentieth-century French philosopher and theologian Emmanuel Mounier, to whom "we owe Peter's and Dorothy's emphasis on personal responsibility in history (as opposed to withdrawal from the world). Peter Maurin's French roots and language helped him to keep abreast of all that was happening in the vital renaissance in the Catholic Church in France, of which personalism was so much a part. He was able to . . . make the religious revival of France immediately present in the United States."[31] In turn, Mounier, the founder of the French school of personalism, was profoundly influenced by Frédéric Ozanam. As a member of the Society of St. Vincent de Paul in Grenoble, Mounier first actively experienced poverty and gained a deeper understanding of the terrible conditions in which many workers lived.[32] Mounier openly praised Ozanam as one of the few Catholic intellectuals of his time to recognize that the Catholic Church had to embrace the issue of poverty. Ozanam's language in insisting that the Church should address the needs of the masses, according to another commentator, "strikingly anticipated not only the general judgment but the precise language of Mounier a century later."[33] Maurin most likely came into contact with Ozanam's thoughts through reading Mounier.

The twentieth-century Catholic philosopher Jacques Maritain has also singled out Ozanam for his daring thought and action in the nineteenth century. According to Maritain, "A living Christianity is necessary to the world. Faith must be actual, practical, existential faith. To believe in God must mean to live in such a manner that life could not possibly be lived if God did not exist. For the practical believer, gospel justice, gospel attentiveness to everything human must inspire not only the deeds of the saints, but the structure and institutions of common life, and must penetrate to the depths of terrestrial existence."[34] For Maritain, the saint plays an important role in the world:

> If we look at the saint, it seems that the inner act through which he achieves his total break with the world and total liberation from the world, making him free from everything but God, will inevitably overflow from the realm of spiritual life onto the realm of temporal life.

Thus, if he is not dedicated solely to a contemplative state of existence, he will be led to act as a ferment of renewal in the structures of the world, as a stimulating and transforming energy in social matters and in the field of the activities of civilization. And this is true, of course. As a matter of fact, it is what has been taking place for centuries. The Fathers of the Church were great revolutionaries. Thomas Aquinas in the order of culture, St. Vincent de Paul in the social field, were eminent examples of genuine radicals, whose initiative brought about decisive changes in the history of civilization. For centuries temporal progress in the world has been furthered by the saints.[35]

Chantelle Olgilvie-Ellis comments that "it is important for Maritain that saints . . . play a distinct role . . . of imbuing the temporal world with Gospel vitality. In this way, the sacred would animate and sanctify the secular and profane."[36] In the world of the Industrial Revolution, unfortunately, few stepped forward: "A particularly inhuman structure of society, caused by the Industrial Revolution, made the problem of social justice manifestly crucial; except for a few men of faith, like Ozanam in France and Toniolo in Italy . . . , the task, as we know, was not conducted by saints. It even happened that atheists, instead of saints, took the lead in social matters, much to the misfortune of all."[37] Ozanam, according to Maritain, was one of the prominent exceptions, stepping forward, taking "the lead in the protest of the poor and . . . the movement of labor toward its historical coming of age."[38]

The term "liberal Catholicism" has often been attached to Ozanam's name. Carol E. Harrison rejects this term as a general label for Ozanam and several other prominent nineteenth-century French figures, in favor of another: "Scholars most commonly refer to the individuals [whom I study] . . . as 'liberal Catholics,' a term that I have rejected in favor of 'romantic Catholics.'"[39] She includes both Amélie and Frédéric Ozanam within the "romantic Catholic" camp, as well Maurice de Guérin, Charles de Montalembert, and Pauline Craven.[40] According to Harrison, Charles de Montalembert and some of his Catholic associates were the first to refer to themselves as a "liberal Catholic opposition." The term "liberal" is misleading, however, because most of these Catholic thinkers found some fault with the liberal tradition that stressed the "autonomous male individual" and that often "willfully denied that the

ties between individuals mattered more than the individuals themselves."[41] Her term "romantic Catholic" refers to Catholics who held an
organic view of society, favored looking to past traditions rather than
abandoning them completely, and favored individual rights but with
clear social responsibilities.

Harrison identifies seven essential characteristics of this group of
"romantic Catholics," including Ozanam. First, they recognized that
"relationships and the sentiments of affection and respect out of which
they grew were the true elements of the social fabric." In particular, they
believed that marriage and the family were the most significant relationships, providing a model for all other social arrangements.[42] Second,
although they were not anti-clerical[43] and welcomed as supporters cler-
ics such as Félicité de Lamennais and Henri Dominique Lacordaire, they
asserted the important role of the laity in the life of the Church. Third,
they were "inclined to trust emotions as the foundation for rational
argument."[44] All of them, including Ozanam, "sought out experiences
that would encourage an emotional connection with the past."[45] Fourth,
they were attracted to the medieval world, not because they wished to
return to those days, but rather as a Christian period that offered valuable lessons for the modern world struggling with faith: "The Middle
Ages was thus an imaginative space to which romantic Catholics could
appeal—less a blueprint than a reservoir of Christian thought."[46] Fifth,
they were cosmopolitan. Most were fluent in numerous languages, most
traveled extensively, and most had an extensive network of international
friends with whom they regularly corresponded.[47] Sixth, because of their
ties with other Catholics, these romantic Catholics avoided the extreme
nationalism of the nineteenth century; they had a genuine respect for
the links among countries and the universal brotherhood of all.[48] Last,
romantic Catholic men "saw no conflict between their gender and their
faith and . . . were not persistently apologizing or compensating for their
membership in a 'feminine' church."[49] The hope of all romantic Catholics was to reconcile faith and modernity in order to bring peace to a
troubled world.[50]

In his public life, Ozanam acknowledged that the contributors to
L'Ère nouvelle such as himself may have "often shown a lack of human
prudence," but he also maintained that "God never allowed them to lack
a love for justice, for the poor people."[51] For him, what mattered was

building a civilization based on Christian love. He hoped his contribution, as quoted earlier, would be "the passionate love of my country, the enthusiasm of common interests, and the alliance of Christianity and freedom."[52] In Harrison's terminology, he was indeed a "romantic Catholic."

LEGACY OF PRAXIS

Ozanam, as this study has amply demonstrated, was not simply a theoretician but also a practitioner. In the words of Fichter, "It would have been much easier to sit at the scholar's desk penning indictments against the sinful world and advising others how to perform the dirty work of reconstruction."[53] That was not Ozanam's way. As John Honner puts it, "His was indeed a life of putting truth into practice."[54] When Ozanam participated in the conference of history in his student days, he had already begun to link theory and practice: "Let's not relegate our beliefs to the domain of speculation and theory; let's take them seriously, and let our life be the continual expression of them."[55] Later in his life he remarked to a friend: "We do not have two lives, one to seek the truth, the other for the practice."[56] He not only wrote about serving those in poverty but was also actively engaged in that service. He used his experiences to shape his practice. He left a model of service that is based on forming relationships, rooted in deep reflection, and connected intimately with charity and justice.

Especially for young people, Ozanam argued, charity constituted an active form of service that leads over time to greater engagement in the struggle for social change. In 1834, at the age of twenty-one, he wrote to his friend and distant cousin Ernest Falconnet: "But . . . we are too young to intervene in the social struggle. Should we remain inactive therefore in the midst of a suffering and groaning world? No, there is a preparatory path open to us; before taking action for the public good we can take action for the good of individuals; before regenerating France, we can solace poor persons."[57] He did not, however, conceive of this service experience as a haphazard undertaking by merely a few: "I would further wish that all young people might unite in head and heart in some charitable work and that there be formed throughout the whole country a vast generous association for the relief of the common people."[58] Ozanam envisioned a transformation of French society by engaging young university students in active service to the common good. Indeed, as Sean McCarty maintains, Ozanam continues to "speak to current proponents of social justice in both theoretical and practical ways. As a teacher and writer, he sought social reform aimed at causes and systems. As leader of the Conference, he worked tirelessly and concretely to bring aid to those in need."[59]

Ozanam has left us a rich legacy of ideas and practices that can enrich discussions of community service. Moreover, his view of "true" charity and his assessment of its effects are profoundly different in several ways from those of major American thinkers such as Jane Addams and John Dewey, whose ideas have widely informed discussions of community service. Both of these seminal American thinkers had a generally negative assessment of charity, its purpose, and its effects. For Dewey, charity was more of a curse than a comfort. In 1908, Dewey claimed that charity may "serve to supply rich persons with a cloak for selfishness in other directions. . . . Charity may even be used as a sop to one's social conscience while at the same time it buys off the resentment which might otherwise grow up in those who suffer from social injustice. Magnificent philanthropy may be employed to cover up brutal exploitation."[60] Indeed, he feared that charity "assumes the continued and necessary existence of a dependent 'lower' class to be the recipient of the kindness of their superiors."[61] His contemporary Jane Addams, who influenced Dewey's thought, was equally critical of the world of charity. The person who visits those in need, according to Addams, exercises "a cruel advantage"[62] and often thinks "more of what a man ought to be than of what he is or what he may become."[63] According to the social historian Roy Lubove, the practice of charity in the late nineteenth century "was essentially a process of character regimentation, not social reform."[64] Poverty was not the fault of society; "the charitable agent really blamed the individual for his poverty."[65] The person receiving charity was "less an equal . . . than an object of character reformation" who had been undone by "ignorance or deviations from middle-class values and patterns of life organization: temperance, industriousness, family cohesiveness, frugality, foresight, moral restraint."[66]

Ozanam's viewpoint differed in several ways. First, he was quick to distinguish charity from philanthropy. He held that true charity is always linked to a community built on bonds of deep friendship and trust, whereas so-called charitable efforts that are outside the boundaries of community (what he would call philanthropy) are often dehumanizing and performed for individual recognition. According to Ozanam, most philanthropic societies, after about a year of existence, have nothing but "meetings, reports, summings-up, bills, and accounts; . . . they have volumes of minutes and so forth."[67] To distinguish philanthropy from charity, Ozanam employed images that would resonate with his intended (primarily male) audience. Philanthropy is like "a vain woman for whom good actions are a piece of jewelry and who loves to look at herself in a mirror," while charity "is a tender mother . . . who no longer thinks of herself, and who forgets her beauty for love."[68] Unlike Dewey and Addams, Ozanam's dilemma was how to restore authentic relationships (his emphasis on regeneration is precisely related to this dilemma) that have failed because of the human inability to recognize and fulfill the need for solidarity. Further, Ozanam never intended to treat those in poverty as inferior. They were the "masters," for they understood poverty better than anyone else and were closest to Christ. Nor, as we have seen, did he blame the poor for their poverty.

Ozanam provides us with a view of charity that is intimately linked to justice. He would argue, in fact, that providing charity can be a matter of basic justice, especially when the need is an essential one such as food, clothing, or shelter. Justice requires the assistance of charity, but charity in turn requires the pursuit of justice. The relationship was one of mutual necessity, with charity "widening the focus of justice to include God and groups of people previously passed over."[69] According to McCarty, "The Vincentian heritage of finding Christ in the person of the poor and the safeguarding of that fundamental charity that informed the works by the practice of humility saved their [the Society members'] efforts from the contamination of selfish pursuit or ambiguous motivations. . . . This kind of charity would seem to embrace a biblical and contemporary understanding of justice, that is, sharing what belongs to the poor by right. Seemingly central to a Vincentian spirit is a charity that makes of the poor masters to those who help them."[70] Craig Mousin adds this additional insight: "Ozanam offered the . . . argument . . . that Christians have an unambiguous duty to engage the powers-that-be to end poverty. . . . Charity heals some wounds . . . but individual and community social engagement to convince those with resources to find equitable distribution methods is necessarily part of one's call to justice."[71]

For Ozanam, justice presupposes love as part of the necessary respect for the rights and freedom of others. Thus a community service organization does not have to choose between charity and justice; as Ozanam demonstrated, a community service organization can and should include both charity and justice in its mission. Indeed, Ozanam was opposed to the Society of St. Vincent de Paul becoming another large bureaucratic organization, because he thought that the concept of the essential dignity of the human person would be lost in the process. His concerns offer considerable food for thought for large nonprofit organizations, which can sometimes contribute unwittingly to the very thing they wish to prevent—the stripping away of a person's dignity.

In his essay "The Irony of Service," Keith Morton maintains that there are three paradigms of service—through charity, projects, and social change. Each paradigm can be exemplified with or without integrity, or, as he terms it, in a thick or thin manner: "Thick versions of each paradigm are grounded in deeply held, internally coherent values; match means and ends; describe a primary way of interpreting and relating to the world; offer a way of defining problems and solutions; and suggest a vision of what a transformed world might look like. At their thickest, the paradigms seem to intersect, or at least complement one another. Insisting on the humanity of another person in the face of sometimes overwhelming pressure to deny that humanity can be a motive for charity, for project and for social change."[72] From the evidence already presented in this biography, it is fair to argue that Ozanam represents the thickest version of service, where the three paradigms intersect or complement each another.

In McCarty's words, "Ozanam demonstrated the compatibility of a passionate love for the Church and orthodoxy (right belief) as well as a profound commitment to development and orthopraxis (right practice), especially toward the poor."[73] There is no doubt that Ozanam valued the orthodox doctrines of the Church: "orthodoxy is the nerve, the strength of religion, and . . . without this vital condition any Catholic association is powerless."[74] Yet his "dedication to social reform enabled him to challenge lovingly the Church and tradition he cherished."[75] Some might emphasize orthopraxis or right practice over right belief; Ozanam reconciled the two, understanding their delicate but essential relationship. Christian orthodoxy and Christian orthopraxy are not incompatible. The latter is the fruit of the former. Moreover, in today's age of excessive individualism, Ozanam "models communitarian dimensions of spirituality and collaborative dimensions of ministry. . . . [He] never meant to accomplish his great work for the Church for the cause of truth and service of the poor as a solitary venture."[76]

Frédéric Ozanam left his most lasting legacy of charitable community service in the Society of St. Vincent de Paul. Begun in Paris in 1833, the Society spread quickly throughout the world. In the United States, it found an early home at the old Saint Louis Cathedral along the banks of the Mississippi in 1845. Today there are more than 4,400 conferences of charity in most of the fifty states. The Society annually helps some 14 million people to the amount of nearly $1 billion in money, goods, volunteer time, and contributed services. It is also actively engaged in advocacy. In the United States, its national committee, known as Voice of the Poor (VOP), guides members on important issues of social justice, prepares key position papers on issues such as homelessness and wages, and works closely with the United States Conference of Catholic Bishops in advocacy initiatives.[77]

The Society was a part of Ozanam's vision of a lay apostolate, which he had enunciated as early as 1835.[78] By the 1840s the Society openly embraced this idea of a lay apostolate, where "the laity participate in the priesthood of priests."[79] As Mousin argues, "The foundation of the Society marked the beginning of what would become known as the Catholic Action movement, which eventually spread across Europe and North America and became one of the key elements in a Catholic renaissance among the laity in subsequent generations. . . . Catholic Action and the Society of St. Vincent de Paul were movements in which lay people felt inspired and were concretely empowered to take on roles which had been traditionally reserved for those who belonged to a kind of professional class of sisters, brothers, and priests evolved over the centuries."[80] The Society of St. Vincent de Paul, for Mousin, "can be characterized as something that is both fundamentally conservative, insofar as it was a charitable outreach to the poor, while, at the same time, it was also something that was radically progressive and disruptive to the status quo due to the fact that it organized lay people in a way that supplemented and supplanted those who occupied positions traditionally reserved for an elite religious class."[81] By envisioning a network of charity and justice and through his inspiration, Frédéric Ozanam, as we have seen, was to a great extent responsible for bringing the Society of St. Vincent de Paul to the world.

PERSONAL LEGACY

A life well-lived is the greatest personal legacy of Frédéric Ozanam to us: "His life demonstrated a genuine integration of professional and spiritual life, theory and practice, faith and works."[82] As shown in earlier chapters, he was a devoted son and brother, a loving husband, a caring father, and an excellent friend. He led others with a deep faith and a compassionate heart.

Family was sacred to him. As we have seen, the deaths of his parents weighed heavily on him. He confided to his friend François Lallier, "May I continue with them in thought, faith, and strength that intimacy that nothing could interrupt, and may there be no family change except two saints more! Pray *for us*, then, excellent friend, for all of us: for me especially, who so greatly loved that sheltered life of the paternal home who, surrounded by my brothers and my numerous confreres, cannot get used to seeing no longer those of the preceding generation, and who find myself so alone!"[83] At his death, his brothers and only surviving siblings, Alphonse and Charles, were at his side supporting and consoling him, as he had supported and consoled them many times.

In Amélie Soulacroix, he found a soul mate. Philippe Charpentier de Beauville claims that her love "enhanced the stature of his life." She was the "'Beatrice' of this great man and the 'guardian angel' of the great Christian."[84] Amélie "strengthened rather than drained his charitable impulses."[85] Like the Christian women of the early centuries, she helped teach her husband "to revere weakness and to care for those who suffered."[86] Frédéric's mother and his devotion to the Virgin Mary had fostered in him a respect for the role of women in God's plan of salvation. However, through his life with Amélie especially, Frédéric recognized that women "possessed extraordinary virtue that should give all

Catholics hope for salvation."[87] According to Carol E. Harrison, once he had married, "Frédéric gradually abandoned the fraternal model of Catholic Society that had been so important to romantic Catholics around 1830. In its place, he elaborated a vision of society in which women represented the bonds that tied individuals together: marriage rather than friendship dominated his mature vision of a Catholic social."[88] There is some truth in this analysis. Ozanam regarded the importance of marriage and the family to society in a new light after his marriage in 1841. At the same time, his friendships and the fraternal bonds forged in the Society of St. Vincent de Paul remained vital aspects of his life.

An avid daily reader of scripture, he would have been familiar with the following passage from the Book of Sirach on friendship: "Faithful friends are a sturdy shelter: whoever finds one has found a treasure. / Faithful friends are beyond price; no amount can balance their worth. / Faithful friends are life-saving medicine; and those who fear the Lord will find them."[89] His own life was a "mosaic of significant relationships of family, friends, models, mentors, peers, students, and followers."[90] Perhaps he excelled in friendships because he saw himself as a servant first. Emulating the models of his Lord, Jesus Christ, and his patron, Saint Vincent de Paul, Ozanam became an authentic servant leader.

Ozanam's life is also a perfect example of the Christian recognition of the subtle but real presence of God in the world and in individual lives. He gave a beautiful testimony to this view of human life and destiny in an address at Saint-Sulpice to a workmen's society:

It is we ourselves who are working out our destiny on earth unknown to us, exactly as the craftsmen of the Gobelins work at their tapestry. Docilely following the design of an unknown artist, they devoted themselves to arranging the several colours indicated by him, on the reverse of the woof, not knowing what the result of their work was to be. It was only afterwards, when the work was completed, that they could admire the flowers, pictures, figures and marvels of art, which then left their hands to adorn the dwellings of kings. Thus, friends, let us work on this earth, docile and submissive to the will of God without knowing what He is accomplishing through us. But He, the divine Artist, sees and knows. When He will show us the finished work of our life, of our toil and of our troubles, we shall be thrown into ecstasy and we shall bless Him for deigning to accept and place our poor works in His eternal mansion.[91]

His view of history, as this passage illustrates, was intimately linked to the Christian conviction that God works out his plan in history while still leaving humankind with freedom of will, one of God's greatest gifts. In his spiritual life, of course, Ozanam was first and foremost a Catholic, and he hoped that Catholicism would find many converts in his nineteenth-century world. He provides an example for all Catholics; in the words of Gérard Cholvy, "Frédéric Ozanam is . . . the model of the Apostolic commitment of the laity in the world. . . . [He] has given a persistent example of love of the Church and attachment to its Roman center."[92] The spirituality of Frédéric Ozanam is also an example for all persons of faith; as quoted earlier, his spirituality was "that of the person in the pew who burns with the desire to love God and neighbor and who, also, wants to put into practice that love."[93]

The cause for the canonization of Frédéric Ozanam was first introduced on March 15, 1925, by the diocese of Paris.[94] It followed the procedures outlined in canons 1999–2141 of the 1917 Code of Canon Law.[95] The first step, the examination of "his reputation for holiness, his virtues, and any alleged miracles," lasted from June 1925[96] until June 1928.[97] Given that the canonization inquiry was initiated seventy-two years after Ozanam's death, of the thirty-one witnesses who were called for this step, only one could claim that she had known him. That witness was Elisabeth Cornudet, the daughter of Léon Cornudet, whom Ozanam had chosen to watch over his daughter in the event of his death.[98] Most of the evidence was based on secondhand knowledge and on important documents, including notes written by Ozanam's widow, Amélie. What had caused such a delay in the start of a canonization process? According to the past postulator general, Reverend Roberto D'Amico, C. M., the delay "was due to the obvious need for an in-depth study of someone so involved, and in so many ways, in the world of the laity, and to the unfavourable political climate in France, and to the World War [World War I]."[99]

The next steps in the canonization process proved to be painfully slow. The numerous documents and writings of Ozanam had to be reviewed. The decree of approval was not issued until November 11, 1949. Four years later, "the promoter of the faith presented his observations."[100] In 1956 the Sacred Congregation permitted the cause to move to the next step: an examination of the virtues of the "Servant of God." Because of the lack of sufficient evidence to make a final judgment, the process was referred to the Historical Section of the Sacred Congregation in 1962. Not until a new postulator, Father Giuseppe Lapalorcia, C. M., was appointed in 1970 did the cause move forward again.[101] Three years later in 1973 an extensive scholarly study (*Disquisitio*) was required to complement the document "Position on the Virtues" (*Positio*) that also had to be prepared. The purpose of the *Disquisitio*, which was undertaken by a vice-postulator, Etienne Diebold, C. M., was to establish as clearly as possible the principal stages of Ozanam's life and activities in view of the canonization cause. It took seven years to complete. When it finally appeared in 1980, it was a massive work, totaling 1,255 pages of research.[102] It was not until December 18, 1992, that all of the materials in both the *Positio* and the *Disquisitio* were reviewed by both historical and theological consultors assigned by the Roman Curia (the Congregation for the Causes of Saints) and a decision reached that was "affirmative and unanimous."[103] As a result, Ozanam was declared "Venerable"—a first stage toward sainthood—by Pope John Paul II on July 6, 1993.

Three years later (June 25, 1996) John Paul II signed a decree that officially recognized the miracle of February 2, 1926, that was attributed to the intercession of Ozanam. An eighteen-month-old Brazilian baby, Fernando Luiz Benedetto Ottoni, who was suffering from a severe case of diphtheria, miraculously recovered after his grandfather, a member of the Society of St. Vincent de Paul, prayed that his grandson would be healed through the intercession of Ozanam. Within hours of the prayer the boy recovered. The date was February 2, the Feast of the Blessed Virgin Mary's Purification.[104] On the basis of this miracle, the Holy Father scheduled the beatification ceremony for August 22, 1997, at Notre Dame Cathedral, Paris. The beatification coincided with the Catholic Church's World Day of Youth. Ozanam was held up as an example for all laity but in particular for young people seeking a social, moral, and spiritual model.[105] In his message delivered at the beatification ceremony, John Paul II included the words: "He went to all those who needed to be loved more than others, those to whom the love of God could not be revealed effectively except through the love of another person. There Ozanam discovered his vocation, the path to which Christ called him. He found his road to sanctity. And he followed it with determination."[106] Although declared "Blessed" in 1997, as of 2016, Frédéric Ozanam's canonization is still under consideration by the Vatican.

When one looks back on the extent of Ozanam's legacy, one might ask: How did he accomplish all that he did, given that for years he was afflicted with a painful kidney disease that prematurely took his life? We can enumerate many reasons: his work ethic; his genuine love for both his academic work and his work for the Society of St. Vincent de Paul; the deep sense of mission that drove him to overcome obstacles; the personal strength rooted in his faith and trust in God's providence; his many friends, who provided him with encouragement and the exchange of ideas; and the love and care of his wife. Amélie's devotion to and support of her husband cannot be overlooked as a crucial element in his success. But in no way do these reasons make his legacy any less remarkable.

Frédéric Ozanam's greatest legacy is thus his life as an example for others—his part in the vast tapestry woven by the divine artist. The epitaph on his tomb is an eloquent tribute:

> Here rests in peace Frederic Ozanam,
> Who stirred the young into action in the
> Service of Christ. Principal founder
> Of the Society of Saint-Vincent de Paul.
>
> By science, history, eloquence, poetry and charity,
> He consecrated himself to transforming everything
> in Christ's name. He enclosed the whole world
> within a network of charity.
>
> His name shall be invoked
> From generation to generation.
> Nations will celebrate his wisdom
> And the Church shall praise him.

A saintly life does not mean perfection; it involves a journey toward perfection over time. Ozanam could be faulted for his occasional naïveté about politics and entrenched interests, or for thinking that all Catholics and Christians, once they grasped the problem, would respond to persistent human misery with the same passion that he displayed. But he cannot be faulted or reproached for the integrity of his principles or for his dedication to a cause once he had committed to it. He had an incisive mind, a confident soul, but most of all, a tender heart. As Mireille Beaup observes, "Until his last breath, Frederic Ozanam lived loving."[107] For forty years Antoine Frédéric Ozanam truly believed in the transformative power of love, and, as a consequence, he became a genuine embodiment of 1 Corinthians 13:4–8 at the end of his short lifetime. He was patient, he was kind. He did not envy, he did not boast, he was not proud. He did not dishonor others, he was not self-seeking, he was not easily angered, he kept no record of wrongs. He did not delight in evil, but rejoiced with the truth. He always protected, always trusted, always hoped, always persevered. He lived a life of abiding love and was the model of charity, because he knew in his heart that love never fails.

NOTES

CHAPTER 1. SON AND SIBLING

1. Marcel Vincent, *Ozanam: Une jeunesse romantique, 1813–1833* (Paris: Médiaspaul, 1994), 42–43.

2. Léonce Curnier, *La jeunesse de Frédéric Ozanam*, 4th ed. (Paris: A. Hennuyer, Imprimateur-Éditeur, 1890), 3–4.

3. Vincent, *Ozanam*, 43.

4. Curnier, *La jeunesse*, 4.

5. Ibid.

6. Lacordaire, quoted in ibid. For another English translation see H. D. Lacordaire, O.P., *My Friend Ozanam*, trans. by a Discalced Carmelite (Sydney, Australia: The Society of St. Vincent de Paul Ozanam House, 1957), 7–8.

7. Right Reverend Monsignor Louis Baunard, *Ozanam in His Correspondence* (Dublin: Catholic Truth Society, 1925), 77.

8. Quoted in ibid.

9. Ibid., 78.

10. Albert Paul Schimberg, *The Great Friend: Frederick Ozanam* (Milwaukee: Bruce Publishing Company, 1946), 15–16.

11. Amin de Tarrazi and Ronald Ramson, C.M., *Ozanam* (Bowling Green, MO: Éditions du Signe, 1997), 12.

12. "To Dominique Meynis," 17 May 1843, in *Lettres de Frédéric Ozanam*, vol. 5, *Supplément et tables*, édition critique sous la direction de Didier Ozanam (Paris: Éditions Klincksieck, 1997), no. 1395, 102. See also Tarrazi and Ramson, *Ozanam*, 12.

13. Quoted in Tarrazi and Ramson, *Ozanam*, 12.

14. Desiderius (Didier) of Vienne died in 607. He was the martyred bishop of Vienne and recognized as a saint by the Catholic Church.

15. Kathleen O'Meara, *Frederic Ozanam, Professor at the Sorbonne: His Life and Works* (New York: Catholic Publication Society Company, 1891), 1–2.

16. Gérard Cholvy, *Frédéric Ozanam: L'engagement d'un intellectuel catholique au XIXe siècle* (Paris: Fayard, 2003), 55.

17. The Berchiny Hussars were a light cavalry unit in the French military.

18. Schimberg, *The Great Friend*, 1–2.

19. Ibid., 3.

20. Baunard, *Ozanam*, 1. See Schimberg, *The Great Friend*, 3n.3. Schimberg points out that one biographer, Heinrich Auer, claims that Jean-Antoine's rank at retirement was that of lieutenant, not captain. He also indicates that another biographer, Ainslie Coates, suggests that Jean-Antoine had some trouble getting his dismissal from the army. See Ainslie Coates, trans., *Letters of Frederic Ozanam* (London: Elliot Stock, 1886), 5. Hereafter cited as Coates, *Ozanam*.

21. Schimberg, *The Great Friend*, 5.

22. Cholvy, *Ozanam: L'engagement*, 39–41.

23. Quoted in Vincent, *Ozanam*, 46.

24. Ibid., 35.

25. Ibid., 46.

26. Cholvy, *Ozanam: L'engagement*, 42. See 39–56 for an excellent and more detailed discussion of Frédéric's father.

27. Ibid., 46.

28. Ibid., 48.

29. Vincent, *Ozanam*, 50.

30. Quoted in Baunard, *Ozanam*, 3.

31. Preceding quotation from Vincent, *Ozanam*, 51. See also Cholvy, *Ozanam: L'engagement*, 59.

32. Vincent, *Ozanam*, 51.

33. Cholvy, *Ozanam: L'engagement*, 59. See also Vincent, *Ozanam*, 50.

34. Schimberg, *The Great Friend*, 14.

35. Ibid. See also Baunard, *Ozanam*, 3.

36. Vincent, *Ozanam*, 51. For more information on Marie Cruziat, see Cholvy, *Ozanam: L'engagement*, 60.

37. Curnier, *La jeunesse*, 2–3.

38. Cholvy, *Ozanam: L'engagement*, 27.

39. Baunard, *Ozanam*, 2. See also Schimberg, *The Great Friend*, 4.

40. Cholvy, *Ozanam: L'engagement*, 28–29, 32.

41. Vincent, *Ozanam*, 42–43.

42. R. R. Palmer, *Twelve Who Ruled: The Year of the Terror in the French Revolution* (Princeton, NJ: Princeton University Press, 1970), 33.

43. Schimberg, *The Great Friend*, 9–10. See also Curnier, *La jeunesse*, 4–5.

44. Palmer, *Twelve Who Ruled*, 101.

45. Ibid., 129.

46. Ibid., 170.

47. Schimberg, *The Great Friend*, 9–10. See also Curnier, *La jeunesse*, 4–5.

48. Schimberg, *The Great Friend*, 9.

49. Baunard, *Ozanam*, 2.

50. Schimberg, *The Great Friend*, 11.

51. "Letter to H. Fortoul et Huchard," 15 January 1831, in "Lettres de Frédéric Ozanam," vol. 2, in Frédéric Ozanam, *Oeuvres complètes* (Paris: Jacques Lecoffre et Cie, Libraires-Éditeurs, 1865), vol. 11, 7. Hereafter cited as "Lettres Ozanam," *Oeuvres complètes* (1865). See also *Lettres de Frédéric Ozanam*, vol. 1, *Lettres de jeunesse (1819–1840)*, ed. Léonce Célier, Jean-Baptiste Duroselle, and Didier Ozanam (Paris: Bloud and Gay, 1960), no. 25, 34.

52. Curnier, *La jeunesse*, 7.

53. See Cholvy, *Ozanam: L'engagement*, 64–65.

54. Schimberg, *The Great Friend*, 14.

55. Baunard, *Ozanam*, 7.

56. Ibid.

57. Cholvy, *Ozanam: L'engagement*, 61.

58. Schimberg, *The Great Friend*, 11.

59. C.-A. Ozanam, *Vie de Frédéric Ozanam* (Paris: Librairie Poussielgue Frères, 1879), 559.

60. Schimberg, *The Great Friend*, 14–15.

61. Ibid., 7. Schimberg mentions that this church was torn down in 1836 and reconstructed in a nearby location. In 1847 it was rededicated to St. Charles Borromeo.

62. Ibid., 10.

63. Cholvy, *Ozanam: L'engagement*, 57–58.

64. Ibid., 58. High infant mortality was not unusual for this period.

65. Quoted in Baunard, *Ozanam*, 4.

66. C.-A. Ozanam, *Frédéric Ozanam*, 81–82.

67. Ibid., 82. It is interesting that Frédéric indicates in one of his letters that he was seven years old when this fever occurred. That implies that it happened in 1820, not 1819. Marcel Vincent appears to accept this interpretation and places Frédéric's illness in the same year that his sister Élisa died—1820, contradicting other accounts. See Vincent, *Ozanam*, 53–54.

68. Quoted in O'Meara, *Ozanam*, 6.

69. C.-A. Ozanam, *Frédéric Ozanam*, 82–83.

70. Ibid., 79.

71. Cholvy, *Ozanam: L'engagement*, 35.

72. Schimberg, *The Great Friend*, 14; Curnier, *La jeunesse*, 23.

73. O'Meara, *Ozanam*, 6. See also Schimberg, *The Great Friend*, 14.

74. "Letter to Auguste Materne," 5 June 1830, in Joseph I. Dirvin, C. M., trans. and ed., *Frederic Ozanam: A Life in Letters* (St. Louis: Society of St. Vincent de Paul, Council of the United States, 1986), 11. Hereafter cited as Dirvin, *A Life in Letters*. For the original French text see *Lettres*, vol. 1, no. 12, 13.

75. Ibid., 10. For the original French text see *Lettres*, vol. 1, no. 12, 13.

76. Austin Fagan, *Through the Eye of a Needle: Frédéric Ozanam* (Middlegreen and Bowling Green Lane, England: St. Paul Publications and Universe Publications Co., 1989), 19–20. Hereafter cited as Fagan, *Frédéric Ozanam*.

77. Vincent, *Ozanam*, 53.

78. Quoted in ibid.

79. Fagan, *Frédéric Ozanam*, 21.

80. Quoted in Vincent, *Ozanam*, 53. See also Baunard, *Ozanam*, 9. For the original French text see A. F. Ozanam, "Avant-Propos," *La civilisation au cinquième siècle*, in *Oeuvres complètes*, 2nd ed. (Paris: Jacques Lecoffre et Cie, 1862), vol. 1, 2. Hereafter cited as Ozanam, "Avant-Propos," *Oeuvres complètes* (1862).

81. Fagan, *Frédéric Ozanam*, 22.

82. Tarrazi and Ramson, *Ozanam*, 6. Tarrazi and Ramson assign her the age of eighty-nine when she died, but Alphonse Ozanam indicates that she was eighty-seven. See C.-A. Ozanam, *Frédéric Ozanam*, 57. She was born in 1768 according to Cholvy. See Cholvy, *Ozanam: L'engagement*, 60.

83. C.-A. Ozanam, *Frédéric Ozanam*, 57.

84. Tarrazi and Ramson, *Ozanam*, 6.

85. Cholvy, *Ozanam: L'engagement*, 60–61.

86. Ibid., 61.

87. Fagan, *Frédéric Ozanam*, 22–23.

88. "Letter to Auguste Materne," 5 June 1830, in Dirvin, *A Life in Letters*, 12. For the original French text see *Lettres*, vol. 1, no. 12, 15.

89. "Letter to his mother," 8 April 1832, in Dirvin, *A Life in Letters*, 25. For the original French text see *Lettres*, vol. 1, no. 45, 78.

90. C.-A. Ozanam, *Frédéric Ozanam*, 552.

91. Ibid.; Lacordaire, *My Friend*, 8.

92. "Letter to his mother," 19 June 1833, in Dirvin, *A Life in Letters*, 40. For the original French text see *Lettres*, vol. 1, no. 58, 106.

93. Ibid., 42n.8.

94. Thomas E. Jordan, *Ireland's Children: Quality of Life, Stress, and Child Development in the Famine Era* (Westport, CT: Greenwood Press, 1998), 138.

95. C.-A. Ozanam, *Frédéric Ozanam*, 552; Lacordaire, *My Friend*, 8.

96. "Letter to his mother," 19 June 1833, in Dirvin, *A Life in Letters*, 40. The phrase "au nez large" can also mean a wide, broad, or big nose. For the original French text see *Lettres*, vol. 1, no. 58, 105. See also Lacordaire, *My Friend*, 8; C.-A. Ozanam, *Frédéric Ozanam*, 552–53.

97. C.-A. Ozanam, *Frédéric Ozanam*, 552.

98. Ibid., 553.

99. Ibid., 556.

100. Lacordaire, *My Friend*, 8.

101. C.-A. Ozanam, *Frédéric Ozanam*, 553.

102. Ibid.

103. Didier Ozanam, "Frederic Ozanam," in Mary Ann Garvie Hess, trans., *Frédéric Ozanam*, special issue, *Cahiers Ozanam*, nos. 37/38/39, January–June (Paris: Society of Saint Vincent de Paul, Council General, 1974), 11. Hereafter cited as Hess, *Cahiers Ozanam*.

104. C.-A. Ozanam, *Frédéric Ozanam*, 555.

105. Ibid.

106. Ibid.

107. "Letter to Auguste Materne," 5 June 1830, in Dirvin, *A Life in Letters*, 12. For the original French text see *Lettres*, vol. 1, no. 12, 15.

108. Schimberg, *The Great Friend*, 14–15.

109. "Letter to his mother," 11 April 1837, in Dirvin, *A Life in Letters*, 110. For the original French text see *Lettres*, vol. 1, no. 146, 260.

110. Baunard, *Ozanam*, 7.

111. Tarrazi and Ramson, *Ozanam*, 5.

112. C.-A. Ozanam, *Frédéric Ozanam*, 64.

113. Coates, *Ozanam*, 189.

114. C.-A. Ozanam, *Frédéric Ozanam*, 65.

115. Coates, *Ozanam*, 189.

116. Ibid., 190.

117. Ibid.

118. Curnier, *La jeunesse*, 129.

119. See *Lettres*, vol. 1, no. 154, 271.

120. Coates, *Ozanam*, 190–91. For the original French text see *Lettres*, vol. 1, no. 154, 271.

121. Ibid., 191. For the original French text see *Lettres*, vol. 1, no. 154, 271.

122. Ibid. For the original French text see *Lettres*, vol. 1, no. 154, 271.

123. Ibid., 191–92. For the original French text see *Lettres*, vol. 1, no. 154, 271.

124. Ibid., 192. For the original French text see *Lettres*, vol. 1, no. 154, 272.

125. "Letter to Emmanuel Bailly," 20 May 1837, in Dirvin, *A Life in Letters*, 111. For the original French text see *Lettres*, vol. 1, no. 150, 267.

126. Ibid. For the original French text see *Lettres*, vol. 1, no. 150, 267.

127. Ibid., 112. For the original French text see *Lettres*, vol. 1, no. 150, 268.

128. Ibid. For the original French text see *Lettres*, vol. 1, no. 150, 267–68.

129. Schimberg, *The Great Friend*, 123.

130. Ibid.

131. Coates, *Ozanam*, 190.

132. "Letter to his mother," 19 March 1833, in Dirvin, *A Life in Letters*, 36. For the original French text see *Lettres*, vol. 1, no. 55, 100.

133. Ibid., 34. For the original French text see *Lettres*, vol. 1, no. 55, 98.

134. "Letter to his mother," 23 July 1836, in Dirvin, *A Life in Letters*, 75. For the original French text see *Lettres*, vol. 1, no. 121, 219.

135. "Letter to his mother," 11 April 1837, in Dirvin, *A Life in Letters*, 110. For the original French text see *Lettres*, vol. 1, no. 146, 260.

136. "Letter to his mother," 26 July 1839, in Dirvin, *A Life in Letters*, 165. For the original French text see *Lettres*, vol. 1, no. 207, 356.

137. C.-A. Ozanam, *Frédéric Ozanam*, 327–28. See also Cholvy, *Ozanam: L'engagement*, 352.

138. C.-A. Ozanam, *Frédéric Ozanam*, 328.

139. "Letter to François Lallier," 25 December 1839, in Dirvin, *A Life in Letters*, 171. For the original French text see *Lettres*, vol. 1, no. 221, 375.

140. Ibid. For the original French text see *Lettres*, vol. 1, no. 221, 375.

141. Ibid., 171–72. For the original French text see *Lettres*, vol. 1, no. 221, 375. See also Curnier, *La jeunesse*, 184–85.

142. Quoted in Baunard, *Ozanam*, 155. This was the date of his father's death.

143. "Letter to François Lallier," 25 December 1839, in Dirvin, *A Life in Letters*, 172. For the original French text see *Lettres*, vol. 1, no. 221, 376.

144. "Letter to Léonce Curnier," 10 October 1836, in Dirvin, *A Life in Letters*, 82. For the original French text see *Lettres*, vol. 1, no. 133, 231.

145. "Letter to Joseph Arnaud," 9 July 1839, in Dirvin, *A Life in Letters*, 164. For the original French text see *Lettres*, vol. 1, no. 205, 354.

146. See for example "Letter to his mother," 26 July 1839, in Dirvin, *A Life in Letters*, 166. For the original French text see *Lettres*, vol. 1, no. 207, 356–57.

147. Cholvy, *Ozanam: L'engagement*, 353.

148. Ibid.

149. Ibid., 354.

150. "Letter to Charles Ozanam," 28 March 1842, in Dirvin, *A Life in Letters*, 284–86. For the original French text see "Letter to Charles Ozanam," in *Lettres de Frédéric Ozanam*, vol. 2, *Premières années à la Sorbonne (1841–1844)*, édition critique de Jeanne Caron (Paris: Celse, 1978), no. 387, 271–72.

151. "Letter to Charles Ozanam," 28 March 1842, in Dirvin, *A Life in Letters*, 286. For the original French text see *Lettres*, vol. 2, no. 387, 272. Abbé Joseph Mathias Noirot was a philosophy teacher who helped Ozanam through a difficult crisis of faith in his early school days, discussed in the next chapter. See Cholvy, *Ozanam: L'engagement*, 87–91.

152. "Letter to Charles Ozanam," 28 March 1842, in Dirvin, *A Life in Letters*, 286. For the original French text see *Lettres*, vol. 2, no. 387, 272.

153. Ibid. For the original French text see *Lettres*, vol. 2, no. 387, 272.

154. Ibid. For the original French text see *Lettres*, vol. 2, no. 387, 272.

155. Quoted in O'Meara, *Ozanam*, 159. For the original French text see "Letter to Charles Ozanam," 23 June 1842, in *Lettres*, vol. 2, no. 415, 310–11.

156. "Letter to Ernest Falconnet," 22 May 1844, in Dirvin, *A Life in Letters*, 369 (emphasis in Dirvin). For the original French text see *Lettres*, vol. 2, no. 539, 535.

157. Ibid. For the original French text see *Lettres*, vol. 2, no. 539, 535–36.

CHAPTER 2. STUDENT

1. Vincent, *Ozanam*, 59.

2. "The knights of the clos Willermoz." Although Marcel Vincent uses the term "Willermoz," Ozanam refers to it as the "clos Villermez" in a letter to his mother. See "Letter to his mother," 24 February 1835, in *Lettres*, vol. 1, no. 91, 169.

3. Vincent, *Ozanam*, 61.

4. Ibid., 59–60, 63. Schimberg mistakenly locates the Ozanam home at rue Pizay no. 14. See Schimberg, *The Great Friend*, 27.

5. Vincent, *Ozanam*, 63.

6. Ibid., 64.

7. C.-A. Ozanam, *Frédéric Ozanam*, 83.

8. Vincent, *Ozanam*, 65.

9. Ibid., 64.

10. Ibid.

11. Ibid., 66.

12. Ibid., 67.

13. "Letter to Auguste Materne," 5 June 1830, in Dirvin, *A Life in Letters*, 11. For the original French text see *Lettres*, vol. 1, no. 12, 14.

14. Ibid. For the original French text see *Lettres*, vol. 1, no. 12, 14.

15. Baunard, *Ozanam*, 8.

16. Vincent, *Ozanam*, 87.

17. O'Meara, *Ozanam*, 7.

18. Vincent, *Ozanam*, 88.

19. O'Meara, *Ozanam*, 7. For samples of these verses, see C.-A. Ozanam, *Frédéric Ozanam*, 88–114.

20. Quoted in O'Meara, *Ozanam*, 7.

21. Ibid., 9. See also Vincent, *Ozanam*, 108.

22. Quoted in O'Meara, *Ozanam*, 9.

23. "Letter to Auguste Materne," 5 June 1830, in Dirvin, *A Life in Letters*, 11. For the original French text see *Lettres*, vol. 1, no. 12, 14.

24. Ozanam, *La civilisation*, in *Oeuvres complètes* (1862), vol. 1, 2. See Vincent, *Ozanam*, 112; Schimberg, *The Great Friend*, 24; C.-A. Ozanam, *Frédéric Ozanam*, 116–18.

25. O'Meara, *Ozanam*, 10.

26. Schimberg, *The Great Friend*, 26–27.

27. O'Meara, *Ozanam*, 10.

28. Quoted in Schimberg, *The Great Friend*, 27. For the original French text see "Letter to his mother," 7 May 1834, in *Lettres*, vol. 1, no. 72, 137.

29. C.-A. Ozanam, *Frédéric Ozanam*, 121.

30. Gérard Cholvy, *Frédéric Ozanam: Le christianisme a besoin de passeurs* (Perpignan: Éditions Artège, 2012), 30.

31. Schimberg, *The Great Friend*, 19.

32. Ibid., 18.

33. Ibid., 19.

34. O'Meara, *Ozanam*, 11.

35. Baunard, *Ozanam*, 14.

36. Ibid.

37. Quoted in ibid. For the original French text see Curnier, *La jeunesse*, 20–23.

38. Vincent, *Ozanam*, 116.

39. Quoted in Baunard, *Ozanam*, 14–15. For the original French text see Curnier, *La jeunesse*, 23; 26–27.

40. Quoted in ibid., 15. For the original French text see Curnier, *La jeunesse*, 27.

41. Quoted in ibid. For the original French text see Curnier, *La jeunesse*, 27–29.

42. Quoted in ibid. For the original French text see Curnier, *La jeunesse*, 29–30.

43. "Letter to Hippolyte Fortoul and Huchard," 15 January 1831, in *Lettres*, vol. 1, no. 25, 34. See Vincent, *Ozanam*, 154.

44. "Letter to Hippolyte Fortoul and Claude Huchard," 21 February 1831, in *Lettres*, vol. 5, no. 1341 [26], 17. See also "Letter to Hippolyte Fortoul and Huchard," 21 February 1831, in *Lettres*, vol. 1, no. 26, 36, and "Letter to Hippolyte Fortoul and Huchard," 15 January 1831, in *Lettres*, vol. 1, no. 25, 34–35.

45. Vincent, *Ozanam*, 154.

46. Gordon Wright, *France in Modern Times: From the Enlightenment to the Present* (Chicago: Rand McNally College Publishing Company, 1974), 182.

47. Quoted in Parker Thomas Moon, *The Labor Problem and the Social Catholic Movement in France: A Study in the History of Social Politics* (New York: Macmillan Company, 1921), 26.

48. Wright, *France in Modern Times*, 182.

49. Schimberg, *The Great Friend*, 29. See also Vincent, *Ozanam*, 158–59.

50. See chapter 6 for more information about the unrest of Lyon silk workers between 1831 and 1834.

51. Antoine Frédéric Ozanam, *An Unending Feast: A Critique of the Document of Saint-Simon*, ed. J. A. Morley (New South Wales, Australia: State Council of the Society of Saint Vincent de Paul, 1982), 6. Hereafter cited as Ozanam, *A Critique*. For the original French text see Antoine Frédéric Ozanam, "Réflexions sur la doctrine de Saint-Simon," in *Oeuvres complètes*, seconde édition (Paris: Jacques Lecoffre et Cie, 1859), vol. 7, 275.

52. Ozanam, *A Critique*, 6. For the original French text see Ozanam, "Réflexions," *Oeuvres complètes* (1859), vol. 7, 277.

53. Ibid., 17. For the original French text see Ozanam, "Réflexions," *Oeuvres complètes* (1859), vol. 7, 307.

54. Ibid., 20. For the original French text see Ozanam, "Réflexions," *Oeuvres complètes* (1859), vol. 7, 315.

55. Ibid. For the original French text see Ozanam, "Réflexions," *Oeuvres complètes* (1859), vol. 7, 315.

56. Ibid. For the original French text see Ozanam, "Réflexions," *Oeuvres complètes* (1859), vol. 7, 316.

57. Ibid. For the original French text see Ozanam, "Réflexions," *Oeuvres complètes* (1859), vol. 7, 316.

58. Ibid. For the original French text see Ozanam, "Réflexions," *Oeuvres complètes* (1859), vol. 7, 316.

59. Ibid., 29. For the original French text see Ozanam, "Réflexions," *Oeuvres complètes* (1859), vol. 7, 337–39.

60. Ibid., 30. For the original French text see Ozanam, "Réflexions," *Oeuvres complètes* (1859), vol. 7, 340.

61. Ibid., 34. For the original French text see Ozanam, "Réflexions," *Oeuvres complètes* (1859), vol. 7, 351.

62. Ibid. For the original French text see Ozanam, "Réflexions," *Oeuvres complètes* (1859), vol. 7, 351.

63. Cholvy, *Ozanam: Le christianisme*, 37. See also Schimberg, *The Great Friend*, 32.

64. Quoted in Baunard, *Ozanam*, 19. See also Schimberg, *The Great Friend*, 32, and Coates, *Ozanam*, 30.

65. Baunard, *Ozanam*, 19. *L'Avenir* was the paper of Lamennais, whose ideas inspired both Frédéric and his father. For *L'Avenir*'s review see Vincent, *Ozanam*, 163–64.

66. Quoted in Baunard, *Ozanam*, 19. François-René Châteaubriand, the famous French writer, politician, diplomat, and historian, is considered by many to be the founder of Romanticism in French literature.

67. Quoted in Baunard, *Ozanam*, 19–20.

68. Moon, *The Labor Problem*, 26. For another account of this incident, see Cholvy, *Ozanam: Le christianisme*, 36–38.

69. Baunard, *Ozanam*, 20. Baunard translates this as "what is to occupy my life." But when one looks at the original French text—"De l'idée qui doit occuper notre vie"—it appears that Ozanam is including his cousin. See "Letter to Ernest Falconnet," 4 September 1831, in *Lettres*, vol. 1, no. 32, 47. See also Coates, *Ozanam*, 29. Coates translates the phrase as "which must occupy our life."

70. Vincent, *Ozanam*, 156.

71. Quoted in Baunard, *Ozanam*, 13.

72. Jean-Claude Caron, "Frédéric Ozanam, Catholic Student (1831–1836)," *Vincentian Heritage* 30, no. 1 (2010): 29. Caron provides a figure of 5,000 in 1830 and 7,500 in 1835.

73. Ibid.

74. "Letter to his mother," 7 November 1831, in *Lettres*, vol. 1, no. 37, 54. See J.-C. Caron, "Catholic Student," 36.

75. "Letter to his father," November 1831, in *Lettres*, vol. 1, no. 40, 61. See J.-C. Caron, "Catholic Student," 36.

76. Quoted in Coates, *Ozanam*, 47. For the original French text see "Letter to Ernest Falconnet," 18 December 1831, in *Lettres*, vol. 1, no. 42, 68. This letter was started on December 18 and continued on December 29.

77. J.-C. Caron, "Catholic Student," 36–37.

78. Dirvin, *A Life in Letters*, 17n.1.

79. "Letter to his father," 12 November 1831, in Dirvin, *A Life in Letters*, 16–17. For the original French text see *Lettres*, vol. 1, no. 38, 56–57.

80. O'Meara, *Ozanam*, 48.

81. Ibid.

82. Ibid., 49.

83. Ibid., 21.

84. Curnier, *La jeunesse*, 78.

85. O'Meara, *Ozanam*, 21–22.

86. J.-C. Caron, "Catholic Student," 31. See also Louis de Carné, *Souvenirs de ma jeunesse au temps de la Restauration* (Paris: Didier et Cie, 1873), and Edmond d'Alton-Shee, *Mes Memoires (1826–1848)* (Paris: Lacroix-Verboecken, 1869), cited by Caron.

87. "Letter to Ernest Falconnet," 10 February 1832, in Dirvin, *A Life in Letters*, 17–18. For the original French text see *Lettres*, vol. 1, no. 43, 72–73.

88. Ibid., 18. For the original French text see *Lettres*, vol. 1, no. 43, 73.

89. "Letter to Ernest Falconnet," 25 March 1832, in Dirvin, *A Life in Letters*, 20. Jouffroy (1796–1842) was a philosopher who introduced Scottish philosophy to France. See ibid., 22n.1. For the original French text see *Lettres*, vol. 1, no. 44, 75.

90. Ibid., 20–21. For the original French text see *Lettres*, vol. 1, no. 44, 75.

91. Ibid., 21. For the original French text see *Lettres*, vol. 1, no. 44, 75.

92. Ibid. For the original French text see *Lettres*, vol. 1, no. 44, 76.

93. "Letter to Ernest Falconnet," 10 February 1832, in Dirvin, *A Life in Letters*, 18. For the original French text see *Lettres*, vol. 1, no. 43, 73. The original French text includes "Le système lamennaisien." Dirvin appears to make a common spelling error in his translation.

94. "Letter to Ernest Falconnet," 5–8 January 1833, in Dirvin, *A Life in Letters*, 27–28. For the original French text see *Lettres*, vol. 1, no. 53, 91–92.

95. Ibid., 27. For the original French text see *Lettres*, vol. 1, no. 53, 91.

96. Ibid. For the original French text see *Lettres*, vol. 1, no. 53, 92.

97. Ibid. For the original French text see *Lettres*, vol. 1, no. 53, 92.

98. Ibid., 28. For the original French text see *Lettres*, vol. 1, no. 53, 92.

99. Ibid. For the original French text see *Lettres*, vol. 1, no. 53, 92.

100. "Letter to Ernest Falconnet," 19 March 1833, in Dirvin, *A Life in Letters*, 31–32. For the original French text see *Lettres*, vol. 1, no. 54, 95–96.

101. J.-C. Caron, "Catholic Student," 37. For more on Ozanam and his friendships, see chapter 7 in this volume.

102. J.-C. Caron, "Catholic Student," 39.

103. O'Meara, *Ozanam*, 81–82.

104. "Letter to Henri Pessonneaux," 2 November 1834, in Dirvin, *A Life in Letters*, 50–51. For the original French text see *Lettres*, vol. 1, no. 80, 150.

105. "Letter to Ernest Falconnet," 7 January 1834, in Dirvin, *A Life in Letters*, 43. For the original French text see *Lettres*, vol. 1, no. 67, 122.

106. Thomas Auge, *Frederic Ozanam and His World* (Milwaukee: The Bruce Publishing Company, 1966), 16.

107. Baunard, *Ozanam*, 48–49.

108. Auge, *Frederic Ozanam*, 16.

109. Baunard, *Ozanam*, 49–51.

110. Ibid., 52. Lacordaire, a diocesan priest at the time, entered the Order of Preachers in 1839.

111. Auge, *Frederic Ozanam*, 18.

112. Ibid.

113. "Letter to Ferdinand Velay," 2 May 1835, in *Lettres*, vol. 1, no. 96, 180.

114. Ibid.

115. Ibid. On this episode leading to the Lenten series, see also Cholvy, *Ozanam: Le christianisme*, 54–58.

116. Ozanam recalled this later in a letter to Lallier. See "Letter to François Lallier," 17 May 1838, in Dirvin, *A Life in Letters*, 139. For the original French text see *Lettres*, vol. 1, no. 175, 305.

117. "Letter to Ernest Falconnet," 21 July 1834, in Dirvin, *A Life In Letters*, 47. For the original French text see *Lettres*, vol. 1, no. 77, 143.

118. Baunard, *Ozanam*, 86–87.

119. Quoted in O'Meara, *Ozanam*, 82. For the original French text see "Letter to his mother," 16 May 1834, in *Lettres*, vol. 1, no. 73, 135–36.

120. Baunard, *Ozanam*, 88, 91.

121. Quoted in Baunard, *Ozanam*, 90. For the original French text see "Letter to his mother," 8 February 1835, in *Lettres*, vol. 1, no. 89, 163–64.

122. Quoted in Hess, *Cahiers Ozanam*, 100. For the original French text see "Letter to his parents," 12 August 1835, in *Lettres*, vol. 1, no. 101, 187.

123. "Letter to his parents," 12 August 1835, in *Lettres*, vol. 1, no. 101, 186–87.

124. Hess, *Cahiers Ozanam*, 99. For the original French text see "Letter to his mother," 26 May 1832, in *Lettres*, vol. 1, no. 47, 81.

125. J.-C. Caron, "Catholic Student," 38.

126. Ibid.

127. Ibid., 33.

128. Hess, *Cahiers Ozanam*, 99. For the original French text see "Letter to his mother," 24 February 1835, in *Lettres*, vol. 1, no. 91, 171.

129. Ibid. For the original French text see "Letter to his mother," 23 May 1835, in *Lettres*, vol. 1, no. 98, 184.

130. James Patrick Derum, *Apostle in a Top Hat: The Inspiring Story of Frederick Ozanam, Founder of the Society of Saint Vincent de Paul* (St. Clair, MI: Fidelity Publishing Company, 1962).

131. Ibid., 22.

132. See "Top Hat," *Fashion Encyclopedia*. http://www.fashionencyclopedia.com/.

133. Baunard, *Ozanam*, 114–15.

134. O'Meara, *Ozanam*, 99.

135. "Letter to François Lallier," 5 November 1836, in Dirvin, *A Life in Letters*, 92. For the original French text see *Lettres*, vol. 1, no. 136, 239–40.

136. "Letter to Louis Janmot," 13 November 1836, in Dirvin, *A Life in Letters*, 97. For the original French text see *Lettres*, vol. 1, no. 137, 244–45.

137. "Letter to François Lallier," 5 October 1837, in Dirvin, *A Life in Letters*, 116. For the original French text see *Lettres*, vol. 1, no. 160, 279.

138. Ibid. For the original French text see *Lettres*, vol. 1, no. 160, 279–80. The term *écu* originally refers to various gold and silver coins of France that were issued between the thirteenth and eighteenth centuries and bore the image of a shield. The *écu* disappeared during the French Revolution, but five-franc silver coins minted in the nineteenth century were still referred to as *écu* by the French people. See John Porteous, *Coins in History* (New York: Putnam Publishing Group, 1969).

139. "Letter to Henri Pessonneaux," 7 February 1838, in Dirvin, *A Life in Letters*, 132. For the original French text see *Lettres*, vol. 1, no. 170, 297.

140. "Letter to François Lallier," 9 April 1838, in Dirvin, *A Life in Letters*, 134. For the original French text see *Lettres*, vol. 1, no. 173, 300–301. *Res angusta domi* is a Latin phrase that means narrowed circumstances at home, that is, limited means.

141. Ibid. For the original French text see *Lettres*, vol. 1, no. 173, 301.

142. Baunard, *Ozanam*, 155.

143. See Eugène Galopin, *Essai de bibliographie chronologique sur Antoine-Frédéric Ozanam (1813–1853)* (Paris: Société D'Édition "Les Belles Lettres," 1933), 63, 70, 73–75, respectively. These works will be discussed at greater length in chapter 5, on Ozanam as a scholar.

CHAPTER 3. THE SOCIETY OF ST. VINCENT DE PAUL

1. Cholvy, *Ozanam: Le christianisme*, 62. The address is today 38 and is marked by a commemorative plaque on the side of the building.

2. Vincent, *Ozanam*, 264.

3. C.-A. Ozanam, *Frédéric Ozanam*, 187–89. See also Cholvy, *Ozanam: Le christianisme*, 59–60, and O'Meara, *Ozanam*, 59–60.

4. Cholvy, *Ozanam: Le christianisme*, 62.

5. See Joseph H. Fichter, S.J., *Roots of Change* (New York and London: D. Appleton-Century Company, 1939), 125.

6. Cholvy, *Ozanam: Le christianisme*, 47, 62. See also Ralph Middlecamp, "Lives of Distinction—Ozanam's Cofounders of the Society of St. Vincent de Paul," available at http://famvin.org/wiki/SVDP_-_Founders. Ralph Middlecamp, a member of the Society of St. Vincent de Paul for over thirty years, has spent many years researching the early days of the Society and has contributed to the Vincentian Encyclopedia on the Vincentian Family website (Famvin).

7. Cholvy, *Ozanam: Le christianisme*, 60.

8. Charles L. Souvay, C.M., "The Society of St. Vincent de Paul as an Agency of Reconstruction," *Catholic Historical Review* 7:4 (1922): 443.

9. Louise Sullivan, D.C., *Sister Rosalie Rendu: A Daughter of Charity on Fire with Love for the Poor* (Chicago: Vincentian Studies Institute, 2006), 201–2. See also Middlecamp, "Lives of Distinction," 3.

10. Baunard, *Ozanam*, 57.

11. Sullivan, *Sister Rosalie*, 200–201. See also Cholvy, *Ozanam: Le christianisme*, 47, and Middlecamp, "Lives of Distinction," 3–5.

12. One historian, Catherine Duprat, sees the Society of St. Vincent de Paul as originally an exact replica of the Society of Good Works. See Cholvy, *Ozanam: Le christianisme*, 60. See also Matthieu Brejon de Lavergnée, *La Société de Saint-Vincent de-Paul au XIXe siècle: Un fleuron du catholicisme social* (Paris: Les Éditions du Cerf, 2008), 118.

13. Baunard, *Ozanam*, 71.

14. Vincent, *Ozanam*, 265.

15. Gérard Cholvy, "Frédéric Ozanam and the Challenges of the Times," *Society of St. Vincent de Paul Bulletin of News* (13 February 2009), 2.

16. Cholvy, *Ozanam: Le christianisme*, 61–62.

17. Ibid., 62–63.

18. Sullivan, *Sister Rosalie*, 206. See also Middlecamp, "Lives of Distinction," 12.

19. Middlecamp, "Lives of Distinction," 6. See also Cholvy, *Ozanam: Le christianisme*, 63. "Lazarist" is the name given in France to the Congregation of the Mission priests who were founded by Saint Vincent de Paul. In Paris they were originally located in the priory of St. Lazarus.

20. Baunard, *Ozanam*, 67.

21. Cholvy, *Ozanam: Le christianisme*, 63.

22. Sullivan, *Sister Rosalie*, 205.

23. "Letter to Léonce Curnier," 4 November 1834, in Dirvin, *A Life in Letters*, 56. For the original French text see *Lettres*, vol. 1, no. 82, 155.

24. Lacordaire, *My Friend*, 32–33.

25. Cholvy, *Ozanam: Le christianisme*, 65.

26. See *Lettres de Frédéric Ozanam: Deuxième supplément*, édition critique sous la direction de Didier Ozanam (Paris: Société de Saint-Vincent-De-Paul, 2013), vol. 6, no. 1457 [76 bis], 1n.1.

27. "Report On Charity, Friday, June 27, 1834," 3. http://famvin.org /wiki/Society_of_St._Vincent_de_Paul_First_Written_Report. For the original French text see "Rapport sur les travaux de la Société de Saint-Vincent-De-Paul depuis les origines," in *Lettres*, vol. 6, no. 1457 [76 bis], 3.

28. "Report On Charity, 1834," 3. For the original French text see "Rapport," *Lettres*, vol. 6, no. 1457 [76 bis], 3.

29. Souvay, "The Society of St. Vincent de Paul," 445.

30. Ibid., 446.

31. Brejon de Lavergnée, *La Société de Saint-Vincent de-Paul*, 599–600.

32. "Report On Charity, 1834," 3–4. For the original French text see "Rapport," *Lettres*, vol. 6, no. 1457 [76 bis], 4.

33. Ibid., 4–5. For the original French text see "Rapport," *Lettres*, vol. 6, no. 1457 [76 bis], 5–6.

34. Ibid., 5. For the original French text see "Rapport," *Lettres*, vol. 6, no. 1457 [76 bis], 7.

35. Ibid., 6. For the original French text see "Rapport," *Lettres*, vol. 6, no. 1457 [76 bis], 8. Bracketed translation is mine.

36. Sullivan, *Sister Rosalie*, 215.

37. Ibid., 219.

38. "Letter to François Lallier," 17 May 1838, in Dirvin, *A Life in Letters*, 143. For the original French text see *Lettres*, vol. 1, no. 175, 308–9.

39. Sullivan, *Sister Rosalie*, 215.

40. See also *Rules of the Society of St. Vincent de Paul, and Indulgences*, Printed for the Council of New York (New York: D. & J. Sadlier & Co., 1869), 10. This

publication includes the original Rule of 1835 in translation. Hereafter cited as *Rules of the Society 1835*. http://archive.org/stream/rulesandindulge00paulgoog #page/n4/mode/2up.

41. "Letter to Emmanuel Bailly," 20 November 1834, in Dirvin, *A Life in Letters*, 59. For the original French text see *Lettres*, vol. 1, no. 85, 158.

42. Cholvy, *Ozanam: Le christianisme*, 67.

43. Sullivan, *Sister Rosalie*, 214.

44. Baunard, *Ozanam*, 93.

45. Ibid., 93–94.

46. Ibid., 94–95.

47. Fagan, *Frédéric Ozanam*, 69.

48. Sister Louise Sullivan suggests that Bailly, Lallier, and Ozanam "were charged with the task." And she further emphasizes that as early as 1834 Ozanam "had clearly seen the need for greater organization." See Sullivan, *Sister Rosalie*, 221. Edward O'Connor argues convincingly that, at the very least, the concluding portion of the Rule was composed by Ozanam. See Edward O'Connor, S. J., *The Secret of Frederick Ozanam: Founder of the Society of St. Vincent de Paul* (Dublin: M. H. Gill and Son, 1953), 56. According to Baunard, Ozanam "was actively engaged in conjunction with Lallier, in the drawing-up of the Rule of the Society of St. Vincent de Paul." See Baunard, *Ozanam*, 106.

49. *Rules of the Society 1835*, 9. Quoted also in Sullivan, *Sister Rosalie*, 222. Original in Society of Saint Vincent de Paul, *Règlement de la Société de Saint Vincent de Paul* (Paris: Imprimerie de E-J Bailly et Compagnie, 1835), 5–6. Hereafter cited as *Règlement de la Société*.

50. During the seventeenth century both Vincent de Paul and Louise de Marillac collaborated on various charitable works. Their practice was to see what worked first, in order to be certain of its efficacy and its divine approval, before forming any rules or guidelines.

51. *Rules of the Society 1835*, 11–12. Quoted also in Sullivan, *Sister Rosalie*, 223. Original in *Règlement de la Société*, 8–9.

52. *Rules of the Society 1835*, 13–14.

53. Ibid., 14.

54. Ibid. Discussion of this matter appears from time to time in the minutes of meetings. Carol E. Harrison is rather critical of the Society's concerns over this issue. See her *Romantic Catholics: France's Postrevolutionary Generation in Search of a Modern Faith* (Ithaca, NY: Cornell University Press, 2014), 205–6.

55. *Rules of the Society 1835*, 20–21. For a fuller discussion of this issue see chapter 6 in this volume.

56. *Rules of the Society 1835*, 14–15.

57. Ibid., 15–16.

58. Ibid., 16–17. On these virtues see also Sullivan, *Sister Rosalie*, 222–24; *Règlement de la Société*, 7–10.

59. *Rules of the Society 1835*, 17.

60. Ibid., 20.

61. For the source of the original French text see Amélie Ozanam-Soulacroix, *Notes biographique sur Frédéric Ozanam*, edition established by Raphaëlle Chevalier-Motariol, in Faculté de théologie Université catholique de Lyon, *Frédéric Ozanam: Actes du Colloque des 4 et 5 décembre 1998* (Paris: Bayard, 2001), 334. Hereafter cited as Amélie Ozanam-Soulacroix, *Notes biographique*, and *Actes du Colloque*, respectively. "Septembrist Jacobin": The Jacobins were a radical political group during the French Revolution. Septembrist refers to the September Massacres of 1792 during the French Revolution. Mob violence broke out and the prisons were emptied, with many prisoners massacred. Some twelve hundred prisoners, including many women and young children, lost their lives. One classic study of this event is Pierre Caron, *Les massacres de septembre* (Paris: La Maison du Livre Français, 1935).

62. Amélie Ozanam-Soulacroix, *Notes biographique*, in *Actes du Colloque*, 334.

63. Article 3 in *Rules of the Society 1835*, 25. Brejon de Lavergnée provides an excellent organizational diagram or flowchart based on the Rule in his *La Société de Saint-Vincent de-Paul*, 219.

64. Article 2 in *Rules of the Society 1835*, 25.

65. Article 4 in ibid., 25–26.

66. The conference could have more than one vice-president. See Articles 8 and 27 in ibid., 26–27 and 32, respectively.

67. Articles 27 and 29 in ibid., 32–33. Special works are those activities intended to support the work of the conference, such as a special outreach to prisoners, a library for soldiers, apprenticeship programs, and so forth.

68. Article 5 in ibid., 26.

69. Articles 36 and 37 in ibid., 34–35.

70. Article 38 in ibid., 35.

71. Article 45 in ibid., 37. Pope Paul VI moved his feast day from July 19 to September 27.

72. Article 48 in ibid., 38.

73. *Rules of the Society 1835*, 12.

74. Article 53 in ibid., 39.

75. Brejon de Lavergnée, *La Société de Saint-Vincent de-Paul*, 53.

76. "Letter to his mother," 23 July 1836, in Dirvin, *A Life in Letters*, 76. For the original French text see *Lettres*, vol. 1, no. 121, 220.

77. Ibid. For the original French text see *Lettres*, vol. 1, no. 121, 220.

78. Ibid. For the original French text see *Lettres*, vol. 1, no. 121, 220.

79. Brejon de Lavergnée, *La Société de Saint-Vincent de-Paul*, 93.

80. "Letter to François Lallier," 5 October 1837, in Dirvin, *A Life in Letters*, 120. For the original French text see *Lettres*, vol. 1, no. 160, 283.

81. Cholvy, *Ozanam: Le christianisme*, 77.

82. C.-A. Ozanam, *Frédéric Ozanam*, 229.

83. Not all conferences were officially aggregated with the Council-General. Following is a list of cities of the United States in the order of official aggregation of their older conferences over the fifteen-year period from 1846 to 1861. This list is found in Souvay, "The Society of St. Vincent de Paul," 451.

St. Louis, MO, Conference of the Cathedral	February 2, 1846
New York, NY, Conference of St. Patrick	March 27, 1848
Lockport, NY	October 28, 1848
Buffalo, NY, Conference of the Cathedral	November 28, 1848
Utica, NY	September 17, 1849
Milwaukee, WI, Conference of the Cathedral	March 25, 1850
New Orleans, LA, Conference of St. Patrick	June 20, 1853
Brooklyn, NY, Conference of St. James	May 26, 1856
Seneca Falls, NY	January 25, 1858
Rochester, NY, Conference of St. Patrick	January 25, 1858
Philadelphia, PA, Conference of St. Joseph	February 22, 1858
Albany, NY, Conference of the Immaculate Conception	July 12, 1858
Jersey City, NJ, Conference of St. Peter	July 12, 1858
St. Paul, MN	October 4, 1858
Chicago, IL	November 1, 1858
Cincinnati, OH, Conference of St. Peter	January 3, 1859
Dubuque, IA, Conference of St. Raphael	April 11, 1859
Newark, NJ	June 27, 1859
Washington, DC	January 16, 1860
Louisville, KY, Conference of the Cathedral	August 25, 1861

84. C.-A. Ozanam, *Frédéric Ozanam*, 225. See also Auge, *Frederic Ozanam*, 25.

85. Brejon de Lavergnée, *La Société de Saint-Vincent de-Paul*, 598.

86. "Letter to his mother," 23 July 1836, in Dirvin, *A Life in Letters*, 77. For the original French text see *Lettres*, vol. 1, no. 121, 221.

87. Brejon de Lavergnée, *La Société de Saint-Vincent de-Paul*, 416.

88. Ibid., 353. The *petite bourgeoisie* were the lower middle class, such as small business owners, tradespeople, artisans, and craft workers.

89. For a fuller treatment of the backgrounds of members, see ibid., 354–417.

90. Ibid., 417.

91. Ibid., 478.

92. "Letter to Léonce Curnier," 23 February 1835, in Dirvin, *A Life in Letters*, 64. For the original French text see *Lettres*, vol. 1, no. 90, 166.

93. "Letter to Mademoiselle Soulacroix," 1 May 1841, in Dirvin, *A Life in Letters*, 243. For the original French text see *Lettres*, vol. 2, no. 310, 137.

94. Quoted in Hess, *Cahiers Ozanam*, 116. For the original French text see "Letter to his wife," 6–7 August 1842, in *Lettres*, vol. 2, no. 430, 344.

95. Ibid. For the original French text see *Lettres*, vol. 2, no. 430, 344.

96. Ibid., 116–17. For the original French text see Amélie Ozanam-Soulacroix, *Notes biographique*, in *Actes du Colloque*, 333–34.

97. Ibid., 117. For the original French text see Amélie Ozanam-Soulacroix, *Notes biographique*, in *Actes du Colloque*, 332–33.

98. Ibid., 117–18. For the original French text see Amélie Ozanam-Soulacroix, *Notes biographique*, in *Actes du Colloque*, 334–35.

99. Ibid., 118. For the original French text see Amélie Ozanam-Soulacroix, *Notes biographique*, in *Actes du Colloque*, 335.

100. Didier Ozanam, "Frederic Ozanam," in Hess, *Cahiers Ozanam*, 17.

101. Pope Paul VI, *Decree on the Apostolate of the Laity, Apostolicam Actuositatem*, November 18, 1965, no. 2. http://www.vatican.va/.

102. "Letter to Léonce Curnier," 23 February 1835, in Dirvin, *A Life in Letters*, 64. For the original French text see *Lettres*, vol. 1, no. 90, 166–67.

103. Ibid., 64–65. For the original French text see *Lettres*, vol. 1, no. 90, 167.

104. Ibid., 65. For the original French text see *Lettres*, vol. 1, no. 90, 167.

105. "Letter to Léonce Curnier," 29 October 1835, in Dirvin, *A Life in Letters*, 72. For the original French text see *Lettres*, vol. 1, no. 107, 197.

106. Quoted in O'Meara, *Ozanam*, 191. For the original French text see "Letter to François Lallier," 7 August 1846, in *Lettres de Frédéric Ozanam*, vol. 3, *L'engagement (1845–1849)*, édition critique sous la direction de Didier Ozanam (Paris: Celse, 1978), no. 694, 207.

107. Brejon de Lavergnée, *La Société de Saint-Vincent de-Paul*, 172–73.

108. Ibid., 172. For this phrase of Ozanam's, see "Letter to Dominique Meynis," 25 August 1845, in *Lettres*, vol. 3, no. 638, 122. The Society for the Propagation of the Faith had been started in Lyon by Pauline Jaricot in 1822 to advance the faith through missionary activity. Ozanam edited its *Annals* or reports until 1848. For more information see Edward John Hickey, *The Society for the Propagation of the Faith: Its Foundation, Organization, and Success (1822–1922)* (Washington, DC: Catholic University of America, 1922).

109. The biretta is the name given to a hat once regularly worn by priests. *Paroles d'un croyant* is a work written by Lamennais in 1834 that was condemned by the pope; see also chapter 6.

110. "Letter to François Lallier," 1 August 1838, in Dirvin, *A Life in Letters*, 150–51. For the original French text see *Lettres*, vol. 1, no. 181, 319–20.

111. "Letter to François Lallier," 11 August 1838, in Dirvin, *A Life in Letters*, 151–52. For the original French text see *Lettres*, vol. 1, no. 182, 320.

112. Ibid., 152. For the original French text see *Lettres*, vol. 1, no. 182, 320.

113. Ibid. For the original French text see *Lettres*, vol. 1, no. 182, 320.

114. For these five recommendations see ibid., 152–53. For the original French text see *Lettres*, vol. 1, no. 182, 320–21.

115. "Letter to Joseph Arthaud," 9 July 1839, in Dirvin, *A Life in Letters*, 163. For the original French text see *Lettres*, vol. 1, no. 205, 353.

116. *Rules of the Society 1835*, 10–11.

117. "Aux Conférences de Saint-Vincent-De-Paul," 11 June 1844, in *Lettres*, vol. 5, no. 1403 [540 bis], 112. On the issue of the founding see also Sacra Congregatio Pro Causis Sanctorum Officium Historicum, *Frederici Ozanam, Patris Familias Primarii Fondatoris Societatis Conferentiarum S. Vincentii a Paulo, Disquisitio de Vita et Actuositate Servi Dei* (Rome, 1980), 309–45. Hereafter cited as *Disquisitio*.

118. Vincent, *Ozanam*, 267. For a fuller discussion of the controversy that ensued see 260–73.

119. Lacordaire, *My Friend*, 32. Brejon de Lavergnée looks at the founding time (1833–35) and the collective acts of the founding group as a way of examining the early history of the Society. He thus bypasses the controversial debate on the exact date of foundation and the selection of the founder, although he recognizes Ozanam's premier contribution. See his *La Société de Saint-Vincent de-Paul*, 335–630.

120. Charles Mercier, *La Société de Saint-Vincent-de-Paul: Une mémoire des origins en movement, 1833–1914* (Paris: L'Harmattan, 2006), 38. Mercier looks at three periods in the development of the Society: 1833–53, 1853–56, and 1856–1913. Each period has its own story, with 1853–56 being the period of controversy over the foundation.

121. In 1842 Louis Veuillot became editor of the Paris daily *L'Univers*. For nearly four decades he was a highly influential figure in modern French religious history. A convert to Catholicism, he became a fanatical champion of the Catholic cause and saw himself as the opponent of any kind of liberal thought or free-thinking. For more on Veuillot see chapter 6.

122. Léonce Celier, "Ozanam and the Society of Saint Vincent de Paul," in Hess, *Cahiers Ozanam*, 64–65. For the original French text see Antoine Frédéric Ozanam, "Des devoirs littéraires des chrétiens," in *Oeuvres complètes*, quatrième édition (Paris: Lecoffre Fils et Cie, 1872), vol. 7, 165.

123. Celier, "Ozanam and the Society of Saint Vincent de Paul," in Hess, *Cahiers Ozanam*, 65.

124. Ibid., 66.

125. Ibid.

126. Ibid.

127. Quoted in Baunard, *Ozanam*, 70. For the original French text see C.-A. Ozanam, *Frédéric Ozanam*, 208–9.

128. Quoted in Baunard, *Ozanam*, 66–67.

129. Middlecamp, "Lives of Distinction," 9.

130. Léonce Celier, "Ozanam and the Society of Saint Vincent de Paul," in Hess, *Cahiers Ozanam*, 63.

131. In the *Disquisitio* this letter is dated 1883, but Baunard dates the letter 1888 and indicates that it was written to Ozanam's brother Alphonse. The *Disquisitio* contains the following remark about Lamache's letter: "We think that Lamache touched upon the heart of this history of the Society of Saint Vincent de Paul." See *Disquisitio*, 345. See also Baunard, *Ozanam*, 70.

132. Léonce Celier, "Ozanam and the Society of Saint Vincent de Paul," in Hess, *Cahiers Ozanam*, 67. For a fuller discussion of this issue see Léon De Lanzac de Laborie, "Le Fondateur de la Société de Saint-Vincent-de-Paul," in G. Goyau et al., *Ozanam, Livre du Centenaire* (Paris: Gabriel Beauchesne, 1913), 97–150.

133. Cholvy, "Ozanam and the Challenges," 2.

134. Society of Saint Vincent de Paul, *Rule of the International Confederation of the Society of St. Vincent De Paul* (2003), I, 6. Hereafter cited as *International Rule*. For other discussions of this episode see Charles Mercer, "Frédéric Ozanam: Constructions et déconstructions d'une image," in *Frédéric Ozanam (1813–1853): Un universitaire chrétien face à la modernité*, ed. Bernard Barbiche and Christine Franconnet (Paris: Les Éditions du Cerf; Bibliothèque Nationale de France, 2006), 137–62. See also Cholvy, *Ozanam: L'engagement*, 296–309.

135. Mercier, *La Société*, 119–20.

136. Ibid., 120.

137. "Letter to Léonce Curnier," 4 November 1834, in Dirvin, *A Life in Letters*, 56. For the original French text see *Lettres*, vol. 1, no. 82, 155.

138. "Letter to Gustav Colas de la Noue," 24 November 1835, in *Lettres*, vol. 1, no. 111, 206.

CHAPTER 4. HUSBAND AND FATHER

1. "Letter to François Lallier," 28 June 1841, in Dirvin, *A Life in Letters*, 269. For the original French text see *Lettres*, vol. 2, no. 331, 184.

2. Some genealogies place Amélie's birth on August 14, 1821. Gérard Cholvy indicates that she was born on August 15. See his *Ozanam: L'engagement*, 418. But at least one scholar suggests that she was born in 1820. For the latter position see Agnès Walch, "Frédéric et Amélie Ozanam: Un itinéraire matrimonial exemplaire," in Barbiche and Franconnet, *Frédéric Ozanam (1813–1853)*, 77.

3. "Letter to Léonce Curnier," 29 October 1835, in Dirvin, *A Life in Letters*, 72. For the original French text see *Lettres*, vol. 1, no. 107, 197–98.

4. Ibid. For the original French text see *Lettres*, vol. 1, no. 107, 198.

5. Ibid. For the original French text see *Lettres*, vol. 1, no. 107, 198.

6. Ibid. For the original French text see *Lettres*, vol. 1, no. 107, 198.

7. Ibid. For the original French text see *Lettres*, vol. 1, no. 107, 198.

8. Quoted in Baunard, *Ozanam*, 177. For the original French text see "Letter to Henri Pessonneaux," 21 September 1835, in *Lettres*, vol. 1, no. 103, 188.

9. "Letter to François Lallier," 5 October 1837, in Dirvin, *A Life in Letters*, 117–18. For the original French text see *Lettres*, vol. 1, no. 160, 280–81.

10. Cholvy, *Ozanam: L'engagement*, 228.

11. "Letter to François Lallier," 10 November 1834, in *Lettres*, vol. 5, no. 1347 [84 bis], 28.

12. Cholvy, *Ozanam: L'engagement*, 229–31, 330–33.

13. "Letter to Auguste Le Taillandier," 19 August 1838, in Dirvin, *A Life in Letters*, 154. For the original French text see *Lettres*, vol. 1, no. 183, 322–23.

14. "Letter to François Lallier," 25 December 1839, in Dirvin, *A Life in Letters*, 172. For the original French text see *Lettres*, vol. 1, no. 221, 376.

15. See "Letter to Lacordaire," 26 August 1839, in Dirvin, *A Life in Letters*, 167–69. For the original French text see *Lettres*, vol. 1, no. 211, 359–61.

16. Cholvy, *Ozanam: L'engagement*, 330–31. English text quoted in Reverend Yves Danjou, C.M., "Fr. Eugène Boré, C.M. (1809–1878): Scholarship in the Service of the Faith," trans. John E. Rybolt, C.M., *Vincentiana* 50:5 (September–October 2006): 363. http://cmglobal.org/vincentiana-novus-en/files/downloads/2006_5/vt_2006_05_12_en.pdf.

17. Quoted in Cholvy, *Ozanam: L'engagement*, 331.

18. Baunard, *Ozanam*, 180.

19. "Letter to Henri Pessonneaux," 13 March 1840, in Dirvin, *A Life in Letters*, 177. For the original French text see *Lettres*, vol. 1, no. 227, 393–94.

20. "Letter to François Lallier," 21–28 June 1840, in Dirvin, *A Life in Letters*, 187. For the original French text see *Lettres*, vol. 1, no. 241, 408.

21. Baunard, *Ozanam*, 181. See also C.-A. Ozanam, *Frédéric Ozanam*, 355–56.

22. Baunard, *Ozanam*, 181.

23. Ibid., 182. There is direct evidence that this description is quite accurate. Ozanam reiterates these strong feelings for Amélie in a letter written on December 22, 1840, when he was in Paris and separated from her. He speaks of the "charm of her presence." He refers to her as an "adored image" in his mind and as "an angelic figure who has taken possession of the sanctuary of his heart." At the end of the letter, he proclaims that he is her "obedient servant." See *Lettres*, vol. 2, no. 272, 35–38.

24. Baunard, *Ozanam*, 182.

25. Schimberg, *The Great Friend*, 154.

26. Baunard, *Ozanam*, 182.

27. Ibid., 183.

28. Schimberg, *The Great Friend*, 132.

29. O'Meara, *Ozanam*, 134. For the original French text of Ozanam's account of this ordeal, quoted in O'Meara, see "Letter to François Lallier," 20 October 1840, in *Lettres*, vol. 1, no. 258, 432–33.

30. Scholiasts were scholars who wrote commentaries on ancient Greek and Latin texts.

31. Schimberg, *The Great Friend*, 133.

32. Cholvy, *Ozanam: Le christianisme*, 90. As described in chapter 2, Jean-Jacques Ampère was the son of André-Marie Ampère, at whose home Ozanam lived when he first came to Paris.

33. Quoted in Baunard, *Ozanam*, 184. For the original French text see "Letter to François Lallier," 14 October 1840, in *Lettres*, vol. 1, no. 257, 425.

34. "Letter to François Lallier," 14 October 1840, in *Lettres*, vol. 1, no. 257, 425.

35. Cholvy, *Ozanam: Le christianisme*, 90. See also Schimberg, *The Great Friend*, 133–34.

36. Baunard, *Ozanam*, 184.

37. Ibid.

38. Quoted in ibid.

39. C.-A. Ozanam, *Frédéric Ozanam*, 356.

40. Cholvy, *Ozanam: Le christianisme*, 91.

41. Quoted in Baunard, *Ozanam*, 183. For the original French text see C.-A. Ozanam, *Frédéric Ozanam*, 357.

42. C.-A. Ozanam, *Frédéric Ozanam*, 357.

43. Tarrazi and Ramson, *Ozanam*, 18.

44. Quoted in Hess, *Cahiers Ozanam*, 101. For the original French text see "Letter to François Lallier," 6 December 1840, in *Lettres*, vol. 1, no. 265, 440.

45. "Letter to François Lallier," 6 December 1840, in *Lettres*, vol. 1, no. 265, 440.

46. "Letter to Antoine Frédéric Ozanam," 7 February 1841. This letter is quoted by Xavier Lacroix, "Frédéric Ozanam, amourex, époux et père," in *Actes du Colloque*, 194.

47. "Letter to Antoine Frédéric Ozanam," 20 February 1841. This letter is quoted by Lacroix, "Frédéric Ozanam, amourex," in *Actes du Colloque*, 196.

48. "Letter to Mademoiselle Soulacroix," 24 January 1841, in Dirvin, *A Life in Letters*, 204. For the original French text see *Lettres*, vol. 2, no. 280, 55.

49. Ibid., 204–5; For the original French text see *Lettres*, vol. 2, no. 280, 56.

50. Ibid., 208; For the original French text see *Lettres*, vol. 2, no. 280, 59–60.

51. "Letter to Mademoiselle Soulacroix," 30 January 1841, in Dirvin, *A Life in Letters*, 210. For the original French text see *Lettres*, vol. 2, no. 281, 62.

52. Ibid. For the original French text see *Lettres*, vol. 2, no. 281, 62.

53. Walch, "Frédéric et Amélie Ozanam," in Barbiche and Franconnet, *Frédéric Ozanam (1813–1853)*, 79–80.

54. "Letter to Mademoiselle Soulacroix," 6 February 1841, in Dirvin, *A Life in Letters*, 211. For the original French text see *Lettres*, vol. 2, no. 282, 63.

55. Ibid., 212. For the original French text see *Lettres*, vol. 2, no. 282, 64.

56. Ibid., 212–13. For the original French text see *Lettres*, vol. 2, no. 282, 64.

57. Ibid., 214–15. For the original French text see *Lettres*, vol. 2, no. 282, 67.

58. "Letter to Mademoiselle Soulacroix," 28 February 1841, in Dirvin, *A Life in Letters*, 225; see also 225n.3. For the original French text see *Lettres*, vol. 2, no. 290, 89.

59. Ibid., 225. For the original French text see *Lettres*, vol. 2, no. 290, 89.

60. "Letter to Mademoiselle Soulacroix," 13 May 1841, in Dirvin, *A Life in Letters*, 254. For the original French text see *Lettres*, vol. 2, no. 313, 149.

61. "Letter to Mademoiselle Soulacroix," 17 March 1841, in Dirvin, *A Life in Letters*, 227. For the original French text see *Lettres*, vol. 2, no. 298, 109.

62. "Letter to Mademoiselle Soulacroix," 26 April 1841, in Dirvin, *A Life in Letters*, 233–34. For the original French text see *Lettres*, vol. 2, no. 307, 126–27.

63. "Letter to Mademoiselle Soulacroix," 1 May 1841, in Dirvin, *A Life in Letters*, 241–42. For the original French text see *Lettres*, vol. 2, no. 310, 135.

64. Ibid., 242. For the original French text see *Lettres*, vol. 2, no. 310, 136.

65. Ibid., 244. For the original French text see *Lettres*, vol. 2, no. 310, 138–39.

66. Ibid., 243. For the original French text see *Lettres*, vol. 2, no. 310, 139.

67. Ibid., 245. For the original French text see *Lettres*, vol. 2, no. 310, 139–40.

68. Ibid., 246. For the original French text see *Lettres*, vol. 2, no. 310, 140.

69. "Letter to Antoine Frédéric Ozanam," 28 February 1841. This letter is quoted by Lacroix, "Frédéric Ozanam, amourex," in *Actes du Colloque*, 193.

70. Quoted in Hess, *Cahiers Ozanam*, 101–2. For the original French text see "Letter to Mademoiselle Soulacroix," 6 March 1841, in *Lettres*, vol. 2, no. 292, 92.

71. See "Letter to Mademoiselle Soulacroix," 2 May 1841, in Dirvin, *A Life in Letters*, 247. For the original French text see *Lettres*, vol. 2, no. 311, 141. This letter is dated 2 May by Ozanam, but is really 3 May.

72. "Letter to Mademoiselle Soulacroix," 8 May 1841, in Dirvin, *A Life in Letters*, 250. For the original French text see *Lettres*, vol. 2, no. 312, 144.

73. Ibid. For the original French text see *Lettres*, vol. 2, no. 312, 144.

74. Quoted in Hess, *Cahiers Ozanam*, 102. For the original French text see "Letter to Mademoiselle Soulacroix," in *Lettres*, vol. 2, no. 327, 179–80.

75. "Letter to Antoine Frédéric Ozanam," 12 June 1841. This letter is quoted by Lacroix, "Frédéric Ozanam, amourex," in *Actes du Colloque*, 198.

76. "Letter of Zélie Soulacroix, mother of Amélie, to her own mother, Joséphine Magagnos," 5 July 1841, in Amélie Ozanam-Soulacroix, *Notes biographique*, in *Actes du Colloque*, 328.

77. Baunard, *Ozanam*, 186. For the original French text see "Letter to François Lallier," 28 June 1841, in *Lettres*, vol. 1, no. 331, 184.

78. "Letter to Auguste Le Taillandier," 19 August 1838, in Dirvin, *A Life in Letters*, 154. For the original French text see *Lettres*, vol. 1, no. 183, 322–23.

79. Baunard, *Ozanam*, 186. For the original French text see "Letter to François Lallier," 28 June 1841, in *Lettres*, vol. 1, no. 331, 184.

80. "Letter of Zélie Soulacroix, mother of Amélie, to her own mother, Joséphine Magagnos," 5 July 1841, in Amélie Ozanam-Soulacroix, *Notes biographique*, in *Actes du Colloque*, 329.

81. Most Reverend Jacques Martin, "The Humour of Pope Pius IX," *L'Osservatore Romano* (23 March 1978), 8. Martin was Prefect of the Pontifical Household. https://www.ewtn.com/library/MARY/P9HUMOR.HTM.

82. O'Meara, *Ozanam*, 143. For the original French text see "Letter to François Lallier," 28 June 1841, in *Lettres*, vol. 1, no. 331, 185.

83. Baunard, *Ozanam*, 186. For the original French text see "Letter to François Lallier," 28 June 1841, in *Lettres*, vol. 1, no. 331, 185. See also Dirvin, *A Life in Letters*, 269.

84. "Letter to François Lallier," 28 June 1841, in *Lettres*, vol. 1, no. 331, 185. See also O'Meara, *Ozanam*, 143, and Dirvin, *A Life in Letters*, 269.

85. Baunard, *Ozanam*, 187–88. See also O'Meara, *Ozanam*, 145–46.

86. "Letter to Henri Pessonneaux," 12 November 1841, in Dirvin, *A Life in Letters*, 277. For the original French text see *Lettres*, vol. 2, no. 365, 233.

87. "Letter to M. and Mme. Soulacroix," 15 November 1841, in Dirvin, *A Life in Letters*, 279. For the original French text see *Lettres*, vol. 2, no. 366, 235–36.

88. Ibid. For the original French text see *Lettres*, vol. 2, no. 366, 236.

89. Baunard, *Ozanam*, 188.

90. Schimberg, *The Great Friend*, 146.

91. Quoted in Hess, *Cahiers Ozanam*, 104. Shagreen is a kind of untanned leather with a granular surface. It is normally prepared from the hide of a horse, shark, seal, and so on.

92. Ibid. For the original French text see Walch, "Frédéric et Amélie Ozanam," in Barbiche and Franconnet, *Frédéric Ozanam (1813–1853)*, 83.

93. Amélie Ozanam-Soulacroix, *Notes biographique*, in *Actes du Colloque*, 331.

94. Ibid., 330–31. See also Hess, *Cahiers Ozanam*, 111.

95. Amélie Ozanam-Soulacroix, *Notes biographique*, in *Actes du Colloque*, 330–31. See also Hess, *Cahiers Ozanam*, 111.

96. Amélie Ozanam-Soulacroix, *Notes biographique*, in *Actes du Colloque*, 331.

97. Ibid.

98. Quoted in Robert Maloney, C.M., *Faces of Holiness: Portraits of Some Saints in the Vincentian Family* (Saint Louis, MO: National Council of

the United States Society of Saint Vincent de Paul, 2008), 98. For the original French text see "Letter to his wife," 20 July 1842, in *Lettres*, vol. 2, no. 419, 316.

99. Quoted in Maloney, *Faces of Holiness*, 98–99. For the original French text see *Lettres*, vol. 2, no. 419, 318.

100. Lacroix, "Frédéric Ozanam, amourex," in *Actes du Colloque*, 199.

101. "Letter to his wife," 13 October 1843, in Dirvin, *A Life in Letters*, 355. For the original French text see *Lettres*, vol. 2, no. 515, 495.

102. Ibid., 356–57. For the original French text see *Lettres*, vol. 2, no. 515, 495–97.

103. Ibid., 358. For the original French text see *Lettres*, vol. 2, no. 515, 498.

104. Walch, "Frédéric et Amélie Ozanam," in Barbiche and Franconnet, *Frédéric Ozanam (1813–1853)*, 81.

105. "Letter to Ernest Falconnet," 22 May 1844, in Dirvin, *A Life in Letters*, 369. For the original French text see *Lettres*, vol. 2, no. 539, 535.

106. Baunard, *Ozanam*, 230. Monsieur Soulacroix had been named Chef de la division de la Comptabilitié au ministère de l'Instruction publique (Head of the division of Accounting in the ministry of Public Instruction). See Barbiche and Franconnet, *Frédéric Ozanam (1813–1853)*, 199 (chronology). See also "Letter to Théophile Foisset," 5 April 1845, in *Lettres*, vol. 3, no. 605, 67. See Cholvy, *Ozanam: Le christianisme*, 210.

107. "Letter to François Lallier," 24 July 1845, in *Lettres*, vol. 3, no. 627, 107.

108. Quoted in Hess, *Cahiers Ozanam*, 106. For the original French text see "Letter to François Lallier," 24 July 1845, in *Lettres*, vol. 3, no. 628, 108.

109. "Letter to François Lallier," 24 July 1845, in *Lettres*, vol. 3, no. 627, 107.

110. "Letter to the Abbé Marc-Antoine Soulacroix," 31 July 1845, in *Lettres*, vol. 3, no. 632, 112. See also Cholvy, *Ozanam: Le christianisme*, 213–14.

111. Quoted in Hess, *Cahiers Ozanam*, 106. For the original French text see "Letter to Ernest Falconnet," 2 January 1846, in *Letters*, vol. 3, no. 659, 160.

112. "Letter to Ernest Falconnet," 2 January 1846, in *Letters*, vol. 3, no. 659, 159.

113. Cholvy, *Ozanam: Le christianisme*, 216–17. See "Letter to François Lallier," 20 May 1847, in *Lettres*, vol. 3, no. 737, 298. Apparently Marie behaved well before the pope, who was charmed by her.

114. Cholvy, *Ozanam: Le christianisme*, 217.

115. Quoted in Hess, *Cahiers Ozanam*, 106–7.

116. Quoted in ibid., 107–8. For the original French text see "Letter to Amélie Soulacroix," 31 July 1850, in *Lettres de Frédéric Ozanam*, vol. 4, *Les dernières années (1850–1853)*, édition critique par Christine Franconnet (Paris: Éditions Klincksieck, 1992), no. 1006, 123–24. The grand prix Gobert is an annual prize in the field of history presented by the Académie française.

117. Quoted in ibid. For the original French text see *Lettres*, vol. 4, no. 1006, 125.

118. This point is convincingly made by Xavier Lacroix. See Lacroix, "Frédéric Ozanam, amourex," in *Actes du Colloque*, 193.

119. Ibid., 204.

120. These ideas are developed in Cholvy, *Ozanam: Le christianisme*, 222–23.

121. Ibid., 223.

122. Amélie Ozanam-Soulacroix, *Notes biographique*, in *Actes du Colloque*, 331. See also Cholvy, *Ozanam: Le christianisme*, 224.

CHAPTER 5. SCHOLAR

1. Schimberg, *The Great Friend*, 21.

2. Cholvy, *Ozanam: Le christianisme*, 37. See also Schimberg, *The Great Friend*, 32. For more details, see chapter 2 in this volume.

3. "Letter to Hippolyte Fortoul and Huchard," 15 January 1831, in *Lettres*, vol. 1, no. 25, 34–35.

4. "Letter to Hippolyte Fortoul and Claude Huchard," 21 February 1831, in *Lettres*, vol. 5, no. 1341 [46], 17. See also "Letter to Hippolyte Fortoul and Huchard," 21 February 1831, in *Lettres*, vol. 1, no. 26, 36, and "Letter to Hippolyte Fortoul and Huchard," 15 January 1831, in *Lettres*, vol. 1, no. 25, 34–35.

5. Dirvin, *A Life in Letters*, 1.

6. Ibid.

7. See Galopin, *Essai de bibliographie*, 63, 70, 73–75, respectively.

8. Baunard, *Ozanam*, 109.

9. Antoine Frédéric Ozanam, *Two Chancellors of England*, trans. John Finlay (Sydney, Australia: The Society of St. Vincent de Paul, 1960), 3. For the original French text see Antoine Frédéric Ozanam, *Deux chanceliers d'Angleterre: Bacon de Vérulam et S. Thomas de Cantorbéry*, in *Oeuvres complètes* (1872), vol. 7, 421.

10. Ozanam, *Two Chancellors*, 3. For the original French text see Ozanam, *Deux chanceliers*, in *Oeuvres complètes* (1872), vol. 7, 421.

11. Ibid., 17. For the original French text see Ozanam, *Deux chanceliers*, in *Oeuvres complètes* (1872), vol. 7, 446.

12. Ibid., 21. For the original French text see Ozanam, *Deux chanceliers*, in *Oeuvres complètes* (1872), vol. 7, 452–53.

13. Ibid., 22. For the original French text see Ozanam, *Deux chanceliers*, in *Oeuvres complètes* (1872), vol. 7, 456.

14. Ibid., 24–25. For the original French text see Ozanam, *Deux chanceliers*, in *Oeuvres complètes* (1872), vol. 7, 458.

15. Ibid., 27. For the original French text see Ozanam, *Deux chanceliers*, in *Oeuvres complètes* (1872), vol. 7, 463–64.

16. Ibid., 36–37. For the original French text see Ozanam, *Deux chanceliers*, in *Oeuvres complètes* (1872), vol. 7, 480–83.

17. Ibid., 41–42. For the original French text see Ozanam, *Deux chanceliers*, in *Oeuvres complètes* (1872), vol. 7, 488–92.

18. Ibid., 45. For the original French text see Ozanam, *Deux chanceliers*, in *Oeuvres complètes* (1872), vol. 7, 498.

19. Ibid., 90. For the original French text see Ozanam, *Deux chanceliers*, in *Oeuvres complètes* (1872), vol. 7, 573.

20. Ibid., 90–91. For the original French text see Ozanam, *Deux chanceliers*, in *Oeuvres complètes* (1872), vol. 7, 573–74.

21. Ibid., 91. For the original French text see Ozanam, *Deux chanceliers*, in *Oeuvres complètes* (1872), vol. 7, 574.

22. Ibid. For the original French text see Ozanam, *Deux chanceliers*, in *Oeuvres complètes* (1872), vol. 7, 574.

23. Ibid., 98. For the original French text see Ozanam, *Deux chanceliers*, in *Oeuvres complètes* (1872), vol. 7, 588.

24. Ibid., 102. For the original French text see Ozanam, *Deux chanceliers*, in *Oeuvres complètes* (1872), vol. 7, 594.

25. Ibid., 104. For the original French text see Ozanam, *Deux chanceliers*, in *Oeuvres complètes* (1872), vol. 7, 597.

26. Antoine Frédéric Ozanam, *Du protestantisme dans ses rapports avec la liberté*, in *Oeuvres complètes* (1872), vol. 8, 277.

27. Ibid., 285.

28. Ibid., 321.

29. Baunard, *Ozanam*, 160. In Cologne there were long-standing tensions between Catholics and Protestants. In 1837 the archbishop of Cologne was arrested and imprisoned for two years after a legal dispute over marriages between Protestants and Roman Catholics.

30. Quoted in ibid., 298.

31. Ozanam, *Dante and Catholic Philosophy in the Thirteenth Century*, trans. Lucia D. Pychowska, 2nd ed. (New York: The Cathedral Library Association, 1913), 47–48. For the original French text see A. F. Ozanam, *Dante et la philosophie catholique au treizième siècle* (Paris: Debécourt, Libraire Éditeur, 1839), 1–2. http://www.archive.org/stream/danteetlaphilos05ozangoog#page /n13/mode/2up. See also Antoine Frédéric Ozanam, *Dante et la philosophie catholique au treizième siècle*, in *Oeuvres complètes*, troisième édition (Paris: Lecoffre Fils et Cie, 1869), vol. 6, 47–48. The two French editions are hereafter cited, respectively, as Ozanam, *Dante et la philosophie catholique*, and Ozanam, *Oeuvres complètes* (1869).

32. Charles L. Souvay, "Ozanam as Historian," *Catholic Historical Review* 19:1 (April 1933): 7–9.

33. Ozanam, *Dante and Catholic Philosophy*, 344. For the original French text see Ozanam, *Dante et la philosophie catholique*, 258. See also Ozanam, *Oeuvres complètes* (1869), vol. 6, 347.

34. Ibid., 354. For the original French text see Ozanam, *Dante et la philosophie catholique*, 265. See also Ozanam, *Oeuvres complètes* (1869), vol. 6, 356.

35. Ibid. For the original French text see Ozanam, *Dante et la philosophie catholique*, 265. See also Ozanam, *Oeuvres complètes* (1869), vol. 6, 356–57.

36. Ibid., 355. For the original French text see Ozanam, *Dante et la philosophie catholique*, 265–66. See also Ozanam, *Oeuvres complètes* (1869), vol. 6, 357.

37. Ibid. For the original French text see Ozanam, *Dante et la philosophie catholique*, 266. See also Ozanam, *Oeuvres complètes* (1869), vol. 6, 357–58.

38. Ibid., 356–57. For the original French text see Ozanam, *Dante et la philosophie catholique*, 266. See also Ozanam, *Oeuvres complètes* (1869), vol. 6, 358.

39. Baunard, *Ozanam*, 155.

40. Quoted in Sister Emmanuel Renner, O.S.B., *The Historical Thought of Frédéric Ozanam* (Washington, DC: Catholic University of America Press, 1959), 13.

41. Baunard, *Ozanam*, 191.

42. Ibid., 175–77.

43. Ibid., 194.

44. Ibid., 195–96. David Friedrich Strauss (1808–74) was a philosopher and theologian at Tübingen; Christian Lassen (1800–76) a professor at Bonn; and Georg Gottfried Gervinus (1805–71) a historian at Göttingen.

45. "Letter to François Lallier," 17 August 1842, in Dirvin, *A Life in Letters*, 314. For the original French text see "Letter to François Lallier," in *Lettres*, vol. 2, no. 433, 350–51.

46. Ibid., 315. For the original French text see *Lettres*, vol. 2, no. 433, 351.

47. Ibid. For the original French text see *Lettres*, vol. 2, no. 433, 351. The review referred to in this passage is most likely *Le Correspondant*. Ozanam and his friends were planning to begin this review in early 1843. See Dirvin, *A Life in Letters*, 316n.7.

48. Galopin, *Essai de bibliographie*, 89, 95, and 99, respectively.

49. Baunard, *Ozanam*, 314.

50. Souvay, "Ozanam as Historian," 13.

51. Ibid. The first work would appear in 1850. A rough translation of the title is "Unpublished (or original) documents for assisting with the literary history of the Italy." This represented a significant research contribution to the field. The second work was originally published in installments, beginning in November 1847. It was published in book form in 1852 and included in this version the *Fioretti*, a collection of Franciscan legends from the medieval era. Ozanam's wife, Amélie, assisted with one of the translations. See ibid., 14. See also Schimberg, *The Great Friend*, 177.

52. Frederick Ozanam, *The Franciscan Poets in Italy of the Thirteenth Century*, trans. A. E. Nellen and N. C. Craig (London: David Nutt, 1914), 56. For

the original French text see A. F. Ozanam, *Les poètes franciscains en Italie au treizième siècle*, troisième édition, in A. F. Ozanam, *Oeuvres complètes*, seconde édition (Paris: Jacques Lecoffre et Cie, 1859), vol. 5, 51.

53. Ozanam, *Franciscan Poets*, 57. For the original French text see Ozanam, *Les poètes franciscains*, in *Oeuvres complètes* (1859), vol. 5, 52.

54. Ibid., 59–61. For the original French text see Ozanam, *Les poètes franciscains*, in *Oeuvres complètes* (1859), vol. 5, 54–55.

55. Ibid., 284–85. For the original French text see Ozanam, *Les poètes franciscains*, in *Oeuvres complètes* (1859), vol. 5, 207–8.

56. Ibid., 186–296. For the original French text see Ozanam, *Les poètes franciscains*, in *Oeuvres complètes* (1859), vol. 5, 131–217.

57. Ibid., 188. For the original French text see Ozanam, *Les poètes franciscains*, in *Oeuvres complètes* (1859), vol. 5, 133.

58. Souvay, "Ozanam as Historian," 14. Ozanam attributes to Jacopone both the *Stabat Mater Dolorosa*, which represents the "lament of the grief-stricken Virgin" for her crucified son, and the *Stabat Mater Speciosa* or the *Stabat* of the Cradle, "in which the Virgin Mother was to figure in all the joy of childbirth." See Ozanam, *Franciscan Poets*, 239–40. For the original French text see Ozanam, *Les poètes franciscains*, in *Oeuvres complètes* (1859), vol. 5, 169–70.

59. Souvay, "Ozanam as Historian," 14–15. For examples see Ozanam, *Franciscan Poets*, 256–65, 277–80. For the original French text see Ozanam, *Les poètes franciscains*, in *Oeuvres complètes* (1859), vol. 5, 185–92, 202–4.

60. Baunard, *Ozanam*, 315.

61. Ozanam, *Franciscan Poets*, 295–96. For the original French text see Ozanam, *Les poètes franciscains*, in *Oeuvres complètes* (1859), vol. 5, 216–17.

62. Some sources claim that Ozanam was a Third Order Franciscan, as was Dante. See "Text of the Decree of Introduction of Ozanam Cause," in *Ozanam: Path to Sainthood* (Melbourne, Australia: National Council of Australia Society of St. Vincent de Paul, 1987), 10. See also Schimberg, *The Great Friend*, 179. For the opposite point of view, see *Lettres*, vol. 4, no. 1323, 669n.550. In this footnote to a letter from a Franciscan leader, the editors of *Lettres* clearly indicate that Ozanam was honored by the Franciscans but also that there is no solid evidence that he was ever made a member of the third order.

63. See Souvay, "Ozanam as Historian," 14.

64. Quoted in Baunard, *Ozanam*, 316–17.

65. Souvay, "Ozanam as Historian," 14.

66. Quoted in Baunard, *Ozanam*, 317. For the original French text see "Letter to Théophile Foisset," 26 January 1848, in *Lettres*, vol. 3, no. 777, 367. Foisset was a respected magistrate in Dijon. He was actively involved in the work of *Le Correspondant* as a trusted advisor and contributor. See George Armstrong Kelly, *The Humane Comedy: Constant, Tocqueville and French Liberalism* (Cambridge: Cambridge University Press, 1992), 174. For further information,

see Henri Beaune, *M. Th. Foisset* (Dijon: Lamarche, Libraire-Éditeur, 1874). A digitized copy can be accessed at http://data.bnf.fr/15537401/joseph_theophile _foisset/.

67. Quoted in Baunard, *Ozanam*, 317. For the original French text see *Lettres*, vol. 3, no. 777, 367. Ozanam had also written on Dante's *Purgatorio*; see *Le Purgatoire de Dante*, in *Oeuvres complètes* (1862), vol. 9.

68. Quoted in Baunard, *Ozanam,*, 317–18. For the original French text see *Lettres*, vol. 3, no. 777, 367.

69. Quoted in ibid., 318. For the original French text see *Lettres*, vol. 3, no. 777, 367–68.

70. Quoted in ibid. For the original French text see *Lettres*, vol. 3, no. 777, 368.

71. Quoted in ibid. For the original French text see *Lettres*, vol. 3, no. 777, 368.

72. Ibid., 318–19.

73. A. Frédéric Ozanam, "Author's Preface," in *History of Civilization in the Fifth Century*, trans. Ashley C. Glyn, 2 vols. (London: Wm. H. Allen & Co., 1868), vol. 1, xi. For the original French text see Ozanam, "Avant-Propos," *Oeuvres complètes* (1862), vol. 1, 1–2.

74. Quoted in Reverend Henry Louis Hughes, *Frederick Ozanam* (Saint Louis, MO: B. Herder Book Company, 1933), 108. For the original French text see Ozanam, "Avant-Propos," *Oeuvres complètes* (1862), vol. 1, 5.

75. Baunard, *Ozanam*, 320–21.

76. Ibid.

77. Ibid.

78. Ibid., 323–24.

79. Ozanam, *History of Civilization*, vol. 1, 295. For the original French text see Ozanam, *La civilisation*, in *Oeuvres complètes* (1862), vol. 1, 395.

80. Ibid., vol. 2, 35–47. For the original French text see Ozanam, *La civilisation*, in *Oeuvres complètes* (1862), vol. 1, 48–62.

81. See ibid., vol. 2, 56–89. For the original French text see Ozanam, *La civilisation*, in *Oeuvres complètes* (1862), vol. 1, 74–115.

82. Ibid., vol. 2, 48. For the original French text see Ozanam, *La civilisation*, in *Oeuvres complètes* (1862), vol. 1, 63.

83. Ibid., vol. 2, 48–49. For the original French text see Ozanam, *La civilisation*, in *Oeuvres complètes* (1862), vol. 1, 63–65.

84. Ibid., vol. 2, 48–49. For the original French text see Ozanam, *La civilisation*, in *Oeuvres complètes* (1862), vol. 1, 64–65.

85. Ibid., vol. 2, 275. For the original French text see Ozanam, *La civilisation*, in *Oeuvres complètes* (1862), vol. 2, 348.

86. Renner, *Historical Thought*, 73.

87. Ozanam, "Avant-Propos," *Oeuvres complètes* (1862), vol. 1, 7.

88. Renner, *Historical Thought*, 37.

89. Marco Bartoli, "Ozanam, historien du Moyen Âge," in *Actes du Colloque*, 254.

90. Renner, *Historical Thought*, 27.

91. Ozanam, *Dante and Catholic Philosophy*, 63. For the original French text see Ozanam, *Dante et la philosophie catholique*, 21. See also Ozanam, *Oeuvres complètes* (1869), vol. 6, 65.

92. Renner, *Historical Thought*, 27. See also Ozanam, *La civilisation*, in *Oeuvres complètes* (1862), vol. 2, 212–13.

93. Renner, *Historical Thought*, 28. See also Ozanam, *La civilisation*, in *Oeuvres complètes* (1862), vol. 2, 206–7.

94. Renner, *Historical Thought*, 28.

95. Ibid., 27.

96. Ibid., 28–29.

97. Quoted in ibid., 29. For the original French text see A. F. Ozanam, *Les Germains avant le christianisme*, vol. 1, troisième édition, in *Oeuvres complètes*, seconde édition (Paris: Jacques Lecoffre et Cie, 1861), vol. 3, 15.

98. Ozanam, *Les Germains*, 15–16.

99. Renner, *Historical Thought*, 61.

100. Ibid., 76. For a fuller treatment of Ozanam as historian, see E. Jordan, "L'historien," in G. Goyau et al., *Ozanam, Livre du Centenaire* (Paris: Gabriel Beauchesne, 1913), 153–258.

101. George Wilhelm Friedrich Hegel, *Introduction to the Philosophy of History*, trans. S. Sibree, in *Hegel Selections*, ed. J. Loewenberg (New York: Charles Scribner's Sons, 1965), 361.

102. "Letter to François Lallier," 9 April 1838, in Dirvin, *A Life in Letters*, 136. For the original French text see *Lettres*, vol. 1, no. 173, 303. Many of the popes named by Ozanam had altercations with civil rulers.

103. "Letter to François Lallier," 17 August 1842, in Dirvin, *A Life in Letters*, 314–15. For the original French text see *Lettres*, vol. 2, no. 433, 351.

104. George Wilhelm Friedrich Hegel, *The Doctrine of Essence*, trans. William Wallace, in *Hegel Selections*, 177.

105. George Wilhelm Friedrich Hegel, *The Philosophy of Mind*, trans. William Wallace, in *Hegel Selections*, 273.

106. Ibid., 274.

107. Renner, *Historical Thought*, 25.

108. Quoted in ibid., 36. For the original French text see "Letter to Ernest Falconnet," 4 September 1831, in *Lettres*, vol. 1, no. 32, 44.

109. Quoted in ibid. For the original French text see "Letter to Ernest Falconnet," 4 September 1831, in *Lettres*, vol. 1, no. 32, 44.

110. Hegel, *Philosophy of History*, in *Hegel Selections*, 379–80.

111. Renner, *Historical Thought*, 44.

112. Quoted in ibid.

113. See Søren Kierkegaard, *Stages on Life's Way*, ed. and trans. Howard V. Hong and Edna H. Hong (Princeton, NJ: Princeton University Press, 1988).

114. "Letter to François Lallier," 5 October 1837, in Dirvin, *A Life in Letters*, 119–20. For the original French text see *Lettres*, vol. 1, no. 160, 283.

115. Daniel Johnson, "On Truth As Subjectivity in Kierkegaard's *Concluding Unscientific Postscript*," *Quodlibet Journal* 5:2–3 (July 2003). http://www .quodlibet.net/articles/johnson-truth.shtml.

116. M. Jamie Ferreira, "Kierkegaard and Levinas on Four Elements of the Biblical Love Commandment," in *Kierkegaard and Levinas: Ethics, Politics, and Religion*, ed. Aaron J Simmons and David Wood (Bloomington: Indiana University Press, 2008), 82–83.

117. Bruce H. Kirmsee, *Sören Kierkegaard and the Common Man* (Grand Rapids, MI: Wm. B. Eerdmans Publishing Co., 2001), xv–xviii, 85.

118. Cholvy, *Ozanam: Le christianisme*, 288.

119. Matthew Mancini, *Alexis de Tocqueville and American Intellectuals: From His Time to Ours* (Lanham, MD: Rowman & Littlefield Publishers, 2006), 134.

120. Ibid., 137.

121. See Cholvy, *Ozanam: L'engagement*, 658. See also Mancini, *Alexis de Tocqueville*, 137.

122. "Letter to J.-J. Ampère," 18 November 1853, in Sacra Congregatio Pro Causis Sanctorum Officium Historicum, *Disquisitio*. See also Jean-Jacques Ampère, *Papiers Ampère de L'Institute*, in *Oeuvres complètes d'Alexis de Tocqueville*, vol. 11, *Correspondence d'Alexis de Tocqueville avec P.-P. Royer-Collard et avec J.-J Ampère*, ed. André Janin (Paris: Gallimard, 1970), no. 67, 227.

123. "A Romish Brotherhood: The Founder of the St. Vincent De Paul. Prof. Frederic Ozanam's Life and Works. The History of the Brotherhood, An Interesting Memoir," *New York Times*, 18 August 1878, ProQuest Historical Newspapers, *The New York Times* (1851–2003), 8.

124. "Letter to Doctor Édouard Dufresne," 28 August 1851, in *Lettres*, vol. 4, no. 1104, 277. Newman converted to Catholicism in 1845, and Henry Edward Manning converted in 1850.

125. Thomas W. O'Brien, "Pioneer and Prophet: Frédéric Ozanam's Influence on Modern Catholic Social Theory," *Vincentian Heritage Journal* 31:1 (2012): 41.

126. Ibid.

127. Ibid., 42.

128. Ibid.

129. Ibid., 40.

130. Schimberg, *The Great Friend*, 162.

131. Quoted in ibid.

132. Quoted in Baunard, *Ozanam*, 217. Montalembert's publication can be found online at https://archive.org/details/1843dudevoirdes00mont.

133. "Letter to Théophile Foisset," 21 October 1843, in Dirvin, *A Life in Letters*, 360. See also Baunard, *Ozanam*, 218. For the original French text see *Lettres*, vol. 2, no. 516, 500.

134. "Letter to Théophile Foisset," 21 October 1843, in Dirvin, *A Life in Letters*, 360–61. See also Baunard, *Ozanam*, 218. For the original French text see *Lettres*, vol. 2, no. 516, 500–501.

135. "Letter to Théophile Foisset," 21 October 1843, in Dirvin, *A Life in Letters*, 361. See also Baunard, *Ozanam*, 218. For the original French text see *Lettres*, vol. 2, no. 516, 501.

136. Baunard, *Ozanam*, 216. Edgar Quinet (1803–1875) was a French poet, historian, and political philosopher. Jules Michelet (1798–1874) was a French nationalist historian. His most famous work was *Histoire de France*.

137. "Letter to Théophile Foisset," 21 October 1843, in Dirvin, *A Life in Letters*, 361. See also Baunard, *Ozanam*, 218–19. For the original French text see *Lettres*, vol. 2, no. 516, 501.

138. Schimberg, *The Great Friend*, 164.

139. Ibid. See also Baunard, *Ozanam*, 12.

140. O'Meara, *Ozanam*, 168–70.

141. Lacordaire, *My Friend*, 56.

142. Ibid., 57.

143. Gérard Cholvy, "Frédéric Ozanam et la liberté de l'enseignement," in Barbiche and Franconnet, *Frédéric Ozanam (1813–1853)*, 119–20.

144. Cholvy, *Ozanam: Le christianisme*, 186–87.

145. Cholvy, "Frédéric Ozanam et la liberté de l'enseignement," in Barbiche and Franconnet, *Frédéric Ozanam (1813–1853)*, 120.

146. O'Meara, *Ozanam*, 150. It is interesting that O'Meara refers to his eyes as "dark," perhaps referring to the intensity. Ozanam actually had "grey eyes." See "Letter to his mother," 19 June 1833, in Dirvin, *A Life in Letters*, 40. For the original French text see *Lettres*, vol. 1, no. 58, 105.

147. O'Meara, *Ozanam*, 151.

148. Quoted in Baunard, *Ozanam*, 200–201.

149. Ibid., 201.

150. Ibid., 205.

151. Quoted in ibid., 224. For the original French text see Amélie Ozanam-Soulacroix, *Notes biographique*, in *Actes du Colloque*, 328.

152. Ibid., 207.

153. O'Meara, *Ozanam*, 155.

154. Ibid., 153–54.

155. Ibid., 155.

156. "Letter to Alexandre Dufieux," 16 May 1846, in *Lettres*, vol. 3, no. 679, 189. These are similar to the B.A., M.A., and doctoral degrees.

157. Baunard, *Ozanam*, 207.

158. Quoted in O'Meara, *Ozanam*, 191. For the original French text see "Letter to François Lallier," 7 August 1846, in *Lettres*, vol. 3, no. 694, 207.

159. O'Meara, *Ozanam*, 155.

160. As noted in the previous chapter, the Ozanams had moved to a house on the rue de Fleurus at the invitation of Emmanuel Bailly because their previous quarters were uncomfortably hot in the summer. Ozanam referred to the location as a "palace" because the house Bailly owned "had been built originally for Murat, afterwards King of Naples." Baunard, *Ozanam*, 203.

161. Quoted in ibid., 204.

162. Jeremy D. Popkin, *A History of Modern France*, 2nd ed. (Upper Saddle River, NJ: Prentice-Hall, 2001), 127.

163. Quoted in Hughes, *Ozanam*, 87.

164. Quoted in Christian Verheyde, *15 Days of Prayer with Blessed Frédéric Ozanam*, trans. John E. Rybolt, C.M. (New York: New City Press, 2011), 115. For the original French text see "Letter to Charles Benoît," 28 February 1853, in *Lettres*, vol. 4, no. 1245, 531.

165. "Letter to Ernest Falconnet," 22 May 1844, in Dirvin, *A Life in Letters*, 369. For the original French text see *Lettres*, vol. 2, no. 539, 535.

166. Quoted in Baunard, *Ozanam*, 297.

CHAPTER 6. SPOKESPERSON FOR THE PEOPLE

1. Popkin, *Modern France*, 79–80.

2. Leo A. Loubère, *Nineteenth-Century Europe: The Revolution of Life* (Englewood Cliffs, NJ: Prentice-Hall, 1994), 56.

3. Sally Waller, *France in Revolution, 1776–1830* (Oxford: Heinemann Education Publishers, 2002), 127. Loubère suggests that approximately 10,000 could serve as deputies. See Loubère, *Nineteenth-Century Europe*, 56.

4. Loubère, *Nineteenth-Century Europe*, 54–55.

5. Waller, *France in Revolution*, 127.

6. Popkin, *Modern France*, 80.

7. Loubère, *Nineteenth-Century Europe*, 55–56.

8. Popkin, *Modern France*, 82.

9. Loubère, *Nineteenth-Century Europe*, 58.

10. Popkin, *Modern France*, 82.

11. Loubère, *Nineteenth-Century Europe*, 60.

12. Ibid.

13. Popkin, *Modern France*, 87.

14. Loubère, *Nineteenth-Century Europe*, 60.

15. Popkin, *Modern France*, 87–88.

16. Ibid., 88.

17. Loubère, *Nineteenth-Century Europe*, 61.

18. Ibid., 63. François Guizot was a major opponent of Charles X's regime as a liberal deputy. He became the chief spokesperson for Louis-Philippe's regime and became prime minister in 1847. See Popkin, *Modern France*, 86, 92.

19. Popkin, *Modern France*, 88.

20. Loubère, *Nineteenth-Century Europe*, 61.

21. Popkin, *Modern France*, 88.

22. Ibid., 93.

23. Loubère, *Nineteenth-Century Europe*, 62.

24. Popkin, *Modern France*, 90.

25. Ibid., 91.

26. Gregory XVI, *Mirari Vos:* Encyclical Letter of His Holiness Pope Gregory XVI, On Liberalism and Religious Indifferentism, 1832. http://www .papalencyclicals.net/Greg16/g16mirar.htm.

27. Popkin, *Modern France*, 91.

28. Loubère, *Nineteenth-Century Europe*, 61.

29. Roger Magraw, *France, 1815–1914: The Bourgeois Century* (New York and Oxford: Oxford University Press, 1986), 96.

30. Popkin, *Modern France*, 90.

31. Jean-Antoine Ozanam, *Histoire de Lyon pendant les journées des 21, 22 et 23 novembre 1831, contenant les causes, les conséquences et les suites de ces déplorables événements* (Lyon: Auguste Baron; Paris: Moutardier, 1832).

32. Ibid., 16. The English translation can be found in J.-C. Caron, "Catholic Student," 40–41.

33. J.-C. Caron, "Catholic Student," 41.

34. Popkin, *Modern France*, 93.

35. Magraw, *France, 1815–1914*, 96–97.

36. Quoted in Philip Spencer, "'Barbarian Assault': The Fortunes of a Phrase," *Journal of the History of Ideas* 16:2 (1955): 232. See also Saint-Marc Girardin, *Souvenirs et réflexions politiques d'un journaliste*, 2nd ed. (Paris: Michel Lévy Frères, Éditeurs, 1873), 143. http://babel.hathitrust.org/cgi/pt?id= mdp.39015058482236;seq=163;view=1up;num=143.

37. The article is reprinted in Saint-Marc Girardin, *Souvenirs*, 144–51.

38. Spencer, "'Barbarian Assault,'" 233; Saint-Marc Girardin, *Souvenirs*, 147.

39. Spencer, "'Barbarian Assault,'" 233; Saint-Marc Girardin, *Souvenirs*, 147–48.

40. Spencer, "'Barbarian Assault,'" 234.

41. Ibid.

42. Popkin, *Modern France*, 93.

43. Ibid.

44. Loubère, *Nineteenth-Century Europe*, 63.

45. Quoted in Hess, *Cahiers Ozanam*, 107. For the original French text see "Letter to his wife," in *Lettres*, vol. 2, no. 509, 481.

46. Popkin, *Modern France*, 97.

47. Ibid., 97–98.

48. Ibid., 98–99 (the *bourgeoisie à talent* of chapter 1).

49. Ibid., 99.

50. Ibid., 101.

51. Ibid.

52. Magraw, *France, 1815–1914*, 46.

53. Popkin, *Modern France*, 102.

54. Ibid.

55. Ibid., 100.

56. Ibid., 101.

57. Wright, *France in Modern Times*, 169–70.

58. Popkin, *Modern France*, 102–3.

59. Kathryn E. Amdur, "The Making of the French Working Class," in *The Transformation of Modern France: Essays in Honor of Gordon Wright*, ed. William B. Cohen (New York and Boston: Houghton Mifflin Company, 1997), 72.

60. Quoted in ibid., 74.

61. Ibid.

62. Peter N. Stearns, *1848: The Revolutionary Tide in Europe* (New York: W. W. Norton & Company, 1974), 34.

63. Quoted in Popkin, *Modern France*, 107. See also Alexis de Tocqueville, *Recollections*, trans. George Lawrence (Garden City, NY: Doubleday, 1970), 14.

64. Popkin, *Modern France*, 107.

65. "Letter to Prosper Dugas," 11 March 1849, in "Lettres Ozanam," *Oeuvres complètes* (1865), vol. 11, 236. See also *Lettres*, vol. 3, no. 870, 495–96. This is also quoted in Derum, *Apostle in a Top Hat*, 202. Some of what follows in this chapter is based upon information in my article "Faith, Charity, Justice, and Civic Learning: The Lessons and Legacy of Frédéric Ozanam," *Vincentian Heritage* 30:1 (2010).

66. Quoted in Hess, *Cahiers Ozanam*, 27. See also "Letter to Théophile Foisset," 24 September 1848, in *Lettres*, vol. 3, no. 839, 459. Théophile Foisset, also mentioned in the previous chapter, was born in 1800 and died in 1873. He "was a friend of Ozanam and biographer of Lacordaire." Dirvin, *A Life in Letters*, 161n.1. See Henry Boissard, *Théophile Foisset (1800–1873)* (Paris: E. Plon, Nourrit et Cie, 1891); Beaune, *M. Th. Foisset*.

67. "Letter to Auguste Materne," August 1830, in *Lettres*, vol. 1, no. 21, 27. Cholvy indicates that in 1831, Ozanam associated the republic with the Reign of

Terror that began in 1793 and referred to the republic as a "hideous phantom." See Cholvy, *Ozanam: L'engagement*, 600. See also "Letter to Auguste Materne," 19 March 1831, in *Lettres*, vol. 1, no. 28, 39. It is in this letter that Ozanam uses the phrase "fantôme hideux."

68. "Letter to his mother," 23 December 1831, in *Lettres*, vol. 1, no. 42, 71.

69. Ibid.

70. "Letter to Ernest Falconnet," 10 February 1832, in Dirvin, *A Life in Letters*, 18. For the original French text see *Lettres*, vol. 1, no. 43, 73.

71. "Letter to Ernest Falconnet," 21 July 1834, in Dirvin, *A Life in Letters*, 46. For the original French text see *Lettres*, vol. 1, no. 77, 142.

72. Ibid., 46. For the original French text see *Lettres*, vol. 1, no. 77, 142.

73. Ibid., 46–47. For the original French text see *Lettres*, vol. 1, no. 77, 143. Saint Louis was Louis IX, the only canonized king of France (r. 1226–70).

74. Ibid. For the original French text see *Lettres*, vol. 1, no. 77, 143.

75. Ozanam, *Dante and Catholic Philosophy*, 63. For the original French text see Ozanam, *Dante et la philosophie catholique*, 17. See also Ozanam, *Oeuvres complètes* (1869), vol. 6, 65.

76. Ozanam, *Dante and Catholic Philosophy*, 17; Ozanam, *Dante et la philosophie catholique*, x; Ozanam, *Oeuvres complètes* (1869), vol. 6, 16.

77. Antoine Frédéric Ozanam, *Two Chancellors*, 98. The original work appeared in 1836. For the original French text see Antoine Frédéric Ozanam, *Deux chanceliers*, in *Oeuvres complètes* (1872), vol. 7, 588.

78. "Letter to François Lallier," 9 April 1838, in Dirvin, *A Life in Letters*, 136. For the original French text see *Lettres*, vol. 1, no. 173, 303.

79. Ozanam, *Dante and Catholic Philosophy*, 241. For the original French text see Ozanam, *Dante et la philosophie catholique*, 163, and Ozanam, *Oeuvres complètes* (1869), vol. 6, 243.

80. Quoted in Hess, *Cahiers Ozanam*, 19. See also "Letter to François Lallier," 17 June 1845, in *Lettres*, vol. 3, no. 615, 86.

81. Thomas Bokenkotter, *Church and Revolution: Catholics in the Struggle for Democracy and Social Justice* (New York: Doubleday, 1998), 131.

82. Cholvy, "Ozanam and the Challenges," 2.

83. "Letter to his mother," 8 April 1832, in Dirvin, *A Life In Letters*, 23–24. For the original French text see *Lettres*, vol. 1, no. 45, 77.

84. Quoted in O'Meara, *Ozanam*, 83. See "Letter to Ernest Falconnet," 21 July 1834, in Dirvin, *A Life in Letters*, 47. For the original French text see *Lettres*, vol. 1, no. 77, 143.

85. All of these quotations are from "Letter to Léonce Curnier," 9 March 1837, in Dirvin, *A Life in Letters*, 106. For the original French text see *Lettres*, vol. 1, no. 142, 254.

86. O'Meara, *Ozanam*, 246. For the original French text see Ozanam, *Oeuvres complètes* (1872), vol. 7, 269.

87. Ibid., 246. For the original French text see Ozanam, *Oeuvres complètes* (1872), vol. 7, 268.

88. Katherine A. Lynch, *Family, Class, and Ideology in Early Industrial France: Social Policy and the Working-Class Family, 1825–1848* (Madison: University of Wisconsin Press, 1988), 44.

89. O'Meara, *Ozanam*, 246. For the original French text see Ozanam, *Oeuvres complètes*, vol. 7, 269.

90. Spencer, " 'Barbarian Assault,' " 237.

91. Ibid.

92. Quoted in ibid. For the original French text see Ozanam, "Les dangers de Rome et ses espérances," *Le Correspondant* (10 February 1848), 412–35.

93. Ibid.

94. Hess, *Cahiers Ozanam*, 19. See also "Letter to Théophile Foisset," 22 February 1848, in *Lettres*, vol. 3, no. 784, 379.

95. Ibid. See also "Letter to Théophile Foisset," 22 February 1848, in *Lettres*, vol. 3, no. 784, 379.

96. Quoted in Hess, *Cahiers Ozanam*, 19. For the original French text see "Letter to L'Abbé Alphonse Ozanam," 6 March 1848, in *Lettres*, vol. 3, no. 787, 388.

97. Ibid., 27. For the original French text see "Letter to L'Abbé Alphonse Ozanam," 15 March 1848, in *Lettres*, vol. 3, no. 789, 391.

98. Ibid. For the original French text see "Letter to L'Abbé Alphonse Ozanam," 12–21 April 1848, in *Lettres*, vol. 3, no. 802, 413.

99. "Letter to L'Abbé Alphonse Ozanam," 12–21 April 1848, in *Lettres*, vol. 3, no. 802, 414.

100. "To the Constitutents of the Department of the Rhone" (original title "Aux électeurs du Department de Rhone"), 15 April 1848, in Hess, *Cahiers Ozanam*, 51.

101. Many of these ideas will be discussed in more depth in the chapter on solidarity as well as elsewhere throughout this book.

102. Hess, *Cahiers Ozanam*, 51.

103. Ibid.

104. Ibid., 51–52.

105. Ibid., 52. See also Cholvy, *Ozanam: L'engagement*, 601–5.

106. Auge, *Frederic Ozanam*, 86.

107. Ibid., 86–87.

108. "Letter to Léonce Curnier," 4 November 1834, in Dirvin, *A Life In Letters*, 55. See also *Lettres*, vol. 1, no. 82, 154.

109. *Rules of the Society 1835*, 20–21.

110. "Circular-letter of M. Gossin, President-General," 15 August 1844, in *The Manual of the Society of St. Vincent de Paul*, 21st ed. (Dublin: The Superior Council of Ireland, 1958), 131. Hereafter cited as *Manual of the SVP* (Dublin).

111. See "À L'Assemblée Générale de la Société de Saint-Vincent-de-Paul," 11 April 1839, in *Lettres*, vol. 5, no. 1347 [84 bis], 85–86. See also "Letter of Frederic Ozanam," 11 April 1839, in *Manual of the SVP* (Dublin), 113.

112. *International Rule*, I, 17.

113. Ibid., 16–17.

114. "Letter to Louis Janmot," 13 November 1836, in Dirvin, *A Life In Letters*, 96–97. See also *Lettres*, vol. 1, no. 137, 243–44.

115. Jay P. Corrin, *Catholic Intellectuals and the Challenge of Democracy* (Notre Dame, IN: University of Notre Dame Press, 2002), 16.

116. Two interesting sources for this work and Ozanam's contribution to it are Chr. Morel [Christine Franconnet], "Un journal démocrate chrétien en 1848–1849: *L'Ère nouvelle*," *Revue d'histoire de l'Église de France* 63:170 (1977), and Claude Bressolette, "Frédéric Ozanam et *L'Ère nouvelle*," *Revue d'histoire de l'Église de France* 85:214 (1999). Hereafter cited as Morel, "Un journal: *L'Ère nouvelle*," and Bressolette, "Ozanam et *L'Ère nouvelle*," respectively.

117. Morel, "Un journal: *L'Ère nouvelle*," 42.

118. Ibid., 28. Maret was a noted theologian of his day and a proponent of Christian democracy. He wrote, "Daughter of Christianity and of reason, modern democracy is the final end of social progress." Quoted in ibid., 39. For more on Maret see Claude Bressolette, *L'abbé Maret: Le combat de théologien pour une démocratie chrétienne, 1830–1851* (Paris: Broche, 1997).

119. Moon, *The Labor Problem*, 35. The first quote is from Moon, and the second is from the prospectus itself.

120. Bressolette, "Ozanam et *L'Ère nouvelle*," 76–77.

121. Harrison, *Romantic Catholics*, 225.

122. Ibid., 226.

123. Morel, "Un journal: *L'Ère nouvelle*," 25.

124. Harrison, *Romantic Catholics*, 225.

125. Bressolette, "Ozanam et *L'Ère nouvelle*," 76–77.

126. Ibid., 75, 87.

127. Morel, "Un journal: *L'Ère nouvelle*," 52. Morel provides an excellent appendix with the numbers and dates of the chief contributors' articles.

128. Quoted in Bressolette, "Ozanam et *L'Ère nouvelle*," 79.

129. Quoted in ibid.

130. Ibid.

131. Quoted in ibid.

132. Morel, "Un journal: *L'Ère nouvelle*," 36.

133. Ibid., 36–37.

134. Quoted in Schimberg, *The Great Friend*, 238–39. See also O'Meara, *Ozanam*, 235.

135. Alexandre Dufieux (1806–57) was a "Lyon friend of Ozanam, born at Vaise, entered his father's firm, took part in literary circles, urged on by the wish

to defend his political and religious beliefs. Collaborated in *Reparateur* and the *Gazette de Lyon.*" Dirvin, *A Life in Letters*, 94n.5.

136. Wright, *France in Modern Times*, 126.

137. Quoted in ibid.

138. Schimberg, *The Great Friend*, 237.

139. Quoted in Hess, *Cahiers Ozanam*, 21. For the original French text see "Letter to Alexandre Dufieux," 31 May 1848, in *Lettres*, vol. 3, no. 814, 432.

140. Wright, *France in Modern Times*, 171.

141. Popkin, *Modern France*, 111–12.

142. Ibid., 112. Schimberg offers a higher figure, 16,000, for those slain, but this seems too high. See Schimberg, *The Great Friend*, 219.

143. Quoted in Schimberg, *The Great Friend*, 219. For the original French text see "Letter to L'Abbé Alphonse Ozanam," in *Lettres*, vol. 3, no. 825, 443. By this time Ozanam was married and the father of Marie.

144. Affre was an opponent of Louis-Philippe's policies and had also sponsored clerical reforms. Most likely the two men with Ozanam were Monsieur Emmanuel Bailly and Cornudet. Léon Cornudet (1808–76) was a close friend of Ozanam. In fact, when he was dying, Ozanam placed his daughter in Cornudet's protection, as described in chapter 12. Cornudet belonged to the Society of St. Vincent de Paul as one of its early members and was vice-president in 1844. See Dirvin, *A Life in Letters*, 149n.1; Schimberg, *The Great Friend*, 219–20; "Letter to L'Abbé Alphonse Ozanam," in *Lettres*, vol. 3, no. 825, 444.

145. Schimberg, *The Great Friend*, 220–21.

146. Bressolette, "Ozanam et *L'Ère nouvelle*," 79.

147. Morel, "Un journal: *L'Ère nouvelle*," 52.

148. Bressolette, "Ozanam et *L'Ère nouvelle*," 79.

149. Ibid., 79–80.

150. Ibid., 80.

151. "Letter to Léonce Curnier," 9 March 1837, in Dirvin, *A Life in Letters*, 106. For the original French text see *Lettres*, vol. 1, no. 142 , 254.

152. "Letter to Léonce Curnier," 23 February 1835, in Dirvin, *A Life in Letters*, 64–65. For the original French text see *Lettres*, vol. 1, no. 90, 167. See also O'Meara, *Ozanam*, 87–88.

153. "Letter to François Lallier," 5 November 1836, in Dirvin, *A Life in Letters*, 92. For the original French text see *Lettres*, vol. 1, no. 136, 239.

154. Ibid. For the original French text see *Lettres*, vol. 1, no. 136, 239.

155. Bressolette, "Ozanam et *L'Ère nouvelle*," 87.

156. Morel, "Un journal: *L'Ère nouvelle*," 47. See also Moon, *The Labor Problem*, 28. Moon's work lists five planks shared by the social Catholic movement: opposition to the liberal school of political economy; Christian charity and morality as the foundation of economy and social philosophy; support of labor

organization; support of a wage that would be adequate to support a worker and his family; and advocacy of social legislation.

157. Morel, "Un journal: *L'Ère nouvelle*," 47.

158. Ibid., 48.

159. Ibid., 52.

160. Bressolette, "Ozanam et *L'Ère nouvelle*," 78.

161. Ibid.

162. Morel, "Un journal: *L'Ère nouvelle*," 48.

163. Harrison, *Romantic Catholics*, 227–28.

164. Ibid., 229.

165. Ibid.

166. Quoted in Ronald W. Ramson, C.M., *Hosanna! Blessed Frederic Ozanam: Family and Friends* (Bloomington, IN: Westbow Press, 2013), 50. See also Ozanam, *History of Civilization*, vol. 2, 66–67. For the original French text see Ozanam, *La civilisation*, in *Oeuvres complètes* (1862), vol. 2, 85–86. For similar views see Ozanam, "Du divorce," in *Oeuvres complètes* (1872), vol. 7, 176–78.

167. Quoted in Harrison, *Romantic Catholics*, 230. For the original French text see Ozanam, "Du divorce," in *Oeuvres complètes* (1872), vol. 7, 177. See also Harrison, *Romantic Catholics*, 229–30.

168. Ozanam, "Du divorce," in *Oeuvres complètes* (1872), vol. 7, 179.

169. Bressolette, "Ozanam et *L'Ère nouvelle*," 81. See also Ozanam, "Du divorce," in *Oeuvres complètes* (1872), vol. 7, 209.

170. Bressolette, "Ozanam et *L'Ère nouvelle*," 81. See also Ozanam, "Du divorce," in *Oeuvres complètes* (1872), vol. 7, 209–10.

171. Bressolette, "Ozanam et *L'Ère nouvelle*," 81.

172. Ozanam, "Les origines du socialisme," in *Oeuvres complètes* (1872), vol. 7, 402–3.

173. Ibid., 407.

174. Quoted in Bressolette, "Ozanam et *L'Ère nouvelle*," 82.

175. Ibid., 75.

176. Loubère, *Nineteenth-Century Europe*, 129–30.

177. Bressolette, "Ozanam et *L'Ère nouvelle*," 86.

178. Schimberg, *The Great Friend*, 231.

179. Ibid.

180. Popkin, *Modern France*, 113.

181. Ibid.

182. Ibid., 114–15.

183. Ibid., 116–17.

184. "Letter to Alexandre Dufieux," 9 April 1851, in *Lettres*, vol. 4, no. 1069, 228.

185. Ibid. English translation quoted in Baunard, *Ozanam*, 304.

CHAPTER 7. FRIENDSHIP

1. Schimberg, *The Great Friend*, 313.

2. Dirvin, *A Life in Letters*, 7n.1.

3. Vincent, *Ozanam*, 99.

4. Ibid. *L'Abeille française* (The French Bee) was "a little review founded in Lyons by Fathers Noiret [*sic*] and Legeay of the Royal College. Its purpose was to give alumni . . . a means of expression, and Frederick availed himself of the opportunity, commenting on current events, indulging in poetic flights, treating of historical and philosophical subjects" (Schimberg, *The Great Friend*, 29).

5. "Letter to Auguste Materne," 12 September 1829, in Dirvin, *A Life in Letters*, 6. For the original French text see *Lettres*, vol. 1, no. 6, 3.

6. "Letter to Auguste Materne," 5 May 1830, in Dirvin, *A Life in Letters*, 7. For the original French text see *Lettres*, vol. 1, no. 11, 10. Because of an insult to the French consul in Algiers in 1827, the French government instituted a blockade of Algiers that lasted for three years. The failure of the blockade was used as an excuse for a military expedition against Algiers in 1830. The letter refers to this incident. The young Ozanam took the side of the French against the Algerians in his poem.

7. Ibid., 9. For the original French text see *Lettres*, vol. 1, no. 11, 12.

8. "Letter to Auguste Materne," 5 June 1830, in Dirvin, *A Life in Letters*, 12. For the original French text see *Lettres*, vol. 1, no. 12, 15.

9. "Letter to Auguste Materne," 8 June 1830, in Dirvin, *A Life in Letters*, 14. For the original French text see *Lettres*, vol. 1, no. 13, 16–17.

10. Vincent, *Ozanam*, 102.

11. O'Meara, *Ozanam*, 17.

12. Ibid., 17–18.

13. Caron, "Catholic Student," 36.

14. Ibid., 36–37.

15. Dirvin, *A Life in Letters*, 17n.1.

16. O'Meara, *Ozanam*, 20.

17. "Letter to his father," 12 November 1831, in Dirvin, *A Life in Letters*, 17. For the original French text see *Lettres*, vol. 1, no. 38, 57.

18. O'Meara, *Ozanam*, 21.

19. J.-C. Caron, "Catholic Student," 37.

20. "Letter to his mother," 19 March 1833, in Dirvin, *A Life in Letters*, 35. For the original French text see *Lettres*, vol. 1, no. 55, 99. "Henri" most likely refers to Ozanam's cousin Henri Pessonneaux.

21. For further information on these three, see Dirvin, *A Life in Letters*, 38–39, nn.2–4.

22. "Letter to his mother," 19 March 1833, in Dirvin, *A Life in Letters*, 36. For the original French text see *Lettres*, vol. 1, no. 38, 100.

23. Ibid. For the original French text see *Lettres*, vol. 1, no. 38, 99.

24. Ibid. For the original French text see *Lettres*, vol. 1, no. 38, 99–100.

25. "Letter to François Lallier," 9 April 1838, in Dirvin, *A Life in Letters*, 135. For the original French text see *Lettres*, vol. 1, no. 173, 301.

26. "Ernest Falconnet (1815–91), distant cousin of Ozanam, was substitute of the tribunal of Saint-Etienne (1839) and of Bourg (1842) before going in the same capacity to Lyon, February 5, 1844. [A substitute stands in for the *procureur de la République*, who is a magistrate of the French ministry of justice.] Falconnet then pursued his career as substitute at the court of Rouen (1846), advocate general (1849), first advocate general (1852) at Lyon, procurator general at Pau, and councilor of the Supreme Court from 1875 until his retirement in 1890." See Dirvin, *A Life in Letters*, 19n.1.

27. "Letter to Ernest Falconnet," 5–8 January 1833, in Dirvin, *A Life in Letters*, 26. For the original French text see *Lettres*, vol. 1, no. 53, 90–91.

28. "Letter to Ernest Falconnet," 19 March 1833, in Dirvin, *A Life in Letters*, 31–33. For the original French text see *Lettres*, vol. 1, no. 54, 95–97.

29. "Letter to Ernest Falconnet," 7 January 1834, in Dirvin, *A Life in Letters*, 44–45. For the original French text see *Lettres*, vol. 1, no. 67, 122–23.

30. Ibid., 43. For the original French text see *Lettres*, vol. 1, no. 67, 121.

31. Baunard, *Ozanam*, 349. For the original French text see "Letter to Ernest Falconnet," 30 July 1851, in *Lettres*, vol. 4, no. 1088, 248–50.

32. Ibid. For the original French text see *Lettres*, vol. 4, no. 1088, 249–50.

33. Ibid., 349–50. For the original French text see *Lettres*, vol. 4, no. 1088, 249.

34. For the original French text see "Letter to Ernest Falconnet," 30 July 1851, in *Lettres*, vol. 4, no. 1088, 250, and "Letter to M. Falconnet," 30 July 1851, in "Lettres Ozanam," *Oeuvres complètes* (1865), vol. 11, 334. The complete letter is on pp. 331–34.

35. Schimberg, *The Great Friend*, 57.

36. Ibid., 82.

37. "Letter to Louis Janmot," 13 November 1836, in Dirvin, *A Life in Letters*, 96. For the original French text see *Lettres*, vol. 1, no. 137, 243.

38. Quoted in Baunard, *Ozanam*, 349. For the original French text see "Letter to Louis Janmot," 4 October 1852, in *Lettres*, vol. 4, no. 1176, 394–95.

39. Dirvin, *A Life in Letters*, 49n.3.

40. See chapter 2 for more details of their friendship.

41. See "Letter to Léonce Curnier," 4 November 1834, in Dirvin, *A Life in Letters*, 55–57. For the original French text see *Lettres*, vol. 1, no. 82, 153–55.

42. For further information on Léonce Curnier, see the entry on him in Adolphe Robert, Edgar Bourloton, and Gaston Cougny, *Dictionnaire des Parlementaires français de 1789 à 1889* (Paris: Bourloton, 1891). The reference to Curnier can also be accessed at http://www.assemblee-nationale.fr/sycomore/fiche.asp?num_dept=9576.

43. "Letter to Léonce Curnier," 9 March 1837, in Dirvin, *A Life in Letters*, 105. For the original French text see *Lettres*, vol. 1, no. 142, 253.

44. "Circular-letter of M. Lallier, Secretary-General," 1 March 1837, in *Manual of the SVP* (Dublin), 120.

45. Curnier, *La jeunesse*, 112.

46. O'Connor, *The Secret of Frederick Ozanam*, 31. Quoted in O'Meara, *Ozanam*, 177. For the original French text see Ozanam, *Oeuvres complètes* (1872), vol. 7, 293.

47. O'Connor, *The Secret of Frederick Ozanam*, 31.

48. "Circular-letter of M. Lallier, Secretary-General," August 1837, in *Manual of the SVP* (Dublin), 205–6.

49. Ibid., 207.

50. Quoted in O'Meara, *Ozanam*, 176–77. For the original French text see Ozanam, *Oeuvres complètes* (1872), vol. 7, 293.

51. Baunard, *Ozanam*, 347.

52. Cholvy, *Ozanam: L'engagement*, 223, 225. Cholvy refers to their friendship as "une grande amitié." He notes that there is a remarkable richness in the correspondence between these two men.

53. Baunard, *Ozanam*, 347.

54. "Letter to François Lallier," 17 May 1838, in Dirvin, *A Life in Letters*, 139–40. For the original French text see *Lettres*, vol. 1, no. 175, 304–6.

55. Baunard, *Ozanam*, 347. See "Letter to François Lallier," 21 June 1840, in Dirvin, *A Life in Letters*, 187. For the original French text see *Lettres*, vol. 1, no. 241, 409.

56. Baunard, *Ozanam*, 347. This letter, described and quoted by Baunard as from 1842, is from 1844. Baunard is clearly mistaken about the date. See "Letter to François Lallier," 27 August 1844, in *Lettres*, vol. 2, no. 573, 599–600.

57. Baunard, *Ozanam*, 347–48. For the original French text see *Lettres*, vol. 2, no. 573, 600.

58. "Letter to François Lallier," 16 May 1843, in Dirvin, *A Life in Letters*, 339, 340. For the original French text see *Lettres*, vol. 2, no. 488, 450, 452.

59. Baunard, *Ozanam*, 231.

60. For the original French text see "Letter to M. Lallier," 27 August 1845, in "Lettres Ozanam," *Oeuvres complètes* (1865), vol. 11, 89, and also *Lettres*, vol. 3, no. 639, 122. See also Baunard, *Ozanam*, 231.

61. For the original French text see "Letter to M. Lallier," 27 August 1845, in "Lettres Ozanam," *Oeuvres complètes* (1865), vol. 11, 91, and also *Lettres*, vol. 3, no. 639, 123. See also Baunard, *Ozanam*, 348.

62. Baunard, *Ozanam*, 231–32. See "Letter to M. Lallier," 30 December 1845, in "Lettres Ozanam," *Oeuvres complètes* (1865), vol. 11, 95. See also *Lettres*, vol. 3, no. 656, 150.

63. Baunard, *Ozanam*, 348. For the original French text see *Lettres*, vol. 4, no. 1133, 322.

64. Ibid.

65. Schimberg, *The Great Friend*, 115; Dirvin, *A Life in Letters*, 17n.2.

66. Christine Franconnet, "Jean-Jacques Ampère et Frédéric Ozanam: La Construction d'une amitié," in Barbiche and Franconnet, *Frédéric Ozanam (1813–1853)*, 64–65.

67. Ibid., 69–74.

68. Schimberg, *The Great Friend*, 33. See also Baunard, *Ozanam*, 20.

69. Baunard, *Ozanam*, 169–70. For the original French text, see "Letter to Jean-Jacques Ampère," 21 February 1840, in *Lettres*, vol. 1, no. 225, 386.

70. Ibid., 222–23. See also O'Meara, *Ozanam*, 182–83.

71. Baunard, *Ozanam*, 223.

72. Ibid., 334.

73. See Cholvy, *Ozanam: L'engagement*, 658. See also Mancini, *Alexis de Tocqueville*, 137.

74. Baunard, *Ozanam*, 334.

75. Ibid., 336.

76. Franconnet, "Ampère et Ozanam," in Barbiche and Franconnet, *Frédéric Ozanam (1813–1853)*, 62.

77. O'Meara, *Ozanam*, 263.

78. Schimberg, *The Great Friend*, 313.

79. Franconnet, "Ampère et Ozanam," in Barbiche and Franconnet, *Frédéric Ozanam (1813–1853)*, 62.

80. Baunard, *Ozanam*, 353–54. For the original French text see "Letter to M. Ampère," 24 August 1851, in "Lettres Ozanam," *Oeuvres complètes* (1865), vol. 11, 340–41. See also *Lettres*, vol. 4, no. 1101, 266–67.

81. Ibid., 354. For the original French text see "Letter to M. Ampère," 24 August 1851, in "Lettres Ozanam," *Oeuvres complètes* (1865), vol. 11, 341. See also *Lettres*, vol. 4, no. 1101, 267.

82. Ibid. For the original French text see "Letter to M. Ampère," 24 August 1851, in "Lettres Ozanam," *Oeuvres complètes* (1865), vol. 11, 341. See also *Lettres*, vol. 4, no. 1101, 267.

83. Ibid. For the original French text see "Letter to M. Ampère," 24 August 1851, in "Lettres Ozanam," *Oeuvres complètes* (1865), vol. 11, 341–42. See also *Lettres*, vol. 4, no. 1101, 267.

84. Ibid. For the original French text see "Letter to M. Ampère," 24 August 1851, in "Lettres Ozanam," *Oeuvres complètes* (1865), vol. 11, 342. See also *Lettres*, vol. 4, no. 1101, 267.

85. Ibid., 354–55; Baunard's emphasis. By "us four," Ampère is referring to himself, Frédéric, Amélie, and Marie.

86. "Letter to Jean-Jacques Ampère," 13 January 1853, in *Lettres*, vol. 4, no. 1224, 490.

87. Ibid.

88. Franconnet, "Ampère et Ozanam," in Barbiche and Franconnet, *Frédéric Ozanam (1813–1853)*, 74.

89. Baunard, *Ozanam*, 355n.

90. Quoted in John E. Rybolt, C.M., "The Virtuous Personality of Blessed Frederick Ozanam," *Vincentian Heritage* 17:1 (1996): 35.

91. Lacordaire, *My Friend*, 45.

92. Ibid., 84.

93. Ibid., 7.

94. "Letter to Lacordaire," 26 August 1839, in Dirvin, *A Life in Letters*, 167. For the original French text see *Lettres*, vol. 1, no. 211, 359–60.

95. Ibid., 168–69. For the original French text see *Lettres*, vol. 1, no. 211, 360–61.

96. On Lacordaire's position concerning democracy, see Lancelot C. Sheppard, *Lacordaire: A Biographical Essay* (New York: Macmillan Company, 1964), 102–3. See also Morel, "Un journal: *L'Ère nouvelle*," 37–40.

97. Baunard, *Ozanam*, 352. For the original French text see "Letter to Father Henri Lacordaire," 29 September 1851, in *Lettres*, vol. 4, no. 1113, 289.

98. Lacordaire, *My Friend*, 87.

99. "Letter to Auguste Materne," 5 June 1830, in Dirvin, *A Life in Letters*, 12. For the original French text see *Lettres*, vol. 1, no. 12, 15.

100. Schimberg, *The Great Friend*, 149.

101. O'Meara, *Ozanam*, 153–54.

102. Quoted in O'Connor, *The Secret of Frederick Ozanam*, 36.

103. Schimberg, *The Great Friend*, 275. The expression "perfection of kindness" most likely came from Baunard. See Baunard, *Ozanam*, 390.

104. Schimberg, *The Great Friend*, 275–76.

105. Ibid., 276.

106. Baunard, *Ozanam*, 390. For the original French text see "Letter to M. Jérusalemy," 6 May 1853, in "Lettres Ozanam," *Oeuvres complètes* (1865), vol. 11, 503–5, and *Lettres*, vol. 4, no. 1286, 597–98. See also Cholvy, *Ozanam: L'engagement*, 699.

107. Franconnet, "Ampère et Ozanam," in Barbiche and Franconnet, *Frédéric Ozanam (1813–1853)*, 61.

108. Baunard, *Ozanam*, 347.

109. Ozanam, *Dante and Catholic Philosophy*, 108. For the original French text see Ozanam, *Oeuvres complètes*, troisième édition (1869), vol. 6, 112.

110. Schimberg, *The Great Friend*, 313.

CHAPTER 8. SPIRITUALITY AND SANCTIFICATION

1. "Letter to Ernest Falconnet," 21 July 1834, in Dirvin, *A Life in Letters*, 46. For the original French text see *Lettres*, vol. 1, no. 77, 142.

2. Ronald W. Ramson, C.M., "Frédéric Ozanam: His Piety and Devotion," *Vincentiana* 41:3 (May–June 1997), 149 (3). *Vincentiana* is online at http://

cmglobal.org/vincentiana/. Hereafter cited as Ramson, "His Piety and Devotion"; the online page numbers are given in parentheses.

3. Quoted in Baunard, *Ozanam*, 342. For the original French text see "Letter to Charles Hommais," 16 June 1842, in *Lettres*, vol. 4, no. 1143, 335.

4. Cholvy, *Ozanam: Le christianisme*, 230.

5. Quoted in Hess, *Cahiers Ozanam*, 128. See also Baunard, *Ozanam*, 342.

6. Cholvy, *Ozanam: Le christianisme*, 226. The *Imitation of Christ* (*De Imitatione Christi*) by Thomas à Kempis, written in Latin during the early fifteenth century, is a guide for spiritual life and one of the most widely read works of Christian devotion. For more on Thomas à Kempis, see Robert S. Miola, *Early Modern Catholicism: An Anthology of Primary Sources* (New York: Oxford University Press, 2007), 285.

7. "Letter to Ernest Falconnet," 11 April 1834, in *Lettres*, vol. 1, no. 70, 129.

8. "Letter to Mademoiselle Soulacroix," 1 May 1841, in Dirvin, *A Life in Letters*, 245. For the original French text see *Lettres*, vol. 2, no. 310, 139–40.

9. Vincent, *Ozanam*, 65; Cholvy, *Ozanam: Le christianisme*, 227.

10. Baunard, *Ozanam*, 40. For the original French text see C.-A. Ozanam, *Frédéric Ozanam*, 639.

11. Ramson, "His Piety and Devotion," 150 (3). See also Baunard, *Ozanam*, 40. For the original French text see "Letter to his mother," 16 May 1834, in *Lettres*, vol. 1, no. 73, 136.

12. "Letter to Mademoiselle Soulacroix," 26 April 1841, in Dirvin, *A Life in Letters*, 236. For the original French text see *Lettres*, vol. 2, no. 307, 129–30.

13. The Chapel of Saint Vincent de Paul is the site of the remains of the famous French saint and is owned by the Congregation of the Mission. It is located on 95 rue de Sèvres 75007, Paris.

14. By "that double family," Ozanam is referring to the priests of the Congregation of the Mission (Vincentian fathers) and the Daughters of Charity.

15. "Letter to his wife," 23 July 1842, in Dirvin, *A Life in Letters*, 302. For the original French text see *Lettres*, vol. 2, no. 421, 322.

16. Ramson, "His Piety and Devotion," 148 (1).

17. Rybolt, "Virtuous Personality," 37.

18. "Letter to Emmanuel Bailly," 22 October 1836, in Dirvin, *A Life in Letters*, 88. For the original French text see *Lettres*, vol. 1, no. 135, 236.

19. "Letter to François Lallier," 5 October 1837, in Dirvin, *A Life in Letters*, 120. For the original French text see *Lettres*, vol. 1, no. 160, 283–84.

20. "Letter to his wife," 13 October 1841, in Dirvin, *A Life in Letters*, 356–57. For the original French text see *Lettres*, vol. 2, no. 515, 496.

21. Quoted in Ramson, "His Piety and Devotion," 154–55 (7). See also Saint Vincent de Paul, *Correspondance, Entretiens, Documents*, ed. Reverend Pierre Coste, C.M. (Paris: Gabalda, 1921–1925), vol. 2, 453, 456.

22. Ramson, "His Piety and Devotion," 156 (8). Ramson does not identify the source of his quote.

23. Not far from the Chapel of Saint Vincent de Paul is the motherhouse of the Daughters of Charity on the rue du Bac. The Blessed Mother appeared here to Saint Catherine Labouré, a member of the order, whose body still lies in state in the chapel of the Miraculous Medal at this location. According to Joseph I. Dirvin, C.M., in 1933 an exhumation ordered by the Catholic Church revealed the following: "Catherine lay there, as fresh and serene as the day she was buried [56 years earlier]. Her skin had not darkened in the least; the eyes which had looked on Our Lady were as intensely blue as ever, and—most remarkable of all—her arms and legs were as supple as if she were merely asleep." See his *Saint Catherine Labouré of the Miraculous Medal* (Rockford, IL: Tan Books and Publishers, 1984), 228–29.

24. Dirvin, *Saint Catherine Labouré*, 116–17.

25. "History of the Medal," *The Chapel Pamphlets* (July 2004), section 5, 2. See http://www.chapellenotredamedelamedaillemiraculeuse.com/Carnets /carnetEN/HistoireMedaille-AN.pdf.

26. "Letter to Dominique Meynis," 14 April 1842, in Dirvin, *A Life in Letters*, 289. For the original French text see *Lettres*, vol. 2, no. 392, 280. The miraculous conversion of a French Jew who was an outspoken critic of the Catholic Church is recounted in Dirvin, *Saint Catherine Labouré*, 166–71.

27. "Letter to Dominique Meynis," 22 June 1842, in Dirvin, *A Life in Letters*, 301. For the original French text see *Lettres*, vol. 2, no. 414, 310.

28. "Letter to Théophile Foisset," 7 August 1845, in *Lettres*, vol. 3, no. 636, 118.

29. "Letter to Ernest Falconnet," 5–8 January 1833, in Dirvin, *A Life in Letters*, 25–26. For the original French text see *Lettres*, vol. 1, no. 53, 90.

30. Corpus Christi was traditionally celebrated on the Thursday after Trinity Sunday, which is the Sunday after the feast of Pentecost. The procession carried the Blessed Sacrament, usually in a monstrance, through the streets. Nanterre is about seven miles west of the center of Paris.

31. "Letter to his mother," 19 June 1833, in *Lettres*, vol. 1, no. 58, 106. See also Dirvin, *A Life in Letters*, 40.

32. "Letter to Charles Ozanam," 28 March 1842, in Dirvin, *A Life in Letters*, 284–85. For the original French text see *Lettres*, vol. 2, no. 387, 270. A *Te Deum* is a special hymn of praise to God.

33. Cholvy, *Ozanam: Le christianisme*, 228.

34. "Letter to Léonce Curnier," 16 May 1835, in Dirvin, *A Life in Letters*, 67. For the original French text see *Lettres*, vol. 1, no. 97, 182.

35. Quoted in Baunard, *Ozanam*, 99. For the original French text see "Letter to Alexandre Dufieux," 2 March 1835, in *Lettres*, vol. 1, no. 92, 172.

36. Quoted in ibid. For the original French text see *Lettres*, vol. 1, no. 92, 173.

37. "Letter to François Lallier," 5 November 1836, in Dirvin, *A Life in Letters*, 93. For the original French text see *Lettres*, vol. 1, no. 136, 241.

38. Quoted in O'Meara, *Ozanam*, 176–77. For the original French text see Ozanam, *Oeuvres complètes* (1872), vol. 7, 293.

39. "Letter to Mademoiselle Soulacroix," 1 May 1841, in Dirvin, *A Life in Letters*, 242. For the original French text see *Lettres*, vol. 2, no. 310, 136–37.

40. "Letter to Charles Ozanam," 25 June 1843, in Dirvin, *A Life in Letters*, 347. For the original French text see *Lettres*, vol. 2, no. 496, 465–66.

41. Quoted in Ramson, *Hosanna!*, 27. For the original French text see "Letter to Father Tommaso Pendola," 9 July 1853, in *Lettres*, vol. 4, no. 1319, 659.

42. Cholvy, *Ozanam: Le christianisme*, 231–39.

43. Ozanam published articles on the religions of India and China. He was fascinated with the idea of a common origin of all religions. See Dirvin, *A Life in Letters*, 288n.1.

44. Ferdinand Holböck, *Married Saints and Blesseds through the Centuries* (San Francisco: Ignatius Press, 2002), 479.

45. See Dirvin, *A Life in Letters*, 2. See also "Letter to Dominique Meynis," 31 January 1843, in Dirvin, *A Life in Letters*, 325–26. For the original French text, see *Lettres*, vol. 2, no. 468, 414–15.

46. Ramson, "His Piety and Devotion," 159–60 (12).

47. Rybolt, "Virtuous Personality," 44.

CHAPTER 9. SOLIDARITY

1. Pope John Paul II, *On Social Concern* (*Sollicitudo Rei Socialis*), December 30, 1987, no. 38. http://www.vatican.va/.

2. Ibid., no. 39.

3. Meghan J. Clark, "The Complex but Necessary Union of Charity and Justice: Insights from the Vincentian Tradition for Contemporary Catholic Social Teaching," *Vincentian Heritage Journal* 31:2 (2012): 39.

4. O'Brien, "Pioneer and Prophet," 45.

5. "Letter to Léonce Curnier," 23 February 1835, in Dirvin, *A Life in Letters*, 63. For the original French text see *Lettres*, vol. 1, no. 90, 166.

6. Ibid., 64. For the original French text see *Lettres*, vol. 1, no. 90, 166.

7. "Letter to Louis Janmot," in Dirvin, *A Life in Letters*, 96. For the original French text see *Lettres*, vol. 1, no. 137, 243.

8. Ibid. For the original French text see *Lettres*, vol. 1, no. 137, 243.

9. Ibid. For the original French text see *Lettres*, vol. 1, no. 137, 243.

10. Clark, "Complex but Necessary Union," 26–27. Clark also remarks that *caritas* as friendship with God was part of Thomas Aquinas's views. See Meghan

J. Clark, "Love of God and Neighbor: Living Charity in Aquinas' Ethics," *New Blackfriars* 92:1040 (2011).

11. "Letter to Emmanuel Bailly," 22 October 1836, in Dirvin, *A Life in Letters*, 88. For the original French text see *Lettres*, vol. 1, no. 135, 236.

12. "Letter to François Lallier," 5 November 1836, in Dirvin, *A Life in Letters*, 92. For the original French text see *Lettres*, vol. 1, no. 136, 239.

13. "Letter to Léonce Curnier," 9 March 1837, in Dirvin, *A Life in Letters*, 106. For the original French text see *Lettres*, vol. 1, no. 142, 254.

14. For the original French text see Antoine Frédéric Ozanam, *Notes d'un cours de droit commercial*, in *Oeuvres complètes* (1872), vol. 8, 586.

15. Quoted in Clark, "Complex but Necessary Union," 26–27. The quote is from Thomas Shubeck, *Love that Does Justice* (Maryknoll, NY: Orbis Books, 2007), 131.

16. Ozanam, *La civilisation*, in *Oeuvres complètes* (1862), vol. 1, 24.

17. Quoted in John Looby, S.J., "Ozanam and Marx," *The Irish Monthly* 81:964 (1953): 476–77.

18. I have organized my discussion of Catholic social teaching according to the ten themes suggested by Byron and Maloney. The United States Catholic Conference of Bishops (USCCB) has identified seven, but differences are minor. For example, Byron and Maloney suggest that the first two principles are the dignity of the human person and the respect for human life. The USCCB combines these into one theme: the life and dignity of the human person. See William J. Byron, "Ten Building Blocks of Catholic Social Teaching," *America* 179:13 (1998): 9–12. See also Robert P. Maloney, C.M., "Ten Foundational Principles in the Social Teaching of the Church," *Vincentiana* 43:3 (1999). http://cmglobal.org/vincentiana/.

19. United States Catholic Conference of Bishops (USCCB), *Sharing Catholic Social Teaching: Challenges and Directions—Reflections of the U.S. Catholic Bishops* (Washington, DC, 1998), 2. http://www.usccb.org/.

20. Byron, "Ten Building Blocks," 10. See also Maloney, "Ten Foundational Principles."

21. Byron, "Ten Building Blocks," 10. See also Maloney, "Ten Foundational Principles."

22. "Letter to Louis Janmot," 13 November 1836, in Dirvin, *A Life in Letters*, 96. For the original French text see *Lettres*, vol. 1, no. 137, 243. Ozanam refers to the apostle Thomas, who originally doubted that the other apostles had seen Christ.

23. Quoted in O'Meara, *Ozanam*, 176–77. For the original French text see Ozanam, *Oeuvres complètes* (1872), vol. 7, 292–93.

24. USCCB, *Sharing Catholic Social Teaching*, 2.

25. Byron, "Ten Building Blocks," 10. See also Maloney, "Ten Foundational Principles."

26. Quoted in O'Meara, *Ozanam*, 245. For the original French text see Ozanam, *Oeuvres complètes* (1872), vol. 7, 265–66.

27. USCCB, *Sharing Catholic Social Teaching*, 4. Byron's and Maloney's two principles—association and participation—are included in the second USCCB theme: call to family, community, and participation.

28. Byron, "Ten Building Blocks," 10. See also Maloney, "Ten Foundational Principles."

29. USCCB, *Sharing Catholic Social Teaching*, 5.

30. Byron, "Ten Building Blocks," 10. See also Maloney, "Ten Foundational Principles."

31. United States Catholic Conference of Bishops, *Forming Consciences for Faithful Citizenship: A Call to Political Responsibility from the Catholic Bishops of the United States* (Washington, DC, 2007), no. 13, 4. http://www .usccb.org/.

32. *Catechism of the Catholic Church*, 2nd ed., no. 1913. http://www.usccb .org/.

33. Schimberg, *The Great Friend*, 219. See also "Letter to L'Abbé Alphonse Ozanam," in *Lettres*, vol. 3, no. 825, 443; Hess, *Cahiers Ozanam*, 51.

34. "Letter to Théophile Foisset," 22 February 1848, in *Lettres*, vol. 3, no. 784, 379.

35. Ozanam, *Dante and Catholic Philosophy*, 241. For original French text see Ozanam, *Oeuvres complètes* (1869), vol. 6, 243.

36. Quoted in Spencer, "'Barbarian Assault,'" 237. See also Ozanam, "Les dangers de Rome."

37. Auge, *Frederic Ozanam*, 86.

38. USCCB, *Sharing Catholic Social Teaching*, 5. The USCCB identifies a separate theme: the dignity of work and the rights of workers.

39. Ozanam, *Oeuvres complètes* (1872), vol. 8, 579–80.

40. Ibid., 580–81.

41. Quoted in John A. Ryan and Joseph Husslein, S.J., *The Church and Labor* (New York: Macmillan Company, 1920), vii. For the original French text see Ozanam, *Oeuvres complètes* (1872), vol. 7, 246–47.

42. Quoted in ibid., 11. For the original French text see Ozanam, *Oeuvres complètes* (1872), vol. 7, 280. This selection is from "Les causes de la misère," published in *L'Ère nouvelle*, October 1848.

43. Quoted in ibid., 11–12. For the original French text see Ozanam, *Oeuvres complètes* (1872), vol. 7, 280.

44. Quoted in ibid., 12. For the original French text see Ozanam, *Oeuvres complètes* (1872), vol. 7, 280.

45. Quoted in ibid., 11. For the original French text see Ozanam, *Oeuvres complètes* (1872), vol. 7, 247.

46. Ozanam, *Oeuvres complètes* (1872), vol. 8, 588–89.

47. Quoted in Ryan and Husslein, *The Church and Labor*, 20. For the original French text see Ozanam, *Oeuvres complètes* (1872), vol. 8, 582–87. The helots were the slaves of the ancient Greek city-state of Sparta.

48. David L. Gregory, "Antoine Frederic Ozanam: Building the Good Society," *University of St. Thomas Law Journal* 3:1 (2005): 39.

49. Ibid., 36.

50. Byron, Maloney, and the USCCB include this as one of their principles.

51. USCCB, *Sharing Catholic Social Teaching*, 5.

52. Byron, "Ten Building Blocks," 11. See also Maloney, "Ten Foundational Principles."

53. Hess, *Cahiers Ozanam*, 27. For the original French text, see "Letter to L'Abbé Alphonse Ozanam," 12–21 April 1848, in *Lettres*, vol. 3, no. 802, 413.

54. Quoted in O'Meara, *Ozanam*, 248. For the original French text see Ozanam, *Oeuvres complètes* (1872), vol. 7, 282–84.

55. O'Meara, *Ozanam*, 177.

56. USCCB, *Sharing Catholic Social Teaching*, 5. Byron, Maloney, and the USCCB include this as one of their principles.

57. Byron, "Ten Building Blocks," 11. See also Maloney, "Ten Foundational Principles."

58. Gregory, "Ozanam: Building the Good Society," 39.

59. Sister Louise Sullivan indicates that Ozanam wrote the letter to Léonce Curnier rather than vice versa, and cites a letter of 3 November 1834, in *Lettres de Frédéric Ozanam*, 1:152. See Sullivan, *Sister Rosalie*, 212. But unfortunately no such letter exists in the collected work of letters. There is, however, a letter of November 4 to Léonce, in which Ozanam responds to a letter sent to him by Léonce on November 3. See 4 November 1834, *Lettres*, vol. 1, no. 82, 153. It is in the letter of November 3 to Ozanam (not from Ozanam) that Léonce mentions how inspired he was by Ozanam's vision of a "network of Charity" for France. Concerning this letter, see Baunard, *Ozanam*, 89. For this latter view see Auge, *Frederic Ozanam*, 24.

60. O'Brien, "Pioneer and Prophet," 44.

61. For the original French text see Ozanam, *Oeuvres complètes* (1872), vol. 8, 51.

62. USCCB, *Sharing Catholic Social Teaching*, 5. Byron and Maloney include the USCCB's theme of care for God's creation in their principle of stewardship.

63. Byron, "Ten Building Blocks," 11. See also Maloney, "Ten Foundational Principles."

64. Frédéric Ozanam, *A Pilgrimage to the Land of the Cid*, trans. Pauline Stump (New York: Christian Press Association Publishing Company, 1895), 8–9. For the original French text see Antoine Frédéric Ozanam, *Un pèlerinage au pays du Cid*, in *Oeuvres complètes* (1872), vol. 7, 5.

65. Ozanam, *Franciscan Poets*, 70. For the original French text see Ozanam, *Les poètes franciscains*, in *Oeuvres complètes* (1859), vol. 5, 65.

66. Ozanam, *Pilgrimage*, 18. For the original French text Ozanam, *Un pèlerinage*, in *Oeuvres complètes*, vol. 7, 10.

67. "Letter to Emmanuel Bailly," 22 October 1836, in Dirvin, *A Life in Letters*, 89. For the original French text see *Lettres*, vol. 1, no. 135, 237.

68. Designed by Joseph Paxton, the Crystal Palace was erected to house the Great Exhibition of 1851.

69. O'Meara, *Ozanam*, 265–66. For the original French text see "Letter to Charles Ozanam," 25 August 1851, in *Lettres*, vol. 4, no. 1102, 269–69.

70. "Letter to Henri Pessonneaux," 6 September 1851, in *Lettres*, vol. 4, no. 1107, 282.

71. Byron, "Ten Building Blocks," 11. See also Maloney, "Ten Foundational Principles."

72. See chapter 12 on suffering.

73. Baunard, *Ozanam*, 259. For the original French text see "Letter to Théophile Foisset," 22 March 1848, in *Lettres*, vol. 3, no. 792, 397.

74. See Amélie Ozanam-Soulacroix, *Notes biographique*, in *Actes du Colloque*, 332.

75. Byron's and Maloney's principles of equality, subsidiarity, and the common good are all included under the USCCB theme: rights and responsibilities.

76. Byron, "Ten Building Blocks," 11. See also Maloney, "Ten Foundational Principles."

77. USCCB, *Sharing Catholic Social Teaching*, 6.

78. Byron, "Ten Building Blocks," 11. See also Maloney, "Ten Foundational Principles."

79. Byron, "Ten Building Blocks," 11. See also Maloney, "Ten Foundational Principles."

80. Morel, "Un journal: *L'Ère nouvelle*," 48.

81. O'Brien, "Pioneer and Prophet," 30.

82. Ozanam, *Oeuvres complètes* (1872), vol. 8, 51.

83. Pope Benedict XVI, *Caritas in Veritate*, June 29, 2009, no. 1. http://www.vatican.va/.

84. Ibid., no. 6.

85. Ibid., no. 7. Emphasis in original.

86. Clark, "Complex but Necessary Union," 26.

87. Pope Francis I, "Address of Holy Father Francis," Cathedral of Cagliari, Sunday, September 22, 2013, no. 1. http://www.vatican.va/.

88. Pope Francis I, "Address of Holy Father Francis," Largo Carlo Felice, Cagliari, September 22, 2013. http://www.vatican.va/.

89. Ryan and Husslein, *The Church and Labor*, 17.

90. O'Brien, "Pioneer and Prophet," 34.

CHAPTER 10. SERVANT LEADERSHIP

1. Ozanam, *La civilisation*, in *Oeuvres complètes* (1862), vol. 1, 24.

2. Robert K. Greenleaf, *Servant Leadership: A Journey into the Nature of Legitimate Power and Greatness* (New York: Paulist Press, 1977).

3. Ibid., 13.

4. Ibid.

5. Ibid., 13–14.

6. For the original French text see Ozanam, *Oeuvres complètes* (1872), vol. 8, 47.

7. The Gospels indicate this. See Mark 10:42–45, Matthew 23:8–12, Luke 22:24–27, and John 13:12–17, and the discussion in Shane D. Lavery, "Religious Educators: Promoting Servant Leadership," 3–6. Originally published in *Religious Education Journal of Australia* 25:1 (2009): 31–36. Accessible at http://researchonline.nd.edu.au/; page nos. refer to this online version.

8. "Letter to François Lallier," 17 May 1838, in Dirvin, *A Life in Letters*, 143. For the original French text see *Lettres*, vol. 1, no. 175, 308–9.

9. See J. P. Murphy, C.M., "Servant Leadership in the Manner of Saint Vincent de Paul," *Vincentian Heritage* 19:1 (1998): 121–34.

10. Ibid.

11. Ibid., 124.

12. Ibid., 132.

13. Larry C. Spears, "Character and Servant Leadership: Ten Characteristics of Effective, Caring Leaders," *Journal of Virtues & Leadership* 1:1 (2010): 27. Larry C. Spears is the president and CEO of The Larry C. Spears Center for Servant-Leadership. He served as the president and CEO of the Robert K. Greenleaf Center for Servant-Leadership from 1990 to 2007.

14. Greenleaf, *Servant Leadership*, 17.

15. O'Meara, *Ozanam*, 150.

16. Ibid., 173.

17. Spears, "Character and Servant Leadership," 27.

18. Shaun McCarty, S.T., "Frederick Ozanam: Lay Evangelizer," *Vincentian Heritage* 17:1 (1996): 34.

19. English translation quoted in Baunard, *Ozanam*, 304. For the original French text see "Letter to Alexandre Dufieux," 9 April 1851, in *Lettres*, vol. 4, no. 1069, 228.

20. Spears, "Character and Servant Leadership," 27. Vincent de Paul would have called this compassion.

21. Hess, *Cahiers Ozanam*, 116. For the original French text see Amélie Ozanam-Soulacroix, *Notes biographique*, in *Actes du Colloque*, 333.

22. Amélie Ozanam-Soulacroix, *Notes biographique*, in *Actes du Colloque*, 332.

23. Spears, "Character and Servant Leadership," 27. See also Greenleaf, *Servant Leadership*, 36.

24. Spears, "Character and Servant Leadership," 27. See also Greenleaf, *Servant Leadership*, 27–29.

25. Quoted in Hess, *Cahiers Ozanam*, 114. See also "Letter to François Lallier," 5 November 1836, in Dirvin, *A Life in Letters*, 91–92. For the original French text see *Lettres*, vol. 1, no. 136, 239.

26. Quoted in Hess, *Cahiers Ozanam*, 118. See also "Letter to Léonce Curnier," 23 February 1835, in Dirvin, *A Life in Letters*, 63. For the original French text see *Lettres*, vol. 1, no. 90, 166.

27. Spears, "Character and Servant Leadership," 28. See also Greenleaf, *Servant Leadership*, 29–30.

28. Quoted in Hess, *Cahiers Ozanam*, 19. For the original French text see "Letter to Théophile Foisset," 22 March 1848, in *Lettres*, vol. 4, no. 792, 397.

29. Reverend Craig B. Mousin, "Frédéric Ozanam—Beneficent Deserter: Mediating the Chasm of Income Inequality through Liberty, Equality, and Fraternity," *Vincentian Heritage* 30:1 (2010): 63.

30. Quoted in Hess, *Cahiers Ozanam*, 19. For the original French text see "Letter to L'Abbé Alphonse Ozanam," 6 March 1848, in *Lettres*, vol. 4, no. 787, 388.

31. Ibid., 66. See also O'Meara, *Ozanam*, 230.

32. Spears, "Character and Servant Leadership," 28. See also Greenleaf, *Servant Leadership*, 30–32.

33. C.-A. Ozanam, *Frédéric Ozanam*, 210. See also Coates, *Ozanam*, 81.

34. Quoted in Ramson, *Hosanna!*, 27. For the original French text see "Letter to Father Tommaso Pendola," 9 July 1853, in *Lettres*, vol. 4, no. 1319, 659.

35. Spears, "Character and Servant Leadership," 28. See also Greenleaf, *Servant Leadership*, 24–27.

36. Corrin, *Catholic Intellectuals*, 16.

37. Spears, "Character and Servant Leadership," 29. See also Greenleaf, *Servant Leadership*, 94, 97.

38. "Report On Charity, 1834," 3. For the original French text see "Rapport," *Lettres*, vol. 6, no. 1457 [76 bis], 3.

39. "Letter to Louis Janmot," in Dirvin, *A Life in Letters*, 96. For the original French text see *Lettres*, vol. 1, no. 135, 243.

40. Spears, "Character and Servant Leadership," 29.

41. Greenleaf, *Servant Leadership*, 13–14.

42. "Letter to Léonce Curnier," 4 November 1834, in Dirvin, *A Life in Letters*, 56. For the original French text see *Lettres*, vol. 1, no. 82, 155.

43. Greenleaf, *Servant Leadership*, 13–14.

44. Quoted in Baunard, *Ozanam*, 261. See also Mousin, "Frédéric Ozanam—Beneficent Deserter," 68.

45. Spears, "Character and Servant Leadership," 29.

46. Greenleaf, *Servant Leadership*, 39.

47. "Letter to Henri Pessonneaux," 13 March 1840, in Dirvin, *A Life in Letters*, 178. For the original French text see *Lettres*, vol. 1, no. 227, 394.

48. "Letter to Mademoiselle Soulacroix," 28 February 1841, in Dirvin, *A Life in Letters*, 224. For the original French text see *Lettres*, vol. 2, no. 290, 88.

49. "Letter to Léonce Curnier," 4 November 1834, in Dirvin, *A Life in Letters*, 55. For the original French text see *Lettres*, vol. 1, no. 82, 154.

50. Ibid. For the original French text see *Lettres*, vol. 1, no. 82, 154.

51. *International Rule*, I, 3.11.

52. "Letter to François Lallier," 5 November 1836, in Dirvin, *A Life in Letters*, 93. For the original French text see *Lettres*, vol. 1, no. 136, 241.

53. "Letter to François Lallier," 5 October 1837, in Dirvin, *A Life in Letters*, 121. For the original French text see *Lettres*, vol. 1, no. 160, 284.

54. Murphy, "Servant Leadership," 128.

55. "Circular Letter of the Vice-Presidents-General," 11 June 1844, in *Manual of the SVP* (Dublin), 257. For the original French text see "Aux Conférences de Saint-Vincent-De-Paul," 11 June 1844, in *Lettres*, vol. 5, no. 1403 [540 bis], 112–13.

56. McCarty, "Frederick Ozanam," 10.

57. O'Meara, *Ozanam*, 175.

58. Murphy, "Servant Leadership," 132.

CHAPTER 11. SYSTEMIC THINKING AND SYSTEMIC CHANGE

I am grateful to the Vincentian Studies Institute at De Paul University for allowing me to use my article "Frédéric Ozanam: Systemic Thinking, and Systemic Change," *Vincentian Heritage Journal* 32:1 (2014), as the basis for this chapter.

1. See O'Meara, *Ozanam*, 64; Baunard, *Ozanam*, 72; O'Connor, *The Secret of Frederick Ozanam*, 32.

2. O'Meara, *Ozanam*, 64; Baunard, *Ozanam*, 72; O'Connor, *The Secret of Frederick Ozanam*, 32.

3. Peter M. Senge, *The Fifth Discipline: The Art and Practice of the Learning Organization* (New York: Doubleday, 1990), 13.

4. Ibid.

5. Ibid.

6. Ibid.

7. Robert P. Maloney, C.M., "Commission for Promoting Systemic Change," *Vincentiana* 52:1–2 (January–April 2008): 66. http://via.library.depaul.edu/cgi/viewcontent.cgi?article=1470&context=vincentiana.

8. James Keane, S.J., ed., *Seeds of Hope: Stories of Systemic Change* (St. Louis, MO: The Society of St.Vincent de Paul for the Commission for Promoting Systemic Change, 2008), 3.

9. Ibid., 43–48, 76–85, 118–26, and 162–69, respectively. See also the Vincentian Family News Blog's *Systemic Change: Seeds of Change* series. This twenty-week series was offered by the members of the Commission for Promoting Systemic Change. It highlights the most significant strategies. Cited hereafter as the *Seeds of Change* series. http://www.famvin.org/wiki/Systemic_Change:_Seeds_of_Change.

10. "Letter to François Lallier," 7 February 1838, in Dirvin, *A Life in Letters*, 131. For the original French text see *Lettres*, vol. 1, no. 169, 295.

11. "Letter to Mademoiselle Soulacroix," 28 February 1841, in Dirvin, *A Life in Letters*, 224. For the original French text see *Lettres*, vol. 2, no. 290, 88.

12. Keane, *Seeds of Hope*, 118–19; also 77, 83. See also *Seeds of Change* series, chapters 4 and 14.

13. Keane, *Seeds of Hope*, 164–65. See also *Seeds of Change* series, chapter 18.

14. Senge, *The Fifth Discipline*, 13.

15. Keane, *Seeds of Hope*, 118–19.

16. Baunard, *Ozanam*, 278.

17. Quoted in ibid., 279. See also Schimberg, *The Great Friend*, 210; Hughes, *Ozanam*, 60.

18. Quoted in Baunard, *Ozanam*, 65. For the original French text see Antoine Frédéric Ozanam, "Discours à la conférence de Florence," in *Oeuvres complètes* (1872), vol. 8, 4. See also C.-A. Ozanam, *Frédéric Ozanam*, 187.

19. *International Rule*, I, 6.

20. Keane, *Seeds of Hope*, 44–47. See also *Seeds of Change* series, chapters 2 and 3.

21. Quoted in Sullivan, *Sister Rosalie*, 210–11. See also Armand de Melun, *Vie de la sœur Rosalie, Fille de la Charité*, 13th ed. (Paris, 1929), 99–100.

22. Quoted in Sullivan, *Sister Rosalie*, 211.

23. Senge, *The Fifth Discipline*, 13.

24. "Letter to his mother," 23 July 1836, in Dirvin, *A Life in Letters*, 76. For the original French text see *Lettres*, vol. 1, no. 121, 220.

25. "Letter to his mother," 11 April 1837, in Dirvin, *A Life in Letters*, 110. For the original French text see *Lettres*, vol. 1, no. 146, 260.

26. Dirvin, *A Life in Letters*, 111n.4.

27. "Letter to Mademoiselle Soulacroix," 28 February 1841, in Dirvin, *A Life in Letters*, 224. For the original French text see *Lettres*, vol. 2, no. 290, 88.

28. "Letter of Frédéric Ozanam," December 1837, in *Manual of the SVP* (Dublin), 223–24. For the original French text see "À L'Assemblée Général de la Société de Saint-Vincent-De Paul," 8 December 1837, in *Lettres*, vol. 5, no. 1369 [164 bis], 64. The location of this report is Lyon. The original French report indicates 266 soldiers rather than 268. The General Assembly was typically an annual gathering of members.

29. "Letter to François Lallier," 5 October 1837, in Dirvin, *A Life in Letters*, 120. For the original French text see *Lettres*, vol. 1, no. 160, 283.

30. Conference 164, "Love for the Poor, January 1657," in Vincent de Paul, *Correspondence, Conferences, Documents*, ed. and trans. Jacqueline Kilar, D.C., Marie Poole, D.C., et al., 1-13a & 13b (New York: New City Press, 1985–2010), 11:349.

31. Keane, *Seeds of Hope*, 76, 78–79. See also *Seeds of Change* series, chapters 10 and 11.

32. Lacordaire, *My Friend*, 35.

33. Keane, *Seeds of Hope*, 76, 80–81. See also *Seeds of Change* series, chapters 12 and 13.

34. "Letter to Emmanuel Bailly," 22 October 1836, in Dirvin, *A Life in Letters*, 88. For the original French text see *Lettres*, vol. 1, no. 135, 236.

35. "Letter to François Lallier," 17 May 1838, in Dirvin, *A Life in Letters*, 143. For the original French text see *Lettres*, vol. 1, no. 175, 308–9.

36. *International Rule*, I, 11.

37. Brejon de Lavergnée suggests that there is insufficient evidence to conclude that Sister Rosalie was an ongoing mentor. See his *La Société de Saint-Vincent de-Paul*, 42, 44.

38. The Vincentian Family often refers to theological reflection as "apostolic reflection."

39. Sullivan, *Sister Rosalie*, 211. Sullivan does make this claim.

40. *International Rule*, I, 9.

41. "Letter of Frédéric Ozanam," 27 April 1838, in *Manual of the SVP* (Dublin), 121. For the original French text see "À L'Assemblée Général de la Société de Saint-Vincent-De Paul," 27 April 1838, in *Lettres*, vol. 5, no. 1372 [173 bis], 71.

42. Ibid., 209. For the original French text see *Lettres*, vol. 5, no. 1372 [173 bis], 72. The quote at the end is from Conference 164, "Love for the Poor, January 1657," the accepted modern English translation of which can be found in Vincent de Paul, *Correspondence, Conferences, Documents*, 11:349.

43. Antoine Frédéric Ozanam, "De l'aumône," *Oeuvres complètes* (1872), vol. 7, 299.

44. *Seeds of Change* series, chapter 13.

45. McCarty, "Frederick Ozanam," 34.

46. "Letter to Léonce Curnier," 23 February 1835, in Dirvin, *A Life in Letters*, 65. For the original French text see *Lettres*, vol. 1, no. 90, 167.

47. "Letter to Ernest Falconnet," 7 January 1834, in Dirvin, *A Life in Letters*, 43. For the original French text see *Lettres*, vol. 1, no. 67, 122.

48. "Letter to Mademoiselle Soulacroix," 1 May 1841, in Dirvin, *A Life in Letters*, 243. For the original French text see *Lettres*, vol. 2, no. 310, 137.

49. This quotation is from Vincent de Paul's *Common Rules* in General Curia of the Congregation of the Mission, *Constitutions and Statutes of the*

Congregation of the Mission (Philadelphia, 1989), 109. Originally published Rome, 1984.

50. The first quote is from Ellen Flynn, D.C., *Seeds of Change* series, chapter 6. See also *International Rule*, I, 10.

51. "Aux Conférences de Saint-Vincent-de-Paul," 11 June 1844, in *Lettres*, vol. 5, no. 1403 [540 bis], 112–13.

52. "Letter to François Lallier," 7 February 1838, in Dirvin, *A Life in Letters*, 131. For the original French text see *Lettres*, vol. 1, no. 169, 296.

53. Keane, *Seeds of Hope*, 118, 119, 122, 123. See also *Seeds of Change* series, chapters 6 and 7.

54. "Letter of Frédéric Ozanam," 27 April 1838, in *Manual of the SVP* (Dublin), 120. For the original French text see "À L'Assemblée Général de la Société de Saint-Vincent-De Paul," 27 April 1838, in *Lettres*, vol. 5, no. 1372 [173 bis], 71.

55. Ibid., 121. For the original French text see *Lettres*, vol. 5, no. 1372 [173 bis], 71.

56. Keane, *Seeds of Hope*, 119, 124. See also *Seeds of Change* series, chapter 8.

57. Quoted in O'Connor, *The Secret of Frederick Ozanam*, 56. See also *Rules of the Society 1835*, 43.

58. Quoted in Sullivan, *Sister Rosalie*, 222. Original in *Règlement de la Société*, 5–6. See also *Rules of the Society 1835*, 9–10.

59. Quoted in Sullivan, *Sister Rosalie*, 222–24. Original in *Règlement de la Société*, 7–10. See also *Rules of the Society 1835*, 12–13.

60. Senge, *The Fifth Discipline*, 13.

61. *International Rule*, I, 9.

62. Quoted in O'Connor, *The Secret of Frederick Ozanam*, 57. See also Baunard, *Ozanam*, 343–44. Original French text in Ozanam, *Oeuvres complètes* (1872), vol. 8, 55, 57.

63. Keane, *Seeds of Hope*, 77, 85, 119, 125. See also *Seeds of Change* series, chapters 9 and 16.

64. "Letter to François Lallier," 5 October 1837, in Dirvin, *A Life in Letters*, 120–21. For the original French text see *Lettres*, vol. 1, no. 160, 283–84.

65. Senge, *The Fifth Discipline*, 13.

66. "Letter of Frédéric Ozanam," 27 April 1838, in *Manual of the SVP* (Dublin), 120. For the original French text see "À L'Assemblée Général de la Société de Saint-Vincent-De Paul," 27 April 1838, in *Lettres*, vol. 5, no. 1372 [173 bis], 71.

67. William Hartenbach, C.M., "Vincentian Spirituality," *Vincentian Heritage* 17:1 (1996): 46.

68. Keane, *Seeds of Hope*, 77, 84, 164, 166, 167. See also *Seeds of Change* series, chapters 15, 19, and 20.

69. "Letter to Prosper Dugas," 11 March 1849, in "Lettres Ozanam," *Oeuvres complètes* (1865), vol. 11, 236. See also *Lettres*, vol. 3, no. 870, 495–96. This is also quoted in Derum, *Apostle in a Top Hat*, 202.

70. Baunard, *Ozanam*, 278. For the original French text see *Oeuvres complètes* (1872), vol. 7, 212.

71. Mousin, "Frédéric Ozanam—Beneficent Deserter," 80.

72. Keane, *Seeds of Hope*, 44–45, 118–20. See also *Seeds of Change* series, chapters 1 and 5.

73. Ozanam, "De l'assistance qui humilie et de celle qui honore," *L'Ère nouvelle*, no. 187, 22 October 1848. See Morel, "Un journal: *L'Ère nouvelle*," 52.

74. See Moon, *The Labor Problem*, 25–28. See also Gregory, "Ozanam: Building the Good Society," 33–41.

75. Keane, *Seeds of Hope*, 163–65. See also *Seeds of Change* series, chapters 17 and 18.

76. Ozanam, *Oeuvres complètes* (1872), vol. 8, 49, 51, 53.

77. Ozanam, *History of Civilization*, vol. 1, 3.

78. See O'Meara, *Ozanam*, 175, and Sullivan, *Sister Rosalie*, 210, respectively.

79. Senge, *The Fifth Discipline*, 13.

80. For these five criteria see Keane, *Seeds of Hope*, 9.

81. *International Rule*, I, 16.

82. See "Circular-letter of M. Gossin, President-General," 2 July 1845, in *Manual of the SVP* (Dublin), 218–21.

83. Brejon de Lavergnée emphasizes that the Society did not hesitate to multiply its works. See his *La Société de Saint-Vincent de-Paul*, 44.

84. C.-A. Ozanam, *Frédéric Ozanam*, 225.

85. Keane, *Seeds of Hope*, 9.

86. Thomas McKenna, C.M., "Frédéric Ozanam's Tactical Wisdom for Today's Consumer Society," *Vincentian Heritage* 30:1 (2010): 28.

87. Senge, *The Fifth Discipline*, 13.

88. Keane, *Seeds of Hope*, 188.

89. Quoted in O'Connor, *The Secret of Frederick Ozanam*, 60.

CHAPTER 12. SUFFERING

1. Quoted in Baunard, *Ozanam*, 292. For the original French text see "Letter to Madame Soulacroix," 7 April 1949, in *Lettres*, vol. 3, no. 875, 501.

2. Ramson, *Hosanna!*, 27.

3. Ibid., 27–28.

4. "Letter to his mother," 19 March 1833, in Dirvin, *A Life in Letters*, 37. For the original French text see *Lettres*, vol. 1, no. 55, 100. See also "Letter to his mother," in Dirvin, *A Life in Letters*, 41. For the original French text see *Lettres*, vol. 1, no. 58, 107.

5. "Letter to Mademoiselle Soulacroix," 8 May 1841, in Dirvin, *A Life in Letters*, 249. For the original French text see *Lettres*, vol. 2, no. 312, 143.

6. "Letter to Madame Soulacroix," 20 May 1841, in Dirvin, *A Life in Letters*, 262. For the original French text see *Lettres*, vol. 2, no. 316, 156–57.

7. Ibid. For the original French text see *Lettres*, vol. 2, no. 316, 156–57.

8. "Letter to Joseph Arthaud," 20 May 1841, in Dirvin, *A Life in Letters*, 264. For the original French text see *Lettres*, vol. 2, no. 317, 159.

9. "Letter to Dominique Meynis," 9 June 1841, in Dirvin, *A Life in Letters*, 267. For the original French text see *Lettres*, vol. 2, no. 326, 177.

10. "Bright Disease," *Encyclopedia Britannica* (Encyclopedia Britannica, 2015). https://www.britannica.com/science/Bright-disease.

11. Others have suggested that the disease may have been tubercular in origin. See Tarrazi and Ramson, *Ozanam*, 36. See also *Lettres*, vol. 4, no. 331, 590.

12. Quoted in Baunard, *Ozanam*, 82. For the original French text see "Letter to his parents," 30 December 1833, in *Lettres*, vol. 1, no. 66, 118–19.

13. Quoted in ibid., 82. For the original French text see "Letter to Ernest Falconnet," 11 April 1834, in *Lettres*, vol. 1, no. 70, 130–31.

14. "Letter to François Lallier," 5 October 1837, in Dirvin, *A Life in Letters*, 118. For the original French text see *Lettres*, vol. 1, no. 160, 281.

15. Ibid. For the original French text see *Lettres*, vol. 1, no. 160, 281.

16. Ibid. For the original French text see *Lettres*, vol. 1, no. 160, 281.

17. Ibid. For the original French text see *Lettres*, vol. 1, no. 160, 281.

18. Ibid. For the original French text see *Lettres*, vol. 1, no. 160, 281.

19. Baunard, *Ozanam*, 97.

20. "Letter to Léonce Curnier," 23 February 1835, in Dirvin, *A Life in Letters*, 64. For the original French text see *Lettres*, vol. 1, no. 90, 166.

21. Quoted in Ramson, "His Piety and Devotion," 151 (4).

22. "Letter to Louis Janmot," 13 November 1836, in Dirvin, *A Life in Letters*, 96. For the original French text see *Lettres*, vol. 1, no. 137, 243.

23. Keith Morton, "The Irony of Service: Charity, Project and Social Change in Service-Learning," *Michigan Journal of Community Service Learning* 2:1 (1995): 26.

24. Ramson, "His Piety and Devotion," 160 (11).

25. "Letter to Doctor Joseph Arthaud," 3 November 1849, in *Lettres*, vol. 3, no. 947, 601. See also Tarrazi and Ramson, *Ozanam*, 36.

26. Quoted in Tarrazi and Ramson, *Ozanam*, 36. For the original French text see "Letter to Doctor Joseph Arthaud," 3 November 1849, in *Lettres*, vol. 3, no. 947, 602.

27. Baunard, *Ozanam*, 340. For the original French text see "Letter to Jean-Jacques Ampère," 22 October 1851, in *Lettres*, vol. 4, no. 1115, 292.

28. Ibid. For the original French text see "Letter to Alexander Dufieux," 16 February 1852, in *Lettres*, vol. 4. no. 1123, 308.

29. Quoted in Baunard, *Ozanam*, 357. See "Letter to Jean-Jacques Ampère," 18 February 1852, in *Lettres*, vol. 4, no. 1125, 311.

30. Baunard, *Ozanam*, 358–59. See also O'Meara, *Ozanam*, 275–76.

31. Quoted in Frédéric Ozanam, *The Book of the Sick* (Paris: Society of St. Vincent de Paul International Council General, 2013), 26. For the original French text see "Letter to François Lallier," 19 October 1852, in *Lettres*, vol. 4, no. 1180, 403. As stated in the foreword, the 2013 edition is based on "the original adaptation of the book in the French version." It is divided into three parts, consisting of an anthology, the *Book of the Sick* itself, and information on the miracle attributed to Ozanam.

32. Baunard, *Ozanam*, 230.

33. "Letter to Monsieur and Madame Soulacroix," 19 March 1847, in *Lettres*, vol. 3, no. 719, 254.

34. Ibid.

35. "Letter to Prosper Dugas," 4–20 April 1847, in *Lettres*, vol. 3, no. 726, 273. See also Cholvy, *Ozanam: L'engagement*, 541.

36. Baunard, *Ozanam*, 368, 373–75. See also O'Meara, *Ozanam*, 324–26; Amélie Ozanam-Soulacroix, *Notes biographique*, in *Actes du Colloque*, 335–36.

37. See "Au Conseil Général de la Société de Saint-Vincent-De-Paul," 10 July 1853, in *Lettres*, vol. 4, no. 1320, 661–66.

38. "Letter to Alexandre Dufieux," 2 December 1852, in Hess, *Cahiers Ozanam*, 126. For the original French text see *Lettres*, vol. 4, no. 1203, 446.

39. Ibid., in Hess, *Cahiers Ozanam*, 126. For the original French text see *Lettres*, vol. 4, no. 1203, 446–47.

40. "Letter to Charles Ozanam," 5 December 1852, in Hess, *Cahiers Ozanam*, 126. For the original French text see *Lettres*, vol. 4, no. 1205, 452.

41. Quoted in Holböck, *Married Saints*, 479. See also Amélie Ozanam-Soulacroix, *Notes biographique*, in *Actes du Colloque*, 343.

42. See Madeleine des Rivières, *Ozanam*, trans. James Parry (Montreal: Les Éditions Bellarmin, 1989), 149.

43. "Letter to Father Henri Maret," 4 March 1853, in *Lettres*, vol. 4, no. 1249, 538. See also Ramson, *Hosanna!*, 163–64.

44. "Letter to Doctor Salvat Franchisteguy," 3 April 1853, and "Letter to Father Alphonse Ozanam," 30 April 1853, in *Lettres*, vol. 4, no. 1269, 572, and no. 1281, 590, respectively.

45. "Letter to Doctor Salvat Franchisteguy," 3 April 1853, in *Lettres*, vol. 4, no. 1269, 573. See also Baunard, *Ozanam*, 383; Ramson, *Hosanna!*, 162; Amélie Ozanam-Soulacroix, *Notes biographique*, in *Actes du Colloque*, 343.

46. Quoted in Ramson, *Hosanna!*, 167. For the original French text see "Letter to Doctor Salvat Franchisteguy," 3 April 1853, in *Lettres*, vol. 4, no. 1269, 572–73.

47. Amélie Ozanam-Soulacroix, *Notes biographique*, in *Actes du Colloque*, 350.

48. Des Rivières, *Ozanam*, 138.

49. Ibid., 110, 114. For the original French text of the quote see "Letter to Prosper Dugas," 4–20 April 1847, in *Lettres*, vol. 3, no. 726, 278.

50. Ramson, *Hosanna!*, 56.

51. Des Rivières, *Ozanam*, 117. For the original French text of the quote see "Letter to François Lallier," 31 December 1847, in *Lettres*, vol. 3, no. 775, 359.

52. Des Rivières, *Ozanam*, 156.

53. Baunard, *Ozanam*, 386. For the original French text see Amélie Ozanam-Soulacroix, *Notes biographique*, in *Actes du Colloque*, 349–50.

54. "Letter to Charles Ozanam," 14 November 1852, and "Letter to Théophile Foisset," 25 September 1851, in *Lettres*, vol. 4, no. 1195 and no. 1111, 428 and 285, respectively. See also Ramson, *Hosanna!*, 115.

55. Ramson, *Hosanna!*, 115–16.

56. Antoine Frédéric Ozanam, *The Bible for the Sick* (Dunwoodie, NY: St. Joseph's Seminary, 1901), "Introduction," p. C. I am grateful for receiving a copy of this English translation from the archives of the Council of Manhattan, Society of St. Vincent de Paul. This work has been republished in 2013 as *The Book of the Sick*, with a newer English translation by the International Society (see note 31 above).

57. Quoted in Tarrazi and Ramson, *Ozanam*, 39. For the original French text see Amélie Ozanam-Soulacroix, *Notes biographique*, in *Actes du Colloque*, 351–54. See also Cholvy, *Ozanam: L'engagement*, 711–12.

58. Amélie Ozanam-Soulacroix, *Notes biographique*, in *Actes du Colloque*, 352–53.

59. Cholvy, *Ozanam: L'engagement*, 712. Ozanam wrote this phrase to Lallier in 1845. See "Letter to François Lallier," 30 December 1845, in *Lettres*, vol. 3, no. 656, 151.

60. Ozanam, *Bible for the Sick*, "Introduction," p. B. For the original French text see "Letter to M. Jérusalemy," 6 May 1853, in "Lettres," vol. 2, in *Oeuvres Complètes* (1865), vol. 11, 503–5; and *Lettres*, vol. 4, no. 1286, 597–98. In the copy of the *Bible for the Sick* that I have used (1901), the date of this letter is incorrectly identified as 3 April. See also Baunard, *Ozanam*, 390; Cholvy, *Ozanam: L'engagement*, 699.

61. Ozanam, *Bible for the Sick*, "Introduction," p. A.

62. Amélie Ozanam-Soulacroix, *Notes biographique*, in *Actes du Colloque*, 339.

63. Ibid. Amélie notes that this young priest "died at sea while returning to France, his zeal has killed him."

64. Des Rivières, *Ozanam*, 149.

65. Ibid., 147, 158.

66. Baunard, *Ozanam*, 391.

67. Ibid., 391–92. For the original French text of the poem see 392n.

68. Amélie Ozanam-Soulacroix, *Notes biographique*, in *Actes du Colloque*, 342.

69. Baunard, *Ozanam*, 392.

70. Ibid., 397.

71. Ibid., 399. See also des Rivières, *Ozanam*, 158.

72. Baunard, *Ozanam*, 400.

73. Amélie Ozanam-Soulacroix, *Notes biographique*, in *Actes du Colloque*, 345.

74. Ibid., 344. For the prayer and translation see Baunard, *Ozanam*, 401.

75. Amélie Ozanam-Soulacroix, *Notes biographique*, in *Actes du Colloque*, 344. Amélie suggests that adding the codicil requiring an autopsy occurred around August 26 or 27, but others have suggested a much earlier date of April 18, 1853. See *Frédéric Ozanam à Marseille*, special issue, *Cahiers Ozanam*, no. 79, January–March (Paris: Society of Saint Vincent de Paul, Council General, 1983), 14. Hereafter cited as *Cahiers Ozanam*, no. 79.

76. Amélie Ozanam-Soulacroix, *Notes biographique*, in *Actes du Colloque*, 345. See also C.-A. Ozanam, *Frédéric Ozanam*, 531.

77. *Cahiers Ozanam*, no. 79, 10.

78. Amélie Ozanam-Soulacroix, *Notes biographique*, in *Actes du Colloque*, 345. See also Baunard, *Ozanam*, 403; *Cahiers Ozanam*, no. 79, 10; C.-A. Ozanam, *Frédéric Ozanam*, 532.

79. *Cahiers Ozanam*, no. 79, 13.

80. Amélie Ozanam-Soulacroix, *Notes biographique*, in *Actes du Colloque*, 346–47.

81. C.-A. Ozanam, *Frédéric Ozanam*, 535.

82. Ibid.

83. *Cahiers Ozanam*, no. 79, 13.

84. Ramson, *Hosanna!*, 168–69.

85. Ibid. See also Baunard, *Ozanam*, 403.

86. Ramson, *Hosanna!*, 170. La chapelle des Carmes is at 70 rue de Vaugirard, very close to the rue de Fleurus, where the Ozanam family resided in 1852. Today it is in the perimeter of L'Institut catholique de Paris, rue d'Aras. See *L'inhumation aux Carmes*, in *Actes du Colloque*, 361.

87. *L'inhumation aux Carmes*, in *Actes du Colloque*, 361.

88. Des Rivières, *Ozanam*, 163.

89. Quoted in O'Meara, *Ozanam*, 335–56. For the original French text see "Letter to Father Tomasso Pendola," 9 July 1853, in *Lettres*, vol. 4, no. 1319, 659–60.

90. Ozanam, *Bible for the Sick*, "Introduction," p. A.

CHAPTER 13. AN ENDURING LEGACY

1. Quoted in Amin de Tarrazi, "Frédéric Ozanam, A Lay Saint for Our Times," *Vincentiana* 41:3 (May–June 1997): 140. http://cmglobal.org

/vincentiana/. For the original French text see "Letter to Alexandre Dufieux," 14 July 1850, in *Lettres*, vol. 4, no. 999, 110.

2. Quoted in Baunard, *Ozanam*, 408.

3. John Paul II, "Beatification of Frédéric Ozanam, Homily of John Paul II," Notre-Dame de Paris, August 22, 1997, nos. 1 and 6. http://www.vatican.va/.

4. Mousin, "Frédéric Ozanam—Beneficent Deserter," 59.

5. O'Meara, *Ozanam*, 168–70.

6. Quoted in Baunard, *Ozanam*, 168. Ozanam expressed these ideas in an article written for *Le Contemporain* in 1840.

7. Cholvy, *Ozanam: Le christianisme*, 282.

8. Quote from Francisque Sarsky, later a French journalist, in Baunard, *Ozanam*, 201.

9. Renner, *Historical Thought*, 73.

10. Ibid., 61.

11. Baunard, *Ozanam*, 149.

12. Mousin, "Frédéric Ozanam—Beneficent Deserter," 64.

13. Ibid., 65.

14. Ozanam, *Dante and Catholic Philosophy*, 381–82. See also Mousin, "Frédéric Ozanam—Beneficent Deserter," 66. For the original French text see Ozanam, *Oeuvres complètes* (1869), vol. 6, 383.

15. Mousin, "Frédéric Ozanam—Beneficent Deserter," 66.

16. Ibid. See also Baunard, *Ozanam*, 149.

17. Baunard, *Ozanam*, 149.

18. Cholvy, "Ozanam and the Challenges," 1–2.

19. McCarty, "Frederick Ozanam," 33.

20. Léonce Celier, *Frédéric Ozanam, 1813–1853* (Paris: P. Lethielleux, Éditeur, 1956), 130.

21. Fichter, *Roots of Change*, 126.

22. Edward O'Connor, *The Secret of Frederick Ozanam*, 58.

23. Wright, *France in Modern Times*, 124.

24. McCarty, "Frederick Ozanam," 34.

25. Fichter, *Roots of Change*, 127.

26. Eugène Duthoit, *Frédéric Ozanam et la civilisation de l'amour* (Paris: Beauchesne, 1997), 94.

27. Ryan and Husslein, *The Church and Labor*, vii.

28. Mousin, "Frédéric Ozanam—Beneficent Deserter," 80.

29. Dorothy Day, *House of Hospitality* (New York: Sheed & Ward, 1939), 54.

30. Ibid., 55–56.

31. Mark Zwick and Louise Zwick, *The Catholic Worker Movement: Intellectual and Spiritual Origins* (New York: Paulist Press, 2005), 101.

32. Ibid., 103.

33. R. W. Rauch, Jr., *Politics and Belief in Contemporary France* (The Hague: Martinus Nijhoff, 1972), 16.

34. Jacques Maritain, *The Range of Reason* (New York: Scribner, 1952), 100.

35. Ibid., 113.

36. Chantelle Ogilvie-Ellis, "Jacques Maritain and a Spirituality of Democratic Participation," *Solidarity: The Journal of Catholic Social Thought and Secular Ethics* 3:1 (2013): 83.

37. Maritain, *Range of Reason*, 113.

38. Ibid.

39. Harrison, *Romantic Catholics*, 3.

40. Ibid., 4.

41. Ibid., 3.

42. Ibid., 3, 6.

43. Ibid., 6–7.

44. Ibid., 9.

45. Ibid.

46. Ibid., 10.

47. Ibid., 11.

48. Ibid.

49. Ibid., 19.

50. Ibid., 27.

51. "Letter to Niccolò Tommaseo," 5 April 1851, in *Lettres*, vol. 4, no. 1068, 226.

52. "To the Constitutents of the Department of the Rhone," 15 April 1848, in Hess, *Cahiers Ozanam*, 51.

53. Fichter, *Roots of Change*, 124.

54. John Honner, *Love and Politics: The Revolutionary Frederic Ozanam* (Melbourne, Australia: David Lovell Publishing, 2007), 86.

55. "Letter to Ernest Falconnet," 5–8 January 1833, in Dirvin, *A Life in Letters*, 26. For the original French text see *Lettres*, vol. 1, no. 53, 91. See also McCarty, "Frederick Ozanam," 18.

56. "Letter to Charles Hommais," 16 June 1852, in *Lettres*, vol. 4, no. 1143, 336.

57. "Letter to Ernest Falconnet," 21 July 1834, in Dirvin, *A Life in Letters*, 47. For the original French text see *Lettres*, vol. 1, no. 77, 143.

58. Ibid. For the original French text see *Lettres*, vol. 1, no. 77, 143.

59. McCarty, "Frederick Ozanam," 34.

60. John Dewey, *Ethics: The Middle Works of John Dewey*, vol. 5, ed. Jo Ann Boydston (Carbondale: Southern Illinois University Press, 1978), 301.

61. Ibid., 348.

62. Jane Addams, "The Subtle Problems of Charity," *Atlantic Monthly* 83:496 (1899): 163–78.

63. Ibid., 177.

64. Roy Lubove, *The Professional Altruist: The Emergence of Social Work as a Career, 1880–1930* (Cambridge, MA: Harvard University Press, 1965), 12.

65. Addams, "Subtle Problems," 163.

66. Lubove, *The Professional Altruist*, 16.

67. Quoted in O'Meara, *Ozanam*, 86. For the original French text see "Letter to Léonce Curnier," 23 February 1835, in *Lettres*, vol. 1, no. 90, 166.

68. "Letter to Léonce Curnier," 23 February 1835, quoted in Dirvin, *A Life in Letters*, 63. For the original French text see *Lettres*, vol. 1, no. 90, 166.

69. Quoted in Clark, "Complex but Necessary Union," 26–27. The quote is from Shubeck, *Love that Does Justice*, 131.

70. McCarty, "Frederick Ozanam," 34.

71. Mousin, "Frédéric Ozanam—Beneficent Deserter," 76.

72. Morton, "The Irony of Service," 28.

73. McCarty, "Frederick Ozanam," 33.

74. "Letter to Gustave Colas de la Noue," 24 November 1835, in *Lettres*, vol. 1, no. 111, 207.

75. McCarty, "Frederick Ozanam," 33.

76. Ibid., 33–34.

77. For information on VOP, see https://www.svdpusa.org/members /Programs-Tools/Programs/Voice-of-the-Poor.

78. "Letter to Léonce Curnier," 23 February 1835, in Dirvin, *A Life in Letters*, 64. For the original French text see *Lettres*, vol. 1, no. 90, 166–67. See also Didier Ozanam, "Frederic Ozanam," in Hess, *Cahiers Ozanam*, 17.

79. Brejon de Lavergnée, *La Société de Saint-Vincent de-Paul*, 172–73.

80. Mousin, "Frédéric Ozanam—Beneficent Deserter," 36–37.

81. Ibid., 37.

82. McCarty, "Frederick Ozanam," 33.

83. "Letter to François Lallier," 25 December 1839, in Dirvin, *A Life in Letters*, 172. For the original French text see *Lettres*, vol. 1, no. 221, 376.

84. Philippe Charpentier de Beauville, *Frédéric Ozanam, 1813–1853: Histoire d'une vocation* (Paris: Salvator, 2013), 170.

85. Harrison, *Romantic Catholics*, 215.

86. Amélie Ozanam-Soulacroix, *Notes biographique*, in *Actes du Colloque*, 233.

87. Harrison, *Romantic Catholics*, 235.

88. Ibid.

89. Sirach 6:14–16, New Revised Standard Version.

90. McCarty, "Frederick Ozanam," 34.

91. Quoted in Baunard, *Ozanam*, 235–36. For the French text see Cholvy, *Ozanam: Le christianisme*, 291.

92. Cholvy, *Ozanam: Le christianisme*, 279, 285.

93. Ramson, "His Piety and Devotion," 159 (12).

94. Tarrazi, "Frédéric Ozanam," 143.

95. William W. Sheldon, C.M., "Canonization of Frederick Ozanam: History of the Cause," *Vincentian Heritage* 17:1 (1996): 52.

96. Roberto D'Amico, C.M., "The History of the Cause for the Beatification of Frederick Ozanam," *Vincentiana* 41:3 (May–June 1997): 163. http://cmglobal.org/vincentiana/.

97. Sheldon, "Canonization," 56.

98. Ibid.

99. D'Amico, "History of the Cause," 162–63.

100. Sheldon, "Canonization," 57.

101. Ibid., 58.

102. Ibid., 59.

103. Ibid., 61.

104. For a brief history of this case, see Ozanam, *Book of the Sick*, 113–20.

105. D'Amico, "History of the Cause," 163–64.

106. John Paul II, "Beatification of Frédéric Ozanam, Homily," no. 1.

107. Mireille Beaup, *Frédéric Ozanam: La sainteté d'un laïc* (Paris: Paroles et Silence, 2003), 135.

WORKS CITED

LETTERS OF OZANAM

See also the two collections of Ozanam's letters, including biographical material, listed under Ainslie Coates and Joseph I. Dirvin in the section "Other Works Cited."

"Lettres de Frédéric Ozanam." 2 vols. In Antoine Frédéric Ozanam, *Oeuvres complètes*. Vols. 10 and 11. Paris: Jacques Lecoffre et Cie, Libraires-Éditeurs, 1865.

Lettres de Frédéric Ozanam. Vol. 1. *Lettres de jeunesse (1819–1840)*. Léonce Célier, Jean-Baptiste Duroselle, and Didier Ozanam, éditeurs. Paris: Bloud and Gay, 1960.

Lettres de Frédéric Ozanam. Vol. 2. *Premières années à la Sorbonne (1841–1844)*. Édition critique de Jeanne Caron. Paris: Celse, 1978.

Lettres de Frédéric Ozanam. Vol. 3. *L'engagement (1845–1849)*. Édition critique sous la direction de Didier Ozanam. Paris: Celse, 1978.

Lettres de Frédéric Ozanam. Vol. 4. *Les Dernières Années (1850–1853)*. Édition critique par Christine Franconnet. Paris: Éditions Klincksieck, 1992.

Lettres de Frédéric Ozanam. Vol. 5. *Supplément et tables*. Édition critique sous la direction de Didier Ozanam. Paris: Éditions Klincksieck, 1997.

Lettres de Frédéric Ozanam. Vol. 6. *Deuxième supplément*. Édition critique sous la direction de Didier Ozanam. Paris: Société de Saint-Vincent-De-Paul, 2013.

WORKS OF OZANAM

The works by Ozanam listed below are published, variously, under the names A. F. Ozanam, A. Frédéric Ozanam, Antoine Frédéric Ozanam, and Frédéric or Frederick Ozanam.

The Bible for the Sick. Dunwoodie, NY: St. Joseph's Seminary, 1901.

The Book of the Sick. Paris: Society of St. Vincent de Paul International Council General, 2013.

La civilisation au cinquième siècle. In *Oeuvres complètes*. Seconde édition. Vol. 1. Paris: Jacques Lecoffre et Cie, 1862.

"Les dangers de Rome et ses espérances." *Le Correspondant* (10 February 1848).

Dante and Catholic Philosophy in the Thirteenth Century. Translated by Lucia D. Pychowska. 2nd ed. New York: The Cathedral Library Association, 1913.

Dante et la philosophie catholique au treizième siècle. Paris: Debécourt, Libraire Éditeur, 1839. http://www.archive.org/stream/danteetlaphilos05ozangoog #page/n13/mode/2up.

Dante et la philosophie catholique au treizième siècle. Cinquième édition. In *Oeuvres complètes*. Troisième édition. Vol. 6. Paris: Paris: Lecoffre Fils et Cie, 1869.

"Des devoirs littéraires des chrétiens." In *Oeuvres complètes*. Quatrième édition. Vol. 7. Paris: Lecoffre Fils et Cie, 1872.

Deux chanceliers d'Angleterre: Bacon de Vérulam et S. Thomas de Cantorbéry. In *Oeuvres complètes*. Quatrième édition. Vol. 7. Paris: Lecoffre Fils et Cie, 1872.

Du protestantisme dans ses rapports avec la liberté. In *Oeuvres complètes*. Quatrième édition. Vol. 8. Paris: Lecoffre Fils et Cie, 1872.

The Franciscan Poets in Italy of the Thirteenth Century. Translated by A. E. Nellen and N. C. Craig. London: David Nutt, 1914.

Les Germains avant le christianisme. Troisième édition. Vol. 1. In *Oeuvres complètes*. Seconde édition. Vol. 3. Paris: Jacques Lecoffre et Cie, 1861.

History of Civilization in the Fifth Century. Translated by Ashley C. Glyn. 2 vols. London: Wm. H. Allen & Co., 1868.

Notes d'un cours de droit commercial. In *Oeuvres complètes*. Quatrième édition. Vol. 8. Paris: Lecoffre Fils et Cie, 1872.

Oeuvres complètes. Seconde édition. 11 vols. Paris: Jacques Lecoffre et Cie, 1859.

Oeuvres complètes, Seconde édition. 11 vols. Paris: Jacques Lecoffre et Cie, 1861.

Oeuvres complètes. Seconde édition. 11 vols. Paris: Jacques Lecoffre et Cie, 1862.

Oeuvres complètes. 11 vols. Paris: Jacques Lecoffre et Cie, Libraires-Éditeurs, 1865.

Oeuvres complètes. Troisième édition. 11 vols. Paris: Lecoffre Fils et Cie, 1869.

Oeuvres complètes. Quatrième édition. 11 vols. Paris: Lecoffre Fils et Cie, 1872.

Un pèlerinage au pays du Cid. In *Oeuvres complètes*. Quatrième édition. Vol. 7. Paris: Lecoffre Fils et Cie, 1872.

A Pilgrimage to the Land of the Cid. Translated by Pauline Stump. New York: Christian Press Association Publishing Company, 1895.

Les poètes franciscains en Italie au treizième siècle. Troisième édition. In *Oeuvres complètes*. Seconde édition. Vol. 5. Paris: Jacques Lecoffre et Cie, 1859.

Le Purgatoire de Dante. In *Oeuvres complètes*. Seconde édition. Vol. 9. Paris: Jacques Lecoffre et Cie, 1862.

"Réflexions sur la doctrine de Saint-Simon." In *Oeuvres complètes*. Seconde édition. Vol. 7. Paris: Jacques Lecoffre et Cie, 1859.

Two Chancellors of England. Translated by John Finlay. Sydney, Australia: The Society of St. Vincent de Paul, 1960.

An Unending Feast: A Critique of the Document of Saint-Simon. Edited by J. A. Morley. New South Wales, Australia: State Council of the Society of Saint Vincent de Paul, 1982.

OTHER WORKS CITED

Addams, Jane. "The Subtle Problems of Charity." *Atlantic Monthly* 83:496 (1899).

Alton-Shee, Edmond d'. *Mes Memoires (1826–1848).* Paris: Lacroix-Verboecken, 1869.

Amdur, Kathryn E. "The Making of the French Working Class." In *The Transformation of Modern France: Essays in Honor of Gordon Wright,* edited by William B. Cohen. New York and Boston: Houghton Mifflin Company, 1997.

Ampère, Jean-Jacques. *Papiers Ampère de L'Institute.* In *Oeuvres complètes d'Alexis de Tocqueville.* Vol. 11. *Correspondence d'Alexis de Tocqueville avec P.-P. Royer-Collard et avec J.-J Ampère.* Paris: Gallimard, 1970.

Auge, Thomas. *Frederic Ozanam and His World.* Milwaukee: Bruce Publishing Company, 1966.

Barbiche, Bernard, and Christine Franconnet, eds. *Frédéric Ozanam (1813–1853): Un universitaire chrétien face à la modernité.* Paris: Les Éditions du Cerf; Bibliothèque Nationale de France, 2006.

Baunard, Louis, Right Reverend Monsignor. *Ozanam in His Correspondence.* Dublin: Catholic Truth Society, 1925.

Beaune, Henri. *M. Th. Foisset.* Dijon: Lamarche, Libraire-Éditeur, 1874. http://data.bnf.fr/15537401/joseph_theophile_foisset/.

Beaup, Mireille. *Frédéric Ozanam: La sainteté d'un laïc.* Paris: Paroles et Silence, 2003.

Benedict XVI. *Caritas in Veritate.* June 29, 2009. http://www.vatican.va/.

Boissard, Henry. *Théophile Foisset (1800–1873).* Paris: E. Plon, Nourrit et Cie, 1891.

Bokenkotter, Thomas. *Church and Revolution: Catholics in the Struggle for Democracy and Social Justice.* New York: Doubleday, 1998.

Brejon de Lavergnée, Matthieu. *La Société de Saint-Vincent de-Paul au XIXe siècle: Un fleuron du catholicisme social.* Paris: Les Éditions du Cerf, 2008.

Bressolette, Claude. *L'abbé Maret: Le combat de théologien pour une démocratie chrétienne, 1830–1851.* Paris: Broche, 1997.

———. "Frédéric Ozanam et *L'Ère nouvelle.*" *Revue d'histoire de l'Église de France* 85:214 (1999).

Byron, William J. "Ten Building Blocks of Catholic Social Teaching." *America* 179:13 (1998).

Carné, Louis de. *Souvenirs de ma jeunesse au temps de hi Restauration*. Paris: Didier et Cie, 1873.

Caron, Jean-Claude. "Frédéric Ozanam, Catholic Student (1831–1836)." *Vincentian Heritage* 30:1 (2010).

Caron, Pierre. *Les massacres de septembre*. Paris: La Maison du Livre Français, 1935.

Catechism of the Catholic Church. 2nd ed. http://www.usccb.org.

Celier, Léonce. *Frédéric Ozanam, 1813–1853*. Paris: P. Lethielleux, Éditeur, 1956.

Charpentier de Beauville, Philippe. *Frédéric Ozanam, 1813–1853: Histoire d'une vocation*. Paris: Salvator, 2013.

Cholvy, Gérard. "Frédéric Ozanam and the Challenges of the Times." *Society of St. Vincent de Paul Bulletin of News* (13 February 2009).

———. *Frédéric Ozanam: Le christianisme a besoin de passeurs*. Perpignan: Éditions Artège, 2012.

———. *Frédéric Ozanam: L'engagement d'un intellectual catholique au XIXe siècle*. Paris: Fayard, 2003.

Clark, Meghan J. "The Complex but Necessary Union of Charity and Justice: Insights from the Vincentian Tradition for Contemporary Catholic Social Teaching." *Vincentian Heritage* 31:2 (2012).

———. "Love of God and Neighbor: Living Charity in Aquinas' Ethics." *New Blackfriars* 92:1040 (2011).

Coates, Ainslie, trans. *Letters of Frederic Ozanam*. London: Elliot Stock, 1886.

Corrin, Jay P. *Catholic Intellectuals and the Challenge of Democracy*. Notre Dame, IN: University of Notre Dame Press, 2002.

Curnier, Léonce. *La jeunesse de Frédéric Ozanam*. 4th ed. Paris: A. Hennuyer, Imprimateur-Éditeur, 1890.

D'Amico, Roberto, C.M. "The History of the Cause for the Beatification of Frederick Ozanam." *Vincentiana* 41:3 (May–June 1997). http://cmglobal .org/vincentiana/.

Danjou, Yves, C.M. "Fr. Eugène Boré, C.M. (1809–1878): Scholarship in the Service of the Faith." Translated by John E. Rybolt, C.M. *Vincentiana* 50:5 (September–October 2006). http://cmglobal.org/vincentiana-novus-en/files /downloads/2006_5/vt_2006_05_12_en.pdf.

Day, Dorothy. *House of Hospitality*. New York: Sheed & Ward, 1939.

Derum, James Patrick. *Apostle in a Top Hat: The Inspiring Story of Frederick Ozanam, Founder of the Society of Saint Vincent de Paul*. St. Clair, MI: Fidelity Publishing Company, 1962.

Dewey, John. *Ethics: The Middle Works of John Dewey*. Vol. 5. Edited by Jo Ann Boydston. Carbondale: Southern Illinois University Press, 1978.

Dirvin, Joseph I., C.M., trans. and ed. *Frederic Ozanam: A Life in Letters*. St. Louis: Society of Saint Vincent de Paul Council of the United States, 1986.

————. *Saint Catherine Labouré of the Miraculous Medal*. Rockford, IL: Tan Books and Publishers, 1984.

Duthoit, Eugène. *Frédéric Ozanam et la civilisation de l'amour*. Paris: Beauchesne, 1997.

Faculté de théologie Université catholique de Lyon. *Frédéric Ozanam: Actes du Colloque des 4 et 5 décembre 1998*. Paris: Bayard, 2001.

Fagan, Austin. *Through the Eye of a Needle: Frédéric Ozanam*. Middlegreen and Bowling Green Lane, England: St. Paul Publications and Universe Publications Co., 1989.

Ferreira, M. Jamie. "Kierkegaard and Levinas on Four Elements of the Biblical Love Commandment." In *Kierkegaard and Levinas: Ethics, Politics, and Religion*, edited by Aaron J. Simmons and David Wood. Bloomington: Indiana University Press, 2008.

Fichter, Joseph H., S.J. *Roots of Change*. New York and London: D. Appleton-Century Company, 1939.

Francis I. "Address of Holy Father Francis." Cathedral of Cagliari, Sunday. September 22, 2013. http://www.vatican.va/.

————. "Address of Holy Father Francis." Largo Carlo Felice, Cagliari. 22 September 2013. http://www.vatican.va/.

Frédéric Ozanam à Marseille. Special issue, *Cahiers Ozanam*, no. 79. January–March. Paris: Society of Saint Vincent de Paul, Council General, 1983.

Galopin, Eugène. *Essai de bibliographie chronologique sur Antoine-Frédéric Ozanam (1813–1853)*. Paris: Société D'Édition "Les Belles Lettres," 1933.

Girardin, Saint-Marc. *Souvenirs et réflexions politiques d'un journaliste*. 2nd ed. Paris: Michel Lévy Frères, Éditeurs, 1873. http://babel.hathitrust.org/cgi/pt?id=mdp.39015058482236;seq=163;view=1up;num=143.

Goyau, G., et al. *Ozanam, Livre du Centenaire*. Paris: Gabriel Beauchesne, 1913.

Greenleaf, Robert K. *Servant Leadership: A Journey into the Nature of Legitimate Power and Greatness*. New York: Paulist Press, 1977.

Gregory XVI. *Mirari Vos: Encyclical Letter of His Holiness Pope Gregory XVI, On Liberalism and Religious Indifferentism*, 1832. http://www.papalencyclicals.net/Greg16/g16mirar.htm.

Gregory, David L. "Antoine Frederic Ozanam: Building the Good Society." *University of St. Thomas Law Journal* 3:1 (2005).

Harrison, Carol E. *Romantic Catholics: France's Postrevolutionary Generation in Search of a Modern Faith*. Ithaca, NY: Cornell University Press, 2014.

Hartenbach, William, C.M. "Vincentian Spirituality." *Vincentian Heritage* 17:1 (1996).

Hegel, George Wilhelm Friedrich. *The Doctrine of Essence*. Translated by William Wallace. In *Hegel Selections*, edited by J. Loewenberg. New York: Charles Scribner's Sons, 1965.

———. *Introduction to the Philosophy of History.* Translated by S. Sibree. In *Hegel Selections,* edited by J. Loewenberg. New York: Charles Scribner's Sons, 1965.

———. *The Philosophy of Mind.* Translated by William Wallace. In *Hegel Selections,* edited by J. Loewenberg. New York: Charles Scribner's Sons, 1965.

Hess, Mary Ann Garvie, trans. *Frédéric Ozanam.* Special issue, *Cahiers Ozanam,* nos. 37/38/39. January–June. Paris: Society of Saint Vincent de Paul, Council General, 1974.

Hickey, Edward John. *The Society for the Propagation of the Faith: Its Foundation, Organization, and Success (1822–1922).* Washington, DC: Catholic University of America, 1922.

"History of the Medal." *The Chapel Pamphlets.* July 2004. http://www.chapellenotredamedelamedaillemiraculeuse.com/Carnets/carnetEN/HistoireMedaille-AN.pdf.

Holböck, Ferdinand. *Married Saints and Blesseds through the Centuries.* San Francisco: Ignatius Press, 2002.

Honner, John. *Love and Politics: The Revolutionary Frederic Ozanam.* Melbourne, Australia: David Lovell Publishing, 2007.

Hughes, Reverend Henry Louis. *Frederick Ozanam.* Saint Louis, MO: B. Herder Book Company, 1933.

John Paul II. "Beatification of Frédéric Ozanam, Homily of Pope John Paul II." Notre-Dame de Paris, August 22, 1997. http://www.vatican.va/.

———. *On Social Concern (Sollicitudo Rei Socialis).* December 30, 1987. http://www.vatican.va/.

Johnson, Daniel. "On Truth As Subjectivity in Kierkegaard's *Concluding Unscientific Postscript.*" *Quodlibet Journal* 5:2–3 (July 2003). http://www.quodlibet.net/articles/johnson-truth.shtml.

Jordan, Thomas E. *Ireland's Children: Quality of Life, Stress, and Child Development in the Famine Era.* Westport, CT: Greenwood Press, 1998.

Keane, James, S.J., ed. *Seeds of Hope: Stories of Systemic Change.* St. Louis, MO: The Society of St. Vincent de Paul for the Commission for Promoting Systemic Change, 2008.

Kelly, George Armstrong. *The Humane Comedy: Constant, Tocqueville and French Liberalism.* Cambridge: Cambridge University Press, 1992.

Kierkegaard, Søren. *Stages on Life's Way.* Edited and translated by Howard V. Hong and Edna H. Hong. Princeton, NJ: Princeton University Press, 1988.

Kirmsee, Bruce H. *Sören Kierkegaard and the Common Man.* Grand Rapids, MI: Wm. B. Eerdmans Publishing Co., 2001.

Lacordaire, H. D., O.P. *My Friend Ozanam.* Translated by a Discalced Carmelite. Sydney, Australia: The Society of St. Vincent de Paul Ozanam House, 1957.

Lavery, Shane D. "Religious Educators: Promoting Servant Leadership." *Religious Education Journal of Australia* 25:1 (2009). http://researchonline.nd.edu.au/.

Looby, John, S.J. "Ozanam and Marx." *The Irish Monthly* 81:964 (1953).

Loubère, Leo A. *Nineteenth-Century Europe: The Revolution of Life.* Englewood Cliffs, NJ: Prentice-Hall, 1994.

Lubove, Roy. *The Professional Altruist: The Emergence of Social Work as a Career, 1880–1930.* Cambridge, MA: Harvard University Press, 1965.

Lynch, Katherine A. *Family, Class, and Ideology in Early Industrial France: Social Policy and the Working-Class Family, 1825–1848.* Madison: University of Wisconsin Press, 1988.

Magraw, Roger. *France, 1815–1914: The Bourgeois Century.* New York and Oxford: Oxford University Press, 1986.

Maloney, Robert P., C.M. "Commission for Promoting Systemic Change." *Vincentiana* 52:1–2 (January–April 2008). http://via.library.depaul.edu/cgi/viewcontent.cgi?article=1470&context=vincentiana.

———. *Faces of Holiness: Portraits of Some Saints in the Vincentian Family.* Saint Louis, MO: National Council of the United States Society of Saint Vincent de Paul, 2008.

———. "Ten Foundational Principles in the Social Teaching of the Church." *Vincentiana* 43:3 (1999). http://cmglobal.org/vincentiana/.

Mancini, Matthew. *Alexis de Tocqueville and American Intellectuals: From His Time to Ours.* Lanham, MD: Rowman & Littlefield Publishers, 2006.

The Manual of the Society of St. Vincent de Paul. 21st ed. Dublin: The Superior Council of Ireland, 1958.

Maritain, Jacques. *The Range of Reason.* New York: Scribner, 1952.

Martin, Most Reverend Jacques. "The Humour of Pope Pius IX." *L'Osservatore Romano* (23 March 1978). https://www.ewtn.com/library/MARY/P9HUMOR.HTM.

McCarty, Shaun, S.T. "Frederick Ozanam: Lay Evangelizer." *Vincentian Heritage* 17:1 (1996).

McKenna, Thomas, C.M. "Frédéric Ozanam's Tactical Wisdom for Today's Consumer Society." *Vincentian Heritage* 30:1 (2010).

Melun, Armand de. *Vie de la soeur Rosalie, Fille de la Charité.* 13th ed. Paris, 1929.

Mercier, Charles. *La Société de Saint-Vincent-de-Paul: Une mémoire des origins en movement, 1833–1914.* Paris: L'Harmattan, 2006.

Middlecamp, Ralph. "Lives of Distinction—Ozanam's Cofounders of the Society of St. Vincent de Paul." http://famvin.org/wiki/SVDP_-_Founders.

Miola, Robert S. *Early Modern Catholicism: An Anthology of Primary Sources.* New York: Oxford University Press, 2007.

Moon, Parker Thomas. *The Labor Problem and the Social Catholic Movement in France: A Study in the History of Social Politics.* New York: Macmillan Company, 1921.

Morel, Chr. [Christine Franconnet]. "Un journal démocrate chrétien en 1848–1849: *L'Ère nouvelle*." *Revue d'histoire de l'Église de France* 63:170 (1977).

Morton, Keith. "The Irony of Service: Charity, Project and Social Change in Service-Learning." *Michigan Journal of Community Service Learning* 2:1 (1995).

Mousin, Reverend Craig B. "Frédéric Ozanam—Beneficent Deserter: Mediating the Chasm of Income Inequality through Liberty, Equality, and Fraternity." *Vincentian Heritage* 30:1 (2010).

Murphy, J. P., C.M. "Servant Leadership in the Manner of Saint Vincent de Paul." *Vincentian Heritage* 19:1 (1998).

O'Brien, Thomas W. "Pioneer and Prophet: Frédéric Ozanam's Influence on Modern Catholic Social Theory." *Vincentian Heritage* 31:1 (2012).

O'Connor, Edward, S.J. *The Secret of Frederick Ozanam: Founder of the Society of St. Vincent de Paul*. Dublin: M. H. Gill and Son, 1953.

Ogilvie-Ellis, Chantelle. "Jacques Maritain and a Spirituality of Democratic Participation." *Solidarity: The Journal of Catholic Social Thought and Secular Ethics* 3:1 (2013).

O'Meara, Kathleen. *Frederic Ozanam, Professor at the Sorbonne: His Life and Works*. New York: Catholic Publication Society Company, 1891.

Ozanam, C.-A. *Vie de Frédéric Ozanam*. Paris: Librairie Poussielgue Frères, 1879.

Ozanam, Jean-Antoine. *Histoire de Lyon pendant les journées des 21, 22 et 23 novembre 1831, contenant les causes, les conséquences et les suites de ces déplorables événements*. Lyon: Auguste Baron; Paris: Moutardier, 1832.

Ozanam-Soulacroix, Amélie. *Notes biographique sur Frédéric Ozanam*. Edition established by Raphaëlle Chevalier-Motariol. In Faculté de théologie Université catholique de Lyon, *Frédéric Ozanam: Actes du Colloque des 4 et 5 décembre 1998*. Paris: Bayard, 2001.

Palmer, R. R. *Twelve Who Ruled: The Year of the Terror in the French Revolution*. Princeton, NJ: Princeton University Press, 1970.

Paul VI. *Decree on the Apostalate of the Laity, Apostolicam Actuositatem*. November 18, 1965. http://www.vatican.va/.

Popkin, Jeremy D. *A History of Modern France*. 2nd ed. Upper Saddle River, NJ: Prentice-Hall, 2001.

Porteous, John. *Coins in History*. New York: Putnam Publishing Group, 1969.

Ramson, Ronald W., C.M. "Frédéric Ozanam: His Piety and Devotion." *Vincentiana* 41:3 (May–June 1997). http://cmglobal.org/vincentiana/.

———. *Hosanna! Blessed Frederic Ozanam: Family and Friends*. Bloomington, IN: Westbow Press, 2013.

Rauch, R. W., Jr. *Politics and Belief in Contemporary France*. The Hague: Martinus Nijhoff, 1972.

Renner, Sister Emmanuel, O.S.B. *The Historical Thought of Frédéric Ozanam*. Washington, DC: Catholic University of America Press, 1959.

"Report On Charity, Friday, June 27, 1834." http://famvin.org/wiki/Society_of _St._Vincent_de_Paul_First_Written_Report.

Rivières, Madeleine, des. *Ozanam*. Translated by James Parry. Montreal: Les Éditions Bellarmin, 1989.

Robert, Adolphe, Edgar Bourloton, and Gaston Cougny. *Dictionnaire des Parlementaires français de 1789 à 1889*. Paris: Bourloton, 1891.

"A Romish Brotherhood: The Founder of the St. Vincent De Paul. Prof. Frederic Ozanam's Life and Works. The History of the Brotherhood, An Interesting Memoir." *New York Times*, 18 August 1878, ProQuest Historical Newspapers, *The New York Times* (1851–2003).

Rules of the Society of St. Vincent de Paul, and Indulgences. Printed for the Council of New York. New York: D. & J. Sadlier & Co., 1869. http://archive.org /stream/rulesandindulge00paulgoog#page/n4/mode/2up.

Ryan, John A., and Joseph Husslein, S.J. *The Church and Labor*. New York: Macmillan Company, 1920.

Rybolt, John E., C.M. "The Virtuous Personality of Blessed Frederick Ozanam." *Vincentian Heritage* 17:1 (1996).

Sacra Congregatio Pro Causis Sanctorum Officium Historicum. *Frederici Ozanam, Patris Familias Primarii Fondatoris Societatis Conferentiarum S. Vincentii a Paulo, Disquisitio de Vita et Actuositate Servi Dei*. Rome, 1980.

Schimberg, Albert Paul. *The Great Friend: Frederick Ozanam*. Milwaukee: Bruce Publishing Company, 1946.

Senge, Peter M. *The Fifth Discipline: The Art and Practice of the Learning Organization*. New York: Doubleday, 1990.

Sheldon, William W., C.M. "Canonization of Frederick Ozanam: History of the Cause." *Vincentian Heritage* 17:1 (1996).

Sheppard, Lancelot C. *Lacordaire: A Biographical Essay*. New York: Macmillan Company, 1964.

Shubeck, Thomas. *Love that Does Justice*. Maryknoll, NY: Orbis Books, 2007.

Sickinger, Raymond L. "Faith, Charity, Justice, and Civic Learning: The Lessons and Legacy of Frédéric Ozanam." *Vincentian Heritage* 30:1 (2010).

———. "Frédéric Ozanam: Systemic Thinking, and Systemic Change." *Vincentian Heritage* 32:1 (2014).

Society of Saint Vincent de Paul. *Règlement de la Société de Saint Vincent de Paul*. Paris: Imprimerie de E-J Bailly et Compagnie, 1835.

———. *Rule of the International Confederation of the Society of St. Vincent De Paul* (2003).

Souvay, Charles L., C.M. "Ozanam as Historian." *Catholic Historical Review* 19:1 (April 1933).

———. "The Society of St. Vincent de Paul as an Agency of Reconstruction." *Catholic Historical Review* 7:4 (1922).

Spears, Larry C. "Character and Servant Leadership: Ten Characteristics of Effective, Caring Leaders." *Journal of Virtues & Leadership* 1:1 (2010).

Spencer, Philip. "'Barbarian Assault': The Fortunes of a Phrase." *Journal of the History of Ideas* 16:2 (1955).

Stearns, Peter N. *1848: The Revolutionary Tide in Europe.* New York: W. W. Norton & Company, 1974.

Sullivan, Louise, D.C. *Sister Rosalie Rendu: A Daughter of Charity on Fire with Love for the Poor.* Chicago: Vincentian Studies Institute, 2006.

Tarrazi, Amin de. "Frédéric Ozanam, A Lay Saint for Our Times." *Vincentiana* 41:3 (May–June 1997). http://cmglobal.org/vincentiana/.

Tarrazi, Amin de, and Ronald Ramson, C.M. *Ozanam.* Bowling Green, MO: Éditions du Signe, 1997.

"Text of the Decree of Introduction of Ozanam Cause." In *Ozanam: Path to Sainthood.* Melbourne, Australia: National Council of Australia Society of St. Vincent de Paul, 1987.

Tocqueville, Alexis de. *Recollections.* Translated by George Lawrence. Garden City, NY: Doubleday, 1970.

United States Catholic Conference of Bishops. *Forming Consciences for Faithful Citizenship: A Call to Political Responsibility from the Catholic Bishops of the United States.* Washington, DC, 2007. http://www.usccb.org/.

———. *Sharing Catholic Social Teaching: Challenges and Directions—Reflections of the U.S. Catholic Bishops.* Washington, DC, 1998. http://www.usccb.org/.

Verheyde, Christian. *15 Days of Prayer with Blessed Frédéric Ozanam.* Translated by John E. Rybolt, C.M. New York: New City Press, 2011.

Vincent, Marcel. *Ozanam: Une jeunesse romantique, 1813–1833.* Paris: Médiaspaul, 1994.

Vincent de Paul. *Common Rules.* In General Curia of the Congregation of the Mission, *Constitutions and Statutes of the Congregation of the Mission.* Philadelphia, 1989. Originally published Rome, 1984.

———. *Correspondance, Entretiens, Documents.* Edited by Reverend Pierre Coste, C.M. Paris: Gabalda, 1921–1925.

———. *Correspondence, Conferences, Documents.* Edited and translated by Jacqueline Kilar, D.C., Marie Poole, D.C., et al. New York: New City Press, 1985–2010.

Vincentian Family News Blog. *Systemic Change: Seeds of Change* series. http://www.famvin.org/wiki/Systemic_Change:_Seeds_of_Change.

Waller, Sally. *France in Revolution, 1776–1830.* Oxford: Heinemann Education Publishers, 2002.

Wright, Gordon. *France in Modern Times: From the Enlightenment to the Present.* Chicago: Rand McNally College Publishing Company, 1974.

Zwick, Mark, and Louise Zwick. *The Catholic Worker Movement: Intellectual and Spiritual Origins.* New York: Paulist Press, 2005.

INDEX

"AFO" and "Society" refer respectively to Antoine Frédéric Ozanam and the Society of St. Vincent de Paul.

Raymond Sickinger is professor of history at Providence College.

CPSIA information can be obtained
at www.ICGtesting.com
Printed in the USA
LVOW13*2028310317

529227LV00007B/8/P